MARK TWAIN

ADVENTURES OF HUCKLEBERRY FINN

THE MARK TWAIN LIBRARY

The Library offers for the first time popular editions of Mark Twain's best works just as he wanted them to be read. These moderately priced volumes, faithfully reproduced from the California scholarly editions and printed on acid-free paper, are expertly annotated and include all the original illustrations that Mark Twain commissioned and enjoyed.

"Huck waited for no particulars. He sprang away
and sped down the hill as fast as his
legs could carry him."

—THE ADVENTURES OF TOM SAWYER

Mark Twain

FROM THE BUST BY KARL GERHARDT.

E·W·Kemble
·1884·

HUCKLEBERRY FINN.

MARK TWAIN

ADVENTURES OF HUCKLEBERRY FINN

TOM SAWYER'S COMRADE

SCENE: THE MISSISSIPPI VALLEY
TIME: FORTY TO FIFTY YEARS AGO

Illustrated by E. W. Kemble and John Harley

125th Anniversary Edition

Editors
Victor Fischer and Lin Salamo

with Harriet Elinor Smith
and the late Walter Blair

A publication of the
Mark Twain Project of The Bancroft Library

University of California Press
Berkeley   Los Angeles   London

The text of this Mark Twain Library edition of *Adventures of Huckleberry Finn* is identical with the text of the scholarly edition of *Adventures of Huckleberry Finn*, edited by Victor Fischer and Lin Salamo (University of California Press, 2003). It is based on the complete author's manuscript now in the Buffalo and Erie County Public Library, and was established in accord with the standards of the Committee on Scholarly Editions (CSE). Editorial work was supported by generous grants from the Barkley Fund, the Hedco Foundation, and the National Endowment for the Humanities.

University of California Press, one of the most distinguished university presses in the United States, enriches lives around the world by advancing scholarship in the humanities, social sciences, and natural sciences. Its activities are supported by the UC Press Foundation and by philanthropic contributions from individuals and institutions. For more information, visit www.ucpress.edu.

University of California Press
Berkeley and Los Angeles, California

University of California Press, Ltd.
London, England

ISBN 978-0-520-26609-4 (cloth: alk. paper)
ISBN 978-0-520-26610-0 (pbk.: alk. paper)

The Library of Congress has cataloged an earlier edition of this book as follows:

Library of Congress Cataloging-in-Publication Data

Twain, Mark, 1835–1910.
  Adventures of Huckleberry Finn / Mark Twain ; illustrated by E. W. Kemble and John Harley ; editors, Victor Fischer . . . [et al.].
    p. cm.—(The Mark Twain Library)
  "A publication of the Mark Twain Project of the Bancroft Library."
  Includes bibliographical references (p.).
  ISBN 978-0-520-22838-2 (pbk. : alk. paper)
  1. Finn, Huckleberry (Fictitious character)—Fiction.   2. Mississippi River—Fiction.   3. Fugitive slaves—Fiction.   4. Male friendship—Fiction.   5. Missouri—Fiction.   6. Boys—Fiction. I. Fischer, Victor, 1942–   II. Bancroft Library.   III. Title.

PS1305.A2 F5   2001
813'.4—dc21   2001027448

Manufactured in the United States of America

19 18 17 16 15 14 13 12 11 10
10 9 8 7 6 5 4 3 2 1

The Mark Twain Library is designed by Steve Renick.

The text of this Mark Twain Library edition of
Adventures of Huckleberry Finn
is drawn from the Mark Twain Project's complete edition of
The Works and Papers of Mark Twain.
*Editorial work for this volume has been supported by grants
to the Friends of The Bancroft Library from the*

BARKLEY FUND

and the

HEDCO FOUNDATION

and by matching funds from the

NATIONAL ENDOWMENT FOR THE HUMANITIES,

an independent federal agency.

*Without such generous support, these editions could
not have been produced.*

*The Mark Twain Project
dedicates this volume to*

WALTER BLAIR

*in appreciation of his contributions
to the field of Mark Twain studies*

and also to the

TEACHERS OF AMERICAN LITERATURE

*who have continued to find new ways
to bring* Huckleberry Finn *alive
in their classrooms.*

CONTENTS

ILLUSTRATIONS

FOREWORD

Mark Twain began writing *Adventures of Huckleberry Finn* in July 1876. Working "by fits and starts," he gradually added to his stack of manuscript pages—sometimes after intervals of two or three years—for a total of 1,361 pages in a little more than seven years. During that same period he actually finished and published three other long books: *A Tramp Abroad* (1880), *The Prince and the Pauper* (1881), and *Life on the Mississippi* (1883). When he finally published *Huckleberry Finn* in February 1885, he issued it by subscription through his own publishing house, Charles L. Webster and Company, run by his nephew, Charlie Webster. At the time, Mark Twain was just nine months shy of fifty. He was at the height of his powers, and even though he lived and wrote for another twenty-five years, he never wrote anything as good as *Huckleberry Finn*.

Since the 1940s, *Huckleberry Finn* has risen so far in the academic canon of American literature that one recent critic has complained of its "hyper-canonization." This new edition, replacing the Mark Twain Project's edition of 1985, assumes that *Huckleberry Finn* is indeed Mark Twain's masterpiece, and that the very widest audience will want to know what has been learned about the text following the discovery, in 1990, of the long-lost manuscript for the entire first half of the story. (For some details, see the Note on the Text.)

Shortly before the book's first publication, Mark Twain wrote the following dedication for it, prompted perhaps by having seen many of his Hannibal friends the previous year when he revisited the Mississippi River, preparing to write *Life on the Mississippi*:

> *To the Once Boys & Girls*
> who comraded with me in the morning of time
> & the youth of antiquity, in the village of
> *Hannibal, Missouri,*
> this book is inscribed, with affection for themselves,
> respect for their virtues, & reverence for their honorable gray hairs.
> The Author.

Almost immediately he decided against using this nostalgic salute to the people and the place that had served him as models for many of his characters and for the town of St. Petersburg. He decided instead to begin the book with the ironic "Notice," with its mock threat to persons attempting to find a motive, moral, or plot in it. This notice was signed by the mysterious "G. G., Chief of Ordnance," who it turns out was probably meant for George Griffin, the Clemenses' butler, a former slave and veteran of the Civil War who had become a virtual member of the family. The rhetorical distance between these two ways of introducing his book suggests that Mark Twain was not entirely sure at the time which aspect of his creation he wanted to emphasize—its seemingly innocent evocation of the past, or its highly ironic and humorous condemnation of that past, especially the race-based social system that persisted in the South.

Not surprisingly, some of the book's earliest readers, including the author's own Hannibal family, followed the simpler of these two strains. They found themselves easily able to recognize real people behind the fictional characters, not to mention the real speech and manner and popular culture of Hannibal, and of the Mississippi Valley generally—cultural details that suffuse the novel. John Milton Hay, a native of Illinois who had served as Lincoln's private secretary during the war, and who had long admired Mark Twain's work, wrote to him shortly after publication:

It is a strange life you have described, one which I imagine must be already pretty nearly obsolete in most respects. I, who grew up in the midst of it, have almost forgotten it, except when I read of it in your writings—the only place, I think, where a faithful record of it survives. To me the great interest of this, and your other like books, independent of their wit and humor and pathos, which everybody can see, is "documentary." Without them I should not know today, the speech and the way of living, with which I was familiar as a child. Huck Finns and Tom Sawyers were my admired and trusted friends—though I had to cultivate them as the early Christians did their religion—in out of the way places. I am glad to meet them again in your luminous pages.

One hundred and twenty-five years after its publication, critics and scholars are still scouring the book for what is real—for clues to the actual counterparts of its fiction—attempting somehow to grasp the essence of what it says about American history and culture. But one of the reasons *Huckleberry Finn* has endured is that while it struck readers like John Hay and Clemens's own family as portraying a recently vanished way of life, it still strikes today's reader as real, and as remarkably relevant to modern life.

The book *is* real to its readers, which is just another way of saying it was profoundly imagined. Another perennial subject of critical essays on *Huckleberry Finn* is the search for what makes it seem so real. Part of the answer, most would now agree, lies in the way it is told. In 1875, just after he finished *The Adventures of Tom Sawyer*, Mark Twain wrote to William Dean Howells:

I have finished the story & didn't take the chap beyond boyhood. I believe it would be fatal to do it in any shape but autobiographically—like Gil Blas. I perhaps made a mistake in not writing it in the first person. . . .

By & by I shall take a boy of twelve & run him on through life (in the first person) but not Tom Sawyer—he would not be a good character for it.

One year after he wrote this letter, Mark Twain had decided that a "good character" to tell his own story "in the first person" was in fact Huckleberry Finn, Tom Sawyer's comrade, and he began writing what he then called "Huck Finn's Autobiography." Huck was based on a Hannibal childhood contemporary of Clemens's, Tom Blankenship, from a family of poor whites whose father was the town drunkard. Mark Twain later described Tom Blankenship as "ignorant, unwashed, insufficiently fed; but he had as good a heart as ever any boy had."

Huck's voice, its tone and idiom, its "dialect" pronunciation, were among the things that seemed literally "real" to Mollie Clemens, Mark Twain's sister-in-law, when she first read the text. But the voice was also the product of Mark Twain's genius. Huck's voice in the finished novel seems so natural that it almost appears to have been "found" or simply remembered and copied down. From the opening sentence until the last, Huck *talks* to us, and we share his thoughts and feelings, and seem to share his very *experience*. Here is Huck, telling us what it is like to be lost in the fog on the river:

I kept quiet, with my ears cocked, about fifteen minutes, I reckon. I was floating along, of course, four or five mile an hour; but you don't ever think of that. No, you *feel* like you are laying dead still on the water; and if a little glimpse of a snag slips by, you don't think to yourself how fast *you're* going, but you catch your breath and think, My! how that snag's tearing along. If you think it ain't dismal and lonesome out in a fog that way, by yourself, in the night, you try it once—you'll see.

Mark Twain's memories of real Pike County speech certainly played their part in this literary illusion, but having the *whole* manuscript at last makes it possible to trace how Mark Twain learned, slowly over several years, in hundreds of pages, and thousands of small and large revisions, to render Huck's voice on the page.

By comparing this manuscript with the first edition, we can see that Mark Twain made innumerable changes in Huck's voice, not just in the manuscript itself, but on a document that probably no longer exists, the typed copy of the manuscript which he revised extensively and eventually placed in the hands of the typesetter. For example, in chapter 8, when Huck is planning to spend the night on Jackson's Island, Mark Twain wrote in the manuscript: "it got sort of lonesome, & I . . . looked at the stars, & out over the river watching the rafts come down. So for an hour, & then to bed." But in the published text, this passage reads: "it got sort of lonesome, and so I . . . counted the stars and drift-logs and rafts that come down, and then went to bed; there ain't no better way to put in time when you are lonesome; you can't stay so, you soon get over it." Later in the chapter, when Huck is on the Illinois shore, the manuscript has him say: "I had about made up my mind to stay there all night, when I heard horses." But in the book he says: "I had about made up my mind I would stay there all night, when I hear a *plunkety-plunk, plunkety-plunk*, and says to myself, horses coming."

Mark Twain developed Huck's voice, but also his sensibility, his capacity for articulating his thoughts. When Huck is castigating himself at the end of chapter 16 for not turning in Jim to the slave-hunters, leading them instead to think the raft is infected with smallpox, he says in the manuscript:

> They went off & I hopped aboard the raft, saying to myself, I've done wrong again, & was trying as hard as I could to do right, too; but when it come right down to telling them it was a nigger on the raft, & I opened my mouth a-purpose to do it, I couldn't. I am a mean, low coward, & it's the fault of them that brung me up. If I had been raised right, I wouldn't said anything about anybody being sick, but the more I try to do right, the more I can't. I reckon I won't ever try again, because it ain't no sort of use & only makes me feel bad. From this out I mean to do everything as wrong as I can do it, & just go straight to the dogs & done with it. I don't see why people's put here, anyway.

But in the text as Mark Twain revised and published it, Huck's narration shows a clear advance in his ability to identify and rationalize his moral dilemma. He says:

> They went off, and I got aboard the raft, feeling bad and low, because I knowed very well I had done wrong, and I see it warn't no use for me to try to learn to do right; a body that don't get *started* right when he's little, ain't got no show—when the pinch comes there ain't nothing to back him up and keep him to his work, and so he gets beat. Then I thought a minute, and says to myself, hold on,—s'pose you'd a done right and give Jim up; would you felt better than what you do now? No, says I, I'd feel bad—I'd feel just the same way I do now. Well, then, says I, what's the use you learning to do right, when it's troublesome to do right and ain't no trouble to do wrong, and the wages is just the same? I was stuck. I couldn't answer that. So I reckoned I wouldn't bother no more about it, but after this always do whichever come handiest at the time.

In 1895, when he chose the episode from chapter 16 ("Small-pox & a lie save Jim") for public reading in his "morals" lecture, he sketched an introduction in his notebook which provides a key not just to that episode, but to the moral and philosophical dilemma that lies at the heart of *Huckleberry Finn*:

> Next, I should exploit the proposition that in a crucial moral emergency a sound heart is a safer guide than an ill-trained conscience. I sh'd support this doctrine with a chapter from a book of mine where a sound heart & a deformed conscience come into collision & conscience suffers defeat. Two persons figure in this chapter: Jim, a middle-aged slave, & Huck Finn, a boy of 14, son of the town drunkard. These two

are close friends, bosom friends, drawn together by community of misfortune. Huck is the child of neglect & acquaint[e]d with cold, hunger, privation, humiliation, & with the unearned aversion of the upper crust of the community. The respectable boys were not allowed to play with him—so they played with him all the time—preferred his company to any other. There was nothing against him but his rags, & to a boy's untutored eye rags don't count if the person in them is satisfactory.

In those old slave-holding days the whole community was agreed as to one thing—the awful sacredness of slave property. To help steal a horse or a cow was a low crime, but to help a hunted slave, or feed him or shelter him, or hide him, or comfort him, in his troubles, his terrors, his despair, or hesitate to promptly betray him to the slave-catcher when opportunity offered was a much baser crime, & carried with it a stain, a moral smirch which nothing could wipe away. That this sentiment should exist among slave-owners is comprehensible—there were good commercial reasons for it—but that it should exist & did exist among the paupers, the loafers the tag-rag & bobtail of the community, & in a passionate & uncompromising form, is not in our remote day realizable. It seemed natural enough to me then; natural enough that Huck & his father the worthless loafer should feel it & approve it, though it seems now absurd. It shows that that strange thing, the conscience—that unerring monitor—can be trained to approve any wild thing you *want* it to approve if you begin its education early & stick to it.

Readers lulled by Huck's voice just talking his story, and lulled by Mark Twain's loving evocation of the sights, sounds, and smells of idyllic life on and along the river, are sometimes jolted by the discomfort they feel at Huck's language, and at the people and incidents Huck encounters. Readers long to be on that raft, eating that catfish, experiencing that sunrise, but the people and incidents that soon crowd the story—the violence of Pap Finn, the feud between the Grangerfords and Shepherdsons, the murder of Boggs, the bilking of the orphan Wilks girls, the betrayal of Jim—belong to a world profoundly flawed and uncomfortably real. Readers have come to the book not only for the story, but for a distillation of pre–Civil War culture, for commentary on and insight into black and white race relations. In it they find a satirical portrait of bigots and confidence men, an evocation of the violence and false courtliness at the heart of the Southern aristocracy, and they find in even the kindest people Huck meets, not to mention Huck himself, an unquestioning acceptance of slavery.

Because in its plot and its narrative details the book brings up issues of class and violence and racism in American society (issues Huck does not always seem able to recognize even as he reports them), and because these issues are still familiar in American life, the book remains almost as controversial as it is celebrated. In the nineteenth century, critics were shocked at Huck's "low" language, his rationalization of lying and stealing, and his undisguised skepticism toward such things as prayer and religious doctrine. They sought to ban the book lest it set a bad example for children. In the twentieth century, critics angry about Mark Twain's realistic language and impatient with his ironic condemnation of racism, have accused *him* of it, confusing the messenger with the message.

Huckleberry Finn is one of the funniest books ever written, a fact sometimes forgotten in discussions of its more serious side. Among its humorous riches are jokes hidden behind Huck's invariable deadpan ("Jim he found a . . . wooden leg. The straps was broke off of it, but barring that, it was a good enough leg, though it was too long for me and not long enough for Jim, and we couldn't find the other one, though we hunted all around"). The difference between this kind of joke and a more traditional use of "deadpan" is that only the reader and Mark Twain "get it": Huck is entirely humorless. Mark Twain is thereby able to comment indirectly on matters that are beyond Huck's understanding ("There was some books, too. . . . One was 'Pilgrim's Progress,' about a man that left his family, it didn't say why. I read considerable in it, now and then. The statements was interesting, but tough"). Huck frankly admires the sentimental poetry that Mark Twain designed as burlesque ("And did young Stephen sicken, | And did young Stephen die? | And did the sad hearts thicken, | And did the mourners cry?"). He admires Shakespearean lines that were never written by Shakespeare ("To be, or not to be: that is the bare bodkin"). And he is impressed by things that should make the reader only smile ("This table had a cover made out of beautiful oil cloth, with a red and blue spread-eagle painted on it, and a painted border all around. It come all the way from Philadelphia, they said").

In 1883 Mark Twain first published in chapter 3 of *Life on the Mississippi* the so-called "raft episode," taken from his *Huckleberry Finn* manuscript. Other excerpts from the book began appearing in the *Century Magazine* at the end of 1884, two months before the book itself was issued. Comments on these excerpts ranged from the *Atlantic Monthly*'s "a wonderful transcript from nature . . . that will not easily be surpassed in the future" to the Boston *Herald*'s "pitched in but one key, and that is the key of a vulgar and abhorrent life."

The book was first published in England in December 1884, and American publication followed in February 1885. Almost immediately an argument about its literary merit broke out in the newspapers. One of the members of the Concord Public Library, who removed it from the shelves, wrote: "It deals with a series of adventures of a very low grade of morality; it is couched in the language of a rough, ignorant dialect, and all through its pages there is a systematic use of bad grammar and an employment of rough, coarse, inelegant expressions. It is also very irreverent." Some like-minded reviewers called it "a pitiable exhibition of irreverence and vulgarity" and "a pot-boiler in its baldest form," reporting that "a search expedition for . . .

humorous qualities" yielded nothing but blood-curdling and unfunny episodes. Others, though, called it the crowning achievement of "a literary artist of a very high order," a "*tour de force*," a "minute and faithful picture," and
hailed its evocation of the "lawless, mysterious, wonderful Mississippi" and
of the "startlingly real" riverside people who "do not have the air of being
invented, but of being found."

The *way* Huck tells his story, without any direct comment from Mark
Twain, proved to be a new way to write, resembling actual speech more than
what Mark Twain would have called "book talk." From the outset this bold
experiment seems to have been embraced with special fervor by other writers—perhaps most famously by Hemingway and Faulkner. But even earlier
than that, Robert Louis Stevenson said in February 1885 that *Huckleberry
Finn* "contains many excellent things; above all, the whole story of a healthy
boy's dealings with his conscience, incredibly well done." Three years later
he wrote to Clemens that he had read it "four times," and was "quite ready
to begin again tomorrow." William L. Alden, another contemporary author
and literary critic, wrote to Clemens:

I have read the extracts from the book in the *Century* & enjoyed them more than I
ever enjoyed any magazine articles anywhere. I want to tell you that the Grangerford
feud lays over anything you ever wrote. The deceased painter of pathetic pictures:—
the boy who was always ready to bet that he'd "get one of them"—and that exhaustive criticism of the Pilgrim's Progress—"the statements were interesting but
tough"—are simply heavenly.

And after reading the whole book, he wrote again: "I have just read Huck
through in course. It is the best book ever written," a judgment Clemens
carefully noted on the envelope. Joel Chandler Harris (Uncle Remus) wrote
to Clemens, saying that "its value as a picture of life and as a study in philology will yet come to be recognized by those whose recognition is worth anything. It is the most original contribution that has yet been made to American literature." And later Harris wrote for publication that "there is not in
our fictive literature a more wholesome book than 'Huckleberry Finn.' It is
history, it is romance, it is life. Here . . . we see people growing and living; we
laugh at their humor, share their griefs; and . . . we are taught the lesson of
honesty, justice and mercy."

In the twentieth century, the book's reputation continued to grow among
writers. In 1907, George Bernard Shaw wrote Clemens, in part:

Once, when I was in [William] Morris's house, a superior anti-Dickens sort of man
(sort of man that thinks Dickens no gentleman) was annoyed by Morris disparaging
Thackeray. With studied gentleness he asked whether Morris could name a greater
master of English. Morris promptly said "Mark Twain." This delighted me extremely,
as it was my own opinion; and I then found that Morris was an incurable Huckfino-
maniac. . . . I am persuaded that the future historian of America will find your works

as indispensable to him as a French historian finds the political tracts of Voltaire. I tell you so because I am the author of a play in which a priest says "Telling the truth's the funniest joke in the world," a piece of wisdom which you helped to teach me.

In 1910, H. L. Mencken wrote:

The pictures of the mighty Mississippi, as the immortal Huck presents them, do not belong to buffoonery or to pretty writing, but to universal and almost flawless art. Where, in all fiction, will you find another boy as real as Huck himself? In sober truth, his equals, young or old, are distressingly few in the world. Rabelais created two, Fielding one, Thackeray three or four and Shakespeare a roomful; but you will find none of them in the pages of Hawthorne or Poe or Cooper or Holmes. In Kipling's phrase, Huck stands upon his feet. Not a freckle is missing, not a scar, not a trick of boyish fancy, not a habit of boyish mind.

Ralph Ellison wrote in 1970 about "the spoken idiom of Negro Americans":

Its flexibility, its musicality, its rhythms, freewheeling diction and metaphors, as projected in Negro American folklore, were absorbed by the creators of our great 19th-century literature even when the majority of blacks were still enslaved. Mark Twain celebrated it in the prose of *Huckleberry Finn*; without the presence of blacks, the book could not have been written. No Huck and Jim, no American novel as we know it.

In 1996, Toni Morrison wrote:

Although its language—sardonic, photographic, persuasively aural—and the structural use of the river as control and chaos seem to me quite the major feats of *Huckleberry Finn*, much of the novel's genius lies in its quiescence, the silences that pervade it and give it a porous quality that is by turns brooding and soothing. It lies in the approaches to and exits from action; the byways and inlets seen out of the corner of the eye; the subdued images in which the repetition of a simple word, such as "lonesome," tolls like an evening bell; the moments when nothing is said, when scenes and incidents swell the heart unbearably precisely because unarticulated, and force an act of imagination almost against the will. . . . It is classic literature.

Charles Kuralt declared on television in the early 1980s: "If I had to say as much about America as I possibly could in only two words, I would say . . . 'Huck Finn.' " One Russian writer and critic, a boy during World War II, remembered in 1986: "When the enemy was advancing on Moscow, my mother and I were evacuated from the city to a safe area in the Ural Mountains. We could take only a few necessities. Among these necessities was a copy of 'Huckleberry Finn,' with the original [Kemble] illustrations. I learned it by heart." Japanese author Kenzaburo Oe has said *Huckleberry Finn* was his greatest inspiration and the book that convinced him to become a writer.

The list of writers and critics who have praised *Huckleberry Finn* goes on and on. But are all these accolades too much? Can a book's reputation stand in the way of a reader's ability to discover it for himself? Apparently not. Well over a hundred editions of *Huckleberry Finn* are currently in print in the

United States alone. The novel is issued on compact disk, in e-book format, in more than a score of audio tapes, and in nearly a dozen adaptations for film and video. It has been translated into more than fifty-three languages, and has appeared in more than seven hundred foreign editions; it is currently in print in scores of languages worldwide.

In August 1909, substantially before academics ever wrote very much about *Huckleberry Finn*, let alone assigned it to their students, H. L. Mencken said that Mark Twain was,

by great odds, the most noble figure America has ever given to English literature. Having him, we may hold up our heads when Spaniards boast of Cervantes and Frenchmen of Molière. His one book, *Huckleberry Finn*, is worth, I believe, the complete works of Poe, Hawthorne, Cooper, Holmes, Howells, and James, with the entire literary output to date of Indiana, Pennsylvania and all the States south of the Potomac thrown in as makeweight.

Mencken, like a boasting raftsman, exaggerated to make a point. Nonetheless, it seems safe to concede that *Huckleberry Finn* is indeed something special, not just for Americans, but for readers worldwide.

Victor Fischer
Lin Salamo

Berkeley, January 2001

MARK TWAIN ON TOUR

During the last months of 1884 and early 1885, while the first American edition of *Adventures of Huckleberry Finn* was being readied for publication and book agents were selling subscriptions door-to-door, Mark Twain (Samuel L. Clemens) went on a reading tour in the East and Midwest with his friend and fellow author George Washington Cable. Among Mark Twain's most popular readings were selections from *Huckleberry Finn*, extracted episodes of which were currently running in the *Century Magazine*. Reproduced here are the publisher's advertisement for subscription agents, an advertisement for Mark Twain's books currently in print, an official portrait of Mark Twain and Cable made for the reading tour, and three of the reading programs. Four letters from Clemens written while the two authors were on the road follow. In March 1885, one month after the official American publication, the book was banned from the Concord (Massachusetts) Public Library. Mark Twain's first reaction, in a letter to his publisher, is reproduced at the end.

"Confidential Terms to Agents." This flyer, meant to attract local agents to sell *Adventures of Huckleberry Finn* door-to-door, offered for seventy-five cents an "Outfit for Canvassing," which contained a prospectus (illustrated pages from the book and sample bindings), advertising notices and reviews, and a "Private Instruction-Book teaching the agent how to proceed with the business." The Occidental Publishing Company of San Francisco acted as territorial agents for Mark Twain's publisher, Charles L. Webster & Company. Courtesy of Ron Randall.

MARK TWAIN'S
COMPLETE WORKS.

On the back of the flyer, the Occidental Publishing Company also provided a list of "Mark Twain's Complete Works," published by the American Publishing Company and James R. Osgood and Company, and offered local agents a 40 percent discount, which would effectively give them a profit of 40 percent of the cover price upon sale of the books. Courtesy of Ron Randall.

Mark Twain and George Washington Cable in 1884, prior to their joint speaking tour. Photograph by Napoleon Sarony, New York. Mark Twain Papers, The Bancroft Library (CU-MARK).

THE
"MARK TWAIN"–CABLE
READINGS,
New Haven Opera House,
WEDNESDAY EVG., NOV. 5, 1884.

1.

The Music of Place Congo.
MR. GEO. W. CABLE.

2.

**ADVANCE SHEETS FROM "THE ADVEN-
TURES OF HUCKLEBERRY FINN.**

a. "King Sollermunn."
b. "How come a Frenchman doan' talk like a man?"
MARK TWAIN.

Bret Harte's tale

3.

SCENES FROM DR. SEVIER.

a. Narcisse, Kate Riley, Richling and Ristofalo—
(Borrowing and Courtship Scenes).
b. Narcisse puts on Mourning for "Lady Byron."
c. A Sound of Drums—Off for the Wars.
d. Mary's Night Ride.
MR. GEO. W. CABLE.

4.

a. A Ghost Story.
b. Tragic Tale of the Fishwife.
c. A Trying Situation.
MARK TWAIN.

J. B. POND, Manager,

Carriages at 10 o'clock.   EVERETT HOUSE, NEW YORK.

"The 'Mark Twain'–Cable Readings." Program from the New Haven, Connecticut, Opera House, 5 November 1884, the first reading of the tour (5 Nov 84 to Chatto and Windus, ViU). Mark Twain wrote "Bret Harte's tale" in faint pencil. Mark Twain Papers, The Bancroft Library (CU-MARK).

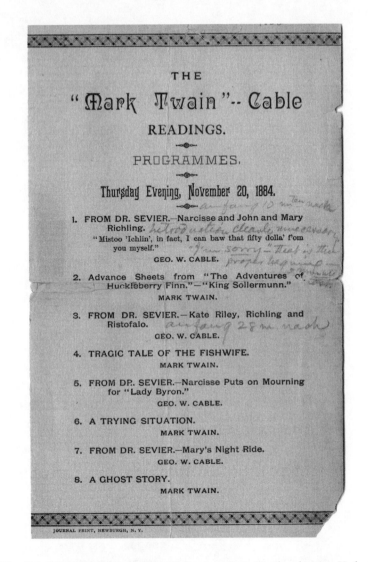

THE
"Mark Twain"-- Cable
READINGS.
PROGRAMMES.

Thursday Evening, November 20, 1884.

1. FROM DR. SEVIER.—Narcisse and John and Mary
   Richling.
   "Mistoo 'Ichlin', in fact, I can baw that fifty dolla' f'om
   you myself."
   GEO. W. CABLE.

2. Advance Sheets from "The Adventures of
   Huckleberry Finn."—"King Sollermunn."
   MARK TWAIN.

3. FROM DR. SEVIER.—Kate Riley, Richling and
   Ristofalo.
   GEO. W. CABLE.

4. TRAGIC TALE OF THE FISHWIFE.
   MARK TWAIN.

5. FROM DR. SEVIER.—Narcisse Puts on Mourning
   for "Lady Byron."
   GEO. W. CABLE.

6. A TRYING SITUATION.
   MARK TWAIN.

7. FROM DR. SEVIER.—Mary's Night Ride.
   GEO. W. CABLE.

8. A GHOST STORY.
   MARK TWAIN.

JOURNAL PRINT, NEWBURGH, N. Y.

"The 'Mark Twain'–Cable Readings." Program from Newburgh, New York, 20
November 1884. Cable wrote his wife that he had struck "a new streak" at that
night's reading, while Clemens showed some annoyance at the growing length of
the program, as witnessed by his notes written here (loosely translated): "anfang
10 mᵗᵉⁿ nach" (begun 10 minutes behind); "Introduction clearly unnecessary.";
"'I'm *sorry*'—that is the proper beginning—5 minute[s] lost."; "anfang 28 m.
nach" (begun 28 minutes behind) (Cardwell, 21–22; Bikle, 133; see *HF2003*,
578–616). Mark Twain Papers, The Bancroft Library (CU-MARK).

CENTRAL MUSIC HALL.

THE

"Mark Twain"—Cable Readings,

Saturday Afternoon, January 17th, 1885.

PROGRAMME.

1. FROM DR. SEVIER,—*Narcisse and John and Mary Richling.*
   "Mistoo 'Ichlin', in fact, I can baw that fifty dolla' f'om you myself."
   GEO. W. CABLE.

2. ADVANCE SHEETS FROM "THE ADVENTURES OF
   HUCKLEBERRY FINN."—"*King Sollermunn.*"
   MARK TWAIN. *ended at 3.*

3. FROM DR. SEVIER.—*Kate Riley, Richling and Ristofalo.*
   GEO. W. CABLE. *ended at 3.16*

4. *Tragic Tale of the Fishwife.*
   MARK TWAIN.

5. FROM DR. SEVIER.—*Narcisse puts on mourning for "Lady
   Byron."*
   GEO. W. CABLE.

6. *A Trying Situation.*
   MARK TWAIN.

7. FROM DR. SEVIER.—*Mary's Night Ride.*
   GEO. W. CABLE.

8. *Selection.*
   MARK TWAIN.

"MARK TWAIN" and MR. CABLE will appear for the last time in Chicago,
this evening, with an entirely new programme.

J. B. POND, MANAGER, EVERETT HOUSE, NEW YORK.

CARRIAGES AT 10.

"The 'Mark Twain'–Cable Readings." Program from the Central Music Hall,
Chicago, 17 January 1885. Mark Twain wrote "ended at 3." after his first
selection, and "ended at 3.16" after Cable's second selection. Mark Twain Papers,
The Bancroft Library (CU-MARK).

FOUR LETTERS FROM MARK TWAIN

Samuel Clemens wrote three of the following four letters to his wife, Olivia, and the fourth to his eldest daughter, Susy, while on his speaking tour with George Washington Cable in 1884–85. Mentioned in the letters are his three daughters, Olivia Susan (Susy), Clara (Ben), and Jean; the Congregationalist minister and social reformer Henry Ward Beecher; the lawyer and lumber merchant Dean Sage and his wife, Sarah Manning Sage, who acted as Clemens's hostess in Rochester in December; the former president Ulysses S. Grant and his wife, Julia Dent Grant; and the author and Civil War general Lew Wallace. All the letters are in the Mark Twain Papers, The Bancroft Library (CU-MARK).

To Olivia L. Clemens
23 November 1884 • New York, N.Y.

N.Y., Nov. '84.
Saturday, after midnight.

Livy dear, only a line to say we finished the *eighth* performance for this week in Brooklyn Academy of Music at 10 this evening, & then came over the Bridge & home. Tired to death, & hungry. Disposed of two great chops, 3 eggs, fried potatoes, & a bottle of ale. I eat a big breakfast every morning & a big supper every night, & am growing fat. We got up at 6 this morning, & have talked to two huge houses in Brooklyn today. Mr. Beecher & the Sages were there tonight, & Dean came behind the scenes.

Thank those dear sweet children for me, for their welcome letters. I love them & their mother.   Saml

To Olivia Susan (Susy) Clemens
23 November 1884 • New York, N.Y.

New York Nov. 23/84.

Susie dear, I don't know how to sufficiently thank you & Ben for writing me such good letters & so faithfully. And I want to thank you both for making Jean say things to be sent to me, too. I called at Gen. Grant's the other morning, & when I saw all his swords, & medals, & collections of beautiful & rare things from Japan & China, I was so sorry I hadn't made Mamma go with me. And Mrs. Grant was sorry, too, & made me promise that I would bring Mamma there to luncheon, some time. Gen. Lew Wallace was there—he has an article in this month's Century about the great Victory of Fort Donelson—& when I told him Mamma was at the reading the other night & was sorry I didn't make her acquainted with the author of Ben Hur, he was very sorry I was so heedless himself. Mrs. Grant got up & stood between Gen Wallace & me, & said, "There, there's many a woman in this land that would like to be in my place & be able to tell her children that she had stood once elbow to elbow between two such great authors as Mark Twain & General Wallace." We all laughed & I said to Gen. Grant; "Don't look so cowed, General; you have written a book, too, & when it is published you can hold up your head & let on to be a person of consequence yourself."

Kiss 'em all for me, sweetheart—& I send love & kisses to you, too.

Papa

To Olivia L. Clemens
6 December 1884 • 2nd of 2 • Rochester, N.Y.

Rochester, Dec. 6./84

Poor Mrs. Sage, she keeps a temperance house, but she had put her principles into the background for my sake, & bought some Scotch whisky & got everything ready for my traditional punch. It almost tempted me to take a drink, but she allowed me to decline without any serious urging.

It has rained cats & dogs here all day—& of course it was one of those accursed Matinée days. The houses were good but not crowded, & we made them shout. I wore that coat for the first time—& the last. It will go back to you by express. I shall never wear anything but evening dress again. I will not defer to fashion to the destruction of my comfort.

Goodbye, I love you darling,   Saml

To Olivia L. Clemens
9 December 1884 • 1st of 2 • Toronto, Canada

Toronto, midnight, Dec. 8/84.
I ate a hearty breakfast at 9 this morning. On the hotel car at 1 p.m., I took a sirloin steak & mushrooms, sweet potatoes, Irish ditto, plate of trout, bowl of tomato soup, 3 cups of coffee, 4 pieces of apple pie (or one complete pie), 2 plates of ice cream & 1 orange. But I stopped then, on account of the expense, although still hungry.

To-night a noble hall to talk in, & an audience befitting it. Both of us had a gorgeously good time. I saw ladies swabbing their eyes freely & undisguisedly after Cable's "Night Ride." He did it well.

After the performance we came down & tagged along behind the audience, halting to be introduced to people, & a most gentle-faced attractive girl in black kept looking back as if she were trying to muster pluck enough to speak to me; & finally she stopped, hesitated, her party heartened her up, & she came to me & put out her hand & said with a little tremor of fright in her voice, "Don't you remember me, Mr. Clemens?" (It was her joke—I had been reciting "A Trying Situation"). I said, "No, but I do wish I did. But I'll remember you next time— don't you be afraid about that." Then she thanked me timidly but very nicely for the evening's entertainment, & then re-joined her father & sister, & they all seemed pleased with her—& so was I. It was a very pleasant adventure.

I got Susie's letter, which was ever so welcome; & yours, too, which was also most welcome; & so I have sent you a telegram to tell you the hoarseness is utterly gone—I filled that huge hall to-night with not even an effort.

I love you my darling, I do indeed. And I send love to mother & to those little chaps, too.

Saml.

I have just finished a robust supper, of beefsteak &c. I travel 6 or 8 hours by rail without the slightest touch of weariness.

(*Opposite*)
Dear Charley—
The Committee of the Public Library of Concord, Mass., have given us a rattling tip-top puff which will go into every paper in the country. They have expelled Huck from their library as "trash & suitable only for the slums." That will sell 25,000 copies for us, sure.   Ys
SLC

On 18 March 1885, just after the newspapers reported that *Adventures of Huckleberry Finn* had been removed from the shelves of the Concord Public Library, Clemens wrote this letter to his publisher, Charles L. Webster. Subsequently, however, when a nationwide debate broke out about the book's (and the author's) morality, Clemens was less amused. Mark Twain Papers, The Bancroft Library (CU-MARK). The writing in the top margin is by Mark Twain's biographer, Albert Bigelow Paine, who wrote and canceled "Huck out of Concord," and by subsequent editors.

MARK TWAIN

ADVENTURES
OF
HUCKLEBERRY
FINN

NOTICE

PERSONS attempting to find a Motive in this narrative will be prosecuted; persons attempting to find a Moral in it will be banished; persons attempting to find a Plot in it will be shot.

By Order of the Author
Per G. G., Chief of Ordnance.

EXPLANATORY

In this book a number of dialects are used, to wit: the Missouri negro dialect; the extremest form of the backwoods South-Western dialect; the ordinary "Pike-County" dialect; and four modified varieties of this last. The shadings have not been done in a hap-hazard fashion, or by guess-work; but pains-takingly, and with the trustworthy guidance and support of personal familiarity with these several forms of speech.

I make this explanation for the reason that without it many readers would suppose that all these characters were trying to talk alike and not succeeding.

The Author.

The Adventures of Huckleberry Finn.

Chapter I.

THE WIDOW'S.

YOU don't know about me, without you have read a book by the name of "The Adventures of Tom Sawyer," but that ain't no matter. That book was made by Mr. Mark Twain, and he told the truth, mainly. There was things which he stretched, but mainly he told the truth. That is nothing. I never seen anybody but lied, one time or another, without it was aunt Polly, or the widow, or maybe Mary. Aunt Polly,—Tom's aunt Polly, she is—and Mary, and the widow Douglas, is all told about in that book—which is mostly a true book; with some stretchers, as I said before.

Now the way that the book winds up, is this: Tom and me found the money that the robbers hid in the cave, and it made us rich. We got six thousand dollars apiece—all gold. It was an awful sight of money when it was piled up. Well, Judge Thatcher, he took it and put it out at interest, and it fetched us a dollar a day apiece, all the year round—more than a body could tell what to do with. The widow Douglas she took me for her son, and allowed she would sivilize me; but it was rough living in the house all the time, considering how dismal regular and decent the widow was in all her ways; and so when I couldn't stand it no longer, I lit out. I got into my old rags, and my sugar hogshead again, and was free and satisfied. But Tom Sawyer he hunted me up and said he was going to

start a band of robbers, and I might join if I would go back to the
widow and be respectable. So I went back.

The widow she cried over me, and called me a poor lost lamb, and
she called me a lot of other names, too, but she never meant no harm
by it. She put me in them new clothes again, and I couldn't do
nothing but sweat and sweat, and feel all cramped up. Well, then,
the old thing commenced again. The widow rung a bell for supper,
and you had to come to time. When you got to the table you couldn't
go right to eating, but you had to wait for the widow to tuck down

LEARNING ABOUT MOSES AND THE "BULRUSHERS."

her head and grumble a little over the victuals; though there warn't
really anything the matter with them. That is, nothing only everything was cooked by itself. In a barrel of odds and ends it is different;
things get mixed up, and the juice kind of swaps around, and the
things go better.

After supper she got out her book and learned me about Moses
and the bulrushers, and I was in a sweat to find out all about him;
but by and by she let it out that Moses had been dead a considerable
long time; so then I didn't care no more about him; because I don't
take no stock in dead people.

Pretty soon I wanted to smoke, and asked the widow to let me. But she wouldn't. She said it was a mean practice and wasn't clean, and I must try to not do it any more. That is just the way with some people. They get down on a thing when they don't know nothing about it. Here she was a-bothering about Moses, which was no kin to her, and no use to anybody, being gone, you see, yet finding a power of fault with me for doing a thing that had some good in it. And she took snuff too; of course that was all right, because she done it herself.

Her sister, Miss Watson, a tolerable slim old maid, with goggles

Miss Watson

on, had just come to live with her, and took a set at me now, with a spelling-book. She worked me middling hard for about an hour, and then the widow made her ease up. I couldn't stood it much longer. Then for an hour it was deadly dull, and I was fidgety. Miss Watson would say, "Don't put your feet up there, Huckleberry," and "Don't scrunch up like that, Huckleberry—set up straight;" and pretty soon she would say, "Don't gap and stretch like that, Huckleberry— why don't you try to behave?" Then she told me all about the bad place, and I said I wished I was there. She got mad, then, but I didn't mean no harm. All I wanted was to go somewheres; all I wanted was a change—I warn't particular. She said it was wicked to say what I said; said she wouldn't say it for the whole world; *she* was going to live so as to go to the good place. Well, I couldn't see no advantage in going where she was going, so I made up my mind I wouldn't try for it. But I never said so, because it would only make trouble, and wouldn't do no good.

Now she had got a start, and she went on and told me all about the good place. She said all a body would have to do there was to go around all day long with a harp and sing, forever and ever. So I didn't think much of it. But I never said so. I asked her if she reckoned Tom Sawyer would go there, and she said not by a considerable sight. I was glad about that, because I wanted him and me to be together.

Miss Watson she kept pecking at me and it got tiresome and lonesome. By and by they fetched the niggers in and had prayers, and then everybody was off to bed. I went up to my room with a piece of candle and put it on the table. Then I set down in a chair by the window and tried to think of something cheerful, but it warn't no use. I felt so lonesome I most wished I was dead. The stars was shining, and the leaves rustled in the woods ever so mournful; and I heard an owl, away off, who-whooing about somebody that was dead, and a whippowill and a dog crying about somebody that was going to die; and the wind was trying to whisper something to me and I couldn't make out what it was, and so it made the cold shivers run over me. Then away out in the woods I heard that kind of a sound that a ghost makes when it wants to tell about something that's on its mind and can't make itself understood, and so can't rest easy in its grave and has to go about that way every night, grieving. I got so down-hearted and scared, I did wish I had some company. Pretty soon a spider went crawling up my shoulder, and I flipped it off and it lit in the candle; and before I could budge it was all shriveled up. I didn't need anybody to tell me that that was an awful bad sign and would fetch me some bad luck, so I was scared and most shook the clothes off of me. I got up and turned around in my tracks three times and crossed my breast every time; and then I tied up a little lock of my hair with a thread to keep witches away. But I hadn't no confidence. You do that when you've lost a horse-shoe that you've found, instead of nailing it up over the door, but I hadn't ever heard anybody say it was any way to keep off bad luck when you'd killed a spider.

I set down again, a-shaking all over, and got out my pipe for a smoke; for the house was all as still as death, now, and so the widow wouldn't know. Well, after a long time I heard the clock away off in the town go Boom—boom—boom—twelve licks—and all still again—stiller than ever. Pretty soon I heard a twig snap, down in the dark amongst the trees—something was a-stirring. I set still and listened. Directly I could just barely hear a *"Me-yow! me-yow!"* down there. That was good! Says I, *"Me-yow! me-yow!"* as soft as I could, and then I put out the light and scrambled out of the window onto the shed. Then I slipped down to the ground and crawled in amongst the trees, and sure enough there was Tom Sawyer waiting for me.

HUCK STEALING AWAY.

Chapter II.

THEY TIP-TOED ALONG.

We went tip-toeing along a path amongst the trees back towards the end of the widow's garden, stooping down so as the branches wouldn't scrape our heads. When we was passing by the kitchen, I fell over a root and made a noise. We scrouched down and laid still. Miss Watson's big nigger, named Jim, was setting in the kitchen door; we could see him pretty clear, because there was a light behind him. He got up and stretched his neck out about a minute, listening. Then he says,

"Who dah?"

He listened some more; then he come tip-toeing down and stood right between us; we could a touched him, nearly. Well, likely it was minutes and minutes that there warn't a sound, and we all there so close together. There was a place on my ancle that got to itching; but I dasn't scratch it; and then my ear begun to itch; and next my back, right between my shoulders. Seemed like I'd die if I couldn't scratch. Well, I've noticed that thing plenty of times, since. If you are with the quality, or at a funeral, or trying to go to sleep when you ain't sleepy—if you are anywheres where it won't do for you to scratch, why you will itch all over in upwards of a thousand places. Pretty soon Jim says:

"Say—who is you? Whar is you? Dog my cats ef I didn' hear sumf'n. Well, I knows what I's gwyne to do. I's gwyne to set down here and listen tell I hears it agin."

So he set down on the ground betwixt me and Tom. He leaned his back up against a tree, and stretched his legs out till one of them most touched one of mine. My nose begun to itch. It itched till the tears come into my eyes. But I dasn't scratch. Then it begun to itch on the inside. Next I got to itching underneath. I didn't know how I was going to set still. This miserableness went on as much as six or seven minutes; but it seemed a sight longer than that. I was itching in eleven different places, now. I reckoned I couldn't stand it more'n a minute longer, but I set my teeth hard and got ready to try. Just then Jim begun to breathe heavy; next he begun to snore—and then I was pretty soon comfortable again.

Tom he made a sign to me,—kind of a little noise with his mouth—and we went creeping away on our hands and knees. When we was ten foot off, Tom whispered to me and wanted to tie Jim to the tree for fun; but I said no; he might wake and make a disturbance, and then they'd find out I warn't in. Then Tom said he hadn't got candles enough, and he would slip in the kitchen and get some more. I didn't want him to try. I said Jim might wake up and come. But Tom wanted to resk it; so we slid in there and got three candles, and Tom laid five cents on the table for pay. Then we got out, and I was in a sweat to get away; but nothing would do Tom but he must crawl to where Jim was, on his hands and knees, and play something on him. I waited, and it seemed a good while, everything was so still and lonesome.

As soon as Tom was back, we cut along the path, around the garden fence and by and by fetched up on the steep top of the hill the other side of the house. Tom said he slipped Jim's hat off of his head and hung it on a limb right over him, and Jim stirred a little, but he didn't wake. Afterwards Jim said the witches bewitched him and put him in a trance, and rode him all over the State, and then set him under the trees again and hung his hat on a limb to show who done it. And next time Jim told it he said they rode him down to New Orleans; and after that, every time he told it he spread it more and more, till by and by he said they rode him all over the world, and tired him most to death, and his back was all over saddle-boils. Jim was monstrous proud about it, and he got so he wouldn't hardly notice the other niggers. Niggers would come miles to hear Jim tell about it, and he was more looked up to than any nigger in that country. Strange niggers would stand with their mouths open and look him all over, same as if he was a wonder. Niggers is always talking about witches in the dark by the kitchen fire; but whenever one was talking and letting on to know all about such things, Jim would happen in and say, "Hm! what you know 'bout witches?"— and that nigger was corked up and had to take a back seat. Jim always kept that five-center piece around his neck with a string and said it

JIM.

was a charm the devil give to him with his own hands and told him he could cure anybody with it and fetch witches whenever he wanted to, just by saying something to it; but he never told what it was he said to it. Niggers would come from all around there and give Jim anything they had, just for a sight of that five-center piece; but they wouldn't touch it, because the devil had had his hands on it. Jim was most ruined, for a servant, because he got so stuck up on account of having seen the devil and been rode by witches.

Well, when Tom and me got to the edge of the hill-top, we looked away down into the village and could see three or four lights twinkling, where there was sick folks, maybe; and the stars over us was sparkling ever so fine; and down by the village was the river, a whole mile broad, and awful still and grand. We went down the hill and found Jo Harper, and Ben Rogers, and two or three more of the boys, hid in the old tan yard. So we unhitched a skiff and pulled down the river two mile and a half, to the big scar on the hill side, and went ashore.

We went to a clump of bushes, and Tom made everybody swear to keep the secret, and then showed them a hole in the hill, right in the thickest part of the bushes. Then we lit the candles and crawled in on our hands and knees. We went about two hundred yards, and then the cave opened up. Tom poked about amongst the passages and pretty soon ducked under a wall where you wouldn't a noticed that there was a hole. We went along a narrow place and got into a kind of room, all damp and sweaty and cold, and there we stopped. Tom says:

"Now we'll start this band of robbers and call it Tom Sawyer's Gang. Everybody that wants to join has got to take an oath, and write his name in blood."

Everybody was willing. So Tom got out a sheet of paper that he had wrote the oath on, and read it. It swore every boy to stick to the band, and never tell any of the secrets; and if anybody done anything to any boy in the band, whichever boy was ordered to kill that person and his family must do it, and he mustn't eat and he mustn't sleep till he had killed them and hacked a cross in their breasts, which was the sign of the band. And nobody that didn't belong to the band could use that mark, and if he did he must be sued; and if he done it again he must be killed. And if anybody that belonged to the band told the secrets, he must have his throat cut, and then have his carcase burnt up and the ashes scattered all around, and his name blotted off of the list with blood and never mentioned again by the Gang, but have a curse put on it and be forgot, forever.

TOM SAWYER'S BAND OF ROBBERS.

Everybody said it was a real beautiful oath, and asked Tom if he got it out of his own head. He said, some of it, but the rest was out of pirate books, and robber books, and every Gang that was high-toned had it.

Some thought it would be good to kill the *families* of boys that told the secrets. Tom said it was a good idea, so he took a pencil and wrote it in. Then Ben Rogers says:

"Here's Huck Finn, he hain't got no family—what you going to do 'bout him?"

"Well, hain't he got a father?" says Tom Sawyer.

"Yes, he's got a father, but you can't never find him, these days. He used to lay drunk with the hogs in the tanyard, but he hain't been seen in these parts for a year or more."

They talked it over, and they was going to rule me out, because they said every boy must have a family or somebody to kill, or else it wouldn't be fair and square for the others. Well, nobody could think of anything to do—everybody was stumped, and set still. I was most ready to cry; but all at once I thought of a way, and so I offered them Miss Watson—they could kill her. Everybody said:

"O, she'll do, she'll do. That's all right. Huck can come in."

Then they all stuck a pin in their fingers to get blood to sign with, and I made my mark on the paper.

"Now," says Ben Rogers, "what's the line of business of this Gang?"

"Nothing only robbery and murder," Tom said.

"But who are we going to rob? Houses—or cattle—or—"

"Stuff! stealing cattle and such things ain't robbery, it's bur-glary," says Tom Sawyer. "We ain't burglars. That ain't no sort of style. We are highwaymen. We stop stages and carriages on the road, with masks on, and kill the people and take their watches and money."

"Must we always kill the people?"

"O, certainly. It's best. Some authorities think different, but mostly it's considered best to kill them. Except some that you bring to the cave here and keep till they're ransomed."

"Ransomed? What's that?"

"I don't know. But that's what they do. I've seen it in books; and so of course that's what we've got to do."

"But how can we do it if we don't know what it is?"

"Why blame it all, we've *got* to do it. Don't I tell you it's in the books? Do you want to go to doing different from what's in the books, and get things all muddled up?"

"O, that's all very fine to *say*, Tom Sawyer, but how in the nation are these fellows going to be ransomed if we don't know how to do it to them? That's the thing *I* want to get at. Now what do you *reckon* it is?"

"Well I don't know. But per'aps if we keep them till they're ransomed, it means that we keep them till they're dead."

"Now, that's something *like*. That'll answer. Why couldn't you said that before? We'll keep them till they're ransomed to death— and a bothersome lot they'll be, too, eating up everything and always trying to get loose."

"How you talk, Ben Rogers. How can they get loose when there's a guard over them, ready to shoot them down if they move a peg?"

"A guard. Well that *is* good. So somebody's got to set up all night and never get any sleep, just so as to watch them. I think that's foolishness. Why can't a body take a club and ransom them as soon as they get here?"

"Because it ain't in the books so—that's why. Now Ben Rogers, do you want to do things regular, or don't you?—that's the idea. Don't you reckon that the people that made the books knows what's the correct thing to do? Do you reckon *you* can learn 'em anything? Not by a good deal. No sir, we'll just go on and ransom them in the regular way."

"All right. I don't mind; but I say it's a fool way, anyhow. Say—do we kill the women, too?"

"Well Ben Rogers, if I was as ignorant as you I wouldn't let on. Kill the women? No—nobody ever saw anything in the books like that. You fetch them to the cave, and you're always as polite as pie to them; and by and by they fall in love with you and never want to go home any more."

"Well, if that's the way, I'm agreed, but I don't take no stock in it. Mighty soon we'll have the cave so cluttered up with women, and fellows waiting to be ransomed that there won't be no place for the robbers. But go ahead, I ain't got nothing to say."

Little Tommy Barnes was asleep, now, and when they waked him up he was scared, and cried, and said he wanted to go home to his ma, and didn't want to be a robber any more.

So they all made fun of him, and called him cry-baby, and that made him mad, and he said he would go straight and tell all the secrets. But Tom give him five cents to keep quiet, and said we would all go home and meet next week and rob somebody and kill some people.

Ben Rogers said he couldn't get out much, only Sundays, and so he wanted to begin next Sunday; but all the boys said it would be wicked to do it on Sunday, and that settled the thing. They agreed to get together and fix a day as soon as they could, and then we elected Tom Sawyer first captain and Jo Harper second captain of the Gang, and so started home.

I clumb up the shed and crept into my window just before day was breaking. My new clothes was all greased up and clayey and I was dog-tired.

HUCK CREEPS INTO HIS WINDOW.

Chapter III.

MISS WATSON'S LECTURE.

WELL, I got a good going-over in the morning, from old Miss Watson, on account of my clothes; but the widow she didn't scold, but only cleaned off the grease and clay and looked so sorry that I thought I would behave a while if I could. Then Miss Watson she took me in the closet and prayed, but nothing come of it. She told me to pray every day, and whatever I asked for I would get it. But it warn't so. I tried it. Once I got a fish-line, but no hooks. It warn't any good to me without hooks. I tried for the hooks three or four times, but somehow I couldn't make it work. By and by, one day, I asked Miss Watson to try for me, but she said I was a fool. She never told me why, and I couldn't make it out no way.

I set down, one time, back in the woods, and had a long think about it. I says to myself, if a body can get anything they pray for, why don't deacon Winn get back the money he lost on pork? why can't the widow get back her silver snuff box that was stole? why can't Miss Watson fat up? No, says I to myself, there ain't nothing in it. It stands to reason there ain't nothing in it. I went and told the widow about it, and she said the thing a body could get by praying for it was "spiritual gifts." This was too many for me, but she told me what she meant—I must help other people, and do everything I could for other people, and look out for them all the time, and never think about myself. This was including Miss Watson, as I took it. I went out in the woods and turned it over in my mind a long time, but I couldn't see no advantage about it—except for the other people—so at last I reckoned I wouldn't worry about it any more, but just let it go. Sometimes the widow would take me one side and talk about Providence in a way to make a body's mouth water; but maybe next day Miss Watson would take hold and knock it all down again. I judged I could see that there was two Providences, and a poor chap would stand considerable show with the widow's Providence, but if Miss Watson's got him there warn't no help for him any more. I thought it all out, and reckoned I would belong to the widow's, if he wanted me, though I couldn't make out how he was agoing to be any better off then than what he was before, seeing I was so ignorant and so kind of low-down and ornery.

Pap he hadn't been seen for more than a year, and that was comfortable for me; I didn't want to see him no more. He used to always whale me when he was sober and could get his hands on me; though I used to take to the woods most of the time when he was around. Well, about this time he was found in the river drownded, about twelve mile above town, so people said. They judged it was him, anyway; said this drownded man was just his size, and was ragged, and had uncommon long hair—which was all like pap—but they couldn't make nothing out of the face, because it had been in the water so long it warn't much like a face at all. They said he was floating on his back in the water. They took him and buried him on the bank. But I warn't comfortable long, because I happened to think of something. I knowed mighty well that a drownded man don't float on his back, but on his face. So I knowed, then, that this warn't pap, but a woman dressed up in a man's clothes. So I was uncomfortable again. I judged the old man would turn up again by and by, though I wished he wouldn't.

We played robber now and then about a month, and then I resigned. All the boys did. We hadn't robbed nobody, we hadn't killed any people, but only just pretended. We used to hop out of the woods and go charging down on hog-drovers and women in carts taking garden stuff to market, but we never hived any of them. Tom Sawyer called the hogs "ingots," and he called the turnips and stuff "julery," and we would go to the cave and pow-wow over what we had done and how many people we had killed and marked. But I couldn't see no profit in it. One time Tom sent a boy to run about town with a blazing stick, which he called a slogan (which was the sign for the

Gang to get together) and then he said he had got secret news by his spies that next day a whole parcel of Spanish merchants and rich A-rabs was going to camp in Cave Hollow with two hundred elephants, and six hundred camels, and over a thousand "sumter" mules, all loaded down with di'monds, and they didn't have only a guard of four hundred soldiers, and so we would lay in ambuscade, as he called it, and kill the lot and scoop the things. He said we must slick up our swords and guns, and get ready. He never could go after even a turnip cart but he must have the swords and guns all scoured up for it; though they was only lath and broomsticks, and you might scour at them till you rotted and then they warn't worth a mouthful of ashes more than what they was before. I didn't believe we could lick such a crowd of Spaniards and A-rabs, but I wanted to see the camels and elephants, so I was on hand next day, Saturday, in the ambuscade; and when we got the word, we rushed out of the woods and down the hill. But there warn't no Spaniards and A-rabs, and there warn't no camels nor no elephants. It warn't anything but a Sunday School picnic, and only a primer-class at that. We busted it up, and chased the children up the Hollow; but we never got

anything but some doughnuts and jam, though Ben Rogers got a rag doll, and Jo Harper got a hymn-book and a tract; and then the teacher charged in and made us drop everything and cut. I didn't see no dimonds, and I told Tom Sawyer so. He said there was loads of them there, anyway; and he said there was A-rabs there, too, and elephants and things. I said, why couldn't we see them, then? He said if I warn't so ignorant, but had read a book called "Don Quixote," I would know without asking. He said it was all done by enchantment. He said there was hun-

THE ROBBERS DISPERSED.

dreds of soldiers there, and elephants, and treasure, and so on, but
we had enemies which he called magicians, and they had turned
the whole thing into an infant Sunday School—just out of spite. I
said, all right, then the thing for us to do was to go for the magicians.
Tom Sawyer said I was a numscull.

"Why," says he, "a magician could call up a lot of genies, and
they would hash you up like nothing, before you could say Jack
Robinson. They are as tall as a tree and as big around as a church."

"Well," I says, "s'pose we got some genies to help *us*—can't we
lick the other crowd then?"

"How you going to get them?"

"I don't know. How do *they* get them?"

"Why they rub an old tin lamp or an iron ring, and then the genies
come tearing in, with the thunder and lightning a-ripping around
and the smoke a-rolling, and everything they're told to do they up
and do it. They don't think nothing of pulling a shot tower up by the
roots and belting a Sunday School superintendent over the head
with it—or any other man."

"Who makes them tear around so?"

"Why, whoever rubs the lamp or the ring. They belong to whoever
rubs the lamp or the ring, and they've got to do whatever he says. If
he tells them to build a palace forty miles long, out of dimonds, and
fill it full of chewing gum, or whatever you want, and fetch an
emperor's daughter from China for you to marry, they've got to do
it—and they've got to do it before sun-up next morning, too. And
more—they've got to waltz that palace around over the country
wherever you want it, you understand."

"Well," says I, "I think they are a pack of flatheads for not keeping
the palace themselves 'stead of fooling them away like that. And
what's more—if I was one of them I would see a man in Jericho
before I would drop my business and come to him for the rubbing of
an old tin lamp."

"How you talk, Huck Finn. Why, you'd *have* to come when he
rubbed it, whether you wanted to or not."

"What, and I as high as a tree and as big as a church? All right,
then; I *would* come; but I lay I'd make that man climb the highest
tree there was in the country."

"Shucks, it ain't no use to talk to you, Huck Finn. You don't seem to know anything, somehow—perfect sap-head."

I thought all this over for two or three days, and then I reckoned I would see if there was anything in it. I got an old tin lamp and an iron ring and went out in the woods and rubbed and rubbed till I sweat like an Injun, calculating to build a palace and sell it; but it warn't no use, none of the genies come. So then I judged that all that stuff was only just one of Tom Sawyer's lies. I reckoned he believed in the A-rabs and the elephants, but as for me I think different. It had all the marks of a Sunday school.

RUBBING THE LAMP.

Chapter IV.

!!!!!

WELL, three or four months run along, and it was well into the winter, now. I had been to school most all the time, and could spell, and read, and write just a little, and could say the multiplication table up to six times seven is thirty-five, and I don't reckon I could ever get any further than that if I was to live forever. I don't take no stock in mathematics, any-way.

At first I hated the school, but by and by I got so I could stand it. Whenever I got un-common tired I played hookey, and the hiding I got next day done me good and cheered me up. So the longer I went to school the easier it got to be. I was getting sort of used to the widow's ways, too, and they warn't so raspy on me. Living in a house and sleeping in a bed pulled on me pretty tight, mostly, but before the cold weather I used to slide out and sleep in the woods, sometimes, and so that was a rest to me. I liked the old ways best, but I was getting so I liked the new ones, too, a little bit. The widow said I was coming along slow but sure, and doing very satisfactory. She said she warn't ashamed of me.

One morning I happened to turn over the salt-cellar at breakfast. I reached for some of it as quick as I could, to throw over my left shoulder and keep off the bad luck, but Miss Watson was in ahead of me, and crossed me off. She says, "Take your hands away, Huckleberry—what a mess you are always making." The widow put in a good word for me, but that warn't going to keep off the bad luck, I knowed that well enough. I started out, after breakfast, feeling worried and shaky, and wondering where it was going to fall on me and what it was going to be. There is ways to keep off some kinds of bad luck, but this wasn't one of them kind; so I never tried to do anything, but just poked along low-spirited and on the watch-out.

I went down the front garden and clumb over the stile, where you go through the high board fence. There was an inch of new snow on the ground, and I seen somebody's tracks. They had come up from the quarry and stood around the stile awhile, and then went on around the garden fence. It was funny they hadn't come in, after standing around so. I couldn't make it out. It was very curious, somehow. I was going to follow around, but I stooped down to look at the tracks first. I didn't notice anything, at first, but next I did. There was a cross in the left boot heel, made with big nails, to keep off the devil.

I was up in a second and shinning down the hill. I looked over my shoulder every now and then, but I didn't see nobody. I was at Judge Thatcher's as quick as I could get there. He said:

"Why, my boy, you are all out of breath. Did you come for your interest?"

"No sir," I says, "is there some for me?"

"Oh, yes, a half-yearly is in, last night. Over a hundred and fifty dollars. Quite a fortune for you. You better let me invest it along with your six thousand, because if you take it you'll spend it."

"No, sir," I says, "I don't want to spend it. I don't want it at all—nor the six thousand, nuther. I want you to take it; I want to give it to you—the six thousand and all."

He looked surprised. He couldn't seem to make it out. He says:

"Why what can you mean, my boy?"

I says, "Don't you ask me no questions about it, please. You'll take it—won't you?"

He says:

"Well, I'm puzzled. Is something the matter?"

"Please take it," says I, "and don't ask me nothing—then I won't have to tell no lies."

He studied a while, and then he says:

"Oho-o. I think I see. You want to *sell* all your property to me—not give it. That's the correct idea."

JUDGE THATCHER SURPRISED.

Then he wrote something on a paper and read it over, and says:

"There—you see it says 'for a consideration.' That means I have bought it of you and paid you for it. Here's a dollar for you. Now you sign it."

So I signed it, and left.

Miss Watson's nigger, Jim, had a hair-ball as big as your fist, which had been took out of the fourth stomach of an ox, and he used to do magic with it. He said there was a spirit inside of it and it knowed everything. So I went to him that night and told him pap was here again, for I found his tracks in the snow. What I wanted to know, was, what he was going to do, and was he going to stay? Jim got out his hair-ball, and said something over it, and then he held it up and dropped it on the floor. It fell pretty solid, and only rolled about an inch. Jim tried it again, and then another time, and it acted just the same. Jim got down on his knees and put his ear against it and listened. But it warn't no use; he said it wouldn't talk. He said sometimes it wouldn't talk without money. I told him I had an old slick, counterfeit quarter that warn't no good because the brass showed through the silver a little, and it wouldn't pass nohow, even if the brass didn't show, because it was so slick it felt greasy and so that would tell on it every time. (I reckoned I wouldn't say nothing about the dollar I got from the judge.) I said it was pretty bad money, but maybe the hair-ball would take it, because maybe it wouldn't know the difference. Jim smelt it and bit it and rubbed it and said he would manage so the hair-ball would think it was good. He said he would split open a raw Irish potato and stick the quarter in between and keep it there all night, and next morning you couldn't see no brass, and it wouldn't feel greasy no more, and so anybody in town would take it in a minute, let alone a hair-ball. Well, I knowed a potato would do that, before, but I had forgot it.

Jim put the quarter under the hair-ball and got down and listened again. This time he said the hair-ball was all right. He said it would tell my whole fortune if I wanted it to. I says, go on. So the hair-ball talked to Jim, and Jim told it to me. He says:

"Yo' ole father doan' know, yit, what he's agwyne to do. Sometimes he spec he'll go 'way, en den agin he spec he'll stay. De bes'

JIM LISTENING.

way is to res' easy en let de ole man take his own way. Dey's two angels hoverin' roun' 'bout him. One uv 'em is white en shiny en t'other one is black. De white one gits him to go right, a little while, den de black one sail in en bust it all up. A body can't tell, yit, which one gwyne to fetch him at de las'. But you is all right. You gwyne to have considable trouble in yo' life, en considable joy. Sometimes you gwyne to git hurt, en sometimes you gwyne to git sick; but every time you's gwyne to git well agin. Dey's two gals flyin' 'bout you in yo' life. One uv 'em's light en t'other one is dark. One is rich en t'other is po'. You's gwyne to marry de po' one fust en de rich one by en by. You wants to keep 'way fum de water as much as you kin, en don't run no resk, 'kase it's down in de bills dat you's gwyne to git hung."

When I lit my candle and went up to my room that night, there set pap, his own self!

Chapter V.

I HAD SHUT the door to. Then I turned around, and there he was. I used to be scared of him all the time, he tanned me so much. I reckoned I was scared now, too; but in a minute I see I was mistaken. That is, after the first jolt, as you may say, when my breath sort of hitched—he being so unexpected; but right away after, I see I warn't scared of him worth bothering about.

He was most fifty, and he looked it. His hair was long and tangled and greasy, and hung down, and you could see his eyes shining through, like he was behind vines. It was all black; no gray; so was his long, mixed-up whiskers. There warn't no color in his face where his face showed; it was white; not like another man's white, but a white to make a body sick, a white to make a body's flesh crawl—a tree-toad white, a fish-belly white. As for his clothes—just rags, that was all. He had one ancle resting on t'other knee; the boot on that foot was busted, and two of his toes stuck through, and he worked them, now and then. His hat was laying on the floor; an old black slouch with the top caved in, like a lid.

"PAP."

I stood, a-looking at him; he set there a-looking at me, with his chair tilted back a little. I set the candle down. I noticed the window was up; so he had clumb in by the shed. He kept a-looking me all over. By and by he says:

"Starchy clothes—very. You think you're a good deal of a big-bug, *don't* you?"

"Maybe I am, maybe I ain't," I says.

"Don't you give me none o' your lip," says he. "You've put on considerble many frills since I been away. I'll take you down a peg before I git done with you. You're educated, too, they say; can read and write. You think you're better'n your father, now, don't you, because he can't? *I'll* take it out of you. Who told you you might meddle with such hifalut'n foolishness, hey?—who told you you could?"

"The widow. She told me."

"The widow, hey?—and who told the widow she could put in her shovel about a thing that ain't none of her business?"

"Nobody never told her."

"Well I'll learn her how to meddle. And looky-here—you drop that school, you hear? I'll learn people to bring up a boy to put on airs over his own father and let on to be better'n what *he* is. You lemme catch you fooling around that school again, you hear? Your mother couldn't read, and she couldn't write, nuther, before she died. None of the family couldn't, before *they* died. *I* can't; and here you're a-swelling yourself up like this. I ain't the man to stand it— you hear? Say—lemme hear you read."

I took up a book and begun something about General Washington and the wars. When I'd read about a half a minute, he fetched the book a whack with his hand and knocked it across the house. He says:

"It's so. You can do it. I had my doubts when you told me. Now looky-here; you stop that putting on frills. I won't have it. I'll lay for you, my smarty; and if I catch you about that school I'll tan you good. First you know you'll get religion, too. I never see such a son."

He took up a little blue and yaller picture of some cows and a boy, and says—

"What's this?"

"It's something they give me for learning my lessons good."

He tore it up, and says—

"I'll give you something better—I'll give you a cowhide."

He set there a-mumbling and a-growling a minute, and then he says—

"*Ain't* you a sweet-scented dandy, though? A bed; and bed-clothes; and a look'n-glass; and a piece of carpet on the floor—and your own father got to sleep with the hogs in the tanyard. I never see such a son. I bet I'll take some o' these frills out o' you before I'm done with you. Why there ain't no end to your airs—they say you're rich. Hey?—how's that?"

"They lie—that's how."

"Looky-here—mind how you talk to me; I'm a-standing about all I can stand, now—so don't gimme no sass. I've been in town two

HUCK AND HIS FATHER.

days, and I hain't heard nothing but about you bein' rich. I heard about it away down the river, too. That's why I come. You git me that money to-morrow—I want it."

"I hain't got no money."

"It's a lie. Judge Thatcher's got it. You git it. I want it."

"I hain't got no money, I tell you. You ask Judge Thatcher; he'll tell you the same."

"All right. I'll ask him; and I'll make him pungle, too, or I'll know the reason why. Say—how much you got in your pocket? I want it."

"I hain't got only a dollar, and I want that to—"

"It don't make no difference what you want it for—you just shell it out."

He took it and bit it, to see if it was good, and then he said he was going down town to get some whisky; said he hadn't had a drink all day. When he had got out on the shed, he put his head in again, and cussed me for putting on frills and trying to be better than him; and when I reckoned he was gone he come back and put his head in again, and told me to mind about that school, because he was going to lay for me and lick me if I didn't drop that.

Next day he was drunk, and he went to Judge Thatcher's and bullyragged him and tried to make him give up the money, but he couldn't, and then he swore he'd make the law force him.

The judge and the widow went to law to get the court to take me away from him and let one of them be my guardian; but it was a new judge that had just come, and he didn't know the old man; so he said courts mustn't interfere and separate families if they could help it; said he'd druther not take a child away from its father. So Judge Thatcher and the widow had to quit on the business.

That pleased the old man till he couldn't rest. He said he'd cowhide me till I was black and blue if I didn't raise some money for him. I borrowed three dollars from Judge Thatcher and pap took it and got drunk and went a-blowing around and cussing and whooping and carrying on; and he kept it up all over town, with a tin pan till most midnight; then they jailed him, and next day they had him before court and jailed him again for a week. But he said *he* was satisfied; said he was boss of his son and he'd make it warm for *him*.

When he got out the new judge said he was agoing to make a man of him. So he took him to his own house, and dressed him up clean and nice, and had him to breakfast and dinner and supper with the family, and was just old pie to him, so to speak. And after supper he talked to him about temperance and such things till the old man cried, and said he'd been a fool, and fooled away his life; but now he was agoing to turn over a new leaf and be a man nobody wouldn't be ashamed of, and he hoped the judge would help him and not look down on him. The judge said he could hug him for them words; so *he* cried, and his wife she cried, and the old man cried again; said he'd been a man that had always been misunderstood, before, and the judge said he believed it. The old man said that what a man wanted that was down, was sympathy; and the judge said it was so;

so they cried again. And when it was bedtime, the old man rose up and held out his hand and says:

"Look at it, gentlemen and ladies all; take a-hold of it; shake it. There's a hand that was the hand of a hog; but it ain't so no more; it's the hand of a man that's started in on a new life and 'll die before he'll go back. You mark them words—don't forget I said them. It's a clean hand, now; shake it—don't be afeard."

So they shook it, one after the other, all around, and cried. The judge's wife she kissed it. Then the old man he signed a pledge—

REFORMING THE DRUNKARD.

made his mark. The judge said it was the holiest time on record, or something like that. Then they tucked the old man into a beautiful room, which was the spare room, and in the night some time he got powerful thirsty and clumb out onto the porch-roof and slid down a stanchion and traded his new coat for a jug of forty-rod, and clumb back again and had a good old time; and towards daylight he crawled out again, drunk as a fiddler, and rolled off the porch and broke his left arm in two places and was most froze to death when somebody found him after sun-up. And when they come to look at that spare room, they had to take soundings before they could navigate it.

The judge he felt kind of sore. He said he reckoned a body could reform the old man with a shot-gun, maybe, but he didn't know no other way.

FALLING FROM GRACE.

Chapter VI

GETTING OUT OF THE WAY.

WELL, pretty soon the old man was up and around again, and then he went for Judge Thatcher in the courts to make him give up that money, and he went for me, too, for not stopping school. He catched me a couple of times and thrashed me, but I went to school just the same, and dodged him or out-run him most of the time. I didn't want to go to school, much, before, but I reckoned I'd go now to spite pap. That law trial was a slow business; appeared like they warn't ever going to get started on it; so every now and then, all winter, the old man would lay for me and catch me, and then I'd borrow two or three dollars off of the judge for him, to keep from getting a cowhiding. Every time he got money he got drunk; and every time he got drunk he raised Cain around town; and every time he raised Cain he got jailed. He was just suited—this kind of thing was right in his line.

He got to hanging around the widow's too much, and so she told him, at last, that if he didn't quit using around there she would make trouble for him. Well, *wasn't* he mad? He said he would show who was Huck Finn's boss. So he watched out for me one day in the spring, and catched me, and took me up the river about three mile in a skiff and crossed over to the Illinois shore where it was woody and there warn't no houses but an old log hut in a place where the timber was so thick you couldn't find it if you didn't know where it was.

He kept me with him all the time and I never got a chance to run off. We lived in that old cabin, and he always locked the door and put the key under his head, nights. He had a gun, which he had stole, I reckon, and we fished and hunted, and that was what we lived on. Every little while he locked me in and went down to the store, three miles, to the ferry, and traded fish and game for whisky and fetched it home and got drunk and had a good time, and licked me. The widow she found out where I was, by and by, and she sent a man over to try to get hold of me, but pap drove him off with the

SOLID COMFORT.

gun, and it warn't long after that till I was used to being where I was, and liked it, all but the cowhide part.

It was kind of lazy and jolly, laying off comfortable, all day, smoking and fishing, and no books nor study. Two months or more run along, and my clothes got to be all rags and dirt, and I didn't see how I'd ever got to like it so well at the widow's where you had to wash, and eat on a plate, and comb up, and go to bed and get up regular, and be forever bothering over a book and have old Miss Watson pecking at you all the time. I didn't want to go back no more. I had stopped cussing, because the widow didn't like it; but now I took to it again, because pap hadn't no objections. It was pretty good times up in the woods there, take it all around.

But by and by pap got too handy with his hick'ry, and I couldn't stand it. I was all over welts. He got to going away so much, too, and locking me in. Once he locked me in and was gone three days. It was dreadful lonesome. I judged he had got drownded and I wasn't ever going to get out any more. I was scared. I made up my mind I would fix up some way to leave there. I had tried to get out of that cabin many a time, but I couldn't find no way. There warn't a window to it big enough for a dog to get through. I couldn't get up the chimbly, it was too narrow. The door was thick, solid oak slabs. Pap was pretty careful not to leave a knife or anything in the cabin when he was away; I reckon I had hunted the place over as much as a hundred times; well, I was most all the time at it, because it was about the only way to put in the time. But this time I found something at last; I found an old rusty wood-saw without any handle; it was laid in between a rafter and the clapboards of the roof. I greased it up and went to work. There was an old horse-blanket nailed against the logs at the far end of the cabin behind the table, to keep the wind from blowing through the chinks and putting the candle out. I got under the table and raised the blanket and went to work to saw a section of the big bottom log out, big enough to let me through. Well, it was a good long job, but I was getting towards the end of it when I heard pap's gun in the woods. I got rid of the signs of my work, and dropped the blanket and hid my saw, and pretty soon pap come in.

Pap warn't in a good humor—so he was his natural self. He said he was down to town, and everything was going wrong. His lawyer said he reckoned he would win his lawsuit and get the money, if they ever got started on the trial, but then there was ways to put it off a long time and Judge Thatcher knowed how to do it. And he said people allowed there'd be another trial to get me away from him and give me to the widow for my guardian, and they guessed it would win, this time. This shook me up considerable, because I didn't want to go back to the widow's any more and be so cramped up and sivilized, as they called it. Then the old man got to cussing, and cussed everything and everybody he could think of, and then cussed them all over again to make sure he hadn't skipped any, and after that he polished off with a kind of a general cuss all round, including a considerable parcel of people which he didn't know the names of, and so called them What's-his-name, when he got to them, and went right along with his cussing.

He said he would like to see the widow get me. He said he would watch out, and if they tried to come any such game on him he knowed of a place six or seven mile off, to stow me in, where they might hunt till they dropped and they couldn't find me. That made me pretty uneasy again, but only for a minute; I reckoned I wouldn't stay on hand till he got that chance.

The old man made me go to the skiff and fetch the things he had got. There was a fifty-pound sack of corn meal, and a side of bacon, ammunition, and a four-gallon jug of whisky, and an old book and two newspapers for wadding, besides some tow. I toted up a load, and went back and set down on the bow of the skiff to rest. I thought it all over and I reckoned I would walk off with the gun and some fishing lines, and take to the woods when I run away. I guessed I wouldn't stay in one place, but just tramp right across the country,

THINKING IT OVER.

mostly night-times, and hunt and fish to keep alive, and so get so far away that the old man nor the widow couldn't ever find me any more. I judged I would saw out and leave that night if pap got drunk enough, and I reckoned he would. I got so full of it I didn't notice how long I was staying till the old man hollered and asked me whether I was asleep or drownded.

I got the things all up to the cabin, and then it was about dark. While I was cooking supper the old man took a swig or two and got sort of warmed up, and went to ripping again. He had been drunk over in town, and laid in the gutter all night, and he was a sight to look at. A body would a thought he was Adam, he was just all mud. Whenever his liquor begun to work, he most always went for the govment. This time he says:

"Call this a govment! Why, just look at it and see what it's like. Here's the law a-standing ready to take a man's son away from him—a man's own son, which he has had all the trouble and all the anxiety and all the expense of raising. Yes, just as that man has got that son raised at last, and ready to go to work and begin to do suthin' for *him* and give him a rest, the law up and goes for him. And they call *that* govment! That ain't all, nuther. The law backs that old Judge Thatcher up and helps him to keep me out o' my property. Here's what the law does. The law takes a man worth six thousand dollars and up'ards, and jams him into an old trap of a cabin like this, and lets him go round in clothes that ain't fitten for a hog. They call that govment! A man can't git his rights in a govment like this. Sometimes I've a mighty notion to just leave the country for good and all. Yes, and I *told* 'em so; I told old Thatcher so, to his face. Lots of 'em heard me, and can tell what I said. Says I, for two cents I'd leave the blamed country and never come a-near it agin. Them's the very words. I says, look at my hat—if you call it a hat—but the lid raises up and the rest of it goes down till it's below my chin, and then it ain't rightly a hat at all, but more like my head was shoved up through a j'int o' stove pipe. Look at it, says I—such a hat for me to wear—one of the wealthiest men in this town, if I could git my rights.

"O, yes, this is a wonderful govment, wonderful. Why looky-here. There was a free nigger there, from Ohio; a mulatter, most as white as a white man. He had the whitest shirt on you ever see, too, and the shiniest hat; and there ain't a man in that town that's got as fine clothes as what he had; and he had a gold watch and chain, and a silver-headed cane—the awfulest old gray-headed nabob in the State. And what do you think? they said he was a p'fessor in a

college, and could talk all kinds of languages, and knowed everything. And that ain't the wust. They said he could *vote*, when he
was at home. Well that let me out. Thinks I, what is the country a-
coming to? It was 'lection day, and I was just about to go and vote,
myself, if I warn't too drunk to git there; but when they told me
there was a state in this country where they'd let that nigger vote, I
drawed out. I says I'll never vote agin. Them's the very words I said;
they all heard me; and the country may rot, for all me—I'll never
vote agin as long as I live. And to see the cool way of that nigger—
why he wouldn't a give me the road if I hadn't shoved him out o' the
way. I says to the people, why ain't this nigger put up at auction and
sold?—that's what I want to know. And what do you reckon they
said? Why they said he couldn't be sold till he'd been in the State
six months, and he hadn't been there that long yet. There, now—
that's a specimen. They call that a govment that can't sell a free nigger till he's been in the State six months. Here's a govment that
calls itself a govment, and lets on to be a govment, and thinks it
is a govment, and yet's got to set stock still for six whole months
before it can take a-hold of a prowling, thieving, infernal, white-
shirted free nigger and—"

Pap was agoing on so, he never noticed where his old limber legs
was taking him to, so he went head over heels over the tub of salt
pork and barked both shins, and the rest of his speech was all the
hottest kind of language—mostly hove at the nigger and the govment, though he give the tub some, too, all along, here and there.
He hopped around the cabin considerable, first on one leg and then
on the other, holding first one shin and then the other one, and at
last he let out with his left foot all of a sudden and fetched the tub a
rattling kick. But it warn't good judgment, because that was the
boot that had a couple of his toes leaking out of the front end of it;
so now he raised a howl that fairly made a body's hair raise, and
down he went in the dirt, and rolled there, and held his toes; and the
cussing he done then laid over anything he had ever done previous.
He said so his own self, afterwards. He had heard old Sowberry Ha-
gan in his best days, and he said it laid over him, too; but I reckon
that was sort of piling it on, maybe.

After supper pap took the jug and said he had enough whisky
there for two drunks and one delirium tremens. That was always

his word. I judged he would be blind drunk in about an hour, and then I would steal the key, or saw myself out, one or t'other. He drank and drank, and tumbled down on his blankets, by and by; but

RAISING A HOWL.

luck didn't run my way. He didn't go sound asleep, but was uneasy. He groaned and moaned and thrashed around this way and that for a long time. At last I got so sleepy I couldn't keep my eyes open, all I could do, and so before I knowed what I was about I was sound asleep, and the candle burning.

I don't know how long I was asleep, but all of a sudden there was an awful scream, and I was up. There was pap, looking wild and skipping around every which way and yelling about snakes. He said they was crawling up his legs; and then he would give a jump and scream, and say one had bit him on the cheek—but I couldn't see no snakes. He started, and run round and round the cabin, hollering "Take him off! take him off! he's biting me on the neck!" I never see a man look so wild in the eyes. Pretty soon he was all fagged out and fell down, panting; then he rolled over and over, wonderful fast, kicking things every which way, and striking and grabbing at the air with his hands, and screaming, and saying there was devils ahold of him. He wore out, by and by, and laid still a while, moaning. Then he laid stiller, and didn't make a sound. I could hear the owls and the wolves, away off in the woods, and it seemed terrible still. He was laying over by the corner. By and by he raised up, part way, and listened, with his head to one side. He says, very low:

"Tramp—tramp—tramp; that's the dead; tramp—tramp—tramp; they're coming after me; but I won't go— O, they're here! don't touch me—don't! hands off—they're cold; let go— O, let a poor devil alone!"

Then he went down on all fours and crawled off begging them to let him alone, and he rolled himself up in his blanket and wallowed in under the old pine table, still a begging; and then he went to crying. I could hear him through the blanket.

By and by he rolled out and jumped up on his feet looking wild, and he see me and went for me. He chased me round and round the place, with a clasp-knife, calling me the angel of death and saying he would kill me and then I couldn't come for him no more. I begged, and told him I was only Huck, but he laughed *such* a screechy laugh, and roared and cussed, and kept on chasing me up. Once when I turned short and dodged under his arm he made a grab and got me by the jacket between my shoulders and I thought I was gone; but I slid out of the jacket quick as lightning, and saved myself. Pretty soon he was all tired out and dropped down with his back against the door, and said he would rest a minute and then kill me. He put his knife under him, and said he would sleep and get strong, and then he would see who was who.

So he dozed off, pretty soon. By and by I got the old split-bottom chair and clumb up, as easy as I could, not to make any noise, and got down the gun. I slipped the ramrod down it to make sure it was loaded, and then I laid it across the turnip barrel, pointing towards pap, and set down behind it to wait for him to stir. And how slow and still the time did drag along.

CHAPTER VII.

"GIT UP!"

"Git up! What you 'bout!"

I opened my eyes and looked around, trying to make out where I was. It was after sun-up, and I had been sound asleep. Pap was standing over me, looking sour—and sick, too. He says—

"What you doin' with this gun?"

I judged he didn't know nothing about what he had been doing, so I says:

"Somebody tried to get in, so I was laying for him."

"Why didn't you roust me out?"

"Well I tried to, but I couldn't; I couldn't budge you."

"Well, all right. Don't stand there palavering all day, but out with you and see if there's a fish on the lines for breakfast. I'll be along in a minute."

He unlocked the door and I cleared out, up the river bank. I noticed some pieces of limbs and such things floating down, and a sprinkling of bark; so I knowed the river had begun to rise. I reckoned I would have great times, now, if I was over at the town. The June rise used to be always luck for me; because as soon as that rise begins, here comes cord-wood floating down, and pieces of log rafts—sometimes a dozen logs together; so all you have to do is to catch them and sell them to the wood yards and the sawmill.

I went along up the bank with one eye out for pap and t'other one out for what the rise might fetch along. Well all at once, here comes a canoe; just a beauty, too, about thirteen or fourteen foot long, riding high like a duck. I shot head first off of the bank, like a frog, clothes and all on, and struck out for the canoe. I just expected

there'd be somebody laying down in it, because people often done
that to fool folks, and when a chap had pulled a skiff out most to it
they'd raise up and laugh at him. But it warn't so this time. It was a
drift-canoe, sure enough, and I clumb in and paddled her ashore.
Thinks I, the old man will be glad when he sees this—she's worth
ten dollars. But when I got to shore pap wasn't in sight yet, and as I
was running her into a little creek like a gully, all hung over with
vines and willows, I struck another idea; I judged I'd hide her good,
and then, 'stead of taking to the woods when I run off, I'd go down
the river about fifty mile and camp in one place for good, and not
have such a rough time tramping on foot.

It was pretty close to the shanty, and I thought I heard the old
man coming all the time; but I got her hid and then I out and looked
around a bunch of willows; and there was the old man down the
path apiece just drawing a bead on a bird with his gun. So he hadn't
seen anything.

When he got along I was hard at it taking up a trot-line. He
abused me a little for being so slow, but I told him I fell in the river
and that was what made me so long. I knowed he would see I was
wet, and then he would be asking questions. We got five cat-fish off
of the lines and went home.

THE SHANTY.

While we laid off, after breakfast, to sleep up, both of us being about wore out, I got to thinking that if I could fix up some way to keep pap and the widow from trying to follow me, it would be a certainer thing than trusting to luck to get far enough off before they missed me; you see, all kinds of things might happen. Well, I didn't see no way for a while, but by and by pap raised up, a minute, to drink another barrel of water, and he says:

"Another time a man comes a-prowling round here, you roust me out, you hear? That man warn't here for no good. I'd a shot him. Next time, you roust me out, you hear?"

Then he dropped down and went to sleep again—but what he had been saying give me the very idea I wanted. I says to myself, I can fix it now so nobody won't think of following me.

About twelve o'clock we turned out and went along up the bank. The river was coming up pretty fast, and lots of drift-wood going by on the rise. By and by, along comes part of a log raft—nine logs fast together. We went out with the skiff and towed it ashore. Then we had dinner. Anybody but pap would a waited and seen the day through, so as to catch more stuff; but that warn't pap's style. Nine logs was enough for one time; he must shove right over to town and sell. So he locked me in and took the skiff and started off towing the raft about half past three. I judged he wouldn't come back that night. I waited till I reckoned he had got a good start, then I out with my saw and went to work on that log again. Before he was t'other side of the river I was out of the hole; him and his raft was just a speck on the water away off yonder.

I took the sack of corn meal and took it to where the canoe was hid, and shoved the vines and branches apart and put it in; then I done the same with the side of bacon; then the whisky jug; I took all the coffee and sugar there was, and all the ammunition; I took the wadding; I took the bucket and gourd, I took a dipper and a tin cup, and my old saw, and two blankets, and the skillet and the coffee pot. I took fish lines and matches and other things—everything that was worth a cent. I cleaned out the place. I wanted an ax, but there wasn't any, only the one out at the wood pile, and I knowed why I was going to leave that. I fetched out the gun, and now I was done.

I had wore the ground a good deal crawling out of the hole and dragging out so many things. So I fixed that as good as I could from the outside by scattering dust on the place, which covered up the smoothness and the sawdust. Then I fixed the piece of log back into its place and put two rocks under it and one against it to hold it there,—for it was bent up, at that place, and didn't quite touch ground. If you stood four or five foot away and didn't know it was sawed, you wouldn't ever notice it; and besides, this was the back of the cabin and it warn't likely anybody would go fooling around there.

It was all grass, clear to the canoe; so I hadn't left a track. I followed around to see. I stood on the bank and looked out over the river. All safe. So I took the gun and went up a piece into the woods and was hunting around for some birds, when I see a wild pig; hogs soon went wild in them bottoms after they had got away from the prairie farms. I shot this fellow and took him into camp.

I took the ax and smashed in the door—I beat it and hacked it considerable, a-doing it. I fetched the pig in and took him back nearly to the table and hacked into his throat with the ax, and laid him down on the ground to bleed—I say ground, because it *was* ground—hard packed, and no boards. Well, next I took an old sack and put a lot of big rocks in it,—all I could drag—and I started it from the pig and dragged it to the door and through the woods down

SHOOTING THE PIG.

to the river and dumped it in, and down it sunk, out of sight. You could easy see that something had been dragged over the ground. I did wish Tom Sawyer was there, I knowed he would take an interest in this kind of business, and throw in the fancy touches. Nobody could spread himself like Tom Sawyer in such a thing as that.

Well, last I pulled out some of my hair, and bloodied the ax good and stuck it on the back side, and slung the ax in the corner. Then I took up the pig and held him to my breast with my jacket (so he couldn't drip,) till I got a good piece below the house and then dumped him into the river. Now I thought of something else. So I went and got the bag of meal and my old saw out of the canoe and fetched them to the house. I took the bag to where it used to stand and ripped a hole in the bottom of it with the saw, for there warn't no knives and forks on the place—pap done everything with his clasp-knife, about the cooking. Then I carried the sack about a hundred yards across the grass and through the willows east of the house, to a shallow lake that was five mile wide and full of rushes—and ducks too, you might say, in the season. There was a slough or a creek leading out of it on the other side, that went miles away, I don't know where, but it didn't go to the river. The meal sifted out and made a little track all the way to the lake. I dropped pap's whetstone there, too, so as to look like it had been done by accident. Then I tied up the rip in the meal sack with a string, so it wouldn't leak no more, and took it and my saw to the canoe again.

It was about dark, now; so I dropped the canoe down the river under some willows that hung over the bank, and waited for the moon to rise. I made fast to a willow; then I took a bite to eat, and by and by laid down in the canoe to smoke a pipe and lay out a plan. I says to myself, they'll follow the track of that sackful of rocks to the shore and then drag the river for me. And they'll follow that meal track to the lake and go browsing down the creek that leads out of it to find the robbers that killed me and took the things. They won't ever hunt the river for anything but my dead carcass. They'll soon get tired of that, and won't bother no more about me. All right; I can stop anywhere I want to. Jackson's Island is good enough for me; I know that island pretty well, and nobody ever comes there. And then I can paddle over to town, nights, and slink around and pick up things I want. Jackson's Island's the place.

I was pretty tired, and the first thing I knowed, I was asleep. When I woke up I didn't know where I was, for a minute. I set up and looked around, a little scared. Then I remembered. The river looked miles and miles across. The moon was so bright I could a counted the drift logs that went a-slipping along, black and still, hundreds of yards out from shore. Everything was dead quiet, and it looked late, and *smelt* late. You know what I mean—I don't know the words to put it in.

I took a good gap and a stretch and was just going to unhitch and start when I heard a sound away over the water. I listened. Pretty soon I made it out. It was that dull kind of a regular sound that comes from oars working in rowlocks when it's a still night. I peeped out through the willow branches, and there it was—a skiff, away across the water. I couldn't tell how many was in it. It kept a-coming, and when it was abreast of me I see there warn't but one man in it. Thinks I, maybe it's pap, though I warn't expecting him. He dropped below me, with the current, and by and by he come a-swinging up shore in the easy water and he went by so close I could a reached out the gun and touched him. Well, it *was* pap, sure enough—and sober, too, by the way he laid to his oars.

I didn't lose no time. The next minute I was a-spinning down stream, soft but quick, in the shade of the bank. I made two mile and a half and then struck out a quarter of a mile or more towards the middle of the river, because pretty soon I would be passing the ferry landing and people might see me and hail me. I got out amongst the drift wood and then laid down in the bottom of the canoe and let her float. I laid there and had a good rest and a smoke out of my pipe, looking away into the sky, not a cloud in it. The sky looks ever so deep when you lay down on your back in the moonshine; I never knowed it before. And how far a body can hear on the water such nights! I heard people talking at the ferry landing. I heard what they said, too, every word of it. One man said it was getting towards the long days and the short nights, now. T'other one said *this* warn't one of the short ones, he reckoned—and then they laughed, and he said it over again and they laughed again; then they waked up another fellow and told him, and laughed, but he didn't laugh; he ripped out something brisk and said let him alone. The first fellow said he 'lowed to tell it to his old woman—she would think it was pretty good; but he said that warn't nothing to some things he had said in his time. I heard one man say it was nearly three o'clock and he hoped daylight wouldn't wait more than about a week longer. After that the talk got further and further away and I couldn't make out the words any more but I could hear the mumble; and now and then a laugh, too, but it seemed a long ways off.

I was away below the ferry now. I rose up and there was Jackson's Island, about two mile and a half down stream, heavy-timbered and

TAKING A REST.

standing up out of the middle of the river, big and dark and solid, like a steamboat without any lights. There warn't any signs of the bar at the head—it was all under water, now.

It didn't take me long to get there. I shot past the head at a ripping rate, the current was so swift, and then I got into the dead water and landed on the side towards the Illinois shore. I run the canoe into a deep dent in the bank that I knowed about; I had to part the willow branches to get in; and when I made fast nobody could a seen the canoe from the outside.

I went up and set down on a log at the head of the island and looked out on the big river and the black drift wood, and away over to the town, three mile away, where there was three or four lights twinkling. A monstrous big lumber-raft was about a mile up stream, coming along down, with a lantern in the middle of it. I watched it come creeping down, and when it was most abreast of where I stood I heard a man say, "Stern oars, there!—heave her head to stabboard!" I heard that just as plain as if the man was by my side.

There was a little gray in the sky, now; so I stepped into the woods and laid down for a nap before breakfast.

Chapter VIII.

The sun was up so high when I waked, that I judged it was after eight o'clock. I laid there in the grass and the cool shade, thinking about things and feeling rested and ruther comfortable and satisfied. I could see the sun out at one or two holes, but mostly it was big trees all about, and gloomy in there amongst them. There was freckled places on the ground where the light sifted down through the leaves, and the freckled places swapped about, a little, showing there was a little breeze up there. A couple of squirrels set on a limb and jabbered at me very friendly.

IN THE WOODS.

I was powerful lazy and comfortable—didn't want to get up and cook breakfast. Well, I was dozing off again when I thinks I hears a deep sound of "Boom!" away up the river. I rouses up and rests on my elbow and listens; pretty soon I hears it again. I hopped up and went and looked out at a hole in the leaves, and I see a bunch of smoke laying on the water a long ways up—about abreast the ferry. And there was the ferry boat full of people, floating along down. I knowed what was the matter, now. "Boom!" I see the white smoke squirt out of the ferryboat's side. You see, they was firing cannons over the water, trying to make my carcass come to the top.

I was pretty hungry, but it warn't going to do for me to start a fire, because they might see the smoke. So I set there and watched the cannon-smoke and listened to the boom. The river was a mile wide, there, and it always looks pretty on a summer morning—so I was having a good enough time seeing them hunt for my remainders, if I only had a bite to eat. Well, then I happened to think how they always put quicksilver in loaves of bread and float them off because they always go right to the drownded carcass and stop there. So says I, I'll keep a look-out; and if any of them's floating around after me, I'll give them a show. I changed to the Illinois edge of the island to see what luck I could have, and I warn't disappointed. A big double-

WATCHING THE BOAT.

loaf come along, and I most got it, with a long stick, but my foot slipped and she floated out further. Of course I was where the current set in the closest to the shore—I knowed enough for that. But by and by along comes another one, and this time I won. I took out the plug and shook out the little dab of quicksilver, and set my teeth in. It was "baker's bread"—what the quality eat—none of your low-down corn-pone.

I got a good place amongst the leaves, and set there on a log munching the bread, and watching the ferry-boat, and very well satisfied. And then something struck me. I says, now I reckon the widow or the parson or somebody prayed that this bread would find me, and here it has gone and done it. So there ain't no doubt but there is something in that thing. That is, there's something in it when a body like the widow or the parson prays, but it don't work for me, and I reckon it don't work for only just the right kind.

I lit a pipe and had a good long smoke and went on watching. The ferry-boat was floating with the current, and I allowed I'd have a chance to see who was aboard when she come along, because she would come in close, where the bread did. When she'd got pretty well along down towards me, I put out my pipe and went to where I fished out the bread and laid down behind a log on the bank in a little open place. Where the log forked I could peep through.

By and by she come along, and she drifted in so close that they could a run out a plank and walked ashore. Most everybody was on the boat. Pap, and Judge Thatcher, and Becky Thatcher, and Jo Harper, and Tom Sawyer and his old aunt Polly, and Sid and Mary, and plenty more. Everybody was talking about the murder, but the captain broke in and says:

"Look sharp, now; the current sets in the closest here, and maybe he's washed ashore and got tangled amongst the brush at the water's edge—I hope so, anyway."

I didn't hope so. They all crowded up and leaned over the rails, nearly in my face, and kept still, watching with all their might. I could see them first-rate, but they couldn't see me. Then the captain sung out:

"Stand away!" and the cannon let off such a blast right before me that it made me deef with the noise and pretty near blind with the smoke, and I judged I was gone. If they'd a had some bullets in I reckon they'd a got the corpse they was after. Well, I see I warn't hurt, thanks to goodness. The boat floated on and went out of sight around the shoulder of the island. I could hear the booming, now and then, further and further off, and by and by after an hour, I didn't hear it no more. The island was three mile long. I judged they had got to the foot, and was giving it up. But they didn't, yet awhile. They turned around the foot of the island and started up the channel on the Missouri side, under steam, and booming once in a while as they went. I crossed over to that side and watched them. When they got abreast the head of the island they quit shooting and dropped over to the Missouri shore and went home to the town.

I knowed I was all right now. Nobody else would come a-hunting after me. I got my traps out of the canoe and made me a nice camp in the thick woods. I made a kind of a tent out of my blankets to put my things under so the rain couldn't get at them. I catched a catfish and haggled him open with my saw, and towards sundown I started my camp fire and had supper. Then I set out a line to catch some fish for breakfast.

When it was dark I set by my camp fire smoking, and feeling pretty satisfied; but by and by it got sort of lonesome, and so I went and set on the bank and listened to the currents washing along, and counted the stars and drift-logs and rafts that come down, and then went to bed; there ain't no better way to put in time when you are lonesome; you can't stay so, you soon get over it.

And so for three days and nights. No difference—just the same thing. But the next day I went exploring around down through the island. I was boss of it; it all belonged to me, so to say, and I wanted to know all about it; but mainly I wanted to put in the time. I found plenty strawberries, ripe and prime; and green summer-grapes, and green razberries; and the green blackberries was just beginning to show. They would all come handy by and by, I judged.

Well, I went fooling along in the deep woods till I judged I warn't far from the foot of the island. I had my gun along, but I hadn't shot nothing; it was for protection; thought I would kill some game nigh home. About this time I mighty near stepped on a good sized snake, and it went sliding off through the grass and flowers, and I after it, trying to get a shot at it. I clipped along, and all of a sudden I bounded right onto the ashes of a camp fire that was still smoking.

My heart jumped up amongst my lungs. I never waited for to look further, but uncocked my gun and went sneaking back on my tip-toes as fast as ever I could. Every now and then I stopped, a second, amongst the thick leaves, and listened; but my breath come so hard I couldn't hear nothing else. I slunk along another piece further, then listened again; and so on, and so on; if I see a stump, I took it for a man; if I trod on a stick and broke it, it made me feel like a person had cut one of my breaths in two and I only got half, and the short half, too.

When I got to camp I warn't feeling very brash, there warn't much sand in my craw; but I says, this ain't no time to be fooling around. So I got all my traps into my canoe again so as to have them out of sight, and I put out the fire and scattered the ashes around to look like an old last-year's camp, and then clumb a tree.

I reckon I was up in the tree two hours; but I didn't see nothing, I didn't hear nothing—I only *thought* I heard and seen as much as a

DISCOVERING THE CAMP FIRE.

thousand things. Well I couldn't stay up there forever; so at last I got down, but I kept in the thick woods and on the lookout all the time. All I could get to eat was berries and what was left over from breakfast.

By the time it was night I was pretty hungry. So when it was good and dark I slid out from shore before moonrise and paddled over to the Illinois bank—about a quarter of a mile. I went out in the woods and cooked a supper, and I had about made up my mind I would stay there all night, when I hear a *plunkety-plunk*, *plunkety-plunk*, and says to myself, horses coming; and next I hear people's voices. I got everything into the canoe as quick as I could, and then went creeping through the woods to see what I could find out. I hadn't got far when I hear a man say:

"We better camp here, if we can find a good place; the horses is about beat out. Let's look around."

I didn't wait, but shoved out and paddled away easy. I tied up in the old place, and reckoned I would sleep in the canoe.

I didn't sleep much. I couldn't, somehow, for thinking. And every time I waked up I thought somebody had me by the neck. So the sleep didn't do me no good. By and by I says to myself, I can't live this way; I'm agoing to find out who it is that's here on the island with me; I'll find it out or bust. Well, I felt better, right off.

So I took my paddle and slid out from shore just a step or two and then let the canoe drop along down amongst the shadows. The moon was shining, and outside of the shadows it made it most as light as day. I poked along well onto an hour, everything still as rocks and sound asleep. Well by this time I was most down to the foot of the island. A little ripply cool breeze begun to blow, and that was as good as saying the night was about done. I give her a turn with the paddle and brung her nose to shore; then I got my gun and slipped out and into the edge of the woods. I set down there on a log and looked out through the leaves. I see the moon go off watch and the darkness begin to blanket the river. But in a little while I see a pale streak over the tree tops, and knowed the day was coming. So I took my gun and slipped off towards where I had run across that camp fire, stopping every minute or two to listen. But I hadn't no luck, somehow; I couldn't seem to find the place. But by and by, sure enough, I catched a glimpse of fire, away through the trees. I went for it, cautious and slow. By and by I was close enough to have a look, and there laid a man on the ground. It most give me the fantods. He had a blanket around his head, and his head was nearly in the fire. I set there behind a clump of bushes, in about six foot of him, and kept my eyes on him steady. It was getting gray daylight, now. Pretty soon he gapped, and stretched himself, and hove off the blanket, and it was Miss Watson's Jim! I bet I was glad to see him. I says:

"Hello, Jim!" and skipped out.

He bounced up and stared at me wild. Then he drops down on his knees and puts his hands together and says:

"Doan' hurt me—don't! I hain't ever done no harm to a ghos'. I awluz liked dead people, en done all I could for 'em. You go en git in

JIM AND THE GHOST.

de river agin, whah you b'longs, en doan' do nuffn to ole Jim, 'at 'uz awluz yo' fren'."

Well, I warn't long making him understand I warn't dead. I was ever so glad to see Jim. I warn't lonesome now. I told him I warn't afraid of *him* telling the people where I was. I talked along, but he only set there and looked at me; never said nothing. Then I says:

"It's good daylight. Le's get breakfast. Make up your camp fire good."

"What's de use er makin' up de camp fire to cook strawbries en sich truck? But you got a gun—hain't you? Den we kin git sumfn better den strawbries."

"Strawberries and such truck," I says. "Is that what you live on?"

"I couldn' git nuffn else," he says.

"Why, how long you been on the island, Jim?"

"I come heah de night arter you's killed."

"What, all that time?"

"Yes-indeedy."

"And ain't you had nothing but that kind of rubbage to eat?"

"No, sah—nuffn else."

"Well, you must be most starved, ain't you?"

"I reck'n I could eat a hoss. I think I could. How long you ben on de islan'?"

"Since the night I got killed."

"No! W'y what has you lived on? But you got a gun. O, yes, you got a gun. Dat's good. Now you kill sumfn, en I'll make up de fire."

So we went over to where the canoe was, and while he built a fire in a grassy open place amongst the trees, I fetched meal and bacon and coffee, and coffee pot and frying pan, and sugar and tin cups, and the nigger was set back considerable, because he reckoned it was all done with witchcraft. I catched a good big catfish, too, and Jim cleaned him with his knife and fried him.

When breakfast was ready, we lolled on the grass and eat it smoking hot. Jim laid it in with all his might, for he was most about starved. Then when we had got pretty well stuffed, we laid off and lazied.

By and by Jim says:

"But looky-here, Huck, who wuz it dat 'uz killed in dat shanty, ef it warn't you?"

Then I told him the whole thing, and he said it was smart. He said Tom Sawyer couldn't get up no better plan than what I had. Then I says:

"How do you come to be here, Jim, and how'd you get here?"

He looked pretty uneasy, and didn't say nothing for a minute. Then he says:

"Maybe I better not tell."

"Why, Jim?"

"Well, dey's reasons. But you wouldn' tell on me ef I 'uz to tell you, would you, Huck?"

"Blamed if I would, Jim."

"Well, I b'lieve you, Huck. I—I *run off*."

"Jim!"

"But mind, you said you wouldn't tell—you know you said you wouldn't tell, Huck."

"Well, I did. I said I wouldn't, and I'll stick to it. Honest *injun*, I will. People would call me a low-down ablitionist and despise me for keeping mum—but that don't make no difference. I ain't agoing to tell, and I ain't agoing back there, anyways. So now, le's know all about it."

"Well, you see, it 'uz dis way. Ole missus—dat's Miss Watson—she pecks on me all de time, en treats me pooty rough, but she awluz said she wouldn' sell me down to Orleans. But I noticed dey wuz a nigger trader roun' de place considable, lately, en I begin to git oneasy. Well, one night I creeps to de do', pooty late, en de do' warn't quite shet, en I hear ole missus tell de widder she gwyne to sell me down to Orleans, but she didn' want to, but she could git eight hund'd dollars for me en it 'uz sich a big stack o' money she couldn' resis'. De widder she try to git her to say she wouldn' do it, but I never waited to hear de res'. I lit out, mighty quick, I tell you.

"I tuck out en shin down de hill en 'spec to steal a skift 'long de sho' som'ers 'bove de town, but dey wuz people a-stirrin', yit, so I hid in de ole tumble-down cooper shop on de bank to wait for everybody to go 'way. Well, I wuz dah all night. Dey wuz somebody roun' all de time. 'Long 'bout six in de mawnin' skifts begin to go by, en 'bout eight er nine every skift dat went 'long wuz talkin' 'bout how yo' pap come over to de town en say you's killed. Dese las' skifts wuz full o' ladies en genlmen agoin' over for to see de place. Sometimes dey'd pull up at de sho' en take a res' b'fo' dey started acrost, so by de talk I got to know all 'bout de killin'. I 'uz powerful sorry you's killed, Huck, but I ain't no mo', now.

"I laid dah under de shavin's all day. I 'uz hungry, but I warn't afeard; bekase I knowed ole missus en de widder wuz goin' to start to de camp-meetn' right arter breakfas' en be gone all day, en dey knows I goes off wid de cattle 'bout daylight, so dey wouldn' 'spec to see me roun' de place, en so dey wouldn' miss me tell arter dark in de evenin'. De yuther servants wouldn' miss me, kase dey'd shin out en take holiday, soon as de ole folks 'uz out'n de way.

"Well, when it come dark I tuck out up de river road en went 'bout two mile er more, to whah dey warn't no houses. I'd made up my mine 'bout what I's agwyne to do. You see, ef I kep' on tryin' to git away afoot, de dogs 'ud track me; ef I stole a skift to cross over, dey'd miss dat skift, you see, en dey'd know 'bout whah I'd lan' on de yuther side en whah to pick up my track. So I says, a raff is what I's arter; it doan' *make* no track.

"I see a light a-comin' roun' de p'int, bymeby, so I wade' in en shove' a log ahead o' me en swum more'n half way acrost de river en got in 'mongst de drift wood en kep' my head down low en kinder swum agin de current tell de raff come along. Den I swum to de stern uv it en tuck aholt. It clouded up en 'uz pooty dark for a little while. So I clumb up en laid down on de planks. De men 'uz all 'way yonder in de middle, whah de lantern wuz. De river wuz arisin' en dey wuz a good current; so I reck'n'd 'at by fo' in de mawnin' I'd be twenty-five mile down de river, en den I'd slip in, jis' b'fo' daylight, en swim asho' en take to de woods on de Illinoi side.

"But I didn' have no luck. When we 'uz mos' down to de head er de islan', a man begin to come aft wid de lantern. I see it warn't no use fer to wait, so I slid overboad, en struck out fer de islan'. Well, I had a notion I could lan' mos' anywhers, but I couldn't—bank too bluff. I 'uz mos' to de foot er de islan' b'fo' I foun' a good place. I went into de woods en jedged I wouldn' fool wid raffs no mo', long as dey move de lantern roun' so. I had my pipe en a plug er dog-leg en some matches in my cap, en dey warn't wet, so I 'uz all right."

"And so you ain't had no meat nor bread to eat all this time? Why didn't you get mud turkles?"

"How you gwyne to git'm? You can't slip up on um en grab um; en how's a body gwyne to hit um wid a rock? How could a body do it in de night? En I warn't gwyne to show mysef on de bank in de daytime."

"Well, that's so. You've had to keep in the woods all the time, of course. Did you hear 'em shooting the cannon?"

"O yes. I knowed dey was arter you. I see um go by heah; watched um thoo de bushes."

Some young birds come along, flying a yard or two at a time and lighting. Jim said it was a sign it was going to rain. He said it was a sign when young chickens flew that way, and so he reckoned it was the same way when young birds done it. I was going to catch some of them, but Jim wouldn't let me. He said it was death. He said his father laid mighty sick once, and some of them catched a bird, and his old granny said his father would die, and he did.

And Jim said you mustn't count the things you are going to cook for dinner, because that would bring bad luck. The same if you shook the table-cloth after sundown. And he said if a man owned a bee hive, and that man died, the bees must be told about it before sun-up next morning, or else the bees would all weaken down and quit work and die. Jim said bees wouldn't sting idiots; but I didn't believe that, because I had tried them lots of times myself, and they wouldn't sting me.

I had heard about some of these things before, but not all of them. Jim knowed all kinds of signs. He said he knowed most everything. I said it looked to me like all the signs was about bad luck, and so I asked him if there warn't any good-luck signs. He says:

"Mighty few—an' *dey* ain' no use to a body. What you want to know when good luck's a-comin' for? Want to keep it off?" And he said: "Ef you's got hairy arms en a hairy breas', it's a sign dat you's agwyne to be rich. Well, dey's some use in a sign like dat, 'kase it's so fur ahead. You see, maybe you's got to be po' a long time fust, en so you might git discourage' en kill yo'sef 'f you didn' know by de sign dat you gwyne to be rich bymeby."

"Have you got hairy arms and a hairy breast, Jim?"

"What's de use to ax dat question? Don' you see I has?"

"Well, are you rich?"

"No; but I ben rich wunst and gwyne to be rich agin. Wunst I had foteen dollars, but I tuck to specalat'n', en got busted out."

"What did you speculate in, Jim?"

"Well, fust I tackled stock."

"What kind of stock?"

"Why, live stock. Cattle, you know. I put ten dollars in a cow. But I ain' gwyne to resk no mo' money in stock. De cow up 'n' died on my han's."

"So you lost the ten dollars."

"No, I didn' lose it all. I on'y los' 'bout nine of it. I sole de hide en taller for a dollar en ten cents."

"You had five dollars and ten cents left. Did you speculate any more?"

"Yes. You know dat one-laigged nigger dat b'longs to ole Misto Bradish? Well, he sot up a bank, en say anybody dat put in a dollar would git fo' dollars mo' at de en' er de year. Well, all de niggers went in, but dey didn' have much. I wuz de on'y one dat had much. So I stuck out for mo' dan fo' dollars, en I said 'f I didn' git it I'd start a bank mysef. Well o' course dat nigger want to keep me out er de business, bekase he say dey warn't business 'nough for two banks, so he say I could put in my five dollars en he pay me thirty-five at de en' er de year.

"So I done it. Den I reck'n'd I'd inves' de thirty-five dollars right off en keep things a-movin'. Dey wuz a nigger name' Bob, dat had ketched a wood-flat, en his marster didn' know it; en I bought it off'n him en tole him to take de thirty-five dollars when de en' er de

MISTO BRADISH'S NIGGER.

year come; but somebody stole de wood-flat dat night, en nex' day de one-laigged nigger say de bank 's busted. So dey didn' none uv us git no money."

"What did you do with the ten cents, Jim?"

"Well, I 'uz gwyne to spen' it, but I had a dream, en de dream tole me to give it to a nigger name' Balum—Balum's Ass dey call him for short,—he's one er dem chuckleheads, you know. But he's lucky, dey say, en I see I warn't lucky. De dream say let Balum inves' de ten cents en he'd make a raise for me. Well, Balum he tuck de money, en when he wuz in church he hear de preacher say dat whoever give to de po' len' to de Lord, en boun' to git his money back a hund'd times. So Balum he tuck en give de ten cents to de po' en laid low to see what wuz gwyne to come of it."

"Well, what did come of it, Jim?"

"Nuffn' never come of it. I couldn' manage to k'leck dat money no way; en Balum he couldn'. I ain' gwyne to len' no mo' money 'dout I see de security. Boun' to git yo' money back a hund'd times, de preacher says! Ef I could git de ten *cents* back, I'd call it squah, en be glad er de chanst."

"Well, it's all right, anyway, Jim, long as you're going to be rich again some time or other."

"Yes—en I's rich now, come to look at it. I owns mysef, en I's wuth eight hund'd dollars. I wisht I had de money, I wouldn' want no mo'."

Chapter IX.

I WANTED to go and look at a place right about the middle of the island, that I'd found when I was exploring; so we started, and soon got to it, because the island was only three miles long and a quarter of a mile wide.

This place was a tolerable long, steep hill or ridge, about forty foot high. We had a rough time getting to the top, the sides was so steep and the bushes so thick. We tramped and clumb around all over it and by and by found a good big cavern in the rock, most up to the top on the side towards Illinois. The cavern was as big as two or three rooms bunched together, and Jim could stand up straight in it. It was cool in there. Jim was for putting our traps in there, right away, but I said we didn't want to be climbing up and down there all the time.

EXPLORING THE CAVE.

Jim said if we had the canoe hid in a good place and had all the traps in the cavern we could rush there if anybody was to come to the island, and they would never find us without dogs. And besides, he said them little birds had said it was going to rain, and did I want the things to get wet?

So we went back and got the canoe and paddled up abreast the cavern and lugged all the traps up there. Then we hunted up a place close by to hide the canoe in, amongst the thick willows. We took some fish off of the lines and set them again, and begun to get ready for dinner.

The door of the cavern was big enough to roll a hogshead in, and on one side of the door the floor stuck out a little bit and was flat and a good place to build a fire on. So we built it there and cooked dinner.

We spread the blankets inside for a carpet and eat our dinner in there. We put all the other things handy at the back of the cavern. Pretty soon it darkened up and begun to thunder and lighten; so the birds was right about it. Directly it begun to rain, and it rained like all fury, too, and I never see the wind blow so. It was one of these regular summer storms. It would get so dark that it looked all blue-black outside, and lovely; and the rain would thrash along by so thick that the trees off a little ways looked dim and spider-webby; and here would come a blast of wind that would bend the trees down and turn up the pale underside of the leaves; and then a perfect ripper of a gust would follow along and set the branches to tossing their arms as if they was just wild; and next, when it was just about the bluest and blackest—*fst!* it was as bright as glory and you'd have a little glimpse of tree-tops a-plunging about, away off yonder in the storm, hundreds of yards further than you could see before; dark as sin again in a second, and now you'd hear the thunder let go with an awful crash and then go rumbling, grumbling, tumbling down the sky towards the underside of the world, like rolling empty barrels

IN THE CAVE.

down stairs, where it's long stairs and they bounce a good deal, you know.

"Jim, this is nice," I says. "I wouldn't want to be nowhere else but here. Pass me along another hunk of fish and some hot corn-bread."

"Well, you wouldn't a ben here, 'f it hadn't a ben for Jim. You'd a ben down dah in de woods widout any dinner, en gittn' mos' drownded, too, dat you would, honey. Chickens knows when it's gwyne to rain, en so do de birds, chile."

The river went on raising and raising for ten or twelve days, till at last it was over the banks. The water was three or four foot deep on the island in the low places and on the Illinois bottom. On that side it was a good many miles wide; but on the Missouri side it was the same old distance across—a half a mile—because the Missouri shore was just a wall of high bluffs.

Daytimes we paddled all over the island in the canoe. It was mighty cool and shady in the deep woods even if the sun was blazing outside. We went winding in and out amongst the trees; and some-times the vines hung so thick we had to back away and go some other way. Well, on every old broken-down tree you could see rab-bits, and snakes, and such things; and when the island had been overflowed a day or two, they got so tame, on account of being hun-gry, that you could paddle right up and put your hand on them if you wanted to; but not the snakes and turtles—they would slide off in the water. The ridge our cavern was in, was full of them. We could a had pets enough if we'd wanted them.

One night we catched a little section of a lumber raft—nice pine planks. It was twelve foot wide and about fifteen or sixteen foot long, and the top stood above water six or seven inches, a solid level floor. We could see saw-logs go by in the daylight, sometimes, but we let them go; we didn't show ourselves in daylight.

Another night, when we was up at the head of the island, just before daylight, here comes a frame house down, on the west side. She was a two-story, and tilted over, considerable. We paddled out and got aboard—clumb in at an up-stairs window. But it was too dark to see, yet, so we made the canoe fast and set in her to wait for daylight.

The light begun to come before we got to the foot of the island.

Then we looked in at the window. We could make out a bed, and a table, and two old chairs, and lots of things around about on the floor; and there was clothes hanging against the wall. There was something laying on the floor in the far corner that looked like a man. So I says:

"Hello, you!"

But it didn't budge. So I hollered again, and then Jim says:

"De man ain't asleep—he's dead. You hold still—I'll go en see."

He went and bent down and looked, and says:

"It's a dead man. Yes, indeedy; naked, too. He's ben shot in de

JIM SEES A DEAD MAN.

back. I reck'n he's ben dead two er three days. Come in, Huck, but doan' look at his face—it's too gashly."

I didn't look at him at all. Jim throwed some old rags over him, but he needn't done it; I didn't want to see him. There was heaps of old greasy cards scattered around over the floor, and old whisky bottles, and a couple of masks, made out of black cloth; and all over the walls was the ignorantest kind of words and pictures, made with charcoal. There was two old dirty calico dresses and a sun bonnet and some women's under-clothes hanging against the wall, and some men's clothing, too. We put the lot into the canoe; it might come good. There was a boy's old speckled straw hat on the floor; I took that, too. And there was a bottle that had had milk in it; and it had a rag stopper for a baby to suck. We would a took the bottle, but it was broke. There was a seedy old chest and an old hair trunk with the hinges broke. They stood open, but there warn't nothing left in them that was any account. The way things was scattered about, we reckoned the people left in a hurry and warn't fixed so as to carry off most of their stuff.

We got an old tin lantern, and a butcher knife without any handle, and a bran-new Barlow knife worth two bits in any store, and a lot of tallow candles, and a tin candlestick, and a gourd, and a tin cup, and a ratty old bed quilt off the bed, and a reticule with needles and pins and beeswax and buttons and thread and all such truck in it, and a hatchet and some nails, and a fish-line as thick as my little finger, with some monstrous hooks on it, and a roll of buckskin, and a leather dog-collar, and a horseshoe, and some vials of medicine that didn't have no label on them; and just as we was leaving I found a tolerable good curry-comb and Jim he found a ratty old fiddle-bow and a wooden leg. The straps was broke off of it, but barring that, it was a good enough leg, though it was too long for me and not long enough for Jim, and we couldn't find the other one, though we hunted all around.

And so, take it all around, we made a good haul. When we was ready to shove off we was a quarter of a mile below the island and it was pretty broad day; so I made Jim lay down in the canoe and cover up with the quilt, because if he set up, people could tell he was a nigger a good ways off. I paddled over to the Illinois shore, and drifted down most a half a mile doing it. I crept up the dead water under the bank and hadn't no accidents and didn't see nobody. We got home all safe.

Chapter X.

THEY FOUND EIGHT DOLLARS.

AFTER breakfast I wanted to talk about the dead man and guess out how he come to be killed, but Jim didn't want to. He said it would fetch bad luck; and besides, he said, he might come and ha'nt us; he said a man that warn't buried was more likely to go a-ha'nting around than one that was planted and comfortable. That sounded pretty reasonable, so I didn't say no more; but I couldn't keep from studying over it and wishing I knowed who shot the man, and what they done it for.

We rummaged the clothes we'd got, and found eight dollars in silver sewed up in the lining of an old blanket overcoat. Jim said he reckoned the people in that house stole the coat, because if they'd a knowed the money was there they wouldn't a left it. I said I reckoned they killed him, too; but Jim didn't want to talk about that. I says:

"Now you think it's bad luck; but what did you say when I fetched in the snake-skin that I found on the top of the ridge day before yesterday? You said it was the worst bad luck in the world to touch a snake-skin with my hands. Well, here's your bad luck! We've raked in all this truck and eight dollars besides. I wish we could have some bad luck like this every day, Jim."

"Never you mind, honey, never you mind. Don't you git too peart. It's a-comin'. Mind I tell you, it's a-comin'."

It did come, too. It was a Tuesday that we had that talk. Well,

after dinner, Friday, we was laying around in the grass at the upper
end of the ridge, and got out of tobacco. I went to the cavern to get
some, and found a rattlesnake in there. I killed him, and curled him
up on the foot of Jim's blanket, ever so natural, thinking there'd be
some fun when Jim found him there. Well, by night I forgot all about
the snake, and when Jim flung himself down on the blanket while I
struck a light, the snake's mate was there, and bit him.

He jumped up yelling, and the first thing the light showed was
the varmint curled up and ready for another spring. I laid him out in

JIM AND THE SNAKE.

a second with a stick, and Jim grabbed pap's whisky jug and begun
to pour it down.

He was barefooted, and the snake bit him right on the heel. That
all comes of my being such a fool as to not remember that wherever
you leave a dead snake its mate always comes there and curls around

it. Jim told me to chop off the snake's head and throw it away, and then skin the body and roast a piece of it. I done it and he eat it and said it would help cure him. He made me take off the rattles and tie them around his wrist, too. He said that that would help. Then I slid out quiet and throwed the snakes clear away amongst the bushes; for I warn't going to let Jim find out it was all my fault, not if I could help it.

Jim sucked and sucked at the jug, and now and then he got out of his head and pitched around and yelled; but every time he come to himself he went to sucking at the jug again. His foot swelled up pretty big, and so did his leg; but by and by the drunk begun to come, and so I judged he was all right; but I'd druther been bit with a snake than pap's whisky.

Jim was laid up for four days and nights. Then the swelling was all gone and he was around again. I made up my mind I wouldn't ever take aholt of a snake-skin again with my hands, now that I see what had come of it. Jim said he reckoned I would believe him, next time. And he said that handling a snake-skin was such awful bad luck that maybe we hadn't got to the end of it yet. He said he druther see the new moon over his left shoulder as much as a thousand times than take up a snake-skin in his hand. Well I was getting to feel that way myself, though I've always reckoned that looking at the new moon over your left shoulder is one of the carelessest and foolishest things a body can do. Old Hank Bunker done it once, and bragged about it; and in less than two years he got drunk and fell off of the shot tower and spread himself out so that he was just a kind of a layer, as you may say; and they slid him edgeways between two barn doors for a coffin, and buried him so, so they say, but I didn't see it. Pap told me. But anyway, it all come of looking at the moon that way, like a fool.

Well, the days went along, and the river went down between its banks again; and about the first thing we done was to bait one of the big hooks with a skinned rabbit and set it and catch a catfish that was as big as a man, being six foot two inches long, and weighed over two hundred pounds. We couldn't handle him, of course; he would a flung us into Illinois. We just set there and watched him rip and tear around till he drownded. We found a brass button in his stomach, and a round ball, and lots of rubbage. We split the ball open with the hatchet, and there was a spool in it. Jim said he'd had it there a long time, to coat it over so and make a ball of it. It was as big a fish as was ever catched in the Mississippi, I reckon. Jim said he hadn't ever seen a bigger one. He would a been worth a good deal, over at the village. They peddle out such a fish as that by the pound in the market house there; everybody buys some of him; his meat's as white as snow and makes a good fry.

Next morning I said it was getting slow and dull, and I wanted to

OLD HANK BUNKER.

get a stirring up, some way. I said I reckoned I would slip over the river and find out what was going on. Jim liked that notion; but he said I must go in the dark and look sharp. Then he studied it over and said, couldn't I put on some of them old things and dress up like a girl? That was a good notion, too. So we shortened up one of the calico gowns and I turned up my trowser-legs to my knees and got into it. Jim hitched it behind with the hooks, and it was a fair fit. I put on the sun bonnet and tied it under my chin, and then for a body to look in and see my face was like looking down a joint of stove-pipe. Jim said nobody would know me, even in the daytime, hardly. I practiced around all day to get the hang of the things, and by and by I could do pretty well in them, only Jim said I didn't walk like a girl; and he said I must quit pulling up my gown to get at my britches pocket. I took notice, and done better.

I started up the Illinois shore in the canoe just after dark.

I started across to the town from a little below the ferry landing, and the drift of the current fetched me in at the bottom of the town. I tied up and started along the bank. There was a light burning in a little shanty that hadn't been lived in for a long time, and I wondered who had took up quarters there. I slipped up and peeped in at the

"A FAIR FIT."

window. There was a woman about forty year old, in there, knitting by a candle that was on a pine table. I didn't know her face; she was a stranger, for you couldn't start a face in that town that I didn't know. Now this was lucky, because I was weakening; I was getting afraid I had come; people might know my voice and find me out. But if this woman had been in such a little town two days she could tell me all I wanted to know; so I knocked at the door, and made up my mind I wouldn't forget I was a girl.

Chapter XI.

"Come in," says the woman, and I did. She says:

"Take a cheer."

I done it. She looked me all over with her little shiny eyes, and says:

"What might your name be?"

"Sarah Williams."

"Where 'bouts do you live? In this neighborhood?"

"No'm. In Hookerville, seven mile below. I've walked all the way and I'm all tired out."

"Hungry, too, I reckon. I'll find you something."

"No'm, I ain't hungry. I was so hungry I had to stop two mile below here at a farm; so I ain't hungry no more. It's what makes me so late. My mother's down sick, and out of money and everything, and I come to tell my uncle Abner Moore. He lives at the upper end of the town, she says. I hain't ever been here before. Do you know him?"

"No; but I don't know everybody yet. I haven't lived here quite two weeks. It's a considerable ways to the upper end of the town. You better stay here all night. Take off your bonnet."

"No," I says, "I'll rest a while, I reckon, and go on. I ain't afeard of the dark."

She said she wouldn't let me go by myself, but her husband would be in by and by, maybe in a hour and a half, and she'd send him along with me. Then she got to talking about her husband, and about her relations up the river, and her relations down the river, and about how much better off they used to was, and how they didn't know

"COME IN."

but they'd made a mistake coming to our town, instead of letting well alone—and so on and so on, till I was afeard *I* had made a mistake coming to her to find out what was going on in the town; but by and by she dropped onto pap and the murder and then I was pretty willing to let her clatter right along. She told about me and Tom Sawyer finding the six thousand dollars (only she got it ten,) and all about pap and what a hard lot he was, and what a hard lot I was, and at last she got down to where I was murdered. I says:

"Who done it? We've heard considerable about these goings on, down in Hookerville, but we don't know who 'twas that killed Huck Finn."

"Well I reckon there's a right smart chance of people *here* that 'd like to know who killed him. Some thinks old Finn done it, himself."

"No—is that so?"

"Most everybody thought it at first. He'll never know how nigh he come to getting lynched. But before night they changed around and judged it was done by a runaway nigger named Jim."

"Why *he*—"

I stopped. I reckoned I better keep still. She run on, and never noticed I had put in at all.

"The nigger run off the very night Huck Finn was killed. So there's a reward out for him—three hundred dollars. And there's a reward out for old Finn, too—two hundred dollars. You see, he come to town the morning after the murder, and told about it, and was out with 'em on the ferry-boat hunt, and right away after he up and left. Before night they wanted to lynch him, but he was gone, you see. Well, next day they found out the nigger was gone; they found out he hadn't ben seen sence ten o'clock the night the murder was done. So then they put it on him, you see, and while they was full of it, next day back comes old Finn and went boo-hooing to Judge Thatcher to get money to hunt for the nigger all over Illinois with. The judge give him some, and that evening he got drunk and was around till after midnight with a couple of mighty hard look-ing strangers, and then went off with them. Well, he hain't come back sence, and they ain't looking for him back till this thing blows over a little, for people thinks now that he killed his boy and fixed things so folks would think robbers done it, and then he'd get

Huck's money without having to bother a long time with a lawsuit. People do say he warn't any too good to do it. O, he's sly, I reckon. If he don't come back for a year, he'll be all right. You can't prove anything on him, you know; everything will be quieted down, then, and he'll walk into Huck's money as easy as nothing."

"Yes, I reckon so, 'm. I don't see nothing in the way of it. Has everybody quit thinking the nigger done it?"

"O, no, not everybody. A good many thinks he done it. But they'll get the nigger pretty soon, now, and maybe they can scare it out of him."

"Why, are they after him yet?"

"Well, you're innocent, ain't you! Does three hundred dollars lay round every day for people to pick up? Some folks thinks the nigger ain't far from here. I'm one of them—but I hain't talked it around. A few days ago I was talking with an old couple that lives next door in the log shanty and they happened to say hardly anybody ever goes to that island over yonder that they call Jackson's island. Don't anybody live there? says I. No, nobody, says they. I didn't say any more, but I done some thinking. I was pretty near certain I'd seen smoke, over there, about the head of the island, a day or two before that, so I says to myself, like as not that nigger's hiding over there; anyway, says I, it's worth the trouble to give the place a hunt. I hain't seen any smoke sence, so I reckon maybe he's gone, if it was him; but husband's going over to see—him and another man. He was gone up the river; but he got back to-day and I told him as soon as he got here two hours ago."

I had got so uneasy I couldn't set still. I had to do something with my hands; so I took up a needle off of the table and went to threading it. My hands shook, and I was making a bad job of it. When the woman stopped talking, I looked up, and she was looking at me pretty curious, and smiling a little. I put down the needle and thread and let on to be interested—and I was, too—and says:

"Three hundred dollars is a power of money. I wish my mother could get it. Is your husband going over there to-night?"

"O, yes. He went up town with the man I was telling you of, to get a boat and see if they could borrow another gun. They'll go over after midnight."

"Couldn't they see better if they was to wait till daytime?"

"Yes. And couldn't the nigger see better, too? After midnight he'll likely be asleep, and they can slip around through the woods and hunt up his camp fire all the better for the dark, if he's got one."

"I didn't think of that."

"HIM AND ANOTHER MAN."

The woman kept looking at me pretty curious, and I didn't feel a bit comfortable. Pretty soon she says:

"What did you say your name was, honey?"

"M—Mary Williams."

Somehow it didn't seem to me that I said it was Mary, before; so I didn't look up; seemed to me I said it was Sarah; so I felt sort of cornered, and was afeard maybe I was looking it, too. I wished the woman would say something more; the longer she set still, the uneasier I was. But now she says:

"Honey, I thought you said it was Sarah when you first come in?"

"O yes'm, I did. Sarah Mary Williams. Sarah's my first name. Some calls me Sarah, some calls me Mary."

"O, that's the way of it?"

"Yes'm."

I was feeling better, then, but I wished I was out of there, anyway. I couldn't look up, yet.

Well, the woman fell to talking about how hard times was, and how poor they had to live, and how the rats was as free as if they owned the place, and so forth and so on, and then I got easy again. She was right about the rats. You'd see one stick his nose out of a hole in the corner every little while. She said she had to have things handy to throw at them when she was alone, or they wouldn't give her no peace. She showed me a bar of lead, twisted up into a knot, and said she was a good shot with it generly, but she'd wrenched her arm a day or two ago, and didn't know whether she could throw true, now. But she watched for a chance, and directly she banged away at a rat, but she missed him wide, and said "Ouch!" it hurt her arm so. Then she told me to try for the next one. I wanted to be getting away before the old man got back, but of course I didn't let on. I got the thing, and the first rat that showed his nose I let drive, and if he'd a stayed where he was he'd a been a tolerable sick rat. She said that that was first rate, and she reckoned I would hive the next one. She went and got the lump of lead and fetched it back and brought along a hank of yarn, which she wanted me to help her with. I held up my two hands and she put the hank over them and went on talking about her and her husband's matters. But she broke off to say:

"Keep your eye on the rats. You better have the lead in your lap, handy."

So she dropped the lump into my lap, just at that moment, and I clapped my legs together on it and she went on talking. But only about a minute. Then she took off the hank and looked me straight in the face, but very pleasant, and says:

"Come, now—what's your real name?"

"Wh-what, mum?"

"What's your real name? Is it Bill, or Tom, or Bob?—or what is it?"

I reckon I shook like a leaf, and I didn't know hardly what to do. But I says:

"Please to don't poke fun at a poor girl like me, mum. If I'm in the way, here, I'll—"

"No you won't. Set down, and stay where you are. I ain't going to hurt you, and I ain't going to tell on you, nuther. You just tell me your secret, and trust me. I'll keep it; and what's more, I'll help you. So'll my old man, if you want him to. You see, you're a runaway 'prentice—that's all. It ain't anything. There ain't any harm in it. You've been treated bad, and you made up your mind to cut. Bless you, child, I wouldn't tell on you. Tell me all about it, now—that's a good boy."

So I said it wouldn't be no use to try to play it any longer, and I would just make a clean breast and tell her everything, but she mustn't go back on her promise. Then I told her my father and mother was dead, and the law had bound me out to a mean old farmer in the country thirty mile back from the river and he treated me so bad I couldn't stand it no longer; he went away to be gone a couple of days, and so I took my chance, and stole some of his daughter's old clothes and cleared out, and I had been three nights coming the thirty miles; I traveled nights, and hid daytimes and slept, and the bag of bread and meat I carried from home lasted me all the way and I had a plenty. I said I believed my uncle Abner Moore would take care of me and so that was why I struck out for this town of Goshen.

"Goshen, child? This ain't Goshen. This is St. Petersburg. Goshen's ten mile further up the river. Who told you this was Goshen?"

"Why a man I met, at daybreak this morning, just as I was going to turn into the woods for my regular sleep. He told me when the roads forked I must take the right hand, and five mile would fetch me to Goshen."

"He was drunk, I reckon. He told you just exactly wrong."

"Well, he did act like he was drunk, but it ain't no matter now. I got to be moving along. I'll fetch Goshen before daylight."

"Hold on a minute. I'll put you up a snack to eat. You might want it."

So she put me up a snack and says:

"Say—when a cow's laying down, which end of her gets up first? Answer up prompt, now—don't stop to study over it. Which end gets up first?"

"The hind end, mum."

"Well, then, a horse?"

"The for'rard end, mum."

"Which side of a tree does the most moss grow on?"

"North side."

"If fifteen cows is browsing on a hillside, how many of them eats with their heads pointed the same direction?"

"The whole fifteen, mum."

SHE PUTS UP A SNACK.

"Well, I reckon you *have* lived in the country. I thought maybe you was trying to hocus me again. What's your real name, now?"

"George Peters, mum."

"Well, try to remember it, George. Don't forget and tell me it's Elexander before you go, and then get out by saying it's George-Elexander when I catch you. And don't go about women in that old calico. You do a girl tolerable poor, but you might fool men, maybe. Bless you, child, when you set out to thread a needle, don't hold the thread still and fetch the needle up to it; hold the needle still and poke the thread at it—that's the way a woman most always does;

but a man always does t'other way. And when you throw at a rat or anything, hitch yourself up a tip-toe, and fetch your hand up over your head, as awkard as you can, and miss your rat about six or seven foot. Throw stiff-armed, from the shoulder, like there was a pivot there for it to turn on—like a girl; not from the wrist and elbow, with your arm out to one side, like a boy. And mind you, when a girl tries to catch anything in her lap, she throws her knees apart; she don't clap them together, the way you did when you catched the lump of lead. Why, I spotted you for a boy when you was threading the needle; and I contrived the other things just to make certain. Now trot along to your uncle, Sarah Mary Williams George Elexander Peters, and if you get into trouble, you send word to Mrs. Judith Loftus, which is me, and I'll do what I can to get you out of it. Keep the river road, all the way, and next time you tramp take shoes and socks with you. The river road's a rocky one, and your feet 'll be in a condition when you get to Goshen, I reckon."

I went up the bank about fifty yards and then I doubled on my tracks and slipped back to where my canoe was, a good piece below the house. I jumped in and was off in a hurry. I went up stream far enough to make the head of the island, and then started across. I took off the sun-bonnet, for I didn't want no blinders on, then. When I was about the middle, I hear the clock begin to strike; so I stops and listens; the sound come faint over the water, but clear—eleven. When I struck the head of the island I never waited to blow, though I was most winded, but I shoved right into the timber where my old camp used to be, and started a good fire there on a high-and-dry spot.

Then I jumped in the canoe and dug out for our place a mile and a half below, as hard as I could go. I landed and slopped through the timber and up the ridge and into the cavern. There Jim laid, sound asleep on the ground. I roused him out and says:

"Git up and hump yourself, Jim! There ain't a minute to lose. They're after us!"

Jim never asked no questions, he never said a word; but the way he worked for the next half an hour showed about how he was scared. By that time everything we had in the world was on our raft and she was ready to be shoved out from the willow cove where she was hid. We put out the camp fire at the cavern the first thing, and didn't show a candle outside after that.

I took the canoe out from shore a little piece and took a look, but if there was a boat around I couldn't see it, for stars and shadows ain't good to see by. Then we got out the raft and slipped along down in the shade, past the foot of the island dead still, never saying a word.

"HUMP YOURSELF!"

Chapter XII.

ON THE RAFT.

MUST a been close onto one o'clock when we got below the island at last, and the raft did seem to go mighty slow. If a boat was to come along we was going to take to the canoe and break for the Illinois shore; and it was well a boat didn't come, for we hadn't ever thought to put the gun into the canoe, or a fishing-line, or anything to eat. We was in ruther too much of a sweat to think of so many things. It warn't good judgment to put *everything* on the raft.

If the men went to the island, I just expect they found the camp fire I built, and watched it all night for Jim to come. Anyways, they stayed away from us, and if my building the fire never fooled them it warn't no fault of mine. I played it as low-down on them as I could.

When the first streak of day begun to show, we tied up to a tow-head in a big bend on the Illinois side, and hacked off cottonwood branches with the hatchet and covered up the raft with them so she looked like there had been a cave-in in the bank there. A tow-head is a sand-bar that has cottonwoods on it as thick as harrow-teeth.

We had mountains on the Missouri shore and heavy timber on the Illinois side, and the channel was down the Missouri shore at that place, so we warn't afraid of anybody running across us. We laid there all day and watched the rafts and steamboats spin down the Missouri shore, and up-bound steamboats fight the big river in the middle. I told Jim all about the time I had jabbering with that woman; and Jim said she was a smart one, and if she was to start after us herself *she* wouldn't set down and watch a camp fire—no, sir, she'd fetch a dog. Well, then, I said, why couldn't she tell her husband to fetch a dog? Jim said he bet she did think of it by the time the men was ready to start, and he believed they must a gone up town to get a dog and so they lost all that time, or else we wouldn't be here on a tow-head sixteen or seventeen mile below the village— no indeedy, we would be in that same old town again. So I said I didn't care what was the reason they didn't get us, as long as they didn't.

When it was beginning to come on dark we poked our heads out of the cottonwood thicket and looked up, and down, and across; nothing in sight; so Jim took up some of the top planks of the raft and built a snug wigwam to get under in blazing weather and rainy, and to keep the things dry. Jim made a floor for the wigwam and raised it a foot or more above the level of the raft, so now the blankets and all the traps was out of the reach of steamboat waves. Right in the middle of the wigwam we made a layer of dirt about five or six inches deep with a frame around it for to hold it to its place; this was to build a fire on in sloppy weather or chilly; the wigwam would keep it from being seen. We made an extra steering oar, too, because one of the others might get broke, on a snag or something. We fixed up a short forked stick to hang the old lantern on; because we must always light the lantern whenever we see a steamboat coming down stream, to keep from getting run over; but we wouldn't have to light it for up-stream boats unless we see we was in what they call a "crossing;" for the river was pretty high, yet, very low banks being still a little under water; so up-bound boats didn't always run the channel, but hunted easy water.

This second night we run between seven and eight hours, with a current that was making over four mile an hour. We catched fish, and talked, and we took a swim now and then to keep off sleepiness. It was kind of solemn, drifting down the big still river, laying on our backs looking up at the stars, and we didn't ever feel like talking loud, and it warn't often that we laughed, only a little kind of a low chuckle. We had mighty good weather, as a general thing, and nothing ever happened to us at all, that night, nor the next nor the next.

Every night we passed towns, some of them away up on black hill sides, nothing but just a shiny bed of lights, not a house could you see. The fifth night we passed St. Louis, and it was like the whole world lit up. In St. Petersburg they used to say there was twenty or thirty thousand people in St. Louis, but I never believed it till I see that wonderful spread of lights at two o'clock that still night. There warn't a sound there; everybody was asleep.

HE SOMETIMES LIFTED A CHICKEN.

Every night, now, I used to slip ashore towards ten o'clock at some little village and buy ten or fifteen cents' worth of meal or bacon or other stuff to eat; and sometimes I lifted a chicken that warn't roosting comfortable, and took him along. Pap always said, take a chicken when you get a chance, because if you don't want him yourself you can easy find somebody that does, and a good deed ain't ever forgot. I never see pap when he didn't want the chicken himself, but that is what he used to say, anyway.

Mornings, before daylight, I slipped into corn-fields and borrowed a watermelon, or a mushmelon, or a punkin, or some new corn, or things of that kind. Pap always said it warn't no harm to borrow things, if you was meaning to pay them back, sometime, but the widow said it warn't anything but a soft name for stealing and no decent body would do it. Jim said he reckoned the widow was partly right and pap was partly right; so the best way would be for us to pick out two or three things from the list and say we wouldn't borrow them any more—then he reckoned it wouldn't be no harm to borrow the others. So we talked it over all one night, drifting along down the river, trying to make up our minds whether to drop the watermelons, or the cantelopes, or the mushmelons, or what. But towards daylight we got it all settled satisfactory, and concluded to drop crabapples and p'simmons. We warn't feeling just right, before that, but it was all comfortable now. I was glad the way it come out, too, because crabapples ain't ever good, and the p'simmons wouldn't be ripe for two or three months yet.

We shot a water-fowl, now and then, that got up too early in the morning or didn't go to bed early enough in the evening. Take it all around, we lived pretty high.

The fifth night below St. Louis we had a big storm after midnight, with a power of thunder and lightning, and the rain poured down in a solid sheet. We staid in the wigwam and let the raft take care of itself. When the lightning glared out we could see a big straight river ahead, and high rocky bluffs on both sides. By and by says I, "Hel-*lo*, Jim, looky yonder!" It was a steamboat that had killed herself on a rock. We was drifting straight down for her. The lightning showed her very distinct. She was leaning over, with part of her upper deck above water, and you could see every little chimbly-guy clean and clear, and a chair by the big bell, with an old slouch hat hanging on the back of it when the flashes come.

Well, it being away in the night, and stormy, and all so mysterious-like, I felt just the way any other boy would a felt, when I see that wreck laying there so mournful and lonesome in the middle of the river. I wanted to get aboard of her and slink around a little, and see what there was there. So I says:

"Le's land on her, Jim."

But Jim was dead against it, at first. He says:

"I doan want to go fool'n 'long er no wrack. We's doin' blame' well, en we better let blame' well alone, as de good book says. Like as not dey's a watchman on dat wrack."

"Watchman your grandmother," I says; "there ain't nothing to watch but the texas and the pilot house; and do you reckon anybody's going to resk his life for a texas and a pilot house such a night as this, when it's likely to break up and wash off down the river any minute?" Jim couldn't say nothing to that, so he didn't try. "And besides," I says, "we might borrow something worth having, out of the captain's stateroom. Seegars, *I* bet you—and cost five cents apiece, solid cash. Steamboat captains is always rich, and get sixty dollars a month, and *they* don't care a cent what a thing costs, you know, long as they want it. Stick a candle in your pocket; I can't rest, Jim, till we give her a rummaging. Do you reckon Tom Sawyer would ever go by this thing? Not for pie, he wouldn't. He'd call it an adventure—that's what he'd call it; and he'd land on that wreck if it was his last act. And wouldn't he throw style into it?— wouldn't he spread himself, nor nothing? Why, you'd think it was Christopher C'lumbus discovering Kingdom-Come. I wish Tom Sawyer *was* here."

Jim he grumbled a little, but give in. He said we mustn't talk any more than we could help, and then talk mighty low. The lightning showed us the wreck again, just in time, and we fetched the starboard derrick, and made fast there.

The deck was high out, here. We went sneaking down the slope of it to labboard, in the dark, towards the texas, feeling our way slow with our feet, and spreading our hands out to fend off the guys, for it was so dark we couldn't see no sign of them. Pretty soon we struck the forward end of the skylight, and clumb onto it; and the next step fetched us in front of the captain's door, which was open; and by jimminy, away down through the texas hall we see a light! and all in the same second we seem to hear low voices in yonder!

Jim whispered and said he was feeling powerful sick; and told me to come along. I says, all right; and was going to start for the raft; but just then I heard a voice wail out and say:

"O, please don't, boys; I swear I won't ever tell!"

Another voice said, pretty loud:

"It's a lie, Jim Turner. You've acted this way before. You always want more'n your share of the truck, and you've always got it, too, because you've swore 't if you didn't you'd tell. But this time you've said it jist one time too many. You're the meanest, treacherousest hound in this country."

By this time Jim was gone for the raft. I was just a-biling with curiosity; and I says to myself, Tom Sawyer wouldn't back out now, and so I won't either; I'm agoing to see what's going on here. So I dropped on my hands and knees, in the little passage, and crept aft in the dark, till there warn't but about one stateroom betwixt me and the cross-hall of the texas. Then, in there I see a man stretched on the floor and tied hand and foot, and two men standing over him, and one of them had a dim lantern in his hand, and the other one had a pistol. This one kept pointing the pistol at the man's head on the floor and saying,—

"I'd *like* to! And I orter, too, a mean skunk!"

The man on the floor would shrivel up and say, "O, please don't, Bill—I hain't ever goin' to tell."

And every time he said that, the man with the lantern would laugh, and say:

" 'Deed you *ain't!* You never said no truer thing 'n that, you bet you." And once he said: "Hear him beg! and yit if we hadn't got the best of him and tied him, he'd a killed us both. And what *for?* Jist for noth'n'. Jist because we stood on our *rights*—that's what for. But I lay you ain't agoin' to threaten nobody any more, Jim Turner. Put *up* that pistol, Bill."

"PLEASE DON'T, BILL."

Bill says:

"I don't want to, Jake Packard. I'm for killin' him—and didn't he kill old Hatfield jist the same way—and don't he deserve it?"

"But I don't *want* him killed, and I've got my reasons for it."

"Bless yo' heart for them words, Jake Packard!—I'll never forgit you, long's I live!" says the man on the floor, sort of blubbering.

Packard didn't take no notice of that, but hung up his lantern on a nail, and started towards where I was, there in the dark, and motioned Bill to come. I crawfished as fast as I could, about two yards, but the boat slanted so that I couldn't make very good time; so, to keep from getting run over and catched, I crawled into a stateroom on the upper side. The men come a-pawing along in the dark, and when Packard got to my stateroom, he says:

"Here—come in here."

And in he come, and Bill after him. But before they got in, I was up in the upper berth, cornered, and sorry I come. Then they stood there, with their hands on the ledge of the berth, and talked. I couldn't see them, but I could tell where they was, and how close they was, by the whisky they'd been having. I was glad I didn't drink whisky; but it wouldn't made much difference, anyway, because most of the time they couldn't a treed me, because I didn't breathe. I was too scared. And besides, a body *couldn't* breathe, and hear such talk. They talked low and earnest. Bill wanted to kill Turner. He says:

"He's said he'll tell, and he will. If we was to give both our shares to him, *now*, it wouldn't make no difference, after the row, and the way we've served him. Shore's you're born, he'll turn State's evidence, now you hear *me*. I'm for putting him out of his troubles."

"So'm I," says Packard, very quiet.

"Blame it, I'd sorter begun to think you wasn't. Well, then, that's all right. Le's go and do it."

"Hold on, a minute; I hain't had my say, yit. You listen to me. Shooting's good, but there's quieter ways, if the thing's *got* to be done. But what *I* say, is this: it ain't good sense to go court'n around after a halter, if you can git at what you're up to in some way that's jist as good and at the same time don't bring you into no resks. Ain't that so?"

"You bet it is. But how you goin' to manage it this time?"

"Well, my idea is this: we'll rustle around and gether up whatever pickins we've overlooked in the staterooms, and shove for shore and hide the truck. Then we'll wait. Now I say it ain't agoin' to be more'n two hours befo' this wrack breaks up and washes off down the river. See? He'll be drownded, and won't have nobody to blame for it but his own self. I reckon that's a considerble sight better'n killin' of him. I'm unfavorable to killin' a man as long as you can git around it; it ain't good sense, it ain't good morals. Ain't I right?"

"IT AIN'T GOOD MORALS."

"Yes—I reck'n you are. But s'pose she *don't* break up and wash off?"

"Well, we can wait the two hours, anyway, and see, can't we?"

"All right, then; come along."

So they started, and I lit out, all in a cold sweat, and scrambled forward. It was dark as pitch there; but I said, in a kind of a coarse whisper, "Jim!" and he answered up, right at my elbow, with a sort of a moan, and I says:

"Quick, Jim, it ain't no time for fooling around and moaning; there's a gang of murderers in yonder, and if we don't hunt up their boat and set her drifting down the river so these fellows can't get away from the wreck, there's one of 'em going to be in a bad fix. But if we find their boat we can put *all* of 'em in a bad fix—for the Sheriff 'll get 'em. Quick—hurry! I'll hunt the labboard side, you hunt the stabboard. You start at the raft, and—"

"O my lordy, lordy! *Raf'*? Dey ain' no raf' no mo', she done broke loose en gone!—en here we is!"

"O MY LORDY, LORDY!"

Chapter XIII

IN A FIX.

WELL, I catched my breath, and most fainted. Shut up on a wreck with such a gang as that! But it warn't no time to be sentimentering. We'd *got* to find that boat, now—had to have it for ourselves. So we went a-quaking and shaking down the stabboard side, and slow work it was, too—seemed a week before we got to the stern. No sign of a boat. Jim said he didn't believe he could go any further—so scared he hadn't hardly any strength left, he said. But I said come on, if we get left on this wreck, we are in a fix, sure. So on we prowled, again. We struck for the stern of the texas, and found it, and then scrabbled along forwards on the skylight, hanging on from shutter to shutter, for the edge of the skylight was in the water. When we got pretty close to the cross-hall door, there was the skiff, sure enough!—I could just barely see her. I felt ever so thankful. In another second I would a been aboard of her; but just then the door opened. One of the men stuck his head out, only about a couple of foot from me, and I thought I was gone; but he jerked it in again, and says:

"Heave that blame lantern out o' sight, Bill!"

He flung a bag of something into the boat, and then got in, himself, and set down. It was Packard. Then Bill *he* come out and got in. Packard says, in a low voice:

"All ready—shove off!"

I couldn't hardly hang onto the shutters, I was so weak. But Bill says:

"Hold on—'d you go through him?"

"No. Didn't you?"

"No. So he's got his share o' the cash, yet."

"Well, then, come along—no use to take truck and leave money."

"Say—won't he suspicion what we're up to?"

"Maybe he won't. But we got to have it anyway. Come along."

So they got out and went in.

The door slammed to, because it was on the careened side; and in a half second I was in the boat, and Jim come a-tumbling after me. I out with my knife and cut the rope, and away we went!

We didn't touch an oar, and we didn't speak nor whisper, nor hardly even breathe. We went gliding swift along, dead silent, past the tip of the paddle-box, and past the stern; then in a second or two more we was a hundred yards below the wreck, and the darkness soaked her up, every last sign of her, and we was safe, and knowed it.

When we was three or four hundred yards down stream, we see the lantern show like a little spark at the texas door, for a second, and we knowed by that that the rascals had missed their boat, and was beginning to understand that they was in just as much trouble, now, as Jim Turner was.

Then Jim manned the oars, and we took out after our raft. Now was the first time that I begun to worry about the men—I reckon I hadn't had time to, before. I begun to think how dreadful it was, even for murderers, to be in such a fix. I says to myself, there ain't no telling but I might come to be a murderer myself, yet, and then how would I like it? So says I to Jim:

"The first light we see, we'll land a hundred yards below it or above it, in a place where it's a good hiding place for you and the skiff, and then I'll go and fix up some kind of a yarn, and get somebody to go for that gang and get them out of their scrape, so they can be hung when their time comes."

But that idea was a failure; for pretty soon it begun to storm again, and this time worse than ever. The rain poured down, and never a light showed; everybody in bed, I reckon. We boomed along down the river, watching for lights and watching for our raft. After a long time the rain let up, but the clouds staid, and the lightning kept whimpering, and by and by a flash showed us a black thing ahead, floating, and we made for it.

It was the raft, and mighty glad was we to get aboard of it again. We seen a light, now, away down to the right, on shore. So I said I would go for it. The skiff was half full of plunder which that gang had stole, there on the wreck. We hustled it onto the raft in a pile, and I told Jim to float along down, and show a light when he judged he had gone about two mile and keep it burning till I come; then I manned my oars and shoved for the light. As I got down towards it, three or four more showed—up on a hillside. It was a village. I closed in above the shore-light, and laid on my oars and floated. As I went by, I see it was a lantern hanging on the jackstaff of a double-hull ferry boat. Everything was dead still, nobody stirring. I floated in under the stern, made fast, and clumb aboard. I skimmed around for the watchman, a-wondering whereabouts he slept; and by and by I found him roosting on the bitts, forward, with his head down between his knees. I give his shoulder two or three little shoves, and begun to cry.

He stirred up, in a kind of a startlish way; but when he see it was only me, he took a good gap and stretch, and then he says:

"Hello, what's up? Don't cry, bub. What's the trouble?"

I says:

"Pap, and mam, and sis, and—"

Then I broke down. He says:

"O, dang it, now, *don't* take on so, we all has to have our troubles, and this'n 'll come out all right. What's the matter with 'em?"

"They're—they're—are you the watchman of the boat?"

"Yes," he says, kind of pretty-well-satisfied like. "I'm the captain, and the owner, and the mate, and the pilot, and watchman, and head deck-hand; and sometimes I'm the freight and passengers. I ain't as rich as old Jim Hornback, and I can't be so blame' generous and good to Tom, Dick and Harry as what he is, and slam around money the way he does, but I've told him a many a time 't I wouldn't trade places with him; for, says I, a sailor's life's the life for me, and I'm derned if I'd live two mile out o' town, where there ain't nothing ever goin' on, not for all his spondulicks and as much more on top of it. Says I—"

I broke in and says:

"They're in an awful peck of trouble, and—"

"*Who* is?"

"Why, pap, and mam, and sis, and Miss Hooker; and if you'd take your ferry boat and go up there—"

"Up where? Where are they?"

"On the wreck."

"HELLO, WHAT'S UP?"

"What wreck?"

"Why, there ain't but one."

"What, you don't mean the *Walter Scott*!"

"Yes."

"Good land! what are they doin' *there*, for gracious sakes?"

"Well, they didn't go there a-purpose."

"I bet they didn't! Why, great goodness, there ain't no chance for 'em if they don't git off mighty quick! Why, how in the nation did they ever git into such a scrape?"

"Easy enough. Miss Hooker was a-visiting, up there to the town—"

"Yes, Booth's Landing—go on."

"She was a visiting, there at Booth's Landing, and just in the edge of the evening she started over with her nigger woman in the horse-ferry, to stay all night at her friend's house, Miss What-you-may-call-her, I disremember her name, and they lost their steering-oar, and swung around and went a-floating down, stern-first, about two mile, and saddle-baggsed on the wreck, and the ferry man and the nigger woman and the horses was all lost, but Miss Hooker she made a grab and got aboard the wreck. Well, about an hour after dark, we come along down in our trading-scow, and it was so dark we didn't notice the wreck till we was right on it; and so *we* saddle-baggsed; but all of us was saved but Bill Whipple—and oh, he *was* the best cretur!—I most wish't it had been me, I do."

"My George! it's the beatenest thing I ever struck. And *then* what did you all do?"

"Well, we hollered and took on, but it's so wide, there, we couldn't make nobody hear. So pap said somebody got to get ashore and get help, somehow. I was the only one that could swim; so I made a dash for it, and Miss Hooker she said if I didn't strike help sooner, come here and hunt up her uncle, and he'd fix the thing. I made the land about a mile below, and been fooling along ever since, trying to get people to do something, but they said, 'What, in such a night and such a current? there ain't no sense in it; go for the steam-ferry.' Now if you'll go, and—"

"By Jackson, I'd *like* to, and blame it I don't know but I will; but who in the dingnation's agoin' to *pay* for it? Do you reckon your pap—"

"Why *that*'s all right. Miss Hooker she told me, *particular*, that her uncle Hornback—"

"Great guns! is *he* her uncle? Looky here, you break for that light over yonder-way, and turn out west when you git there, and about a quarter of a mile out you'll come to the tavern; tell 'em to dart you out to Jim Hornback's, and he'll foot the bill. And don't you fool around any, because he'll want to know the news. Tell him I'll have his niece all safe before he can get to town. Hump yourself, now; I'm agoing up around the corner, here, to roust out my engineer."

I struck for the light, but as soon as he turned the corner I went back and got into my skiff and bailed her out and then pulled up shore in the easy water about six hundred yards, and tucked myself in among some woodboats; for I couldn't rest easy till I could see the ferryboat start. But take it all around, I was feeling ruther comfortable, on accounts of taking all this trouble for that gang, for not many would a done it. I wished the widow knowed about it. I judged she would be proud of me for helping these rapscallions, because rapscallions and dead beats is the kind the widow and good people takes the most interest in.

Well, before long, here comes the wreck, dim and dusky, sliding

THE WRECK.

along down! A kind of cold shiver went through me, and then I struck out for her. She was very deep, and I see in a minute there warn't much chance for anybody being alive in her. I pulled all around her, and hollered a little, but there wasn't any answer; all dead still. I felt a little bit heavy-hearted about the gang, but not much, for I reckoned if they could stand it, I could.

Then here comes the ferryboat; so I shoved for the middle of the river on a long down-stream slant; and when I judged I was out of eye-reach, I laid on my oars, and looked back and see her go and smell around the wreck for Miss Hooker's remainders, because the captain would know her uncle Hornback would want them; and then pretty soon the ferryboat give it up and went for shore, and I laid into my work and went a-booming down the river.

It did seem a powerful long time before Jim's light showed up; and when it did show, it looked like it was a thousand mile off. By the time I got there the sky was beginning to get a little gray in the east; so we struck for an island, and hid the raft, and sunk the skiff, and turned in and slept like dead people.

WE TURNED IN AND SLEPT.

Chapter XIV.

B<small>Y AND BY</small>, when we got up, we turned over the truck the gang had stole off of the wreck, and found boots, and blankets, and clothes, and all sorts of other things, and a lot of books, and a spyglass and three boxes of see-gars. We hadn't ever been this rich before, in neither of our lives. The seegars was prime. We laid off all the afternoon in the woods, talking, and me reading the books, and having a general good time. I told Jim all about what happened inside the wreck, and at the ferryboat; and I said these kinds of things was

TURNING OVER THE TRUCK.

adventures; but he said he didn't want no more adventures. He said that when I went in the texas and he crawled back to get on the raft and found her gone, he nearly died; because he judged it was all up with *him*, anyway it could be fixed; for if he didn't get saved he would get drownded; and if he did get saved, whoever saved him would send him back home so as to get the reward, and then Miss Watson would sell him south, sure. Well, he was right; he was most always right; he had an uncommon level head, for a nigger.

I read considerable to Jim about kings, and dukes, and earls and such, and how gaudy they dressed and how much style they put on, and called each other your majesty, and your grace, and your lord-ship, and so on, 'stead of mister; and Jim's eyes bugged out, and he was interested. He says:

"I didn' know dey was so many un um. I hain't hearn 'bout none

un um, skasely, but ole king Sollermun, onless you counts dem
kings dat's in a pack er k'yards. How much do a king git?"

"Get?" I says; "why, they get a thousand dollars a month if they
want it; they can have just as much as they want; everything belongs
to them."

"*Ain'* dat gay? En what dey got to do, Huck?"

"*They* don't do nothing! Why, how you talk. They just set
around."

"No—is dat so?"

"Of course it is. They just set around. Except maybe when there's
a war; then they go to the war. But other times they just lazy around;
or go hawking—just hawking and sp— Sh!—d' you hear a noise?"

We skipped out and looked; but it warn't nothing but the flutter
of a steamboat's wheel away down coming around the point; so we
come back.

"Yes," says I, "and other times, when things is dull, they fuss
with the parlyment; and if everybody don't go just so, he whacks
their heads off. But mostly they hang round the harem."

"Roun' de which?"

"Harem."

"What's de harem?"

"The place where he keep his wives. Don't you know about the
harem? Solomon had one; he had about a million wives."

"Why, yes, dat's so; I—I'd done forgot it. A harem's a bo'd'n house,
I reck'n. Mos' likely dey has rackety times in de nussery. En I reck'n
de wives quarrels considable; en dat 'crease de racket. Yit dey say
Sollermun de wises' man dat ever live'. I doan' take no stock in dat.
Bekase why: would a wise man want to live in de mids' er sich a
blimblammin' all de time? No—'deed he wouldn't. A wise man 'ud
take en buil' a biler-factry; en den he could shet *down* de biler-factry
when he want to res'."

"Well, but he *was* the wisest man, anyway; because the widow
she told me so, her own self."

"I doan k'yer what de widder say, he *warn't* no wise man, nuther.
He had some er de dad-fetchedes' ways I ever see. Does you know
'bout dat chile dat he 'uz gwyne to chop in two?"

"Yes; the widow told me all about it."

"*Well*, den! Warn' dat de beatenes' notion in de worl'? You jis'

take en look at it a minute. Dah's de stump, dah—dat's one er de
women; heah's you—dat's de yuther one; I's Sollermun; en dish-
yer dollar bill's de chile. Bofe un you claims it. What does I do? Does
I shin aroun' mongs' de neighbors en fine out which un you de bill
do b'long to, en han' it over to de right one, all safe en soun', de way

SOLOMON AND HIS MILLION WIVES.

dat anybody dat had any gumption would? No—I take en whack de
bill in *two*, en give half un it to you, en de yuther half to de yuther
woman. Dat's de way Sollermun was gwyne to do wid de chile. Now
I want to ast you: what's de use er dat half a bill?—can't buy noth'n
wid it. En what use is a half a chile? I wouldn' give a dern for a
million un um."

"But hang it, Jim, you've clean missed the point—blame it,
you've missed it a thousand mile."

"Who? me? Go 'long. Doan talk to *me* 'bout yo' pints. I reck'n I
knows sense when I sees it; en dey ain' no sense in sich doin's as
dat. De 'spute warn't 'bout a half a chile, de 'spute was 'bout a whole
chile; en de man dat think he kin settle a 'spute 'bout a whole chile
wid a half a chile, doan know enough to come in out'n de rain. Doan
talk to me 'bout Sollermun, Huck, I knows him by de back."

"But I tell you you don't get the point."

"Blame de pint! I reck'n I knows what I knows. En mine you, de *real* pint is down furder—it's down deeper. It lays in de way Sollermun was raised. You take a man dat's got on'y one er two chillen: is dat man gwyne to be waseful o' chillen? No, he ain't; he can't 'ford it. *He* know how to value 'em. But you take a man dat's got 'bout

THE STORY OF "SOLLERMUN."

five million chillen runnin' roun' de house, en it's diffunt. *He* as soon chop a chile in two as a cat. Dey's plenty mo'. A chile er two, mo' er less, warn't no consekens to Sollermun, dad fetch him!"

I never see such a nigger. If he got a notion in his head once, there warn't no getting it out again. He was the most down on Solomon of any nigger I ever see. So I went to talking about other kings, and let Solomon slide. I told about Louis Sixteenth that got his head cut off in France long time ago; and about his little boy the dolphin, that would a been a king, but they took and shut him up in jail, and some say he died there.

"Po' little chap."

"But some says he got out and got away, and come to America."

"Dat's good! But he'll be pooty lonesome—dey ain' no kings here, is dey, Huck?"

"No."

"Den he cain't git no situation. What he gwyne to do?"

"Well, I don't know. Some of them gets on the police, and some of them learns people how to talk French."

"Why, Huck, doan de French people talk de same way we does?"

"*No*, Jim; you couldn't understand a word they said—not a single word."

"Well, now, I be ding-busted! How do dat come?"

"*I* don't know; but it's so. I got some of their jabber out of a book. Spose a man was to come to you and say *Polly-voo-franzy*—what would you think?"

"I wouldn' think nuff'n; I'd take en bust him over de head. Dat is, ef he warn't white. I wouldn't 'low no nigger to call me dat."

"Shucks, it ain't calling you anything. It's only saying, do you know how to talk French."

"Well, den, why couldn't he *say* it?"

"Why, he *is* a-saying it. That's a Frenchman's *way* of saying it."

"Well, it's a blame' ridicklous way, en I doan want to hear no mo' 'bout it. Dey ain' no sense in it."

"Looky here, Jim, does a cat talk like we do?"

"No, a cat don't."

"Well, does a cow?"

"No, a cow don't, nuther."

"Does a cat talk like a cow, or a cow talk like a cat?"

"No, dey don't."

"It's natural and right for 'em to talk different from each other, ain't it?"

" 'Course."

"And ain't it natural and right for a cat and a cow to talk different from *us?*"

"Why, mos' sholy it is."

"Well, then, why ain't it natural and right for a *Frenchman* to talk different from us?—you answer me that."

"Is a cat a man, Huck?"

"No."

"Well, den, dey ain't no sense in a cat talkin' like a man. Is a cow a man?—er is a cow a cat?"

"No, she ain't either of them."

"Well, den, she ain' got no business to talk like either one er the yuther of 'em. Is a Frenchman a man?"

"Yes."

"*Well*, den! Dad blame it, why doan he *talk* like a man?—you answer me *dat!*"

I see it warn't no use wasting words—you can't learn a nigger to argue. So I quit.

Chapter XV.

"WE WOULD SELL THE RAFT."

WE JUDGED that three nights more would fetch us to Cairo, at the bottom of Illinois, where the Ohio river comes in, and that was what we was after. We would sell the raft and get on a steamboat and go way up the Ohio amongst the free States, and then be out of trouble.

Well, the second night a fog begun to come on, and we made for a tow-head to tie to, for it wouldn't do to try to run in fog, but when I paddled ahead in the canoe, with the line, to make fast, there warn't anything but little saplings to tie to. I passed the line around one of them right on the edge of the cut bank, but there was a stiff current and the raft come booming down so lively she tore it out by the roots and away she went. I see the fog closing down and it made me so sick and scared I couldn't budge for most a half a minute it seemed to me—and then there warn't no raft in sight; you couldn't see twenty yards. I jumped into the canoe and run back to the stern and grabbed the paddle and set her back a stroke. But she didn't come. I was in such a hurry I hadn't untied her. I got up and tried to untie her, but I was so excited my hands shook so I couldn't hardly do anything with them.

As soon as I got started I took out after the raft, hot and heavy, right down the tow-head. That was all right, as far as it went, but the tow-head warn't sixty yards long, and the minute I flew by the foot of it I shot out into the solid white fog and hadn't no more idea which way I was going than a dead man.

Thinks I, it won't do to paddle; first I know I'll run into the bank or a tow-head or something; I got to set still and float, and yet it's mighty fidgety business to have to hold your hands still at such a time. I whooped, and listened. Away down there, somewheres, I hears a small whoop and up comes my spirits. I went tearing after it, listening sharp to hear it again. The next time it come, I see I warn't heading for it but heading away to the right of it. And the next time, I was heading away to the left of it—and not gaining on it much, either, for I was flying around, this way and that and t'other, but it was going straight ahead all the time.

I did wish the fool would think to beat a tin pan, and beat it all the time, but he never did, and it was the still places between the whoops that was making the trouble for me. Well, I fought along, and directly I hears the whoop *behind* me. I was tangled good, now. That was somebody else's whoop, or else I was turned around.

I throwed the paddle down. I heard the whoop again; it was behind me yet, but in a different place; it kept coming, and kept changing its place, and I kept answering, till by and by it was in front of me again and I knowed the current had swung the canoe's head down stream and I was all right, if that was Jim and not some other raftsman hollering. I couldn't tell nothing about voices in a fog, for nothing don't look natural nor sound natural in a fog.

The whooping went on, and in about a minute I come a booming down on a cut bank with smoky ghosts of big trees on it and the current throwed me off to the left and shot by, amongst a lot of snags that fairly roared, the current was tearing by them so swift.

In another second or two it was solid white and still again. I set perfectly still then, listening to my heart thump, and I reckon I didn't draw a breath while it thumped a hundred.

I just give up, then. I knowed what the matter was. That cut bank was an island and Jim had gone down t'other side of it. It warn't no tow-head, that you could float by in ten minutes. It had the big timber of a regular island; it might be five or six mile long and more than a half a mile wide.

I kept quiet, with my ears cocked, about fifteen minutes, I reckon. I was floating along, of course, four or five mile an hour; but you don't ever think of that. No, you *feel* like you are laying dead still on the water; and if a little glimpse of a snag slips by, you don't think to yourself how fast *you're* going, but you catch your breath and

AMONG THE SNAGS.

think, My! how that snag's tearing along. If you think it ain't dismal and lonesome out in a fog that way, by yourself, in the night,
you try it once—you'll see.

Next, for about a half an hour, I whoops now and then; at last I
hears the answer a long ways off, and tries to follow it, but I couldn't
do it, and directly I judged I'd got into a nest of tow-heads, for I had
little dim glimpses of them on both sides of me, sometimes, just a
narrow channel between; and some that I couldn't see, I knowed
was there, because I'd hear the wash of the current against the old
dead brush and trash that hung over the banks. Well, I warn't long
losing the whoops down amongst the tow-heads and I only tried to
chase them a little while, anyway, because it was worse than chasing a jack-o-lantern. You never knowed a sound dodge around so,
and swap places so quick and so much.

I had to claw away from the bank pretty lively, four or five times,
to keep from knocking the islands out of the river, and so I judged
the raft must be butting into the bank every now and then, or else it
would get further ahead and clear out of hearing—it was floating a
little faster than what I was.

Well, I seemed to be in the open river again, by and by, but I
couldn't hear no sign of a whoop nowheres. I reckoned Jim had

fetched up on a snag, maybe, and it was all up with him. I was good and tired, so I laid down in the canoe and said I wouldn't bother no more. I didn't want to go to sleep, of course; but I was so sleepy I couldn't help it; so I thought I would take just one little cat-nap.

But I reckon it was more than a cat nap, for when I waked up the stars was shining bright, the fog was all gone and I was spinning down a big bend stern first. First I didn't know where I was; I thought I was dreaming; and when things begun to come back to me, they seemed to come up dim out of last week.

It was a monstrous big river here, with the tallest and the thickest kind of timber on both banks; just a solid wall, as well as I could see, by the stars. I looked away down stream, and seen a black speck on the water. I took out after it; but when I got to it it warn't nothing but a couple of saw-logs made fast together. Then I see another speck, and chased that; then another, and this time I was right. It was the raft.

ASLEEP ON THE RAFT.

When I got to it Jim was setting there with his head down between his knees, asleep, with his right arm hanging over the steering oar. The other oar was smashed off, and the raft was littered up with leaves and branches and dirt. So she'd had a rough time.

I made fast and laid down under Jim's nose on the raft, and begun to gap, and stretch my fists out against Jim, and says:

"Hello, Jim, have I been asleep? Why didn't you stir me up?"

"Goodness gracious, is dat you, Huck? En you ain' dead—you ain' drownded—you's back agin? It's too good for true, honey, it's too good for true. Lemme look at you, chile, lemme feel o' you. No, you ain' dead! you's back agin, 'live en soun', jis' de same ole Huck—de same ole Huck, thanks to goodness!"

"What's the matter with you, Jim? You been a drinking?"

"Drinkin'? Has I ben a drinkin'? Has I had a chance to be a drinkin'?"

"Well, then, what makes you talk so wild?"

"How does I talk wild?"

"*How?* Why, hain't you been talking about my coming back, and all that stuff, as if I'd been gone away?"

"Huck—Huck Finn, you look me in de eye; look me in de eye. *Hain't* you ben gone away?"

"Gone away? Why what in the nation do you mean? *I* hain't been gone anywheres. Where would I go to?"

"Well, looky-here, boss, dey's sumf'n wrong, dey is. Is I *me*, or who *is* I? Is I heah, or whah *is* I? Now dat's what I wants to know."

"Well I think you're here, plain enough, but I think you're a tangle-headed old fool, Jim."

"I is, is I? Well you answer me dis. Didn't you tote out de line in de canoe, fer to make fas' to de tow-head?"

"No, I didn't. What tow-head? I hain't seen no tow-head."

"You hain't seen no tow-head? Looky-here—didn't de line pull loose en de raf' go a hummin' down de river, en leave you en de canoe behine in de fog?"

"What fog?"

"Why *de* fog. De fog dat's ben aroun' all night. En didn't you whoop, en didn't I whoop, tell we got mix' up in de islands en one un us got los' en t'other one was jis' as good as los', 'kase he didn' know whah he wuz? En didn't I bust up agin a lot er dem islands en have a turrible time en mos' git drownded? Now ain' dat so, boss—ain't it so? You answer me dat."

"Well this is too many for me, Jim. I hain't seen no fog, nor no islands, nor no troubles, nor nothing. I been setting here talking with you all night till you went to sleep about ten minutes ago, and I reckon I done the same. You couldn't a got drunk in that time, so of course you've been dreaming."

"Dad fetch it, how is I gwyne to dream all dat in ten minutes?"

"Well, hang it all, you did dream it, because there didn't any of it happen."

"But Huck, it's all jis' as plain to me as—"

"It don't make no difference how plain it is, there ain't nothing in it. I know, because I've been here all the time."

Jim didn't say nothing for about five minutes, but set there studying over it. Then he says:

"Well, den, I reck'n I did dream it, Huck, but dog my cats ef it ain't de powerfullest dream I ever see. En I hain't ever had no dream b'fo' dat's tired me like dis one."

"O, well, that's all right, because a dream does tire a body like everything sometimes. But this one was a staving dream—tell me all about it Jim."

So Jim went to work and told me the whole thing right through, just as it happened, only he painted it up considerable. Then he said he must start in and " 'terpret" it, because it was sent for a warning. He said the first tow-head stood for a man that would try to do us some good, but the current was another man that would get us away from him. The whoops was warnings that would come to us every now and then, and if we didn't try hard to make out to understand them they'd just take us into bad luck, 'stead of keeping us out of it. The lot of tow-heads was troubles we was going to get into with quarrelsome people and all kinds of mean folks, but if we minded our business and didn't talk back and aggravate them, we would pull through and get out of the fog and into the big clear river, which was the free States, and wouldn't have no more trouble.

It had clouded up pretty dark just after I got onto the raft, but it was clearing up again, now.

"O, well, that's all interpreted well enough, as far as it goes, Jim," I says, "but what does *these* things stand for?"

It was the leaves and rubbish on the raft, and the smashed oar. You could see them first rate, now.

Jim looked at the trash, and then looked at me, and back at the trash again. He had got the dream fixed so strong in his head that he couldn't seem to shake it loose and get the facts back into its place again, right away. But when he did get the thing straightened around, he looked at me steady, without ever smiling, and says:

"What do dey stan' for? I's gwyne to tell you. When I got all wore out, wid work, en wid de callin' for you, en went to sleep, my heart wuz mos' broke bekase you wuz los', en I didn' k'yer no mo' what become er me en de raf'. En when I wake' up en fine you back agin, all safe en soun', de tears come en I could a got down on my knees en kiss' yo' foot I's so thankful. En all you wuz thinkin' 'bout, wuz how you could make a fool uv ole Jim wid a lie. Dat truck dah is *trash;* en trash is what people is dat puts dirt on de head er dey fren's en makes 'em ashamed."

Then he got up, slow, and walked to the wigwam, and went in there, without saying anything but that. But that was enough. It made me feel so mean I could almost kissed *his* foot to get him to take it back.

It was fifteen minutes before I could work myself up to go and humble myself to a nigger—but I done it, and I warn't ever sorry for it afterwards, neither. I didn't do him no more mean tricks, and I wouldn't done that one if I'd a knowed it would make him feel that way.

Chapter XVI

"IT *AMOUNTED* TO SOMETHING
BEING A RAFTSMAN."

WE SLEPT most all day, and started out, at night, a little ways behind a monstrous long raft that was as long going by as a procession. She had four long sweeps at each end, so we judged she carried as many as thirty men, likely. She had five big wigwams aboard, wide apart, and an open camp fire in the middle, and a tall flag pole at each end. There was a power of style about her. It *amounted* to something being a raftsman on such a craft as that.

We went drifting down into a big bend, and the night clouded up and got hot. The river was very wide and was walled with solid timber on both sides; you couldn't see a break in it, hardly ever, or a light. We talked about Cairo, and wondered whether we would know it when we got to it. I said likely we wouldn't, because I had heard say there warn't but about a dozen houses there, and if they didn't happen to have them lit up, how was we going to know we was passing a town? Jim said if the two big rivers joined together there, that would show. But I said maybe we might think we was passing the foot of an island and coming into the same old river again. That disturbed Jim—and me too. So the question was, what to do? I said, paddle ashore the first time a light showed, and tell them pap was behind, coming along with a trading scow, and was a green hand at the business, and wanted to know how far it was to Cairo. Jim thought it was a good idea, so we took a smoke on it and waited.

But you know a young person can't wait very well when he is impatient to find a thing out. We talked it over, and by and by Jim said it was such a black night, now, that it wouldn't be no resk to swim down to the big raft and crawl aboard and listen—they would talk about Cairo, because they would be calculating to go ashore there for a spree, maybe, or anyway they would send boats ashore to buy whisky or fresh meat or something. Jim had a wonderful level head, for a nigger; he could most always start a good plan when you wanted one.

I stood up and shook my rags off and jumped into the river, and struck out for the raft's light. By and by, when I got down nearly to

"I SWUM DOWN ALONG
THE RAFT."

her I eased up and went slow and cautious. But everything was all right—nobody at the sweeps. So I swum down along the raft till I was most abreast the camp fire in the middle. Then I crawled aboard and inched along and got in amongst some bundles of shingles on the weather side of the fire. There was thirteen men there— they was the watch on deck, of course. And a mighty rough looking lot, too. They had a jug, and tin cups, and they kept the jug moving. One man was singing—roaring, you may say; and it warn't a nice song—for a parlor, anyway. He roared through his nose, and strung out the last word of every line very long. When he was done they all fetched a kind of Injun war-whoop, and then another was sung. It begun:

"There was a woman in our towdn,
   In our towdn did dwed'l (dwell,)
She loved her husband dear-i-lee,
   But another man twyste as wed'l.

Singing too, riloo, riloo, riloo,
   Ri-too, riloo, rilay - - - - e,
She loved her husband dear-i-lee,
   But another man twyste as wed'l."

And so on—fourteen verses. It was kind of poor, and when he was
going to start on the next verse one of them said it was the tune the
old cow died on; and another one said, "O, give us a rest;" and
another one told him to take a walk. They made fun of him till he
got mad and jumped up and begun to cuss the crowd, and said he
could lam any thief in the lot.

They was all about to make a break for him, but the biggest man
there jumped up and says:

"Set whar you are, gentlemen. Leave him to me; he's my meat."

Then he jumped up in the air three times and cracked his heels

"HE JUMPED UP IN THE AIR."

together every time. He flung off a buckskin coat that was all hung with fringes, and says, "You lay thar tell the chawin-up's done;" and flung his hat down, which was all over ribbons, and says, "You lay thar tell his sufferins is over."

Then he jumped up in the air and cracked his heels together again and shouted out:

"Whoo-oop! I'm the old original iron-jawed, brass-mounted, copper-bellied corpse-maker from the wilds of Arkansaw! Look at me! I'm the man they call Sudden Death and General Desolation! Sired by a hurricane, dam'd by an earthquake, half-brother to the cholera, nearly related to the small-pox on the mother's side! Look at me! I take nineteen alligators and a bar'l of whisky for breakfast when I'm in robust health, and a bushel of rattlesnakes and a dead body when I'm ailing! I split the everlasting rocks with my glance and I squench the thunder when I speak! Whoo-oop! stand back and give me room according to my strength! Blood's my natural drink, and the wails of the dying is music to my ear! Cast your eye on me, gentlemen!—and lay low, and hold your breath, for I'm 'bout to turn myself loose!"

All the time he was getting this off, he was shaking his head and looking fierce, and kind of swelling around in a little circle, tucking up his wristbands, and now and then straightening up and beating his breast with his fist, saying "Look at me, gentlemen!" When he got through, he jumped up and cracked his heels together three times, and let off a roaring "whoo-oop! I'm the bloodiest son of a wildcat that lives!"

Then the man that had started the row tilted his old slouch hat down over his right eye; then he bent,

"WENT AROUND IN A LITTLE CIRCLE."

stooping forward, with his back sagged and his south end sticking out far, and his fists a-shoving out and drawing in in front of him, and so went around in a little circle about three times, swelling himself up and breathing hard. Then he straightened, and jumped up and cracked his heels together three times before he lit again (that made them cheer) and he begun to shout like this:

"Whoo-oop! Bow your neck and spread, for the kingdom of sorrow's a-coming! Hold me down to the earth, for I feel my powers a-working! whoo-oop! I'm a child of sin, *don't* let me get a start! Smoked glass, here, for all! don't attempt to look at me with the naked eye, gentlemen! When I'm playful I use the meridians of longitude and parallels of latitude for a seine, and drag the Atlantic ocean for whales! I scratch my head with the lightning and purr myself to sleep with the thunder! When I'm cold, I bile the Gulf of Mexico and bathe in it; when I'm hot I fan myself with an equinoctial storm; when I'm thirsty I reach up and suck a cloud dry like a sponge; when I range the earth hungry, famine follows in my tracks! Whoo-oop! Bow your neck and spread! I put my hand on the sun's face and make it night in the earth; I bite a piece out of the moon and hurry the seasons; I shake myself and crumble the mountains! Contemplate me through leather—*don't* use the naked eye! I'm the man with a petrified heart and biler-iron bowels! The massacre of isolated communities is the pastime of my idle moments, the destruction of nationalities the serious business of my life! The boundless vastness of the great American desert is my enclosed property, and I bury my dead on my own premises!"

He jumped up and cracked his heels together three times before he lit (they cheered him again), and as he come down he shouted out: "Whoo-oop! Bow your neck and spread, for the pet child of Calamity's a-coming!"

Then the other one went to swelling around and blowing again—the first one—the one they called Bob; next, the Child of Calamity chipped in again, bigger than ever; then they both got at it at the same time, swelling round and round each other and punching their fists most into each other's faces, and whooping and jawing like Injuns; then Bob called the Child names, and the Child called him names back again; next, Bob called him a heap rougher names and the Child come back at him with the very worst kind of language;

next, Bob knocked the Child's hat off, and the Child picked it up and kicked Bob's ribbony hat about six foot; Bob went and got it and said never mind, this warn't going to be the last of this thing, because he was a man that never forgot and never forgive, and so the Child better look out, for there was a time a-coming, just as sure as he was a living man, that he would have to answer to him with the best blood in his body. The Child said no man was willinger than he was, for that time to come, and he would give Bob fair warning, *now*, never to cross his path again, for he could never rest till he had waded in his blood, for such was his nature, though he was sparing him now on account of his family, if he had one.

Both of them was edging away in different directions, growling and shaking their heads and going on about what they was going to do; but a little black-whiskered chap skipped up and says:

"Come back here, you couple of chicken-livered cowards, and I'll thrash the two of ye!"

And he done it, too. He snatched them, he jerked them this way and that, he booted them around, he knocked them sprawling faster than they could get up. Why, it warn't two minutes till they begged like dogs—and how the other lot did yell and laugh and clap their hands all the way through, and shout "Sail in, Corpse-Maker!" "Hi! at him again, Child of Calamity!" "Bully for you, little Davy!"

Well, it was a perfect pow-wow for a while. Bob and the Child had red noses and black eyes when they got through. Little Davy made them own up that they was sneaks and cowards and not fit to eat with a dog or drink with a nigger; then Bob and the Child shook hands with each other, very solemn, and said they had always respected each other and was willing to let bygones be bygones. So then they washed their faces in the river, and just then there was a loud order to stand by for a crossing, and some of them went forward to man the sweeps there, and the rest went aft to handle the after sweeps.

I laid still and waited for fifteen minutes, and had a smoke out of a pipe that one of them left in reach; then the crossing was finished and they stumped back and had a drink around and went to talking and singing again.

Next they got out an old fiddle, and one played, and another patted Juba, and the rest turned themselves loose on a regular old-fashioned keel-boat break-down. They couldn't keep that up very long without getting winded, so by and by they settled around the jug again.

They sung "Jolly, jolly raftsman's the life for me," with a rousing chorus, and then they got to talking about differences betwixt hogs, and their different kind of habits; and next about women and their different ways; and next about the best ways to put out houses that was afire; and next about what ought to be done with the Injuns; and next about what a king had to do, and how much he got; and next about how to make cats fight; and next about what to do when a man has fits; and next about differences betwixt clear-water rivers and muddy-water ones. The man they called Ed, said the muddy Mississippi water was wholesomer to drink than the clear water of the Ohio; he said if you let a pint of this yaller Mississippi water settle, you would have about a half to three-quarters of an inch of mud in the bottom, according to the stage of the river, and then it warn't no better than Ohio water—what you wanted to do was to

"HE KNOCKED THEM SPRAWLING."

keep it stirred up—and when the river was low, keep mud on hand to put in and thicken the water up the way it ought to be.

The Child of Calamity said that was so; he said there was nutritiousness in the mud, and a man that drunk Mississippi water could grow corn in his stomach if he wanted to. He says:

"You look at the graveyards; that tells the tale. Trees won't grow worth shucks in a Cincinnati graveyard, but in a Sent Louis graveyard they grow upwards of eight hundred foot high. It's all on

AN OLD-FASHIONED BREAK-DOWN.

account of the water the people drunk before they laid up. A Cincinnati corpse don't richen a soil any."

And they talked about how Ohio water didn't like to mix with Mississippi water. Ed said if you take the Mississippi on a rise when the Ohio is low, you'll find a wide band of clear water all the way down the east side of the Mississippi for a hundred mile or more, and the minute you get out a quarter of a mile from shore and pass the line, it is all thick and yaller the rest of the way across.

Then they talked about how to keep tobacco from getting mouldy, and from that they went into ghosts and told about a lot that other folks had seen; but Ed says:

"Why don't you tell something that you've seen yourselves? Now let me have a say. Five years ago I was on a raft as big as this, and right along here it was a bright moonshiny night, just after midnight, and I was on watch and boss of the stabboard oar forrard, and one of my pards was a man named Dick Allbright, and he come along to where I was setting, forrard—gaping and stretching, he was—and stooped down on the edge of the raft and washed his face in the river, and come and set down by me and got out his pipe, and had just got it filled, when he looks up and says, 'Why looky-here,' he says, 'ain't that Buck Miller's place, over yander in the bend?' 'Yes,' says I, 'it is—why?' He laid his pipe down and leant his head on his hand, and says, 'I thought we'd be furder down.' I says, 'I thought it too, when I went off watch'—we was standing six hours on and six off—'but the boys told me,' I says, 'that the raft didn't seem to hardly move, for the last hour,' says I, 'though she's a slipping along all right, now,' says I. He give a kind of a groan and says, 'I've seed a raft act so before, along here,' he says; ' 'pears to me the current has most quit, above the head of this bend durin' the last two years,' he says.

"Well, he raised up two or three times, and looked away off and around on the water. That started me at it, too. A body is always doing what he sees somebody else doing, though there mayn't be no sense in it. Pretty soon I see a black something floating on the water away off to stabboard and quartering behind us. I see he was looking at it, too. I says, 'What's that?' He says, sort of pettish, ''Tain't nothing but an old empty bar'l.' 'An empty bar'l!' says I, 'why,' says I, 'a spy-glass is a fool to *your* eyes. How can you tell it's an empty bar'l?' He says, 'I don't know; I reckon it ain't a bar'l; but I thought it might be,' says he. 'Yes,' I says, 'so it might be; and it might be anything else, too; a body can't tell nothing about it, such a distance as that,' I says.

"We hadn't nothing else to do, so we kept on watching it. By and by I says, 'Why looky-here, Dick Allbright, that thing's a-gaining on us, I believe.' He never said nothing. The thing gained and gained, and I judged it must be a dog that was about tired out. Well, we swung down into the crossing, and the thing floated across the bright streak of the moonshine, and by George it *was* a bar'l.

"Says I, 'Dick Allbright, what made you think that thing was a bar'l, when it was a half a mile off,' says I. Says he, 'I don't know.' Says I, 'You tell me, Dick Allbright.' He says, 'Well, I knowed it was a bar'l; I've seen it before; lots has seen it; they says it's a ha'nted bar'l.' I called the rest of the watch and they come and stood there, and I told them what Dick said. It floated right along abreast, now, and didn't gain any more. It was about twenty foot off. Some was for having it aboard, but the rest didn't want to. Dick Allbright said rafts that had fooled with it had got bad luck by it. The captain of the watch said he didn't believe in it. He said he reckoned the bar'l gained on us because it was in a little better current than what we was; he said it would leave by and by.

"So then we went to talking about other things, and we had a song, and then a breakdown; and after that the captain of the watch called for another song; but it was clouding up, now, and the bar'l stuck right thar in the same place, and the song

THE MYSTERIOUS BARREL.

didn't seem to have much warm-up to it, somehow, and so they didn't finish it, and there warn't any cheers, but it sort of dropped flat, and nobody said anything for a minute. Then everybody tried to talk at once, and one chap got off a joke, but it warn't no use, they didn't laugh, and even the chap that made the joke didn't laugh at it, which ain't usual. We all just settled down glum, and watched the bar'l, and was oneasy and oncomfortable. Well sir, it shut down black and still, and then the wind begin to moan around, and next the lightning begin to play and the thunder to grumble. And pretty soon there was a regular storm, and in the middle of it a man that was running aft stumbled and fell and sprained his ancle so bad he had to lay up. This made the boys shake their heads. And every time the lightning come, there was that bar'l, with the blue lights

winking around it. We was always on the lookout for it. But by and
by, towards dawn, she was gone. When the day come we couldn't
see her anywhere, and we warn't sorry, neither.

"But next night about half past nine, when there was songs and
high jinks going on, here she comes again, and took her old roost on
the stabboard side. There warn't no more high jinks. Everybody got
solemn; nobody talked; you couldn't get anybody to do anything
but set around moody and look at the bar'l. It begun to cloud up
again. When the watch changed, the off watch stayed up, 'stead of
turning in. The storm ripped and roared around all night, and in the
middle of it another man tripped and sprained his ancle and had to
knock off. The bar'l left, towards day, and nobody see it go.

"SOON THERE WAS A REGULAR STORM."

"Everybody was sober and down in the mouth all day. I don't
mean the kind of sober that comes of leaving liquor alone. Not that.
They was quiet, but they all drunk more than usual—not together,
but each man sidled off and took it private, by himself.

"After dark the off watch didn't turn in; nobody sung, nobody
talked; the boys didn't scatter around, neither; they sort of huddled

together, forrard, and for two hours they set there, perfectly still, looking steady in the one direction, and heaving a sigh once in a while. And then, here comes the bar'l again. She took up her old place. She staid there all night; nobody turned in. The storm come on again, after midnight. It got awful dark; the rain poured down; hail, too; the thunder boomed and roared and bellowed; the wind blowed a hurricane; and the lightning spread over everything in big sheets of glare, and showed the whole raft as plain as day, and the river lashed up white as milk as far as you could see for miles, and there was that bar'l jiggering along, same as ever. The captain ordered the watch to man the after sweeps for a crossing, and nobody would go—no more sprained ancles for them, they said. They wouldn't even *walk* aft. Well then, just then the sky split wide open, with a crash, and the lightning killed two men of the after watch and crippled two more. Crippled them how, says you? Why, *sprained their ancles!*

"THE LIGHTNING KILLED TWO MEN."

"The bar'l left, in the dark betwixt lightnings, towards dawn. Well not a body eat a bite at breakfast that morning. After that the men loafed around, in twos and threes, and talked low together. But none of them herded with Dick Allbright. They all give him the cold shake. If he come around where any of the men was, they split up and sidled away. They wouldn't man a sweep with him. The captain had all the skiffs hauled up on the raft, alongside of his wigwam, and wouldn't let the dead men be took ashore to be planted; he didn't believe a man that got ashore would come back; and he was right.

"After night come, you could see pretty plain that there was going to be trouble if that bar'l come again, there was such a muttering going on. A good many wanted to kill Dick Allbright, because he'd seen the bar'l on other trips and that had an ugly look. Some wanted to put him ashore. Some said, let's all go ashore in a pile, if the bar'l comes again.

"This kind of whispers was still going on, the men being bunched together forrard watching for the bar'l, when lo and behold you, here she comes again. Down she comes, slow and steady, and settles into her old tracks. You could a heard a pin drop. Then up comes the captain, and says: 'Boys, don't be a pack of children and fools; I don't want this bar'l to be dogging us all the way to Orleans, and *you* don't; well, then, how's the best way to stop it? Burn it up—that's the way. I'm going to fetch it aboard,' he says. And before anybody could say a word, in he went.

"He swum to it, and as he come pushing it to the raft, the men spread to one side. But the old man got it aboard and busted in the head, and there was a baby in it! Yes sir, a stark naked baby. It was Dick Allbright's baby; he owned up and said so. 'Yes,' he says, a leaning over it, 'Yes, it is my own lamented darling, my poor lost Charles William Allbright deceased,' says he—for he could curl his tongue around the bulliest words in the language when he was a mind to, and lay them before you without a j'int started, anywheres. Yes, he said he used to live up at the head of this bend, and one night he choked his child, which was crying, not intending to kill it, which was prob'ly a lie, and then he was scared, and buried it in a bar'l, before his wife got home, and off he went, and struck the northern trail and went to rafting, and this was the third year that the bar'l had chased him. He said the bad luck always begun light, and lasted till four men was killed, and then the bar'l didn't come any more after that. He said if the men would stand it one more night—and was agoing on like that, but the men had got enough. They started to get out a boat to take him ashore and lynch him, but he grabbed the little child all of a sudden and jumped overboard with it hugged up to his breast and shedding tears, and we never see him again in this life, poor old suffering soul, nor Charles William neither."

"*Who* was shedding tears?" says Bob; "was it Allbright, or the baby?"

"Why, Allbright, of course; didn't I tell you the baby was dead? Been dead three years—how could it cry?"

"Well, never mind how it could cry—how could it *keep*, all that time?" says Davy. "You answer me that."

"I don't know how it done it," says Ed. "It done it, though,—that's all I know about it."

"Say—what did they do with the bar'l?" says the Child of Calamity.

"Why, they hove it overboard and it sunk like a chunk of lead."

"Edward, did the child look like it was choked?" says one.

"Did it have its hair parted?" says another.

"What was the brand on that bar'l, Eddy?" says a fellow they called Bill.

"Have you got the papers for them statistics, Edmund?" says Jimmy.

"Say, Edwin, was you one of the men that was killed by the lightning?" says Davy.

"Him? O, no, he was both of 'em," says Bob. Then they all haw-hawed.

"GRABBED THE LITTLE CHILD."

"Say, Edward, don't you reckon you'd better take a pill? You look bad—don't you feel pale?" says the Child of Calamity.

"O, come, now, Eddy," says Jimmy, "show up; you must a kept part of that bar'l to prove the thing by. Show us the bunghole—*do*—and we'll all believe you."

"Say, boys," says Bill, "less divide it up. Thar's thirteen of us. I can swaller a thirteenth of the yarn, if you can worry down the rest."

Ed got up mad and said they could all go to some place which he ripped out pretty savage, and then walked off aft cussing to himself, and they yelling and jeering at him and roaring and laughing so you could hear them a mile.

"Boys, we'll split a watermelon on that," says the Child of Calamity, and he come rummaging around in the dark amongst the shingle bundles where I was, and put his hand on me. I was warm and soft and naked; so he says "Ouch!" and jumped back.

"Fetch a lantern or a chunk of fire here, boys—there's a snake here as big as a cow!"

So they run there with a lantern and crowded up and looked in on me.

"ED GOT UP MAD."

"Come out of that, you beggar!" says one.

"Who are you?" says another.

"What are you after here? Speak up prompt, or overboard you go."

"Snake him out, boys. Snatch him out by the heels."

I began to beg, and crept out amongst them trembling. They looked me over, wondering, and the Child of Calamity says:

"A cussed thief! Lend a hand and less heave him overboard!"

"No," says Big Bob, "less get out the paint pot and paint him a sky blue all over from head to heel, and *then* heave him over!"

"Good! That's it. Go for the paint, Jimmy."

When the paint come, and Bob took the brush and was just going to begin, the others laughing and rubbing their hands, I begun to cry, and that sort of worked on Davy and he says:

" 'Vast there! He's nothing but a cub. I'll paint the man that tetches him!"

So he looked around on them, and some of them grumbled and growled, and Bob put down the paint and the others didn't take it up.

"Come here to the fire, and less see what you're up to here," says Davy. "Now set down there and give an account of yourself. How long

"WHO ARE YOU?"

have you been aboard here?"

"Not over a quarter of a minute, sir," says I.

"How did you get dry so quick?"

"I don't know, sir. I'm always that way, mostly."

"O, you are, are you? What's your name?"

I warn't going to tell my name. I didn't know what to say, so I just says:

"Charles William Allbright, sir."

Then they roared—the whole crowd; and I was mighty glad I said that, because maybe laughing would get them in a better humor.

When they got done laughing, Davy says:

"It won't hardly do, Charles William. You couldn't have growed this much in five year, and you was a baby when you come out of the bar'l, you know, and dead at that. Come, now, tell a straight story, and nobody 'll hurt you, if you ain't up to anything wrong. What *is* your name?"

"Aleck Hopkins, sir. Aleck James Hopkins."

"Well, Aleck, where did you come from, here?"

"From a trading scow. She lays up the bend yonder. I was born on her. Pap has traded up and down here all his life; and he told me to

"CHARLES WILLIAM ALLBRIGHT, SIR."

swim off here, because when you went by he said he would like to get some of you to speak to a Mr. Jonas Turner, in Cairo, and tell him—"

"O, come!"

"Yes, sir, it's as true as the world; Pap he says—"

"O, your grandmother!"

They all laughed, and I tried again to talk, but they broke in on me and stopped me.

"Now looky-here," says Davy; "you're scared, and so you talk wild. Honest, now, do you live in a scow, or is it a lie?"

"Yes, sir, in a trading scow. She lays up at the head of the bend. But I warn't born in her. It's our first trip."

"Now you're talking! What did you come aboard here, for? To steal?"

"No, sir, I didn't. It was only to get a ride on the raft. All boys does that."

"Well, I know that. But what did you hide, for?"

"Sometimes they drive the boys off."

"So they do. They might steal. Looky-here; if we let you off this time, will you keep out of these kind of scrapes hereafter?"

" 'Deed I will, boss. You try me."

"All right, then. You ain't but little ways from shore. Overboard with you, and don't you make a fool of yourself another time this way. Blast it, boy, some raftsmen would rawhide you till you were black and blue!"

I didn't wait to kiss good-bye, but went overboard and broke for shore. When Jim come along by and by, the big raft was away out of sight around the point. I swum out and got aboard, and was mighty glad to see home again.

I had to tell Jim I didn't find out how far it was to Cairo. He was pretty sorry. There warn't nothing to do now but to look out sharp for the town and not pass it without seeing it. He said he'd be mighty sure to see it, because he'd be a free man the minute he seen it, but if he missed it he'd be in the slave country again and no more show for freedom. Every little while he jumps up and says:

"Dah she is!"

But it warn't. It was jack-o'-lanterns, or lightning bugs; so he set down again, and went to watching, same as before. Jim said it made him all over trembly and feverish to be so close to freedom. Well, I can tell you it made me all over trembly and feverish, too, to hear him, because I begun to get it through my head that he *was* most free—and who was to blame for it? Why, *me*. I couldn't get that out of my conscience, no how nor no way. It got to troubling me so I couldn't rest, I couldn't stay still in one place. It hadn't ever come home to me before what this thing was that I was doing. But now it did; and it staid with me, and scorched me more and more. I tried to make out to myself that *I* warn't to blame, because *I* didn't run Jim off from his rightful owner; but it warn't no use, conscience up and says, every time, 'But you knowed he was running for his freedom and you could a paddled ashore and told somebody.' That was so— I couldn't get around that, no way. That was where it pinched. Conscience says to me, 'What had poor Miss Watson done to you, that you could see her nigger go off right under your eyes and never say one single word? What did that poor old woman do to you, that you could treat her so mean? Why she tried to learn you your book, she tried to learn you your manners, she tried to be good to you every way she knowed how. *That's* what she done.'

I got to feeling so mean and so miserable I most wished I was dead. I fidgeted up and down the raft, abusing myself to myself, and Jim was fidgeting up and down past me. We neither of us could keep still. Every time he danced around and says 'Dah's Cairo!' it went through me like a shot, and I thought if it *was* Cairo I reckoned I would die of miserableness.

Jim talked out loud all the time while I was talking to myself. He was saying how the first thing he would do when he got to a free State he would go to saving up money and never spend a single cent, and when he got enough he would buy his wife, which was owned on a farm close to where Miss Watson lived; and then they would both work to buy the two children; and if their master wouldn't sell them, they'd get an ab'litionist to go and steal them.

It most froze me to hear such talk. He wouldn't ever dared to talk such talk in his life before. Just see what a difference it made in him the minute he judged he was about free. It was according to the old saying, 'Give a nigger an inch and he'll take an ell.' Thinks I, this is what comes of my not thinking. Here was this nigger which I had as good as helped to run away, coming right out flat-footed and saying he would steal his children—children that belonged to a man I didn't even know; a man that hadn't ever done me no harm.

I was sorry to hear Jim say that, it was such a lowering of him. My conscience got to stirring me up hotter than ever, until at last I says to it, 'Let up on me—it ain't too late, yet—I'll paddle ashore at the first light and tell.' I felt easy and happy and light as a feather right off. All my troubles was gone. I went to looking out sharp for a light and sort of singing to myself. By and by one showed. Jim sings out:

"We's safe, Huck, we's safe! Jump up and crack yo' heels, dat's de good ole Cairo at las' I jis' knows it!"

I says:

"I'll take the canoe and go see, Jim. It mightn't be, you know."

He jumped and got the canoe ready, and put his old coat in the bottom for me to set on, and give me the paddle; and as I shoved off he says:

"Pooty soon I'll be a-shout'n for joy, en I'll say, it's all on accounts o' Huck; I's a free man, en I couldn't ever ben free ef it hadn' ben for Huck; Huck done it. Jim won't ever forgit you, Huck; you's de bes' fren' Jim's ever had; en you's de *only* fren' ole Jim's got, now."

I was paddling off, all in a sweat to tell on him; but when he says this it seemed to kind of take the tuck all out of me. I went along slow, then, and I warn't right down certain whether I was glad I started or whether I warn't. When I was fifty yards off, Jim says:

"Dah you goes, de ole true Huck; de on'y white genlman dat ever kep' his promise to ole Jim."

Well, I just felt sick. But I says, I *got* to do it—I can't get *out* of it. Right then, along comes a skiff with two men in it, with guns, and they stopped and I stopped. One of them says:

"What's that, yonder?"

"A piece of a raft," I says.

"Do you belong on it?"

"Yes, sir."

"Any men on it?"

"Only one, sir."

"Well, there's five niggers run off, to-night, up yonder above the head of the bend. Is your man white, or black?"

I didn't answer up prompt. I tried to, but the words wouldn't come. I tried, for a second or two, to brace up, and out with it, but I warn't man enough—hadn't the spunk of a rabbit. I see I was weakening; so I just give up trying, and up and says—

"He's white."

"I reckon we'll go and see for ourselves."

"I wish you would," says I, "because it's pap that's there, and maybe you'd help me tow the raft ashore where the light is. He's sick—and so is mam and Mary Ann."

"Oh, the devil! We're in a hurry, boy. But I s'pose we've got to. Come—buckle to your paddle, and let's get along."

I buckled to my paddle and they laid to their oars. When we had made a stroke or two, I says:

"Pap 'll be mighty much obleeged to you, I can tell you. Everybody goes away when I want them to help me tow the raft ashore and I can't do it by myself."

"Well, that's infernal mean. Odd, too. Say, boy, what's the matter with your father?"

"It's the—a—the—well, it ain't anything, much."

They stopped pulling. It warn't but a mighty little ways to the raft, now. One says:

"Boy, that's a lie. What *is* the matter with your pap? Answer up square, now, and it'll be the better for you."

"I will, sir, I will, honest—but don't leave us, please. It's the—the—gentlemen, if you'll only pull ahead, and let me heave you the head-line, you won't have to come a-near the raft—please do."

"Set her back, John, set her back!" says one. They backed water. "Keep away, boy—keep to looard. Confound it, I just expect the wind has blowed it to us. Your pap's got the small-pox, and you know it precious well. Why didn't you come out and say so? Do you want to spread it all over?"

"Well," says I, a-blubbering, "I've told everybody before, and then they just went away and left us."

"Poor devil, there's something in that. We are right down sorry for you, but we—well, hang it, we don't want the small-pox, you

"BOY, THAT'S A LIE."

see. Look here, I'll tell you what to do. Don't you try to land by yourself, or you'll smash everything to pieces. You float along down about twenty miles and you'll come to a town on the left hand side of the river. It will be long after sun-up, then, and when you ask for help, you tell them your folks are all down with chills and fever. Don't be a fool again and let people guess what is the matter. Now we're trying to do you a kindness; so you just put twenty miles between us, that's a good boy. It wouldn't do any good to land yonder where the light is—it's only a wood yard. Say—I reckon your father's poor, and I'm bound to say he's in pretty hard luck. Here—I'll put a twenty-dollar gold piece on this board, and you get it when it floats by. I feel mighty mean to leave you, but my kingdom! it won't do to fool with small-pox, don't you see?"

"Hold on, Parker," says the other man, "here's a twenty to put on the board for me. Good-bye, boy, you do as Mr. Parker told you and you'll be all right."

"That's so, my boy—good-bye, good-bye. If you see any runaway niggers, you get help and nab them, and you can make some money by it."

"Good-bye, sir," says I, "I won't let no runaway niggers get by me if I can help it."

They went off, and I got aboard the raft, feeling bad and low, because I knowed very well I had done wrong, and I see it warn't no use for me to try to learn to do right; a body that don't get *started* right when he's little, ain't got no show—when the pinch comes there ain't nothing to back him up and keep him to his work, and so he gets beat. Then I thought a minute, and says to myself, hold on,—s'pose you'd a done right and give Jim up; would you felt better than what you do now? No, says I, I'd feel bad—I'd feel just the same way I do now. Well, then, says I, what's the use you learning to do right, when it's troublesome to do right and ain't no trouble to do wrong, and the wages is just the same? I was stuck. I couldn't answer that. So I reckoned I wouldn't bother no more about it, but after this always do whichever come handiest at the time.

I went into the wigwam; Jim warn't there. I looked all around; he warn't anywhere. I says:

"Jim!"

"Here I is, Huck. Is dey out o' sight, yit? Don't talk loud."

He was in the river, under the stern-oar, with just his nose out. I told him they was out of sight, so he come aboard. He says:

"I was a-listenin' to all de talk, en I slips into de river en was gwyne to shove for sho' if dey come aboard. Den I was gwyne to swim to de raf' agin when dey was gone. But lawsy, how you did fool 'em, Huck! Dat *wuz* de smartes' dodge! I tell you, chile, I 'speck it save' ole Jim—ole Jim ain't gwyne to forgit you for dat, honey."

"HERE I IS, HUCK."

Then we talked about the money. It was a pretty good raise, twenty dollars apiece. Jim said we could take deck passage on a steamboat, now, and the money would last us as far as we wanted to go in the free States. He said twenty mile more warn't far for the raft to go, but he wished we was already there.

Towards daybreak we tied up, and Jim was mighty particular about hiding the raft good. Then he worked all day fixing things in bundles and getting all ready to quit rafting.

That night about ten we hove in sight of the lights of a town away down in a left-hand bend.

I went off in the canoe, to ask about it. Pretty soon I found a man out in the river with a skiff, setting a trot-line. I ranged up and says:

"Mister, is that town Cairo?"

"Cairo? No. You must be a blame' fool."

"What town is it, mister?"

"If you want to know, go and find out. If you stay here botherin' around me for about a half a minute longer, you'll get something you won't want."

I paddled to the raft. Jim was awful disappointed, but I said never mind, Cairo would be the next place, I reckoned.

We passed another town before daylight and I was going out again; but it was high ground, so I didn't go. No high ground about Cairo, Jim said. I had forgot it. We laid up for the day, on a tow-head tolerable close to the left-hand bank. I begun to suspicion something. So did Jim. I says:

"Maybe we went by Cairo in the fog that night."

He says:

"Doan' less talk about it, Huck. Po' niggers can't have no luck. I awluz 'spected dat rattle-snake skin warn't done wid its work."

"I wish I'd never seen that snake-skin, Jim—I do wish I'd never laid eyes on it."

"It ain't yo' fault, Huck; you didn' know. Don't you blame yo'self 'bout it."

When it was daylight, here was the clear Ohio water in shore, sure enough, and outside was the old regular Muddy! So it was all up with Cairo.

We talked it all over. It wouldn't do to take to the shore; we couldn't take the raft up stream, of course. There warn't no way but to wait for dark and start back in the canoe and take the chances. So we slept all day amongst the cottonwood thicket, so as to be fresh for the work, and when we went back to the raft about dark the canoe was gone!

We didn't say a word for a good while. There warn't anything to say. We both knowed well enough it was some more work of the rattlesnake skin; so what was the use to talk about it? It would only look like we was finding fault, and that would be bound to fetch more bad luck—and keep on fetching it, too, till we knowed enough to keep still.

By and by we talked about what we better do, and found there warn't no way but just to go along down with the raft till we got a chance to buy a canoe to go back in. We warn't going to borrow it when there warn't anybody around, the way pap would do, for that might set people after us.

So we shoved out, after dark, on the raft.

Anybody that don't believe, yet, that it's foolishness to handle a snake-skin, after all that that snake-skin done for us, will believe it now, if they read on and see what more it done for us.

The place to buy canoes is off of rafts laying up at shore. But we didn't see no rafts laying up; so we went along, during three hours and more. Well, the night got gray and ruther thick, which is the next meanest thing to fog. You can't tell the shape of the river, and you can't see no distance. It got to be very late and still, and then along comes a steamboat up the river. We lit the lantern, and judged she would see it. Up-stream boats didn't generly come close to us; they go out and follow the bars and hunt for easy water under the reefs; but nights like this they bull right up the channel against the whole river.

We could hear her pounding along, but we didn't see her good till she was close. She aimed right for us. Often they do that and try to see how close they can come without touching; sometimes the wheel bites off a sweep, and then the pilot sticks his head out and laughs and thinks he's mighty smart. Well, here she comes and we said she was going to try to shave us; but she didn't seem to be sheering off a bit. She was a big one and she was coming in a hurry, too—looking like a black cloud with rows of glow-worms around it; but all of a sudden she bulged out, big and scary, with a long row of wide-open furnace-doors shining like red-hot teeth, and her monstrous bows and guards hanging right over us. There was a yell at us, and a jingling of bells to stop the engines, a pow-wow of cussing, and whistling of steam—and as Jim went overboard on one side and I on the other, she come smashing straight through the raft.

I dived—and I aimed to find the bottom, too, for a thirty-foot wheel had got to go over me and I wanted it to have plenty of room. I could always stay under water a minute; this time I reckon I staid under water a minute and a half. Then I bounced for the top in a hurry, for I was nearly busting. I popped out to my arm-pits and blowed the water out of my nose and puffed a bit. Of course there was a booming current; and of course that boat started her engines again ten seconds after she stopped them, for they never cared much for raftsmen; so now she was churning along up the river, out of sight in the thick weather, though I could hear her.

I sung out for Jim about a dozen times, but I didn't get any answer, so I grabbed a plank that touched me while I was "treading water," and struck out for shore, shoving it ahead of me. But I made out to see that the drift of the current was towards the left-hand shore, which meant that I was in a crossing; so I changed off and went that way.

It was one of these long, slanting, two-mile crossings; so I was a good long time in getting over. I made a safe landing and clumb up the bank. I couldn't see but a little ways, but I went poking along over rough ground for a quarter of a mile or more, and then I run across a big old-fashioned double log house before I noticed it. I was going to rush by and get away, but a lot of dogs jumped out and went to howling and barking at me and I knowed better than to move another peg.

CLIMBING UP THE BANK.

Chapter XVII.

"WHO'S THERE?"

IN ABOUT half a minute somebody spoke out of a window, without putting his head out, and says:

"Be done, boys! Who's there?"

I says:

"It's me."

"Who's me?"

"George Jackson, sir."

"What do you want?"

"I don't want nothing, sir. I only want to go along by, but the dogs won't let me."

"What are you prowling around here this time of night for—hey?"

"I warn't prowling around, sir; I fell overboard off of the steamboat."

"O, you did, did you? Strike a light there, somebody. What did you say your name was?"

"George Jackson, sir. I'm only a boy."

"Look here; if you're telling the truth, you needn't be afraid—nobody'll hurt you. But don't try to budge; stand right where you are. Rouse out Bob and Tom, some of you, and fetch the guns. George Jackson, is there anybody with you?"

"No, sir, nobody."

I heard the people stirring around in the house, now, and see a light. The man sung out:

"Snatch that light away, Betsy, you old fool—ain't you got any sense? Put it on the floor behind the front door. Bob, if you and Tom are ready, take your places."

"All ready."

"Now, George Jackson, do you know the Shepherdsons?"

"No, sir—I never heard of them."

"Well, that may be so, and it mayn't. Now, all ready. Step forward, George Jackson. And mind, don't you hurry—come mighty slow. If there's anybody with you, let him keep back—if he shows himself he'll be shot. Come along, now. Come slow; push the door open, yourself—just enough to squeeze in, d'you hear?"

I didn't hurry. I couldn't, if I'd a wanted to. I took one slow step at a time, and there warn't a sound, only I thought I could hear my heart. The dogs were as still as the humans, but they followed a little behind me. When I got to the three log door-steps I heard them unlocking and unbarring and unbolting. I put my hand on the door and pushed it a little and a little more, till somebody said, "There, that's enough—put your head in." I done it, but I judged they would take it off.

The candle was on the floor, and there they all was, looking at me and me at them, for about a quarter of a minute. Three big men, with guns pointed at me, which made me wince I tell you; the oldest gray and about sixty, the other two thirty or more—all of them fine and handsome—and the sweetest old gray-headed lady, and back of her two young women which I couldn't see right well. The old gentleman says:

"There—I reckon it's all right. Come in."

As soon as I was in, the old gentleman he locked the door and barred it and bolted it, and told the young men to come in with their guns, and they all went in a big parlor that had a new rag carpet on the floor and got together in a corner that was out of range of the front windows—there warn't none on the side. They held the candle and took a good look at me and all said, "Why, *he* ain't a Shepherdson—no, there ain't any Shepherdson about him." Then the old man said he hoped I wouldn't mind being searched for arms because he didn't mean no harm by it—it was only to make sure. So he didn't pry into my pockets, but only felt outside with his hands and said it was all right. He told me to make myself easy and at home, and tell all about myself, but the old lady says:

"Why bless you, Saul, the poor thing's as wet as he can be; and don't you reckon it may be he's hungry?"

"True for you, Rachel—I forgot."

So the old lady says:

"Betsy," (this was a nigger woman,) "you fly around and get him something to eat, as quick as you can, poor thing, and one of you girls go and wake up Buck and tell him— O, here he is himself.

"BUCK."

Buck, take this little stranger and get the wet clothes off from him and dress him up in some of yours that's dry."

Buck looked about as old as me—thirteen or fourteen or along there, though he was a little bigger than me. He hadn't on anything but a shirt, and he was very frowsy-headed. He come in gaping and digging one fist into his eyes, and he was dragging a gun along with the other one. He says:

"Ain't they no Shepherd-sons around?"

They said, no, 'twas a false alarm.

"Well," he says, "if they'd a ben some I reckon I'd a got one."

They all laughed, and Bob says:

"Why, Buck, they might have scalped us all, you've been so slow in coming."

"Well, nobody come after me, and it ain't right. I'm always kep' down; I don't get no show."

"Never mind, Buck, my boy," says the old man, "you'll have show enough, all in good time, don't you fret about that. Go 'long with you, now, and do as your mother told you."

When we got up stairs to his room, he got me a coarse shirt and a roundabout and pants of his, and I put them on. While I was at it he asked me what my name was, but before I could tell him he started to telling me about a blue jay and a young rabbit he had catched in the woods day before yesterday, and he asked me where Moses was when the candle went out. I said I didn't know; I hadn't heard about it before, no way.

"Well, guess," he says.

"How'm I going to guess," says I, "when I never heard tell about it before?"

"But you can guess, can't you? It's just as easy."

"*Which* candle?" I says.

"Why, any candle," he says.

"I don't know where he was," says I, "where was he?"

"Why he was in the *dark!* That's where he was!"

"Well if you knowed where he was, what did you ask me for?"

"Why, blame it, it's a riddle, don't you see? Say—how long are you going to stay here? You got to stay always. We can just have booming times—they don't have no school now. Do you own a dog? I've got a dog—and he'll go in the river and bring out chips that you throw in. Do you like to comb up, Sundays, and all that kind of foolishness? You bet I don't, but ma she makes me. Confound these ole britches, I reckon I'd better put 'em on, but I'd ruther not, it's so warm. Are you all ready? All right—come along, old hoss."

Cold corn-pone, cold corn beef, butter and buttermilk—that is what they had for me down there, and there ain't nothing better that ever I've come across yet. Buck and his ma and all of them smoked cob pipes, except the nigger woman, which was gone, and the two young women. They all smoked and talked, and I eat and talked. The young women had quilts around them and their hair down their backs. They all asked me questions, and I told them how pap and me and all the family was living on a little farm down at the bottom of Arkansaw, and my sister Mary Ann run off and got married and never was heard of no more, and Bill went to hunt them and he warn't heard of no more, and Tom and Mort died, and by and by mam died, and then there warn't nobody but just me and pap left, and he was just trimmed down to nothing, on account of his troubles; so when he died I took what there was left, because the farm didn't belong to us, and started up the river deck passage and fell overboard and that was how I come to be here. So they said I could have a home there as long as I wanted it. Then it was most daylight, and everybody went to bed, and I went to bed with Buck, and when I waked up, in the morning, drat it all I had forgot what my name was. So I laid there about an hour trying to think, and when Buck waked up, I says:

"Can you spell, Buck?"

"Yes," he says.

"I bet you can't spell my name," says I.

"I bet you what you dare I can," says he.

"All right," says I, "go ahead."

"G-o-r-g-e J-a-x-o-n—there, now," he says.

"Well," says I, "you done it, but I didn't think you could. It ain't no slouch of a name to spell—right off without studying."

I set it down, private, because somebody might want *me* to spell it, next, and so I wanted to be handy with it and rattle it off like I was used to it.

It was a mighty nice family, and a mighty nice house, too. I hadn't seen no house out in the country before that was so nice and had so much style. It didn't have an iron latch on the front door, nor a wooden one with a buckskin string, but a brass knob to turn, the same as houses in a town. There warn't no bed in the parlor, not a sign of a bed; but heaps of parlors in towns has beds in them. There was a big fire place that was bricked on the bottom, and the bricks was kept clean and red by pouring water on them and scrubbing them with another brick; sometimes they washed them over with red water-paint that they call Spanish brown, same as they do in town. They had big brass dog-irons that could hold up a saw-log. There was a clock on the middle of the mantel piece with a picture of a town painted on the bottom half of the glass front, and a round place in the middle of it for the sun, and you could see the pendulum swing behind it. It was beautiful to hear that clock tick; and sometimes when one of these pedlers had been along and scoured her up and got her in good shape she would start in and strike a hundred and fifty before she got tuckered out. They wouldn't took any money for her.

Well, there was a big outlandish parrot on each side of the clock, made out of something like chalk, and painted up gaudy. By one of the parrots was a cat made of crockery and a crockery dog by the other; and when you pressed down on them they squeaked but didn't open their mouths nor look different nor interested. They squeaked through underneath. There was a couple of big wild-turkey-wing fans spread out behind those things. On a table in the middle of the room was a kind of a lovely crockery basket that had apples and oranges and peaches and grapes piled up in it which was much redder and yellower and prettier than real ones is, but they warn't real, because you could see where pieces had got chipped off and showed the white chalk or whatever it was, underneath.

This table had a cover made out of beautiful oil cloth, with a red and blue spread-eagle painted on it, and a painted border all around. It come all the way from Philadelphia, they said. There was some books, too, piled up perfectly exact, on each corner of the table. One was a big family Bible, full of pictures. One was "Pilgrim's Progress," about a man that left his family, it didn't say why. I read considerable in it, now and then. The statements was interesting, but tough. Another was "Friendship's Offering," full of beautiful stuff and poetry; but I didn't read the poetry. Another was Henry Clay's Speeches, and another was Dr. Gunn's Family Medicine, which told you all about what to do if a body was sick or dead. There was a hymn book, and a lot of other books. And there was nice split-bottom chairs, and perfectly sound, too—not bagged down in the middle and busted, like an old basket.

They had pictures hung on the walls—mainly Washingtons, and Lafayettes, and battles, and Highland Marys, and one called "Signing the Declaration." There was some that they called crayons, which one of the daughters which was dead made her own self when she was only fifteen years old. They was different from any pictures I ever see before; blacker, mostly, than is common. One was a woman in a slim black dress, belted small under the arm-pits, with bulges like a cabbage in the middle of the sleeves, and a large black scoop-shovel bonnet with a black veil, and white slim ancles crossed about with black tape, and very wee black slippers, like a chisel, and she was leaning pensive on a tombstone on her right elbow, under a weeping willow, and her other hand hanging down her side holding a white handkerchief and a reticule, and underneath the picture it said "Shall I Never See Thee More Alas." Another one was a young lady with her hair all combed up straight to the top of her head and knotted there in front of a comb like a chair-back, and she was crying into a handkerchief and had a dead bird laying on its back in her other hand with its heels up, and underneath the picture it said "I Shall Never Hear Thy Sweet Chirrup More Alas." There was one where a young lady was at a window, looking up at the moon, and tears running down her cheeks; and she had an open letter in one hand with black sealing-wax showing on one edge of it, and she was mashing a locket with a chain to it against her mouth, and underneath the picture it said "And Art Thou Gone Yes Thou Art Gone Alas." These was all nice pictures, I reckon, but I didn't somehow seem to take to them, because if ever I was down a little, they always give me the fan-tods. Everybody was sorry she died, because she had laid out a lot more of these pictures to do, and a body could see by what she had done what they had lost. But I reckoned, that with her disposition, she was having a better time in the graveyard. She was at work on what they said was her greatest picture when she took sick, and every day and every night it was her prayer to be allowed to live till she got it done, but she

"IT MADE HER LOOK TOO SPIDERY."

never got the chance. It was a picture of a young woman in a long white gown, standing on the rail of a bridge all ready to jump off, with her hair all down her back, and looking up to the moon, with the tears running down her face, and she had two arms folded across her breast, and two arms stretched out in front, and two more reaching up towards the moon—and the idea was, to see which pair would look best and then scratch out all the other arms; but as I was saying, she died before she got her mind made up, and now they kept this picture over the head of the bed in her room, and every time her birthday come they hung flowers on it. Other times it was hid with a little curtain. The young woman in the picture had a kind of a nice sweet face, but there was so many arms it made her look too spidery, seemed to me.

This young girl kept a scrap-book when she was alive, and used to paste obituaries and accidents, and cases of patient suffering in it out of the *Presbyterian Observer* and write poetry after them out of her own head. It was very good poetry. This is what she wrote about a boy by the name of Stephen Dowling Bots that fell down a well and was drownded:

ODE TO STEPHEN DOWLING BOTS, DEC'D.

And did young Stephen sicken,
    And did young Stephen die?
And did the sad hearts thicken,
    And did the mourners cry?

No; such was not the fate of
    Young Stephen Dowling Bots;
Though sad hearts round him thickened,
    'Twas not from sickness' shots.

No whooping-cough did rack his frame,
    Nor measles drear, with spots;
Not these impaired the sacred name
    Of Stephen Dowling Bots.

Despisèd love struck not with woe
    That head of curly knots,
Nor stomach troubles laid him low,
    Young Stephen Dowling Bots.

O no. Then list with tearful eye,
    Whilst I his fate do tell.
His soul did from this cold world fly,
    By falling down a well.

They got him out and emptied him;
    Alas it was too late;
His spirit was gone for to sport aloft
    In the realms of the good and great.

"THEY GOT HIM OUT AND EMPTIED HIM."

If Emmeline Grangerford could make poetry like that before she was fourteen, there ain't no telling what she could a done by and by. Buck said she could rattle off poetry like nothing. She didn't ever have to stop to think. He said she would slap down a line, and if she couldn't find anything to rhyme with it she would just scratch it out and slap down another one, and go ahead. She warn't particular, she could write about anything you choose to give her to write about, just so it was sadful. Every time a man died, or a woman died, or a child died, she would be on hand with her "Tribute" before he was cold. She called them Tributes. The neighbors said it was the doctor first, then Emmeline, then the undertaker—the undertaker never got in ahead of Emmeline but once, and then she hung fire on a rhyme for the dead person's name, which was Whistler. She warn't ever the same, after that; she never complained, but she kind of pined away and did not live long. Poor thing, many's the time I made myself go up to the little room that used to be hers and get out her poor old scrap book and read in it when her pictures had been aggravating me and I had soured on her a little. I liked all that family, dead ones and all, and warn't going to let anything come between us. Poor Emmeline made poetry about all the dead people when she was alive, and it didn't seem right that there warn't nobody to make some about her, now she was gone; so I tried to sweat out a verse or two myself but I couldn't seem to make it go, somehow. They kept Emmeline's room trim and nice, and all the things fixed in it just the way she liked to have them when she was alive, and nobody ever slept there. The old lady took care of the room herself, though there was plenty of niggers, and she sewed there a good deal and read her Bible there, mostly.

Well, as I was saying about the parlor, there was beautiful curtains on the windows, white, with pictures painted on them, of castles with vines all down the walls, and cattle coming down to drink. There was a little old piano, too, that had tin pans in it, I reckon, and nothing was ever so lovely as to hear the young ladies sing "The Last Link is Broken" and play "The Battle of Prague" on it. The walls of all the rooms was plastered, and most had carpets on the floors, and the whole house was whitewashed on the outside.

It was a double house and the big open place betwixt them was roofed and floored, and sometimes the table was set there in the middle of the day and it was a cool, comfortable place. Nothing couldn't be better. And warn't the cooking good and just bushels of it, too!

THE HOUSE.

Chapter XVIII.

COL. GRANGERFORD.

Col. Grangerford was a gentleman, you see. He was a gentleman all over; and so was his family. He was well born, as the saying is, and that's worth as much in a man as it is in a horse, so the widow Douglas said, and nobody ever denied that she was of the first aristocracy in our town; and pap he always said it too, though he warn't no more quality than a mud-cat, himself. Col. Grangerford was very tall and very slim, and had a darkish-paly complexion, not a sign of red in it anywheres; he was clean-shaved every morning, all over his thin face, and he had the thinnest kind of lips, and the thinnest kind of nostrils, and a high nose, and heavy eyebrows, and the blackest kind of eyes, sunk so deep back that they seemed like they was looking out of caverns at you, as you may say. His forehead was high and his hair was black and straight and hung to his shoulders. His hands was long and thin, and every day of his life he put on a clean shirt and a full suit from head to foot made out of linen so white it hurt your eyes to look at it; and on Sundays he wore a blue tail-coat with brass buttons on it. He carried a mahogany cane with a silver head to it. There warn't no frivolishness about him, not a bit, and he warn't ever loud. He was as kind as he could be—you could feel that, you know, and so you had confidence. Sometimes he smiled, and it was good to see; but when he straightened himself up like a liberty-pole and the lightning begun to flicker out from under his eyebrows, you wanted to climb a tree

first, and find out what the matter was afterwards. He didn't ever
have to tell anybody to mind their manners—everybody was always good mannered where he was. Everybody loved to have him
around, too; he was sunshine most always—I mean he made it
seem like good weather. When he turned into a cloud-bank it was
awful dark for a half a minute, and that was enough; there wouldn't
nothing go wrong again for a week.

When him and the old lady come down in the morning, all the
family got up out of their chairs and give them good day and didn't
set down again till they had set down. Then Tom and Bob went to
the sideboard where the decanters was, and mixed a glass of bitters
and handed it to him, and he held it in his hand and waited till Tom's
and Bob's was mixed, and then they bowed and said "Our duty to
you, sir, and madam;" and *they* bowed the least bit in the world and
said thank you, and so they drank, all three, and Bob and Tom poured
a spoonful of water on the sugar and the mite of whisky or apple
brandy in the bottom of their tumblers, and give it to me and Buck
and we drank to the old people too.

Bob was the oldest and Tom next. Tall, beautiful men with very
broad shoulders, and brown faces and long black hair and black eyes.
They dressed in white linen from head to foot, like the old gentleman, and wore broad Panama hats.

Then there was Miss Charlotte, she was twenty-five, and tall and
proud and grand, but as good as she could be, when she warn't stirred
up; but when she was, she had a look that would make you wilt in
your tracks, like her father. She was beautiful.

So was her sister, Miss Sophia, but it was a different kind. She
was gentle and sweet, like a dove, and she was only twenty.

Each person had their own nigger to wait on them—Buck, too.
My nigger had a monstrous easy time, because I warn't used to
having anybody do anything for me, but Buck's was on the jump
most of the time.

This was all there was of the family, now; but there used to be
more—three sons—they got killed; and Emmeline, that died.

The old gentleman owned a lot of farms and over a hundred niggers. Sometimes a stack of people would come there, horseback,
from ten or fifteen mile around, and stay five or six days, and have
such junketings round about and on the river, and dances and

picnics in the woods, daytimes, and balls at the house, nights. These people was mostly kin-folks of the family. The men brought their guns with them. It was a handsome lot of quality, I tell you.

There was another clan of aristocracy around there—five or six families—mostly of the name of Shepherdson. They was as high-toned, and well born, and rich and grand as the tribe of Granger-fords. The Shepherdsons and the Grangerfords used the same

YOUNG HARNEY SHEPHERDSON.

steamboat landing, which was about two mile above our house; so sometimes when I went up there with a lot of our folks I used to see a lot of the Shepherdsons there, on their fine horses.

One day Buck and me was away out in the woods hunting, and heard a horse coming. We was crossing the road. Buck says:

"Quick! Jump for the woods!"

We done it, and then peeped down the woods through the leaves. Pretty soon a splendid young man come galloping down the road, setting his horse easy and looking like a soldier. He had his gun across his pommel. I had seen him before. It was young Harney

Shepherdson. I heard Buck's gun go off at my ear, and Harney's hat tumbled off from his head. He grabbed his gun and rode straight to the place where we was hid. But we didn't wait. We started through the woods on a run. The woods warn't thick, so I looked over my shoulder, to dodge the bullet, and twice I seen Harney cover Buck with his gun, and then he rode away the way he come—to get his hat, I reckon, but I couldn't see. We never stopped running till we got home. The old gentleman's eyes blazed a minute—'twas pleasure, mainly, I judged—then his face sort of smoothed down and he says kind of gentle:

"I don't like that shooting from behind a bush. Why didn't you step into the road, my boy?"

"The Shepherdsons don't, father. They always take advantage."

Miss Charlotte she held her head up like a queen while Buck was telling his tale, and her nostrils spread and her eyes snapped. The two young men looked dark but never said nothing. Miss Sophia she turned pale, but the color come back when she found the man warn't hurt.

MISS CHARLOTTE.

Soon as I could get Buck down by the corn-cribs under the trees by ourselves, I says:

"Did you want to kill him, Buck?"

"Well I bet I did."

"What did he do to you?"

"Him? He never done nothing to me."

"Well then, what did you want to kill him for?"

"Why nothing—only it's on account of the feud."

"What's a feud?"

"Why where was you raised? Don't you know what a feud is?"

"Never heard of it before—tell me about it."

"Well," says Buck, "a feud is this way. A man has a quarrel with another man, and kills him; then that other man's brother kills *him*; then the other brothers, on both sides, goes for one another; then the *cousins* chip in—and by and by everybody's killed off, and there ain't no more feud. But it's kind of slow and takes a long time."

"Has this one been going on long, Buck?"

"Well I should *reckon!* It started thirty year ago, or som'ers along there. There was trouble 'bout something, and then a lawsuit to settle it; and the suit went agin one of the men, and so he up and shot the man that won the suit—which he would naturally do, of course. Anybody would."

"What was the trouble about, Buck?—land?"

"I reckon maybe—I don't know."

"Well who done the shooting?—was it a Grangerford, or a Shepherdson?"

"Laws, how do *I* know? It was so long ago."

"Don't anybody know?"

"O, yes, pa knows, I reckon, and some of the other old folks; but they don't know, now, what the row was about in the first place."

"Has there been many killed, Buck?"

"Yes—right smart chance of funerals. But they don't always kill. Pa's got a few buck-shot in him; but he don't mind it, 'cuz he don't weigh much anyway. Bob's been carved up some with a Bowie, and Tom's been hurt once or twice."

"Has anybody been killed this year, Buck?"

"Yes, we got one, and they got one. 'Bout three months ago, my cousin Bud, fourteen year old, was riding through the woods, on t'other side of the river, and didn't have no weapon with him, which was blame' foolishness, and in a lonesome place he hears a horse a-coming, behind him, and sees old Baldy Shepherdson a-linkin' after him with his gun in his hand and his white hair a-flying in the wind; and 'stead of jumping off and taking to the brush, Bud 'lowed he could outrun him; so they had it, nip and tuck, for five mile or more, the old man a-gaining all the time; so at last Bud seen it warn't any use, so he stopped and faced around, so as to have the bullet holes in front, you know, and the old man he rode up and shot him down. But he didn't git much chance to enjoy his luck, for inside of a week our folks laid *him* out."

"I reckon that old man was a coward, Buck."

"I reckon he *warn't* a coward. Not by a blame' sight. There ain't a coward amongst them Shepherdsons—not a one. And there ain't no cowards amongst the Grangerfords, either. Why that old man kep' up his end in a fight, one day, for a half an hour, against three Grangerfords, and come out winner. They was all a-horseback; he lit off of his horse and got behind a little woodpile, and kep' his horse before him to stop the bullets; but the Grangerfords staid on their horses and capered around the old man, and peppered away at him, and he peppered away at them. Him and his horse both went home pretty leaky and crippled, but the Grangerfords had to be *fetched* home—and one of 'em was dead, and another died the next day. No, sir, if a body's out hunting for cowards, he don't want to fool away any time amongst them Shepherdsons, becuz they don't breed any of that *kind*."

Next Sunday we all went to church, about three mile, everybody a-horseback. The men took their guns along, so did Buck, and kept them between their knees or stood them handy against the wall. The Shepherdsons done the same. It was pretty ornery preaching— all about brotherly love and such-like tiresomeness, but everybody said it was a good sermon, and they all talked it over, going home, and had such a powerful lot to say about faith, and good works, and free grace, and preforeordestination, and I don't know what all, that it did seem to me to be one of the roughest Sundays I had run across yet.

About an hour after dinner everybody was dozing around, some in their chairs and some in their rooms, and it got to be pretty dull. Buck and a dog was stretched out on the grass in the sun, sound asleep. I went up to our room, and judged I would take a nap myself. I found that sweet Miss Sophia standing in her door, which was next to ours, and she took me in her room and shut the door very soft, and asked me if I liked her, and I said I did; and she asked me if I

"AND ASKED ME IF I LIKED HER."

would do something for her and not tell anybody, and I said I would. Then she said she'd forgot her Testament, and left it in the seat at church, between two other books, and would I slip out quiet and go there and fetch it to her, and not say nothing to nobody. I said I would. So I slid out and slipped off up the road, and there warn't anybody at the church, except maybe a hog or two, for there warn't any lock on the door, and hogs likes a puncheon floor in summer time because it's cool. If you notice, most folks don't go to church only when they've got to; but a hog is different.

Says I to myself, something's up—it ain't natural for a girl to be in such a sweat about a Testament; so I give it a shake, and out drops a little piece of paper with "*Half-past two*" wrote on it with a pencil. I ransacked it, but couldn't find anything else. I couldn't make anything out of that, so I put the paper in the book again, and when I got home and up stairs, there was Miss Sophia in her door waiting for me. She pulled me in and shut the door; then she looked in the Testament till she found the paper, and as soon as she read it she looked glad; and before a body could think, she grabbed me and give me a squeeze, and said I was the best boy in the world, and not to tell anybody. She was mighty red in the face, for a minute, and her eyes lighted up, and it made her powerful pretty. I was a good deal astonished, but when I got my breath I asked her what the paper was about, and she asked me if I had read it, and I said no, and she asked me if I could read writing, and I told her "no, only coarse-hand," and then she said the paper warn't anything but a book-mark to keep her place, and I might go and play, now.

I went off down to the river, studying over this thing, and pretty soon I noticed that my nigger was following along behind. When we was out of sight of the house, he looked back and around, a second, and then comes a-running and says—

"Mars Jawge, if you'll come down into de swamp, I'll show you a whole stack o' water-moccasins."

Thinks I, that's mighty curious; he said that yesterday. He ought-er know a body don't love water-moccasins enough to go around hunting for them. What is he up to, anyway? So I says—

"All right—trot ahead."

I followed a half a mile, then he struck out over the swamp and waded ancle deep as much as another half mile. We come to a little flat piece of land which was dry, and very thick with trees and bushes and vines, and he says—

"You shove right in dah, jist a few steps, mars Jawge, dah's whah dey is. I's seed 'm befo', I don't k'yer to see 'em no mo'."

Then he slopped right along and went away, and pretty soon the trees hid him. I poked into the place a ways, and come to a little open patch as big as a bedroom, all hung around with vines, and found a man laying there asleep—and by jings it was my old Jim!

I waked him up, and I reckoned it was going to be a grand surprise to him to see me again, but it warn't. He nearly cried, he was so glad, but he warn't surprised. Said he swum along behind me, that night, and heard me yell, every time, but dasn't answer, because he didn't want nobody to pick *him* up, and take him into slavery again. Says he—

"I got hurt a little, en couldn't swim fas', so I wuz a considable ways behine you, towards de las'; when you landed I reck'ned I could ketch up wid you on de lan' 'dout havin' to shout at you, but when I see dat house I begin to go slow. I 'uz off too fur to hear what dey say to you—I wuz 'fraid o' de dogs—but when it 'uz all quiet agin, I knowed you's in de house, so I struck out for de woods to wait for day. Early in de mawnin' some er de niggers come along, gwyne to de fields, en dey tuck me en showed me dis place, whah de dogs can't track me on accounts o' de water, en dey brings me truck to eat every night, en tells me how you's a gitt'n along."

"Why didn't you tell my Jack to fetch me here sooner, Jim?"

"Well, 'twarn't no use to 'sturb you, Huck, tell we could do sumfn—but we's all right, now. I ben a-buyin' pots en pans en vittles, as I got a chanst, en a-patchin' up de raf', nights when—"

"*What* raft, Jim?"

"Our ole raf'."

"You mean to say our old raft warn't smashed all to flinders?"

"No, she warn't. She was tore up a good deal—one en' of her was—but dey warn't no great harm done, on'y our traps was mos' all los'. Ef we hadn' dive' so deep en swum so fur under water, en de night hadn' ben so dark, en we warn't so sk'yerd, en ben sich punkin-heads, as de sayin' is, we'd a seed de raf'. But it's jis' as well we didn't, 'kase now she's all fixed up agin mos' as good as new, en we's got a new lot o' stuff, too, in de place o' what 'uz los'."

"Why how did you get hold of the raft again, Jim—did you catch her?"

"How I gwyne to ketch her, en I out in de woods? No, some er de niggers foun' her ketched on a snag along heah in de ben', en dey hid her in a crick, 'mongst de willows, en dey wuz so much jawin' 'bout which un 'um she b'long to de mos', dat I come to heah 'bout it pooty soon, so I ups en settles de trouble by tellin' 'um she don't b'long to none uv um, but to you en me; en I ast 'm if dey gwyne to grab a young white genlman's propaty, en git a hid'n for it? Den I gin 'm ten cents apiece, en dey 'uz mighty well satisfied, en wisht some mo' raf's 'ud come along en make 'm rich agin. Dey's mighty good to me, dese niggers is, en whatever I wants 'm to do fur me, I doan' have to ast 'm twice, honey. Dat Jack's a good nigger, en pooty smart."

"Yes, he is. He ain't ever told me you was here; told me to come, and he'd show me a lot of water-moccasins. If anything happens, *he* ain't mixed up in it. He can say he never seen us together, and it'll be the truth."

I don't want to talk much about the next day. I reckon I'll cut it pretty short. I waked up about dawn, and was agoing to turn over and go to sleep again, when I noticed how still it was—didn't seem to be anybody stirring. That warn't usual. Next I noticed that Buck was up and gone. Well, I gets up, a-wondering, and goes down stairs—nobody around; everything as still as a mouse. Just the same outside; thinks I, what does it mean? Down by the woodpile I comes across my Jack, and says—

"What's it all about?"

Says he—

"Don't you know, mars Jawge?"

"No," says I, "I don't."

"Well, den, Miss Sophia's run off! 'Deed she has. She run off in de night, some time—nobody don't know jis' when—run off to git married to dat young Harney Shepherdson, you know—leastways, so dey 'spec. De fambly foun' it out, 'bout half an hour ago—maybe a little mo'—en I *tell* you dey warn't no time los'. Sich another hurryin' up guns en hosses *you* never see! De women folks has gone for to stir up de relations, en ole mars Saul en de boys tuck dey guns en rode up de river road for to try to ketch dat young man en kill him 'fo' he kin git acrost de river wid Miss Sophia. I reck'n dey's gwyne to be mighty rough times."

"Buck went off 'thout waking me up."

"Well I reck'n he *did!* Dey warn't gwyne to mix you up in it. Mars Buck he loaded up his gun en 'lowed he's gwyne to fetch home a Shepherdson or bust. Well, dey'll be plenty un 'm dah, I reck'n, en you bet you he'll fetch one ef he gits a chanst."

I took up the river road as hard as I could put. By and by I begin to hear guns a good ways off. When I come in sight of the log store and

the woodpile where the steamboats lands, I worked along under the
trees and brush till I got to a good place, and then I clumb up into
the forks of a cottonwood that was out of reach, and watched. There
was a wood-rank, four foot high, a little ways in front of the tree,
and first I was going to hide behind that; but maybe it was luckier
I didn't.

There was four or five men cavorting around on their horses in
the open place before the log store, cussing and yelling, and trying
to get at a couple of young chaps that was behind the wood-rank
alongside of the steamboat landing—but they couldn't come it.

"BEHIND THE WOOD-RANK."

Every time one of them showed himself on the river side of the
wood pile he got shot at. The two boys was squatting back to back
behind the pile, so they could watch both ways.

By and by the men stopped cavorting around, and yelling. They
started riding towards the store; then up gets one of the boys, draws
a steady bead over the wood-rank, and drops one of them out of his
saddle. All the men jumped off of their horses and grabbed the hurt
one and started to carry him to the store; and that minute the two
boys started on the run. They got half way to the tree I was in, before the men noticed. Then the men see them, and jumped on their

horses and took out after them. They gained on the boys, but it didn't do no good, the boys had too good a start; they got to the wood pile that was in front of my tree, and slipped in behind it, and so they had the bulge on the men again. One of the boys was Buck, and the other was a slim young chap about nineteen years old.

The men ripped around a while, and then rode away. As soon as they was out of sight, I sung out to Buck and told him. He didn't know what to make of my voice coming out of the tree, at first. He was awful surprised. He told me to watch out sharp and let him know when the men come in sight again; said they was up to some devilment or other—wouldn't be gone long. I wished I was out of that tree, but I dasn't come down. Buck begun to cry and rip, and 'lowed that him and his cousin Joe (that was the other young chap) would make up for this day, yet. He said his father and his two brothers was killed, and two or three of the enemy. Said the Shepherdsons laid for them, in ambush. Buck said his father and brothers ought to waited for their relations—the Shepherdsons was too strong for them. I asked him what was become of young Harney and Miss Sophia. He said they'd got across the river and was safe. I was glad of that; but the way Buck did take on because he didn't manage to kill Harney that day he shot at him—I hain't ever heard anything like it.

All of a sudden, bang! bang! bang! goes three or four guns—the men had slipped around through the woods, and come in from behind without their horses! The boys jumped for the river—both of them hurt—and as they swum down the current the men run along the bank shooting at them and singing out, "Kill them, kill them!" It made me so sick, I most fell out of the tree. I ain't agoing to tell *all* that happened—it would make me sick again if I was to do that. I wished I hadn't ever come ashore that night, to see such things. I ain't ever going to get shut of them—lots of times I dream about them.

I staid in the tree till it begun to get dark, afraid to come down. Sometimes I heard guns away off in the woods; and twice I seen little gangs of men gallop past the log store with guns; so I reckoned the trouble was still agoing on. I was mighty down-hearted; so I made up my mind I wouldn't ever go anear that house again, because I reckoned I was to blame, somehow. I judged that that piece of paper meant that Miss Sophia was to meet Harney somewheres at half-past two and run off; and I judged I ought to told her father about that paper and the curious way she acted, and then maybe he would a locked her up and this awful mess wouldn't ever happened.

When I got down out of the tree I crept along down the river bank a piece, and found the two bodies laying in the edge of the water, and tugged at them till I got them ashore; then I covered up their faces, and got away as quick as I could. I cried a little when I was covering up Buck's face, for he was mighty good to me.

It was just dark, now. I never went near the house, but struck through the woods and made for the swamp. Jim warn't on his island, so I tramped off in a hurry for the crick, and crowded through the willows, red-hot to jump aboard and get out of that awful country—the raft was gone! My souls, but I was scared! I couldn't get my breath for most a minute. Then I raised a yell. A voice not twenty-five foot from me says—

"Good lan'! is dat you, honey? Doan' make no noise."

It was Jim's voice—nothing ever sounded so good before. I run along the bank a piece and got aboard, and Jim he grabbed me and hugged me, he was so glad to see me. He says—

"Laws bless you, chile, I 'uz right down sho' you's dead agin. Jack's ben heah, en he say he reck'n you's ben shot, kase you didn' come home no mo'; so I's jes' dis minute a startin' de raf' down towards de mouf er de crick, so's to be all ready for to shove out en leave soon as Jack comes agin en tells me for certain you *is* dead. Lawsy, I's mighty glad to git you back agin, honey."

I says—

"All right—that's mighty good; they won't find me, and they'll think I've been killed, and floated down the river—there's something up there that'll help them to think so—so don't you lose no time, Jim, but just shove off for the big water as fast as ever you can."

I never felt easy till the raft was two mile below there and out in the middle of the Mississippi. Then we hung up our signal lantern, and judged that we was free and safe once more. I hadn't had a bite to eat since yesterday; so Jim he got out some corn-dodgers, and buttermilk, and pork and cabbage, and greens—there ain't nothing in the world so good, when it's cooked right—and whilst I eat my supper we talked, and had a good time. I was powerful glad to get away from the feuds, and so was Jim to get away from the swamp. We said there warn't no home like a raft, after all. Other places do seem so cramped up and smothery, but a raft don't. You feel mighty free and easy and comfortable on a raft.

Chapter XIX

HIDING DAYTIMES.

TWO OR THREE days and nights went by; I reckon I might say they swum by, they slid along so quiet and smooth and lovely. Here is the way we put in the time. It was a monstrous big river down there—sometimes a mile and a half wide; we run, nights, and laid up and hid, daytimes; soon as night was most gone, we stopped navigating, and tied up—nearly always in the dead water under a tow-head; and then cut young cottonwoods and willows and hid the raft with them. Then we set out the lines. Next we slid into the river and had a swim, so as to freshen up and cool off; then we set down on the sandy bottom where the water was about knee deep, and watched the daylight come. Not a sound, anywheres—perfectly still—just like the whole world was asleep, only sometimes the bull-frogs a-cluttering, maybe. The first thing to see, looking away over the water, was a kind of dull line—that was the woods on t'other side—you couldn't make nothing else out; then a pale place in the sky; then more paleness, spreading around; then the river softened up, away off, and warn't black any more, but gray; you could see little dark spots drifting along, ever so far away— trading scows, and such things; and long, black streaks—rafts; sometimes you could hear a sweep screaking; or jumbled up voices, it was so still, and sounds come so far; and by and by you could see a streak on the water which you know by the look of the streak that there's a snag there in a swift current which breaks on it and makes that streak look that way; and you see the mist curl up off of the water, and the east reddens up, and the river, and you make out a log cabin in the edge of the woods, away on the bank on t'other side of the river, being a wood-yard, likely, and piled by them cheats so you can throw a dog through it anywheres; then the nice breeze springs up, and comes fanning you from over there, so cool and fresh, and sweet to smell, on account of the woods and the flowers; but sometimes not that way, because they've left dead fish laying around, gars, and such, and they do get pretty rank; and next you've got the full day, and everything smiling in the sun, and the song-birds just going it!

A little smoke couldn't be noticed, now, so we would take some fish off of the lines, and cook up a hot breakfast. And afterwards we would watch the lonesomeness of the river, and kind of lazy along, and by and by lazy off to sleep. Wake up, by and by, and look to see what done it, and maybe see a steamboat, coughing along up stream, so far off towards the other side you couldn't tell nothing about her only whether she was stern-wheel or side-wheel; then for about an hour there wouldn't be nothing to hear nor nothing to see—just solid lonesomeness. Next you'd see a raft sliding by, away off yonder, and maybe a galoot on it chopping, because they're most always doing it on a raft; you'd see the axe flash, and come down—you don't hear nothing; you see that axe go up again, and by the time it's above the man's head, then you hear the *k'chunk!*—it had took all that time to come over the water. So we would put in the day, lazying around, listening to the stillness. Once there was a thick fog, and the rafts and things that went by was beating tin pans so the steamboats wouldn't run over them. A scow or a raft went by so close we could hear them talking and cussing and laughing—heard them plain; but we couldn't see no sign of them; it made you feel crawly, it was like spirits carrying on that way in the air. Jim said he believed it was spirits; but I says:

"No, spirits wouldn't say, 'Dern the dern fog.'"

Soon as it was night, out we shoved; when we got her out to about the middle, we let her alone, and let her float wherever the current wanted her to; then we lit the pipes and dangled our legs in the water and talked about all kinds of things—we was always naked, day and night, whenever the mosquitoes would let us—the new clothes Buck's folks made for me was too good to be comfortable, and besides I didn't go much on clothes, nohow.

Sometimes we'd have that whole river all to ourselves, for the longest time. Yonder was the banks and the islands, across the water; and maybe a spark—which was a candle in a cabin window—and sometimes on the water you could see a spark or two—on a raft or a scow, you know; and maybe you could hear a fiddle or a song coming over from one of them crafts. It's lovely to live on a raft. We had the sky, up there, all speckled with stars, and we used to lay on our backs and look up at them, and discuss about whether they was made, or only just happened—Jim he allowed they was made, but I allowed they happened; I judged it would have took too long to *make* so many. Jim said the moon could a *laid* them; well, that looked kind of reasonable, so I didn't say nothing against it, because I've seen a frog lay most as many, so of course it could be done. We used to watch the stars that fell, too, and see them streak down. Jim allowed they'd got spoiled and was hove out of the nest.

Once or twice of a night we would see a steamboat slipping along in the dark, and now and then she would belch a whole world of sparks up out of her chimbleys, and they would rain down in the river and look awful pretty; then she would turn a corner and her lights would wink out and her pow-wow shut off and leave the river still again; and by and by her waves would get to us, a long time after she was gone, and joggle the raft a bit, and after that you wouldn't hear nothing for you couldn't tell how long, except maybe frogs or something.

After midnight the people on shore went to bed, and then for two or three hours the shores was black—no more sparks in the cabin windows. These sparks was our clock—the first one that showed, again, meant morning was coming, so we hunted a place to hide and tie up, right away.

One morning about daybreak, I found a canoe and crossed over a chute to the main shore—it was only two hundred yards—and paddled about a mile up a crick amongst the cypress woods, to see if I couldn't get some berries. Just as I was passing a place where a kind of a cow-path crossed the crick, here comes a couple of men tearing up the path as tight as they could foot it. I thought I was a goner, for whenever anybody was after anybody, I judged it was *me*—or

maybe Jim. I was about to dig out from there in a hurry, but they
was pretty close to me, then, and sung out and begged me to save
their lives—said they hadn't been doing nothing, and was being

"AND DOGS A-COMING."

chased for it—said there was men and dogs a-coming. They wanted
to jump right in, but I says—

"Don't you do it. I don't hear the dogs and horses, yet; you've got
time to crowd through the brush and get up the crick a little ways;
then you take to the water and wade down to me and get in—that'll
throw the dogs off the scent."

They done it, and soon as they was aboard I lit out for our tow-
head, and in about five or ten minutes we heard the dogs and the
men away off, shouting. We heard them come along towards the
crick, but couldn't see them; they seemed to stop and fool around a
while; then, as we got further and further away all the time, we
couldn't hardly hear them at all; by the time we had left a mile of

woods behind us and struck the river, everything was quiet, and we paddled over to the towhead and hid in the cottonwoods and was safe.

One of these fellows was about seventy, or upwards, and had a bald head and very gray whiskers. He had an old battered-up slouch hat on, and a greasy blue woolen shirt, and ragged old blue jeans britches stuffed into his boot tops, and home-knit galluses—no he only had one. He had an old long-tailed blue jeans coat with slick brass buttons, flung over his arm, and both of them had big fat ratty-looking carpet-bags.

The other fellow was about thirty and dressed about as ornery. After breakfast we all laid off and talked, and the first thing that come out was that these chaps didn't know one another.

"What got you into trouble?" says the bald-head to t'other chap.

"Well, I'd been selling an article to take the tartar off the teeth—and it does take it off, too, and generly the enamel along with it—but I staid about one night longer than I ought to, and was just in the act of sliding out when I ran across you on the trail this side of town, and you told me they were coming, and begged me to help you to get off. So I told you I was expecting trouble myself and would scatter out *with* you. That's the whole yarn—what's yourn?"

"Well, I'd ben a-runnin' a little temperance revival thar, 'bout a week, and was the pet of the women-folks, big and little, for I was makin' it mighty warm for the rummies, I *tell* you, and takin' as much as five or six dollars a night,—ten cents a head, children and niggers free—and business a growin', all the time; when somehow or another a little report got around, last night, that I had a way of puttin' in my time with a private jug, on the sly. A nigger rousted me out, this mornin', and told me the people was getherin' on the quiet, with their dogs and horses, and they'd be along pretty soon and give me 'bout half an hour's start, and then run me down, if they could; and if they got me they'd tar and feather me and ride me on a rail, sure. I didn't wait for no breakfast—I warn't hungry."

"Old man," says the young one, "I reckon we might double-team it together; what do you think?"

"I ain't undisposed. What's your line—mainly?"

"Jour printer, by trade; do a little in patent medicines; theatre-actor—tragedy, you know; take a turn at mesmerism and phrenology when there's a chance; teach singing-geography school for a change; sling a lecture, sometimes—O, I do lots of things—most anything that comes handy, so it ain't work. What's your lay?"

"I've done considerble in the doctoring way, in my time. Layin' on o' hands is my best holt—for cancer, and paralysis, and sich things; and I k'n tell a fortune pretty good, when I've got somebody along to find out the facts for me. Preachin's my line, too; and workin' camp-meetin's; and missionaryin' around."

Nobody never said anything for a while; then the young man hove a sigh and says—

"Alas!"

"What 're you alassin' about?" says the bald-head.

"To think I should have lived to be leading such a life and be degraded down into such company." And he begun to wipe the corner of his eye with a rag.

"Dern your skin, ain't the company good enough for you?" says the bald-head, pretty pert and uppish.

"Yes, it *is* good enough for me; it's as good as I deserve; for who fetched me so low, when I was so high? *I* did myself. I don't blame *you*, gentlemen—far from it; I don't blame anybody. I deserve it all. Let the cold world do its worst; one thing I know—there's a grave somewhere for me. The world may go on just as it's always done, and take everything from me—loved ones, property, everything—but it can't take that. Some day I'll lie down in it and forget it all, and my poor broken heart will be at rest." He went on a wiping.

"Drot your pore broken heart," says the bald-head; "what are you heaving your pore broken heart at *us*, f'r? *we* hain't done nothing."

"No, I know you haven't. I ain't blaming you, gentlemen. I brought myself down—yes, I did it myself. It's right I should suffer—perfectly right—I don't make any moan."

"Brought you down from whar? Whar was you brought down from?"

"Ah, you would not believe me; the world never believes—let it pass—'tis no matter. The secret of my birth—"

"The secret of your birth? Do you mean to say—"

"Gentlemen," says the young man, very solemn, "I will reveal it to you, for I feel I may have confidence in you. By rights I am a duke!"

Jim's eyes bugged out when he heard that; and I reckon mine did, too. Then the bald-head says: "No! You can't mean it?"

"Yes. My great-grandfather, eldest son of the duke of Bridgewater, fled to this country about the end of the last century, to breathe the pure air of freedom; married here, and died, leaving a son, his own father dying about the same time. The second son of the late duke seized the title and estates—the infant real duke was ignored. I am the lineal descendant of that infant—I am the rightful duke of

"BY RIGHTS I AM A DUKE!"

Bridgewater; and here am I, forlorn, torn from my high estate, hunted of men, despised by the cold world, ragged, worn, heartbroken, and degraded to the companionship of felons on a raft!"

Jim pitied him ever so much, and so did I. We tried to comfort him, but he said it warn't much use, he couldn't be much comforted; said if we was a mind to acknowledge him, that would do him more good than most anything else; so we said we would, if he would tell us how. He said we ought to bow, when we spoke to him, and say "Your Grace" or "My Lord," or "Your Lordship"—and he wouldn't mind it if we called him plain "Bridgewater," which he said was a title, anyway, and not a name; and one of us ought to wait on him at dinner, and do any little thing for him he wanted done.

Well, that was all easy, so we done it. All through dinner Jim stood around and waited on him, and says "Will yo' grace have some o' dis, or some o' dat?" and so on, and a body could see it was mighty pleasing to him.

But the old man got pretty silent, by and by—didn't have much to say, and didn't look pretty comfortable over all that petting that was going on around that duke. He seemed to have something on his mind. So, along in the afternoon, he says—

"Looky here, Bilgewater," he says, "I'm nation sorry for you, but you ain't the only person that's had troubles like that."

"No?"

"No, you ain't. You ain't the only person that's ben snaked down wrongfully out'n a high place."

"Alas!"

"No, you ain't the only person that's had a secret of his birth." And by jings, *he* begins to cry.

"Hold! What do you mean?"

"Bilgewater, kin I trust you?" says the old man, still sort of sobbing.

"To the bitter death!" He took the old man by the hand and squeezed it, and says,—"The secret of your being: speak!"

"Bilgewater, I am the late Dauphin!"

You bet you Jim and me stared, this time. Then the duke says: "You are what?"

"Yes, my friend, it is too true—your eyes is lookin' at this very moment on the pore disappeared Dauphin, Looy the Seventeen, son of Looy the Sixteen and Marry Antonette."

"You! At your age! No! you mean you're the late Charlemagne; you must be six or seven hundred years old, at the very least."

"Trouble has done it, Bilgewater, trouble has done it; trouble has brung these gray hairs and this premature balditude. Yes, gentlemen, you see before you, in blue jeans and misery, the wanderin', exiled, trampled-on and sufferin' rightful King of France."

Well, he cried and took on so, that me and Jim didn't know hardly what to do, we was so sorry—and so glad and proud we'd got him with us, too. So we set in, like we done before with the duke, and tried to comfort *him*. But he said it warn't no use, nothing but to be dead and done with it all could do him any good; though he said it often made him feel easier and better for a while if people treated him according to his rights, and got down on one knee to speak to him, and always called him "Your Majesty," and waited on him first, at meals, and didn't set down in his presence till he asked them. So Jim and me set to majestying him, and doing this and that and t'other for him, and standing up till he told us we might set down.

"I AM THE LATE DAUPHIN!"

This done him heaps of good, and so he got cheerful and comfortable. But the duke kind of soured on him, and didn't look a bit satisfied with the way things was going; still, the king acted real friendly towards him, and said the duke's great-grandfather and all the other dukes of Bilgewater was a good deal thought of by *his* father and was allowed to come to the palace considerable; but the duke staid huffy a good while, till by and by the king says—

"Like as not we got to be together a blamed long time, on thish-yer raft, Bilgewater, and so what's the use o' your bein' sour? it'll only make things oncomfortable. It ain't my fault I warn't born a duke, it ain't your fault you warn't born a king—so what's the use to worry? Make the best o' things the way you find 'em, says I—

that's my motto. This ain't no bad thing that we've struck here—plenty grub and an easy life—come, give us your hand, duke, and less all be friends."

The duke done it, and Jim and me was pretty glad to see it. It took away all the uncomfortableness, and we felt mighty good over it, because it would a been a miserable business to have any unfriendliness on the raft; for what you want, above all things, on a raft, is for everybody to be satisfied, and feel right and kind towards the others.

It didn't take me long to make up my mind that these liars warn't no kings nor dukes, at all, but just low-down humbugs and frauds. But I never said nothing, never let on; kept it to myself; it's the best way; then you don't have no quarrels, and don't get into no trouble. If they wanted us to call them kings and dukes, I hadn't no objections, long as it would keep peace in the family; and it warn't no use to tell Jim, so I didn't tell him. If I never learnt nothing else out of pap, I learnt that the best way to get along with his kind of people is to let them have their own way.

Chapter XX

ON THE RAFT.

THEY ASKED US considerable many questions; wanted to know what we covered up the raft that way, for, and laid by in the day-time instead of running—was Jim a runaway nigger? Says I—

"Goodness sakes, would a runaway nigger run *south?*"

No, they allowed he wouldn't. I had to account for things some way, so I says—

"My folks was living in Pike county, in Missouri, where I was born, and they all died off but me, and pa, and my brother Ike. Pa, he 'lowed he'd break up and go down and live with uncle Ben, who's got a little one-horse place on the river forty-four mile below Orleans. Pa was pretty poor, and had some debts; so when he'd squared up there warn't nothing left but sixteen dollars and our nigger, Jim. That warn't enough to take us fourteen hundred mile, deck passage nor no other way. Well, when the river rose, pa had a streak of luck, one day; he ketched this piece of a raft; so we reckoned we'd go down to Orleans on it. Pa's luck didn't hold out; a steamboat run over the forrard corner of the raft one night, and we all went overboard and dove under the wheel; Jim and me come up, all right, but pa was drunk, and Ike was only four years old, so they never come up no more. Well, for the next day or two we had considerable trouble, because people was always coming out in skiffs and trying to take Jim away from me, saying they believed he was a runaway nigger. We don't run daytimes no more, now; nights they don't bother us."

The duke says—

"Leave me alone to cipher out a way so we can run in the day time if we want to. I'll think the thing over—I'll invent a plan that'll fix it. We'll let it alone for to-day, because of course we don't want to go by that town yonder in daylight—it mightn't be healthy."

Towards night it begun to darken up and look like rain; the heat lightning was squirting around, low down in the sky, and the leaves was beginning to shiver—it was going to be pretty ugly, it was easy to see that. So the duke and the king went to overhauling our wigwam, to see what the beds was like. My bed was a straw tick— better than Jim's, which was a corn-shuck tick; there's always cobs around about in a shuck tick, and they poke into you and hurt; and when you roll over, the dry shucks sound like you was rolling over in a pile of dead leaves; it makes such a rustling that you wake up. Well, the duke allowed he would take my bed; but the king allowed he wouldn't. He says—

"I should a reckoned the difference in rank would a sejested to you that a corn-shuck bed warn't jest fitten for me to sleep on. Your grace'll take the shuck bed yourself."

Jim and me was in a sweat again, for a minute, being afraid there was going to be some more trouble amongst them; so we was pretty glad when the duke says—

"'Tis my fate to be always ground into the mire under the iron heel of oppression. Misfortune has broken my once haughty spirit; I yield, I submit; 'tis my fate. I am alone in the world—let me suffer; I can bear it."

We got away as soon as it was good and dark. The king told us to stand well out towards the middle of the river, and not show a light till we got a long ways below the town. We come in sight of the little bunch of lights by and by—that was the town, you know—and slid by, about a half a mile out, all right. When we was three-quarters of a mile below, we hoisted up our signal lantern; and about ten o'clock it come on to rain and blow and thunder and lighten like everything; so the king told us to both stay on watch till the weather got better; then him and the duke crawled into the wigwam and turned in for the night. It was my watch below, till twelve, but I wouldn't a turned in, anyway, if I'd had a bed; because a body don't see such a storm as that every day in the week, not by a long sight. My souls, how the wind did scream along! and every second or two there'd

come a glare that lit up the white-caps for a half a mile around, and
you'd see the islands looking dusty through the rain, and the trees
thrashing around in the wind; then comes a H-WACK!—bum! bum!
bumble-umble-um-bum-bum-bum-bum—and the thunder would
go rumbling and grumbling away, and quit—and then *rip* comes
another flash and another sockdolager. The waves most washed me
off the raft, sometimes, but I hadn't any clothes on, and didn't mind.
We didn't have no trouble about snags; the lightning was glaring
and flittering around so constant that we could see them plenty
soon enough to throw her head this way or that and miss them.

I had the middle watch, you know, but I was pretty sleepy by that
time, so Jim he said he would stand the first half of it for me; he was
always mighty good, that way, Jim was. I crawled into the wigwam,
but the king and the duke had their legs sprawled around so there
warn't no show for me; so I laid outside—I didn't mind the rain,
because it was warm, and the waves warn't running so high, now.
About two they come up again, though, and Jim was going to call
me, but he changed his mind because he reckoned they warn't high
enough yet to do any harm; but he was mistaken about that, for
pretty soon, all of a sudden along comes a regular ripper, and washed
me overboard. It most killed Jim a-laughing. He was the easiest
nigger to laugh that ever was, anyway.

I took the watch, and Jim he laid down and snored away; and by
and by the storm let up for good and all; and the first cabin-light
that showed, I rousted him out and we slid the raft into hiding-
quarters for the day.

The king got out an old ratty deck of cards, after breakfast, and
him and the duke played seven-up a while, five cents a game. Then
they got tired of it and allowed they would "lay out a campaign," as
they called it. The duke went down into his carpet-bag and fetched
up a lot of little printed bills, and read them out loud. One bill said
"the celebrated Dr. Armand de Montalban, of Paris," would "lecture on the science of phrenology" at such-and-such a place, on the
blank day of blank, at ten cents admission, and "furnish charts of
character at twenty-five cents apiece." The duke said that was *him*.
In another bill he was the "world-renowned Shaksperean tragedian, Garrick the Younger, of Drury Lane, London." In other bills
he had a lot of other names, and done other wonderful things, like

finding water and gold with a "divining rod," "dissipating witch-spells," and so on. By and by he says—

"But the histrionic muse is the darling. Have you ever trod the boards, Royalty?"

"No," says the king.

"You shall, then, before you're three days older, Fallen Grandeur," says the duke. "The first good town we come to, we'll hire a hall and do the sword-fight in Richard III, and the balcony scene in Romeo and Juliet. How does that strike you?"

"I'm in, up to the hub, for anything that will pay, Bilgewater, but you see I don't know nothing about play-actn', and hain't ever seen much of it. I was too small when pap used to have 'em at the palace. Do you reckon you can learn me?"

"Easy!"

"All right. I'm jest a-freezn' for something fresh, anyway. Less commence, right away."

So the duke he told him all about who Romeo was, and who Juliet was, and said he was used to being Romeo, so the king could be Juliet.

"But if Juliet's such a young gal, duke, my peeled head and my white whiskers is goin' to look oncommon odd on her, maybe."

"No, don't you worry—these country jakes won't ever think of that. Besides, you know, you'll be in costume, and that makes all the difference in the world; Juliet's in a balcony, enjoying the moonlight before she

THE KING AS JULIET.

goes to bed, and she's got on her night-gown and her ruffled night-cap. Here are the costumes for the parts."

He got out two or three curtain-calico suits which he said was meedyevil armor, for Richard III and t'other chap, and a long white cotton night shirt and a ruffled night-cap to match. The king was satisfied; so the duke got out his book and read the parts over in the most splendid spread-eagle way, prancing around and acting at the same time, to show how it had got to be done; then he give the book to the king and told him to get his part by heart.

There was a little one-horse town about three mile down the bend, and after dinner the duke said he had ciphered out his idea about how to run in daylight without it being dangersome for Jim; so he allowed he would go down to the town and fix that thing. The king allowed he would go, too, and see if he couldn't strike something. We was out of coffee, so Jim said I better go along with them in the canoe and get some.

When we got there, there warn't nobody stirring; streets empty, and perfectly dead and still, like Sunday. We found a sick nigger sunning himself in a back yard, and he said everybody that warn't too young or too sick or too old, was gone to camp-meeting, about two mile back in the woods. The king got the directions, and allowed he'd go and work that camp meeting for all it was worth, and I might go, too.

The duke said what he was after was a printing office. We found it; a little bit of a concern, up over a carpenter shop—carpenters and printers all gone to the meeting, and no doors locked. It was a dirty, littered-up place, and had ink-marks, and handbills with pictures of horses and runaway-niggers on them, all over the walls. The duke shed his coat and said he was all right, now. So me and the king lit out for the camp meeting.

We got there in about a half an hour, fairly dripping, for it was a most awful hot day. There was as much as a thousand people there, from twenty mile around. The woods was full of teams and wagons, hitched everywheres, feeding out of the wagon troughs and stomping to keep off the flies. There was sheds made out of poles and roofed over with branches, where they had lemonade and ginger-bread to sell, and piles of watermelons and green corn and such-like truck.

The preaching was going on under the same kinds of sheds, only they was bigger and held crowds of people. The benches was made out of outside slabs of logs, with holes bored in the round side to drive sticks into for legs. They didn't have no backs. The preachers had high platforms to stand on, at one end of the sheds. The women

"COURTING ON THE SLY."

had on sun-bonnets; and some had linsey-woolsey frocks, some gingham ones, and a few of the young ones had on calico. Some of the young men was barefooted, and some of the children didn't have on any clothes but just a tow-linen shirt. Some of the old women was knitting, and some of the young folks was courting on the sly.

The first shed we come to, the preacher was lining-out a hymn. He lined out two lines, everybody sung it, and it was kind of grand to hear it, there was so many of them and they done it in such a rousing way; then he lined out two more for them to sing—and so on. The people woke up more and more, and sung louder and louder; and towards the end, some begun to groan, and some begun to shout.

Then the preacher begun to preach; and begun in earnest, too; and
went weaving first to one side of the platform and then the other,
and then a-leaning down over the front of it, with his arms and his
body going all the time, and shouting his words out with all his
might; and every now and then he would hold up his Bible and
spread it open, and kind of pass it around this way and that, shouting,
"It's the brazen serpent in the wilderness! look upon it and live!"
and people would shout out, "Glory!—A-a-*men!*" And so he went
on, and the people groaning and crying and saying amen:

"O, come to the mourners' bench! Come, black with sin!
[*Amen!*] come, sick and sore! [*Amen!*] come, lame and halt, and
blind! [*Amen!*] come, pore and needy, sunk in shame! [*A-a-*MEN!]
come all that's worn, and soiled, and suffering!—come with a broken spirit! come with a contrite heart! come, in your rags and sin and
dirt! the waters that cleanse is free, the door of heaven stands open
—O, enter in and be at rest!" [*A-a-*MEN! *Glory, glory hallelujah!*]

And so on. You couldn't make out what the preacher said, any
more, on account of the shouting and crying. Folks got up, everywheres in the crowd, and worked their way, just by main strength,
to the mourners' bench, with the tears running down their faces;
and when all the mourners had got up there to the front benches in
a crowd, they sung, and shouted, and flung themselves down on the
straw, just crazy and wild.

Well, the first I knowed, the king got agoing; and you could hear
him over everybody; and next he went a-charging up onto the platform and the preacher he begged him to speak to the people, and he
done it. He told them he was a pirate—been a pirate for thirty years,
out in the Indian ocean, and his crew was thinned out considerable,
last spring in a fight, and he was home, now, to take out some fresh
men, and thanks to goodness he'd been robbed last night and put
ashore off of a steamboat without a cent, and he was glad of it, it was
the blessedest thing that ever happened to him, because he was a
changed man now, and happy for the first time in his life; and, poor
as he was, he was going to start right off and work his way back to
the Indian ocean and put in the rest of his life trying to turn the
pirates into the true path; for he could do it better than anybody
else, being acquainted with all the pirate crews in that ocean; and
though it would take him a long time to get there, without money,

he would get there, anyway, and every time he convinced a pirate, he would say to him, "Don't you thank me, don't you give me no credit, it all belongs to them dear people in Pokeville camp meeting, natural brothers and benefactors of the race—and that dear preacher there, the truest friend a pirate ever had!"

"A PIRATE FOR THIRTY YEARS."

And then he busted into tears, and so did everybody. Then somebody sings out "Take up a collection for him, take up a collection!" Well, a half a dozen made a jump to do it, but somebody sings out, "Let *him* pass the hat around!" Then everybody said it, the preacher, too.

So the king went all through the crowd with his hat, swabbing his eyes, and blessing the people and praising them and thanking them for being so good to the poor pirates away off there; and every little while the prettiest kind of girls, with the tears running down their cheeks, would up and ask him would he let them kiss him, for to remember him by; and he always done it; and some of them he hugged and kissed as many as five or six times—and he was invited to stay a week; and everybody wanted him to live in their houses, and said they'd think it was an honor; but he said as this was the last day of the camp meeting he couldn't do no good, and besides he was in a sweat to get to the Indian ocean right off and go to work on the pirates.

When we got back to the raft and he come to count up, he found he had collected eighty-seven dollars and seventy-five cents. And then he had fetched away a three-gallon jug of whisky, too, that he found under a wagon when we was starting home through the woods. The king said, take it all around, it laid over any day he'd ever put in in the missionarying line. He said it warn't no use talking, heathens don't amount to shucks, alongside of pirates, to work a camp meeting with.

The duke was thinking *he'd* been doing pretty well, till the king come to show up, but after that he didn't think so so much. He had set up and printed off two little jobs for farmers, in that printing office—horse-bills—and took the money, four dollars. And he had got in ten dollars worth of advertisements for the paper, which he said he would put in for four dollars if they would pay in advance—so they done it. The price of the paper was two dollars a year, but he took in three subscriptions for half a dollar apiece on condition of them paying him in advance; they were going to pay in cord-wood and onions, as usual, but he said he had just bought the concern and knocked down the price as low as he could afford it, and was going to run it for cash. He set up a little piece of poetry, which he made, himself, out of his own head,—three verses—kind of sweet and saddish—the name of it was, "Yes, Crush, Cold World, this Breaking Heart"—and he left that all set up and ready to print in the paper and didn't charge nothing for it. Well, he took in nine dollars and a half, and said he'd done a pretty square day's work for it.

Then he showed us another little job he'd printed and hadn't charged for, because it was for us. It had a picture of a runaway nigger, with a bundle on a stick, over his shoulder, and "$200 REWARD" under it. The reading was all about Jim, and just described him to a dot. It said he run away from St. Jacques plantation, forty mile below New Orleans, last winter, and likely went north, and whoever would catch him and send him back, he could have the reward and expenses.

ANOTHER LITTLE JOB.

"Now," says the duke, "after to-night we can run in the daytime
if we want to. Whenever we see anybody coming, we can tie Jim
hand and foot with a rope and lay him in the wigwam and show
this handbill and say we captured him up the river, and were too
poor to travel on a steamboat, so we got this little raft on credit from
our friends and are going down to get the reward. Handcuffs and
chains would look still better on Jim, but it wouldn't go well with
the story of us being so poor. Too much like jewelry. Ropes are the
correct thing—we must preserve the unities, as we say on the
boards."

We all said the duke was pretty smart, and there couldn't be no
trouble about running daytimes. We judged we could make miles
enough that night to get out of the reach of the pow-wow we
reckoned the duke's work in the printing office was going to make
in that little town—then we could boom right along, if we wanted
to.

We laid low and kept still, and never shoved out till nearly ten o'clock; then we slid by, pretty wide away from the town, and didn't hoist our lantern till we was clear out of sight of it.

When Jim called me to take the watch at four in the morning, he says—

"Huck, does you reck'n we gwyne to run acrost any mo' kings on dis trip?"

"No," I says, "I reckon not."

"Well," says he, "dat's all right, den. I doan' mine one er two kings, but dat's enough. Dis one's powerful drunk, en de duke ain' much better."

I found Jim had been trying to get him to talk French, so he could hear what it was like; but he said he had been in this country so long, and had so much trouble, he'd forgot it.

Chapter XXI

PRACTICING.

IT was after sun-up, now, but we went right on, and didn't tie up. The king and the duke turned out, by and by, looking pretty rusty; but after they'd jumped overboard and took a swim it chippered them up a good deal. After breakfast the king he took a seat on a corner of the raft, and pulled off his boots and rolled up his britches, and let his legs dangle in the water, so as to be comfortable, and lit his pipe, and went to getting his Romeo and Juliet by heart. When he had got it pretty good, him and the duke begun to practice it together. The duke had to learn him over and over again, how to say every speech; and he made him sigh, and put his hand on his heart; and after a while he said he done it pretty well; "only," he says, "you *mustn't* bellow out ROMEO! that way, like a bull—you must say it soft, and sick, and languishy, so—R–o–o–meo!—that is the idea—for Juliet's a dear sweet mere child of a girl, you know, and she don't bray like a jackass."

Well, next they got out a couple of long swords that the duke made out of oak laths, and begun to practice the sword-fight—the duke called himself Richard III; and the way they laid on, and pranced around the raft was grand to see. But by and by the king tripped and fell overboard, and after that they took a rest, and had a talk about all kinds of adventures they'd had in other times along the river.

After dinner, the duke says—

"Well, Capet, we'll want to make this a first class show, you know, so I guess we'll add a little more to it. We want a little something to answer encores with, anyway."

"What's onkores, Bilgewater?"

The duke told him; and then says—

"I'll answer by doing the Highland Fling or the Sailor's Hornpipe; and you—well let me see—O, I've got it—you can do Hamlet's Soliloquy."

"Hamlet's which?"

"Hamlet's Soliloquy, you know; the most celebrated thing in Shakspeare. Ah, it's sublime, sublime! Always fetches the house. I haven't got it in the book—I've only got one volume—but I reckon I can piece it out from memory. I'll just walk up and down, a minute, and see if I can call it back from recollection's vaults."

So he went to marching up and down, thinking—and frowning, horrible, every now and then; then he would hoist up his eyebrows; next he would squeeze his hand on his forehead and stagger back

HAMLET'S SOLILOQUY.

and kind of moan; next he would sigh, and next he'd let on to drop a
tear. It was beautiful to see him. By and by he got it. He told us to
give attention. Then he strikes a most noble attitude, with one leg
shoved forwards, and his arms stretched away up, and his head tilted
back, looking up at the sky—and then he begins to rip and rave and
grit his teeth—and after that, all through his speech he howled, and
spread around, and swelled up his chest, and just knocked the spots
out of any acting ever *I* see before. This is the speech—I learned it,
easy enough, while he was learning it to the king:

> To be, or not to be: that is the bare bodkin
> That makes calamity of so long life;
> For who would fardels bear, till Birnam wood do come to
>   Dunsinane,
> But that the fear of something after death
> Murders the innocent sleep,
> Great nature's second course,
> And makes us rather sling the arrows of outrageous fortune
> Than fly to others that we know not of.
> There's the respect must give us pause:
> Wake Duncan with thy knocking! I would thou couldst;
> For who would bear the whips and scorns of time,
> The oppressor's wrong, the proud man's contumely,
> The law's delay, and the quietus which his pangs might take,
> In the dead waste and middle of the night, when churchyards
>   yawn
> In customary suits of solemn black,
> But that the undiscovered country from whose bourne no
>   traveler returns,
> Breathes forth contagion on the world,
> And thus the native hue of resolution, like the poor cat i' the
>   adage,
> Is sicklied o'er with care,
> And all the clouds that lowered o'er our housetops,
> With this regard their currents turn awry,
> And lose the name of action.
> 'Tis a consummation devoutly to be wished. But soft you, the
>   fair Ophelia:
> Ope not thy ponderous and marble jaws,
> But get thee to a nunnery—go!

Well, the old man he liked that speech, and he mighty soon got it
so he could do it first rate. It seemed like he was just born for it; and

when he had his hand in, and was excited, it was perfectly lovely the way he would rip and tear and rair up behind when he was getting it off.

The first chance we got, the duke he had some show bills printed; and after that, for two or three days, as we floated along, the raft was a most uncommon lively place, for there warn't nothing but sword-fighting and rehearsing—as the duke called it—going on, all the time. One morning, when we was pretty well down the State of Arkansaw, we come in sight of a little one-horse town in a big bend; so we tied up about three-quarters of a mile above it, in the mouth of a crick which was shut in like a tunnel by the cypress trees, and all of us but Jim took the canoe and went down there to see if there was any chance in that place for our show.

We struck it mighty lucky: there was going to be a circus there that afternoon, and the country people was already beginning to come in, in all kinds of old shackly wagons, and on horses. The circus would leave before night, so our show would have a pretty good chance. The duke he hired the court house, and we went around and stuck up our bills. They read like this:

SHAKSPEREAN REVIVAL!!!
Wonderful Attraction!

————

For One Night Only!

————

The World-renowned Tragedians,
DAVID GARRICK THE YOUNGER,
of Drury Lane Theatre, London,
and
EDMUND KEAN THE ELDER,
of the Royal Haymarket Theatre, Whitechapel,
Pudding Lane, Piccadilly, London, and the
Royal Continental Theatres,
In their sublime Shaksperean Spectacle entitled
THE BALCONY SCENE
in
ROMEO AND JULIET!!!

Romeo . . . . Mr. Garrick.
Juliet. . . . . Mr. Kean.
Assisted by the whole strength of the Company!
New Costumes, New Scenery, New Appointments!

————

ALSO:
The thrilling, masterly and blood-curdling
BROAD-SWORD CONFLICT
IN RICHARD III.!!!
Richard III. . . . . Mr. Garrick.
Richmond. . . . . Mr. Kean.
ALSO:
(By Special Request,)
HAMLET'S IMMORTAL SOLILOQUY!!!
By the Illustrious Kean!
Done by him 300 Consecutive Nights in Paris!

———

FOR ONE NIGHT ONLY!
On account of imperative European Engagements!

———

Admission 25 cents; children and servants 10 cents.

———

Then we went loafing around the town. The stores and houses
was most all old shackly dried-up frame concerns that hadn't ever
been painted; they was set up three or four foot above ground on
stilts, so as to be out of reach of the water when the river was
overflowed. The houses had little gardens around them, but they
didn't seem to raise hardly anything in them but jimpson weeds,
and sunflowers, and ash-piles, and old curled-up boots and shoes,
and pieces of bottles, and rags, and played-out tin-ware. The fences
was made of different kinds of boards, nailed on at different times;
and they leaned every-which-way, and had gates that didn't generly
have but one hinge—a leather one. Some of the fences had been
whitewashed, some time or another, but the duke said it was in
Clumbus's time, like enough. There was generly hogs in the garden,
and people driving them out.

All the stores was along one street. They had white domestic
awnings in front, and the country people hitched their horses to the
awning posts. There was empty dry-goods boxes under the awnings,
and loafers roosting on them all day long, whittling them with their
Barlow knives; and chawing tobacco, and gaping and yawning and
stretching—a mighty ornery lot. They generly had on yellow straw
hats most as wide as an umbrella, but didn't wear no coats nor
waistcoats; they called one another Bill, and Buck, and Hank, and
Jo, and Andy, and talked lazy and drawly, and used considerable
many cuss-words. There was as many as one loafer leaning up

against every awning post, and he most always had his hands in his britches pockets, except when he fetched them out to lend a chaw of tobacco or scratch. What a body was hearing amongst them, all the time, was,—

"Gimme a chaw 'v tobacker, Hank."

"Cain't—I hain't got but one chaw left. Ask Bill."

Maybe Bill he gives him a chaw; maybe he lies and says he ain't got none. Some of them kinds of loafers never has a cent in the world, nor a chaw of tobacco of their own. They get all their chawing by borrowing—they say to a fellow, "I wisht you'd len' me a chaw, Jack, I jist this minute give Ben Thompson the last chaw I had"— which is a lie, pretty much every time; it don't fool nobody but a stranger; but Jack ain't no stranger, so he says—

"GIMME A CHAW."

"You give him a chaw, did you? So did your sister's cat's grand-mother. You pay me back the chaws you've awready borry'd off'n me, Lafe Buckner, then I'll loan you one or two ton of it, and won't charge you no back-intrust, nuther."

"Well, I did pay you back some of it wunst."

"Yes, you did—'bout six chaws. You borry'd store tobacker and paid back nigger-head."

Store tobacco is flat, black plug, but these fellows mostly chaws the natural leaf twisted. When they borrow a chaw, they don't generly cut it off with a knife, but they set the plug in between their teeth, and gnaw with their teeth and tug at the plug with their hands till they get it in two—then sometimes the one that owns the tobacco looks mournful at it when it's handed back, and says, sarcastic—

"Here, gimme the *chaw*, and you take the *plug*."

All the streets and lanes was just mud, they warn't nothing else *but* mud—mud as black as tar, and nigh about a foot deep, in some places; and two or three inches deep in *all* the places. The hogs loafed and grunted around, everywheres. You'd see a muddy sow and a litter of pigs come lazying along the street and whollop herself right down in the way, where folks had to walk around her, and she'd stretch out and shut her eyes, and wave her ears, whilst the pigs was milking her, and look as happy as if she was on salary. And pretty soon you'd hear a loafer sing out, "Hi! *so* boy! sick him, Tige!" and away the sow would go, squealing most horrible, with a dog or two swinging to each ear, and three or four dozen more a-coming; and then you would see all the loafers get up and watch the thing out of sight, and laugh at the fun and look grateful for the noise. Then they'd settle back again, till there was a dog-fight. There couldn't anything wake them up all over, and make them happy all over, like a dog-fight—unless it might be putting turpentine on a stray dog and setting fire to him, or tying a tin pan to his tail and seeing him run himself to death.

On the river front some of the houses was sticking out over the bank, and they was bowed and bent, and about ready to tumble in. The people had moved out of them. The bank was caved away under one corner of some others, and that corner was hanging over. People lived in them, yet, but it was dangersome, because sometimes a strip of land as wide as a house caves in at a time. Sometimes a belt of land a quarter of a mile deep will start in and cave along and cave along till it all caves into the river in one summer. Such a town as that has to be always moving back, and back, and back, because the river's always gnawing at it.

The nearer it got to noon, that day, the thicker and thicker was the wagons and horses in the streets, and more coming, all the time. Families fetched their dinners with them, from the country, and eat them in the wagons. There was considerable whisky drinking going on, and I seen three fights. By and by somebody sings out,—

"Here comes old Boggs!—in from the country for his little old monthly drunk—here he comes, boys!"

All the loafers looked glad—I reckoned they was used to having fun out of Boggs. One of them says—

"Wonder who he's a gwyne to chaw up this time. If he'd a chawed up all the men he's ben a gwyne to chaw up in the last twenty year, he'd have considerble ruputation, now."

Another one says, "I wisht old Boggs 'd threaten me—'cuz then I'd know I warn't gwyne to die for a thousan' year."

Boggs comes a-tearing along on his horse, whooping and yelling like an Injun, and singing out—

"Cler the track, thar. I'm on the waw path, and the price uv coffins is a gwyne to raise."

He was drunk, and weaving about in his saddle; he was over fifty year old, and had a very red face. Everybody yelled at him, and laughed at him, and sassed him, and he sassed back, and said he'd attend to them and lay them out in their regular turns, but he couldn't wait, now, because he'd come to town to kill old Colonel Sherburn, and his motto was, "meat first, and spoon-vittles to top off on."

He see me, and rode up and says—

"Whar'd you come f'm, boy? You prepared to die?"

Then he rode on. I was scared; but a man says—

"He don't mean nothing; he's always a carryin' on like that, when he's drunk. He's the best-naturedest old fool in Arkansaw—never hurt nobody, drunk nor sober."

Boggs rode up before the biggest store in town and bent his head down so he could see under the curtain of the awning, and yells—

"Come out here, Sherburn!—come out and meet the man you've swindled. You're the houn' I'm after, and I'm a gwyne to have you, too!"

And so he went on, calling Sherburn everything he could lay his tongue to, and the whole street packed with people listening and

A LITTLE MONTHLY DRUNK.

laughing and going on. By and by a proud looking man about fifty-five,—and he was a heap the best dressed man in that town, too—steps out of the store, and the crowd drops back on each side to let him come. He says to Boggs, mighty ca'm and slow—he says:

"I'm tired of this; but I'll endure it till one o'clock. Till one o'clock, mind—no longer. If you open your mouth against me only once, after that time, you can't travel so far but I will find you."

Then he turns and goes in. The crowd looked mighty sober; nobody stirred, and there warn't no more laughing. Boggs rode off blackguarding Sherburn as loud as he could yell, all down the street; and pretty soon back he comes and stops before the store, still keeping it up. Some men crowded around him and tried to get him to shut up, but he wouldn't; they told him it would be one o'clock in about fifteen minutes, and so he *must* go home—he must go right away. But it didn't do no good. He cussed away, with all his might, and threwed his hat down in the mud and rode over it, and pretty soon away he went a-raging down the street again with his gray hair a flying. Everybody that could get a chance at him tried their best to coax him off of his horse so they could lock him up and get him sober; but it warn't no use—up the street he would tear again, and give Sherburn another cussing. By and by, somebody says—

"Go for his daughter!—quick, go for his daughter; sometimes he'll listen to her. If anybody can persuade him, she can."

So somebody started on a run. I walked down street a ways, and stopped. In about five or ten minutes, here comes Boggs again—but not on his horse. He was a-reeling across the street towards me, bareheaded, with a friend on both sides of him a-holt of his arms and hurrying him along. He was quiet, and looked uneasy; and he warn't hanging back, any, but was doing some of the hurrying, himself. Somebody sings out—

"Boggs!"

I looked over there to see who said it, and it was that Colonel Sherburn. He was standing perfectly still, in the street, and had a pistol raised, in his right hand,—not aiming it, but holding it out with the barrel tilted up towards the sky. The same second, I see a young girl coming on the run, and two men with her. Boggs and the men turned round, to see who called him, and when they see the pistol the men jumped to one side, and the pistol barrel come down slow and steady to a level—both barrels cocked. Boggs throws up both of his hands and says, "O Lord, don't shoot!" Bang! goes the first shot, and he staggers back, clawing at the air—bang! goes the second one, and he tumbles backwards onto the ground, heavy and solid, with his arms spread out. That young girl screamed out, and comes rushing, and down she throws herself on her father, crying, and saying, "O, he's killed him, he's killed him!" The crowd closed up around them, and shouldered and jammed one another, with their necks stretched, trying to see, and people on the inside trying to shove them back, and shouting, "Back, back! give him air, give him air!"

Colonel Sherburn he tossed his pistol onto the ground and turned around on his heel and walked off.

They took Boggs to a little drug store—the crowd pressing around, just the same, and the whole town following, and I rushed and got a good place at the window, where I was close to him and could see in. They laid him on the floor, and put one large Bible under his head, and opened another one and spread it on his breast—but they tore open his shirt, first, and I seen where one of the bullets went in. He made about a dozen long gasps, his breast lifting the Bible up when he drawed in his breath, and letting it down again when he breathed it out—and after that he laid still; he was dead. Then they pulled his daughter away from him, screaming and crying, and took her off. She was about sixteen, and very sweet and gentle-looking, but awful pale and scared.

Well, pretty soon the whole town was there, squirming and scrouging and pushing and shoving to get at the window and have a look, but people that had the places wouldn't give them up, and folks behind them was saying all the time, "Say, now, you've looked enough, you fellows; 'tain't right, and 'tain't fair, for you to stay thar all the time, and never give nobody a chance; other folks has their rights, as well as you."

There was considerable jawing back, so I slid out, thinking maybe there was going to be trouble. The streets was full, and everybody was excited. Everybody that seen the shooting was telling how it happened, and there was a big crowd packed around each one of these fellows, stretching their necks and listening. One long lanky man with long hair and a big white fur stove-pipe hat on the back of his head and a crooked-handled cane, marked out the places on the

THE DEATH OF BOGGS.

ground where Boggs stood, and where Sherburn stood—and the people following him around from one place to t'other and watching everything he done, and bobbing their heads to show they understood, and stooping a little and resting their hands on their thighs to watch him mark the places on the ground with his cane; and then he stood up straight and stiff where Sherburn had stood, frowning, and having his hat brim down over his eyes, and sung out, "Boggs!" and then fetched his cane down slow, to a level, and says "Bang!" staggered backwards, says "Bang!" again, and fell down flat on his back. The people that had seen the thing said he done it perfect; said it was just exactly the way it all happened. Then as much as a dozen people got out their bottles and treated him.

Well, by and by somebody said Sherburn ought to be lynched. In about a minute everybody was saying it; so away they went, mad and yelling, and snatching down every clothes line they come to, to do the hanging with.

Chapter XXII.

SHERBURN STEPS OUT.

They swarmed up the street, towards Sherburn's house, a-whooping and yelling and raging like Injuns, and everything had to clear the way or get run over and tromped to mush, and it was awful to see. Children was heeling it ahead of the mob, screaming and trying to get out of the way; and every window along the road was full of women's heads, and there was nigger boys in every tree, and bucks and wenches looking over every fence; and as soon as the mob would get nearly to them they would break and skaddle back out of reach. Lots of the women and girls was crying and taking on, scared most to death.

They swarmed up in front of Sherburn's palings as thick as they could jam together, and you couldn't hear yourself think for the noise. It was a little twenty-foot yard. Some sung out, "Tear down the fence! tear down the fence!" Then there was a racket of ripping and tearing and smashing, and down she goes, and the front wall of the crowd begins to roll in like a wave.

Just then Sherburn steps out onto the roof of his little front porch, with a double-barrel gun in his hand, and takes his stand, perfectly ca'm and deliberate, not saying a word. The racket stopped, and the wave sucked back.

Sherburn never said a word—just stood there, looking down. The stillness was awful creepy and uncomfortable. Sherburn run his eye slow along the crowd; and wherever it struck, the people tried a little to outgaze him, but they couldn't; they dropped their eyes and looked sneaky. Then pretty soon Sherburn sort of laughed; not the pleasant kind, but the kind that makes you feel like when you are eating bread that's got sand in it.

Then he says, slow and scornful:

"The idea of *you* lynching anybody! It's amusing. The idea of you thinking you had pluck enough to lynch a *man!* Because you're brave enough to tar and feather poor friendless cast-out women that come along here, did that make you think you had grit enough to lay your hands on a *man!* Why, a *man's* safe in the hands of ten thousand of your kind—as long as it's daytime and you're not behind him.

"Do I know you? I know you clear through. I was born and raised in the south, and I've lived in the north; so I know the average all around. The average man's a coward. In the north he lets anybody walk over him that wants to, and goes home and prays for a humble spirit to bear it. In the south one man, all by himself, has stopped a stage full of men, in the daytime, and robbed the lot. Your newspapers call you a brave people so much that you think you *are* braver than any other people—whereas you're just *as* brave, and no braver. Why don't your juries hang murderers? Because they're afraid the man's friends will shoot them in the back, in the dark—and it's just what they *would* do.

"So they always acquit; and then a *man* goes in the night, with a hundred masked cowards at his back, and lynches the rascal. Your mistake is, that you didn't bring a man with you; that's one mistake, and the other is that you didn't come in the dark, and fetch your masks. You brought *part* of a man—Buck Harkness, there—and if you hadn't had him to start you, you'd a taken it out in blowing.

"You didn't want to come. The average man don't like trouble and danger. *You* don't like trouble and danger. But if only *half* a man—like Buck Harkness, there—shouts 'Lynch him, lynch him!' you're afraid to back down—afraid you'll be found out to be what you are—*cowards*—and so you raise a yell, and hang yourselves onto that half-a-man's coat tail, and come raging up here, swearing what big things you're going to do. The pitifulest thing out is a mob;

that's what an army is—a mob; they don't fight with courage that's
born in them, but with courage that's borrowed from their mass,
and from their officers. But a mob without any *man* at the head of
it, is *beneath* pitifulness. Now the thing for *you* to do, is to droop
your tails and go home and crawl in a hole. If any real lynching's
going to be done, it will be done in the dark, southern fashion; and
when they come, they'll bring their masks, and fetch a *man* along.
Now *leave*—and take your half-a-man with you"—tossing his gun
up across his left arm and cocking it, when he says this.

The crowd washed back sudden, and then broke all apart and
went tearing off every which way, and Buck Harkness he heeled it
after them, looking tolerable cheap. I could a staid, if I'd a wanted
to, but I didn't want to.

I went to the circus, and loafed around the back side till the
watchman went by, and then dived in under the tent. I had my

A DEAD HEAD.

twenty-dollar gold piece and some other money, but I reckoned I
better save it, because there ain't no telling how soon you are going
to need it, away from home and amongst strangers, that way. You
can't be too careful. I ain't opposed to spending money on circuses,
when there ain't no other way, but there ain't no use in *wasting* it
on them.

It was a real bully circus. It was the splendidest sight that ever
was, when they all come riding in, two and two, a gentleman and

lady, side by side, the men just in their drawers and undershirts, and no shoes nor stirrups, and resting their hands on their thighs, easy and comfortable,—there must a been twenty of them—and every lady with a lovely complexion, and perfectly beautiful, and looking just like a gang of real sure-enough queens, and dressed in clothes that cost millions of dollars, and just littered with dimonds. It was a powerful fine sight; I never see anything so lovely. And then one by one they got up and stood, and went a-weaving around the ring so gentle, and wavy and graceful, the men looking ever so tall and airy and straight, with their heads bobbing and skimming along, away up there under the tent-roof, and every lady's rose-leafy dress flapping soft and silky around her hips, and she looking like the most loveliest parasol.

And then faster and faster they went, all of them dancing, first one foot stuck out in the air and then the other, the horses leaning more and more, and the ring-master going round and round the centre-pole, cracking his whip and shouting "Hi!—hi!" and the clown cracking jokes behind him; and by and by, all hands dropped the reins, and every lady put her knuckles on her hips and every gentleman folded his arms, and then how the horses did lean over and hump themselves! And so, one after the other they all skipped off into the ring, and made the sweetest bow I ever see, and then scampered out, and everybody clapped their hands and went just about wild.

Well, all through the circus they done the most astonishing things; and all the time, that clown carried on so it most killed the people. The ring-master couldn't ever say a word to him but he was back at him quick as a wink with the funniest things a body ever said; and how he ever *could* think of so many of them, and so sudden and so pat, was what I couldn't no way understand. Why, I couldn't a thought of them in a year. And by and by a drunk man tried to get into the ring—said he wanted to ride; said he could ride as well as anybody that ever was. They argued and tried to keep him out, but he wouldn't listen, and the whole show come to a standstill. Then the people begun to holler at him and make fun of him, and that made him mad, and he begun to rip and tear; so that stirred up the people, and a lot of men begun to pile down off of the benches and swarm towards the ring, saying, "Knock him down! throw him out!" and one or two women begun to scream. So, then, the ring-

master he made a little speech, and said he hoped there wouldn't be
no disturbance, and if the man would promise he wouldn't make
no more trouble, he would let him ride, if he thought he could stay
on the horse. So everybody laughed and said all right, and the man
got on. The minute he was on, the horse begun to rip and tear and
jump, and cavort around, with two circus men hanging onto his bridle trying to hold him, and the drunk man hanging onto his neck,
and his heels flying in the air every jump, and the whole crowd of
people standing up shouting and laughing till the tears rolled down.
And at last, sure enough, all the circus men could do, the horse
broke loose, and away he went like the very nation, round and round
the ring, with that sot laying down on him and hanging to his neck,
with first one leg hanging most to the ground on one side, and then
t'other one on t'other side, and the people just crazy. It warn't funny
to me, though; I was all of a tremble to see his danger. But pretty
soon he struggled up astraddle and grabbed the bridle, a-reeling this
way and that; and the next minute he sprung up and dropped the

HE SHED SEVENTEEN SUITS.

bridle and stood! and the horse agoing like a house afire, too. He just stood up there, a-sailing around as easy and comfortable as if he warn't ever drunk in his life—and then he begun to pull off his clothes and fling them. He shed them so thick they kind of clogged up the air, and altogether he shed seventeen suits. And then, there he was, slim and handsome, and dressed the gaudiest and prettiest you ever saw, and he lit into that horse with his whip and made him fairly hum—and finally skipped off, and made his bow and danced off to the dressing room, and everybody just a-howling with pleasure and astonishment.

Then the ring-master he see how he had been fooled, and he *was* the sickest ring-master you ever see, I reckon. Why, it was one of his own men! He had got up that joke all out of his own head, and never let on to nobody. Well, I felt sheepish enough, to be took in so, but I wouldn't a been in that ring-master's place not for a thousand dollars. I don't know; there may be bullier circuses than what that one was, but I never struck them yet. Anyways it was plenty good enough for *me*; and wherever I run across it, it can have all of *my* custom, every time.

Well, that night we had *our* show, but there warn't only about twelve people there; just enough to pay expenses. And they laughed all the time, and that made the duke mad; and everybody left, anyway, before the show was over, but one boy which was asleep. So the duke said these Arkansaw lunkheads couldn't come up to Shakspeare: what they wanted was low comedy—and maybe something ruther worse than low comedy, he reckoned. He said he could size their style. So next morning he got some big sheets of wrapping paper and some black paint, and drawed off some handbills and stuck them up all over the village. The bills said:

AT THE COURT HOUSE!
FOR 3 NIGHTS ONLY!
The World-Renowned Tragedians
DAVID GARRICK THE YOUNGER!
AND
EDMUND KEAN THE ELDER!
*Of the London and Continental
Theatres,*

In their Thrilling Tragedy of
THE KING'S CAMELOPARD
OR
THE ROYAL NONESUCH!!!
Admission 50 cents.

Then at the bottom was the biggest line of all—which said:

LADIES AND CHILDREN NOT ADMITTED.

"There," says he, "if that line don't fetch them, I don't know Arkansaw!"

Chapter XXIII

TRAGEDY.

'Well, all day him and the king was hard at it, rigging up a stage, and a curtain, and a row of candles for footlights; and that night the house was jam full of men in no time. When the place couldn't hold no more, the duke he quit tending door and went around the back way and come onto the stage and stood up before the curtain, and made a little speech, and praised up this tragedy, and said it was the most thrillingest one that ever was; and so he went on, a-bragging about the tragedy, and about Edmund Kean the Elder, which was to play the main principal part in it; and at last when he'd got everybody's expectations up high enough, he rolled up the curtain, and the next minute the king come a-prancing out on all fours, naked; and he was painted, all over, ring-streaked-and-striped, all sorts of colors, as splendid as a rain-bow. And—but never mind the rest of his outfit, it was just wild, but it was awful funny. The people most killed themselves laughing; and when the king got done capering, and capered off behind the scenes, they roared and clapped and stormed and haw-hawed till he come back and done it over again; and after that, they made him do it another time. Well, it would a made a cow laugh, to see the shines that old idiot cut.

Then the duke he lets the curtain down, and bows to the people, and says the great tragedy will be performed only two nights more, on accounts of pressing London engagements, where the seats is all sold aready for it in Drury Lane; and then he makes them another bow, and says if he has succeeded in pleasing them and instructing them, he will be deeply obleeged if they will mention it to their friends and get them to come and see it.

Twenty people sings out:

"What, is it over? Is that *all?*"

The duke says yes. Then there was a fine time. Everybody sings out "Sold!" and rose up mad, and was agoing for that stage and them tragedians. But a big fine looking man jumps up on a bench and shouts:

"Hold on! Just a word, gentlemen." They stopped to listen. "We are sold—mighty badly sold. But we don't want to be the laughing-stock of this whole town, I reckon, and never hear the last of this thing as long as we live. *No.* What we want, is to go out of here quiet, and talk this show up, and sell the *rest* of the town! Then we'll all be in the same boat. Ain't that sensible?" ["You bet it is!— the jedge is right!" everybody sings out.] "All right, then— not a word about any sell. Go along home, and advise everybody to come and see the tragedy."

Next day you couldn't hear nothing around that town but how splendid that show was. House was jammed again, that night, and we sold this crowd the same way. When me and the king and the duke got home to the raft, we all had a supper; and by and by, about midnight, they made Jim and me back her out and float her down the middle of the river and fetch her in and hide her about two mile below town.

THEIR POCKETS BULGED.

The third night the house was crammed again—and they warn't newcomers, this time, but people that was at the show the other two nights. I stood by the duke at the door, and I see that every man that went in had his pockets bulging, or something muffled up under his coat—and I see it warn't no perfumery, neither, not by a long sight. I smelt sickly eggs by the barrel, and rotten cabbages, and such things; and if I know the signs of a dead cat being around, and I bet I do, there was sixty-four of them went in. I shoved in there for a minute, but it was too various for me, I couldn't stand it. Well, when the place couldn't hold no more people, the duke he give a fellow a quarter and told him to tend door for him a minute, and then he started around for the stage door, I after him; but the minute we turned the corner and was in the dark, he says:

"Walk fast, now, till you get away from the houses, and then shin for the raft like the dickens was after you!"

I done it, and he done the same. We struck the raft at the same time, and in less than two seconds we was gliding down stream, all dark and still, and edging towards the middle of the river, nobody saying a word. I reckoned the poor king was in for a gaudy time of it with the audience; but nothing of the sort: pretty soon he crawls out from under the wigwam, and says:

"Well, how'd the old thing pan out this time, duke?"

He hadn't been up town at all.

We never showed a light till we was about ten mile below that village. Then we lit up and had a supper, and the king and the duke fairly laughed their bones loose over the way they'd served them people. The duke says:

"Greenhorns, flatheads! *I* knew the first house would keep mum and let the rest of the town get roped in; and I knew they'd lay for us the third night, and consider it was *their* turn now. Well, it *is* their turn, and I'd give something to know how much they'd take for it. I *would* just like to know how they're putting in their opportunity. They can turn it into a picnic, if they want to—they brought plenty provisions."

Them rapscallions took in four hundred and sixty-five dollars in that three nights. I never see money hauled in by the wagon load like that, before.

By and by, when they was asleep and snoring, Jim says:

"Don't it sprise you, de way dem kings carries on, Huck?"

"No," I says, "it don't."

"Why don't it, Huck?"

"Well, it don't, because it's in the breed. I reckon they're all alike."

"But Huck, dese kings o' ourn is reglar rapscallions; dat's jist what dey is; dey's reglar rapscallions."

"Well, that's what I'm a-saying; all kings is mostly rapscallions, as fur as I can make out."

"Is dat so?"

"You read about them once—you'll see. Look at Henry the Eight; this'n 's a Sunday School superintendent to *him*. And look at Charles Second, and Louis Fourteen, and Louis Fifteen, and James Second, and Edward Second, and Richard Third, and forty more; besides all them Saxon heptarchies that used to rip around so in old times and raise Cain. My, you ought to seen old Henry the Eight when he was in bloom. He *was* a blossom. He used to marry a new wife every day, and chop off her head next morning. And he would do it just as indifferent as if he was ordering up eggs. 'Fetch up Nell Gwynn,' he says. They fetch her up. Next morning, 'Chop off her head!' And they chop it off. 'Fetch up Jane Shore,' he says; and up she comes. Next morning, 'Chop off her head'—and they chop it off. 'Ring up Fair Rosamun.' Fair Rosamun answers the bell. Next morning, 'Chop off her head.' And he made every one of them tell him a tale every night; and he kept that up till he had hogged a thousand and one tales that way, and then he put them all in a book, and called it Domesday Book—which was a good name, and stated the case. You don't know kings, Jim, but I know them; and this old rip of ourn is one of the cleanest I've struck in history. Well, Henry he takes a notion he wants to get up some trouble with this country. How does he go at it—give notice?—give the country a show? No. All of a sudden he heaves all the tea in Boston harbor overboard, and whacks out a declaration of independence, and dares them to come on. That was *his* style—he never give anybody a chance. He had suspicions of his father, the duke of Wellington. Well, what did he do?—ask him to show up? No—drownded him in a butt of mamsey, like a cat. Spose people left money laying around where he was—what did he do? He collared it. Spose he contracted to do a thing; and you paid him, and didn't set down there and see that he done it—what did he do? He always done the other thing. Spose he opened his mouth—what then? If he didn't shut it up powerful quick, he'd lose a lie, every time. That's the kind of a bug Henry was; and if we'd a had him along stead of our kings, he'd a fooled that town a heap

HENRY THE EIGHTH IN BOSTON HARBOR.

worse than ourn done. I don't say that ourn is lambs, because they ain't, when you come right down to the cold facts; but they ain't nothing to *that* old ram, anyway. All I say, is, kings is kings, and you got to make allowances. Take them all around, they're a mighty ornery lot. It's the way they're raised."

"But dis one do *smell* so like de nation, Huck."

"Well, they all do, Jim. *We* can't help the way a king smells; history don't tell no way."

"Now de duke, he's a tolerble likely man, in some ways."

"Yes, a duke's different. But not very different. This one's a middling hard lot,—for a duke. When he's drunk, there ain't no near-sighted man could tell him from a king."

"Well, anyways, I doan hanker for no mo' un um, Huck. Dese is all I kin stan'."

"It's the way I feel, too, Jim. But we've got them on our hands, and we got to remember what they are, and make allowances. Sometimes I wish we could hear of a country that's out of kings."

What was the use to tell Jim these warn't real kings and dukes? It wouldn't a done no good; and besides, it was just as I said; you couldn't tell them from the real kind.

I went to sleep, and Jim didn't call me when it was my turn. He often done that. When I waked up, just at daybreak, he was setting there with his head down betwixt his knees, moaning and mourning to himself. I didn't take notice, nor let on. I knowed what it was about. He was thinking about his wife and his children, away up yonder, and he was low and homesick; because he hadn't ever been away from home before in his life; and I do believe he cared just as much for his people as white folks does for theirn. It don't seem natural, but I reckon it's so. He was often moaning and mourning, that way, nights, when he judged I was asleep, and saying "Po' little 'Lizabeth! po' little Johnny! it mighty hard; I spec' I ain't ever gwyne to see you no mo', no mo'!" He was a mighty good nigger, Jim was.

But this time I somehow got to talking to him about his wife and young ones; and by and by he says:

"What make me feel so bad dis time, 'uz bekase I hear sumpn over yonder on de bank like a whack, er a slam, while ago, en it mine me er de time I treat my little 'Lizabeth so ornery. She warn't on'y 'bout fo' year ole, en she tuck de sk'yarlet fever, en had a powful rough spell; but she got well, en one day she was a-stannin' aroun', en I says to her, I says:

"'Shet de do'.'

"She never done it; jis' stood dah, kiner smilin' up at me. It make me mad; en I says agin, mighty loud, I says:

"'Doan you hear me?—shet de do'!'

"She jis' stood de same way, kiner smilin' up. I was a-bilin'! I says:

"'I lay I *make* you mine!'

"En wid dat I fetch' her a slap side de head dat sont her a-sprawlin'. Den I went into de yuther room, en 'uz gone 'bout ten minutes; en when I come back, dah was dat do' a-stannin' open *yit*, en dat chile stannin' mos' right in it, a-lookin' down en mournin', en de tears runnin' down. My, but I *wuz* mad. I was agwyne for de chile, but jis' den—it was a do' dat open' innerds—jis' den, 'long come de wind en slam it to, behine de chile, ker-*blam!*—en my lan', de chile never move'! My breff mos' hop outer me; en I feel so—so—I doan know *how* I feel. I crope out, all a-tremblin', en crope aroun' en open de do' easy en slow, en poke my head in behine de chile, sof' en still, en all uv a sudden I says *pow!* jis' as loud as I could yell. *She never budge!* O, Huck, I bust out a-cryin', en grab her up in my arms en say, 'O de po' little thing! de Lord God Amighty fogive po' ole Jim, kaze he never gwyne to fogive hisseff as long's he live!' O, she was plumb deef en dumb, Huck, plumb deef en dumb—en I'd ben a treat'n her so!"

Chapter XXIV

HARMLESS.

Next day, towards night, we laid up under a little willow towhead out in the middle, where there was a village on each side of the river, and the duke and the king begun to lay out a plan for working them towns. Jim he spoke to the duke, and said he hoped it wouldn't take but a few hours, because it got mighty heavy and tiresome to him when he had to lay all day in the wigwam tied with the rope. You see, when we left him all alone we had to tie him, because if anybody happened on him all by himself and not tied, it wouldn't look much like he was a runaway nigger, you know. So the duke said it *was* kind of hard to have to lay roped all day, and he'd cipher out some way to get around it.

He was uncommon bright, the duke was, and he soon struck it. He dressed Jim up in King Lear's outfit—it was a long curtain-calico gown, and a white horse-hair wig and whiskers; and then he took his theatre-paint and painted Jim's face and hands and ears and neck all over a dead dull solid blue, like a man that's been drownded nine days. Blamed if he warn't the horriblest looking outrage I ever see. Then the duke took and wrote out a sign on a shingle, so—

Sick Arab—but harmless when not out of his head.

And he nailed that shingle to a lath, and stood the lath up four or five foot in front of the wigwam. Jim was satisfied. He said it was a sight better than laying tied a couple of years every day and trembling all over every time there was a sound. The duke told him to make himself free and easy, and if anybody ever come meddling around, he must hop out of the wigwam, and carry on a little, and fetch a howl or two like a wild beast, and he reckoned they would light out and leave him alone. Which was sound enough judgment; but you take the average man, and he wouldn't wait for him to howl. Why, he didn't only look like he was dead, he looked considerable more than that.

These rapscallions wanted to try the Nonesuch again, because there was so much money in it, but they judged it wouldn't be safe, because maybe the news might a worked along down by this time. They couldn't hit no project that suited, exactly; so at last the duke said he reckoned he'd lay off and work his brains an hour or two and see if he couldn't put up something on the Arkansaw village; and the king he allowed he would drop over to t'other village, without any plan, but just trust in Providence to lead him the profitable way—meaning the devil, I reckon. We had all bought store clothes where we stopped last; and now the king put his'n on, and he told me to put mine on. I done it, of course. The king's duds was all black, and he did look real swell and starchy. I never knowed how clothes could change a body before. Why, before, he looked like the orneriest old rip that ever was; but now, when he'd take off his new white beaver and make a bow and do a smile, he looked that grand and good and pious that you'd say he had walked right out of the ark, and maybe was old Leviticus himself. Jim cleaned up the canoe, and I got my paddle ready. There was a big steamboat laying at the shore away up under the point, about three mile above town—been there a couple of hours—taking on freight. Says the king:

"Seein' how I'm dressed, I reckon maybe I better arrive down from St. Louis or Cincinnati, or some other big place. Go for the steamboat, Huckleberry; we'll come down to the village on her."

I didn't have to be ordered twice, to go and take a steamboat ride. I fetched the shore a half a mile above the village, and then went scooting along the bluff bank in the easy water. Pretty soon we come to a nice innocent looking young country jake setting on a log swabbing the sweat off of his face, for it was powerful warm weather; and he had a couple of big carpet bags by him.

"Run her nose in shore," says the king. I done it. "Wher' you bound for, young man?"

"For the steamboat; going to Orleans."

"Git aboard," says the king. "Hold on a minute, my servant 'll he'p you with them bags. Jump out and he'p the gentleman, Adolphus"—meaning me, I see.

I done so, and then we all three started on again. The young chap was mighty thankful; said it was tough work toting his baggage

ADOLPHUS.

such weather. He asked the king where he was going, and the king told him he'd come down the river and landed at the other village this morning, and now he was going up a few mile to see an old friend on a farm up there. The young fellow says:

"When I first see you, I says to myself, 'It's Mr. Wilks, sure, and he come mighty near getting here in time.' But then I says, again, 'No, I reckon it ain't him, or else he wouldn't be paddling up the river.' You *ain't* him, are you?"

"No, my name's Blodgett—Elexander Blodgett—*Reverend* Elexander Blodgett, I spose I must say, as I'm one o' the Lord's poor servants. But still I'm jest as able to be sorry for Mr. Wilks for not arriving in time, all the same, if he's missed anything by it—which I hope he hasn't."

"Well, he don't miss any property by it, because he'll get that, all right; but he 's missed seeing his brother Peter die—which he mayn't mind, nobody can tell, as to that—but his brother would a give anything in this world to see *him* before he died; never talked about nothing else all these three weeks; hadn't seen him since they was boys together—and hadn't ever seen his brother William, at all—that's the deef and dumb one—William ain't more than thirty or thirty-five. Peter and George was the only ones that come out here; George was the married brother; him and his wife both died last year. Harvey and William's the only ones that's left, now; and as I was saying, they haven't got here in time."

"Did anybody send 'em word?"

"O, yes; a month or two ago, when Peter was first took; because Peter said, then, that he sorter felt like he warn't going to get well this time. You see, he was pretty old, and George's g'yirls was too young to be much company for him, except Mary Jane the red-headed one; and so he was kinder lonesome after George and his wife died, and didn't seem to care much to live. He most desperately wanted to see Harvey—and William too, for that matter—because he was one of them kind that can't bear to make a will. He left a letter behind, for Harvey, and said he'd told in it where his money was hid, and how he wanted the rest of the property divided up so George's g'yirls would be all right—for George didn't leave nothing. And that letter was all they could get him to put a pen to."

"Why do you reckon Harvey don't come? Wher' does he live?"

"O, he lives in England—Sheffield—preaches there—hasn't ever been in this country. He hasn't had any too much time—and besides he mightn't a got the letter at all, you know."

"Too bad, too bad he couldn't a lived to see his brothers, poor soul. You going to Orleans, you say?"

"Yes, but that ain't only a part of it. I'm going in a ship, next Wednesday, for Ryo Janeero, where my uncle lives."

"It's a pretty long journey. But it 'll be lovely; I wisht I was agoing. Is Mary Jane the oldest? How old is the others?"

"Mary Jane's nineteen, Susan's fifteen, and Joanna's about fourteen—that's the one that gives herself to good works and has a hare-lip."

"Poor things! to be left alone in the cold world, so."

"Well, they could be worse off. Old Peter had friends, and they ain't going to let them come to no harm. There's Hobson, the Babtis' preacher; and deacon Lot Hovey, and Ben Rucker, and Abner Shackleford; and Levi Bell, the lawyer; and Dr. Robinson; and their wives; and the widow Bartley, and—well, there's a lot of them; but these are the ones that Peter was thickest with, and used to write about, sometimes, when he wrote home; so Harvey'll know where to look for friends when he gets here."

Well, the old man he went on asking questions till he just fairly emptied that young fellow. Blamed if he didn't inquire about everybody and every thing in that blessed town, and all about all the Wilkses; and about Peter's business—which was a tanner; and about George's—which was a carpenter; and about Harvey's—which was a dissentering minister; and so on, and so on. Then he says:

"What did you want to walk all the way up to the steamboat, for?"

"Because she's a big Orleans boat, and I was afeard she mightn't stop there. When they're deep they won't stop for a hail. A Cincinnati boat will, but this is a St. Louis one."

"Was Peter Wilks well off?"

HE FAIRLY EMPTIED THAT YOUNG FELLOW.

"O, yes, pretty well off. He had houses and land, and it's reckoned he left three or four thousand in cash hid up som'ers."

"When did you say he died?"

"I didn't say; but it was last night."

"Funeral to-morrow, likely?"

"Yes, 'bout the middle of the day."

"Well, it's all terrible sad; but we've all got to go, one time or another. So what we want to do is to be prepared; then we're all right."

"Yes, sir, it's the best way. Ma used to always say that."

When we struck the boat, she was about done loading, and pretty soon she got off. The king never said nothing about going aboard, so I lost my ride, after all. When the boat was gone, the king made me paddle up another mile, to a lonesome place, and then he got ashore and says:

"Now hustle back, right off, and fetch the duke up here, and the new carpet-bags. And if he's gone over to t'other side, go over there and git him. And tell him to git himself up regardless. Shove along, now."

I see what *he* was up to; but I never said nothing, of course. When I got back with the duke, we hid the canoe, and then they set down on a log, and the king told him everything, just like the young fellow had said it—every last word of it. And all the time he was a doing it, he tried to talk like an Englishman; and he done it pretty well, too, for a slouch. I can't imitate him, and so I ain't agoing to try to; but he really done it pretty good. Then he says:

"How are you on the deef and dumb, Bilgewater?"

The duke said, leave him alone for that; said he had played a deef and dumb person on the histrionic boards. So then they waited for a steamboat.

About the middle of the afternoon a couple of little boats come along, but they didn't come from high enough up the river; but at last there was a big one, and they hailed her. She sent out her yawl, and we went aboard, and she was from Cincinnati; and when they found we only wanted to go four or five mile, they was booming mad, and give us a cussing, and said they wouldn't land us. But the king was ca'm. He says:

"If gentlemen kin afford to pay a dollar a mile, apiece, to be took on and put off in a yawl, a steamboat kin afford to carry 'em, can't it?"

So they softened down and said it was all right; and when we got to the village, they yawled us ashore. About two dozen men flocked down, when they see the yawl a coming; and when the king says—

"Kin any of you gentlemen tell me wher' Mr. Peter Wilks lives?" they give a glance at one another, and nodded their heads, as much as to say, "What d' I tell you?" Then one of them says, kind of soft and gentle:

"I'm sorry, sir, but the best we can do is to tell you where he *did* live, yesterday evening."

Sudden as winking, the ornery old cretur went all to smash, and fell up against the man, and put his chin on his shoulder, and cried down his back, and says:

"Alas, alas, our poor brother—gone, and we never got to see him; oh, it's too, *too* hard!"

Then he turns around, blubbering, and makes a lot of idiotic signs to the duke on his hands, and blamed if *he* didn't drop a carpet-bag

"ALAS, OUR POOR BROTHER."

and bust out a-crying. If they warn't the beatenest lot, them two frauds, that ever I struck.

Well, the men gethered around, and sympathized with them, and said all sorts of kind things to them, and carried their carpet bags up the hill for them, and let them lean on them and cry, and told the king all about his brother's last moments, and the king he told it all over again on his hands to the duke, and both of them took on about that dead tanner like they'd lost the twelve disciples. Well, if ever I struck anything like it, I'm a nigger. It was enough to make a body ashamed of the human race.

Chapter XXV

"YOU BET IT IS."

The news was all over town in two minutes, and you could see the people tearing down on the run, from every which way, some of them putting on their coats as they come. Pretty soon we was in the middle of a crowd, and the noise of the tramping was like a soldier-march. The windows and door-yards was full; and every minute somebody would say, over a fence:

"Is it *them?*"

And somebody trotting along with the gang would answer back and say:

"You bet it is."

When we got to the house, the street in front of it was packed, and the three girls was standing in the door. Mary Jane *was* red-headed, but that don't make no difference, she was most awful beautiful, and her face and her eyes was all lit up like glory, she was so glad her uncles was come. The king he spread his arms, and Mary Jane she jumped for them, and the hare-lip jumped for the duke, and there they *had* it! Everybody, most, leastways women, cried for joy to see them meet at last and have such good times.

Then the king he hunched the duke, private—I see him do it—and then he looked around and see the coffin, over in the corner on two chairs; so then, him and the duke, with a hand across each other's shoulder, and t'other hand to their eyes, walked slow and solemn over there, everybody dropping back to give them room, and all the talk and noise stopping, people saying "Sh!" and all the men taking their hats off and drooping their heads, so you could a heard a pin fall. And when they got there, they bent over and looked in the coffin, and took one sight, and then they bust out a crying so you could a heard them to Orleans, most; and then they put their arms around each other's necks, and hung their chins over each other's shoulders; and then for three minutes, or maybe four, I never see two men leak the way they done. And mind you, everybody was doing the same; and the place was that damp I never see anything like it. Then one of them got on one side of the coffin, and t'other on t'other side, and they kneeled down and rested their foreheads on the coffin, and let on to pray, all to their selves. Well, when it come to that, it worked the crowd like you never see anything like it, and so everybody broke down and went to sobbing right out loud—the poor girls, too; and every woman, nearly, went up to the girls, without saying a word, and kissed them, solemn, on the forehead, and then put their hand on their head, and looked up towards the sky, with the tears running down, and then busted out and went off sobbing and swabbing, and give the next woman a show. I never see anything so disgusting.

Well, by and by the king he gets up and comes forward a little,

LEAKING.

and works himself up and slobbers out a speech, all full of tears and
flapdoodle about its being a sore trial for him and his poor brother
to lose the diseased, and to miss seeing diseased alive, after the long
journey of four thousand mile, but it's a trial that's sweetened and
sanctified to us by this dear sympathy and these holy tears, and so
he thanks them out of his heart and out of his brother's heart,
because out of their mouths they can't, words being too weak and
cold, and all that kind of rot and slush, till it was just sickening; and
then he blubbers out a pious goody-goody Amen, and turns himself
loose and goes to crying fit to bust.

And the minute the words was out of his mouth somebody over
in the crowd struck up the doxolojer, and everybody joined in with
all their might, and it just warmed you up and made you feel as good
as church letting out. Music *is* a good thing; and after all that soul-
butter and hogwash, I never see it freshen up things so, and sound
so honest and bully.

Then the king begins to work his jaw again, and says how him
and his nieces would be glad if a few of the main principal friends of
the family would take supper here with them this evening, and help
set up with the ashes of the diseased; and says if his poor brother
laying yonder could speak, he knows who he would name, for they
was names that was very dear to him, and mentioned often in his
letters; and so he will name the same, to-wit, as follows, vizz: Rev.
Mr. Hobson, and deacon Lot Hovey, and Mr. Ben Rucker, and Abner
Shackleford, and Levi Bell, and Dr. Robinson, and their wives, and
the widow Bartley.

Rev. Hobson and Dr. Robinson was down to the end of the town,
a-hunting together; that is, I mean the doctor was shipping a sick
man to t'other world, and the preacher was pinting him right.
Lawyer Bell was away up to Louisville on some business. But the
rest was on hand, and so they all come and shook hands with the
king and thanked him and talked to him; and then they shook hands
with the duke, and didn't say nothing, but just kept a-smiling and
bobbing their heads like a passel of sapheads whilst he made all
sorts of signs with his hands and said "Goo-goo—goo-goo-goo," all
the time, like a baby that can't talk.

So the king he blatted along, and managed to inquire about pretty
much everybody and dog in town, by his name, and mentioned all

sorts of little things that happened one time or another in the town, or to George's family, or to Peter; and he always let on that Peter wrote him the things, but that was a lie, he got every blessed one of them out of that young flathead that we canoed up to the steamboat.

Then Mary Jane she fetched the letter her uncle left behind, and the king he read it out loud and cried over it. It give the dwelling house and three thousand dollars, gold, to the girls; and it give the tanyard, (which was doing a good business,) along with some other houses and land (worth about seven thousand,) and three thousand dollars in gold, to Harvey and William, and told where the six thousand cash was hid, down cellar. So these two frauds said they'd go and fetch it up, and have everything square and aboveboard; and told me to come with a candle. We shut the cellar door behind us, and when they found the bag they spilt it out on the floor, and it was a lovely sight, all them yaller-boys. My, the way the king's eyes did shine! He slaps the duke on the shoulder, and says:

"O, *this* ain't bully nor noth'n! O, no, I reckon not! Why, Biljy, it beats the Nonesuch—*don't* it!"

The duke allowed it did. They pawed the yaller-boys, and sifted them through their fingers and let them jingle down on the floor; and the king says:

"It ain't no use talkin': bein' brothers to a rich dead man, and representatives of furrin heirs that's got left, is the line for you and me, Bilge. Thish-yer comes of trust'n to Providence. It's the best way, in the long run. I've tried 'em all, and ther' ain't no better way."

Most everybody would a been satisfied with the pile, and took it on trust; but no, they must count it. So they counts it, and it comes out four hundred and fifteen dollars short. Says the king:

"Dern him, I wonder what he done with that four hunderd and fifteen dollars?"

They worried over that, a while, and ransacked all around for it. Then the duke says:

"Well, he was a pretty sick man, and likely he made a mistake—I reckon that's the way of it. The best way's to let it go, and keep still about it. We can spare it."

"Oh, shucks, yes, we can *spare* it. I don't k'yer noth'n 'bout that—it's the *count* I'm thinkin' about. We want to be awful square and open and aboveboard, here, you know. We want to lug thish-yer

money up stairs and count it before everybody—then ther' ain't
noth'n suspicious. But when the dead man says ther's six thous'n
dollars, you know, we don't want to—"

"Hold on," says the duke. "Less make up the deffisit"—and he
begun to haul out yaller-boys out of his pocket.

MAKING UP THE "DEFFISIT."

"It's a most amaz'n' good idea, duke—you *have* got a rattlin'
clever head on you," says the king. "Blest if the old Nonesuch ain't
a heppin' us out agin"—and *he* begun to haul out yaller-jackets and
stack them up.

It most busted them, but they made up the six thousand clean
and clear.

"Say," says the duke, "I got another idea. Le's go up stairs and
count this money, and then take and *give it to the girls.*"

"Good land, duke, lemme hug you! It's the most dazzling idea 'at
ever a man struck. You have cert'nly got the most astonishin' head
I ever see. O, this is the boss dodge, ther' ain't no mistake 'bout it.

Let 'em fetch along their suspicions, now, if they want to—this 'll lay 'em out."

When we got up stairs, everybody gethered around the table, and the king he counted it and stacked it up, three hundred dollars in a pile—twenty elegant little piles. Everybody looked hungry at it, and licked their chops. Then they raked it into the bag again, and I see the king begin to swell himself up for another speech. He says:

"Friends all, my poor brother that lays yonder, has done generous by them that's left behind in the vale of sorrers. He has done generous by these-yer poor little lambs that he loved and sheltered, and that's left fatherless and motherless. Yes, and we that knowed him, knows that he would a done *more* generous by 'em if he hadn't ben afeard o' woundin' his dear William and me. Now, *wouldn't* he? Ther' ain't no question 'bout it, in *my* mind. Well, then—what kind o' brothers would it be, that 'd stand in his way at sech a time? And what kind o' uncles would it be that 'd rob—yes, *rob*—sech poor sweet lambs as these 'at he loved so, at sech a time? If I know William—and I *think* I do—he—well, I'll jest ask him." He turns around and begins to make a lot of signs to the duke with his hands; and the duke he looks at him stupid and leatherheaded a while, then all of a sudden he seems to catch his meaning, and jumps for the king goo-gooing with all his might for joy, and hugs him about fifteen times before he lets up. Then the king says, "I knowed it; I reckon *that*'ll convince anybody the way *he* feels about it. Here, Mary Jane, Susan, Joanner, take the money—take it *all*. It's the gift of him that lays yonder, cold but joyful."

Mary Jane she went for him, Susan and the hare-lip went for the duke, and then such another hugging and kissing I never see yet. And everybody crowded up, with the tears in their eyes, and most shook the hands off of them frauds, saying all the time:

"You *dear* good souls!—how *lovely!*—how *could* you!"

Well, then, pretty soon all hands got to talking about the diseased again, and how good he was, and what a loss he was, and all that; and before long a big iron-jawed man worked himself in there from outside, and stood a-listening and looking, and not saying anything; and nobody saying anything to him, either, because the king was talking and they was all busy listening. The king was saying—in the middle of something he'd started in on—

"—they bein' partickler friends o' the diseased. That's why they're invited here this evenin'; but to-morrow we want *all* to come—everybody; for he respected everybody, he liked everybody, and so it's fitten that his funeral orgies sh'd be public."

GOING FOR HIM.

And so he went a-mooning on and on, liking to hear himself talk, and every little while he fetched in his funeral orgies again, till the duke he couldn't stand it no more; so he writes on a little scrap of paper, "*obsequies*, you old fool," and folds it up and goes to goo-gooing and reaching it over people's heads to him. The king he reads it, and puts it in his pocket, and says:

"Poor William, afflicted as he is, his *heart's* aluz right. Asks me to invite everybody to come to the funeral—wants me to make 'em all welcome. But he needn't a worried—it was jest what I was at."

Then he weaves along, again, perfectly ca'm, and goes to dropping in his funeral orgies again every now and then, just like he done before. And when he done it the third time, he says:

"I say orgies, not because it's the common term, because it ain't—

obsequies bein' the common term—but because orgies is the right term. Obsequies ain't used in England no more, now—it's gone out. We say orgies, now, in England. Orgies is better, because it means the thing you're after, more exact. It's a word that's made up out'n the Greek *orgo*, outside, open, abroad; and the Hebrew *jeesum*, to plant, cover up; hence in*ter*. So, you see, funeral orgies is an open er public funeral."

He was the *worst* I ever struck. Well, the iron-jawed man he

THE DOCTOR.

laughed right in his face. Everybody was shocked. Everybody says, "Why *doctor!*" and Abner Shackleford says:

"Why, Robinson, hain't you heard the news? This is Harvey Wilks."

The king he smiled, eager, and shoved out his flapper, and says:

"*Is* it my poor brother's dear good friend and physician? I—"

"Keep your hands off of me!" says the doctor. "*You* talk like an Englishman—*don't* you? It's the worst imitation I ever heard. *You* Peter Wilks's brother. You're a fraud, that's what you are!"

Well, how they all took on! They crowded around the doctor, and tried to quiet him down, and tried to explain to him, and tell him how Harvey'd showed in forty ways that he *was* Harvey, and knowed everybody by name, and the names of the very dogs, and begged and *begged* him not to hurt Harvey's feelings and the poor girls' feelings, and all that; but it warn't no use, he stormed right along, and said any man that pretended to be an Englishman and couldn't imitate the lingo no better than what he did, was a fraud and a liar. The poor girls was hanging to the king and crying; and all of a sudden the doctor ups and turns on *them*. He says:

"I was your father's friend, and I'm your friend; and I warn you *as* a friend, and an honest one, that wants to protect you and keep you out of harm and trouble, to turn your backs on that scoundrel, and have nothing to do with him, the ignorant tramp, with his idiotic Greek and Hebrew as he calls it. He is the thinnest kind of an imposter—has come here with a lot of empty names and facts which he has picked up somewheres, and you take them for *proofs*, and are helped to fool yourselves by these foolish friends here, who ought to know better. Mary Jane Wilks, you know me for your friend, and for your unselfish friend, too. Now listen to me: turn this pitiful rascal out—I *beg* you to do it. Will you?"

Mary Jane straightened herself up, and my, but she was handsome! She says:

"*Here* is my answer." She hove up the bag of money, and put it in the king's hands, and says, "Take this six thousand dollars, and invest for me and my sisters any way you want to, and don't give us no receipt for it."

Then she put her arm around the king on one side, and Susan and the hare-lip done the same on the other. Everybody clapped their hands and stomped on the floor like a perfect storm, whilst the king held up his head and smiled proud. The doctor says:

"All right; I wash *my* hands of the matter. But I warn you all that a time's coming when you're going to feel sick whenever you think of this day"—and away he went.

"All right, doctor," says the king, kinder mocking him, "we'll try and git 'em to send for you"—which made them all laugh, and they said it was a prime good hit.

THE BAG OF MONEY.

Chapter XXVI

THE CUBBY.

Well, when they was all gone, the king he asks Mary Jane how they was off for spare rooms, and she said she had one spare room, which would do for uncle William, and she'd give her own room to uncle Harvey, which was a little bigger, and she would turn into the room with her sisters and sleep on a cot; and up garret was a little cubby, with a pallet in it. The king said the cubby would do for his valley—meaning me.

So Mary Jane took us up, and she showed them their rooms, which was plain but nice. She said she'd have her frocks and a lot of other traps took out of her room if they was in uncle Harvey's way, but he said they warn't. The frocks was hung along the wall, and before them was a curtain made out of calico that hung down to the floor. There was an old hair trunk in one corner, and a guitar box in another, and all sorts of little knick-knacks and jimcracks around, like girls brisken up a room with. The king said it was all the more homely and more pleasanter for these fixings, and so don't disturb them. The duke's room was pretty small, but plenty good enough, and so was my cubby.

That night they had a big supper, and all them men and women was there, and I stood behind the king and the duke's chairs and waited on them, and the niggers waited on the rest. Mary Jane she set at the head of the table, with Susan alongside of her, and said how bad the biscuits was, and how mean the preserves was, and how ornery and tough the fried chickens was,—and all that kind of rot, the way women always do for to force out compliments; and the people all knowed everything was tip-top, and said so—said "How *do* you get biscuits to brown so nice?" and "Where, for the land's sake *did* you get these amaz'n pickles?" and all that kind of humbug talky-talk, just the way people always does at a supper, you know.

And when it was all done, me and the hare-lip had supper in the kitchen off of the leavings, whilst the others was helping the niggers clean up the things. The hare-lip she got to pumping me about England, and blest if I didn't think the ice was getting mighty thin, sometimes. She says:

"Did you ever see the king?"

"Who? William Fourth? Well, I bet I have—he goes to our church." I knowed he was dead years ago, but I never let on. So when I says he goes to our church, she says:

"What—regular?"

"Yes—regular. His pew's right over opposite ourn—on t'other side the pulpit."

SUPPER WITH THE HARE-LIP.

"I thought he lived in London?"

"Well, he does. Where *would* he live?"

"But I thought *you* lived in Sheffield?"

I see I was up a stump. I had to let on to get choked with a chicken bone, so as to get time to think how to get down again. Then I says:

"I mean he goes to our church regular when he's in Sheffield. That's only in the summer time, when he comes there to take the sea baths."

"Why, how you talk—Sheffield ain't on the sea."

"Well, who said it was?"

"Why, you did."

"I *didn't*, nuther."

"You did!"

"I didn't."

"You did."

"I never said nothing of the kind."

"Well, what *did* you say, then?"

"Said he come to take the sea *baths*—that's what I said."

"Well then!—how's he going to take the sea baths if it ain't on the sea?"

"Looky here," I says; "did you ever see any Congress-water?"

"Yes."

"Well, did you have to go to Congress to get it?"

"Why, no."

"Well, neither does William Fourth have to go to the sea to get a sea bath."

"How does he get it, then?"

"Gets it the way people down here gets Congress-water—in barrels. There in the palace at Sheffield they've got furnaces, and he wants his water hot. They can't bile that amount of water away off there at the sea. They haven't got no conveniences for it."

"O, I see, now. You might a said that in the first place, and saved time."

When she said that, I see I was out of the woods again, and so I was comfortable and glad. Next, she says:

"Do you go to church, too?"

"Yes—regular."

"Where do you set?"

"Why, in our pew."

"*Whose* pew?"

"Why, *ourn*—your uncle Harvey's."

"His'n? What does *he* want with a pew?"

"Wants it to set in. What did you *reckon* he wanted with it?"

"Why, I thought he'd be in the pulpit."

Rot him, I forgot he was a preacher. I see I was up a stump again; so I played another chicken bone and got another think. Then I says:

"Blame it, do you suppose there ain't but one preacher to a church?"

"Why, what do they want with more?"

"What!—to preach before a king? I never see such a girl as you. They don't have no less than seventeen."

"Seventeen! My land! Why, I wouldn't set out such a string as that, not if I *never* got to glory. It must take 'em a week."

"Shucks, they don't *all* of 'em preach the same day—only *one* of 'em."

"Well, then, what does the rest of 'em do?"

"Oh, nothing much. Loll around, pass the plate—and one thing or another. But mainly they don't do nothing."

"Well, then, what are they *for?*"

"Why, they're for *style.* Don't you know nothing?"

"Well, I don't *want* to know no such foolishness as that. How is servants treated in England? Do they treat 'em better'n we treat our niggers?"

"*No!* A servant ain't nobody, there. They treat them worse than dogs."

"Don't they give 'em holidays, the way we do, Christmas, and New Year's week, and fourth of July?"

"Oh, just listen! A body could tell *you* hain't ever been to England, by that. Why, Hare-l—why, Joanna, they never see a holiday from year's end to year's end; never go to the circus, nor theatre, nor nigger shows, nor nowheres."

"Nor church?"

"Nor church."

"But *you* always went to church."

Well, I was gone up again. I forgot I was the old man's servant. But next minute I whirled in on a kind of an explanation how a valley was different from a common servant, and *had* to go to church whether he wanted to or not, and set with the family, on account of it's being the law. But I didn't do it pretty good, and when I got done I see she warn't satisfied. She says:

"Honest injun, now, hain't you been telling me a lot of lies?"

"Honest injun," says I.

"None of it at all?"

"None of it at all. Not a lie in it," says I.

"Lay your hand on this book and say it."

"HONEST INJUN."

I see it warn't nothing but a dictionary, so I laid my hand on it and said it. So then she looked a little better satisfied, and says:

"Well, then, I'll believe some of it; but I hope to gracious if I'll believe the rest."

"What is it you won't believe, Joe?" says Mary Jane, stepping in, with Susan behind her. "It ain't right nor kind for you to talk so to him, and him a stranger and so far from his people. How would you like to be treated so?"

"That's always your way, Maim—always sailing in to help some-body before they're hurt. I hain't done nothing to him. He's told some stretchers, I reckon; and I said I wouldn't swallow it all; and that's every bit and grain I *did* say. I reckon he can stand a little thing like that, can't he?"

"I don't care whether 'twas little or whether 'twas big, he's here in our house and a stranger, and it wasn't good of you to say it. If you was in his place, it would make you feel ashamed; and so you oughtn't to say a thing to another person that will make *them* feel ashamed."

"Why, Maim, he said—"

"It don't make no difference what he *said*—that ain't the thing. The thing is for you to treat him *kind*, and not be saying things to make him remember he ain't in his own country and amongst his own folks."

I says to myself, *This* is a girl that I'm letting that old reptile rob her of her money!

Then Susan *she* waltzed in; and if you'll believe me, she did give Hare-Lip hark from the tomb!

Says I to myself, And this is *another* one that I'm letting him rob her of her money!

Then Mary Jane she took another inning, and went in sweet and lovely again—which was her way—but when she got done there warn't hardly anything left o' poor Hare-Lip. So she hollered.

"All right, then," says the other girls, "you just ask his pardon."

She done it, too. And she done it beautiful. She done it so beautiful it was good to hear; and I wished I could tell her a thousand lies, so she could do it again.

I says to myself, This is *another* one that I'm letting him rob her of her money. And when she got through, they all just laid their-selves out to make me feel at home and know I was amongst friends. I felt so ornery and low down and mean, that I says to myself, My mind's made up: I'll hive that money for them or bust.

So then I lit out—for bed, I said, meaning some time or another. When I got by myself, I went to thinking the thing over. I says to myself, Shall I go to that doctor, private, and blow on these frauds? No—that won't do. He might tell who told him; then the king and the duke would make it warm for me. Shall I go, private, and tell Mary Jane? No—I dasn't do it. Her face would give them a hint, sure; they've got the money, and they'd slide right out and get away with it. If she was to fetch in help, I'd get mixed up in the business, before it was done with, I judge. No, there ain't no good way but one. I got to steal that money, somehow; and I got to steal it some way that they won't suspicion that I done it. They've got a good thing, here; and they ain't agoing to leave till they've played this family and this town for all they're worth, so I'll find a chance time enough. I'll steal it, and hide it; and by and by, when I'm away down the river, I'll write a letter and tell Mary Jane where it's hid. But I better hive it tonight, if I can, because the doctor maybe hasn't let up as much as he lets on he has; he might scare them out of here, yet.

So, thinks I, I'll go and search them rooms. Up stairs the hall was dark, but I found the duke's room, and started to paw around it with my hands; but I recollected it wouldn't be much like the king to let anybody else take care of that money but his own self; so then I went to his room and begun to paw around there. But I see I couldn't do nothing without a candle, and I dasn't light one, of course. So I judged I'd got to do the other thing—lay for them, and eavesdrop. About that time, I hears their footsteps coming, and was going to skip under the bed; I reached for it, but it wasn't where I thought it would be; but I touched the curtain that hid Mary Jane's frocks, so I jumped in behind that and snuggled in amongst the gowns, and stood there perfectly still.

They come in and shut the door; and the first thing the duke done was to get down and look under the bed. Then I was glad I hadn't found the bed when I wanted it. And yet you know it's kind of natural to hide under the bed when you are up to anything private. They sets down, then, and the king says:

"Well, what is it? And cut it middlin' short, because it's better for us to be down there a whoopin'-up the mournin', than up here givin' 'em a chance to talk us over."

"Well, this is it, Capet. I ain't easy; I ain't comfortable. That doctor lays on my mind. I wanted to know your plans. I've got a notion, and I think it's a sound one."

"What is it, duke?"

"That we better glide out of this, before three in the morning, and clip it down the river with what we've got. Specially, seeing we

THE DUKE LOOKS UNDER THE BED.

got it so easy—*given* back to us, flung at our heads, as you may say, when of course we allowed to have to steal it back. I'm for knocking off and lighting out."

That made me feel pretty bad. About an hour or two ago, it would a been a little different, but now it made me feel bad and disappointed. The king rips out and says:

"What! And not sell out the rest o' the property? March off like a passel o' fools and leave eight or nine thous'n' dollars' worth o' property layin' around jest sufferin' to be scooped in?—and all good saleable stuff, too."

The duke he grumbled; said the bag of gold was enough, and he didn't want to go no deeper—didn't want to rob a lot of orphans of *everything* they had.

"Why, how you talk!" says the king. "We shan't rob 'em of nothing at all but jest this money. The people that *buys* the property is the suff'rers; because as soon's it's found out 'at we didn't own it—which won't be long after we've slid—the sale won't be valid, and it'll all go back to the estate. These-yer orphans 'll git their house back agin, and that's enough for *them*: they're young, and spry, and k'n easy earn a livin'. *They* ain't agoing to suffer. Why, jest think—there's thous'n's and thous'n's that ain't nigh so well off. Bless you, *they* ain't got noth'n to complain of."

Well, the king he talked him blind; so at last he give in, and said all right, but said he believed it was blame' foolishness to stay, and that doctor hanging over them. But the king says:

"Cuss the doctor! What do we k'yer for *him?* Hain't we got all the fools in town on our side? and ain't that a big enough majority in any town?"

So they got ready to go down stairs again. The duke says:

"I don't think we put that money in a good place."

That cheered me up. I'd begun to think I warn't going to get a hint of no kind to help me. The king says:

"Why?"

"Because Mary Jane'll be in mourning from this out; and first you know the nigger that does up the rooms will get an order to box these duds up and put 'em away; and do you reckon a nigger can run across money and not borrow some of it?"

"Your head's level, agin, duke," says the king; and he come a fumbling under the curtain two or three foot from where I was. I stuck tight to the wall, and kept mighty still, though quivery; and I wondered what them fellows would say to me if they catched me; and I tried to think what I'd better do if they did catch me. But the king he got the bag before I could think more than about a half a thought, and he never suspicioned I was around. They took and shoved the bag through a rip in the straw\tick that was under the feather bed, and crammed it in a foot or two amongst the straw, and said it was all right, now, because a nigger only makes up the feather bed, and don't turn over the straw tick only about twice a year, and so it warn't in no danger of getting stole, now.

But I knowed better. I had it out of there before they was half way down stairs. I groped along up to my cubby, and hid it there till I could get a chance to do better. I judged I better hide it outside of the house somewheres, because if they missed it they would give the house a good ransacking. I knowed that very well. Then I turned in, with my clothes all on; but I couldn't a gone to sleep, if I'd a wanted to, I was in such a sweat to get through with the business. By and by I heard the king and the duke come up; so I rolled off of my pallet and laid with my chin at the top of my ladder and waited to see if anything was going to happen. But nothing did.

So I held on till all the late sounds had quit and the early ones hadn't begun, yet; and then I slipped down the ladder.

HUCK TAKES THE MONEY.

Chapter XXVII.

A CRACK IN THE
DINING ROOM DOOR.

I crept to their doors and listened; they was snoring, so I tip-toed along, and got down stairs all right. There warn't a sound anywheres. I peeped through a crack of the dining room door, and see the men that was watching the corpse all sound asleep on their chairs. The door was open into the parlor, where the corpse was laying, and there was a candle in both rooms. I passed along, and the parlor door was open; but I see there warn't nobody in there but the remainders of Peter; so I shoved on by; but the front door was locked, and the key wasn't there. Just then I heard somebody coming down the stairs, back behind me. I run in the parlor, and took a swift look around, and the only place I see to hide the bag, was in the coffin. The lid was shoved along about a foot, showing the dead man's face down in there, with a wet cloth over it, and his shroud on. I tucked the money bag in under the lid, just down beyond where his hands was crossed, which made me creep, they was so cold, and then I run back across the room and in behind the door.

The person coming was Mary Jane. She went to the coffin, very soft, and kneeled down and looked in; then she put up her handkerchief and I see she begun to cry, though I couldn't hear her, and her back was to me. I slid out, and as I passed the dining room I thought I'd make sure them watchers hadn't seen me; so I looked through the crack and everything was all right. They hadn't stirred.

I slipped up to bed, feeling ruther blue, on accounts of the thing playing out that way after I had took so much trouble and run so much resk about it. Says I, if it could stay where it is, all right; because when we get down the river a hundred mile or two, I could write back to Mary Jane, and she could dig him up again and get it; but that ain't the thing that's going to happen; the thing that's going to happen, is, the money'll be found when they come to screw on the lid. Then the king 'll get it again, and it'll be a long day before he gives anybody another chance to smouch it from him. Of course I *wanted* to slide down and get it out of there, but I dasn't try it. Every minute it was getting earlier, now, and pretty soon some of them watchers would begin to stir, and I might get catched—catched with six thousand dollars in my hands that nobody hadn't hired me to take care of. I don't wish to be mixed up in no such business as that, I says to myself.

When I got down stairs in the morning, the parlor was shut up, and the watchers was gone. There warn't nobody around but the family and the widow Bartley and our tribe. I watched their faces to see if anything had been happening, but I couldn't tell.

Towards the middle of the day the undertaker come, with his man, and they set the coffin in the middle of the room on a couple of chairs, and then set all our chairs in rows, and borrowed more from the neighbors till the hall and the parlor and the dining room was full. I see the coffin lid was the way it was before, but I dasn't go to look in under it, with folks around.

Then the people begun to flock in, and the beats and the girls took seats in the front row at the head of the coffin, and for a half an hour the people filed around slow, in single rank, and looked down at the dead man's face a minute, and some dropped in a tear, and it was all very still and solemn, only the girls

THE UNDERTAKER.

and the beats holding handkerchiefs to their eyes and keeping their heads bent, and sobbing a little. There warn't no other sound but the scraping of the feet on the floor, and blowing noses—because people always blows them more at a funeral than they do at other places except church.

When the place was packed full, the undertaker he slid around in his black gloves with his softy soothering ways, putting on the last touches, and getting people and things all ship-shape and comfortable, and making no more sound than a cat. He never spoke; he moved people around, he squeezed in late ones, he opened up passage-ways, and done it all with nods, and signs with his hands. Then he took his place over against the wall. He was the softest, gliding-est, stealthiest man I ever see; and there warn't no more smile to him than there is to a ham.

They had borrowed a melodeum—a sick one; and when everything was ready, a young woman set down and worked it, and it was pretty skreeky and colicky, and everybody joined in and sung, and Peter was the only one that had a good thing, according to my notion. Then the Reverend Hobson opened up, slow and solemn, and begun to talk; and straight off the most outrageous row busted out in the cellar a body ever heard; it was only one dog, but he made a most powerful racket, and he kept it up, right along; the parson he had to stand there, over the coffin, and wait—you couldn't hear yourself think. It was right down awkward, and nobody didn't seem to know what to do. But pretty soon they see that long-legged undertaker make a sign to the preacher as much as to say, "Don't you worry—just depend on me." Then he stooped down and begun to glide along the wall, just his shoulders showing over the people's heads. So he glided along, and the pow-wow and racket getting more and more outrageous all the time; and at last, when he had gone around two sides of the room, he disappears down cellar. Then, in about two seconds we heard a whack, and the dog he finished up with a most amazing howl or two and then everything was dead still, and the parson begun his solemn talk where he left off. In a minute or two here comes this undertaker's back and shoulders gliding along the wall again; and so he glided, and glided, around three sides of the room, and then rose up, and shaded his mouth with his hands, and stretched his neck out towards the preacher, over the people's heads, and says, in a kind of a coarse whisper, *"He had a rat!"* Then he drooped down and glided along the wall again, to his place. You could see it was a great satisfaction to the people, because naturally they wanted to know. A little thing like that don't cost nothing, and it's just the little things that makes a man to be looked up to and liked. There warn't no more popular man in town than what that undertaker was.

"HE HAD A RAT!"

Well, the funeral sermon was very good, but pison-long and tiresome; and then the king he shoved in and got off some of his usual rubbage, and at last the job was through, and the undertaker begun to sneak up on the coffin with his screw-driver. I was in a sweat, then, and watched him pretty keen. But he never meddled at all; just slid the lid along, as soft as mush, and screwed it down tight and fast. So there I was! I didn't know whether the money was in there or not. So, says I, spose somebody has hogged that bag, on the sly?—now how do *I* know whether to write to Mary Jane or not? Spose she dug him up and didn't find nothing—what would she think of me? Blame it, I says, I might get hunted up and jailed; I'd better lay low and keep dark, and not write at all; the thing's awful mixed, now; trying to better it, I've worsened it a hundred times, and I wish to goodness I'd just let it alone, dad fetch the whole business!

They buried him, and we come back home, and I went to watching faces again—I couldn't help it, and I couldn't rest easy. But nothing come of it; the faces didn't tell me nothing.

The king he visited around, in the evening, and sweetened everybody up, and made himself ever so friendly; and he give out the idea that his congregation over in England would be in a sweat about him, so he must hurry and settle up the estate right away, and leave for home. He was very sorry he was so pushed, and so was everybody; they wished he could stay longer, but they said they could see it couldn't be done. And he said of course him and William would take the girls home with them; and that pleased everybody too, because then the girls would be well fixed, and amongst their own relations; and it pleased the girls, too—tickled them so they clean forgot they ever had a trouble in the world, and told him to sell out as quick as he wanted to, they would be ready. Them poor things was that glad and happy it made my heart ache to see them getting fooled and lied to, so, but I didn't see no safe way for me to chip in and change the general tune.

Well, blamed if the king didn't bill the house and the niggers and all the property for auction straight off—sale two days after the funeral; but anybody could buy private beforehand if they wanted to.

So the next day after the funeral, along about noontime, the girls' joy got the first jolt: a couple of nigger traders come along, and the king sold them the niggers reasonable, for three-day drafts as they called it, and away they went—the two sons up the river to Memphis, and their mother down the river to Orleans. I thought them poor girls and them niggers would break their hearts for grief; they cried around each other, and took on so it most made me down sick to see it. The girls said they hadn't ever dreamed of seeing the family separated or sold away from the town. I can't ever get it out of my memory, the sight of them poor miserable girls and niggers hanging around each other's necks and crying; and I reckon I couldn't a stood it all but would a had to bust out and tell on our gang if I hadn't knowed the sale warn't no account and the niggers would be back home in a week or two.

The thing made a big stir in the town, too, and a good many come out flatfooted and said it was scandalous to separate the mother and the children that way. It injured the frauds some, but the old fool he bulled right along, spite of all the duke could say or do, and I tell you the duke was powerful uneasy.

Next day was auction day. About broad-day in the morning, the king and the duke come up in the garret and woke me up, and I see by their look that there was trouble. The king says:

"Was you in my room night before last?"

"No, your majesty"—which was the way I always called him when nobody but our gang warn't around.

"WAS YOU IN MY ROOM?"

"Was you in there yisterday er last night?"

"No, your majesty."

"Honor bright, now—no lies."

"Honor bright, your majesty, I'm telling you the truth. I hain't been anear your room since Miss Mary Jane took you and the duke and showed it to you."

The duke says:

"Have you seen anybody else go in there?"

"No, your grace, not as I remember, I believe."

"Stop and think."

I studied a while, and see my chance; then I says:

"Well, I see the niggers go in there several times."

Both of them give a little jump; and looked like they hadn't ever expected it, and then like they *had*. Then the duke says:

"What, *all* of them?"

"No—leastways not all at once. That is, I don't think I ever see them all come *out* at once but just one time."

"Hello—when was that?"

"It was the day we had the funeral. In the morning. It warn't early, because I overslept. I was just starting down the ladder, and I see them."

"Well, go on, *go* on—what did they do? how'd they act?"

"They didn't do nothing. And they didn't act anyway, much, as fur as I see. They tip-toed away; so, I seen, easy enough, that they'd shoved in there to do up your majesty's room, or something, sposing you was up; and found you *warn't* up, and so they was hoping to slide out of the way of trouble without waking you up, if they hadn't already waked you up."

"Great guns, *this* is a go!" says the king; and both of them looked pretty sick, and tolerable silly. They stood there a thinking and scratching their heads, a minute, and then the duke he bust into a kind of a little raspy chuckle, and says:

"It does beat all, how neat the niggers played their hand. They let on to be *sorry* they was going out of this region! and I believed they *was* sorry. And so did you, and so did everybody. Don't ever tell *me*, any more, that a nigger ain't got any histrionic talent. Why, the way they played that thing, it would fool *anybody*. In my opinion, there's a fortune in 'em. If I had capital and a theatre, I wouldn't want a better layout than that—and here we've gone and sold 'em for a song. Yes, and ain't privileged to sing the song, yet. Say, where *is* that song?—that draft."

"In the bank for to be collected. Where *would* it be?"

"Well, *that's* all right, then, thank goodness."

Says I, kind of timid-like:

"Is something gone wrong?"

The king whirls on me and rips out:

"None o' your business! You keep your head shet, and mind y'r own affairs—if you got any. Long as you're in this town, don't you forget *that*, you hear?" Then he says to the duke, "We got to jest swaller it, and say noth'n: mum's the word, for *us*."

As they was starting down the ladder, the duke he chuckles again, and says:

"Quick sales *and* small profits! It's a good business—yes."

The king snarls around on him and says:

"I was trying to do for the best, in sellin' 'm out so quick. If the profits has turned out to be none, lackin' considable, and none to carry, is it my fault any more'n it's yourn?"

"Well, *they*'d be in this house yet, and we *wouldn't*, if I could a got my advice listened to."

The king sassed back, as much as was safe for him, and then swapped around and lit into *me* again. He give me down the banks for not coming and *telling* him I see the niggers come out of his room acting that way—said any fool would a *knowed* something was up. And then waltzed in and cussed *himself* a while; and said it all come of him not laying late and taking his natural rest that morning, and he'd be blamed if he'd ever do it again. So they went off a-jawing; and I felt dreadful glad I'd worked it all off onto the niggers and yet hadn't done the niggers no harm by it.

JAWING.

Chapter XXVIII

IN TROUBLE.

By and by it was getting-up time; so I come down the ladder and started for down stairs, but as I come to the girls' room, the door was open, and I see Mary Jane setting by her old hair trunk, which was open and she'd been packing things in it—getting ready to go to England. But she had stopped, now, with a folded gown in her lap, and had her face in her hands, crying. I felt awful bad to see it; of course anybody would. I went in there, and says:

"Miss Mary Jane, you can't abear to see people in trouble, and *I* can't—most always. Tell me about it."

So she done it. And it was the niggers—I just expected it. She said the beautiful trip to England was most about spoiled for her; she didn't know *how* she was ever going to be happy there, knowing the mother and the children warn't ever going to see each other no more—and then busted out bitterer than ever, and flung up her hands and says:

"O, dear, dear, to think they ain't *ever* going to see each other any more!"

"But they *will*—and inside of two weeks—and I *know* it!" says I.

Laws, it was out before I could think!—and before I could budge, she throws her arms around my neck, and told me to say it *again*, say it *again*, say it *again!*

I see I had spoke too sudden, and said too much, and was in a close place. I asked her to let me think, a minute; and she set there, very impatient and excited and handsome, but looking kind of happy and eased-up, like a person that's had a tooth pulled out. So I went to studying it out. I says to myself, I reckon a body that ups and tells the truth when he is in a tight place, is taking considerable many resks; though I ain't had no experience, and can't say for certain; but it looks so to me, anyway; and yet here's a case where I'm blest if it don't look to me like the truth is better, and actuly *safer*, than a lie. I must lay it by in my mind, and think it over some time or other, it's so kind of strange and unregular. I never see nothing like it. Well, I says to myself, at last, I'm agoing to chance it; I'll up and tell the truth this time, though it does seem most like setting down on a kag of powder and touching it off, just to see where you'll go to. Then I says:

"Miss Mary Jane, is there any place, out of town a little ways, where you could go and stay three or four days?"

"Yes—Mr. Lothrop's. Why?"

"Never mind why, yet. If I'll tell you how I know the niggers will see each other again—inside of two weeks—here, in this house— and *prove* how I know it—will you go to Mr. Lothrop's and stay four days?"

"Four days!" she says; "I'll stay a year!"

"All right," I says, "I don't want nothing more out of *you* than just your word—I druther have it than another man's kiss-the-Bible." She smiled, and reddened up very sweet, and I says, "if you don't mind it, I'll shut the door—and bolt it."

Then I come back and set down again, and says:

"Don't you holler. Just set still, and take it like a man. I got to tell the truth, and you want to brace up, Miss Mary, because it's a bad kind, and going to be hard to take, but there ain't no help for it. These uncles of yourn ain't no uncles at all—they're a couple of frauds—regular dead-beats. There, now, we're over the worst of it— you can stand the rest middling easy."

It jolted her up, like everything, of course; but I was over the shoal water, now, so I went right along,—her eyes a-blazing higher and higher all the time—and told her every blame thing, from where we first struck that young fool going up to the steamboat, clear through to where she flung herself onto the king's breast at the front door and he kissed her sixteen or seventeen times—and then up she jumps, with her face afire like sunset, and says:

"The brute! Come—don't waste a minute—not a *second*—we'll have them tarred and feathered, and flung in the river!"

Says I:

"Cert'nly. But do you mean, *before* you go to Mr. Lothrop's, or—"

INDIGNATION.

"O," she says, "what am I *thinking* about!" she says, and set right down again. "Don't mind what I said— please don't—you *won't*, now, *will* you?" laying her silky hand on mine in that kind of a way that I said I would die first. "I never thought, I was so stirred up," she says; "now go on, and I won't do so any more. You tell me what to do, and whatever you say, I'll do it."

"Well," I says, "it's a rough gang, them two frauds, and I'm fixed so I got to travel with them a while longer, whether I want to or not—I druther not tell you why—and if you was to blow on them this town would get me out of their claws, and *I'd* be all right, but there'd be another person that you

don't know about who'd be in big trouble. Well, we got to save *him* hain't we? Of course. Well then, we won't blow on them."

Saying them words put a good idea in my head. I see how maybe I could get me and Jim rid of the frauds: get them jailed, here, and then leave. But I didn't want to run the raft in daytime, without anybody aboard to answer questions but me; so I didn't want the plan to begin working till pretty late to-night. I says:

"Miss Mary Jane, I'll tell you what we'll do—and you won't have to stay at Mr. Lothrop's so long, nuther. How fur is it?"

"A little short of four miles—right out in the country, back here."

"Well, that'll answer. Now you go along out there, and lay low till nine or half-past, to-night, and then get them to fetch you home again—tell them you've thought of something. If you get here before eleven, put a candle in this window, and if I don't turn up, wait *till* eleven, and *then* if I don't turn up, it means I'm gone, and out of the way, and safe. Then you come out and spread the news around, and get these beats jailed."

"Good," she says, "I'll do it."

"And if it just happens so that I don't get away, but get took up, along with them, you must up and say I told you the whole thing beforehand, and you must stand by me all you can."

"Stand by you, indeed I will. They shan't touch a hair of your head!" she says, and I see her nostrils spread and her eyes snap when she said it, too.

"If I get away, I shan't be here," I says, "to prove these rapscallions ain't your uncles, and I couldn't do it if I *was* here. I could swear they was beats and bummers, that's all; though that's worth something. Well, there's others can do that, better than what I can—and they're people that ain't going to be doubted as quick as I'd be. I'll tell you how to find them. Gimme a pencil and a piece of paper. There—'*Royal Nonesuch, Bricksville.*' Put it away, and don't lose it. When the court wants to find out something about these two, let them send up to Bricksville and say they've got the men that played the Royal Nonesuch, and ask for some witnesses—why, you'll have that entire town down here before you can hardly wink, Miss Mary. And they'll come a-biling, too."

HOW TO FIND THEM.

I judged we had got everything fixed about right, now. So I says:

"Just let the auction go right along, and don't worry. Nobody don't have to pay for the things they buy till a whole day after the auction, on accounts of the short notice, and they ain't going out of this till they get that money—and the way we've fixed it the sale ain't going to count, and they ain't going to *get* no money. It's just like the way it was with the niggers—it warn't no sale, and the niggers will be back before long. Why, they can't collect the money for the *niggers*, yet—they're in the worst kind of a fix, Miss Mary."

"Well," she says, "I'll run down to breakfast, now, and then I'll start straight for Mr. Lothrop's."

"'Deed, *that* ain't the ticket, Miss Mary Jane," I says, "by no manner of means; go *before* breakfast."

"Why?"

"What did you reckon I wanted you to go at all, for, Miss Mary?"

"Well, I never thought—and come to think, I don't know. What was it?"

"Why, it's because you ain't one of these leather-face people. I don't want no better book than what your face is. A body can set down and read it off like coarse print. Do you reckon you can go and face your uncles, when they come to kiss you good-morning, and never—"

"There, there, don't! Yes, I'll go before breakfast—I'll be glad to. And leave my sisters with them?"

"Yes—never mind about them. They've got to stand it yet awhile. They might suspicion something if all of you was to go. I don't want you to see them, nor your sisters, nor nobody in this town—if a neighbor was to ask how is your uncles this morning, your face would tell something. No, you go right along, Miss Mary Jane, and I'll fix it with all of them. I'll tell Miss Susan to give your love to your uncles and say you've went away for a few hours for to get a little rest and change, or to see a friend, and you'll be back tonight or early in the morning."

"Gone to see a friend is all right, but I won't have my love given to them."

"Well, then, it shan't be." It was well enough to tell *her* so—no harm in it. It was only a little thing to do, and no trouble; and it's the little things that smoothes people's roads the most, down here below; it would make Mary Jane comfortable, and it wouldn't cost nothing. Then I says: "There's one more thing—that bag of money."

"Well, they've got that; and it makes me feel pretty silly to think *how* they got it."

"No, you're out, there. They hain't got it."

"Why, who's got it?"

"I wish I knowed, but I don't. I *had* it, because I stole it from them; and I stole it to give to you; and I know where I hid it, but I'm afraid it ain't there no more. I'm awful sorry, Miss Mary Jane, I'm just as sorry as I can be; but I done the best I could; I did, honest. I come nigh getting caught, and I had to shove it into the first place I come to, and run—and it warn't a good place."

"O, stop blaming yourself—it's too bad to do it, and I won't allow it—you couldn't help it; it wasn't your fault. Where did you hide it?"

I didn't want to set her to thinking about her troubles again; and I couldn't seem to get my mouth to tell her what would make her see that corpse laying in the coffin with that bag of money on his stomach. So, for a minute I didn't say nothing—then I says:

"I'd ruther not *tell* you where I put it, Miss Mary Jane, if you don't mind letting me off; but I'll write it for you on a piece of paper, and you can read it along the road to Mr. Lothrop's, if you want to. Do you reckon that'll do?"

"O, yes."

HE WROTE.

So I wrote: "I put it in the coffin. It was in there when you was crying there, away in the night. I was behind the door, and I was mighty sorry for you, Miss Mary Jane."

It made my eyes water a little, to remember her crying there all by herself in the night, and them devils laying there right under her own roof, shaming her and robbing her; and when I folded it up and give it to her, I see the water come into her eyes, too; and she shook me by the hand, hard, and says:

"*Good*-bye—I'm going to do everything just as you've told me; and if I don't ever see you again, I shan't ever forget you, and I'll think of you a many and a many a time, and I'll *pray* for you, too!"— and she was gone.

Pray for me! I reckoned if she knowed me she'd take a job that was more nearer her size. But I bet she done it, just the same—she was just that kind. She had the grit to pray for Judus if she took the notion—there warn't no back-down to her, I judge. You may say what you want to, but in my opinion she had more sand in her than any girl I ever see; in my opinion she was just full of sand. It sounds like flattery, but it ain't no flattery. And when it comes to beauty— and goodness too—she lays over them all. I hain't ever seen her since that time that I see her go out of that door; no, I hain't ever seen her since; but I reckon I've thought of her a many and a many a million times, and of her saying she would pray for me; and if ever I'd a thought it would do any good for me to pray for *her*, blamed if I wouldn't a done it or bust.

Well, Mary Jane she lit out the back way, I reckon, because nobody see her go. When I struck Susan and the hare-lip, I says:

"What's the name of them people over on t'other side of the river that you-all goes to see sometimes?"

They says:

"There's several; but it's the Proctors, mainly."

"That's the name," I says; "I most forgot it. Well, Miss Mary Jane she told me to tell you she's gone over there in a dreadful hurry— one of them's sick."

"Which one?"

"I don't know; leastways I kinder forget; but I think it's—"

"Sakes alive, I hope it ain't *Hanner*?"

"I'm sorry to say it," I says, "but Hanner's the very one."

"My goodness—and she so well only last week! Is she took bad?"

"It ain't no name for it. They set up with her all night, Miss Mary Jane said, and they don't think she'll last many hours."

"Only think of that, now! What's the matter with her?"

I couldn't think of anything reasonable, right off that way, so I says:

"Mumps."

"Mumps your granny!—they don't set up with people that's got the mumps."

"They don't, don't they? You better bet they do with *these* mumps. These mumps is different. It's a new kind, Miss Mary Jane said."

HANNER WITH THE MUMPS.

"How's it a new kind?"

"Because it's mixed up with other things."

"What other things?"

"Well, measles, and whooping cough, and erysiplas, and consumption, and yaller janders, and brain fever, and I don't know what all."

"My land! And they call it the *mumps?*"

"That's what Miss Mary Jane said."

"Well, what in the nation do they call it the *mumps* for?"

"Why, because it *is* the mumps. That's what it starts with."

"Well, ther' ain't no sense in it. A body might stump his toe, and take pison, and fall down the well, and break his neck, and bust his brains out, and somebody come along and ask what killed him, and some numskull up and say, 'Why, he stumped his *toe*.' Would ther' be any sense in that? *No*. And ther' ain't no sense in *this*, nuther. Is it ketching?"

"Is it *ketching*? Why, how you talk. Is a *harrow* catching?—in the dark? If you don't hitch onto one tooth, you're bound to on another, ain't you? And you can't get away with that tooth without fetching the whole harrow along, can you? Well, these kind of mumps is a kind of a harrow, as you may say—and it ain't no slouch of a harrow, nuther, you come to get it hitched on good."

"Well, it's awful, *I* think," says the hare-lip. "I'll go to uncle Harvey and—"

"O, yes," I says, "I *would*. Of *course* I would. I wouldn't lose no time."

"Well, why wouldn't you?"

"Just look at it a minute, and maybe you can see. Hain't your uncles obleeged to get along home to England as fast as they can? And do you reckon they'd be mean enough to go off and leave you to go all that journey by yourselves? *You* know they'll wait for you. So fur, so good. Your uncle Harvey's a preacher, ain't he? Very well, then; is a *preacher* going to deceive a steamboat clerk? is he going to deceive a *ship clerk*?—so as to get them to let Miss Mary Jane go aboard? Now *you* know he ain't. What *will* he do, then? Why, he'll say, 'It's a great pity, but my church matters has got to get along the best way they can; for my niece has been exposed to the dreadful pluribus-unum mumps, and so it's my bounden duty to set down here and wait the three months it takes to show on her if she's got it.' But never mind, if you think it's best to tell your uncle Harvey—"

"Shucks, and stay fooling around here when we could all be having good times in England whilst we was waiting to find out whether Mary Jane's got it or not? Why, you talk like a muggins."

"Well, anyway, maybe you better tell some of the neighbors."

"Listen at that, now. You do beat all, for natural stupidness. Can't you *see* that *they*'d go and tell? Ther' ain't no way but just to not tell anybody at *all*."

"Well, maybe you're right—yes, I judge you *are* right."

"But I reckon we ought to tell uncle Harvey she's gone out a while, anyway, so he won't be uneasy about her?"

"Yes, Miss Mary Jane she wanted you to do that. She says, 'Tell them to give uncle Harvey and William my love and a kiss, and say I've run over the river to see Mr.—Mr.'—what *is* the name of that rich family your uncle Peter used to think so much of?—I mean the one that—"

"Why, you must mean the Apthorps, ain't it?"

"Of course; bother them kind of names, a body can't ever seem to remember them, half the time, somehow. Yes, she said, say she has run over for to ask the Apthorps to be sure and come to the auction and buy this house, because she allowed her uncle Peter would ruther they had it than anybody else; and she's going to stick

THE AUCTION.

to them till they say they'll come; and then if she ain't too tired, she's coming home; and if she is, she'll be home in the morning, anyway. She said, don't say nothing about the Proctors, but only about the Apthorps—which'll be perfectly true, because she *is* going there to speak about their buying the house; I know it, because she told me so, herself."

"All right," they said, and cleared out to lay for their uncles, and give them the love and the kisses, and tell them the message.

Everything was all right, now. The girls wouldn't say nothing, because they wanted to go to England; and the king and the duke would ruther Mary Jane was off working for the auction than around in reach of doctor Robinson. I felt very good; I judged I had done it pretty neat—I reckoned Tom Sawyer couldn't a done it no neater, himself. Of course he would a throwed more style into it, but I can't do that very handy, not being brung up to it.

Well, they held the auction, in the public square, along towards the end of the afternoon, and it strung along, and strung along, and the old man he was on hand and looking his level piousest, up there longside of the auctioneer, and chipping in a little Scripture, now and then, or a little goody-goody saying, of some kind, and the duke he was around goo-gooing for sympathy all he knowed how, and just spreading himself generly.

But by and by the thing dragged through, and everything was sold. Everything but a little old trifling lot in the graveyard. So they'd got to work *that* off—I never see such a girafft as the king was for wanting to swallow *everything*. Well, whilst they was at it, a steamboat landed, and in about two minutes, up comes a crowd a whooping and yelling and laughing and carrying on, and singing out:

"*Here's* your opposition line! Here's your two sets o' heirs to old Peter Wilks—and you pays your money and you takes your choice!"

Chapter XXIX ·

THE TRUE BROTHERS.

They was fetching a very nice looking old gentleman along, and a nice looking younger one, with his right arm in a sling. And my souls, how the people yelled, and laughed, and kept it up. But I didn't see no joke about it, and I judged it would strain the duke and the king some, to see any. I reckoned they'd turn pale. But no, nary a pale did *they* turn. The duke he never let on he suspicioned what was up, but just went a goo-gooing around, happy and satisfied, like a jug that's googling out buttermilk; and as for the king, he just gazed and gazed down sorrowful on them newcomers like it give him the stomach-ache in his very heart to think there could be such frauds and rascals in the world. O, he done it admirable. Lots of the principal people gethered around the king, to let him see they was on his side. That old gentleman that had just come, looked all puzzled to death. Pretty soon he begun to speak, and I see, straight off, he pronounced *like* an Englishman; not the king's way, though the king's *was* pretty good, for an imitation. I can't give the old gent's words, nor I can't imitate him; but he turned around to the crowd, and says, about like this:

"This is a surprise to me which I wasn't looking for; and I'll acknowledge, candid and frank, I ain't very well fixed to meet it and answer it; for my brother and me has had misfortunes: he's broke his arm, and our baggage got put off at a town above here, last night in the night, by a mistake. I am Peter Wilks's brother Harvey, and this is his brother William, which can't hear nor speak—and can't

even make signs to amount to much, now 't he's only got one hand
to work them with. We are who we say we are; and in a day or two,
when I get the baggage, I can prove it. But, up till then, I won't say
nothing more, but go to the hotel and wait."

So him and the new dummy started off; and the king he laughs,
and blethers out:

"Broke his arm—*very* likely, *ain't* it?—and very convenient, too,
for a fraud that's got to make signs, and hain't learnt how. Lost their
baggage! That's *mighty* good!—and mighty ingenious—under the
circumstances!"

So he laughed again; and so did everybody else, except three or
four, or maybe half a dozen. One of these was that doctor; another
one was a sharp looking gentleman, with a carpet bag of the old-
fashioned kind made out of carpet-stuff, that had just come off of
the steamboat and was talking to him in a low voice, and glancing
towards the king now and then and nodding their heads—it was
Levi Bell, the lawyer that was gone up to Louisville; and another
one was a big rough husky that come along and listened to all the
old gentleman said, and was listening to the king, now. And when
the king got done, this husky up and says:

"Say, looky-here; if you are Harvey Wilks, when'd you come to
this town?"

"The day before the funeral, friend," says the king.

"But what time o' day?"

"In the evenin'—'bout an hour er two before sundown."

"*How'd* you come?"

"I come down on the Susan Powell, from Cincinnati."

"Well, then, how'd you come to be up at the Pint in the *mornin'*—
in a canoe?"

"I warn't up at the Pint in the mornin'."

"It's a lie."

Several of them jumped for him and begged him not to talk that
way to an old man and a preacher.

"Preacher be hanged, he's a fraud and a liar. He was up at the Pint
that mornin'. I live up there, don't I? Well, I was up there, and he
was up there. I *see* him there. He come in a canoe, along with Tim
Collins and a boy."

The doctor he up and says:

"Would you know the boy again if you was to see him, Hines?"

"I reckon I would, but I don't know. Why, yonder he is, now. I know him perfectly easy."

It was me he pointed at. The doctor says:

"Neighbors, I don't know whether the new couple is frauds or not; but if *these* two ain't frauds, I am an idiot, that's all. I think it's our duty to see that they don't get away from here till we've looked into this thing. Come along, Hines; come along, the rest of you. We'll take these fellows to the tavern and affront them with t'other couple, and I reckon we'll find out *something* before we get through."

THE DOCTOR LEADS HUCK.

It was nuts for the crowd, though maybe not for the king's friends; so we all started. It was about sundown. The doctor he led me along by the hand, and was plenty kind enough, but he never let *go* my hand.

We all got in a big room in the hotel, and lit up some candles, and fetched in the new couple.

First, the doctor says:

"I don't wish to be too hard on these two men, but *I* think they're frauds, and they may have complices that we don't know nothing about. If they have, won't the complices get away with that bag of gold Peter Wilks left? It ain't unlikely. If these men ain't frauds, they won't object to sending for that money and letting us keep it till they prove they're all right—ain't that so?"

Everybody agreed to that. So I judged they had our gang in a pretty tight place, right at the outstart. But the king he only looked sorrowful, and says:

"Gentlemen, I wish the money was there, for I ain't got no disposition to throw anything in the way of a fair, open, out-and-out investigation o' this misable business; but alas, the money ain't there; you k'n send and see, if you want to."

"Where is it, then?"

"Well, when my niece give it to me to keep for her, I took and hid it inside o' the straw tick o' my bed, not wishin' to bank it for the few days we'd be here, and considerin' the bed a safe place, we not bein' used to niggers, and suppos'n' 'em honest, like servants in England. The niggers stole it the very next mornin', after I had went down stairs; and when I sold 'em, I hadn't missed the money yit, so they got clean away with it. My servant here k'n tell you 'bout it, gentlemen."

The doctor and several said "Shucks!" and I see nobody didn't altogether believe him. One man asked me if I see the niggers steal it. I said no, but I see them sneaking out of the room and hustling away, and I never thought nothing, only I reckoned they was afraid they had waked up my master and was trying to get away before he made trouble with them. That was all they asked me. Then the doctor whirls on me and says:

"Are *you* English, too?"

I says yes; and him and some others laughed, and said, "Stuff!"

Well, then they sailed in on the general investigation, and there we had it, up and down, hour in, hour out, and nobody never said a word about supper, nor ever seemed to think about it—and so they kept it up, and kept it up; and it *was* the worst mixed-up thing you ever see. They made the king tell his yarn, and they made the old gentleman tell his'n; and anybody but a lot of prejudiced chuckleheads would a *seen* that the old gentleman was spinning truth and t'other one lies. And by and by they had me up to tell what I knowed. The king he give me a left-handed look out of the corner of his eye, and so I knowed enough to talk on the right side. I begun to tell about Sheffield, and how we lived there, and all about the English Wilkses, and so on; but I didn't get pretty fur till the doctor begun to laugh; and Levi Bell, the lawyer, says:

"Set down, my boy, I wouldn't strain myself, if I was you. I reckon you ain't used to lying, it don't seem to come handy; what you want is practice. You do it pretty awkward."

I didn't care nothing for the compliment, but I was glad to be let off, any way.

The doctor he started to say something, and turns and says:

"If you'd been in town at first, Levi Bell—"

The king broke in and reached out his hand and says:

"Why, is this my poor dead brother's old friend that he's wrote so often about?"

The lawyer and him shook hands, and the lawyer smiled, and looked pleased, and they talked right along, a while, and then got to one side and talked low; and at last the lawyer speaks up and says:

"That'll fix it. I'll take the order and send it, along with your brother's, and then they'll know it's all right."

So they got some paper and a pen, and the king he set down and twisted his head to one side, and chawed his tongue, and scrawled off something; and then they give the pen to the duke—and then for the first time, the duke looked sick. But he took the pen and wrote. So then the lawyer turns to the new old gentleman and says:

THE DUKE WROTE.

"You and your brother please write a line or two and sign your names."

The old gentleman wrote, but nobody couldn't read it. The lawyer looked powerful astonished, and says:

"Well, it beats *me*"—and snaked a lot of old letters out of his pocket, and examined them, and then examined the old man's writing, and then *them* again; and then says: "These old letters is from Harvey Wilks; and here's *these* two's handwritings, and anybody can see *they* didn't write them" (the king and the duke looked sold and foolish, I tell you, to see how the lawyer had took them in), "and here's *this* old gentleman's handwriting, and anybody can tell, easy enough, *he* didn't write them—fact is, the scratches he makes ain't properly *writing*, at all. Now here's some letters from—"

The new old gentleman says:

"If you please, let me explain. Nobody can read my hand but my brother there—so he copies for me. It's *his* hand you've got there, not mine."

"*Well!*" says the lawyer, "this *is* a state of things. I've got some of William's letters, too; so if you'll get him to write a line or so we can com—"

"He *can't* write with his left hand," says the old gentleman. "If he could use his right hand, you would see that he wrote his own letters and mine too. Look at both, please—they're by the same hand."

The lawyer done it, and says:

"I believe it's so—and if it ain't so there's a heap stronger resemblance than I'd noticed before, anyway. Well, well, well! I thought we was right on the track of a slution, but it's gone to grass, partly. But anyway, *one* thing is proved—*these* two ain't either of 'em Wilkses"—and he wagged his head towards the king and the duke.

Well, what do you think?—that muleheaded old fool wouldn't give in *then!* Indeed he wouldn't. Said it warn't no fair test. Said his brother William was the cussedest joker in the world, and hadn't *tried* to write—*he* see William was going to play one of his jokes the minute he put the pen to paper. And so he warmed up and went warbling and warbling right along, till he was actly beginning to believe what he was saying, *himself*—but pretty soon the new old gentleman broke in and says:

"I've thought of something. Is there anybody here that helped to lay out my br—helped to lay out the late Peter Wilks for burying?"

"Yes" says somebody, "me and Ab Turner done it. We're both here."

Then the old man turns towards the king and says:

"Peraps this gentleman can tell me what was tattooed on his breast?"

Blamed if the king didn't have to brace up mighty quick, or he'd a squshed down like a bluff bank that the river has cut under, it took him so sudden—and mind you it was a thing that was calculated to make most *anybody* sqush, to get fetched such a solid one as that without any notice—because how was *he* going to know what was tattooed on the man? He whitened a little; he couldn't help it; and it was mighty still, in there, and everybody bending a little forwards and gazing at him. Says I to myself, *Now* he'll throw up the sponge—there ain't no more use. Well, did he? A body can't hardly believe it, but he didn't. I reckon he thought he'd keep the thing up till he tired them people out, so they'd thin out and him and the duke could break loose and get away. Anyway, he set there, and pretty soon he begun to smile, and says:

"Mf! It's a *very* tough question, *ain't* it! *Yes*, sir, I k'n tell you what's tattooed on his breast. It's jest a small, thin, blue arrow—that's what it is; and if you don't look clost, you can't see it. *Now* what do you say—hey?"

Well, *I* never see anything like that old blister, for clean out-and-out cheek.

The new old gentleman turns brisk towards Ab Turner and his pard, and his eye lights up like he judged he'd got the king *this* time, and says:

"There—you've heard what he said! Was there any such mark on Peter Wilks's breast?"

Both of them spoke up and says:

"We didn't see no such mark."

"Good!" says the old gentleman. "Now what you *did* see on his breast was a small dim P, and a B, (which is an initial he dropped when he was young,) and a W, with dashes between them, so: P—B—W"—and he marked them that way on a piece of paper. "Come—ain't that what you saw?"

Both of them spoke up again, and says:

"No, we *didn't*. We never seen any marks, at all."

Well, everybody *was* in a state of mind, now; and they sings out:

"The whole *bilin'* of 'm 's frauds! Le's duck 'em! le's drown 'em! le's ride 'em on a rail!" and everybody was whooping at once, and there was a rattling pow-wow. But the lawyer he jumps on the table and yells, and says:

"Gentlemen—gentle*men!* Hear me just a word—just a *single* word—if you PLEASE! There's one way, yet—let's go and dig up the corpse and look."

That took them.

"GENTLEMEN—GENTLE*MEN!*"

"Hooray!" they all shouted, and was starting right off; but the lawyer and the doctor sung out:

"Hold on, hold on! Collar all these four men and the boy, and fetch *them* along, too!"

"We'll do it!" they all shouted; "and if we don't find them marks, we'll lynch the whole gang!"

I *was* scared, now, I tell you. But there warn't no getting away, you know. They gripped us all, and marched us right along, straight for the graveyard, which was a mile and a half down the river, and the whole town at our heels, for we made noise enough, and it was only nine in the evening.

As we went by our house I wished I hadn't sent Mary Jane out of town; because now if I could tip her the wink, she'd light out and save me, and blow on our dead-beats.

Well, we swarmed along down the river road, just carrying on like wild-cats; and to make it more scary, the sky was darking up, and the lightning beginning to wink and flitter, and the wind to shiver amongst the leaves. This was the most awful trouble and most dangersome I ever was in; and I was kinder stunned, everything was going so different from what I had allowed for: 'stead of being fixed so I could take my own time, if I wanted to, and see all the fun, and have Mary Jane at my back to save me and set me free when the close-fit come, here was nothing in the world betwixt me and sudden death but just them tattoo-marks. If they didn't find them—

I couldn't bear to think about it; and yet, somehow, I couldn't think about nothing else. It got darker and darker, and it was a beautiful time to give the crowd the slip; but that big husky had me by the wrist—Hines—and a body might as well try to give Goliar the slip. He dragged me right along, he was so excited; and I had to run to keep up.

When they got there they swarmed into the graveyard, and washed over it like an overflow. And when they got to the grave, they found they had about a hundred times as many shovels as they wanted, but nobody hadn't thought to fetch a lantern. But they sailed in to digging, anyway, by the flicker of the lightning, and sent a man to the nearest house a half a mile off, to borrow one.

So they dug and dug, like everything; and it got awful dark, and the rain started, and the wind swished and swushed along, and the lightning come brisker and brisker, and the thunder boomed; but them people never took no notice of it, they was so full of this business; and one minute you could see every thing and every face in that big crowd, and the shovelfuls of dirt sailing up out of the grave, and the next second the dark wiped it all out, and you couldn't see nothing at all.

At last they got out the coffin, and begun to unscrew the lid, and

then such another crowding, and shouldering and shoving as there
was, to scrouge in and get a sight, you never see; and in the dark,
that way, it was awful. Hines he hurt my wrist dreadful, pulling and
tugging so, and I reckon he clean forgot I was in the world, he was
so excited and panting.

All of a sudden the lightning let go a perfect sluice of white glare,
and somebody sings out:

"By the living jingo, here's the bag of gold on his breast!"

Hines let out a whoop, like everybody else, and dropped my wrist
and give a big surge to bust his way in and get a look, and the way I
lit out and shinned for the road in the dark, there ain't nobody can
tell.

I had the road all to myself, and I fairly flew—leastways I had it
all to myself except the solid dark, and the now-and-then glares,
and the buzzing of the rain, and the thrashing of the wind, and the
splitting of the thunder; and sure as you are born I did clip it along!

When I struck the town, I see there warn't nobody out in the
storm, so I never hunted for no back streets, but humped it straight
through the main one; and when I begun to get towards our house I
aimed my eye and set it. No light there; the house all dark—which
made me feel sorry and disappointed, I didn't know why. But at last,
just as I was sailing by, *flash* comes the light in Mary Jane's window!
and my heart swelled up sudden, like to bust, and the same second
the house and all was behind me in the dark, and wasn't ever going
to be before me no more in this world. She *was* the best girl I ever
see, and had the most sand.

The minute I was far enough above the town to see I could make
the towhead, I begun to look sharp for a boat to borrow; and the first
time the lightning showed me one that wasn't chained, I snatched
it and shoved. It was a canoe, and warn't fastened with nothing but
a rope. The towhead was a rattling big distance off, away out there
in the middle of the river, but I didn't lose no time; and when I
struck the raft at last, I was so fagged I would a just laid down to
blow and gasp if I could afforded it. But I didn't. As I sprung aboard I
sung out:

"Out with you Jim, and set her loose! Glory be to goodness, we're
shut of them!"

Jim lit out, and was a coming for me with both arms spread, he was so full of joy, but when I glimpsed him in the lightning, my heart shot up in my mouth, and I went overboard backwards; for I forgot he was old King Lear and a drownded A-rab all in one, and it

"JIM LIT OUT."

most scared the livers and lights out of me. But Jim fished me out, and was going to hug me and bless me, and so on, he was so glad I was back and we was shut of the king and the duke, but I says:

"Not now—have it for breakfast, have it for breakfast! Cut loose and let her slide!"

So, in two seconds, away we went, a sliding down the river, and it *did* seem so good to be free again and all by ourselves on the big river and nobody to bother us. I had to skip around a bit, and jump up and crack my heels a few times, I couldn't help it; but about the third crack, I noticed a sound that I knowed mighty well,—and held my breath, and listened and waited—and sure enough, when the next flash busted out over the water, here they come!—and just a laying to their oars and making their skiff hum! It was the king and the duke.

So I wilted right down onto the planks, then, and give up; and it was all I could do to keep from crying.

Chapter XXX.

THE KING SHAKES HUCK.

When they got aboard, the king went for me, and shook me by the collar, and says:

"Tryin' to give us the slip, was ye, you pup! Tired of our company—hey?"

I says:

"No, your majesty, we warn't —*please* don't, your majesty!"

"Quick, then, and tell us what *was* your idea, or I'll shake the insides out o' you!"

"Honest, I'll tell you everything, just as it happened, your majesty. The man that had aholt of me was very good to me, and kept saying he had a boy about as big as me, that died last year, and he was sorry to see a boy in such a dangerous fix; and when they was all took by surprise by finding the gold, and made a rush for the coffin, he lets go of me and whispers, 'Heel it, now, or they'll hang ye, sure!' and I lit out. It didn't seem no good for *me* to stay—*I* couldn't do nothing, and I didn't want to be hung if I could get away. So I never stopped running till I found the canoe; and when I got here I told Jim to hurry, or they'd catch me and hang me, yet, and said I was afeard you and the duke wasn't alive, now, and I was awful sorry, and so was Jim, and was awful glad when we see you coming, you may ask Jim if I didn't."

Jim said it was so; and the king told him to shut up, and said, "O, yes, it's *mighty* likely!" and shook me up again, and said he reckoned he'd drownd me. But the duke says:

"Leggo the boy, you old idiot! Would *you* a done any different? Did you inquire around for *him*, when you got loose? *I* don't remember it."

So the king let go of me, and begun to cuss that town, and everybody in it. But the duke says:

"You better a blame sight give *yourself* a good cussing, for you're the one that's entitled to it most. You hain't done a thing, from the start, that had any sense in it, except coming out so cool and cheeky with that imaginary blue-arrow mark. That *was* bright—it was right down bully; and it was the thing that saved us. For if it hadn't been for that, they'd a jailed us till them Englishmen's baggage come, and then—the penitentiary, you bet! But that trick took 'em to the graveyard, and the gold done us a still bigger kindness; for if the excited fools hadn't let go all holts and made that rush to get a look, we'd a slept in our cravats to-night—cravats warranted to *wear*, too—longer than *we'd* need 'em."

They was still a minute—thinking—then the king says, kind of absent-minded like:

"Mf! And we reckoned the *niggers* stole it!"

That made me squirm!

"Yes," says the duke, kinder slow, and deliberate, and sarcastic. "*We* did."

After about a half a minute, the king drawls out:

"Leastways—*I* did."

The duke says, the same way:

"On the contrary—*I* did."

The king kind of ruffles up, and says:

"Looky here, Bilgewater, what'r you referrin' to?"

The duke says, pretty brisk:

"When it comes to that, maybe you'll let me ask, what was *you* referring to?"

"Shucks!" says the king, very sarcastic; "but *I* don't know—maybe you was asleep, and didn't know what you was about."

The duke bristles right up, now, and says:

"O, let *up* on this cussed nonsense—do you take me for a blame' fool? Don't you reckon *I* know who hid that money in that coffin?"

"*Yes* sir! I know you *do* know—because you done it yourself!"

"It's a lie!"—and the duke went for him. The king sings out:

THE DUKE WENT FOR HIM.

"Take y'r hands off!—leggo my throat!—I take it all back!"

The duke says:

"Well, you just own up, first, that you *did* hide that money there, intending to give me the slip one of these days, and come back and dig it up, and have it all to yourself."

"Wait jest a minute, duke—answer me this one question, honest and fair: if you didn't put the money there, say it, and I'll b'lieve you, and take back everything I said."

"You old scoundrel, I didn't, and you know I didn't. There, now!"

"Well then, I b'lieve you. But answer me only jest this one more— now *don't* git mad: didn't you have it in your *mind* to hook the money and hide it?"

The duke never said nothing for a little bit; then he says:

"Well—I don't care if I *did*, I didn't *do* it, anyway. But you not only had it in mind to do it, but you *done* it."

"I wisht I may never die if I done it, duke, and that's honest. I won't say I warn't *goin'* to do it, because I *was*; but you—I mean somebody—got in ahead o' me."

"It's a lie! You done it, and you got to *say* you done it, or—"

The king begun to gurgle, and then he gasps out:

" 'Nough!—*I own up!*"

I was very glad to hear him say that, it made me feel much more easier than what I was feeling before. So the duke took his hands off, and says:

"If you ever deny it again, I'll drown you. It's *well* for you to set there and blubber like a baby—it's fitten for you, after the way you've acted. I never see such an old ostrich for wanting to gobble everything—and I a trusting you all the time, like you was my own father. You ought to been ashamed of yourself to stand by and hear it saddled onto a lot of poor niggers and you never say a word for 'em. It makes me feel ridiculous to think I was soft enough to *believe* that rubbage. Cuss you, I can see, now, why you was so anxious to make up the deffesit—you wanted to get what money I'd got out of the Nonesuch and one thing or another, and scoop it *all!*"

The king says, timid, and still a snuffling:

"Why, duke, it was you that said make up the deffersit, it warn't me."

"Dry up! I don't want to hear no more *out* of you!" says the duke. "And *now* you see what you *got* by it. They've got all their own money back, and all of *ourn* but a shekel or two, *besides*. G'long to bed—and don't you deffersit *me* no more deffersits, long 's *you* live!"

So the king sneaked into the wigwam, and took to his bottle for comfort; and before long the duke tackled *his* bottle; and so in about a half an hour they was as thick as thieves again, and the tighter they got the lovinger they got; and went off a-snoring in each other's arms. They both got powerful mellow, but I noticed the king didn't get mellow enough to forget to remember to not deny about hiding the money-bag, again. That made me feel easy and satisfied. Of course when they got to snoring, we had a long gabble, and I told Jim everything.

Chapter XXXI.

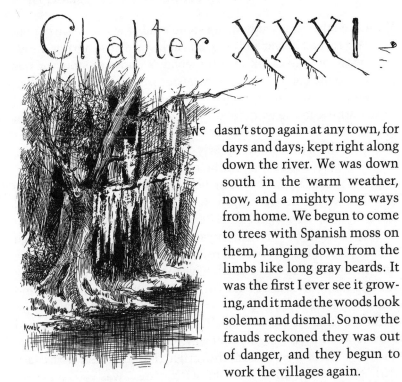

SPANISH MOSS.

We dasn't stop again at any town, for days and days; kept right along down the river. We was down south in the warm weather, now, and a mighty long ways from home. We begun to come to trees with Spanish moss on them, hanging down from the limbs like long gray beards. It was the first I ever see it growing, and it made the woods look solemn and dismal. So now the frauds reckoned they was out of danger, and they begun to work the villages again.

First they done a lecture on temperance; but they didn't make enough for them both to get drunk on. Then in another village they started a dancing school; but they didn't know no more how to dance than a kangaroo does; so the first prance they made, the general public jumped in and pranced them out of town. Another time they tried a go at yellocution; but they didn't yellocute long till the audience got up and give them a solid good cussing and made them skip out. They tackled missionarying, and mesmerizering, and doctoring, and telling fortunes, and a little of everything; but they couldn't seem to have no luck. So at last they got just about dead broke, and laid around the raft, as she floated along, thinking, and thinking, and never saying nothing, by the half a day at a time, and dreadful blue and desperate.

And at last they took a change and begun to lay their heads together in the wigwam and talk low and confidential two or three hours at a time. Jim and me got uneasy. We didn't like the look of it.

We judged they was studying up some kind of worse deviltry than ever. We turned it over and over, and at last we made up our minds they was going to break into somebody's house or store, or was going into the counterfeit money business, or something. So then we was pretty scared, and made up an agreement that we wouldn't have nothing in the world to do with such actions, and if we ever got the least show we would give them the cold shake, and clear out and leave them behind. Well, early one morning we hid the raft in a good safe place about two mile below a little bit of a shabby village, named Pikesville, and the king he went ashore, and told us all to stay hid whilst he went up to town and smelt around to see if anybody had got any wind of the Royal Nonesuch there yet. ("House to rob, you *mean*," says I to myself; "and when you get through robbing it you'll come back here and wonder what's become of me and Jim and the raft—and you'll have to take it out in wondering.") And he said if he warn't back by midday, the duke and me would know it was all right, and we was to come along.

So we staid where we was. The duke he fretted and sweated around, and was in a mighty sour way. He scolded us for everything, and we couldn't seem to do nothing right; he found fault with every little thing. Something was a-brewing, sure. I was good and glad when midday come and no king; we could have a change, anyway—and maybe a chance for *the* change, on top of it. So me and the duke went up to the village, and hunted around there for the king, and by and by we found him in the back room of a little low doggery, very tight, and a lot of loafers bullyragging him for sport, and he a cussing and threatening with all his might, and so tight he couldn't walk, and couldn't do nothing to them. The duke he begun to abuse him for an old fool, and the king begun to sass back; and the minute they was fairly at it, I lit out, and shook the reefs out of my hind legs, and spun down the river road like a deer—for I see our chance; and I made up my mind that it would be a long day before they ever see me and Jim again. I got down there all out of breath but loaded up with joy, and sung out—

"Set her loose, Jim, we're all right, now!"

But there warn't no answer, and nobody come out of the wigwam. Jim was gone! I set up a shout,—and then another—and then another one; and run this way and that in the woods, whooping and screeching; but it warn't no use—old Jim was gone. Then I set down and cried; I couldn't help it. But I couldn't set still long. Pretty soon I went out on the road, trying to think what I better do, and I run across a boy walking, and asked him if he'd seen a strange nigger, dressed so and so, and he says:

"Yes."

"Whereabouts?" says I.

"Down to Silas Phelps's place, two mile below here. He's a runaway nigger, and they've got him. Was you looking for him?"

"You bet I ain't! I run across him in the woods about an hour or two ago, and he said if I hollered he'd cut my livers out—and told me to lay down and stay where I was; and I done it. Been there ever since; afeard to come out."

"Well," he says, "you needn't be afeard no more, becuz they've got him. He run off f'm down south, som'ers."

"It's a good job they got him."

"Well, I *reckon!* There's two hunderd dollars reward on him. It's like picking up money out'n the road."

"Yes, it is—and *I* could a had it if I'd been big enough: I see him *first*. Who nailed him?"

"WHO NAILED HIM?"

"It was an old fellow—a stranger—and he sold out his chance in him for forty dollars, becuz he's got to go up the river and can't wait. Think o' that, now! You bet *I*'d wait, if it was seven year."

"That's me, every time," says I. "But maybe his chance ain't worth no more than that, if he'll sell it so cheap. Maybe there's something ain't straight about it."

"But it *is*, though—straight as a string. I see the handbill myself. It tells all about him, to a dot—paints him like a picture, and tells the plantation he's frum, below Newr*leans*. No-sir-ree-*bob*, they ain't no trouble 'bout *that* speculation, you bet you. Say, gimme a chaw tobacker, won't ye?"

I didn't have none, so he left. I went to the raft, and set down in the wigwam to think. But I couldn't come to nothing. I thought, till I wore my head sore, but I couldn't see no way out of the trouble. After all this long journey, and after all we'd done for them scoundrels, here was it all come to nothing, everything all busted up and ruined, because they could have the heart to serve Jim such a trick as that, and make him a slave again all his life, and amongst strangers, too, for forty dirty dollars.

Once I said to myself it would be a thousand times better for Jim to be a slave at home where his family was, as long as he'd *got* to be a slave, and so I'd better write a letter to Tom Sawyer and tell him to tell Miss Watson where he was. But I soon give up that notion, for two things: she'd be mad and disgusted at his rascality and ungratefulness for leaving her, and so she'd sell him straight down the river again; and if she didn't, everybody naturally despises an ungrateful nigger, and they'd make Jim feel it all the time, and so he'd feel ornery and disgraced. And then think of *me!* It would get all around, that Huck Finn helped a nigger to get his freedom; and if I was to ever see anybody from that town again, I'd be ready to get down and lick his boots for shame. That's just the way: a person does a low-down thing, and then he don't want to take no consequences of it. Thinks as long as he can hide it, it ain't no disgrace. That was my fix exactly. The more I studied about this, the more my conscience went to grinding me, and the more wicked, and low-down and ornery I got to feeling. And at last, when it hit me all of a sudden that here was the plain hand of Providence slapping me in the face and letting me know my wickedness was being watched all the time from up there in heaven, whilst I was stealing a poor old woman's nigger that hadn't ever done me no harm, and now was showing me there's One that's always on the lookout, and ain't agoing to allow no such miserable doings to go only just so fur and no further, I most dropped in my tracks I was so scared. Well, I tried the best I could to kinder soften it up somehow for myself, by saying I was brung up wicked, and so I warn't so much to blame; but something inside of me kept saying, "There was the Sunday School, you could a gone to it; and if you'd a done it they'd a learnt you, there, that people that acts as I'd been acting about that nigger goes to everlasting fire."

It made me shiver. And I about made up my mind to pray; and see if I couldn't try to quit being the kind of a boy I was, and be better. So I kneeled down. But the words wouldn't come. Why wouldn't they? It warn't no use to try and hide it from Him. Nor from *me*, neither. I knowed very well why they wouldn't come. It was because my heart warn't right; it was because I warn't square; it was because I was playing double. I was letting *on* to give up sin, but away inside of me I was holding on to the biggest one of all. I was trying to make my mouth *say* I would do the right thing and the clean thing, and go and write to that nigger's owner and tell where he was; but deep down in me I knowed it was a lie—and He knowed it. You can't pray a lie—I found that out.

So I was full of trouble, full as I could be; and didn't know what to do. At last I had an idea; and I says, I'll go and write the letter—and *then* see if I can pray. Why, it was astonishing, the way I felt as light as a feather, right straight off, and my troubles all gone. So I got a piece of paper and a pencil, all glad and excited, and set down and wrote:

Miss Watson your runaway nigger Jim is down here two mile below Pikesville and Mr. Phelps has got him and he will give him up for the reward if you send. Huck Finn.

I felt good and all washed clean of sin for the first time I had ever felt so in my life, and I knowed I could pray, now. But I didn't do it straight off, but laid the paper down and set there thinking; thinking how good it was all this happened so, and how near I come to being lost and going to hell. And went on thinking. And got to thinking over our trip down the river; and I see Jim before me, all the time, in the day, and in the night-time, sometimes moonlight, sometimes storms, and we a floating along, talking, and singing, and laughing. But somehow I couldn't seem to strike no places to harden me against him, but only the other kind. I'd see him standing my watch on top of his'n, stead of calling me—so I could go on sleeping; and see him how glad he was when I come back out of the fog; and when

THINKING.

I come to him again in the swamp, up there where the feud was; and such-like times; and would always call me honey, and pet me, and do everything he could think of for me, and how good he always was; and at last I struck the time I saved him by telling the men we had small-pox aboard, and he was so grateful, and said I was the best friend old Jim ever had in the world, and the *only* one he's got now; and then I happened to look around, and see that paper.

It was a close place. I took it up, and held it in my hand. I was a trembling, because I'd got to decide, forever, betwixt two things, and I knowed it. I studied a minute, sort of holding my breath, and then says to myself:

"All right, then, I'll *go* to hell"—and tore it up.

It was awful thoughts, and awful words, but they was said. And I let them stay said; and never thought no more about reforming. I shoved the whole thing out of my head; and said I would take up wickedness again, which was in my line, being brung up to it, and the other warn't. And for a starter, I would go to work and steal Jim out of slavery again; and if I could think up anything worse, I would do that, too; because as long as I was in, and in for good, I might as well go the whole hog.

Then I set to thinking over how to get at it, and turned over considerable many ways in my mind; and at last fixed up a plan that suited me. So then I took the bearings of a woody island that was down the river a piece, and as soon as it was fairly dark I crept out with my raft and went for it, and hid it there, and then turned in. I slept the night through, and got up before it was light, and had my breakfast, and put on my store clothes, and tied up some others and one thing or another in a bundle, and took the canoe and cleared for shore. I landed below where I judged was Phelps's place, and hid my bundle in the woods, and then filled up the canoe with water, and loaded rocks into her and sunk her where I could find her again when I wanted her, about a quarter of a mile below a little steam sawmill that was on the bank.

Then I struck up the road, and when I passed the mill I see a sign on it, "Phelps's Sawmill," and when I come to the farm houses, two or three hundred yards further along, I kept my eyes peeled, but didn't see nobody around, though it was good daylight, now. But I didn't mind, because I didn't want to see nobody just yet—I only wanted to get the lay of the land. According to my plan, I was going to turn up there from the village, not from below. So I just took a look, and shoved along, straight for town. Well, the very first man I see, when I got there, was the duke. He was sticking up a bill for the Royal Nonesuch—three-night performance, like that other time. *They* had the cheek, them frauds! I was right on him, before I could shirk. He looked astonished, and says:

"Hel-*lo!* Where'd *you* come from?" Then he says, kind of glad, and eager, "Where's the raft?—got her in a good place?"

I says:

"Why, that's just what I was agoing to ask your grace."

Then he didn't look so joyful—and says:

"What was your idea for asking *me?*" he says.

"Well," I says, "when I see the king in that doggery, yesterday, I says to myself, we can't get him home for hours, till he's soberer; so I went a loafing around town to put in the time, and wait. A man up and offered me ten cents to help him pull a skiff over the river and back to fetch a sheep, and so I went along; but when we was dragging him to the boat, and the man left me aholt of the rope and went behind him to shove him along, he was too strong for me, and jerked loose and run, and we after him. We didn't have no dog, and so we had to chase him all over the country till we tired him out. We never got him till dark, then we fetched him over, and I started down for the raft. When I got there and see it was gone, I says to myself, 'They've got into trouble and had to leave; and they've took my nigger, which is the only nigger I've got in the world, and now I'm in a strange country, and ain't got no property no more, nor nothing, and no way to make my living;' so I set down and cried. I slept in the woods all night. But what *did* become of the raft, then?—and Jim, poor Jim!"

"Blamed if *I* know—that is, what's become of the raft. That old fool had made a trade and got forty dollars, and when we found him in the doggery, the loafers had matched half dollars with him and got every cent but what he'd spent for whisky; and when I got him home late last night and found the raft gone, we said, 'That little rascal has stole our raft and shook us, and run off down the river.'"

"I wouldn't shake my *nigger*, would I?—the only nigger I had in the world, and the only property."

"We never thought of that. Fact is, I reckon we'd come to consider him *our* nigger; yes, we did consider him so—goodness knows we had trouble enough for him. So, when we see the raft was gone, and we flat broke, there warn't anything for it but to try the Royal Nonesuch another shake. And I've pegged along ever since, dry as a powder horn. Where's that ten cents? Give it here."

I had considerable money, so I give him ten cents, but begged him to spend it for something to eat, and give me some, because it was all the money I had, and I hadn't had nothing to eat since yesterday. He never said nothing. The next minute he whirls on me and says:

"Do you reckon that nigger would blow on us? We'd skin him if he done that!"

"How can he blow? Hain't he run off?"

"No! That old fool sold him, and never divided with me, and the money's gone."

"*Sold* him?" I says, and begun to cry: "Why, he was *my* nigger, and that was my money. Where is he?—I want my nigger."

HE GAVE HIM TEN CENTS.

"Well, you can't *get* your nigger, that's all—so dry up your blubbering. Looky-here—do you think *you'd* venture to blow on us? Blamed if I think I'd trust you. Why, if you *was* to blow on us—"

He stopped, but I never see the duke look so ugly out of his eyes before. I went on a-whimpering, and says:

"I don't want to blow on nobody; and I ain't got no time to blow, nohow. I got to turn out and find my nigger."

He looked kinder bothered, and stood there with his bills fluttering on his arm, thinking, and wrinkling up his forehead. At last he says:

"I'll tell you something. We got to be here three days. If you'll promise you won't blow, and won't let the nigger blow, I'll tell you where to find him."

So I promised, and he says:

"A farmer by the name of Silas Ph—" and then he stopped. You see, he started to tell me the truth; but when he stopped, that way, and begun to study and think, again, I reckoned he was changing his mind. And so he was. He wouldn't trust me; he wanted to make sure of having me out of the way the whole three days. So pretty soon he says:

"The man that bought him is named Abram Foster—Abram G. Foster—and he lives forty mile back here in the country, on the road to Lafayette."

"All right," I says, "I can walk it in three days. And I'll start this very afternoon."

"No you won't, you'll start *now*; and don't you lose any time about it, neither, nor do any gabbling by the way. Just keep a tight tongue in your head and move right along, and then you won't get into trouble with *us*, d'ye hear?"

That was the order I wanted, and that was the one I played for. I wanted to be left free to work my plans.

"So clear out," he says; "and you can tell Mr. Foster whatever you want to. Maybe you can get him to believe that Jim *is* your nigger—some idiots don't require documents—leastways I've heard there's such down South here. And when you tell him the handbill and the reward's bogus, maybe he'll believe you when you explain to him what the idea was for getting 'em out. Go 'long, now, and tell him anything you want to; but mind you don't work your jaw any *between* here and there."

So I left, and struck for the back country. I didn't look around, but I kinder felt like he was watching me. But I knowed I could tire him out at that. I went straight out in the country as much as a mile, before I stopped; then I doubled back through the woods towards Phelps's. I reckoned I better start in on my plan straight off, without fooling around, because I wanted to stop Jim's mouth till these fellows could get away. I didn't want no trouble with their kind. I'd seen all I wanted to of them, and wanted to get entirely shut of them.

STRIKING FOR THE BACK COUNTRY.

Chapter XXXII

STILL AND SUNDAY-LIKE.

When I got there it was all still and Sunday-like, and hot and sunshiny—the hands was gone to the fields; and there was them kind of faint dronings of bugs and flies in the air that makes it seem so lonesome and like everybody's dead and gone; and if a breeze fans along and quivers the leaves, it makes you feel mournful, because you feel like it's spirits whispering—spirits that's been dead ever so many years—and you always think they're talking about *you*. As a general thing, it makes a body wish *he* was dead, too, and done with it all.

Phelps's was one of these little one-horse cotton plantations; and they all look alike. A rail fence round a two-acre yard; a stile, made out of logs sawed off and up-ended, in steps, like barrels of a different length, to climb over the fence with, and for the women to stand on when they are going to jump onto a horse; some sickly grass-patches in the big yard, but mostly it was bare and smooth, like an old hat with the nap rubbed off; big double log house for the white folks,— hewed logs, with the chinks stopped up with mud or mortar, and these mud-stripes been whitewashed some time or another; round-log kitchen, with a big broad, open, but roofed passage, joining it to the house; log smoke-house back of the kitchen; three little log nigger-cabins in a row t'other side the smoke-house; one little hut all by itself, away down against the back fence, and some outbuildings down a piece the other side; ash-hopper, and big kettle to bile soap in, by the little hut; bench by the kitchen door, with bucket of water and a gourd; hound asleep there, in the sun; more hounds asleep, round about; about three shade trees, away off in a corner; some currant bushes and gooseberry bushes in one place by the fence; outside of the fence, a garden and a watermelon patch; then the cotton fields begins; and after the fields, the woods.

I went around and clumb over the back stile by the ash-hopper, and started for the kitchen. When I got a little ways, I heard the dim hum of a spinning wheel wailing along up and sinking along down again: and then I knowed for certain I wished I was dead—for that *is* the lonesomest sound in the whole world.

I went right along, not fixing up any particular plan, but just trusting to Providence to put the right words in my mouth when the time come; for I'd noticed that Providence always did put the right words in my mouth, if I left it alone.

When I got half way, first one hound and then another got up and went for me, and of course I stopped, and faced them, and kept still. And such another pow-wow as they made! in a quarter of a minute I was a kind of a hub of a wheel, as you may say—spokes made out of dogs—circle of fifteen of them packed together around me, with their necks and noses stretched up towards me, a-barking and howling; and more a-coming; you could see them sailing over fences and around corners, from everywheres.

A nigger woman come tearing out of the kitchen, with a rolling-pin in her hand, singing out, "Begone! *you* Tige! you Spot! bedone, sah!" and she fetched first one and then another of them a clip and sent him howling, and then the rest followed; and the next second, half of them come back, wagging their tails around me and making friends with me. There ain't no harm in a hound, nohow.

And behind the woman comes a little nigger girl and two little nigger boys, without anything on but tow-linen shirts, and they hung onto their mother's gown, and peeped out from behind her at me, bashful, the way they always do. And here comes the white woman running from the house, about forty-five or fifty year old, bareheaded, and her spinning-stick in her hand; and behind her comes her little white children, acting the same way the little niggers was doing. She was smiling all over so she could hardly stand—and says:

"It's *you*, at last!—*ain't* it?"

I out with a "Yes'm," before I thought.

She grabbed me and hugged me tight; and then gripped me by both hands, and shook and shook; and the tears come in her eyes, and run down over; and she couldn't seem to hug and shake enough, and kept saying, "You don't look as much like your mother as I reckoned you would, but law sakes, I don't care for that, I'm *so* glad to see you! Dear, dear, it does seem like I could eat you up! Childern, it's your cousin Tom!—tell him howdy."

SHE HUGGED HIM TIGHT.

But they ducked their heads, and put their fingers in their mouths, and hid behind her. So she run on:

"Lize, hurry up and get him a hot breakfast, right away—or did you get your breakfast on the boat?"

I said I had got it on the boat. So then she started for the house, leading me by the hand, and the children tagging after. When we got there, she set me down in a split-bottomed chair, and set herself down on a little low stool in front of me, holding both of my hands, and says:

"Now I can have a *good* look at you; and laws-a-me, I've been hungry for it a many and a many a time, all these long years, and it's come at last! We been expecting you a couple of days and more. What's kep' you?—boat get aground?"

"Yes'm—she—"

"Don't say yes'm—say aunt Sally. Where'd she get aground?"

I didn't rightly know what to say, because I didn't know whether the boat would be coming up the river, or down. But I go a good deal on instinct; and my instinct said she would be coming up—from down towards Orleans. That didn't help me much, though; for I didn't know the names of bars down that way. I see I'd got to invent a bar, or forget the name of the one we got aground on—or— Now I struck an idea, and fetched it out:

"It warn't the grounding—that didn't keep us back but a little. We blowed out a cylinder-head."

"Good gracious! anybody hurt?"

"No'm. Killed a nigger."

"Well, it's lucky; because sometimes people do get hurt. Two years ago last Christmas, your uncle Silas was coming up from Newrleans on the old Lally Rook, and she blowed out a cylinder-head and crippled a man. And I think he died, afterwards. He was a Babtist. Your uncle Silas knowed a family in Baton Rouge that knowed his people very well. Yes, I remember, now, he *did* die. Mortification set in, and they had to amputate him. But it didn't save him. Yes, it was mortification—that was it. He turned blue all over, and died in the hope of a glorious resurrection. They say he was a sight to look at. Your uncle's been up to the town every day to fetch you. And he's gone again, not more'n an hour ago; he'll be back any minute, now. You must a met him on the road, didn't you?—oldish man, with a—"

"No, I didn't see nobody, aunt Sally. The boat landed just at daylight, and I left my baggage on the wharfboat and went looking around the town and out a piece in the country, to put in the time and not get here too soon; and so I come down the back way."

"Who'd you give the baggage to?"

"Nobody."

"Why, child, it'll be stole!"

"Not where *I* hid it I reckon it won't," I says.

"How'd you get your breakfast so early on the boat?"

It was kinder thin ice, but I says:

"The captain see me standing around, and told me I better have something to eat before I went ashore; so he took me in the texas to the officers' lunch, and give me all I wanted."

I was getting so uneasy I couldn't listen good. I had my mind on the children all the time; I wanted to get them out to one side, and pump them a little, and find out who I was. But I couldn't get no show, Mrs. Phelps kept it up and run on so. Pretty soon she made the cold chills streak all down my back; because she says:

"But here we're a running on, this way, and you hain't told me a word about Sis, nor any of them. Now I'll rest my works a little, and you start-up yourn; just tell me *everything*—tell me all about 'm all—every one of 'm; and how they are, and what they're doing, and what they told you to tell me; and every last thing you can think of."

Well, I see I was up a stump—and up it good. Providence had stood by me this fur, all right, but I was hard and tight aground, now. I see it warn't a bit of use to try to go ahead—I'd *got* to throw up my hand. So I says to myself, here's another place where I got to resk the truth. I opened my mouth to begin; but she grabbed me and hustled me in behind the bed, and says:

"Here he comes! Stick your head down lower—there, that'll do; you can't be seen, now. Don't you let on you're here. I'll play a joke on him. Childern, don't you say a word."

I see I was in a fix, now. But it warn't no use to worry; there warn't nothing to do but just hold still, and try and be ready to stand from under when the lightning struck.

I had just one little glimpse of the old gentleman when he come in,—then the bed hid him. Mrs. Phelps she jumps for him and says:

"Has he come?"

"No," says her husband.

"Good-*ness* gracious!" she says, "what in the world *can* have become of him?"

"I can't imagine," says the old gentleman; "and I must say, it makes me dreadful uneasy."

"Uneasy!" she says, "I'm ready to go distracted! He *must* a come; and you've missed him along the road. I *know* it's so—something *tells* me so."

"Why Sally, I *couldn't* miss him along the road—*you* know that."

"But oh, dear, dear, what *will* Sis say! He must a come! You must a missed him. He—"

"Oh, don't distress me any more'n I'm already distressed. I don't know what in the world to make of it. I'm at my wit's end, and I don't mind acknowledging 't I'm right down scared. But there's no hope that he's come; for he *couldn't* come and me miss him. Sally it's terrible—just terrible—something's happened to the boat, sure!"

"Why, Silas! Look yonder!—up the road!—ain't that somebody coming?"

He sprung to the window at the head of the bed, and that give Mrs. Phelps the chance she wanted. She stooped down quick, at the foot of the bed, and give me a pull, and out I come; and when he turned back from the window, there she stood, a-beaming and a-smiling like a house afire, and I standing pretty meek and sweaty alongside. The old gentleman stared, and says:

"Why, who's that?"

"Who do you reckon 't is?"

"WHO DO YOU RECKON 'T IS?"

"I hain't no idea. Who *is* it?"

"It's *Tom Sawyer!*"

By jings, I most slumped through the floor. But there warn't no time to swap knives: the old man grabbed me by the hand and shook, and kept on shaking; and all the time, how the woman did dance around and laugh and cry; and then how they both did fire off questions about Sid, and Mary, and the rest of the tribe.

But if they was joyful, it warn't nothing to what I was; for it was like being born again, I was so glad to find out who I was. Well, they froze to me for two hours; and at last when my chin was so tired it couldn't hardly go, any more, I had told them more about my family—I mean the Sawyer family—than ever happened to any six Sawyer families. And I explained all about how we blowed out a cylinder head at the mouth of White river and it took us three days to fix it. Which was all right, and worked first-rate; because *they* didn't know but what it would take three days to fix it. If I'd a called it a bolt-head it would a done just as well.

Now I was feeling pretty comfortable all down one side, and pretty uncomfortable all up the other. Being Tom Sawyer was easy and comfortable; and it staid easy and comfortable till by and by I hear a steamboat coughing along down the river—then I says to myself, spose Tom Sawyer come down on that boat?—and spose he steps in here, any minute, and sings out my name before I can throw him a wink to keep quiet? Well, I couldn't *have* it that way—it wouldn't do, at all. I must go up the road and waylay him. So I told the folks I reckoned I would go up to the town and fetch down my baggage. The old gentleman was for going along with me, but I said no, I could drive the horse myself, and I druther he wouldn't take no trouble about me.

Chapter XXXIII.

"IT WAS TOM SAWYER."

So I started for town, in the wagon, and when I was half way I see a wagon coming, and sure enough it was Tom Sawyer, and I stopped and waited till he come along. I says "Hold on!" and it stopped alongside, and his mouth opened up like a trunk, and staid so; and he swallowed two or three times, like a person that's got a dry throat, and then says:

"I hain't ever done you no harm. You know that. So then, what you want to come back and ha'nt *me*, for?"

I says:

"I hain't come back—I hain't been *gone*."

When he heard my voice, it righted him up, some, but he warn't quite satisfied, yet. He says:

"Don't you play nothing on me, because I wouldn't on you. Honest injun, now, you ain't a ghost?"

"Honest injun, I ain't," I says.

"Well—I—I—well, that ought to settle it, of course; but I can't somehow seem to understand it, no way. Lookyhere, warn't you ever murdered *at all?*"

"No. I warn't ever murdered at all—I played it on them. You come in here and feel of me if you don't believe me."

So he done it; and it satisfied him; and he was that glad to see me again, he didn't know what to do. And he wanted to know all about it, right off; because it was a grand adventure, and mysterious, and so it hit him where he lived. But I said, leave it alone till by and by;

and told his driver to wait, and we drove off a little piece, and I told him the kind of a fix I was in, and what did he reckon we better do? He said, let him alone a minute, and don't disturb him. So he thought and thought, and pretty soon he says:

"It's all right, I've got it. Take my trunk in your wagon, and let on it's your'n; and you turn back and fool along slow, so as to get to the house about the time you ought to; and I'll go towards town a piece, and take a fresh start, and get there a quarter or a half an hour after you; and you needn't let on to know me, at first."

I says:

"All right; but wait a minute. There's one more thing—a thing that *nobody* don't know but me. And that is, there's a nigger here that I'm a trying to steal out of slavery—and his name is *Jim*—old Miss Watson's Jim."

He says:

"What! Why Jim is—"

He stopped, and went to studying. I says:

"*I* know what you'll say. You'll say it's dirty low-down business; but what if it is?—*I'm* low-down; and I'm agoing to steal him, and I want you to keep mum and not let on. Will you?"

His eye lit up, and he says:

"I'll *help* you steal him!"

Well, I let go all holts, then, like I was shot. It was the most astonishing speech I ever heard—and I'm bound to say Tom Sawyer fell, considerable, in my estimation. Only I couldn't believe it. Tom Sawyer a *nigger stealer!*

"Oh, shucks," I says, "you're joking."

"I ain't joking, either."

"Well, then," I says, "joking or no joking, if you hear anything said about a runaway nigger, don't forget to remember that *you* don't know nothing about him, and *I* don't know nothing about him."

Then we took the trunk and put it in my wagon, and he drove off his way, and I drove mine. But of course I forgot all about driving slow, on accounts of being glad and full of thinking; so I got home a heap too quick for that length of a trip. The old gentleman was at the door, and he says:

"Why, this is wonderful. Who ever would a thought it was in that mare to do it. I wish we'd a timed her. And she hain't sweated a hair—not a hair. It's wonderful. Why, I wouldn't take a hunderd dollars for that horse now; I wouldn't, honest; and yet I'd a sold her for fifteen, before, and thought 'twas all she was worth."

That's all he said. He was the innocentest best old soul I ever see. But it warn't surprising; because he warn't only just a farmer, he was a preacher, too, and had a little one-horse log church down back of the plantation, which he built it himself at his own expense, for a church and school house, and never charged nothing for his preaching, and it was worth it, too. There was plenty other farmer-preachers like that, and done the same way, down South.

In about half an hour Tom's wagon drove up to the front stile, and aunt Sally she see it through the window—because it was only about fifty yards—and says:

"Why, there's somebody come! I wonder who 'tis? Why, I do believe it's a stranger. Jimmy," (that's one of the children,) "run and tell Lize to put on another plate for dinner."

Everybody made a rush for the front door—because, of course, a stranger don't come *every* year, and so he lays over the yaller fever, for interest, when he does come. Tom was over the stile and starting for the house; the wagon was spinning up the road for the village, and we was all bunched in the front door. Tom had his store clothes on, and an audience—and that was always nuts for Tom Sawyer. In them circumstances it warn't no trouble to him to throw in an amount of style that was suitable. He warn't a boy to meeky along up that yard like a sheep; no, he come ca'm and important, like the ram. When he got afront of us, he lifts his hat ever so gracious and dainty, like it was the lid of a box that had butterflies asleep in it and he didn't want to disturb them, and says:

"Mr. Archibald Nichols, I presume?"

"No, my boy," says the old gentleman, "I'm sorry to say 't your driver has deceived you; Nichols's place is down a matter of three mile more. Come in, come in."

Tom he took a look back over his shoulder, and says, "Too late— he's out of sight."

"Yes, he's gone, my son, and you must come in and eat your dinner with us; and then we'll hitch up and take you down to Nichols's."

"MR. ARCHIBALD NICHOLS, I PRESUME?"

"Oh, I *can't* make you so much trouble, I couldn't think of it. I'll walk—I don't mind the distance."

"But we won't *let* you walk—it wouldn't be southern hospitality to do it. Come right in."

"Oh, *do*," says aunt Sally; "it ain't a bit of trouble to us, not a bit in the world. You *must* stay. It's a long, dusty three mile, and we *can't* let you walk. And besides, I've already told 'em to put on another plate, when I see you coming; so you mustn't disappoint us. Come right in, and make yourself at home."

So Tom he thanked them very hearty and handsome, and let himself be persuaded, and come in; and when he was in, he said he was a stranger from Hicksville, Ohio, and his name was William Thompson—and he made another bow.

Well, he run on, and on, and on, making up stuff about Hicksville and everybody in it he could invent, and I getting a little nervous, and wondering how this was going to help me out of my scrape; and at last, still talking along, he reached over and kissed aunt Sally right on the mouth, and then settled back again, in his chair, comfortable, and was going on talking; but she jumped up and wiped it off with the back of her hand, and says:

"You owdacious puppy!"

He looked kind of hurt, and says:

"I'm surprised at you, m'am."

"You're s'rp— Why, what do you reckon *I* am? I've a good notion to take and—say, what do you mean by kissing me?"

He looked kind of humble, and says:

"I didn't mean nothing, m'am. I didn't mean no harm. I—I—thought you'd like it."

"Why, you born fool!" She took up the spinning-stick, and it looked like it was all she could do to keep from giving him a crack with it. "What made you think I'd like it?"

"Well, I don't know. Only, they—they—told me you would."

"*They* told you I would. Whoever told you, 's *another* lunatic. I never heard the beat of it. Who's *they?*"

"Why—everybody. They all said so, m'am."

It was all she could do to hold in; and her eyes snapped, and her fingers worked like she wanted to scratch him; and she says:

"Who's 'everybody?' Out with their names—or ther'll be an idiot short."

He got up and looked distressed, and fumbled his hat, and says:

"I'm sorry, and I warn't expecting it. They told me to. They all told me to. They all said kiss her; and said, she'll like it. They all said it—every one of them. But I'm sorry, m'am, and I won't do it no more—I won't, honest."

"You won't, won't you? Well, I sh'd *reckon* you won't!"

"No'm, I'm honest about it; I won't ever do it again. Till you ask me."

"Till I *ask* you! Well, I never see the beat of it in my born days! I lay you'll be the Methusalem-numskull of creation before ever *I* ask you—or the likes of you."

"Well," he says, "it does surprise me so. I can't make it out, somehow. They said you would, and I thought you would. But—" He stopped, and looked around slow, like he wished he could run across a friendly eye, somewheres; and fetched up on the old gentleman's, and says, "Didn't *you* think she'd like me to kiss her, sir?"

"Why, no, I—I—well, no, I b'lieve I didn't."

Then he looks on around, the same way, to me—and says:

"Tom, didn't *you* think aunt Sally'd open out her arms and say, 'Sid Sawyer'—"

"My land!" she says, breaking in and jumping for him, "you impudent young rascal, to fool a body so—" and was going to hug him, but he fended her off, and says:

"No, not till you've asked me, first."

So she didn't lose no time, but asked him; and hugged him and kissed him, over and over again, and then turned him over to the old man, and he took what was left. And after they got a little quiet again, she says:

"Why dear me, I never see such a surprise. We warn't looking for *you*, at all, but only Tom. Sis never wrote to me about anybody coming but him."

"It's because it warn't *intended* for any of us to come but Tom," he says; "but I begged and begged, and at the last minute she let me come, too; so, coming down the river, me and Tom thought it would be a first rate surprise for him to come here to the house first, and for me to by and by tag along and drop in and let on to be a stranger. But it was a mistake, aunt Sally. This ain't no healthy place for a stranger to come."

"No—not impudent whelps, Sid. You ought to had your jaws boxed; I hain't been so put out since I don't know when. But I don't care, I don't mind the terms—I'd be willing to stand a thousand such jokes to have you here. Well, to think of that performance! I don't deny it, I was most putrefied with astonishment when you give me that smack."

We had dinner out in that broad open passage betwixt the house and the kitchen; and there was things enough on that table for seven families—and all hot, too; none of your flabby tough meat that's laid in a cupboard in a damp cellar all night and tastes like a hunk of old cold cannibal in the morning. Uncle Silas he asked a pretty long blessing over it, but it was worth it; and it didn't cool it a bit, neither, the way I've seen them kind of interruptions do, lots of times.

There was a considerable good deal of talk, all the afternoon, and me and Tom was on the lookout all the time, but it warn't no use, they didn't happen to say nothing about any runaway nigger, and we was afraid to try to work up to it. But at supper, at night, one of the little boys says:

"Pa, mayn't Tom and Sid and me go to the show?"

"No," says the old man, "I reckon there ain't going to be any; and you couldn't go if there was; because the runaway nigger told Burton

A PRETTY LONG BLESSING.

and me all about that scandalous show, and Burton said he would tell the people; so I reckon they've drove the owdacious loafers out of town before this time."

So there it was!—but *I* couldn't help it. Tom and me was to sleep in the same room and bed; so, being tired, we bid good night and went up to bed, right after supper, and clumb out of the window and down the lightning rod, and shoved for the town; for I didn't believe anybody was going to give the king and the duke a hint, and so if I didn't hurry up and give them one they'd get into trouble, sure.

On the road Tom he told me all about how it was reckoned I was murdered, and how pap disappeared, pretty soon, and didn't come back no more, and what a stir there was when Jim run away; and I told Tom all about our Royal Nonesuch rapscallions, and as much of the raft-voyage as I had time to; and as we struck into the town and up through the middle of it—it was as much as half after eight, then—here comes a raging rush of people, with torches, and an awful whooping and yelling, and banging tin pans and blowing horns; and we jumped to one side to let them go by; and as they went by, I see they had the king and the duke astraddle of a rail— that is, I knowed it *was* the king and the duke, though they was all over tar and feathers, and didn't look like nothing in the world that was human—just looked like a couple of monstrous big soldier- plumes. Well, it made me sick to see it; and I was sorry for them poor pitiful rascals, it seemed like I couldn't ever feel any hardness against them any more in the world. It was a dreadful thing to see. Human beings *can* be awful cruel to one another.

We see we was too late—couldn't do no good. We asked some stragglers about it, and they said everybody went to the show look- ing very innocent; and laid low and kept dark till the poor old king was in the middle of his cavortings on the stage; then somebody give a signal, and the house rose up and went for them.

So we poked along back home, and I warn't feeling so brash as I was before, but kind of ornery, and humble, and to blame, some- how—though *I* hadn't done nothing. But that's always the way: it don't make no difference whether you do right or wrong, a person's conscience ain't got no sense, and just goes for him *anyway*. If I had a yaller dog that didn't know no more than a person's conscience does, I would pison him. It takes up more room than all the rest of a person's insides, and yet ain't no good, nohow. Tom Sawyer he says the same.

TRAVELING BY RAIL.

Chapter XXXIV.

VITTLES.

We stopped talking, and got to thinking. By and by, Tom says:

"Looky-here, Huck, what fools we are, to not think of it before! I bet I know where Jim is."

"No! Where?"

"In that hut down by the ash-hopper. Why, looky-here. When we was at dinner, didn't you see a nigger man go in there with some vittles?"

"Yes."

"What did you think the vittles was for?"

"For a dog."

"So'd I. Well, it warn't for a dog."

"Why?"

"Because part of it was watermelon."

"So it was—I noticed it. Well, it does beat all, that I never thought about a dog not eating watermelon. It shows how a body can see and don't see, at the same time."

"Well, the nigger unlocked the padlock when he went in, and he locked it again when he come out. He fetched uncle a key, about the time we got up from table—same key, I bet. Watermelon shows man, lock shows prisoner; and it ain't likely there's two prisoners on such a little plantation, and where the people's all so kind and good. Jim's the prisoner. All right—I'm glad we found it out detective fashion; I wouldn't give shucks for any other way. Now you work your mind and study out a plan to steal Jim, and I will study out one, too; and we'll take the one we like the best."

What a head for just a boy to have! If I had Tom Sawyer's head, I wouldn't trade it off to be a duke, nor mate of a steamboat, nor clown in a circus, nor nothing I can think of. I went to thinking out a plan, but only just to be doing something: I knowed very well where the right plan was going to come from. Pretty soon, Tom says:

"Ready?"

"Yes," I says.

"All right,—bring it out."

"My plan is this," I says. "We can easy find out if it's Jim in there. Then get up my canoe tomorrow night, and fetch my raft over from the island. Then the first dark night that comes, steal the key out of the old man's britches, after he goes to bed, and shove off down the river on the raft, with Jim, hiding daytimes and running nights, the way me and Jim used to do before. Wouldn't that plan work?"

"*Work?* Why cert'nly, it would work, like rats a-fighting. But it's too blame' simple; there ain't nothing *to* it. What's the good of a plan that ain't no more trouble than that? It's as mild as goose-milk. Why, Huck, it wouldn't make no more talk than breaking into a soap factory."

I never said nothing, because I warn't expecting nothing different; but I knowed mighty well that whenever he got *his* plan ready it wouldn't have none of them objections to it.

And it didn't. He told me what it was, and I see in a minute it was worth fifteen of mine, for style, and would make Jim just as free a man as mine would, and maybe get us all killed, besides. So I was satisfied, and said we would waltz in on it. I needn't tell what it was, here, because I knowed it wouldn't stay the way it was. I knowed he would be changing it around, every which way, as we went along, and heaving in new bullinesses wherever he got a chance. And that is what he done.

Well, one thing was dead sure; and that was, that Tom Sawyer was in earnest, and was actuly going to help steal that nigger out of slavery. That was the thing that was too many for me. Here was a boy that was respectable, and well brung up; and had a character to lose; and folks at home that had characters; and he was bright and not leatherheaded; and knowing, and not ignorant; and not mean, but kind; and yet here he was, without any more pride, or rightness, or feeling, than to stoop to this business, and make himself a shame, and his family a shame, before everybody. I *couldn't* understand it, no way at all. It was outrageous, and I knowed I ought to just up and tell him so; and so be his true friend, and let him quit the thing right where he was, and save himself. And I *did* start to tell him; but he shut me up, and says:

"Don't you reckon I know what I'm about? Don't I generly know what I'm about?"

"Yes."

"Didn't I *say* I was going to help steal the nigger?"

"Yes."

"*Well*, then."

That's all he said, and that's all I said. It warn't no use to say any more; because when he said he'd do a thing, he always done it. But *I* couldn't make out how he was willing to go into this thing; so I just let it go, and never bothered no more about it. If he was bound to have it so, *I* couldn't help it.

When we got home, the house was all dark and still; so we went on down to the hut by the ash-hopper, for to examine it. We went through the yard, so as to see what the hounds would do. They knowed us, and didn't make no more noise than country dogs is always doing when anything comes by in the night. When we got to the cabin, we took a look at the front and the two sides; and on the side I warn't acquainted with—which was the north side—we found a square window-hole, up tolerable high, with just one stout board nailed across it. I says:

"Here's the ticket. This hole's big enough for Jim to get through, if we wrench off the board."

Tom says:

"It's as simple as tit-tat-toe, three-in-a-row, and as easy as playing hookey. I should *hope* we can find a way that's a little more complicated than *that*, Huck Finn."

"Well, then," I says, "how'll it do to saw him out, the way I done before I was murdered, that time?"

"That's more *like*," he says. "It's real mysterious, and troublesome, and good," he says; "but I bet we can find a way that's twice as long. There ain't no hurry; le's keep on looking around."

Betwixt the hut and the fence, on the backside, was a lean-to, that joined the hut at the eaves, and was made out of plank. It was as long as the hut, but narrow—only about six foot wide. The door

A SIMPLE JOB.

to it was at the south end, and was padlocked. Tom he went to the soap kettle, and searched around and fetched back the iron thing they lift the lid with; so he took it and prized out one of the staples. The chain fell down, and we opened the door and went in, and shut it and struck a match, and see the shed was only built against the cabin and hadn't no connection with it; and there warn't no floor to the shed, nor nothing in it but some old rusty played-out hoes, and spades, and picks and a crippled plow. The match went out, and so did we, and shoved in the staple again, and the door was locked as good as ever. Tom was joyful. He says:

"Now we're all right. We'll *dig* him out. It'll take about a week!"

Then we started for the house, and I went in the back door—you only have to pull a buckskin latch-string, they don't fasten the doors—but that warn't romantical enough for Tom Sawyer: no way would do him but he must climb up the lightning rod. But after he got up half way about three times, and missed fire and fell every time, and the last time most busted his brains out, he thought he'd got to give it up; but after he was rested, he allowed he would give her one more turn for luck, and this time he made the trip.

In the morning we was up at break of day, and down to the nigger cabins to pet the dogs and make friends with the nigger that fed Jim—if it *was* Jim that was being fed. The niggers was just getting through breakfast and starting for the fields; and Jim's nigger was piling up a tin pan with bread and meat and things; and whilst the others was leaving, the key come from the house.

This nigger had a good-natured chuckleheaded face, and his wool was all tied up in little bunches with thread. That was to keep witches off. He said the witches was pestering him awful, these nights, and making him see all kinds of strange things, and hear all kinds of strange words and noises, and he didn't believe he was ever witched so long, before, in his life. He got so worked up, and got to running on so, about his troubles, he forgot all about what he'd been agoing to do. So Tom says:

"What's the vittles for? Going to feed the dogs?"

The nigger kind of smiled around gradually over his face like when you heave a brickbat in a mud puddle, and he says:

"Yes, mars Sid, *a* dog. Cur'us dog, too. Does you want to go en look at 'im?"

"Yes."

I hunched Tom, and whispers:

"You going, right here in the daybreak? *That* warn't the plan."

"No, it warn't—but it's the plan *now.*"

So, drat him, we went along, but I didn't like it much. When we got in, we couldn't hardly see anything, it was so dark; but Jim was there, sure enough, and could see us; and he sings out:

"Why *Huck!* En good *lan'!* ain' dat Misto Tom?"

I just knowed how it would be; I just expected it. *I* didn't know nothing to do; and if I had, I couldn't a done it; because that nigger busted in and says:

"Why, de gracious sakes! do he know you genlmen?"

We could see pretty well, now. Tom he looked at the nigger, steady and kind of wondering, and says:

"Does *who* know us?"

"Why, dish-yer runaway nigger."

"I don't reckon he does; but what put that into your head?"

"What *put* it dar? Didn' he jis' dis minute sing out like he knowed you?"

Tom says, in a puzzled-up kind of way:

"Well, that's mighty curious. *Who* sung out? *When* did he sing out? *What* did he sing out?" And turns to me, perfectly ca'm, and says, "Did *you* hear anybody sing out?"

Of course there warn't nothing to be said but the one thing; so I says:

"No; *I* ain't heard nobody say nothing."

Then he turns to Jim, and looks him over like he never see him before; and says:

"Did you sing out?"

"No, sah," says Jim, "*I* hain't said nothing, sah."

"Not a word?"

"No, sah, I hain't said a word."

"Did you ever see us before?"

"No, sah; not as *I* knows on."

So Tom turns to the nigger, which was looking wild and distressed, and says, kind of severe:

WITCHES.

"What do you reckon's the matter with you, anyway? What made you think somebody sung out?"

"O, it's de dad-blame' witches, sah, en I wisht I was dead, I do. Dey's awluz at it, sah, en dey do mos' kill me, dey sk'yers me so. Please to don't tell nobody 'bout it, sah, er ole mars Silas he'll scole me; 'kase he say dey *ain'* no witches. I jis' wish to goodness he was heah now—*den* what would he say! I jis' bet he couldn' fine no way to git aroun' it *dis* time. But it's awluz jis' so: people dat's *sot*, stays sot; dey won't look into noth'n en fine it out f'r deyselves, en when *you* fine it out en tell um 'bout it, dey doan b'lieve you."

Tom give him a dime, and said we wouldn't tell nobody; and told him to buy some more thread to tie up his wool with; and then looks at Jim and says:

"I wonder if uncle Silas is going to hang this nigger. If I was to catch a nigger that was ungrateful enough to run away, *I* wouldn't give him up, I'd hang him." And whilst the nigger stepped to the door to look at the dime and bite it to see if it was good, he whispers to Jim, and says:

"Don't ever let on to know us. And if you hear any digging going on, nights, it's us: we're going to set you free."

Jim only had time to grab us by the hand and squeeze it, then the nigger come back, and we said we'd come again some time if the nigger wanted us to; and he said he would, more particular if it was dark, because the witches went for him mostly in the dark, and it was good to have folks around, then.

Chapter XXXV.

GETTING WOOD.

It would be most an hour, yet, till breakfast, so we left, and struck down into the woods; because Tom said we got to have *some* light to see how to dig by, and a lantern makes too much, and might get us into trouble; what we must have was a lot of them rotten chunks that's called fox-fire, and just makes a soft kind of a glow when you lay them in a dark place. We fetched an armful and hid it in the weeds, and set down to rest, and Tom says, kind of dissatisfied:

"Blame it, this whole thing is just as easy and awkard as it can be. And so it makes it so rotten difficult to get up a difficult plan. There ain't no watchman to be drugged—now there *ought* to be a watchman. There ain't even a dog, to give a sleeping-mixture to. And there's Jim chained by one leg, with a ten-foot chain, to the leg of his bed: why, all you got to do is to lift up the bedstead and slip off the chain. And uncle Silas he trusts everybody; sends the key to the punkinheaded nigger, and don't send nobody to watch the nigger. Jim could a got out of that window-hole, before this, only there wouldn't be no use trying to travel with a ten-foot chain on his leg. Why, drat it, Huck, it's the stupidest arrangement I ever see. You got to invent *all* the difficulties. Well, we can't help it, we got to do the best we can with the materials we've got. Anyhow, there's one thing—there's more honor in getting him out through a lot of difficulties and dangers, where there warn't one of them furnished to you by the people who it was their duty to furnish them, and you had to contrive them all out of your own head. Now look at just that one thing of the lantern. When you come down to the cold facts, we simply got to *let on* that a lantern's resky. Why, we could work with a torchlight procession if we wanted to, *I* believe. Now whilst I think of it, we got to hunt up something to make a saw out of, the first chance we get."

"What do we want of a saw?"

"What do we *want* of it? Hain't we got to saw the leg of Jim's bed off, so as to get the chain loose?"

"Why, you just said a body could lift up the bedstead and slip the chain off."

"Well, if that ain't just like you, Huck Finn. You *can* get up the infant-schooliest ways of going at a thing. Why, hain't you ever read any books at all?—Baron Trenck, nor Casanova, nor Benvenuto Chelleeny, nor Henri IV, nor none of them heroes? Whoever heard of getting a prisoner loose in such an old-maidy way as that? No; the way all the best authorities does, is to saw the bed-leg in two, and leave it just so, and swallow the sawdust, so it can't be found, and put some dirt and grease around the sawed place so the very keenest seneskal can't see no sign of its being sawed, and thinks the bed-leg is perfectly sound. Then, the night you're ready, fetch the leg a kick, down she goes; slip off your chain, and there you are. Nothing to do but hitch your rope-ladder to the battlements, shin down it, break your leg in the moat—because a rope-ladder is nineteen foot too short, you know—and there's your horses and your trusty vassles, and they scoop you up and fling you across a saddle and away you go, to your native Langudoc, or Navarre, or wherever it is. It's gaudy, Huck. I wish there was a moat to this cabin. If we get time, the night of the escape, we'll dig one."

I says:

"What do we want of a moat, when we're going to snake him out from under the cabin?"

But he never heard me. He had forgot me and everything else. He had his chin in his hand, thinking. Pretty soon, he sighs, and shakes his head; then sighs again, and says:

"No, it wouldn't do—there ain't necessity enough for it."

"For what?" I says.

"Why, to saw Jim's leg off," he says.

"Good land!" I says, "Why, there ain't *no* necessity for it. And what would you want to saw his leg off, for, anyway?"

"Well, some of the best authorities has done it. They couldn't get the chain off, so they just cut their hand off, and shoved. And a leg would be better still. But we got to let that go. There ain't necessity

ONE OF THE BEST AUTHORITIES.

enough in this case; and besides, Jim's a nigger and wouldn't under-stand the reasons for it, and how it's the custom in Europe; so we'll let it go. But there's one thing—he can have a rope ladder; we can tear up our sheets and make him a rope ladder easy enough. And we can send it to him in a pie; it's mostly done that way. And I've et worse pies."

"Why, Tom Sawyer, how you talk," I says; "Jim ain't got no use for a rope ladder."

"He *has* got use for it. How *you* talk, you better say: you don't know nothing about it. He's *got* to have a rope ladder: they all do."

"What in the nation can he *do* with it?"

"*Do* with it? He can hide it in his bed, can't he? That's what they all do; and *he's* got to, too. Huck, you don't ever seem to want to do anything that's regular: you want to be starting something fresh all the time. Spose he *don't* do nothing with it? ain't it there in his bed, for a clew, after he's gone? and don't you reckon they'll want clews? Of course they will. And you wouldn't leave them any? That would be a *pretty* howdy-do, *wouldn't* it! I never heard of such a thing."

"Well," I says, "if it's in the regulations, and he's got to have it, all right, let him have it; because I don't wish to go back on no regulations; but there's one thing, Tom Sawyer—if we go to tearing up our sheets to make Jim a rope ladder, we're going to get into trouble with aunt Sally, just as sure as you're born. Now the way I look at it, a hickry bark ladder don't cost nothing, and don't waste nothing, and is just as good to load up a pie with, and hide in a straw tick, as any rag-ladder you can start; and as for Jim, he ain't had no experience, and so *he* don't care what kind of a—"

"O shucks, Huck Finn, if I was as ignorant as you, I'd keep still— that's what *I'd* do. Who ever heard of a state prisoner escaping by a hickry bark ladder? Why, it's perfectly ridiculous."

"Well, all right, Tom, fix it your own way; but if you'll take my advice, you'll let me borrow a sheet off of the clothes line."

He said that would do. And that give him another idea, and he says:

"Borrow a shirt, too."

"What do we want of a shirt, Tom?"

"Want it for Jim to keep a journal on."

"Journal your granny—*Jim* can't write."

"Spose he *can't* write—he can make marks on the shirt, can't he, if we make him a pen out of an old pewter spoon or a piece of an old iron barrel-hoop?"

"Why, Tom, we can pull a feather out of a goose and make him a better one; and quicker, too."

"*Prisoners* don't have geese running around the donjon-keep to pull pens out of, you muggins. They *always* make their pens out of the hardest, toughest, troublesomest piece of old brass candlestick or something like that they can get their hands on; and it takes them weeks and weeks, and months and months to file it out, too, because they've got to do it by rubbing it on the wall. *They* wouldn't use a goose-quill if they had it. It ain't regular."

"Well, then, what'll we make him the ink out of?"

"Many makes it out of iron-rust and tears; but that's the common sort and women; the best authorities uses their own blood. Jim can do that; and when he wants to send any little common ordinary mysterious message to let the world know where he's captivated, he can write it on the bottom of a tin plate with a fork and throw it out of the window. The Iron Mask always done that, and it's a blame' good way, too."

"Jim ain't got no tin plates. They feed him in a pan."

"That ain't anything; we can get him some."

"Can't nobody *read* his plates."

"That ain't got nothing to *do* with it, Huck Finn. All *he's* got to do is to write on the plate and throw it out. You don't *have* to be able to read it. Why, half the time you can't read anything a prisoner writes on a tin plate, or anywhere else."

"Well, then, what's the sense in wasting the plates?"

"Why, blame it all, it ain't the *prisoner's* plates."

"But it's *somebody's* plates, ain't it?"

THE BREAKFAST HORN.

"Well, spos'n it is? What does the *prisoner* care whose—"

He broke off there, because we heard the breakfast horn blowing. So we cleared out for the house.

Along during that morning I borrowed a sheet and a white shirt off of the clothes line; and I found an old sack and put them in it, and we went down and got the fox-fire, and put that in, too. I called it borrowing, because that was what pap always called it; but Tom said it warn't borrowing, it was stealing. He said we was representing prisoners; and prisoners don't care how they get a thing so they get it, and nobody don't blame them for it, either. It ain't no crime in a prisoner to steal the thing he needs to get away with, Tom said; it's his right; and so, as long as we was representing a prisoner, we had a perfect right to steal anything on this place we had the least use for, to get ourselves out of prison with. He said if we warn't prisoners it would be a very different thing, and nobody but a mean ornery person would steal when he warn't a prisoner. So we allowed we would steal everything there was that come handy. And yet he made a mighty fuss, one day, after that, when I stole a watermelon out of the nigger patch and eat it; and he made me go and give the niggers a dime, without telling them what it was for. Tom said that what he meant was, we could steal anything we *needed*. Well, I says, I needed the watermelon. But he said I didn't need it to get out of prison with, there's where the difference was. He said if I'd a wanted it to hide a knife in, and smuggle it to Jim to kill the seneskal with, it would a been all right. So I let it go at that, though I couldn't see no advantage in my representing a prisoner, if I got to set down and chaw over a lot of gold-leaf distinctions like that, every time I see a chance to hog a watermelon.

Well, as I was saying, we waited, that morning, till everybody was settled down to business, and nobody in sight around the yard; then Tom he carried the sack into the lean-to whilst I stood off a piece to keep watch. By and by he come out, and we went and set down on the woodpile, to talk. He says:

"Everything's all right, now, except tools; and that's easy fixed."

"Tools?" I says.

"Yes."

"Tools for what?"

"Why, to dig with. We ain't agoing to *gnaw* him out, are we?"

"Ain't them old crippled picks and things in there good enough to dig a nigger out with?" I says.

He turns on me looking pitying enough to make a body cry; and says:

"Huck Finn, did you *ever* hear of a prisoner having picks and shovels and all the modern conveniences in his wardrobe to dig himself out with? Now I want to ask you—if you got any reasonableness in you at all—what kind of a show would *that* give him to be a hero? Why they might as well lend him the key, and done with it. Picks and shovels—why they wouldn't furnish 'em to a king."

"Well, then," I says, "if we don't want the picks and shovels, what do we want?"

"A couple of caseknives."

"To dig the foundations out from under that cabin with?"

"Yes."

"Confound it, it's foolish, Tom."

"It don't make no difference how foolish it is, it's the *right* way—and it's the regular way. And there ain't no *other* way, that ever *I* heard of; and I've read all the books that gives any information about these things. They always dig out with a caseknife—and not through dirt, mind you; generly it's through solid rock. And it takes them weeks and weeks and weeks, and forever and ever. Why, look at one of them prisoners in the bottom dungeon of the Castle Deef, in the harbor of Marseilles, that dug himself out that way: how long was *he* at it, you reckon?"

"I don't know."

"Well, guess."

"I don't know. A month and a half?"

"*Thirty-seven year*—and he come out in China. *That's* the kind. I wish the bottom of *this* fortress was solid rock."

"*Jim* don't know nobody in China."

"What's *that* got to do with it? Neither did that other fellow. But you're always a-wandering off on a side issue. Why can't you stick to the main point?"

"All right—*I* don't care where he comes out, so he *comes* out; and Jim don't, either, I reckon. But there's one thing, anyway—Jim's too old to be dug out with a caseknife. He won't last."

"Yes he will *last*, too. You don't reckon it's going to take thirty-seven years to dig out through a *dirt* foundation, do you?"

"How long will it take, Tom?"

"Well, we can't resk being as long as we ought to, because it mayn't take very long for uncle Silas to hear from down there by New Orleans. He'll hear Jim ain't from there. Then his next move will be to advertise Jim, or something like that. So we can't resk being as long digging him out as we ought to. By rights I reckon we ought to be a couple of years; but we can't. Things being so uncertain, what I recommend is this: that we really dig right in, as quick as we can; and after that, we can *let on*, to ourselves, that we was at it thirty-seven years. Then we can snatch him out and rush him away the first time there's an alarm. Yes, I reckon that'll be the best way."

"Now there's *sense* in that," I says. "Letting-on don't cost nothing; letting-on ain't no trouble; and if it's any object, I don't mind letting on we was at it a hundred and fifty year. It wouldn't strain me none, after I got my hand in. So I'll mosey along, now, and smouch a couple of case-knives."

"Smouch three," he says; "we want one to make a saw out of."

"Tom, if it ain't unregular and irreligious to sejest it," I says, "there's an old rusty

SMOUCHING THE KNIVES.

saw-blade around yonder sticking under the weatherboarding behind the smokehouse."

He looked kind of weary and discouraged-like, and says:

"It ain't no use to try to learn you nothing, Huck. Run along and smouch the knives—three of them." So I done it.

Chapter XXXVI ·

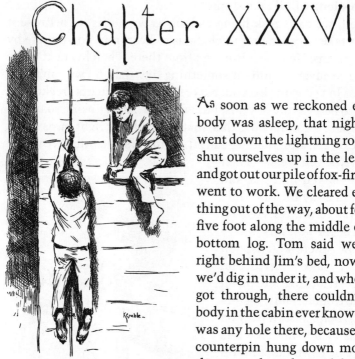

As soon as we reckoned everybody was asleep, that night, we went down the lightning rod, and shut ourselves up in the lean-to, and got out our pile of fox-fire, and went to work. We cleared everything out of the way, about four or five foot along the middle of the bottom log. Tom said we was right behind Jim's bed, now, and we'd dig in under it, and when we got through, there couldn't nobody in the cabin ever know there was any hole there, because Jim's counterpin hung down most to the ground, and you'd have to raise it up and look under, to see the hole. So we dug and dug, with the caseknives, till most midnight; and then we was dog-tired, and our hands was blistered, and yet you couldn't see we'd done anything, hardly. At last I says:

"This ain't no thirty-seven year job, this is a thirty-eight year job, Tom Sawyer."

He never said nothing. But he sighed, and pretty soon he stopped digging, and then for a good little while I knowed he was thinking. Then he says:

"It ain't no use, Huck, it ain't agoing to work. If we was prisoners, it would, because then we'd have as many years as we wanted, and no hurry; and we wouldn't get but a few minutes to dig, every day, while they was changing watches, and so our hands wouldn't get blistered, and we could keep it up right along, year in and year out, and do it right and the way it ought to be done. But *we* can't fool along, we got to rush; we ain't got no time to spare. If we was to put in another night this way, we'd have to knock off for a week to let our hands get well—couldn't touch a caseknife with them sooner."

"Well, then, what we going to do, Tom?"

"I'll tell you. It ain't right, and it ain't moral, and I wouldn't like it to get out—but there ain't only just the one way: we got to dig him out with the picks, and *let on* it's case-knives."

"*Now* you're *talking!*" I says; "Your head gets leveler and leveler all the time, Tom Sawyer," I says. "Picks is the thing, moral or no moral; and as for me, I don't care shucks for the morality of it, nohow. When I start in to steal a nigger, or a watermelon, or a Sunday school book, I ain't no ways particular how it's done, so it's done. What I want is my nigger; or what I want is my watermelon; or what I want is my Sunday school book: and if a pick's the handiest thing, that's the thing I'm agoing to dig that nigger or that watermelon or that Sunday school book out with; and I don't give a dead rat what the authorities thinks about it, nuther."

"Well," he says, "there's excuse for picks and letting-on, in a case like this; if it warn't so, I wouldn't approve of it, nor I wouldn't stand by and see the rules broke—because right is right, and wrong is wrong, and a body ain't got no business doing wrong when he ain't ignorant and knows better. It might answer for *you* to dig Jim out with a pick, *without* any letting-on, because you don't know no better; but it wouldn't for me, because I do know better. Gimme a caseknife."

He had his own by him, but I handed him mine. He flung it down, and says:

"Gimme a *caseknife*."

I didn't know just what to do—but then I thought. I scratched around amongst the old tools, and got a pick-axe and give it to him, and he took it and went to work, and never said a word.

He was always just that particular. Full of principle.

So then I got a shovel, and then we picked and shoveled, turn about, and made the fur fly. We stuck to it about a half an hour, which was as long as we could stand up; but we had a good deal of a hole to show for it. When I got up stairs, I looked out at the window and see Tom doing his level best with the lightning rod, but he couldn't come it, his hands was so sore. At last he says:

"It ain't no use, it can't be done. What you reckon I better do? Can't you think up no way?"

"Yes," I says, "but I reckon it ain't regular. Come up the stairs, and let on it's a lightning rod."

So he done it.

Next day Tom stole a pewter spoon and a brass candlestick in the house, for to make some pens for Jim out of, and six tallow candles; and I hung around the nigger cabins, and laid for a chance, and stole

STEALING SPOONS.

three tin plates. Tom said it wasn't enough; but I said nobody wouldn't ever see the plates that Jim throwed out, because they'd fall in the dog-fennel and jimpson weeds under the window-hole— then we could tote them back and he could use them over again. So Tom was satisfied. Then he says:

"Now, the thing to study out, is, how to get the things to Jim."

"Take them in through the hole," I says, "when we get it done."

He only just looked scornful, and said something about nobody ever heard of such an idiotic idea, and then he went to studying. By and by he said he had ciphered out two or three ways, but there warn't no need to decide on any of them, yet. Said we'd got to post Jim, first.

That night we went down the lightning rod a little after ten, and took one of the candles along, and listened under the window-hole, and heard Jim snoring; so we pitched it in, and it didn't wake him. Then we whirled in with the pick and shovel, and in about two hours and a half the job was done. We crept in under Jim's bed and into the cabin, and pawed around and found the candle and lit it, and stood over Jim awhile, and found him looking hearty and healthy, and then we woke him up, gentle and gradual. He was so glad to see us he most cried; and called us honey, and all the pet names he could think of; and was for having us hunt up a cold chisel to cut the chain off of his leg with, right away, and clearing out without losing any time. But Tom he showed him how unregular it would be, and set down and told him all about our plans, and how we could alter them in a minute any time there was an alarm; and not to be the least afraid, because we would see he got away, *sure.* So Jim he said it was all right, and we set there and talked over old times a while, and then Tom asked a lot of questions, and when Jim told him uncle Silas come in every day or two to pray with him, and aunt Sally come in to see if he was comfortable and had plenty to eat, and both of them was kind as they could be, Tom says:

"*Now* I know how to fix it. We'll send you some things by them."

I said, "Don't do nothing of the kind; it's one of the most jackass ideas I ever struck;" but he never paid no attention to me; went right on. It was his way when he'd got his plans set.

So he told Jim how we'd have to smuggle in the rope-ladder pie, and other large things, by Nat, the nigger that fed him, and he must be on the lookout, and not be surprised, and not let Nat see him open them; and we would put small things in uncle's coat pockets and he must steal them out; and we would tie things to aunt's apron strings or put them in her apron pocket, if we got a chance; and told him what they would be and what they was for. And told him how to keep a journal on the shirt with his blood, and all that. He told him everything. Jim he couldn't see no sense in the most of it, but he allowed we was white folks and knowed better than him; so he was satisfied and said he would do it all just as Tom said.

Jim had plenty corn-cob pipes and tobacco; so we had a right down good sociable time; then we crawled out through the hole, and so home to bed, with hands that looked like they'd been chawed by a dog. Tom was in high spirits. He said it was the best fun he ever had in his life, and the most intellectural; and said if he only could see his way to it we would keep it up all the rest of our lives and leave Jim to our children to get out; for he believed Jim would come to like it better and better the more he got used to it. He said that in that way it could be strung out to as much as eighty year, and would be the best time on record. And he said it would make us all celebrated that had a hand in it.

In the morning we went out to the woodpile and chopped up the brass candlestick into handy sizes, and Tom put them and the pewter spoon in his pocket. Then we went to the nigger cabins, and while I got Nat's notice off, Tom shoved a piece of candlestick into the middle of a corn-pone that was in Jim's pan, and we went along with Nat to see how it would work, and it just worked noble: when Jim bit into it it most mashed all his teeth out; and there warn't ever anything could a worked better. Tom said so himself. Jim he never let on but what it was only just a piece of rock or something like that that's always getting into bread, you know; but after that he never bit into nothing but what he jabbed his fork into it in three or four places, first.

And whilst we was a standing there in the dimmish light, here comes a couple of the hounds bulging in, from under Jim's bed; and they kept on piling in till there was eleven of them, and there warn't hardly room in there to get your breath. By jings we forgot to fasten that lean-to door. The nigger Nat he only just hollered "witches!" once, and keeled over onto the floor amongst the dogs and begun to groan like he was dying. Tom jerked the door open and flung out a slab of Jim's meat, and the dogs went for it; and in two seconds he was out himself and back again and shut the door, and I knowed he'd fixed the other door, too. Then he went to work on the nigger, coaxing him and petting him, and asking him if he'd been imagining he saw something again. He raised up, and blinked his eyes around, and says:

"Mars Sid, you'll say I's a fool, but if I didn' b'lieve I see most a million dogs, er devils, er some'n, I wisht I may die right heah in dese tracks. I did, mos' sholy. Mars Sid, I *felt* um—I *felt* um, sah; dey was all over me. Dad fetch it, I jis' wisht I could git my han's on one er dem witches jis' wunst—on'y jis' wunst—it's all *I*'d ast. But mos'ly I wisht dey'd lemme 'lone, I does."

Tom says:

"Well, I tell you what *I* think. What makes them come here just at this runaway nigger's breakfast time? It's because they're hungry; that's the reason. You make them a witch pie; that's the thing for *you* to do."

TOM ADVISES A WITCH PIE.

"But my lan', mars Sid, how's *I* gwyne to make 'm a witch pie? I doan know how to make it. I hain't ever hearn er sich a thing b'fo'."

"Well, then, I'll have to make it myself."

"Will you do it, honey?—will you? I'll wusshup de groun' und' yo' foot, I will!"

"All right, I'll do it, seeing it's you, and you've been good to us and showed us the runaway nigger. But you got to be mighty careful. When we come around, you turn your back; and then whatever we've put in the pan, don't you let on you see it at all. And don't you look, when Jim unloads the pan—something might happen, I don't know what. And above all, don't you *handle* the witch-things."

"*Hannel* 'm, mars Sid? What *is* you a talkin' 'bout? I wouldn' lay de weight er my finger on um, not f'r ten hund'd thous'n' billion dollars, I wouldn't."

Chapter XXXVII.

THE RUBBAGE PILE.

That was all fixed. So then we went away, and went to the rubbage pile in the back yard where they keep the old boots, and rags, and pieces of bottles, and wore-out tin things, and all such truck, and scratched around and found an old tin washpan and stopped up the holes as well as we could, to bake the pie in, and took it down cellar and stole it full of flour, and started for breakfast, and found a couple of shingle nails that Tom said would be handy for a prisoner to scrabble his name and sorrows on the dungeon walls with, and dropped one of them in aunt Sally's apron pocket which was hanging on a chair, and t'other we stuck in the band of uncle Silas's hat, which was on the bureau, because we heard the children say their pa and ma was going to the runaway nigger's house this morning, and then went to breakfast, and Tom dropped the pewter spoon in uncle Silas's coat pocket, and aunt Sally wasn't come yet, so we had to wait a little while.

And when she come she was hot, and red, and cross, and couldn't hardly wait for the blessing, and then she went to sluicing out coffee with one hand and cracking the handiest child's head with her thimble with the other, and says:

"I've hunted high, and I've hunted low, and it does beat all, what *has* become of your other shirt."

My heart fell down amongst my lungs and livers and things, and a hard piece of corn-crust started down my throat after it and got met on the road with a cough and was shot across the table and took one of the children in the eye and curled him up like a fishing-worm, and let a cry out of him the size of a war-whoop, and Tom he turned kinder blue around the gills, and it all amounted to a considerable state of things for about a quarter of a minute or as much as that, and I would a sold out for half price if there was a bidder. But after that, we was all right again—it was the sudden surprise of it that knocked us so kind of cold. Uncle Silas he says:

"It's most uncommon curious, I can't understand it. I know perfectly well I took it *off*, because—"

"Because you hain't got but one *on*. Just *listen* at the man! *I* know you took it off, and know it by a better way than your wool-gethering memory, too, because it was on the clo'es line yesterday—I see it there myself. But it's gone—that's the long and the short of it, and you'll just have to change to a red flann'l one till I can get time to make a new one. And it'll be the third I've made in two years; it just keeps a body on the jump to keep you in shirts; and whatever you do manage to *do* with 'm all, is more'n *I* can make out. A body'd think you *would* learn to take some sort of care of 'em, at your time of life."

"I know it, Sally, and I do try, all I can. But it oughtn't to be altogether my fault, because you know I don't see them nor have nothing to do with them except when they're on me; and I don't believe I've ever lost one of them *off* of me."

"Well, it ain't *your* fault if you haven't, Silas—you'd a done it if you could, I reckon. And the shirt ain't all that's gone, nuther. Ther's a spoon gone; and *that* ain't all. There was ten, and now ther's only nine. The calf got the shirt, I reckon, but the calf never took the spoon, *that's* certain."

"Why, what else is gone, Sally?"

"Ther's six *candles* gone—that's what. The rats could a got the candles, and I reckon they did; I wonder they don't walk off with the whole place, the way you're always going to stop their holes and don't do it; and if they warn't fools they'd sleep in your hair, Silas—*you'd* never find it out; but you can't lay the *spoon* on the rats, and that I *know*."

"Well, Sally, I'm in fault, and I acknowledge it; I've been remiss; but I won't let to-morrow go by without stopping up them holes."

"O, I wouldn't hurry, next year'll do. Matilda Angelina Araminta *Phelps!*"

Whack comes the thimble, and the child snatches her claws out of the sugar bowl without fooling around any. Just then, the nigger woman steps onto the passage, and says:

"Missus, dey's a sheet gone."

"A *sheet* gone! Well, for the land's sake!"

"I'll stop up them holes *to-day*," says uncle Silas, looking sorrowful.

"O, *do* shet up!—Spose the rats took the *sheet? Where's* it gone, Lize?"

"Clah to goodness I hain't no notion, Miss Sally. She wuz on de clo's line yistiddy, but she done gone; she ain' dah no mo', now."

"I reckon the world *is* coming to an end. I *never* see the beat of it, in all my born days. A shirt, and a sheet, and a spoon, and six can—"

"Missus," comes a young yaller wench, "dey's a brass can-nelstick miss'n."

"Cler out from here, you hussy, er I'll take a skillet to ye!"

Well, she was just a biling. I begun to lay for a chance; I reckoned I would sneak out and go for the woods till the weather moderated. She kept a-raging right along, running her insurrection all by herself, and everybody else mighty meek and quiet; and at

"MISSUS, DEY'S A SHEET GONE."

last uncle Silas, looking kind of foolish, fishes up that spoon out of his pocket. She stopped, with her mouth open and her hands up; and as for me, I wished I was in Jeruslem or somewheres. But not long; because she says:

"It's *just* as I expected. So you had it in your pocket all the time; and like as not you've got the other things there, too. How'd it get there?"

"I reely don't know, Sally," he says, kind of apologizing, "or you know I would tell. I was a-studying over my text in Acts seventeen, before breakfast, and I reckon I put it in there, not noticing, meaning to put my Testament in, and it must be so, because my Testament ain't in, but I'll go and see, and if the Testament is where I had it, I'll know I didn't put it in, and that will show that I laid the Testament down and took up the spoon, and—"

"O, for the land's sake! Give a body a rest! Go 'long, now, the whole kit and biling of ye; and don't come nigh me again till I've got back my peace of mind."

I'd a heard her, if she'd a said it to herself, let alone speaking it out; and I'd a got up and obeyed her, if I'd a been dead. As we was passing through the setting room, the old man he took up his hat, and the shingle nail fell out on the floor, and he just merely picked it up and laid it on the mantel shelf, and never said nothing, and went out. Tom see him do it, and remembered about the spoon, and says:

"Well, it ain't no use to send things by *him* no more, he ain't reliable." Then he says: "But he done us a good turn with the spoon, anyway, without knowing it, and so we'll go and do him one without *him* knowing it—stop up his rat holes."

There was a noble good lot of them, down cellar, and it took us a whole hour, but we done the job tight and good, and ship-shape. Then we heard steps on the stairs, and blowed out our light, and hid; and here comes the old man, with a candle in one hand and a bundle of stuff in t'other, looking as absent-minded as year before last. He went a mooning around, first to one rat hole and then another, till he'd been to them all. Then he stood about five minutes, picking tallow-drip off of his candle and thinking. Then he turns off slow and dreamy towards the stairs, saying:

"Well, for the life of me I can't remember when I done it. I could show her, now, that I warn't to blame on account of the rats. But never mind—let it go. I reckon it wouldn't do no good."

And so he went on a-mumbling up stairs, and then we left. He was a mighty nice old man. And always is.

Tom was a good deal bothered about what to do for a spoon, but he said we'd got to have it; so he took a think. When he had ciphered it out, he told me how we was to do; then we went and waited around the spoon-basket till we see aunt Sally coming, and then

Tom went to counting the spoons and laying them out to one side, and I slid one of them up my sleeve, and Tom says:

"Why, aunt Sally, there ain't but nine spoons, *yet*."

She says:

"Go 'long to your play, and don't bother me. I know better, I counted 'm myself."

"Well, I've counted them twice, aunty, and *I* can't make but nine."

She looked out of all patience, but of course she come to count—anybody would.

"I declare to gracious ther' *ain't* but nine!" she says. "Why, what in the world—plague *take* the things, I'll count 'm again."

So I slipped back the one I had, and when she got done counting, she says:

"Hang the troublesome rubbage, ther's *ten*, now!" and she looked huffy and bothered both. But Tom says:

"Why, aunty, *I* don't think there's ten."

"You numscull, didn't you see me *count* 'm?"

IN A TEARING WAY.

"I know, but—"

"Well, I'll count 'm *again*."

So I smouched one, and they come out nine, same as the other time. Well, she *was* in a tearing way—just a trembling all over, she was so mad. But she counted, and counted, till she got that addled she'd start to count-in the *basket* for a spoon, sometimes: and so, three times they come out right, and three times they come out wrong. Then she grabbed up the basket and slammed it across the house and knocked the cat galley-west; and she said "cle'r out and let her have some peace, and if we come bothering around her again betwixt that and dinner, she'd skin us." So we had the odd spoon; and dropped it in her apron pocket whilst she was a-giving us our sailing-orders, and Jim got it, all right, along with her shingle-nail, before noon. We was very well satisfied with this business, and Tom allowed it was worth twice the trouble it took, because he said *now* she couldn't ever count them spoons twice alike again to save her life; and wouldn't believe she'd counted them right, if she *did*; and said that after she'd about counted her head off, for the next three days, he judged she'd give it up and offer to kill anybody that wanted her to ever count them any more.

So we put the sheet back on the line, that night, and stole one out of her closet; and kept on putting it back and stealing it again, for a couple of days, till she didn't know how many sheets she had, any more, and said she didn't *care*, and warn't agoing to bullyrag the rest of her soul out about it, and wouldn't count them again not to save her life, she druther die first.

So we was all right, now, as to the shirt and the sheet and the spoon and the candles, by the help of the calf and the rats and the mixed-up counting; and as to the candlestick, it warn't no consequence, it would blow over by and by.

But that pie was a job; we had no end of trouble with that pie. We fixed it up away down in the woods, and cooked it there; and we got it done, at last, and very satisfactory, too; but not all in one day; and we had to use up three washpans full of flour, before we got through, and we got burnt pretty much all over, in places, and eyes put out with the smoke; because, you see, we didn't want nothing but a crust, and we couldn't prop it up, right, and she would always cave in. But of course we thought of the right way at last; which was, to cook the ladder, too, in the pie. So then we laid in with Jim, the second night, and tore up the sheet all in little strings, and twisted them together, and long before daylight we had a lovely rope, that you could a hung a person with. We let on it took nine months to make it.

And in the forenoon we took it down to the woods, but it wouldn't go in the pie. Being made of a whole sheet, that way, there was rope enough for forty pies, if we'd a wanted them, and plenty left over for soup, or sausage, or anything you choose. We could a had a whole dinner.

But we didn't need it. All we needed was just enough for the pie, and so we throwed the rest away. We didn't cook none of the pies in the washpan, afraid the solder would melt; but uncle Silas he had a noble brass warming pan which he thought considerable of, because it belonged to one of his ancestors with a long wooden handle that come over from England with William the Conqueror in the Mayflower or one of them early ships and was hid away up garret with a lot of other old pots and things that was valuable, not on account of being any account, because they warn't, but on account of them being relicts, you know, and we snaked her out, private, and took her down there, but she failed on the first pies, because we didn't know how, but she come up smiling on the last one. We took and lined her with dough, and set her in the coals, and loaded her up with rag-rope, and put on a dough roof, and shut down the lid, and

ONE OF HIS ANCESTERS.

put hot embers on top, and stood off five foot, with the long handle, cool and comfortable, and in fifteen minutes she turned out a pie that was a satisfaction to look at. But the person that et it would want to fetch a couple of kags of toothpicks along, for if that rope ladder wouldn't cramp him down to business, I don't know nothing what I'm talking about, and lay him in enough stomach-ache to last him till next time, too.

Nat didn't look, when we put the witch-pie in Jim's pan; and we put the three tin plates in the bottom of the pan under the vittles; and so Jim got everything all right, and as soon as he was by himself he busted into the pie and hid the rope ladder inside of his straw tick, and scratched some marks on a tin plate and throwed it out of the window-hole.

Chapter XXXVIII

JIM'S COAT OF ARMS.

Making them pens was a distressid tough job, and so was the saw; and Jim allowed the inscription was going to be the toughest of all. That's the one which the prisoner has to scrabble on the wall. But we had to have it; Tom said we'd *got* to: there warn't no case of a state prisoner not scrabbling his inscription to leave behind, and his coat of arms.

"Look at lady Jane Grey," he says; "look at Gilford Dudley; look at old Northumberland! Why, Huck, spose it *is* considerble trouble?—what you going to do?—how you going to get around it? Jim's *got* to do his inscription and coat of arms. They all do."

Jim says:

"Why, mars Tom, I hain't got no coat o' arms; I hain't got nuffn but dish-yer ole shirt, en you knows I got to keep de journal on dat."

"O, you don't understand, Jim; a coat of arms is very different."

"Well," I says, "Jim's right, anyway, when he says he hain't got no coat of arms, because he hain't."

"I reckon *I* knowed that," Tom says, "but you bet he'll have one before he goes out of this—because he's going out *right*, and there ain't going to be no flaws in his record."

So whilst me and Jim filed away at the pens on a brickbat apiece, Jim a making his'n out of the brass and I making mine out of the spoon, Tom set to work to think out the coat of arms. By and by he said he'd struck so many good ones he didn't hardly know which to take, but there was one which he reckoned he'd decide on. He says:

"On the scutcheon we'll have a bend *or* in the dexter base, a saltire *murrey* in the fess, with a dog, couchant, for common charge, and under his foot a chain embattled, for slavery, with a chevron *vert* in a chief engrailed, and three invected lines on a field *azure*, with the nombril points rampant on a dancette indented; crest, a runaway nigger, *sable*, with his bundle over his shoulder on a bar sinister; and a couple of gules for supporters, which is you and me; motto, *Maggiore fretta, minore atto.* Got it out of a book—means, the more haste, the less speed."

"Geewhillikins," I says, "but what does the rest of it mean?"

"We ain't got no time to bother over that," he says, "we got to dig in like all git-out."

"Well, anyway," I says, "what's *some* of it? What's a fess?"

"A fess—a fess is—*you* don't need to know what a fess is. I'll show him how to make it when he gets to it."

"Shucks, Tom," I says, "I think you might tell a person. What's a bar sinister?"

"Oh, *I* don't know. But he's got to have it. All the nobility does."

That was just his way. If it didn't suit him to explain a thing to you, he wouldn't do it. You might pump at him a week, it wouldn't make no difference.

He'd got all that coat of arms business fixed, so now he started in to finish up the rest of that part of the work, which was to plan out a mournful inscription—said Jim got to have one, like they all done. He made up a lot, and wrote them out on a paper, and read them off, so:

1. *Here a captive heart busted.*
2. *Here a poor prisoner, forsook by the world and friends, fretted out his sorrowful life.*
3. *Here a lonely heart broke, and a worn spirit went to its rest, after thirty seven years of solitary captivity.*
4. *Here, homeless and friendless, after thirty-seven years of bitter captivity, perished a noble stranger, natural son of Louis XIV.*

Tom's voice trembled, whilst he was reading them, and he most broke down. When he got done, he couldn't no way make up his mind which one for Jim to scrabble onto the wall, they was all so good; but at last he allowed he would let him scrabble them all on. Jim said it would take him a year to scrabble such a lot of truck onto the logs with a nail, and he didn't know how to make letters, besides; but Tom said he would block them out for him, and then he wouldn't have nothing to do but just follow the lines. Then pretty soon he says:

"Come to think, the logs ain't agoing to do; they don't have log walls in a dungeon: we got to dig the inscriptions into a rock. We'll fetch a rock."

Jim said the rock was worse than the logs; he said it would take him such a pison long time to dig them into a rock, he wouldn't ever get out. But Tom said he would let me help him do it. Then he took a look to see how me and Jim was getting along with the pens. It was most pesky tedious hard work and slow, and didn't give my hands no show to get well of the sores, and we didn't seem to make no headway, hardly. So Tom says:

"I know how to fix it. We got to have a rock for the coat of arms and mournful inscriptions, and we can kill two birds with that same rock. There's a gaudy big grindstone down at the mill, and we'll smouch it, and carve the things on it, and file out the pens and the saw on it, too."

It warn't no slouch of an idea; and it warn't no slouch of a grindstone, nuther; but we allowed we'd tackle it. It warn't quite midnight, yet, so we cleared out for the mill, leaving Jim at work. We smouched the grindstone, and set out to roll her home, but it was a most nation tough job. Sometimes, do what we could, we couldn't keep her from falling over, and she come mighty near mashing us, every time. Tom said she was going to get one of us, sure, before we got through. We got her half way; and then we was plumb played out, and most drownded with sweat. We see it warn't no use, we got to go and fetch Jim. So he raised up his bed and slid the chain off of the bed-leg, and wrapt it round and round his neck, and we crawled out through our hole and down there, and Jim and me laid into that grindstone and walked her along like nothing; and Tom superintended. He could out-superintend any boy I ever see. He knowed how to do everything.

A TOUGH JOB.

Our hole was pretty big, but it warn't big enough to get the grindstone through; but Jim he took the pick and soon made it big enough. Then Tom marked out them things on it with the nail, and set Jim to work on them, with the nail for a chisel and an iron bolt from the rubbage in the lean-to for a hammer, and told him to work till the rest of his candle quit on him, and then he could go to bed, and hide the grindstone under his straw tick and sleep on it. Then we helped him fix his chain back, on the bedleg, and was ready for bed ourselves. But Tom thought of something, and says:

"You got any spiders in here, Jim?"

"No, sah, thanks to goodness I hain't, mars Tom."

"All right, we'll get you some."

"But bless you, honey, I doan *want* none. I's afeard un um. I jis' 's soon have rattlesnakes aroun'."

Tom thought a minute or two, and says:

"It's a good idea. And I reckon it's been done. It *must* a been done: it stands to reason. Yes, it's a prime good idea. Where could you keep it?"

"Keep what, mars Tom?"

"Why, a rattlesnake."

"De goodness gracious alive, mars Tom! Why, if dey was a rattlesnake to come in heah, I'd take en bust right out thoo dat log wall, I would, wid my head."

"Why, Jim, you wouldn't be afraid of it, after a little. You could tame it."

"*Tame* it!"

"Yes—easy enough. Every animal is grateful for kindness and petting, and they wouldn't *think* of hurting a person that pets them. Any book will tell you that. You try—that's all I ask; just try for two or three days. Why, you can get him so, in a little while, that he'll love you; and sleep with you; and won't stay away from you a minute; and will let you wrap him round your neck and put his head in your mouth."

"*Please*, mars Tom—*doan'* talk so! I can't *stan'* it! He'd *let* me shove his head in my mouf—fer a favor, hain't it? I lay he'd wait a pow'ful long time 'fo' I *ast* him. En mo' en dat, I doan' *want* him to sleep wid me."

"Jim, don't act so foolish. A prisoner's *got* to have some kind of a dumb pet, and if a rattlesnake hain't ever been tried, why there's more glory to be gained in your being the first to ever try it than any other way you could ever think of to save your life."

"Why, mars Tom, I doan' *want* no sich glory. Snake take 'n bite Jim's chin off, den *whah* is de glory? No, sah, I doan' want no sich doin's."

"Blame it, can't you *try*? I only *want* you to try—you needn't keep it up if it don't work."

"But de trouble all *done*, ef de snake bite me while I's a-tryin' him. Mars Tom, I's willin' to tackle mos' anything 'at ain't onreasonable, but ef you en Huck fetches a rattlesnake in heah for me to tame, I's gwyne to *leave*, dat's *shore*."

"Well, then, let it go, let it go, if you're so bullheaded about it. We can get you some garter-snakes and you can tie some buttons on their tails, and let on they're rattlesnakes, and I reckon that'll have to do."

"I k'n stan' *dem*, mars Tom, but blame' 'f I couldn' git along widout um, I tell you dat. I never knowed, b'fo', 't was so much bother and trouble to be a prisoner."

BUTTONS ON THEIR TAILS.

"Well, it *always* is, when it's done right. You got any rats around here?"

"No, sah, I hain't seed none."

"Well, we'll get you some rats."

"Why, mars Tom, I doan *want* no rats. Dey's de dad-blamedest creturs to 'sturb a body, en rustle roun' over 'im, en bite his feet, when he's tryin' to sleep, I ever see. No, sah, gimme g'yarter snakes, 'f I's got to have 'm, but doan' gimme no rats, I ain' got no use f'r um, skasely."

"But Jim, you *got* to have 'em,—they all do. So don't make no more fuss about it. Prisoners ain't ever without rats. There ain't no instance of it. And they train them, and pet them, and learn them tricks, and they get to be as sociable as flies. But you got to play music to them. You got anything to play music on?"

"I ain' got nuffn but a coase comb en a piece o' paper, en a juice-harp; but I reck'n dey wouldn' take no stock in a juice-harp."

"Yes they would. *They* don't care what kind of music 'tis. A jewsharp's plenty good enough for a rat. All animals likes music— in a prison; they dote on it. Specially, painful music; and you can't get no other kind out of a jewsharp. It always interests them; they come out to see what's the matter with you. Yes, you're all right; you're fixed very well. You want to set on your bed, nights, before you go to sleep, and early in the mornings, and play your jewsharp; play The Last Link is Broken—that's the thing that'll scoop a rat, quicker'n anything else: and when you've played about two minutes, you'll see all the rats, and the snakes, and spiders, and things begin to feel worried about you, and come. And they'll just fairly swarm over you, and have a noble good time."

"Yes, *dey* will, I reck'n, mars Tom, but what kine er time is *Jim* havin'? Blest if I kin see de pint. But I'll do it, ef I got to. I reck'n I better keep de animals satisfied, en not have no trouble in de house."

Tom waited to think over, and see if there wasn't nothing else; and pretty soon he says:

"Oh—there's one thing I forgot. Could you raise a flower here, do you reckon?"

"I doan' know but maybe I could, mars Tom; but it's tolable dark in heah, en I ain' got no use f'r no flower, nohow, en she'd be a powful sight o' trouble."

"Well, you try it, anyway. Some other prisoners has done it."

"One er dem big cat-tail-lookin' mullen-stalks would grow in heah, mars Tom, I reck'n, but she wouldn' be wuth half de trouble she'd coss."

"Don't you believe it. We'll fetch you a little one, and you plant it in the corner, over there, and raise it. And don't call it mullen, call it Pitchiola—that's its right name, when it's in a prison. And you want to water it with your tears."

"Why, I got plenty spring water, mars Tom."

"You don't *want* spring water; you want to water it with your tears. It's the way they always do."

IRRIGATION.

"Why mars Tom, I lay I kin raise one er dem mullen-stalks twyste wid spring water whiles another man's a *start*'n one wid tears."

"That ain't the idea. You *got* to do it with tears."

"She'll die on my han's, mars Tom, she sholy will; kase I doan' skasely ever cry."

So Tom was stumped. But he studied it over, and then said Jim would have to worry along the best he could with an onion. He promised he would go to the nigger cabins and drop one, private, in Jim's coffee pot, in the morning. Jim said he would "jis' 's soon have tobacker in his coffee;" and found so much fault with it, and with the work and bother of raising the mullen, and jewsharping the rats, and petting and flattering up the snakes and spiders and things, on top of all the other work he had to do on pens, and inscriptions, and journals, and things, which made it more trouble and worry and responsibility to be a prisoner than anything he ever undertook, that Tom most lost all patience with him; and said he was just loadened down with more gaudier chances than a prisoner ever had in the world to make a name for himself, and yet he didn't know enough to appreciate them, and they was just about wasted on him. So Jim he was sorry, and said he wouldn't behave so no more, and then me and Tom shoved for bed.

Chapter XXXIX

KEEPING OFF DULL TIMES.

In the morning we went up to the village and bought a wire rat trap and fetched it down, and unstopped the best rat hole, and in about an hour we had fifteen of the bulliest kind of ones; and then we took it and put it in a safe place under aunt Sally's bed. But while we was gone for spiders, little Thomas Franklin Benjamin Jefferson Elexander Phelps found it there, and opened the door of it to see if the rats would come out, and they did; and aunt Sally she come in, and when we got back she was a standing on top of the bed raising Cain, and the rats was doing what they could to keep off the dull times for her. So she took and dusted us both with the hickry, and we was as much as two hours catching another fifteen or sixteen, drat that meddlesome cub, and they warn't the likeliest, nuther, because the first haul was the pick of the flock. I never see a likelier lot of rats than what that first haul was.

We got a splendid stock of sorted spiders, and bugs, and frogs, and caterpillars, and one thing or another; and we like-to got a hornet's nest, but we didn't. The family was at home. We didn't give it right up, but staid with them as long as we could; because we allowed we'd tire them out or they'd got to tire us out, and they done it. Then we got allycumpain and rubbed on the places, and was pretty near all right, again, but couldn't set down convenient. And so we went for the snakes, and grabbed a couple of dozen garters and house-snakes, and put them in a bag, and put it in our room, and by that time it was supper time, and a rattling good honest day's work; and hungry?—oh, no, I reckon not! And there warn't a blessed snake up there, when we went back—we didn't half tie the sack, and they worked out, somehow, and left. But it didn't matter much, because they was still on the premises somewheres. So we judged we could get some of them again. No, there warn't no real scarcity of snakes about the house for a considerble spell. You'd see them dripping from the rafters and places, every now and then; and they generly landed in your plate, or down the back of your neck, and most of the time where you didn't want them. Well, they was handsome, and striped, and there warn't no harm in a million of them; but that never made no difference to aunt Sally, she despised snakes, be the breed what they might, and she couldn't stand them, no way you could fix it; and every time one of them flopped down on her, it didn't make no difference what she was doing, she would just lay that work down and light out. I never see such a woman. And you could hear her whoop to Jericho. You couldn't get her to take aholt of one of them with the tongs. And if she turned over and found one in bed, she would scramble out and lift a howl that you would think the house was afire. She disturbed the old man so, that he said he could most wish there hadn't ever been no snakes created. Why, after every last snake had been gone clear out of the house for as much as a week, aunt Sally warn't over it yet; she warn't near over it; when she was setting thinking about something, you could touch her on the back of her neck with a feather and she would jump right out of her stockings. It was very curious. But Tom said all women was just so. He said they was made that way; for some reason or other.

We got a licking every time one of our snakes come in her way; and she allowed these lickings warn't nothing to what she would do if we ever loaded up the place again with them. I didn't mind the lickings, because they didn't amount to nothing; but I minded the trouble we had, to lay in another lot. But we got them laid in, and all the other things; and you never see a cabin as blithesome as Jim's was when they'd all swarm out for music and go for him. Jim didn't like the spiders, and the spiders didn't like Jim; and so they'd lay for him and make it mighty warm for him. And he said that between the rats, and the snakes, and the grindstone, there warn't no room in bed for him, skasely; and when there was, a body couldn't sleep, it was so lively, and it was always lively, he said, because *they* never all slept at one time, but took turn about, so when the snakes was asleep the rats was on deck, and when the rats turned in the snakes come on watch, so he always had one gang under him, in his way, and t'other gang having a circus over him, and if he got up to hunt a new place, the spiders would take a chance at him as he crossed over. He said if he ever got out, this time, he wouldn't ever be a prisoner again, not for a salary.

Well, by the end of three weeks, everything was in pretty good shape. The shirt was sent in early, in a pie, and every time a rat bit

SAWDUST DIET.

Jim he would get up and write a little in his journal, whilst the ink was fresh; the pens was made, the inscriptions and so-on was all carved on the grindstone; the bed-leg was sawed in two, and we had et up the sawdust, and it give us a most amazing stomach-ache. We reckoned we was all going to die, but didn't. It was the most undigestible sawdust I ever see; and Tom said the same. But as I was saying, we'd got all the work done, now, at last; and we was all pretty much fagged out, too, but mainly Jim. The old man had wrote a couple of times to the plantation below Orleans to come and get their runaway nigger, but hadn't got no answer, because there warn't no such plantation; so he allowed he would advertise Jim in the St. Louis and New Orleans papers; and when he mentioned the St. Louis ones, it give me the cold shivers, and I see we hadn't no time to lose. So Tom said, now for the nonnamous letters.

"What's them?" I says.

"Warnings to the people that something is up. Sometimes it's done one way, sometimes another. But there's always somebody spying around, that gives notice to the governor of the castle. When Louis XVI was going to light out of the Tooleries, a servant girl done it. It's a very good way, and so is the nonnamous letters. We'll use them both. And it's usual for the prisoner's mother to change clothes with him, and she stays in, and he slides out in her clothes. We'll do that, too."

"But lookyhere, Tom, what do we want to *warn* anybody for, that something's up? Let them find it out for themselves—it's their lookout."

"Yes, I know; but you can't depend on them. It's the way they've acted from the very start—left us to do *everything*. They're so confiding and mullet-headed they don't take notice of nothing at all. So if we don't *give* them notice, there won't be nobody nor nothing to interfere with us, and so after all our hard work and trouble this escape 'll go off perfectly flat: won't amount to nothing—won't be nothing *to* it."

"Well, as for me, Tom, that's the way I'd like."

"Shucks," he says, and looked disgusted. So I says:

"But I ain't going to make no complaint. Any way that suits you suits me. What you going to do about the servant girl?"

"You'll be her. You slide in, in the middle of the night, and hook that yaller girl's frock."

"Why, Tom, that'll make trouble, next morning, because of course she prob'ly hain't got any but that one."

"I know; but you don't want it but fifteen minutes, to carry the nonnamous letter and shove it under the front door."

"All right, then, I'll do it; but I could carry it just as handy in my own togs."

"You wouldn't look like a servant girl *then*, would you?"

"No, but there won't be nobody to see what I look like, *anyway*."

"That ain't got nothing to do with it. The thing for us to do, is just to do our *duty*, and not worry about whether anybody *sees* us do it or not. Hain't you got no principle at all?"

"All right, I ain't saying nothing: I'm the servant girl. Who's Jim's mother?"

"I'm his mother. I'll hook a gown from aunt Sally."

"Well, then, you'll have to stay in the cabin when me and Jim leaves."

"Not much. I'll stuff Jim's clothes full of straw and lay it on his bed to represent his mother in disguise, and Jim 'll take aunt Sally's gown off of me and wear it, and we'll all evade together. When a prisoner of style escapes, it's called an evasion. It's always called so when a king escapes, frinstance. And the same with a king's son; it don't make no difference whether he's a natural one or an unnatural one."

So Tom he wrote the nonnamous letter, and I smouched the yaller wench's frock, that night, and put it on, and shoved it under the front door, the way Tom told me to. It said:

TROUBLE IS BREWING.

Beware. Trouble is brewing. Keep a sharp lookout. UNKNOWN FRIEND.

Next night, we stuck a picture which Tom drawed in blood, of a skull and crossbones, on the front door; and next night another one of a coffin, on the back door. I never see a family in such a sweat. They couldn't a been worse scared if the place had a been full of ghosts laying for them behind everything and under the beds and shivering through the air. If a door banged, aunt Sally she jumped, and said "ouch!" if anything fell, she jumped and said "ouch!" if you happened to touch her, when she warn't noticing, she done the same; she couldn't face noway and be satisfied, because she allowed there was something behind her every time—so she was always a whirling around, sudden, and saying "ouch," and before she'd get two-thirds around, she'd whirl back again, and say it again; and she was afraid to go to bed, but she dasn't set up. So the thing was working very well, Tom said; he said he never see a thing work more satisfactory. He said it showed it was done right.

So he said, now for the grand bulge! So the very next morning at the streak of dawn we got another letter ready, and was wondering what we better do with it, because we heard them say at supper they was going to have a nigger on watch at both doors all night. Tom he went down the lightning rod to spy around; and the nigger at the back door was asleep, and he stuck it in the back of his neck and come back. This letter said:

Don't betray me, I wish to be your friend. There is a desprate gang of cutthroats from over in the Ingean Territory going to steal your runaway nigger to-night, and they have been trying to scare you so as you will stay in the house and not bother them. I am one of the gang, but have got relig-gion and wish to quit it and lead a honest life again, and will betray the helish design. They will sneak down from northards, along the fence, at midnight exact, with a false key, and go in the nigger's cabin to get him. I am to be off a piece and blow a tin horn if I see any danger; but stead of that, I will BA *like a sheep soon as they get in and not blow at all; then whilst they are getting his chains loose, you slip there and lock them in, and can kill them at your leasure. Don't do anything but just the way I am telling you, if you do they will suspicion something and raise whoopjam-boreehoo. I do not wish any reward but to know I have done the right thing.* UNKNOWN FRIEND.

Chapter XL

FISHING.

We was feeling pretty good, after breakfast, and took my canoe and went over the river a-fishing, with a lunch, and had a good time, and took a look at the raft and found her all right, and got home late to supper, and found them in such a sweat and worry they didn't know which end they was standing on, and made us go right off to bed the minute we was done supper, and wouldn't tell us what the trouble was, and never let on a word about the new letter, but didn't need to, because we knowed as much about it as anybody did, and as soon as we was half up stairs and her back was turned, we slid for the cellar cubboard and loaded up a good lunch and took it up to our room and went to bed, and got up about half past eleven, and Tom put on aunt Sally's dress that he stole and was going to start with the lunch, but says:

"Where's the butter?"

"I laid out a hunk of it," I says, "on a piece of a corn-pone."

"Well, you *left* it laid out, then—it ain't here."

"We can get along without it," I says.

"We can get along *with* it, too," he says; "just you slide down cellar and fetch it. And then mosey right down the lightning rod and come along. I'll go and stuff the straw into Jim's clothes to represent his mother in disguise, and be ready to *ba* like a sheep and shove, soon as you get there."

So out he went, and down cellar went I. The hunk of butter, big as a person's fist, was where I had left it, so I took up the slab of corn-pone with it on, and blowed out my light, and started up stairs, very stealthy, and got up to the main floor all right, but here comes aunt Sally with a candle, and I clapped the truck in my hat, and clapped my hat on my head, and the next second she see me; and she says:

"You been down cellar?"

"Yes'm."

"What you been doing down there?"

"Noth'n."

"*Noth'n!*"

"No'm."

"Well, then, what possessed you to go down there, this time of night?"

"I don't know'm."

"You don't *know?* Don't answer me that way, Tom, I want to know what you been *doing* down there?"

"I hain't been doing a single thing, aunt Sally, I hope to gracious if I have."

I reckoned she'd let me go, now, and as a generl thing she would; but I spose there was so many strange things going on she was just in a sweat about every little thing that warn't yard-stick straight; so she says, very decided:

"You just march into that setting-room and stay there till I come. You been up to something you no business to, and I lay I'll find out what it is before *I'm* done with you."

So she went away as I opened the door and walked into the setting room. My, but there was a crowd there! Fifteen farmers, and every one of them had a gun. I was most powerful sick, and slunk to a chair and set down. They was setting around, some of them talking a little, in a low voice, and all of them fidgety and uneasy, but trying to look like they warn't; but I knowed they was, because they was always taking off their hats, and putting them on, and scratching their heads, and changing their seats, and fumbling with their buttons. I warn't easy, myself, but I didn't take my hat off, all the same.

I did wish aunt Sally would come, and get done with me, and lick me, if she wanted to, and let me get away and tell Tom how we'd overdone this thing, and what a thundering hornet's nest we'd got ourselves into, so we could stop fooling around, straight off, and clear out with Jim before these rips got out of patience and come for us.

At last she come, and begun to ask me questions, but I *couldn't* answer them straight, I didn't know which end of me was up; because these men was in such a fidget, now, that some was wanting to start right *now* and lay for them desperadoes, and saying it warn't but a few minutes to midnight; and others was trying to get them to hold on and wait for the sheep-signal; and here was aunty pegging away at the questions, and me a shaking all over and ready to sink

EVERY ONE HAD A GUN.

down in my tracks I was that scared; and the place getting hotter and hotter, and the butter beginning to melt and run down my neck and behind my ears; and pretty soon, when one of them says, "*I'm* for going and getting in the cabin *first*, and right *now*, and catching them when they come," I most dropped; and a streak of butter come a trickling down my forehead, and aunt Sally she see it, and turns white as a sheet, and says:

"For the land's sake what *is* the matter with the child!—he's got the brain fever as shore as you're born, and they're oozing out!"

And everybody runs to see, and she snatches off my hat, and out comes the bread, and what was left of the butter, and she grabbed me, and hugged me, and says:

"Oh, what a turn you did give me! and how glad and grateful I am it ain't no worse; for luck's against us, and it never rains but it pours, and when I see that truck I thought we'd lost you, for I knowed by the color and all, it was just like your brains would be if— Dear, dear, whydn't you *tell* me that was what you'd been down there for, *I* wouldn't a cared. Now cler out to bed, and don't lemme see no more of you till morning!"

I was up stairs in a second, and down the lightning rod in another one, and shinning through the dark for the lean-to. I couldn't hardly get my words out, I was so anxious; but I told Tom as quick as I could, we must jump for it, now, and not a minute to lose—the house full of men, yonder, with guns!

His eyes just blazed; and he says:

"No!—is that so? *Ain't* it bully! Why, Huck, if it was to do over again, I bet I could fetch two hundred! If we could put it off till—"

"Hurry! *hurry!*" I says. "Where's Jim?"

"Right at your elbow; if you reach out your arm you can touch him. He's dressed, and everything's ready. Now we'll slide out and give the sheep-signal."

But then we heard the tramp of men, coming to the door, and heard them begin to fumble with the padlock; and heard a man say:

"I *told* you we'd be too soon; they haven't come—the door is locked. Here—I'll lock some of you into the cabin and you lay for 'em in the dark and kill 'em when they come; and the rest scatter around a piece, and listen if you can hear 'em coming."

So in they come, but couldn't see us in the dark, and most trod on us whilst we was hustling to get under the bed. But we got under, all right, and out through the hole, swift but soft—Jim first, me next, and Tom last, which was according to Tom's orders. Now we was in the lean-to, and heard trampings close by, outside. So we crept to the door, and Tom stopped us there and put his eye to the crack, but couldn't make out nothing, it was so dark; and whispered and said he would listen for the steps to get further, and when he nudged us Jim must glide out first, and him last. So he set his ear to the crack and listened, and listened, and listened, and the steps a scraping around, out there, all the time; and at last he nudged us, and we slid out, and stooped down, not breathing, and not making the least noise, and slipped stealthy towards the fence, in Injun file, and got to it, all right, and me and Jim over it; but Tom's britches catched fast on a splinter on the top rail, and then he hear the steps coming, so he had to pull loose, which snapped the splinter and made a noise; and as he dropped in our tracks and started, somebody sings out:

"Who's that? Answer, or I'll shoot!"

But we didn't answer; we just unfurled our heels and shoved.

TOM CAUGHT ON A SPLINTER.

Then there was a rush, and a *bang, bang, bang!* and the bullets fairly whizzed around us! We heard them sing out:

"Here they are! They've broke for the river! after 'em, boys! And turn loose the dogs!"

So here they come, full tilt. We could hear them, because they wore boots, and yelled, but we didn't wear no boots, and didn't yell. We was in the path to the mill; and when they got pretty close onto us, we dodged into the bush and let them go by, and then dropped in behind them. They'd had all the dogs shut up, so they wouldn't scare off the robbers; but by this time somebody had let them loose, and here they come, making pow-wow enough for a million; but they was our dogs; so we stopped in our tracks till they catched up; and when they see it warn't nobody but us, and no excitement to offer them, they only just said howdy, and tore right ahead towards the shouting and clattering; and then we up steam again and whizzed along after them till we was nearly to the mill, and then struck up through the bush to where my canoe was tied, and hopped in and pulled for dear life towards the middle of the river, but didn't make no more noise than we was obleeged to. Then we struck out, easy and comfortable, for the island where my raft was; and we could hear them yelling and barking at each other all up and down the bank, till we was so far away the sounds got dim and died out. And when we stepped onto the raft, I says:

"*Now*, old Jim, you're a free man *again*, and I bet you won't ever be a slave no more."

"En a mighty good job it wuz, too, Huck. It 'uz planned beautiful, en it 'uz *done* beautiful; en dey ain't *nobody* kin git up a plan dat's mo' mixed-up en splendid den what dat one wuz."

We was all as glad as we could be, but Tom was the gladdest of all, because he had a bullet in the calf of his leg.

When me and Jim heard that, we didn't feel so brash as what we did before. It was hurting him considerble, and bleeding; so we laid him in the wigwam and tore up one of the duke's shirts for to bandage him; but he says:

"Gimme the rags, I can do it myself. Don't stop, now; don't fool around here, and the evasion booming along so handsome: man the sweeps, and set her loose! Boys, we done it elegant!—'deed we did. I wish *we*'d a had the handling of Louis XVI, there wouldn't a been no 'Son of Saint Louis, ascend to heaven!' wrote down in *his* biography: no, sir, we'd a whooped him over the *border*—that's what we'd a done with *him*—and done it just as slick as nothing at all, too. Man the sweeps—man the sweeps!"

But me and Jim was consulting—and thinking. And after we'd thought a minute, I says:

"Say it, Jim."

So he says:

"Well, den, dis is de way it look to me, Huck. Ef it wuz *him* dat 'uz bein' sot free, en one er de boys wuz to git shot, would he say, 'Go on en save me, nemmine 'bout a doctor f'r to save dis one?' Is

dat like mars Tom Sawyer? Would he say dat? You *bet* he wouldn't!
Well den—is *Jim* gwyne to say it? No, sah—I doan' budge a step
out'n dis place, 'dout a *doctor;* not ef it's forty year!"

I knowed he was white inside, and I reckoned he'd say what he
did say—so it was all right, now, and I told Tom I was agoing for a

JIM ADVISES A DOCTOR.

doctor. He raised considerble row about it, but me and Jim stuck to
it and wouldn't budge; so he was for crawling out and setting the raft
loose himself; but we wouldn't let him. Then he give us a piece of
his mind—but it didn't do no good.

So when he see me getting the canoe ready, he says:

"Well, then, if you're bound to go, I'll tell you the way to do, when
you get to the village. Shut the door, and blindfold the doctor tight
and fast, and make him swear to be silent as the grave, and put a
purse full of gold in his hand, and then take and lead him all around
the back alleys and everywheres, in the dark, and then fetch him
here in the canoe, in a roundabout way amongst the islands, and

search him and take his chalk away from him, and don't give it back to him till you get him back to the village, or else he will chalk this raft so he can find it again. It's the way they all do."

So I said I would, and left, and Jim was to hide in the woods when he see the doctor coming, till he was gone again.

Chapter XLI

THE DOCTOR.

The doctor was an old man; a very nice, kind looking old man, when I got him up. I told him me and my brother was over on Spanish island hunting, yesterday after noon, and camped on a piece of a raft we found, and about midnight he must a kicked his gun in his dreams, for it went off and shot him in the leg; and we wanted him to go over there and fix it and not say nothing about it, nor let anybody know, because we wanted to come home this evening, and surprise the folks.

"Who is your folks?" he says.

"The Phelpses, down yonder."

"Oh," he says. And after a minute, he says: "How'd you say he got shot?"

"He had a dream," I says, "and it shot him."

"Singular dream," he says.

So he lit up his lantern, and got his saddlebags, and we started. But when he see the canoe, he didn't like the look of her—said she was big enough for one, but didn't look pretty safe for two. I says:

"O, you needn't be afeard, sir, she carried the three of us, easy enough."

"What three?"

"Why, me and Sid, and—and—and *the guns*; that's what I mean."

"Oh," he says.

But he put his foot on the gunnel, and rocked her; and shook his head, and said he reckoned he'd look around for a bigger one. But they was all locked and chained; so he took my canoe, and said for

me to wait till he come back, or I could hunt around further, or
maybe I better go down home and get them ready for the surprise, if
I wanted to. But I said I didn't; so I told him just how to find the raft,
and then he started.

I struck an idea, pretty soon. I says to myself, spos'n he can't fix
that leg just in three shakes of a sheep's tail, as the saying is? spos'n
it takes him three or four days? What are we going to do?—lay
around there till he lets the cat out of the bag? No, sir, I know what
I'll do. I'll wait, and when he comes back, if he says he's got to go
any more, I'll get down there, too, if I swim; and we'll take and tie
him, and keep him, and shove out down the river; and when Tom's
done with him, we'll give him what it's worth, or all we got, and
then let him get ashore.

So then I crept into a lumber pile to get some sleep; and next time
I waked up the sun was away up over my head! I shot out, and went
for the doctor's house, but they told me he'd gone away in the night,
some time or other, and warn't back yet. Well, thinks I, that looks

UNCLE SILAS IN DANGER.

powerful bad for Tom, and I'll dig out for the island, right off. So away I shoved, and turned the corner, and nearly rammed my head into uncle Silas's stomach! He says:

"Why, *Tom!* Where you been, all this time, you rascal?"

"*I* hain't been nowheres," I says, "only just hunting for the runaway nigger—me and Sid."

"Why, where ever did you go?" he says. "Your aunt's been mighty uneasy."

"She needn't," I says, "because we was all right. We followed the men and the dogs, but they outrun us, and we lost them; but we thought we heard them on the water, so we got a canoe and took out after them, and crossed over, but couldn't find nothing of them; so we cruised along up shore till we got kind of tired and beat out; and tied up the canoe and went to sleep, and never waked up till about an hour ago, then we paddled over here to hear the news, and Sid's at the postoffice to see what he can hear, and I'm a-branching out to get something to eat for us, and then we're going home."

So then we went to the postoffice to get 'Sid'; but, just as I suspicioned, he warn't there; so the old man he got a letter out of the office, and we waited a while longer, but Sid didn't come; so the old man said come along, let Sid foot it home, or canoe-it, when he got done fooling around—but we would ride. I couldn't get him to let me stay and wait for Sid; and he said there warn't no use in it, and I must come along, and let aunt Sally see we was all right.

When we got home, aunt Sally was that glad to see me she laughed and cried both, and hugged me, and give me one of them lickings of hern that don't amount to shucks, and said she'd serve Sid the same when he come.

And the place was plumb full of farmers and farmers' wives, to dinner; and such another clack a body never heard. Old Mrs. Hotchkiss was the worst; her tongue was agoing all the time. She says:

"Well, sister Phelps, I've ransacked that-air cabin over, an' I b'lieve the nigger was crazy. I says so to sister Damrell—didn't I, sister Damrell?—s'I, he's crazy, s'I—them's the very words I said. You all hearn me: he's crazy, s'I; everything shows it, s'I. Look at that-air grindstone, s'I: want to tell *me* 't any cretur 'ts in his right mind 's agoin' to scrabble all them crazy things onto a grindstone, s'I? Here sich 'n' sich a person busted his heart; 'n' here so 'n' so pegged along for thirty-seven year, 'n' all that—natcherl son o' Louis somebody, 'n' sich everlast'n rubbage. He's plumb crazy, s'I; it's what I says in the fust place, it's what I says in the middle, 'n' it's what I says last 'n' all the time—the nigger's crazy—crazy 's Nebo-koodneezer, s'I."

"An' look at that-air ladder made out'n rags, sister Hotchkiss," says old Mrs. Damrell, "what in the name o' goodness *could* he ever want of—"

OLD MRS. HOTCHKISS.

"The very words I was a-sayin' no longer ago th'n this minute to sister Utterback, 'n' she'll tell you so herself. Sh-she, look at that-air rag ladder, sh-she; 'n' s'I, yes, *look* at it, s'I—what *could* he a wanted of it, s'I. Sh-she, sister Hotchkiss, sh-she—"

"But how in the nation'd they ever *git* that grindstone *in* there, *any*way? 'n' who dug that-air *hole?* 'n' who—"

"My very *words*, Brer Penrod! I was a-sayin'—pass that-air sasser o' m'lasses, won't ye?—I was a-sayin' to sister Dunlap, jist this minute, how *did* they git that grindstone in there, s'I. Without *help*, mind you—'thout *help! Thar's* wher' 'tis. Don't tell *me*, s'I; there *wuz* help, s'I; 'n' ther' wuz a *plenty* help, too, s'I; ther's ben a *dozen* a-helpin' that nigger, 'n' I lay I'd skin every last nigger on this place, but *I'd* find out who done it, s'I; 'n' moreover, s'I—"

"A *dozen*, says you!—*forty* couldn't a done everything that's been done. Look at them caseknife saws and things, how tedious they've been made; look at that bed-leg sawed off with 'm, a week's work for six men; look at that nigger made out'n straw on the bed; and look at—"

"You may *well* say it, Brer Hightower! It's jist as I was a-sayin' to Brer Phelps, his own self. S'e, what do *you* think of it, sister Hotchkiss, s'e; think o' what, Brer Phelps, s'I; think o' that bed-leg sawed off that a way, s'e; *think* of it? s'I; I lay it never sawed *itself* off, s'I— somebody *sawed* it, s'I; that's my opinion, take it or leave it, it mayn't be no 'count, s'I, but sich as 't is, it's my opinion, s'I, 'n' if anybody k'n start a better one, s'I, let him *do* it, s'I, that's all. I says to sister Dunlap, s'I—"

"Why, dog my cats, they must a ben a house-full o' niggers in there every night for four weeks, to a done all that work, sister Phelps. Look at that shirt—every last inch of it kivered over with secret African writ'n, done with blood! Must a ben a raft uv 'm at it right along, all the time, amost. Why, I'd give two dollars to have it read to me; 'n' as for the niggers that wrote it, I 'low I'd take 'n' lash 'm t'll—"

"People to *help* him, Brother Marples! Well, I reckon you'd *think* so, if you'd a been in this house for a while back. Why, they've stole everything they could lay their hands on—and we a watching, all the time, mind you. They stole that shirt right off o' the line! and as for that sheet they made the rag ladder out of, ther' ain't no telling how many times they *didn't* steal that; and flour, and candles, and candlesticks, and spoons, and the old warming pan, and most a thousand things that I disremember, now, and my new calico dress; and me, and Silas, and my Sid and Tom on the constant watch day *and* night, as I was a-telling you, and not a one of us could catch hide nor hair, nor sight nor sound of them; and here at the last minute, lo and behold you, they slides right in under our noses, and fools us, and not only fools *us* but the Injun Territory robbers too, and actuly gets *away* with that nigger, safe and sound, and that with sixteen men and twenty-two dogs right on their very heels at that very time! I tell you, it just bangs anything I ever *heard* of. Why, *sperits* couldn't a done better, and been no smarter. And I reckon they must a *been* sperits—because, *you* know our dogs, and ther' ain't no better: well, them dogs never even got on the *track* of 'm, once! You explain *that* to me, if you can!—*any* of you!"

"Well, it does beat—"

"Laws alive, I never—"

"So help me, I wouldn't a be—"

"*House*-thieves as well as—"

"Goodnessgracioussakes, I'd a ben afeard to *live* in sich a—"

" 'Fraid to *live!*—why, I was that scared I dasn't hardly go to bed, or get up, or lay down, or *set* down, sister Ridgeway. Why, they'd steal the very—why, goodness sakes, you can guess what kind of a fluster *I* was in by the time midnight come, last night. I hope to gracious if I warn't afraid they'd steal some o' the family! I was just to that pass, I didn't have no reasoning faculties no more. It looks foolish enough, *now*, in the daytime; but I says to myself, there's my two poor boys asleep, 'way up stairs in that lonesome room, and I declare to goodness I was that uneasy 't I crep' up there and locked 'em in! I *did*. And anybody would. Because, you know, when you get scared, that way, and it keeps running on, and getting worse and worse, all the time, and your wits gets to addling, and you get to doing all sorts o' wild things, and by and by you think to yourself, spos'n *I* was a boy, and was away up there, and the door ain't locked, and you—" She stopped, looking kind of wondering, and then she turned her head around slow, and when her eye lit on me—I got up and took a walk.

Says I to myself, I can explain better how we come to not be in that room this morning, if I go out to one side and study over it a little. So I done it. But I dasn't go fur, or she'd a sent for me. And when it was late in the day, the people all went, and then I come in and told her the noise and shooting waked up me and 'Sid,' and the door was locked, and we wanted to see the fun, so we went down the lightning rod, and both of us got hurt a little, and we didn't never want to try *that* no more. And then I went on and told her all what I told uncle Silas before; and then she said she'd forgive us, and maybe it was all right enough, anyway, and about what a body might expect of boys, for all boys was a pretty harum-scarum lot, as fur as she could see; and so, as long as no harm hadn't come of it, she judged she better put in her time being grateful we was alive and well and she had us still, stead of fretting over what was past and done. So then she kissed me, and patted me on the head, and dropped into a kind of a brown study; and pretty soon jumps up and says:

"Why, lawsamercy, it's most night, and Sid not come yet! What *has* become of that boy?"

I see my chance; so I skips up and says:

"I'll run right up to town and get him," I says.

"No you won't," she says. "You'll stay right wher' you are; *one's* enough to be lost at a time. If he ain't here to supper, your uncle 'll go."

Well, he warn't there to supper; so right after supper, uncle went.

He come back about ten, a little bit uneasy; hadn't run across Tom's track. Aunt Sally was a good *deal* uneasy; but uncle Silas he said there warn't no occasion to be—boys will be boys, he said, and you'll see this one turn up in the morning, all sound and right. So she had to be satisfied. But she said she'd set up for him a while, anyway, and keep a light burning, so he could see it.

And then when I went up to bed, she come up with me, and fetched her candle, and tucked me in, and mothered me so good I felt mean and like I couldn't look her in the face; and she set down on the bed and talked with me a long time, and said what a splendid boy Sid was, and didn't seem to want to ever stop talking about him; and kept asking me every now and then, if I reckoned he could a got lost, or hurt, or maybe drownded, and might be laying at this minute, somewheres, suffering or dead, and she not by him to help him; and

AUNT SALLY TALKS TO HUCK.

so the tears would drip down, silent, and I would tell her that Sid was all right, and would be home in the morning, sure; and she would squeeze my hand, or maybe kiss me, and tell me to say it again, and keep on saying it, because it done her good, and she was in so much trouble. And when she was going away, she looked down in my eyes, so steady and gentle, and says:

"The door ain't going to be locked, Tom; and there's the window and the rod; but you'll be good, *won't* you? And you won't go? For *my* sake."

Laws knows I *wanted* to go, bad enough, to see about Tom, and was all intending to go; but after that, I wouldn't a went, not for kingdoms.

But she was on my mind, and Tom was on my mind; so I slept very restless. And twice I went down the rod, away in the night, and slipped around front, and see her setting there by her candle in the window with her eyes towards the road and the tears in them; and I wished I could do something for her, but I couldn't, only to swear that I wouldn't never do nothing to grieve her any more. And the third time, I waked up at dawn, and slid down, and she was there yet, and her candle was most out, and her old gray head was resting on her hand, and she was asleep.

Chapter XLII

TOM SAWYER WOUNDED.

The old man was up town again, before breakfast, but couldn't get no track of Tom; and both of them set at the table, thinking, and not saying nothing, and looking mournful, and their coffee getting cold, and not eating anything. And by and by the old man says:

"Did I give you the letter?"

"What letter?"

"The one I got yesterday, out of the postoffice."

"No, you didn't give me no letter."

"Well, I must a forgot it."

So he rummaged his pockets, and then went off somewheres where he had laid it down, and fetched it, and give it to her. She says:

"Why, it's from St. Petersburg—it's from Sis."

I allowed another walk would do me good; but I couldn't stir. But before she could break it open, she dropped it and run—for she see something. And so did I. It was Tom Sawyer on a mattrass; and that old doctor; and Jim, in *her* calico dress, with his hands tied behind him; and a lot of people. I hid the letter behind the first thing that come handy, and rushed. She flung herself at Tom, crying, and says:

"O, he's dead, he's dead, I know he's dead!"

And Tom he turned his head a little, and muttered something or other, which showed he warn't in his right mind; then she flung up her hands, and says:

"He's alive, thank God! And that's enough!" and she snatched a kiss of him, and flew for the house, to get the bed ready, and scattering orders right and left at the niggers and everybody else, as fast as her tongue could go, every jump of the way.

I followed the men to see what they was going to do with Jim; and the old doctor and uncle Silas followed after Tom into the house. The men was very huffy, and some of them wanted to hang Jim, for an example to all the other niggers around there, so they wouldn't be trying to run away, like Jim done, and making such a raft of trouble, and keeping a whole family scared most to death for days and nights. But the others said, don't do it, it wouldn't answer at all, he ain't our nigger, and his owner would turn up and make us pay for him, sure. So that cooled them down a little, because the people that's always the most anxious for to hang a nigger that hain't done just right, is always the very ones that ain't the most anxious to pay for him when they've got their satisfaction out of him.

They cussed Jim considerble, though, and give him a cuff or two, side the head, once in a while, but Jim never said nothing, and he never let on to know me, and they took him to the same cabin, and put his own clothes on him, and chained him again, and not to no bed-leg, this time, but to a big staple drove into the bottom log, and chained his hands, too, and both legs, and said he warn't to have nothing but bread and water to eat, after this, till his owner come or he was sold at auction because he didn't come in a certain length of time, and filled up our hole, and said a couple of farmers with guns must stand watch around about the cabin every night, and a bulldog tied to the door in the daytime, and about this time they was through with the job and was tapering off with a kind of generl goodbye cussing, and then the old doctor comes, and takes a look, and says:

"Don't be no rougher on him than you're obleeged to, because he ain't a bad nigger. When I got to where I found the boy, I see I couldn't cut the bullet out without some help, and he warn't in no condition for me to leave, to go and get help; and he got a little worse and a little worse, and after a long time he went out of his head, and wouldn't let me come anigh him, any more, and said if I chalked his raft he'd kill me, and no end of wild foolishness like that, and I see I couldn't do anything at all with him; so I says, I got to have *help*, somehow; and the minute I says it, out crawls this nigger from somewheres, and says he'll help; and he done it, too, and done it very well. Of course I judged he must be a runaway nigger, and there I *was!* and there I had to stick, right straight along, all the rest of the day, and all night. It was a fix, I tell you! I had a couple of patients with the chills, and of course I'd of liked to run up to town and see them, but I dasn't, because the nigger might get away, and then I'd be to blame; and yet never a skiff come close enough for me to hail.

THE DOCTOR SPEAKS FOR JIM.

So there I had to stick, plumb till daylight this morning; and I never see a nigger that was a better nuss or faithfuller, and yet he was resking his freedom to do it, and was all tired out, too, and I see plain enough he'd been worked main hard, lately. I liked the nigger for that; I tell you, gentlemen, a nigger like that is worth a thousand dollars—and kind treatment, too. I had everything I needed, and the boy was doing as well there as he would a done at home—better, maybe, because it was so quiet; but there I *was*, with both of 'm on my hands; and there I had to stick, till about dawn this morning; then some men in a skiff come by, and as good luck would have it, the nigger was setting by the pallet with his head propped on his knees, sound asleep; so I motioned them in, quiet, and they slipped up on him and grabbed him and tied him before he knowed what he was about, and we never had no trouble. And the boy being in a kind of a flighty sleep, too, we muffled the oars and hitched the raft on, and towed her over very nice and quiet, and the nigger never made the least row nor said a word, from the start. He ain't no bad nigger, gentlemen; that's what I think about him."

Somebody says:

"Well, it sounds very good, doctor, I'm obleeged to say."

Then the others softened up a little, too, and I was mighty thankful to that old doctor for doing Jim that good turn; and I was glad it was according to my judgement of him, too; because I thought he had a good heart in him and was a good man, the first time I see him. Then they all agreed that Jim had acted very well, and was deserving to have some notice took of it, and reward. So every one of them promised, right out and hearty, that they wouldn't cuss him no more.

Then they come out and locked him up. I hoped they was going to say he could have one or two of the chains took off, because they was rotten heavy, or could have meat and greens with his bread and water, but they didn't think of it, and I reckoned it warn't best for me to mix in, but I judged I'd get the doctor's yarn to aunt Sally, somehow or other, as soon as I'd got through the breakers that was laying just ahead of me. Explanations, I mean, of how I forgot to mention about 'Sid' being shot, when I was telling how him and me put in that dratted night paddling around hunting the runaway nigger.

But I had plenty time. Aunt Sally she stuck to the sick room all day and all night; and every time I see uncle Silas mooning around, I dodged him.

Next morning I heard Tom was a good deal better, and they said aunt Sally was gone to get a nap. So I slips to the sick room and if I found him awake I reckoned we could put up a yarn for the family that would wash. But he was sleeping, and sleeping very peaceful, too; and pale, not fire-faced the way he was when he come. So I set down and laid for him to wake. In about a half an hour, aunt Sally comes gliding in, and there I was, up a stump again! She motioned me to be still, and set down by me, and begun to whisper, and said we could all be joyful, now, because all the symptoms was first rate, and he'd been sleeping like that for ever so long, and looking better and peacefuller all the time, and ten to one he'd wake up in his right mind.

So we set there watching, and by and by, he stirs a bit, and opens his eyes very natural, and takes a look, and says:

"Hello, why I'm at *home!* How's that? Where's the raft?"

"It's all right," I says.

"And *Jim?*"

"The same," I says, but couldn't say it pretty brash. But he never noticed, but says:

"Good! Splendid! *Now* we're all right and safe! Did you tell aunty?"

I was going to say yes; but she chipped in and says:

"About what, Sid?"

"Why, about the way the whole thing was done."

"What whole thing?"

"Why, *the* whole thing—there ain't but one: how we set the runaway nigger free—me and Tom."

"Good land! Set the run—What *is* the child talking about! Dear, dear, out of his head again!"

"*No* I ain't out of my HEAD, I know all what I'm talking about. We *did* set him free—me and Tom. We laid out to do it and we *done* it. And we done it elegant, too." He'd got a start, and she never checked him up, just set and stared and stared, and let him clip along, and I see it warn't no use for *me* to put in. "Why, aunty, it cost us a power of work—weeks of it—hours and hours, every night, whilst you was all asleep. And we had to steal candles, and the sheet and the shirt, and your dress, and spoons, and tin plates, and case-knives, and the warming pan, and the grindstone, and flour, and just no end of things, and you can't think what work it was, to make the saws, and pens, and inscriptions, and one thing or another, and you can't think *half* the fun it was. And we had to make up the pictures of coffins and things, and nonnamous letters from the robbers, and get up and down the lightning rod, and dig the hole into the cabin, and make the rope-ladder and send it in, cooked up in a pie, and send in spoons and things to work with, in your apron pocket"—

"Mercy sakes!"

—"and load up the cabin with rats and snakes and so-on, for company for Jim; and then you kept Tom here so long with the butter in his hat that you come near spiling the whole business, because the men come before we was out of the cabin, and we had to rush, and they heard us and let drive at us, and I got my share, and we dodged out of the path and let them go by, and when the dogs come they warn't interested in us, but went for the most noise, and we got our canoe, and made for the raft, and was all safe, and Jim was a free man, and we done it all by ourselves, and *wasn't* it bully, aunty!"

"Well, I never heard the likes of it in all my born days! So it was *you*, you little rapscallions, that's been making all this trouble, and turned everybody's wits clean inside out and scared us all most to death. I've as good a notion as ever I had in my life, to take it out o' you this very minute. To think, here I've been, night after night, a— *you* just get well, once, you young scamp, and I lay I'll tan the Old Harry out o' both o' ye!"

But Tom, he *was* so proud and joyful, he just *couldn't* hold in, and his tongue just *went* it—she a-chipping in, and spitting fire all along, and both of them going it at once, like a cat-convention; and she says:

"*Well*, you get all the enjoyment you can out of it *now*, for mind I tell you if I catch you meddling with him again—"

"Meddling with *who?*" Tom says, dropping his smile and looking surprised.

"With *who?* Why, the runaway nigger, of course. Who'd you reckon?"

Tom looks at me very grave, and says:

"Tom, didn't you just tell me he was all right? Hasn't he got away?"

"*Him?*" says aunt Sally; "the runaway nigger? 'Deed he hasn't. They've got him back, safe and sound, and he's in that cabin again, on bread and water, and loaded down with chains, till he's claimed or sold!"

Tom rose square up in bed, with his eye hot, and his nostrils opening and shutting like gills, and sings out to me:

"They hain't no *right* to shut him up! *Shove!*—and don't you lose a minute. Turn him loose! he ain't no slave, he's as free as any cretur that walks this earth!"

"What *does* the child mean!"

"I mean every word I *say*, aunt Sally, and if somebody don't go, *I*'ll go. I've knowed him all his life, and so has Tom, there. Old Miss Watson died two months ago, and she was ashamed she ever was going to sell him down the river, and *said* so; and she set him free in her will."

TOM ROSE SQUARE UP IN BED.

"Then what on earth did *you* want to set him free for, seeing he was already free?"

"Well that *is* a question, I must say; and *just* like women! Why, I wanted the *adventure* of it; and I'd a waded neck-deep in blood to— goodness alive, AUNT POLLY!"

If she warn't standing right there, just inside the door, looking as sweet and contented as an angel half-full of pie, I wish I may never!

Aunt Sally jumped for her, and most hugged the head off of her, and cried over her, and I found a good enough place for me under the bed, for it was getting pretty sultry for *us*, seemed to me. And I peeped out, and in a little while Tom's aunt Polly shook herself loose and stood there looking across at Tom over her spectacles— kind of grinding him into the earth, you know. And then she says:

"Yes, you *better* turn y'r head away—I would if I was you, Tom."

"Oh, deary me!" says aunt Sally, "*is* he changed so? Why, that ain't *Tom*, it's Sid; Tom's—Tom's—why, where is Tom? He was here a minute ago."

"You mean where's Huck *Finn*—that's what you mean! I reckon I hain't raised such a scamp as my Tom all these years, not to know him when I *see* him. That *would* be a pretty howdy-do. Come out from under that bed, Huck Finn."

So I done it. But not feeling brash.

Aunt Sally she was one of the mixed-upest looking persons I ever see; except one, and that was uncle Silas, when he come in, and they told it all to him. It kind of made him drunk, as you may say, and he didn't know nothing at all the rest of the day, and preached a prayer meeting sermon that night that give him a rattling ruputation, because the oldest man in the world couldn't a understood it. So Tom's aunt Polly she told all about who I was, and what; and I had to up and tell how I was in such a tight place that when Mrs. Phelps took me for Tom Sawyer—she chipped in and says, "O, go on and call me aunt Sally, I'm used to it, now, and 't ain't no need to change"—that when aunt Sally took me for Tom Sawyer, I had to stand it—there warn't no other way, and I knowed he wouldn't mind, because it would be nuts for him, being a mystery, and he'd make an adventure out of it and be perfectly satisfied. And so it turned out, and he let on to be Sid, and made things as soft as he could for me.

And his aunt Polly she said Tom was right about old Miss Watson setting Jim free in her will; and so, sure enough, Tom Sawyer had gone and took all that trouble and bother to set a free nigger free! and I couldn't ever understand, before, until that minute and that talk, how he *could* help a body set a nigger free, with his bringing-up.

Well, aunt Polly she said that when aunt Sally wrote to her that Tom and *Sid* had come, all right and safe, she says to herself:

"Look at that, now! I might have expected it, letting him go off that way without anybody to watch him. So now I got to go and trapse all the way down the river eleven hundred mile, and find out what that cretur's up to, *this* time; as long as I couldn't seem to get any answer out of *you* about it."

"Why, I never heard nothing from you," says aunt Sally.

"Well, I wonder! Why, I wrote to you twice, to ask you what you could mean by Sid being here."

"Well, I never got 'em, Sis."

Aunt Polly she turns around slow and severe, and says:

"You, Tom!"

"Well—*what?*" he says, kind of pettish.

"Don't you what *me*, you impudent thing—hand out them letters."

"What letters?"

"*Them* letters. I be bound, if I have to take aholt of you I'll—"

"They're in the trunk. There, now. And they're just the same as they was when I got them out of the office. I hain't looked into them, I hain't touched them. But I knowed they'd make trouble, and I thought if you warn't in no hurry, I'd—"

"Well, you *do* need skinning, there ain't no mistake about it. And I wrote another one to tell you I was coming; and I spose he—"

"No, it come yesterday; I hain't read it yet, but *it's* all right, I've got that one."

"HAND OUT THEM LETTERS."

I wanted to offer to bet two dollars she hadn't, but I reckoned maybe it was just as safe to not to. So I never said nothing.

Chapter the Last

OUT OF BONDAGE.

The first time I catched Tom, private, I asked him what was his idea, time of the evasion?—what it was he'd planned to do if the evasion worked all right and he managed to set a nigger free that was already free before? And he said, what he had planned in his head, from the start, if we got Jim out, all safe, was for us to run him down the river, on the raft, and have adventures plumb to the mouth of the river, and then tell him about his being free, and take him back up home on a steamboat, in style, and pay him for his lost time, and write word ahead, and get out all the niggers around, and have them waltz him into town with a torchlight procession, and a brass band, and then he would be a hero, and so would we. But I reckoned it was about as well the way it was.

We had Jim out of the chains in no time, and when aunt Polly and uncle Silas and aunt Sally found out how good he helped the doctor nurse Tom, they made a heap of fuss over him, and fixed him up prime, and give him all he wanted to eat, and a good time, and nothing to do. And we had him up to the sick room; and had a high talk; and Tom give Jim forty dollars for being prisoner for us so patient, and doing it up so good, and Jim was pleased most to death, and busted out, and says:

"*Dah*, now, Huck, what I tell you?—what I tell you up dah on Jackson islan'? I *tole* you I got a hairy breas', en what's de sign un it;

en I *tole* you I ben rich wunst, en gwineter be rich *agin*; en it's come true; en heah she *is! Dah*, now! doan' talk to *me*—signs is *signs*, mine I tell you; en I knowed jis' 's well 'at I 'uz gwineter be rich agin as I's a stannin' heah dis minute!"

And then Tom he talked along, and talked along, and says, le's all three slide out of here, one of these nights, and get an outfit, and go for howling adventures amongst the Injuns, over in the Territory, for a couple of weeks or two; and I says, all right, that suits me, but I ain't got no money for to buy the outfit, and I reckon I couldn't get none from home, because it's likely pap's been back before now, and got it all away from Judge Thatcher and drunk it up.

"No he hain't," Tom says; "it's all there, yet—six thousand dollars and more; and your pap hain't ever been back since. Hadn't when I come away, anyhow."

Jim says, kind of solemn:

"He ain't a comin' back no mo', Huck."

I says:

"Why, Jim?"

"Nemmine why, Huck—but he ain't comin' back no mo'."

But I kept at him; so at last he says:

"Doan' you 'member de house dat was float'n down de river, en dey wuz a man in dah, kivered up, en I went in en unkivered him en

TOM'S LIBERALITY.

didn' let you come in? Well, den, you k'n git yo' money when you wants it; kase dat wuz him."

Tom's most well, now, and got his bullet around his neck on a watch-guard for a watch, and is always seeing what time it is, and so there ain't nothing more to write about, and I am rotten glad of it, because if I'd a knowed what a trouble it was to make a book I wouldn't a tackled it and ain't agoing to no more. But I reckon I got to light out for the Territory ahead of the rest, because aunt Sally she's going to adopt me and sivilize me and I can't stand it. I been there before.

THE END, YOURS TRULY HUCK FINN.

REFERENCE
MATERIAL

MAPS

The title page for *Adventures of Huckleberry Finn* described the book's setting as the Mississippi Valley "forty to fifty years ago," that is, between about 1835 and 1845 (counting back from the book's American publication date in 1885). An earlier version of the title page set the story "forty years ago" or about 1845 (see the note to vii.8). This was the period of Clemens's childhood in Missouri: the family moved to Hannibal in 1839 when Samuel Clemens was four years old. He left in 1853 at the age of seventeen, and made only a few brief return visits. The geography of the fictional St. Petersburg and Jackson's Island, which correspond to Hannibal and Glasscock's Island, borrows from his boyhood memory of the area. His firsthand knowledge of the rest of the river valley dates primarily from the years 1857 to 1861, when he worked as a pilot on steamboats plying between St. Louis and New Orleans. During these years he probably consulted the standard piloting guides of the 1840s and 1850s by George Conclin, Samuel Cummings, and U. P. James. The only river guide he is known to have owned, however, was a much earlier one, Zadok Cramer's *The Navigator*, which went through twelve editions between 1801 and 1824 (Gribben, 2:914).

In 1882, during a three-year gap of work on *Huckleberry Finn*, Mark Twain began work on *Life on the Mississippi*. He revisited the river in April and May. He made copious notes, but he found the river and the towns along its banks transformed since his piloting days. "The river is so thoroughly changed that I can't bring it back to mind even when the changes have been pointed out to me," he noted. "It is like a man pointing out to me a place in the sky where a cloud has been" (*N&J2*, 530). He ordered up-to-date, detailed maps from the Mississippi River Commission and the U.S. Army Corps of Engineers, and he read a number of travel accounts written in the first half of the century. They proved disappointing. "I drudged through all those old books, mainly to find out what the procession of foreign tourists thought of the river towns of the Mississippi. But as a general thing, they forgot to say" (SLC 1944, 411; Kruse 1981, 48–53, 165–66; Blair 1960a, 294–99; Branch and Hirst, 37–38).

When in 1883 he returned to *Huckleberry Finn*, Mark Twain still had the bulk of Huck's adventures on the river below Cairo to write. Despite his stock of memories, his recent river trip, and the research he had done for *Life on the Mississippi,* he made no attempt to further particularize the locations in his early manuscript pages or to include in the later episodes more specific geographic information. He gives us only a few actual place names and unambiguous markers along the raft's route: the raft passes St. Louis and Cairo; the fictional Bricksville is in Arkansas; the Wilkses' village is on the lefthand (east) bank of the river, across from Arkansas and below Memphis, Tennessee; the Phelps farm is below the White River in the region of cotton plantations and Spanish moss, which places it south of Columbia, Arkansas (79.3, 99.1–9, 129.14–24, 180.8–9, 203.1–5, 204.15–16, 234.25–26, 265.6–10, 282.14). The only other specific geographic references are in Clemens's working notes or later statements (see *HF2003,* 480–82, 485, 505, 507 [Mark Twain's Working Notes, nos. 2-2, 2-7, 3-4, and 3-6]; see also the notes to 266.9–267.7 and 358.33–34). He did, however, make specific reference to the speed of the river current and the approximate duration of the raft's nightly travel, in chapters 12 and 15 of the book (78.30–31 and 100.35). This information has encouraged scholars to attempt to calculate the raft's daily mileage, so as to assign actual place names to the deliberately generic Pokeville, Bricksville, and Pikesville. In the early chapters, the raft's journey conforms well to a mathematical model based on an average river current of $4\frac{1}{2}$ miles per hour and a travel time of $7\frac{1}{2}$ hours per night. The model breaks down, however, soon after Cairo is passed; thenceforth the raft's journey can only be traced in broad terms (see Miller, 193–95, 198–200). By the time the raft reaches Pikesville and the Phelps farm, which Mark Twain in several statements firmly located in Arkansas, the disjunction between daily mileage and the passage of time is so great that some scholars argue for a location much further south, deep in Louisiana (see the notes to 266.9–267.7 and 274.15–16).

Throughout the novel, Mark Twain appropriates aspects of real places in his descriptions, without intending a specific identification. His uncle's Missouri farm, for instance, contributes to the descriptions of both the Grangerford house and the Phelps plantation (see the notes to 136.15–17 and 276.18). Similarly, the two towns that Huck and Jim encounter below Cairo recall Columbus and Hickman, Kentucky, in their basic topography and relative positions, but not their distance from Cairo (see the note to 129.23). Bricksville, where the "Royal Nonesuch" is performed, owes something of its character to Napoleon, Arkansas, although new evidence from the manuscript shows that Mark Twain originally located Bricksville in Council Bend, over one hundred miles upriver of Napoleon (see the note to 180.8–9). He eventually deleted the reference to Council Bend, perhaps in accordance with his decision to avoid such specifics. As some scholars have pointed out, this deliberate lack of geographic detail, coupled with the "extraordinary lyrical intensity" of Huck's descriptions of the natural world (Marx 1957, 138), give the raft trip a dream-like dimension: it becomes an "unfettered voyage into an eternal landscape" (Miller, 206; Henry Nash Smith 1958b, x–xii, xvi; Beaver, 62–64, 96–98).

The five maps that follow here are intended to represent some of the real geography on which Mark Twain relied in writing his story. When he used a fictional name for a real place, it appears within parentheses and in capitals and small capitals below the real name: for example, "Hannibal|(St. Petersburg)". Not every fictional place is so readily equated with a real one. When the link is more tentative, the fictional name is preceded by "(Vicinity of," still within parentheses, and the rationale for the identification is discussed in the explanatory notes.

Map Sources

■ *Mississippi River Valley, ca. 1845.* Based on the frontispiece from *Mighty Mississippi* (Childs), this map also draws on plates 19 and 20 of the *Century Atlas* (Benjamin E. Smith, xix, xx), and an 1849 map of the river in *Appletons' Hand-Book* (Hall, following page 428). It shows the valley during the period of the novel and of Clemens's boyhood. (The system of citation used here is discussed at the beginning of the explanatory notes.)

■ *Hannibal, ca. 1845.* This map is based on the following: "Plat of Original Town of Hannibal," dated 1836 (photofacsimile in CU-MARK), which provides the configuration of the town proper; "Map of the Mississippi River from the Falls of St. Anthony to the Junction of the Illinois River" (U.S. Army Corps of Engineers, 1887–88, DLC), which provides the Missouri and Illinois shorelines. No precisely scaled map has been found that shows Glasscock's Island at the time Clemens knew it, and later maps demonstrate no consensus about its size and location. This map, therefore, relies on Mark Twain's description of the island in chapters 7–9 of *Huckleberry Finn* and the virtually identical description, adjusted for the June rise of the river, in *Tom Sawyer,* chapters 13–15.

■ *Bainbridge to Commerce, Mo., ca. 1857 (Vicinity of Walter Scott Wreck).* Based on a river guide contemporary with Clemens's career as a steamboat pilot (James, 25, 27), this map also draws on "Map of the Alluvial Valley of the Upper Mississippi River from the Falls of St. Anthony to the Mouth of the Ohio River" (Mississippi River Commission, 1899, CU-MAPS).

■ *Cairo, ca. 1857.* Based on maps provided in two contemporary river guides (Conclin, 65, 89, and James, 27). This map represents the area as Clemens knew it during his career as a steamboat pilot.

■ *New Madrid Bend (Vicinity of Feud).* Based on "Lloyd's Map of the Lower Mississippi River from St. Louis to the Gulf of Mexico . . . Revised and corrected to the present time, by Captains Bart. and William Bowen" (J. T. Lloyd, 1862, DLC); "Map of a Reconnaissance of the Mississippi River from Cairo, Ill's. to New Orleans, La." (U.S. Army Corps of Engineers, 1878?, DLC); "Preliminary Map of the Lower Mississippi River, from the Mouth of the Ohio River to the Head of the Passes" (Mississippi

River Commission, 1881–85, DLC); "The Mississippi River from St. Louis to the Sea" (J. A. Ockerson, assisted by Charles W. Stewart, 1892, DLC). The stretch of river represented here is a composite of features from the 1850s to the early 1880s. Compromise Landing flourished and vanished in that period, and Island No. 10, hugging the Tennessee shore in Clemens's piloting days, moved closer to the Missouri side (James, 29; SLC 1883, 289; Branch and Hirst, 53–54). The map accurately represents the basic relationship of the Darnell and Watson lands, settled since the late 1820s (Branch and Hirst, 54, 56).

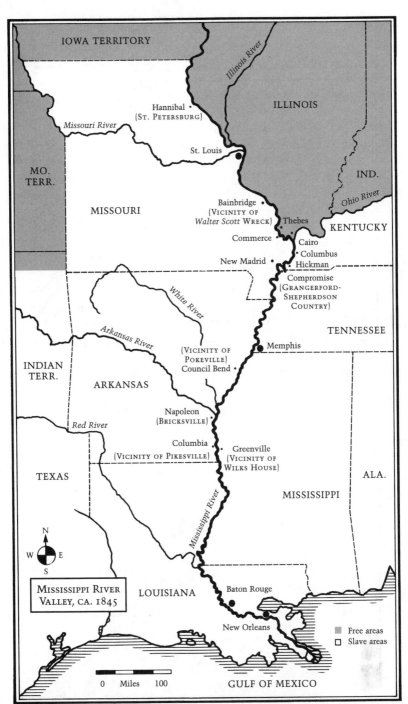

IOWA TERRITORY

ILLINOIS

Illinois River

Hannibal •
(ST. PETERSBURG)

Missouri River

St. Louis

MO.
TERR.

IND.

Ohio River

MISSOURI

Bainbridge
(VICINITY OF
Walter Scott WRECK)

Thebes

KENTUCKY

Commerce •

Cairo
• Columbus

New Madrid •

Hickman

Compromise
(GRANGERFORD-
SHEPHERDSON
COUNTRY)

White River

TENNESSEE

Arkansas River

(VICINITY OF
POKEVILLE)
Council Bend •

Memphis

INDIAN
TERR.

ARKANSAS

Napoleon
(BRICKSVILLE)

Red River

Columbia
(VICINITY OF PIKESVILLE)

Greenville
(VICINITY OF
WILKS HOUSE)

TEXAS

ALA.

MISSISSIPPI

N
W E
S

Mississippi River

MISSISSIPPI RIVER
VALLEY, CA. 1845

LOUISIANA

Baton Rouge

New Orleans

Free areas
Slave areas

0 Miles 100

GULF OF MEXICO

To 10 mi. to Marion City (GOSHEN)

(3 MI. TO PAP'S CABIN)

ILLINOIS

Ferry Landing

Bear Creek

HANNIBAL
(ST. PETERSBURG)

7 mi. to Saverton (HOOKERVILLE)

MISSOURI

GLASSCOCK'S ISLAND
(JACKSON'S ISLAND)

HANNIBAL, CA. 1845

0   Miles   1

Bainbridge

Hamburg

BAINBRIDGE TO COMMERCE, MO., CA. 1857
(VICINITY OF *Walter Scott* WRECK)

Cape Girardeau

MISSOURI

ILLINOIS

Thebes

New York

- - - River Channel
▲▲ Rocks

Commerce

0   Miles   6

Cairo, ca. 1857

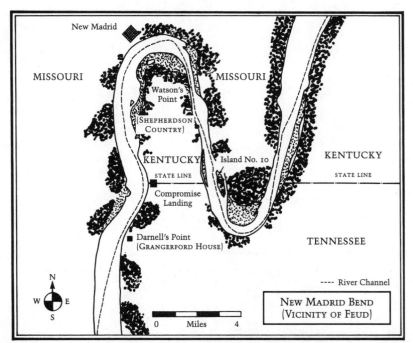

New Madrid Bend (Vicinity of Feud)

EXPLANATORY NOTES

These notes identify real people, places, books, and events that Mark Twain drew upon for *Adventures of Huckleberry Finn*. They document historical, literary, and cultural allusions, parallels, analogues, or influences, both in the text and in E. W. Kemble's illustrations. They identify important moments in the seven-year course of composition and in the process of revision and first publication: when Mark Twain wrote or revised parts of the text, when he stopped or resumed work on them, how he struggled with or commented on them. References to the manuscript may distinguish between its newly discovered first half (MS1) and its long familiar second half (MS2), now both in the Buffalo and Erie County Public Library. References to the typed copies of MS1 and MS2 which Mark Twain had made are to the documents which served as Kemble's and the first edition printer's copy, but the typescripts themselves are not known to survive. What they probably contained and how Mark Twain revised them are matters inferred from the manuscript, the first edition set from the typescripts, and other evidence. For a brief overview of composition, revision, publication, and reception, see the Foreword and the Note on the Text.

References to the text are keyed to this volume by page and line: 3.10 means page 3, line 10. Chapter titles and picture captions are not included in the line count, but when they are referred to, the word *title* or *caption* is substituted for the line number: 3 *caption* means the caption on page 3. Frequently cited books have been assigned an abbreviation, always italicized, which is followed by a page (or volume and page) number: "*MTBus*, 21" or "*MTL*, 1:456–57." But most works are cited by the author's last name, followed by page number, unless there is only one page: "Abbott, 16–17" or simply "Pease." When two or more works by the same author are cited, the year of publication differentiates them: "Budd 1985, 1" or "Budd 1962, 34–76." For works likely to be consulted in any of various editions, citations give chapter numbers (or book, canto, or act numbers) rather than page numbers. Quotations of Mark Twain's published work are from critically edited texts produced by the Mark Twain Project or from the first printings, as necessary. Quotations from original documents follow their wording and punctuation exactly, even when a published form is also cited and may differ slightly from the original. Repositories of unique docu-

ments are identified by the standard Library of Congress abbreviation.
Documents owned by individuals are cited by the owner's last name. All
abbreviations and names used as citations are defined in References, pp.
510–47.

v *frontispiece of Mark Twain*] A week or so after printing had begun on
the first edition, Mark Twain suggested to his publisher, Charles L.
Webster, that they include this frontispiece, saying "I suppose it would
help sell the book" (SLC to Webster, 8 Sept 84, NPV, in *MTBus*, 276). It
is a photograph of a plaster casting of a clay bust sculpted from life by
Karl Gerhardt (1853–1940), who had just returned from Paris after three
years of art study financed by the Clemenses. (Neither Gerhardt's clay
original nor this plaster cast is known to survive; the only known
bronze casting is in the Mark Twain House in Hartford.) Webster agreed
to Mark Twain's suggestion, even as he pointed out that it was too
late to drop the original frontispiece ("Huckleberry Finn") and that
they would therefore "have to face your picture against it," creating a
double frontispiece like that in *A Tramp Abroad* (Webster to SLC, 13
Sept 84, CU-MARK; SLC 1880; *HF2003*, 736–39). As Clemens had
recommended, the photograph was reproduced by the heliotype photo-
gelatine process, which was widely used for art reproductions (Jussim,
341; Pasko, 265). The heliotypes were separately printed, then inserted
into each book and salesman's prospectus before binding. This frontispiece appeared in successive printings of the first edition over the next
six years, but was omitted from the second or "cheap" edition (1891–
1894) and all subsequent lifetime editions. Louis J. Budd has suggested
that Mark Twain may have had more than helping sales in mind when
he decided to include this image of himself: "did the bust say: Don't
confuse me totally with the ragged, naive, barely literate narrator?"
(Budd 1985, 34). The first half of the manuscript found in 1990 tends to
confirm the suggestion that Mark Twain was anxious about such a con-
fusion. The first manuscript page bears the working title, "HUCKLE-
BERRY FINN | Reported by | MARK TWAIN" (see Manuscript Facsimiles, p.
497). In two later works written in Huck's voice, Mark Twain found
other solutions to the problem: "Tom Sawyer Abroad," first published
serially in *St. Nicholas Magazine* in 1893–94, was "BY HUCK FINN. ED-
ITED BY MARK TWAIN," and "Tom Sawyer, Detective," first published
in *Harper's New Monthly Magazine* in 1896, was "BY MARK TWAIN"
but "AS TOLD BY HUCK FINN" (SLC 1893–94, 20; SLC 1896, 344).

vi *frontispiece of Huckleberry Finn*] In early April 1884, Clemens chose
the young cartoonist Edward Windsor Kemble (1861–1933) to illustrate

his book. Although Kemble's sample drawings for the first chapters won him the job, Clemens was not entirely satisfied with the drawings he then began to submit, roughly in sequence, for the book as a whole. He returned the cover design to his publisher on 7 May 1884, saying "All right & good, & will answer; although the boy's mouth is a trifle more Irishy than necessary." On 24 May, having seen the illustrations through chapter 12 and having insisted on some changes to them, Clemens again complained to Webster, concluding with a specific criticism of this frontispiece:

> Some of the pictures are good, but none of them are very *very* good. The faces are generally ugly, & wrenched into ~~inhuman distortions~~ over-expression amounting sometimes to distortion. As a rule (though not always) the people in these pictures are forbidding & repulsive. Reduction will modify them, no doubt, but it can hardly make them pleasant folk to look at. An artist shouldn't follow a book too literally, perhaps—if this is the necessary result. And mind you, much of the drawing, in these pictures is careless & bad.
> The pictures will *do*—they will just barely do—& that is the best I can say for them. ~~Suppose you submit them to t~~
> The frontispiece has the usual blemish—an ugly, ill-drawn face. Huck Finn is an exceedingly good-hearted boy, & should carry a good & good-looking face.

The original drawing for the frontispiece shows numerous and extensive revisions to the arms and face, at least some of which must have been Kemble's effort to respond to Clemens's criticism. Kemble's later drawings were more to Mark Twain's satisfaction, however. On 11 June 1884 the author commented on the illustrations submitted for chapters 13 through 20: "I *knew* Kemble had it *in* him, if he would only modify ~~hims~~ his violences & come down to careful, painstaking work. This batch of pictures is most rattling good. They please me exceedingly" (SLC to Webster: 7 May 84, 24 May 84, 11 June 84, NPV, in *MTBus*, 253, 255–56, 260).

vii.8   TIME: FORTY TO FIFTY YEARS AGO] That is, between about 1835 and 1845. In the typed printer's copy for the title page Mark Twain had specified "Time, forty years ago." But on 24 July 1884, well before printing had begun, he asked his publisher to substitute this more inclusive phrase. Probably at the same time he also inserted the later reading on the manuscript title page, which did not originally have any designation for "scene" or "time" (see the manuscript title page recto and verso in Manuscript Facsimiles, pp. 494–95). Pushing the time back ten years made it consistent with a sequel he was just beginning to write, called "Huck Finn & Tom Sawyer among the Indians 40 or 50 years ago." He had set the sequel on the Oregon Trail prior to the great migration of the 1840s (SLC to Webster, 24 July 84, NPV, in *MTBus*, 271; SLC to Howells, 15 July 84, MH-H, in *MTHL*, 2:496; *HH&T*, 81–140, 372–74; *Inds*, 33–81, 270–72; SLC 1983, 1–2).

xxxi. *title*–6   NOTICE . . . Per G. G., Chief of Ordnance.] Mark Twain's manuscript draft did not include the phrase, "persons attempting to find a Moral in it will be banished," which he added in revision, probably on the typed printer's copy (see Manuscript Facsimiles, p. 496). In "A Little Note to M. Paul Bourget" (1897) Mark Twain quoted this entire "Notice" and indicated that its purpose was ironic, to "playfully warn the public against taking" his book "seriously" (SLC 1897a, 232). If "G. G., Chief of Ordnance" refers to a real person, his identity remains uncertain. The initials could stand for General Grant: Mark Twain had been acquainted with Ulysses S. Grant (1822–85) since 1870, and occasionally, in 1885, referred to him privately by these initials (*N&J3*, 108, 128, 135, 156; *L4*, 167, 168–69 n. 5). But Grant never signed himself in this way, nor was he ever chief of ordnance, the high-ranking officer responsible for the army's munitions and weaponry. The initials "G. G." do not correspond to any actual chief of ordnance from 1815 through 1900 (Heitman, 1:44). More likely, they are a playful (albeit private) reference to George Griffin (1849?–97), who worked in the Hartford household as the family butler from 1875 to 1891. Griffin, born a Maryland slave, had served as body servant to a Union general, Charles Devens (1820–91), during the Civil War (SLC 1906a, 9, 30–31; SLC to Howells, 4 Nov 75, NN-B, in *L6*, 581–85). According to Clemens's "A Family Sketch" (1906), Griffin was "handsome, well built, shrewd, wise, polite, always good-natured, cheerful to gaiety, honest, religious, a cautious truth-speaker, devoted friend to the family, champion of its interests. . . . He was the peace-maker in the kitchen . . . for by his good sense & right spirit & mollifying tongue he adjusted disputes in that quarter before they reached the quarrel-point" (SLC 1906a, 9–10). But it was a combination of Griffin's role as peace-maker and two incidents involving firearms that qualified him playfully as "Chief of Ordnance." He was chief among the household servants, entrusted with the security of the house during the family's absences. During one such absence, in July 1877, Griffin fired from the house upon three "ruffians" in the street who were yelling insults directed at Clemens. "George shot at them twice," Clemens reported to Olivia, "but unluckily failed to get them; they threatened him, then, & he went down in the yard & very gallantly defied the gang" (SLC to OLC, 17 July 77 [1st of 2], CU-MARK, in *LLMT*, 198, and *Letters 1876–1880*). Clemens recalled another occasion, in the "early days" of Griffin's employment at the Hartford house, when George applied to use the family firearm, this time in defense of his own honor:

> One morning he appeared in my study in a high state of excitement, & wanted to borrow my revolver. He had had a rupture with a colored man, & was going to kill him on sight. . . . I saw that at bottom he didn't want to kill anyone—he only wanted some person of known wisdom & high authority to persuade him out of

it; it would save his character with his people; they would see that he was properly bloodthirsty, but had been obliged to yield to wise & righteous counsel. (SLC
1906a, 24–25; see also Hirst)

xxxiii. *title*–12   EXPLANATORY . . . The Author.] Mark Twain was neither joking nor being deliberately obscure, despite the conclusions
drawn by some critics (see, among others, Rulon, and Buxbaum). David
Carkeet has shown that, except for what he characterizes as some inconsistencies overlooked during the long course of composition and revision, Mark Twain indeed made distinctions among "dialects," or
kinds of nonstandard English (Carkeet 1979; see also *HF2003*, 781–90
passim [Introduction]). The seven mentioned in this notice can be
identified with the following speakers:

1.   "the Missouri negro dialect":
            Jim and four other black characters (Jack, Lize, Nat, young
            "wench" at Phelps farm);

2.   "the extremest form of the backwoods South-Western dialect":
            Arkansas gossips (Sister Hotchkiss and others, chapter 41);

3.   "the ordinary 'Pike-County' dialect":
            Huck, Tom, Aunt Polly, Ben Rogers, Pap Finn, Judith Lof-
            tus, the duke, Buck Grangerford, the Wilks daughters, and
            the watchman of the *Walter Scott* passage;

4–7.   "four modified varieties of this last":
            (a) thieves on the *Walter Scott*;
            (b) the king, Tim Collins;
            (c) the Bricksville loafers;
            (d) Aunt Sally and Uncle Silas Phelps, the Pikesville boy.

Editorial work on the complete manuscript and other documents has
shown that many, though not all, of the "inconsistencies" noted by
Carkeet were intentional: Mark Twain regularly had different speakers
within these seven groups use different locutions, and he made fine distinctions within the speech even of a single character, often through
meticulous revision. For instance, Huck always says "again" while Pap
almost always says "agin," even though both are "ordinary" Pike
County speakers. And Jim is made to say *both* "ain' dat" and "ain't it,"
dropping the *t* of "ain't" only when the word following begins with a
consonant. In 1874, preparing to revise "A True Story," Clemens wrote
to William Dean Howells, "I amend dialect stuff by talking & talking
& *talking* it till it sounds right—& I had difficulty with this negro
talk because a negro sometimes (rarely) says 'goin' ' & sometimes
'gwyne,' & they make just such discrepancies in other words—& when

you come to reproduce them on paper they look as if the variation resulted from the writer's carelessness. But I want to work at the proofs & get the dialect as nearly right as possible" (20 Sept 74, NN-B, in *L6*, 233–36). On 17 January 1885, his sister-in-law Mollie wrote from Keokuk, Iowa: "Sam I have just finished Huck Finn. It simply amazes me to see how you kept up the dialects and the underlying moral lesson without a particle of apparent effort. *It is real,* to me" (Jane L. Clemens and Mary E. [Mollie] Clemens to SLC and OLC, 17 Jan 85, CU-MARK). As early as 1872 John Hay publicly praised Mark Twain's *Roughing It* lecture, acknowledging his authority as "the finest living delineator of the true Pike accent." And in 1891 Melville D. Landon (Eli Perkins) expressed a preference for *Huckleberry Finn* over Mark Twain's other books "because it has the truest dialect" (Hay 1872; Landon, 76). Mark Twain himself once told an interviewer, "the only one of my own books that I can ever read with pleasure is . . . 'Huck Finn,' and partly because I know the dialect is true and good" (Blathwait, 26).

1 *illustration*   The Adventures . . . Finn.] Kemble's use of "The" in the title here is mistaken. The definite article was also mistakenly used in the running heads of the first edition, and in some of Webster and Company's advertisements for the book (see *HF2003*, 659–60, 663 [Publisher's Advertisements, 1884–1891]). It appeared throughout the English and Continental editions, as well as the third and fourth American editions, published in 1896 and 1899 (see *HF2003*, 804–5 [Description of Texts]). Just after completing the book manuscript, Clemens himself quoted the title *with* the article in a letter to James R. Osgood, but without it in one to Andrew Chatto, both on 1 September 1883. And probably he, rather than the editor or typesetter, used it in the introductory note for the selections published in the *Century Magazine* (SLC 1884b). Still, there is little room for doubt that he intended the book title to omit the article. Kemble's design for the cover, which was among the first illustrations reviewed and approved by Webster and Clemens, omitted the article, as did Clemens's holograph title page from the summer of 1883 (see Manuscript Facsimiles, p. 494). The printed title page of the first edition, as well as the printed half-title, the illustrated cover and the spine (and both front and back of the prospectus) all agree with the holograph title page in omitting the definite article (SLC to Osgood, 1 Sept 83, WEU; SLC to Chatto, 1 Sept 83, Uk, in Gates, 79; Webster to SLC, 5 May 84, CU-MARK; SLC to Webster, 7 May 84, NPV, in *MTLP*, 174; David and Sapirstein, 38).

1.1–4   You don't know about me . . . "The Adventures of Tom Sawyer,"] In chapter 6 of *Tom Sawyer* (1876) Mark Twain had described Huck Finn as "the juvenile pariah of the village . . . son of the town drunk-

Edward W. Kemble's cover design for the first American edition of *Huckleberry Finn*. Vassar College Library, Poughkeepsie, New York (NPV). See the note to 1 *illustration*.

Title page of the first American edition. Mark Twain Papers, The Bancroft Library (CU-MARK).

ard," adding that he "was cordially hated and dreaded by all the mothers of the town, because he was idle, and lawless, and vulgar and bad—and because all their children admired him so, and delighted in his forbidden society" (*ATS*, 47).

> Huckleberry came and went, at his own free will. He slept on doorsteps in fine weather and in empty hogsheads in wet; he did not have to go to school or to church, or call any being master or obey anybody; he could go fishing or swimming when and where he chose, and stay as long as it suited him; nobody forbade him to fight; he could sit up as late as he pleased; he was always the first boy that went barefoot in the spring and the last to resume leather in the fall; he never had to wash, nor put on clean clothes; he could swear wonderfully. In a word, everything that goes to make life precious, that boy had. So thought every harassed, hampered, respectable boy in St. Petersburg. (*ATS*, 48)

On hearing this passage read aloud, Clemens's sister Pamela said, "Why, that's Tom Blankenship!" (*MTBus*, 265). Mark Twain had said in his preface that "Huck Finn is drawn from life" (*ATS*, xvii), and in 1906 he repeated the assertion in his autobiography. A letter from Alex C. Toncray, an old Hannibal acquaintance, asked him if it were true that Huck Finn was based on his brother, A. O. Toncray. Clemens said:

> I have replied that "Huckleberry Finn" was Tom Blankenship. . . . Tom's father was at one time Town Drunkard, an exceedingly well defined and unofficial office of those days. . . .
> In "Huckleberry Finn" I have drawn Tom Blankenship exactly as he was. He was ignorant, unwashed, insufficiently fed; but he had as good a heart as ever any boy had. His liberties were totally unrestricted. He was the only really independent person—boy or man—in the community, and by consequence he was tranquilly and continuously happy, and was envied by all the rest of us. We liked him; we enjoyed his society. And as his society was forbidden us by our parents, the prohibition trebled and quadrupled its value, and therefore we sought and got more of his society than of any other boy's. (AD, 8 Mar 1906, CU-MARK, in *AutoMT1* and *MTA*, 2:174–75).

One of eight children of Woodson and Mahala Blankenship, Tom was four years older than Clemens (*Inds*, 302–3). Huck's last name was borrowed from another town drunkard—Jimmy Finn, the prototype for Pap Finn (see the note to 10.10–12). The origin of Huck's first name is less clearly documented. Mark Twain certainly knew the derogatory meaning for "huckleberry"—an inconsequential or unimportant person. When he wrote chapter 26 of *Connecticut Yankee*, four years after finishing *Huckleberry Finn*, he had the local reporter for the Camelot *Weekly Hosannah and Literary Volcano* praise two knights, including Sir Palamides the Saracen, "who is no huckleberry himself" (*CY*, 11, 304). Mark Twain doubtless also knew the huckleberry's general connotation: a plain, common fruit, not requiring cultivation in order to flourish, often signifying something backward or rural (Colwell, 71, 74).

1.4   Tom Sawyer] In his preface to *Tom Sawyer*, Mark Twain explained that like Huck Finn, Tom Sawyer was "drawn from life," but not from "an individual—he is a combination of the characteristics of three boys whom I knew" (*ATS*, xvii). Albert Bigelow Paine identified the three boys as John B. Briggs (1837–1907), William Bowen (1836–93), and Clemens himself (*MTB*, 1:54–55). In less guarded moments Clemens sometimes revealed his own role as the primary model for Tom. For example, on 31 May 1902, during his last visit to Hannibal, he reported to his wife that he "went & stood in the door of the old house I lived in when I whitewashed the fence 53 years ago." And on 1 December 1907 he replied to a "nice note" from a young girl, Florence Benson: "[*Private.*] I have always concealed it before, but now I am *compelled* to confess that *I* am Tom Sawyer!" (SLC to OLC, 31 May 1902, CU-MARK, in *LLMT*, 338; SLC to Florence Benson, 1 Dec 1907, MCo). In 1895, Mark Twain reflected on his reasons for naming Tom Sawyer as he did: " 'Tom Sawyer' and 'Huckleberry Finn' were both real characters, but 'Tom Sawyer' was not the real name of the former, nor the name of any person I ever knew, so far as I can remember, but the name was an ordinary one—just the sort that seemed to fit the boy, some way, by its sound, and so I used it" (Pease).

1.12   aunt Polly] Clemens said that his mother, Jane Lampton Clemens, was the prototype for Tom Sawyer's aunt Polly: "I fitted her out with a dialect, & tried to think up other improvements for her, but did not find any" (SLC 1897–98, 49). Aunt Polly bears a striking resemblance, however, to B. P. Shillaber's character Mrs. Partington, who is also a tender-hearted Calvinist widow charged with raising a mischievous nephew. Mark Twain had long known Shillaber's work when he published *Tom Sawyer*, which concluded with an illustration ostensibly of Aunt Polly, but actually reproducing the likeness of Mrs. Partington from the frontispiece of *Life and Sayings of Mrs. Partington* (Blair 1960a, 62–63).

1.13   Mary] Tom Sawyer's cousin (probably not Aunt Polly's daughter, as suggested in previous editions of this book, or at least never so identified by Clemens). She was in part based upon Clemens's older sister, Pamela, known for her "amiable deportment and faithful application to her various studies" (*MTB*, 1:39).

1.15–16   the widow Douglas] In gratitude for Huck's rescuing her from the malevolent designs of Injun Joe, the widow adopted Huck in the last chapters of *Tom Sawyer*. Earlier in that book, Mark Twain had described her as "fair, smart and forty, a generous, good-hearted soul and well-to-do" (chapter 5, *ATS*, 37). Her Hannibal prototype was the twice-widowed Melicent S. (Mrs. Richard T.) Holliday, born ca. 1800, whom the author described in his 1897 "Villagers of 1840–3": "Lived on Holiday's Hill. Well off. Hospitable. Fond of having parties of young people. Widow. Old, but anxious to marry. Always consulting fortune-tellers; always managed to make them understand that she had been promised 3 [husbands] by the first fraud. . . . She finally died before the prophecies had a full chance" (*Inds*, 95–96, 325). She appeared again in "Tom Sawyer's Conspiracy," and as the "widow Guthrie" in Mark Twain's "Schoolhouse Hill" manuscript (*Inds*, 134, 325; *MSM*, 193, 432).

1.22   Judge Thatcher] Father of Tom Sawyer's sweetheart, Becky Thatcher, he was described in chapter 4 of *Tom Sawyer* as "a fine, portly, middle-aged gentleman with iron-gray hair" and as "a prodigious personage—no less a one than the county judge" (*ATS*, 32–33).

2   *illustration*] Kemble used a single model, for Huck and "for every character in the story," a neighbor, sixteen-year-old Courtland P. Morris, hired at four dollars a week. Morris, Kemble wrote, "tallied with my idea of Huck. He was a bit tall for the ideal boy, but I could jam him down a few pegs in my drawing and use him for the other characters. . . . He was always grinning, and one side of his cheek was usually well padded with a 'sour ball' or a huge wad of molasses taffy" (Kemble, 43). Morris recalled:

> The props we used for illustrating the characters in Huckleberry Finn were, for the most part, old clothes belonging to my father and mother, with some of mine thrown in, which I found stored away in trunks up in the attic of our house.
> The battered old straw hat, which was so much a part of Huck, was mine. . . . The old single-barrel shotgun, another of Huck's treasured possessions, was a gun which my aunt had given me a few years before. . . .
> In portraying the female characters in the book, Aunt Polly, Widow Douglas, the woman who caught Huck trying to pass off as a girl, and the others, I would get into an old faded dress of my mother's. Sometimes, if the text called for it, I'd don a sun-bonnet belonging to my mother. (Morris 1930)

Kemble presented his young model with one of the first copies of the book, autographed "To 'Huckleberry Court' " (Morris 1938).

2.15–16   Moses and the bulrushers] In 1861, when Clemens's eight-year-old niece, Annie Moffett, attempted to explain the story of Moses in Exodus 2:1–10 to him, "he just *couldn't* understand" (*MTBus*, 38–39; *L1*, 180). In an 1866 sketch, Mark Twain published a letter from Annie which began, "Uncle Mark, if you was here I could tell you about Moses in the Bulrushers again, I know it better, now" (SLC 1866b, 1).

3.4–7   get down on a thing . . . that had some good in it] Huck's remarks bear more than a passing resemblance to Clemens's own response to similar disapproval from the Langdon family, just before his marriage to Olivia Langdon in 1870: "I cannot attach any weight to either the arguments or the evidence of those who know nothing about the matter personally & so must simply theorize. Theorizing has no effect on me. I have smoked habitually for 26 of my 34 years, & I am the only healthy member our family has. . . . There *is* no argument that can have even a feather's weight with me against smoking . . . for I *know*, & others merely *suppose*" (*L4*, 21).

3.10   Miss Watson] This dour spinster's Hannibal prototype was Mary Ann Newcomb (1809–94), a schoolteacher of Clemens's who for a time boarded with his family. In "Villagers of 1840–3" Clemens described her as an "old maid and thin" (*Inds*, 95, 338). In "Autobiography of a Damned Fool" (1877), Mark Twain based the printer's wife on her: "Mrs. Bangs was three years older than her husband. She was a very thin, tall, Yankee person, who came west when she was thirty, taught school nine years in our town, and then married Mr. Bangs. . . . She had ringlets, and a long sharp nose, and thin, colorless lips, and you could not tell her breast from her back if she had her head up a stove-pipe hole looking for something in the attic. . . . She was a Calvinist and devotedly pious. . . . She had her share of vinegar" (*S&B*, 140, 163).

4.9–10   go around all day long with a harp and sing] Mark Twain had satirized this conventional vision of heaven in a story mapped out in 1869, worked on sporadically during the 1870s, and eventually published as *Extract from Captain Stormfield's Visit to Heaven*: "People take the figurative language of the Bible and the allegories for literal, and the first thing they ask for when they get here is a halo and a harp, and so on. . . . They go and sing and play just about one day, and that's the last you'll ever see them in the choir. They don't need anybody to tell them that that sort of thing wouldn't make a heaven—at least not a heaven that a sane man could stand a week and remain sane" (SLC 1909a, 40). Mark Twain returned to the subject in "Letters from the Earth," written in 1909 (*WIM*, 409).

4.15   fetched the niggers in and had prayers] During the time of Huck's story, "nigger" was a common colloquial term for black person, used by whites and blacks to refer to slave or freeman, both in the North and the South. Colonel Thomas Wentworth Higginson (1823–1911), the white commander of the first regiment of ex-slaves mustered into Union service, noted in 1862 that "This offensive word . . . is almost as common with them as at the North, and far more common than with well-bred slaveholders" (Higginson, 1, 21). Mark Twain was certainly aware of growing objections to its use, and about 1869 he seems to have stopped

using it in print, at least when speaking in his own voice (Pettit, 42–43;
but see the note to 188.13–16). In *Huckleberry Finn*, however, he deliberately reprises it as a literary device to realistically depict the social
class and speech of his characters. Nevertheless, by 1885, he would
probably have agreed with the editor of the *Century Dictionary* (1889–
91) who declared that even though "nigger" was "formerly and to some
extent still is used without opprobrious intent . . . its use is now confined to colloquial or illiterate speech, in which it generally conveys
more or less of contempt" (4:3989). In addition to those who deplored
its implicit "contempt" were those who found it indelicate, vulgar, or
low. In 1884, George Washington Cable advised Mark Twain before
their joint reading tour not to list one of his selections in the printed
program as "Can't learn a nigger to argue" (Huck's rationalization after
losing a debate to Jim in chapter 14) because in isolation it might hint
at a "gross" entertainment:

When we consider that the programme is advertised & becomes cold-blooded
newspaper reading I think we should avoid any risk of appearing—even to the
most thin-skinned and super-sensative and hypercritical matrons and misses—
the faintest bit gross. In the text, whether on the printed page or in the readers
utterances the phrase is absolutely without a hint of grossness; but alone on a
published programme, it invites discreditable conjectures of what the context
may be, from that portion of our public who cannot live without aromatic vinegar. (Cable to SLC, 25 Oct 84, CU-MARK, in Cardwell, 105)

Objections to the use of "nigger" in *Huckleberry Finn* were not made
explicit by even a single newspaper reviewer, north or south, at the
time of first publication, although it is likely that Concord and Boston's
objections to the book's "ignorant dialect" and "vulgarity" tacitly included its use of the term (see Victor Fischer; Budd 1999; Mailloux, 102;
and additional notices and reviews in CU-MARK courtesy of Steven
Mailloux). All three extracts from the book published by the *Century
Magazine* in late 1884 and early 1885 used the word without warning
or apology, unless we count Mark Twain's signed introduction to these
passages which carefully referred to "The negro Jim" (29:268). For an
acute discussion of the different connotations of "nigger" in *Huckleberry Finn*, see David L. Smith, especially 4–6; for a modern lexicog-
rapher's analysis, including four senses distinguished by the color and
intent of the speaker, see Cassidy, 3:788–89; for a personal account of a
black youth's encounter with this loaded word in *Huckleberry Finn*,
see Bradley, xxxix–xlviii; for further critical and factual contributions
to the discussion of Mark Twain's use of the term, see Railton, 393–
99; Sloane, 28–29; Janows and Lee; Rasmussen, 338; and Pettit, 40–50
(despite use of four 1869–70 Buffalo *Express* articles misattributed to
Mark Twain).

4.19–5.12   The stars . . . waiting for me.] Compare chapter 9 of *Tom Sawyer*, which Mark Twain read in proof at about the time he composed the first chapters of *Huckleberry Finn* (*ATS*, 70–72; Blair 1960a, 104–5).

4.20–22   an owl, . . . a whippowill and a dog crying] Folklore held that the cries of the owl, whippoorwill, and dog were signs or portents of death (Hyatt, items 14525, 14577–80, 14680–90, and Thomas and Thomas, items 3340–46, 3617, 3653; for descriptions of the traditions regarding death portents, see Brand, 682–83, 693–94, and Hardwick, 245).

4.25–27   a ghost . . . can't rest easy in its grave] An ancient belief, dating from at least the tenth century. See, for example, *Hamlet*, 1.5.9–13.

4.29–30   a spider . . . lit in the candle] "If a spider is consumed through falling into a lamp, witches are near" (Thomas and Thomas, item 3808). This is apparently a variation of the widespread belief that killing a spider is unlucky (Hazlitt 1905, 2:559).

4.34–35   I . . . turned around in my tracks three times and crossed my breast every time] Two ancient gestures for warding off evil (see, for example, Hardwick, 248). Crossing one's breast is comparable to the Christian sign of the cross invoking the protection of the Trinity.

4.35   I tied up a little lock of my hair] Closely tying one's hair was supposed to protect against the designs of witches, who braided the hair of victims at night in order to possess and ride them (Hoffman, 50; Hughes and Bontemps, 199–200). In 1866, Clemens recorded this superstition in his notebook, and in 1897 he recalled his boyhood awe of "Aunt" Hannah, an aged, "bed-ridden white-headed slave woman" on his uncle John Quarles's farm near Florida, Missouri: "Whenever witches were around she tied up the remnant of her wool in little tufts, with white thread, & this promptly made the witches impotent" (*N&J1*, 160; SLC 1897–98, 43–44).

4.37   when you've lost a horse-shoe that you've found] Hanging a found horseshoe over a doorway was protection against witches: "Dey say de witch got to travel all over de road dat horseshoe been 'fo' she can git in de house" (Minor, 76; see also Thomas and Thomas, item 3435, and Hazlitt 1905, 1:330–31).

6.10   Jim] In 1897, recalling the summers he spent as a boy at his uncle John Quarles's farm, Mark Twain said:

All the negroes were friends of ours, & with those of our own age we were in effect comrades. I say, in effect, using the phrase as a modification. We were comrades, & yet not comrades; color & condition interposed a subtle line which both parties were conscious of, & which rendered complete fusion impossible. We had a faithful & affectionate good friend, ally & adviser in "Uncle Dan'l," a middle-aged slave whose head was the best one in the negro-quarter, whose sympathies were wide & warm, & whose heart was honest & simple & knew no guile. He has served me well, these many, many years. I have not seen him for half a century, & yet spiritually I have had his welcome company a good part of that time, & have staged him in books under his own name & as "Jim," & carted him all around—to Hannibal, down the Mississippi on a raft, & even across the Desert of Sahara in a balloon [in *Tom Sawyer Abroad*]—& he has endured it all with the patience & friendliness & loyalty which were his birthright. It was on the farm that I got my strong liking for his race & my appreciation of certain of its fine qualities. This feeling & this estimate have stood the test of fifty years & have suffered no impairment. (SLC 1897–98, 44–46)

Daniel, or "Dann," was "in the fiftieth year of his age" when John Quarles freed him in 1855, two years after Clemens had left Missouri (Quarles). For an argument that two other black men Clemens knew well—John T. Lewis (1835–1906), who worked on Quarry Farm, and George Griffin, the family butler in Hartford—were also important as models for Jim, see Pettit, 95–106.

7.29–30   witches bewitched him . . . rode him all over the State] The belief that witches could commandeer people or animals to ride at night was common in European as well as American folklore (Hoffman, 50; Dorson, 238; Hughes and Bontemps, 199–200).

8.6–11   Jim always kept that five-center . . . fetch witches] Although wearing a coin around the neck was thought to bring good luck and protect the wearer against evil spirits and disease, Jim's particular beliefs about the coin's powers have not been independently documented (Hazlitt 1905, 1:6–7; Thomas and Thomas, item 3020).

8.27–28   village] As in *Tom Sawyer*, the village of St. Petersburg is modeled on Hannibal, Missouri, a busy river-port on the western bank of the Mississippi, where Clemens lived between the ages of four and seventeen (1839–53). In that time Hannibal nearly tripled its 1839 population of less than one thousand. "St. Petersburg" may be intended to suggest "St. Peter's town," or "heaven," even as it alludes to the American habit of grandiosely naming small towns and villages after the great cities of Europe and Asia: for example, Paris, Cairo, Alexandria, and Constantinople—the hometown of Becky and Judge Thatcher (*ATS*, 33).

8.32   Jo Harper, and Ben Rogers] Mark Twain's working notes for "Tom Sawyer's Conspiracy" (1897–?1902) show that he based Harper on his best friend, Will Bowen, and Rogers on another close friend, John Briggs. Rogers first appears in chapter 2, and Harper in chapter 3 of *Tom Sawyer* (*HH&T*, 383; *Inds*, 289–90, 304–5, 307).

9.15   hacked a cross in their breasts] Tom appears to have read Robert
Montgomery Bird's *Nick of the Woods; or, The Jibbenainosay* (1837), in
which the murderous title character marks his victims with "a knife-
cut, or a brace of 'em, over the ribs in the shape of a cross" (chapter 3).
Mark Twain had probably read this book by the time he was twenty-
three, for in his 1859 sketch "The Mysterious Murders in Risse" he portrayed an assassin who leaves his victim "bearing upon the centre of his
forehead the form of a cross, apparently cut with a knife" (*ET&S1*, 134–
41). In chapter 55 of *Life on the Mississippi*, written in 1882 or 1883, the
author recalled hearing, as a young man, grisly confessions of murder
that turned out to be fabrications inspired by *Nick of the Woods*.

10.10–12   a father . . . lay drunk with the hogs in the tanyard] The chief
model for Pap Finn was the Hannibal town drunkard Jimmy Finn, although Pap may also owe something to "General" Gaines and Woodson
Blankenship: his bellicosity when drunk to Gaines, and his fatherhood
to Blankenship (see the notes to 1.1–4 and 110.7). Mark Twain wrote at
least five separate descriptions of Jimmy Finn: one in 1867 (see the note
to 26.25–26); one in an 1870 letter to Will Bowen (*L4*, 50); one in the
1877 "Autobiography of a Damned Fool," where the character based on
him is said to be "a monument of rags and dirt; he was the profanest
man in town; . . . he slept with the hogs in an abandoned tan-yard"
(*S&B*, 152, 164); a fourth in chapter 23 of *A Tramp Abroad* (1880); and a
fifth in chapter 56 of *Life on the Mississippi* (1883), where Finn is said to
have died "in a tan vat, of a combination of delirium tremens and spon-
taneous combustion" (SLC 1883, 548). He was buried a pauper in 1845,
when Clemens was nine years old (Abbott, 16; Wecter, 150–51; *Inds*,
318–19).

13.8   she took me in the closet and prayed] Miss Watson follows literally
the injunction of Matthew 6:6, "But thou, when thou prayest, enter
into thy closet" (Marx 1967, 21n). Huck's word "closet" means pantry,
as it does in chapter 3 of *Tom Sawyer*, where Aunt Polly took Tom "into
the closet and selected a choice apple and delivered it to him, along
with an improving lecture" and a "happy Scriptural flourish" (*ATS*, 18).

13.10–11   whatever I asked for I would get it] Miss Watson's admonitions
about prayer and Huck's disappointment in it derive from the author's
recollection of his Hannibal schoolteacher Mrs. Elizabeth Horr (1790?–
1873), described in a 1906 dictation as "a New England lady of middle-
age, with New England ways and principles, and she always opened
school with prayer and a chapter from the New Testament; also she explained the chapter with a brief talk. In one of these talks she dwelt
upon the text 'Ask and ye shall receive,' and said that whosoever prayed
for a thing with earnestness and strong desire need not doubt that his

prayer would be answered." Dissatisfied with the result of his prayers, the young Clemens eventually decided the injunction was unsound (AD, 15 Aug 1906, CU-MARK, in *MTE*, 108–9; *Inds*, 326).

14.24–25   a drownded man don't float on his back, but on his face] Folklore held that one would "always find the body of a drowned woman floating face up; the body of a drowned man, face down. Although these positions are occasionally reversed in some sayings, this is the general belief—they are the normal positions in coitus" (Hyatt, item 15134). Mark Twain may well have encountered a variant of this belief in one of his favorite books, W. E. H. Lecky's *History of European Morals from Augustus to Charlemagne*. Lecky quotes the Roman historian Pliny: "It was said that drowned men floated on their backs, and drowned women on their faces; and this, in the opinion of Roman naturalists, was due to the superior purity of the latter" (Lecky, 2:318). Dr. Alvin Tarlov of the University of Chicago Medical School has compared reports by police in Norwalk and Westport, Connecticut, the New York City Harbor Squad, and the Marine Unit of the Chicago Police Department. All agreed with the findings of a veteran of the last unit: "I have been fishing bodies out of Lake Michigan for nine years running, about forty-four a year. . . . Men, women, boys and girls—they all float face down."

14.38   blazing stick, which he called a slogan] Leo Marx has suggested that "Tom has confused two passages from Sir Walter Scott. In *The Lay of the Last Minstrel* (Canto IV, xxvii), 'slogan' is used in its earlier sense to mean a battle cry; in a well-known episode in *The Lady of the Lake* (Canto III), a 'fiery cross' is carried through the countryside to call the clans to battle" (Marx 1967, 23n).

15.3   Cave Hollow] Mark Twain defined "hollow" as "Missourian for 'valley.' " Cave Hollow was the valley containing the entrance to McDowell's cave, south of Hannibal. In *Tom Sawyer*, Mark Twain described it as "a woody hollow" three miles below town, and in 1906, he remembered that "on the Saturday holidays in summertime we used to borrow skiffs whose owners were not present and go down the river three miles to the cave hollow" (AD, 16 Mar 1906, CU-MARK: in *AutoMT1*; *MTA*, 2:215; and SLC 1907, 165; chapters 29 and 33, *ATS*, 204, 243).

15.4–5   "sumter" mules] Tom refers to "sumpter" or pack mules, a term Clemens may have recalled from Cervantes (see also the next note). "Sumpter" mules are twice mentioned in the early pages of Cervantes's picaresque novel about the adventures of two boys, *Rinconete and Cortadillo* (1613). This work was included in the 1855 translation of Cervantes's *Exemplary Novels* which Clemens acquired in 1875. The term also occurs twice in Charles Jarvis's standard translation of *Don Quixote* (1605), first published in 1742, in chapter 19 of part I (Powers, 155, 159, 174 n. 9; Cervantes 1855, 45, 46; Cervantes 1992, xvii, 154, 156; Gribben, 1:136).

15.34–16.3   a book called "Don Quixote," . . . just out of spite] Tom refers to chapter 18 of part I of Cervantes's masterpiece, where "Don Quixote imagines that a herd of sheep, which he sees approaching, is really a motley army of Arabs, Spaniards, Christians and pagans. He attacks the sheep, and the shepherds repulse him, using their slings. Don Quixote explains that his enemy, the magician, has turned the armies into sheep, for spite." The relationship between Tom and Huck, and later between Huck and Jim, is in many ways similar to that between Don Quixote and Sancho Panza (Olin Harris Moore, 327–28, 337–38). In March 1869 Clemens told Olivia Langdon that "Don Quixote is one of the most exquisite books that was ever written, & to lose it from the world's literature would be as the wresting of a constellation from the symmetry & perfection of the firmament" (*L3*, 132).

16.7–8   before you could say Jack Robinson] Mark Twain marked this expression in his copy of Grose's *Classical Dictionary of the Vulgar Tongue* (1785), which he acquired in 1875. Grose defined it as "a saying to express a very short time, originating from a very volatile gentleman of that appellation, who would call on his neighbours, and be gone before his name could be announced" (Grose, 93; Gribben, 1:280).

16.13   they rub an old tin lamp] Aladdin does this, thereby conjuring up a genie, in "History of Aladdin, or the Wonderful Lamp," in *The Arabian Nights' Entertainments* (1839–41). In 1913, one of Clemens's boyhood friends recalled: "In those days, . . . we didn't have much to read. There was but one copy of the Arabian Nights in the village, and that volume was the property of Squire Clemens, Mark Twain's father. Sam knew all the stories. He could hire us, any day, to help him do his chores by merely a promise that, as soon as we were done, he would give us the Forty Thieves or some other yarn" (Abbott, 17).

16.23   chewing gum] Indians taught the New England colonists to chew spruce-tree resins. Spruce gum was first commercially sold in the early 1800s.

17.6   sweat like an Injun] Native American sweat lodges, widely used for health and ceremonial purposes, were described by European colonizers and travelers as early as the sixteenth century (Bruchac, 2, 17–24; Hearn 1981a, 75).

18.3–6   I . . . could spell, and read, and write just a little] Some readers
have questioned whether a boy so unschooled could have written this
long novel (see, for example, O'Connor). In answer, William M. Gibson
has suggested that Huck talked the book, addressing the "reader
orally—for it is a *speaking* letter, dictated or tape-recorded as it
were. . . . the absurdity of the form is glimpsed only momentarily"
(Gibson, 102). Huck's narrative conforms to a centuries-old literary
convention of picaresque "autobiographies" (Blair 1979, 2).

18.28–30   turn over the salt-cellar . . . bad luck] A common superstition,
recorded in Thomas and Thomas, items 1809, 1812, and in Hazlitt
1905, 2:532–33.

19.16   a cross in the left boot heel] In Europe and America a cross was
commonly invoked to ward off evil. For example, to avoid conjuration
blacks in the South made a plus or cross sign on the inner sole of a shoe
or used two needles to make a cross in the crown of a hat (see Hyatt,
items 16508–13, and Hazlitt 1905, 1:156; Puckett, 292).

19.36–37   don't ask me nothing—then I won't have to tell no lies] Huck's
remark echoes the proverb, "Ask me no questions and I'll tell you no
lies," which is the American variant of an English proverb, found, for
instance, in Oliver Goldsmith's *She Stoops to Conquer* (1773, act 3,
scene 1) and in Dickens's *Great Expectations* (1861, chapter 2) (Mieder,
29; Wilson, 20; Hearn 1981a, 77).

20.8   hair-ball] A dense, rounded mass of hair formed in the stomach of an
animal. Jim's divination with the hair-ball of an ox is the only "voodoo
belief . . . of incontestably African origin" in the book (Hoffman, 52).

24.5–6   You think you're better'n your father . . . because he can't] Mark
Twain had read Dickens's *Our Mutual Friend* (1864–65) by 1867. There
(book I, chapter 6) Gaffer Hexam likewise scolds his son after discovering that he has learned to read and write (Gardner, 155–56).

24.21–22   took up a book . . . something about General Washington and
the wars] Anecdotes and praise of George Washington were frequent selections in the textbooks published by William H. McGuffey (1800–73),
and used almost without exception in American schools at the time of
the story. For instance, *The Eclectic Second Reader; Consisting of Pro-
gressive Lessons in Reading and Spelling* (1836) lists "Story about
George Washington" and "More about George Washington," and *The
Eclectic Fourth Reader: Containing Elegant Extracts in Prose and Poetry, from the Best American and English Writers* (1838) includes Daniel Webster's "Washington's Birth Day" (Westerhoff, 126, 148).

26.25–26   new judge said he was agoing to make a man of him] In 1867, having visited Hannibal for the first time since 1861, Mark Twain recalled an incident from his youth when

> Jimmy Finn, the town drunkard, reformed, and that broke up the only saloon in the village. But the temperance people liked it; they were willing enough to sacrifice public prosperity to public morality. And so they made much of Jimmy Finn—dressed him up in new clothes, and had him out to breakfast and to dinner, and so forth, and showed him off as a great living curiosity—a shining example of the power of temperance doctrines when earnestly and eloquently set forth. Which was all very well, you know, and sounded well, and looked well in print, but Jimmy Finn couldn't stand it. He got remorseful about the loss of his liberty; and then he got melancholy from thinking about it so much; and after that, he got drunk. He got awfully drunk in the chief citizen's house, and the next morning that house was as if the swine had tarried in it. That outraged the temperance people and delighted the opposite faction. The former rallied and reformed Jim once more, but in an evil hour temptation came upon him, and he sold his body to a doctor for a quart of whiskey, and that ended all his earthly troubles. He drank it all at one sitting, and his soul went to its long account and his body went to Dr. [Orville] Grant. (SLC 1867)

In 1877 Mark Twain attributed an effort to "reform" the town drunkard to the character based on his brother Orion in "Autobiography of a Damned Fool" (S&B, 152–55). In 1906, he asserted that his father had tried, and failed, to reform both Finn and Injun Joe (AD, 8 Mar 1906, CU-MARK, in AutoMT1 and MTA, 2:175).

33.7   thought he was Adam, he was just all mud] In Genesis 2:7 God creates Adam "of the dust of the ground."

33.8–9   he most always went for the govment] Pap's favorite theme, like his contempt for blacks and literates, would have been recognized by contemporary readers as typical of southern whites who, according to Louis J. Budd, "served the South's reactionaries by opposing education, insisting on white supremacy, and lining up against 'governmental interference of any kind' " (Budd 1962, 96). Travelers in the South both before and after the Civil War deplored a class of shiftless and intemperate "poor whites"—"poor white trash" or "mean whites," as they became known—whose jobs were lost to slave labor and whose sole remaining distinction was the right to vote, "however blindly and ignorantly" (Hundley, 265–66). According to Harriet Beecher Stowe, they were "a material for the most horrible and ferocious of mobs" and "utterly ignorant, and inconceivably brutal. . . . Singular as it may appear, though slavery is the cause of the misery and degradation of this class, yet they are the most vehement and ferocious advocates of slavery" (Stowe 1853, 185; Hundley, 257–58, 265–74; Helper, 43–45; Seabrook; Den Hollander, 403–4, 414–22; Hildreth, 183, 265–66). Shields McIlwaine has traced the "mean white" as a literary type, related to the profane, shiftless characters depicted in the vernacular sketches of Southwest-

ern humor, and discoverable as a minor character in the works of
Harriet Beecher Stowe, William Gilmore Simms, and J. W. De Forest,
among others (McIlwaine, 32–42, 48–74, 96–99). Pap was doubtless recognizable to Mark Twain's readers as an exemplar of a real class, as were
fictional kinsmen such as J. W. De Forest's Selnarten Bowen in "An Independent Ku-Klux" (1872), James Kirke Paulding's backwoodsman,
Ambrose Bushfield, in *Westward Ho!* (1832), and the drunken mob
leader in J. T. Trowbridge's 1864 Civil War novel, *Cudjo's Cave* (De Forest; Paulding, 1:68, 2:182–83; Yellin, 40–41; Trowbridge, 105; Sloane
1988, 46–47).

33.33–34.1   free nigger there, from Ohio . . . talk all kinds of languages]
The learned black professor could hail from Ohio, because slavery had
been banned there by the 1787 Northwest Ordinance long before Ohio
became a state in 1803. Clemens may not have known him, but there
was in fact such a professor in the 1860s: John G. Mitchell (1827–1900),
a light-skinned black, who earned his doctorate of divinity and became
a professor of Greek, Latin, and mathematics at Wilberforce (Ohio)
University. During the Civil War Mitchell raised funds for his university in Missouri (Baker, 17, 28). Clemens did know and greatly admired
Frederick Douglass (1817?–95), whom he met in 1869. Born a slave,
Douglass escaped to freedom in 1838. Although not a professor, he was
an eloquent writer and lecturer against slavery.

34.2–3   he could *vote*, when he was at home] Actually, free blacks were
not allowed to vote in Ohio. Like most states outside the Northeast,
Ohio limited the "elective franchise to white male persons" (Hurd,
2:36, 37, 50, 51, 61, 116, 168).

34.13–14   he couldn't be sold till he'd been in the State six months] By the
1840s all slave states, including Missouri, absolutely prohibited immi-
gration of free blacks. In Hannibal free blacks could be treated as run-
aways if they failed to satisfy stringent legal requirements that they register with the state and have a certificate of freedom. An 1843 Missouri
law further stipulated that free blacks be licensed; and the 1855 statutes, which restricted licensing and length of residence, "were very
severe":

No colored person could live in this State without a license, and these licenses
were to be issued only to certain classes of them; moreover, bond, not exceeding
a thousand dollars, had to be given in security for good behavior. The negro was
not allowed to retain in his possession the license or other free papers, though he
could obtain them in the event of his moving from one county to another, as they
had to be filed with the clerk of the county court where he resided. No free negro
or mulatto could emigrate into the State or enter the State unless in the service

of a white man, or for the purpose of passing through. In either case the time that he could remain in the borders was limited. If he stayed longer he was liable to arrest, a fine of $10, and expulsion. If the fine was not paid he was further liable to not more than twenty lashes, and the court could either order that he immediately leave the State or else hire him out until the fine, costs and expenses of imprisonment had been paid for by his labor. (Conard, 5:604–5)

One Hannibal ordinance made mandatory an annual fee of five dollars, a cash bond, and "evidence of good moral character and behavior" for the required license (Hurd, 2:168n, 169n, 170; Welsh, 38).

35.10–11   pap, looking wild and skipping around] The passage that follows is an accurate description of a delirium tremens attack; indeed, "many clinicians are inclined to think that [it is] the most artful account on record" (Roueché, 96). Mark Twain was certainly familiar with accounts of the horrors of alcohol addiction, which abounded in temperance literature and in newspapers of the day (N&J1, 505; Branch 1983, 577–78). One contemporary temperance lecturer whom he knew, John Bartholomew Gough (1817–86), was famous for his dramatic recreations of alcoholic fits on stage.

36.8   Tramp—tramp—tramp; that's the dead] "Tramp, tramp, tramp," a common nineteenth-century refrain, appears, for instance, in "The Dead March," a temperance song included in an 1882 collection that Clemens owned, *The Treasury of Song for the Home Circle: The Richest, Best-Loved Gems*. The lyrics read in part:

> Tramp, tramp, tramp, in the drunkard's way
> March the feet of a million men.
> If none shall pity and none shall save,
> Where will all this marching end?
> The young, the strong, and the old are there,
> In woeful ranks as they hurry past,
> With not a moment to think or care
> What the fate that comes at last.
>
> Tramp, tramp, tramp . . .
> They are rushing madly on,
> Tramp, tramp, tramp . . .
> What a fearful ghastly throng;
> Rouse, Christian rouse ere it be too late,
> Rescue these souls from the drunkard's fate.
> (D. H. Morrison, 448–49; thanks to Paul
> Baender for this discovery)

37.25   June rise] The June or "Rocky Mountain" rise of the Mississippi resulted from the late outpouring of spring flood waters from the Missouri River (Miller, 194–95, 207 n. 8; Cramer, 133). In an 1875 installment of "Old Times on the Mississippi," written the year before he wrote this passage for *Huckleberry Finn*, Mark Twain described the June rise from the perspective of a cub pilot: "we met a great rise coming down the river. The whole vast face of the stream was black with drifting dead logs, broken boughs, and great trees that had caved in and been washed away. It required the nicest steering to pick one's way through this rushing raft, even in the day-time" (SLC 1875a, 448).

39.33   matches] Described as "new-fangled things" in chapter 33 of *Tom Sawyer* (*ATS*, 242), phosphorus friction matches (sometimes called "lucifer" matches) were patented in 1836 in the United States.

41.35   Jackson's Island] In *Tom Sawyer*, Joe Harper, Tom, and Huck use this island as their pirate refuge (chapters 13–16). Its geographical prototype was Glasscock's Island, near the Illinois shore and, according to Clemens, three miles long and three miles downstream from Hannibal in a mile-wide stretch of the Mississippi (see the map on page 370). At age 62, Clemens wrote Walter Besant of his "longing to go back to the seclusion of Jackson's island & give up the futilities of life. I suppose we all have a Jackson's island somewhere, & dream of it when we are tired" (SLC to Besant, 22 Feb 98, NN-B, in Hearn 1981a, 98).

45.1–16   The sun . . . very friendly] Mark Twain described comparable woodland scenes in *Tom Sawyer*, chapter 14, and *A Tramp Abroad*, chapter 2.

45.25–26   firing cannons over the water . . . carcass come to the top] A common and persistent superstition, both in Great Britain and the United States, was that "a gun fired over a corpse thought to be lying at the bottom of the sea, or a river, will by concussion break the gall bladder, and thus cause the body to float" (Radford and Radford, 87). A similar scene in *Tom Sawyer* (chapter 14) also made use of a boyhood memory. On 6 February 1870, in a letter to his childhood friend Will Bowen, Clemens recalled that "I jumped overboard from the ferry boat in the middle of the river that stormy day to get my hat, & swam two or three miles after it (& *got* it,) while all the town collected on the wharf & for an hour or so looked out across the angry waste of 'white-caps' toward where people said Sam. Clemens was last seen before he went down" (*L4*, 50–51). In a late note to himself, Clemens supplied one further detail of this incident: "fired cannon to raise drowned bodies of Clint Levering & me—when I escaped from ferry boat" (SLC [1902]). Clint Levering (1837?–47), a playmate of Clemens's, did drown in the Mississippi (*Inds*, 331–32).

46.3–4   quicksilver in loaves of bread . . . go right to the drownded carcass] Folklore stipulated: "to locate a drowned person, lay some quicksilver on the middle of a slice of bread and let the bread rest on the water where the person went down. The bread and quicksilver will float and stop above the submerged body" (Hyatt, item 15131). This superstition is "widely held in Britain. . . . A Biblical reference to quicksilver and life is probably the origin" (Radford and Radford, 46). An 1859 St. Louis *Missouri Democrat*, which Clemens might have seen, reports that after a long and fruitless search for the drowned body of a young man, a "loaf of *brown bread*" containing three ounces of quicksilver was thrown into the water and traveled "*against the wind*" to the very spot where the body had sunk (Branch 1983, 579).

47.17   Becky Thatcher] In *Tom Sawyer* Becky is Judge Thatcher's daughter and of course Tom's sweetheart. She is based on one of Clemens's Hannibal contemporaries, Anna Laura Hawkins (1837–1928), generally known as "Laura," who for a time lived across the street from the Clemenses.

47.18   Sid] Sid Sawyer is described in chapter 1 of *Tom Sawyer* as "Tom's younger brother, (or rather, half-brother)," but whether they shared the same mother or father is never specified (*ATS*, 3). Clemens acknowledged elsewhere that Sid was based in part on his own younger brother, Henry (1838–58), "but Sid was not Henry. Henry was a very much finer and better boy than ever Sid was" (AD, 12 Feb 1906, CU-MARK, in *AutoMT1* and *MTA*, 2:92–93).

48.29–30   bounded right onto the ashes of a camp fire . . . still smoking] A comparable scene occurs in Daniel Defoe's *Robinson Crusoe* (1719), where Crusoe finds a footprint on the shore of his island. In chapter 2 of *Life on the Mississippi*, Mark Twain called Marquette and his party's coming upon footprints "a Robinson Crusoe experience which carries an electric shiver with it yet, when one stumbles on it in print" (SLC 1883, 33).

51   *illustration*] Kemble's drawing of Jim quotes unmistakably from one of the most widely known graphic symbols of the campaign to abolish slavery:

> The image is of a kneeling African man, all but naked, his hands and feet chained, his gaze directed heavenward, and is usually captioned, "Am I Not a Man and a Brother?" It was originally adopted in the 1780s as the seal of the Society for the Abolition of Slavery in England. . . . Beginning in the 1820s, American abolitionists blanketed the Northeast with this image. It was printed on countless pamphlets, on stationery (advertised and sold through antislavery newspapers), and on handbills. It was also emblazoned on pottery and other goods.
>
> The most famous version of this image appeared on a broadside of John Greenleaf Whittier's poem "My Countryman in Chains," first published in 1837 and sold, beginning in March of that year, from the Anti-Slavery Offices in Boston and New York. (Reilly, 54–55)

Mark Twain alluded to the slogan ("Am I not a man and a brother?") in chapter 4 of *Tom Sawyer*. When cousin Mary undertakes to wash Tom before church, he emerges from the cleansing as "a man and a brother, without distinction of color" (*ATS*, 28, 263).

"Am I Not a Man and a Brother?" Unknown artist, n.d. Schomburg Center for Research in Black Culture, New York Public Library (NN).

52.39–53.1   People would call me a low-down ablitionist . . . for keeping mum] In 1847, Tom Blankenship's older brother, Benson, shunned the fifty-dollar reward offered for a runaway slave he found hiding on Sny Island, near the Illinois shore. He "kept the runaway over there in the marshes all summer. The negro would fish and Ben would carry him scraps of other food" (*MTB*, 1:63–64; see also Wecter, 148). This kindness must have been the more impressive because Benson's family was itself so poor. "In those old slave-holding days the whole community was agreed as to one thing," Mark Twain wrote in 1895,

the awful sacredness of slave property. To help steal a horse or a cow was a low crime, but to help a hunted slave, or feed him or shelter him, or hide him, or comfort him, in his troubles, his terrors, his despair, or hesitate to promptly betray him to the slave-catcher when opportunity offered was a much baser crime, & carried with it a stain, a moral smirch which nothing could wipe away. That this sentiment should exist among slave-owners is comprehensible—there were good commercial reasons for it—but that it should exist & did exist among the paupers, the loafers the tag-rag & bobtail of the community, & in a passionate & uncompromising form, is not in our remote day realizable. (Notebook 35, TS p. 35, CU-MARK, in Blair 1960a, 144)

The strong local sentiment about "the awful sacredness of slave property" was amply demonstrated in 1841 when three abolitionists from around Quincy, Illinois (across the river from Hannibal), tried to induce three Missouri slaves to escape. The slaves betrayed and helped capture their would-be liberators, who narrowly escaped lynching. After a brief trial, the jury—which included Clemens's father, John Marshall Clemens—found them guilty, and the judge imposed a sentence of twelve years' imprisonment at hard labor. Sharp clashes with abolitionists continued in the 1840s as anti-abolitionist vigilance committees were appointed in every township of Marion County. As a teenager, Clemens clearly shared his community's view of the "infernal abolitionists," as he wrote in an 1853 letter to his mother (24 Aug 53, *L1*, 4). Over the next ten or fifteen years, however, his attitudes underwent a fundamental change. When he died in 1910, William Dean Howells characterized him as "the most desouthernized Southerner I ever knew. No man more perfectly sensed and more entirely abhorred slavery" (Howells, 35; Holcombe, 256–59, 262–64; Blair 1960a, 109–10; Foner, 192–210).

53.6   sell me down to Orleans] Being sold "down the river" was the worst of fates for any slave: not only would he be permanently separated from his family, he would likely face a life of hard labor on a sugar or cotton plantation in Louisiana. In 1890 or 1891, in an attempt to explain how his "kind-hearted and compassionate" mother could tolerate slavery, Mark Twain wrote that

there was nothing about the slavery of the Hannibal region to rouse one's dozing humane instincts to activity. It was the mild domestic slavery, not the brutal plantation article. Cruelties were very rare, and exceedingly and wholesomely unpopular. To separate and sell the members of a slave family to different masters was a thing not well liked by the people, and so it was not often done, except in the settling of estates. . . . The "nigger trader" was loathed by everybody. He was regarded as a sort of human devil who bought and conveyed poor helpless creatures to hell—for to our whites and blacks alike the southern plantation was simply hell; no milder name could describe it. If the threat to sell an incorrigible slave "down the river" would not reform him, nothing would—his case was past cure. ("Jane Lampton Clemens," *Inds*, 88)

Clemens's memory of how slaves and slave families were treated in Hannibal is somewhat at odds with the statistics for Missouri as a whole. In the 1850s, for instance, perhaps thirty percent of Missouri slaves sold locally "were children under fifteen who were sold without either parent" (Tadman, 138).

53.10–11   eight hund'd dollars for me] A price of $800 for Jim is consistent with actual prices on record for young male slaves in Missouri in the 1830s and 1840s (Trexler, 38–39; N. Dwight Harris [1904] 1969, 261).

54.9   swim asho' en take to de woods on de Illinoi side] Jim's initial plan
was fraught with danger. Illinois, though nominally free, would not
have recognized him as a free man, and southern Illinois was a particularly dangerous place for runaway slaves. In compliance with the Fugitive Slave Act of 1793, Illinois authorities arrested blacks who were unable to produce a certificate of freedom, holding them as indentured
laborers until claimed by their owners (McDougall, 105–6; Hurd,
2:134–35). Substantial rewards offered for fugitive slaves made their
capture and return profitable to local residents as well as professional
bounty hunters. Although the law required that blacks be given a certificate of freedom if not claimed within a year, they were always in
danger of being kidnapped, as were all "unattached" or free blacks.
Laws against kidnapping were not enforced, with the result that it "as-
sumed the proportions of an established enterprise" (N. Dwight Harris
[1904] 1969, 54). Mark Twain knew that Jim's best route to freedom
would be northeast, up the Ohio River, which he must reach by first going south (see the note to 99.2–8).

54.31–32   I was going to catch some . . . it was death] Similar superstitions about catching birds are recorded in Hyatt, items 630, 639, 1748,
1756, 1770, 1771, and Thomas and Thomas, items 1908, 3634, 3647,
3658.

54.35–36   you mustn't count . . . bad luck] According to Daniel J. Hoffman, "Counting victuals as an invitation to bad luck would seem a deri-
vation of witch belief, since the witches suffered a fatal compulsion of
counting everything in their way. Hence many charms for the avoid-
ance of witches advised laying brooms, brushes, or bundles of faggots
on the doorstep, since it would take the witches all night to count the
hairs or strands" (Hoffman, 52).

54.37   shook the table-cloth after sundown] Another superstition of European origin (recorded in Hyatt, items 11691–92, and Thomas and
Thomas, item 1657).

54.37–38   if . . . that man died, the bees must be told] This ancient, widely
observed European custom apparently derived from the belief that the
bees are messengers of the gods (Hoffman, 51; Hazlitt 1905, 1:39; Radford and Radford, 30–31; recorded in Thomas and Thomas, item 3669).

55.2   bees wouldn't sting idiots] The innocence of virgins, children,
priests, and idiots was believed to protect them from bee stings. In
1881, five years after first composing this section of the book, Clemens
noted to himself: "Gilbert White, bees & idiots." White gave an account of an idiot boy's obsession with bees and his lack of any "appre-

hensions from their stings" in letter 27 of *The Natural History and Antiquities of Selborne* (1789). Clemens owned an 1875 edition of this work (*N&J2*, 408).

55.11–12 got hairy arms . . . you's agwyne to be rich] This superstition is recorded in Hyatt, items 3584, 3591.

55.20 I tuck to specalat'n', en got busted out] Jim's account is like one in chapter 38 of *History of the Big Bonanza* by William Wright (Dan De Quille), in which a Piute guide named "Capitan" Juan tells how he "was pretty well off once, . . . had *fifty dollars*," but was "burst all to smash" when he married a Spanish woman, "one *mucho* bad spectoolashe" (Wright, 272–73). Clemens, Wright's friend since they worked together on the Virginia City *Territorial Enterprise,* invited him to Hartford in 1875 to write his book and was instrumental in getting it published.

55.32–33 one-laigged nigger dat b'longs to ole Misto Bradish] Higgins, the "one legged mulatto, who belonged to Mr. Garth," was a familiar character in Hannibal (1889 clipping from the Hannibal *Journal,* enclosed in Ben Coontz to SLC, 18 Apr 89, CU-MARK). It may have been fifteen-year-old Sam Clemens who wrote in the Hannibal *Western Union* that when a certain Miss Jemima walked through the town wearing the new "Bloomer costume," Higgins was one of her critics: "Higgins (everybody knows HIGGINS,) plied his single leg with amazing industry and perseverance, keeping up a running fire of comment not calculated to initiate him in the good graces of the person addressed. When the leg became tired, its owner would seat himself and recover a little breath, after which, the indomitable leg would drag off the persevering Higgins at an accelerated pace" (SLC 1851). In a 6 February 1870 letter to Will Bowen, Clemens recalled the time he and Bowen "taught that one-legged nigger, Higgins," to pester another Hannibal resident (*L4*, 50). See also *Inds,* 324–25.

56.12 Balum's Ass] Balaam, an Old Testament prophet, was rebuked by the ass he was riding (Numbers, 22:21–33).

60.6–9 "Well, . . . so do de birds, chile."] In the manuscript for this portion of the book, discovered in 1990, this paragraph is followed by a passage of some fifteen and one-half pages, which contains a "ghost" story told by Jim. Mark Twain wrote the passage in 1876 but deleted it in 1883 or 1884, after it had been typed but before the book was submitted in typescript to the publisher. For the text of this passage and background information, see Three Passages from the Manuscript (pp. 463–70).

62.9–22 We got an old tin lantern . . . hunted all around] T. S. Eliot admired the "consistency and perfect adaptation of the writing" in *Huckleberry Finn*, citing this paragraph as exemplary, partly because "in the details he remembers . . . Huck is true to himself." The paragraph "provides the right counterpoise to the horror of the wrecked house and the corpse; it has a grim precision which tells the reader all he needs to know about the way of life of the human derelicts who had used the house; and (especially the wooden leg, and the fruitless search for its mate) reminds us at the right moment of the kinship of mind and the sympathy between the boy outcast from society and the negro fugitive from the injustice of society" (Eliot 1950, x, xi). Mark Twain had a weakness for "wooden leg" jokes: see, for instance, "Petrified Man," "Whereas," and "Cannibalism in the Cars" (SLC 1862; SLC 1864; SLC 1868).

63.25–26 worst bad luck . . . to touch a snake-skin] One of many superstitions linking snakes with bad luck (Thomas and Thomas, item 3723; Hyatt, item 1607). In 1906 Clemens wrote that "Aunty" Mary Ann Cord, a former slave whom he knew by the early 1870s, believed that snakes were so unlucky they "must be killed on sight, even the harmless ones; & the discoverer of a sloughed snake-skin lying in the road was in for all kinds of calamities" (SLC 1906a, 61, in Pettit, 53–54).

64.10–11 Jim grabbed pap's whisky jug and begun to pour it down] For snakebite the 1867 *Gunn's New Family Physician* prescribed the following remedy:

> Internally, give the patient *all the Whisky he can drink.* From a quart to a gallon should be drunk in six or eight hours. No fears need be entertained of making the patient drunk. You may fill him with Whisky, then let him swim in it, and it will not make him drunk, so long as the poison of the snake remains in the system. . . . It is a complete antidote for Snakebite, if taken freely, and may be relied on in any and all cases. It should be drunk like water for a few hours, and continued, at short intervals, until the patient gives signs of intoxication, when the quantity should gradually be diminished, as the disease is beginning to recede. Keep him "under the influence of liquor," however, until you are sure he is out of danger. (Gunn 1867, 515)

An 1861 newspaper story in the St. Louis *Missouri Democrat,* which Clemens could have read, told of a snakebite victim cured by "a full quart of whisky and ninety drops of hartshorn" given in three doses at five-minute intervals ("Remarkable Case of a Rattlesnake Bite," 11 June 61, in Branch 1983, 578).

64.13–14 wherever you leave a dead snake its mate always comes] A folk belief and frequent observation of travelers: "The friends and relatives of a slain snake would wage war upon the slayer and the latter's friends and relatives" (Hyatt, item 1585; Masterson, 177).

65.20   see the new moon over his left shoulder] Another well-known cause of bad luck (Thomas and Thomas, item 2212; Hazlitt 1905, 2:417).

65.33–35   cat-fish that . . . weighed over two hundred pounds] In *Life on the Mississippi*, Mark Twain said that he had "seen a Mississippi cat-fish that was more than six feet long, and weighed two hundred and fifty pounds" (chapter 2, SLC 1883, 32), and in a late autobiographical note to himself he associated such a fish with the person whose actions were in part the model for the Jackson's Island episode: "Big catfish. Bence Blankenship" (SLC [1897?]). See the note to 52.39–53.1 about Benson Blankenship.

68.11–12   Hookerville, seven mile below] In his working notes for "Tom Sawyer's Conspiracy" (1897–?1902), Mark Twain identified Hooker-ville as Saverton, Missouri, the first river town below Hannibal. In that story, the boys paddle "down the river seven miles in the dugout to Hookerville" (*HH&T*, 383, 180; *Inds*, 151).

73.11–12   my father and mother was dead, and the law had bound me out] In Missouri, male orphans could be indentured as apprentices by court order until the age of twenty-one. Those who helped runaway appren-tices to elude their employers risked a fine of up to $500 (*Revised Stat-utes* 1835, 67, 69; *Revised Statutes* 1845, 116–17, 119).

73.22–23   Goshen's ten mile further up the river] Goshen corresponds to Marion City, Missouri, ten miles upriver from Hannibal. After his 1882 visit, Mark Twain wrote in *Life on the Mississippi*, "When I first saw Marion City, thirty-five years ago, it contained one street, and nearly or quite six houses" (chapter 57, SLC 1883, 555).

74.4–6   "If fifteen cows . . . mum."] Clemens made a similar observation, probably in 1871, in the margin of his copy of *Descent of Man*, next to Darwin's discussion of "sociability" in animals: "sheep eat with their heads all turned the same way on the hillside—cows, mostly, too" (marginal note in Darwin, 71; Sherwood Cummings 1989, 33).

74.14–75.1   child, when you set out to thread a needle . . . t'other way] Nineteenth-century needlework manuals did not regard the manner of threading a needle as gender specific, indicating only that it was cus-tomary to hold the needle and push the thread through the eye, but the reverse method could be used "if preferred" (Hapgood, 6; *Workwoman's Guide*, 1). In 1879 or 1880, about three years after writing this needle-threading episode in *Huckleberry Finn*, Mark Twain gave the opposite gender information in chapter 13 of *The Prince and the Pauper:* Miles

Hendon "did as men have always done, and probably always will do, to the end of time—held the needle still, and tried to thrust the thread through the eye, which is the opposite of a woman's way" (P&P, 5, 148–49).

75.7   a girl . . . throws her knees apart] This gender test has been found in various sources from the eighteenth through the twentieth centuries, both English and American (Charleston Morning Post, 1 May 1786, 2, in Pitcher; Barker, 1:282, in Highfill; Bales, 74). It is also described in chapter 63 of Charles Reade's The Cloister and the Hearth, which Clemens had read and enjoyed in 1869 (L3, 413; see Gribben, 2:571).

78.23–29   stick to hang the old lantern on . . . hunted easy water] In "Old Times on the Mississippi" Mark Twain said that the "law required all such helpless traders to keep a light burning, but it was a law that was often broken" (SLC 1875a, 448). Like the raft, downstream boats followed the current in the river's natural channel, where the water was fastest and safest. Since such boats operated under power, there was always some danger of their overtaking and colliding with a raft, especially at night. Upstream boats, on the other hand, at least during high water, deliberately avoided the resistance of the channel, seeking out "easy water" near the banks. Since the channel itself meandered from one side of the river to the other, in what were called "crossings," upstream boats were sometimes obliged to cross in the opposite direction to avoid it. Huck reasons that upstream boats posed a danger of collision only when their paths intersected the channel.

78.30–31   between seven and eight hours . . . over four mile an hour] The hours traveled and the rate of speed (repeated as "four or five mile an hour" at 100.35) show that Mark Twain was roughly calculating the distance Huck and Jim travel each night as somewhere between twenty-eight and forty miles, the average of which is thirty-four miles. For the part of the trip above Cairo, that distance is realistic enough to make the narrative plausible to anyone familiar with the actual distance between cities such as St. Louis and Cairo. But Mark Twain would soon abandon any attempt to be precise about time and distance traveled. He wrote this portion of his narrative before he had acquired the detailed maps of the Mississippi that he ordered in 1882. So when the following notes refer to actual distances between places, they rely on numbers from U. P. James's River Guide, published in 1857, the year Clemens began to learn the river. Because the course of the river was constantly changing, James's mileage necessarily varies slightly from figures given by earlier and by later river guides.

79.3   The fifth night we passed St. Louis] St. Louis is 137 miles below Hannibal, or "St. Petersburg." The raft's location—after three full nights' and two partial nights' travel—is consistent with an average speed of thirty-four miles a night (see the previous note; James, 3; Miller, 193–98).

80.22–25   big straight river . . . steamboat that had killed herself on a rock] It remains uncertain which section of the river Mark Twain had in mind. The "straight" stretch of river encountered on the "fifth night below St. Louis" corresponds well to the 20-mile stretch that ends about 129 miles below St. Louis and 50 miles above Cairo. In that case, the wreck is about 2 miles below the fictional "Booth's Landing" (90.3–9), which would correspond to the real town of Bainbridge, Missouri, just at the end of the stretch. The hillside village with the ferryboat, on the right-hand shore (88.6–15), would then correspond to Cape Girardeau, Missouri, on a hillside 10 miles beyond Bainbridge (Miller, 198–99). On the other hand, Mark Twain may have had in mind a treacherous section of the river that he navigated in his piloting days. In chapter 25 of *Life on the Mississippi*, he described the "Grand Chain," about 150 miles below St. Louis in the 3-mile section of river between Thebes, Illinois, and Commerce, Missouri, as "a chain of sunken rocks admirably arranged to capture and kill steamboats on bad nights. A good many steamboat corpses lie buried there, out of sight" (SLC 1883, 276; James, 3, 25, 27, 28). See the map, page 370.

80.28–29   chair by the big bell, with an old slouch hat hanging on the back of it] The "big bell" was used to signal arrivals and departures as well as various alarms. It was a standard fixture on the roof of the upper (hurricane) deck. The captain would routinely "come on the roof" and stand beside the three-foot fixed bell, briefly resuming command from his pilot until the boat was again under way (Bates, 67; Way 1943, 260–61, 264; chapter 14, SLC 1883, 163–64). See the steamboat diagrams below.

80.30–98.7   Well, . . . I quit.] In the summer of 1883, Mark Twain inserted this long passage, consisting of sixty pages of manuscript, into his typescript of the first half of the book. The interpolation consists of the remainder of chapter 12 and all of chapters 13 and 14, known collectively as the *Walter Scott* passage after the name of the wrecked steamboat that Huck and Jim board (see the note to 89.12). Mark Twain made this revision a year after his trip down the Mississippi to gather information for *Life on the Mississippi* (April–May 1882), and seven years after he wrote the chapter into which he inserted it. That the new pages were inserted into a typescript rather than the manuscript was first proposed by Bernard DeVoto in 1942, corroborated in 1988 by references to the lost typescript, and is now finally confirmed by the manuscript found in 1990 (see DeVoto 1942, 62, 63; Blair 1958, 18; *HF2003*, 692–94 [Introduction]). See also Manuscript Facsimiles, pages 498–99.

81.20–28   fetched the starboard derrick . . . down through the texas hall
we see a light!] Here and elsewhere (see pages 86–87) Huck's description
of the steamboat is laced with precise river jargon. The steamboat is
pointed upstream, listing to port, with only her hurricane deck, texas,
and pilothouse above water: see the steamboat diagrams below. Huck
and Jim tie the raft to "the starboard derrick," an upright pole that
passes just in front of the hurricane deck, onto which they climb. They
move across this sloping surface, fending off the chimney guy wires, toward the officers' cabin, or "texas." They first reach a slight upward step
in the deck, the front end of the skylight roof (also called the texas deck).
Climbing onto this roof, they find themselves in front of the "captain's
door," at the head of the "texas hall," which bisects the cabin and gives
access to the staterooms on either side of it.

86.19–21   scrabbled along forwards on the skylight . . . to the cross-hall
door] That is, they scramble forward on the left side of the texas, walking on the narrow and sloping skylight roof (or texas deck), holding onto
the stateroom shutters because the edge of this deck is "in the water."
See the steamboat diagrams.

88.36   a sailor's life's the life for me] The ferryman echoes a line from a
song in Isaac Bickerstaff's *Spoil'd Child*, a long-lived two-act farce first
staged in 1790:

> I am a brisk and sprightly lad,
> Just come home from sea, Sir,
> Of all the lives I ever led,
> A sailor's life for me, Sir.
> Yeo, yeo, yeo! yeo, yeo, yeo!
> (act 2, scene 1, in
> Bickerstaff, 3:21)

89.12   *Walter Scott*] Names such as *Walter Scott, Waverley,* and *Ivanhoe*
were common for steamboats during the time of the story (Lytle, 92,
109, 166, 198, 200). In *Life on the Mississippi*, Mark Twain argued that
the South still suffered from "the Sir Walter disease" because antebellum southerners had been influenced by Scott's popular medieval ro-
mances to emulate "decayed and degraded systems of government; . . .
sham chivalries of a brainless and worthless long-vanished society"
(chapter 46, SLC 1883, 467, 468).

91   *illustration*] On 25 June 1884, Clemens wrote to his publisher,
Charles L. Webster, about the proof of this illustration: "It occurs to me,
now, that on the pilot house of that steamboat-wreck the artist has put
TEXAS—having been misled by some of Huck's remarks about the
boat's 'texas'—a thing which is a part of *every* boat. That word had better be removed from that pilot house" (NPV, in *MTBus*, 262). Webster
had the picture corrected before publication.

Bow view of the *Memphis*, a Mississippi steamboat built in 1860, tilted to suggest the position of the wrecked *Walter Scott*. Scale: ½ inch = 20.75 feet. (Reed, plate 14)

Side view of the *Memphis*. Scale: ½ inch = 20.75 feet. (Reed, plate 12)

Plan of the texas of a Mississippi steamboat. (Based on Bates, figures 66, 69, 70, 71; Reed, plate 12; Hilton, Plummer, and Jobé, 88, 94; Way 1972, 24.)

93.26–98.7 I read considerable to Jim about kings . . . I quit.] Comprising
all of chapter 14, this passage is the last part of the long section Mark
Twain inserted into his typescript in 1883 (see the note to 80.30–98.7).
Having already introduced "the king" and "the duke" in 1880, in what
became chapter 19 (158.36), Mark Twain reminded himself to set the
stage for their appearance with this inserted passage: "Back yonder,
Huck reads & tells about monarchies & kings &c. So Jim stares when
he learns the rank of these 2" (see *HF2003*, 505 [Mark Twain's Working Notes, no. 3-4]). The debates are also reminiscent of the comic di-
alogues between the genteel interlocutor and the vernacular end men,
Bones and Tambo, which were a standard feature of minstrel shows of
the mid-nineteenth century. In 1906 Clemens fondly recalled the minstrel shows of his youth, in particular the "delightful jangle of assertion
and contradiction" that characterized them (AD, 30 Nov 1906, CU-
MARK, in *MTE*, 113; Berret 1986, 38–40; Engle, xviii–xxi; Moody, 479–
80, 485–87; *Minstrel Gags*, 5–13, 20–23, and passim). The suggestion of
minstrel show elements in *Huckleberry Finn* has led some critics to describe Jim's character and behavior as a racial stereotype (Woodard and
MacCann 1984 and 1992; Lott; Graff and Phelan, 335–479; Leonard,
Tenney, and Davis, 124–237; and Champion, 143–225). They have been
well answered by critics who recognize how ingeniously Mark Twain
has put minstrel conventions in the service of ridiculing Huck's racism
and giving the reader a lively sense of Jim's intelligence (Mailloux, 72–
87; Fishkin, 79–83; David L. Smith, 8).

94.12 hawking and sp—] A venerable pun, found at least as early as 1639,
but possibly suggested to Mark Twain by Scott's *The Fortunes of Nigel*
(1822), a source for *The Prince and the Pauper*. Scott's Lord Dalgarno
says to Dame Nelly, "you shall ride a hunting and hawking with a lord,
instead of waiting upon an old ship-chandler, who could do nothing but
hawk and spit" (Scott 1822, 3:307; Baetzhold 1970, 94).

94.36 dat chile dat he 'uz gwyne to chop in two] See 1 Kings 3:16–28.

96.14–18 little boy the dolphin . . . come to America] Although Louis
XVII (1785–95?), son of the guillotined Louis XVI, died in a French
prison, he was widely believed to have escaped and come to America
(DeVoto 1932, 318–19). In 1882 Clemens acquired Horace W. Fuller's
Noted French Trials: Impostors and Adventurers, in which one chapter
recounted the stories of "seven impostors [who] have claimed the name
and the rights of the unhappy Louis XVII," some of whom visited the
United States, and one of whom—Eleazar Williams—was born there
(Fuller, 100, in Blair 1957, 27). Mark Twain's 1869 newspaper sketch
"The 'Wild Man' " shows his familiarity with Williams and the contro-
versy surrounding his claims, and Clemens almost certainly had earlier
knowledge of other such impostors: for instance, in 1853 the Hannibal

Journal reprinted a story about the visit to a newspaper office of a Bourbon pretender calling himself "Aminidab Fitz-Louis Dolphin Borebon," whom the staff hailed as the "Dolphin" (SLC 1869c; Ashmead).

97.3   Some of them gets on the police] Mark Twain remarked in *The Innocents Abroad* (chapter 13) that Napoleon III "kept his faithful watch and walked his weary beat a common policeman of London" (SLC 1869a, 127; noted by Henry Nash Smith, personal communication). Napoleon III had joined a special constabulary formed in London in 1848 to prevent Chartist demonstrations (Simpson, 277–78).

97.3–4   some of them learns people how to talk French] In *A Tale of Two Cities*, Charles Darnay, a noble French emigrant, is "established in England as a higher teacher of the French language" before the French Revolution. As Dickens commented, "Princes that had been, and Kings that were to be, were not yet of the Teacher class" (book 2, chapter 10, Dickens 1970, 159, 160).

99.1–2   We judged that three nights more would fetch us to Cairo] In his manuscript, Mark Twain first wrote "two nights," then changed it to "two or three nights," and finally to just "three nights" (MS1, 280.6–7). Although the point is never made explicit, Mark Twain may have intended the estimate of three nights' travel to be their mistaken judgment, which becomes clear when the raft passes Cairo in the fog just *two* nights later (see the note to 129.14).

99.2–8   Cairo . . . was what we was after. We would . . . go way up the Ohio amongst the free States] One leg of Jim's intended flight to freedom was necessarily *south* on the Mississippi. Illinois would not have offered him a true refuge, as the note to 54.9 explains. In notes he made for his 1895–96 lecture tour, Mark Twain accounted for Huck's and Jim's southward journey as follows: "Night after night they kept a sharp lookout for Cairo, where the Ohio river comes in; for there they would land & try to escape far north & east away from the domain of slavery" (SLC 1895a, 1:160; see *HF2003*, 637 [Mark Twain's Revisions for Public Reading, 1895–1896]). In addition to the escape route provided by the Ohio River itself, Ohio had far more Underground Railroad operators than any other state. Most routes of this famed network began at the river and proceeded northward through eastern Indiana and Ohio (Siebert [1898] 1967, map facing 113, 119, appendix E; Siebert 1947, 77, 85, 89).

104.12–13   dog my cats ef it ain't de powerfullest dream I ever see] In chapter 72 of William Wright's *History of the Big Bonanza*, some miners fool a companion, Pike, leading him to believe that an Indian attack that they had staged to frighten him was only a dream. Pike remarks that his "dream" was as "plain" as an actual experience—"the dogonest plainest dream I ever did hev" (Wright, 555; see the note to 55.20).

107.1–123.20   But you know . . . home again.] In 1882 Mark Twain pulled this passage (later called the "raft episode" or "the raft chapter") out of his still unfinished manuscript for *Huckleberry Finn,* and had it typed for publication in *Life on the Mississippi.* He introduced it there as "a chapter from a book which I have been working at, by fits and starts, during the past five or six years, and may possibly finish in the course of five or six more" (chapter 3, SLC 1883, 42; SLC to Webster, 14 Apr 84, NPV, in *MTBus,* 248–49; SLC to Howells, 20 July 83, NN-B, in *MTHL,* 1:435). When the first half of the *Huckleberry Finn* manuscript was typed in late 1882 or 1883, the raft episode pages were apparently not included. As the *Huckleberry Finn* manuscript discovered in 1990 shows, and as other evidence suggests, he eventually put the manuscript of the raft episode back in place and had a typed copy (or tearsheets from *Life on the Mississippi*) inserted into the *Huckleberry Finn* typescript he was revising for publication (MS1, 309–62, NBu; *HF2003,* 705–7; *N&J3,* 60). After Clemens submitted the printer's copy of *Huckleberry Finn* to Charles L. Webster, he began to worry that including any part of the raft episode in the salesmen's prospectus would hurt sales because prospective buyers would regard it as a "reprint." He therefore instructed Webster to "be particular" to exclude the raft episode from the prospectus (SLC to Webster, 14 Apr 84, NPV, in *MTBus,* 248–49). Webster, who was then trying to solve the manufacturing problem of how to make *Tom Sawyer* and *Huckleberry Finn* into matching volumes when the second book was so much longer than the first, suggested leaving it out, not just from the prospectus, but from the book itself. Clemens agreed: "Yes, I think the raft chapter can be left wholly out, by heaving in a paragraph to say Huck visited the raft to find out how far it might be to Cairo, but got no satisfaction. Even *this* is not necessary unless that raft-visit is referred to later in the book. I think it is, but am not certain" (SLC to Webster, 22 Apr 84, NPV, in *MTBus,* 249–50; Webster to SLC, 21 Apr 84, CU-MARK). Webster then removed (or deleted) the episode from the printer's copy, apparently unaware that its omission did indeed create a problem in the text. Huck's plan to "paddle ashore the first time a light showed" and ask "how far it was to Cairo" is agreed to: "Jim thought it was a good idea, so we took a smoke on it and waited." But in the altered text (and ultimately in the first edition) this sentence was followed immediately by an unexplained change of plan, "There warn't nothing to do, now, but to look out sharp for the town" (SLC 1885a, 122–23; see Beidler 1968, 12–13; see also the note to 129.22–24). Until the discovery of the first half of the manuscript in 1990, it was not known what, if any, further change Mark Twain or Webster might have made at the time. The manuscript makes clear, however, that the "raft-visit" was not "referred to later in the book," and that rather than "heaving in a paragraph" as Clemens suggested (a paragraph which Clemens certainly would have written himself if required), Webster most likely attempted to solve any problem of coherence or continuity himself by simply deleting two sentences from the printer's copy. The sentences immediately followed the raft episode and made no sense with the episode left out: "I had to tell Jim I didn't find out how far it was to Cairo. He was pretty sorry" (123.21–22; see Manuscript Facsimiles, p. 501). No illustrations were prepared for the episode, and it never appeared in the novel during the author's lifetime. Because Mark Twain's decision to omit it seems to have been solely to serve the practical convenience of his publisher, the raft episode was restored from the printed text of *Life on the Mississippi* in the 1985 Mark Twain Library and 1988 Works of Mark Twain editions. The 1990 discovery of the first half of the manuscript provided no new evidence that alters the import of the circumstances of omission. In the present editions the raft episode, and the two sentences omitted by Webster, are restored from the manuscript (see *HF2003*, 705–8 [Introduction]). In the absence of Kemble illustrations, the thirteen illustrations made by John Harley for this passage in *Life on the Mississippi* are included here. Mark Twain had seen and approved these two years before publishing *Huckleberry Finn*. In 1885, George Washington Cable urged Mark Twain to restore the episode. In 1907, Mark Twain alluded to practical difficulties rather than aesthetic reasons for continuing to omit it, when the essayist and biographer E. V. Lucas, likewise an advocate of restoration, asked him about it: "I asked him why he had never incorporated in *Huckleberry Finn* the glorious chapter about the boasting bargemen which he dropped into *Life on the Mississippi*. His reasons were not too understandable but I gathered that some copyright question was involved" (*N&J3*, 98; Lucas 1929; Lucas 1910, 116). More recently, Bernard DeVoto, Peter G. Beidler, and William R. Manierre have argued for restoring the passage, on various grounds (SLC 1942, x–xi; Beidler 1968; Manierre), but restoration remains controversial. Hamlin Hill, and more recently Jonathan Arac, have argued against it (see SLC 1962, xii; Arac, 139–42). DeVoto was the first of several editors to publish the passage in place, but he and others who followed his lead all used editorial markers, notes, or a change in type size to set it off (SLC 1942, 120–33; DeVoto 1946, 291–307; Lynn 1961, 42–48; SLC 1996b, 112–29). Other editors have elected to include it as an appendix (see SLC 1958, 247–58; SLC 1967, 331–43). Discussions of the crux can be found in Lynn 1958, 425–27; Leary, 100–103; Rasmussen, 385–86; and SLC 1996b, 377–78.

108.1–8   "There was a woman in our towdn, . . . twyste as wed'l."] This folk-ballad, originally from Britain, was a particular favorite of Mark

Twain's: he had already used it in 1865 in a play which he left unfinished (S&B, 211); his niece remembered his singing it in the family's private railroad car during his wedding journey from Elmira to Buffalo in 1870 (MTBus, 109); he used it in 1876 in this section of the *Huckleberry Finn* manuscript; and he assigned the song to Miles Hendon in the 1880 portion of *The Prince and the Pauper* manuscript (P&P, 5, 148–50). He later recalled his own rendition in an 1885 family parlor performance of *Prince and the Pauper:* "I was great in that song" (MTS 1910, 72). Under various titles, among them "There Was an Old Woman in Ireland," "The Rich Old Lady," and "She Loved Her Husband Dearly," it survives as a folk song in Missouri and neighboring states (Wolford, 93; Sharp, 348–49; Chauncey O. Moore, 218–19; Belden, 238–39). Despite his fondness for the song, Mark Twain wrote "strike out" next to the verses in his manuscript (MS1, 312). But he never did so.

108.10–11   the tune the old cow died on] Although the old cow dies in a great many folk and minstrel songs, the only one found in which she is killed by the tune is a folk song, evidently of English or Irish origin:

> Farmer John from his work came home
> One summer's afternoon,
> And sat himself down by the maple grove
> And sang himself this tune.
> *Chorus:*
> Ri fol de ol, Di ri fol dal di
> Tune the old cow died on.
>   (Musick, 105–6; in Hearn 1981a, 366)

109.7–111.32   "Whoo-oop! I'm the old original . . . after sweeps.] Literary depictions of comic braggarts such as Bob and the Child of Calamity date back at least to Aristophanes' *The Frogs* (405 B.C.). In the United States, early nineteenth-century frontier humor and tall tales were filled with characters such as the legendary keelboatman, Mike Fink, who in an 1842 tale was reported to have said:

I never was particular, about what's called a fair fight, I just ask a half a chance, and the odds against me; and if I then don't keep clear of snags and sawyers, let me spring a leak, and go to the bottom. . . . Well, I walk tall into varmint and Indian, it's a way I've got, and it comes as natural as grinning to a hyena. I'm a regular tornado, tough as a hickory withe, long-winded as a nor'-wester. I can strike a blow like a falling tree, and every lick makes a gap in the crowd that lets in an acre of sunshine. . . . I must fight something, or I'll catch the dry rot, burnt brandy won't save me. (Thorpe 1842, in Estes, 177–78)

Unlike early American swaggerers whose exploits almost justified their threats, typical Old World specimens had been bluffing cowards who ran away from fights. Beginning in the 1850s most American comic writers followed European patterns, as did Clemens in his 1852 sketch "The Dandy Frightening the Squatter" (ET&S1, 63–65), and in the present episode (see Blair 1960a, 115–16; Blair 1960b, 29–31, 154; Blair and Hill, 128–51, 255–62, 314).

110.7   Whoo-oop! Bow your neck and spread] Mark Twain recalled in a
letter to Will Bowen that "old General Gaines used to say, 'Whoop! Bow
your neck & spread!'" (*L4*, 50). Gaines, one of Hannibal's "prominent &
very intemperate neer-do-weels," was the "first town-drunkard before
Jimmy Finn got the place" (SLC 1909c, 5; SLC 1897–98, 54). He appears
in chapter 1 of "Huck Finn and Tom Sawyer among the Indians" (1884),
and in the working notes for "Tom Sawyer's Conspiracy" (1897–?1902),
which show that Mark Twain intended to base another fictional keelboatman on him, "Admiral Grimes" (*HH&T*, 94, 383, 384; *Inds*, 35).

111.37–38   another patted Juba] In patting juba, adapted from African
dances, slaves used their hands in rhythmic accompaniment to music.
According to a former slave, one patted by "striking the hands on the
knees, then striking the hands together, then striking the right shoulder with one hand, the left with the other—all the while keeping time
with the feet, and singing" (Northup, 219). According to another account, "the position was usually a half-stoop or forward bend, with a
slap of one hand on the left knee followed by the same stroke and noise
on the right, and then a loud slap of the two palms together. . . . the left
hand made two strokes in half-time to one for the right. . . . One of the
best-known . . . dance tunes was called 'Juba'" (Wyeth, 59, 62).

111.38–112.1   a regular old-fashioned keel-boat break-down] A break-
down was a boisterous, rapid, shuffling dance in the "Negro style,"
often danced competitively by dancers in succession, and sometimes
accompanied by patting juba (Nathan, 92). Like the music that accompanied them, breakdowns were especially popular among white river-
boatmen. An 1844 St. Louis newspaper reported the boatmen's fondness for "river yarns, boatman songs, and 'nigger break-downs,'
interspersed with wrestling-matches, jumping, laugh, and yell" (Field,
180). But the dance had been observed among slaves as early as 1700:
"The dancers brought along boards, called shingles, upon which they
performed. These wooden planks were usually about five or six feet
long and equally wide, and were kept in place during the dancing by
four of their companions. Rarely in their deft 'turning and shying off'
did they step from the boards" (Ottley and Weatherby, 25–26). Dickens
described a breakdown dancer he saw in 1842: "Single shuffle, double
shuffle, cut and cross-cut: snapping his fingers, rolling his eyes, turning
in his knees, presenting the backs of his legs in front, spinning about
on his toes and heels . . . dancing with two left legs, two right legs, two
wooden legs, two wire legs, two spring legs—all sorts of legs and no
legs" (Dickens 1842, 36).

112.4   "Jolly, jolly raftsman's the life for me,"] An 1844 minstrel song attributed to Daniel Emmett, with lyrics by Andrew Evans (entitled "The
Raftsman," as sung by A. F. Winnemore of the Georgia Champions, and

"The Jolly Raftsman," in *Old Dan Emmit's Original Banjo Melodies*, the latter in Nathan, 302–3).

> *Chorus:*
> My Raft is by the shore
> She's light and free
> To be a jolly Raftsman's the life for me
> And as we glide along
> Our song shall be
> Dearest Dine I love but thee.

112.12–14   the muddy Mississippi water was wholesomer to drink than the clear water of the Ohio] More than one nineteenth-century traveler reported hearing claims about the potability of Mississippi River water. Zadok Cramer, in his early river guide, recommended filtering the muddy water and commented on its usefulness as a "powerful cathartic" and "cure for most cutaneous diseases": "It is upon the whole, after filtration, . . . the most agreeable water I ever drank, and I am led to believe the wholesomest. I have frequently drove off a slight stomach fever after eating, . . . by drinking two, three, or four tumblers of this delightful water" (Cramer, 135–36, 138). Christian Schultz described the water as "thick and turbid" in the record of his 1807–8 travels: "It will deposit a sediment of half an inch deep in a half pint tumbler of water. Yet no other is used for the table." And he noted the water's reputation as a remedy for both sterility and "the itch" (Schultz, 2:199, in Beidler 1990, 58). Charles Murray explained that "a stranger . . . cannot endure the dirty and muddy appearance of the water, although he is told (and with truth) that, when placed in a barrel, or any other vessel, and allowed to settle, it purifies very rapidly and becomes excellent drinking-water" (Murray, 1:233). Dickens in *American Notes* commented on the belief of natives that the water was wholesome (Dickens 1842, 65). And in 1849 Alexander Mackay noted that the "Mississippi water, turgid though it be, is not considered unwholesome, and those long accustomed to it prefer it to any other" (Mackay, 2:128).

113.11–14   Ohio water didn't like to mix with Mississippi water . . . for a hundred mile or more] Alexander Mackay reported that "in passing the Ohio, we were for a few minutes in clear and limpid water; quite a contrast, in this respect, to the turgid and muddy volume with which it mingled. . . . Opposite the northern bank of the Ohio, the line where the two currents mingle is distinctly traceable for some distance into the Mississippi" (Mackay, 2:128).

124.26–27   the old saying, 'Give a nigger an inch and he'll take an ell.'] This variation of a venerable English proverb—"Give an inch and you'll take an ell," recorded as early as 1546—can also be found in Frederick Douglass's 1845 autobiography (Douglass, 29, 31; MacKethan, 259; Burton Stevenson, 1635).

127.11   a twenty-dollar gold piece] A technical anachronism, since coins of this denomination did not begin to circulate until 1850 (Goodyear).

127.24–25   a body that don't get *started* right when he's little, ain't got no show] This passage echoes an opinion Mark Twain held about the moral nature of mankind. According to Albert Bigelow Paine, "Among the books of his summer reading at Quarry Farm, as far back as 1874, there was a copy of [W. E. H.] Lecky's *History of European Morals*, a volume that made a deep impression upon Mark Twain and exerted no small influence upon his intellectual life" (Paine, ix). Lecky distinguished two opposing schools of morality:

> One of them is generally described as the stoical, the intuitive, the independent or the sentimental; the other as the epicurean, the inductive, the utilitarian, or the selfish. The moralists of the former school . . . believe that we have a natural power of perceiving that some qualities, such as benevolence, chastity, or veracity, are better than others. . . . The moralist of the opposite school denies that we have any such natural perception. He maintains that we have by nature absolutely no knowledge of merit and demerit, . . . and that we derive these notions solely from an observation of the course of life which is conducive to human happiness. (Lecky, 1:3)

Lecky favored "the former school," and Huck, in his instinctual desire to help Jim, seems to conform to this point of view. Nevertheless, his statement that he has failed to do the right thing because he didn't "get *started* right" when he was little, illustrates the position of "the opposite school," which held that environment determines morality. In a marginal comment written in his copy of Lecky, Clemens expressed his own belief that "all moral perceptions are acquired by the influences around us; these influences begin in infancy; we never get a chance to find out whether we have any that are innate or not" (Davis, 4; see Blair 1960a, 131–44, and Boewe).

128.6   Dat *wuz* de smartes' dodge] Huck's "dodge"—by which he ingeniously leads the two slave hunters to conclude that his father has smallpox—has an analogue in the autobiography of fugitive slave James Pennington, *The Fugitive Blacksmith* (1849)—a book which Clemens may have read, although decisive evidence has not been found that he either owned or read it (Andrews; MacKethan, 256–58; Pennington, 220–24). He had long been familiar with such accounts, both spoken and printed. By 1869 he knew and admired Frederick Douglass, who in 1838 had been one of many fugitive slaves helped by Clemens's abolitionist in-laws, the Langdons, and who had published his famous *Narrative* in 1845 (*L3*, 426, 428 n. 2). He doubtless heard stories from his good friend James Redpath, a prominent abolitionist, who was both his and Douglass's lecture agent. Redpath collected and published slave narratives in his *Roving Editor: or, Talks with Slaves in the Southern States* in 1859 (*L3*, 217–18 n. 8; *L4*, 315 n. 2). Mark Twain's "A True Story, Repeated

Word for Word as I Heard It" (1874) was based on the personal narrative of Mary Ann Cord, who worked for the Langdons in Elmira. His library included an 1836 pamphlet autobiography of the slave Amos Dresser, as well as the 1883 revised edition of William Still's massive compilation of fugitive slave narratives, *The Underground Rail Road*, first published in 1872 (in which Mark Twain wrote down the story, told by his mother-in-law, of a slave family who escaped to Elmira in the 1840s). He also owned a copy of Charles Ball's autobiographical *Slavery in the United States*, a work he consulted in the late 1880s when writing *A Connecticut Yankee* (Gribben, 1:43, 203, 2:666; *N&J3*, 501; Baetzhold 1970, 151, 349–50 n. 33; MacKethan, 253–54; Fishkin, 96–99).

129.14   "Maybe we went by Cairo in the fog that night."] That is, two nights earlier. In the introduction to the raftsmen's episode in chapter 3 of *Life on the Mississippi*, and in his 1895 notes, Mark Twain confirmed that the raft passed Cairo "in a fog" (SLC 1883, 43; SLC 1895a, 1:174; *HF2003*, 642 [Mark Twain's Revisions for Public Reading, 1895–1896]). Mark Twain clearly did not expect his readers to identify the various villages he mentions either above or below Cairo. Nonetheless, he seems to have drawn on his memory of the geography of some real towns (see the note to 80.22–25). The situation of Columbus and Hickman, Kentucky, twenty-two and forty-two miles *below* Cairo, matches that of the two towns that the raft has just passed—one "in a left-hand bend" and the second on "high ground" (128.17, 129.10) (Miller, 200–201; James, 3, 27–30; see the map on page 369). On his 1882 downriver trip, Mark Twain noted that "Hickman looks about as it always did; and so does Columbus" (*N&J2*, 534).

129.22–24   the clear Ohio water in shore . . . So it was all up with Cairo] In the first edition of *Huckleberry Finn*, which omitted the "raft episode" and consequently the explanation of the difference between Ohio and Mississippi river water (112.12–14 and 113.11–16), the reader was left unintentionally perplexed as to why the contrasting colors meant "it was all up with Cairo," not to mention how Huck suddenly knew what he was clearly ignorant of just pages before (106.20–27; see Beidler 1968, 13–14). Inexplicably, Huck and Jim do not notice the "clear Ohio water" until the third day after they pass Cairo (and the confluence with the Ohio River) in the fog.

130.18–22   She aimed right for us . . . going to try to shave us] In "Old Times on the Mississippi" Mark Twain recalled that the timber rafts, coal barges, and little trading scows heading downstream during the June rise were regarded by steamboat pilots as an "intolerable nuisance." "Pilots bore a mortal hatred" to such "small-fry craft," because the latter often failed to keep a light burning and were difficult to see on a murky night (SLC 1875a, 448, 449; see also the note to 78.23–29).

130.31 I dived—and I aimed to find the bottom] In "Old Times on the Mississippi," Mark Twain told of a cub pilot who "plunged head-first into the river and dived under the wheel" and thus saved himself when his sounding boat was struck in the dark by the steamboat's paddle-wheel (SLC 1875a, 570).

131.6–10 towards the left-hand shore . . . long, slanting, two-mile cross-ings . . . I made a safe landing] Huck apparently comes ashore at the foot of New Madrid Bend where the current crosses from the west (Missouri) side of the river to the east shore, where Kentucky and Tennessee share a narrow neck of land bisected by the state line (James, 3, 29–30; see the map on page 371). In his introductory remarks to the excerpted episode in the December 1884 *Century Magazine*, Mark Twain explained that the raft had "already floated four hundred miles" down river at this point: New Madrid, Missouri, was, in fact, four hundred and two miles below Hannibal, the equivalent of the fictional St. Petersburg (James, 3). This location is also indicated by the incidents described in the next two chapters, based on Mark Twain's recollection of events at Compro-mise, Kentucky, in New Madrid Bend (see the note to 146.12–17). In 1895, when introducing a reading from the upcoming chapters, Mark Twain specified that "Huck swam to the Kentucky side" of the river, that is, the east side (SLC 1895a, 1:174; *HF2003*, 642 [Mark Twain's Revisions for Public Reading, 1895–1896]).

134.10–12 about as old as me—thirteen or fourteen or along there] In 1895, while preparing to read from his book, Mark Twain noted to him-self that Huck was "a boy of 14" (Notebook 35, TS p. 35, CU-MARK, in Blair 1960a, 143). Kemble's illustrations, however, mistakenly suggest a younger boy. In chapter 26, for example, Huck appears diminutive compared with Joanna Wilks, a girl of fourteen (206.35–36 and illustra-tions on pages 221 and 224).

135.2–3 he asked me where Moses was when the candle went out] This "common riddle" inspired an 1878 "popular 'serio-comic song' " by John Stamford, "Where Was Moses When the Lights Went Out?" (Hearn 1981a, 163 n. 7).

136.15–17 hadn't seen no house . . . had so much style] The Grangerford property generally resembles that of John Quarles, Clemens's uncle, who lived in the country near Florida, Missouri, where Clemens re-called he spent "two or three months every year, from the fourth year after we removed to Hannibal till I was eleven or twelve years old" (SLC 1897–98, 37). In many of its furnishings, however, the Grangerford par-lor resembles what Mark Twain described in the "House Beautiful" chapter of *Life on the Mississippi* as the typical "residence of the princi-pal citizen" of towns in the Mississippi Valley, "all the way from the suburbs of New Orleans to the edge of St. Louis" (chapter 38, SLC 1883, 406). Mark Twain almost certainly wrote the description of the Grangerford house and parlor in 1876, six years before he wrote the "House Beautiful" chapter.

136.26–32 There was a clock . . . strike a hundred and fifty before she got tuckered out] The clock of the Sellers household exhibits the same peculiarity in chapter 7 of *The Gilded Age* (SLC 1873–74; Hearn 1981a, 166 n. 17).

137.5–7 prettier than real ones . . . white chalk or whatever it was, underneath] In *Life on the Mississippi*, Mark Twain scorned such decorative fruit, "all done in plaster, rudely, or in wax, and painted to resemble the originals—which they don't" (chapter 38, SLC 1883, 400). The Grangerfords' "apples and oranges and peaches and grapes" were perhaps manufactured by the daughters, acting on the sort of encouragement one could find in articles like "The Art of Making Wax Fruit and Flowers" in *Godey's Lady's Book and Magazine:* "So exact indeed are they, if well made, that the most practised eye cannot sometimes detect the real from the artificial" (Hale and Godey, 20).

137.12–13 "Pilgrim's Progress," about a man that left his family, it didn't say why] John Bunyan's allegory, *The Pilgrim's Progress from This World, to That Which Is to Come* (1678). Clemens owned several copies, including a facsimile of the first edition, published in 1875 (Gribben, 1:111–12).

137.15–16 "Friendship's Offering," . . . but I didn't read the poetry] In *Life on the Mississippi*, Mark Twain included *Friendship's Offering*, with its "sappy inanities illustrated in die-away mezzotints," among the books arranged "with cast-iron exactness" on the center table of the House Beautiful (chapter 38, SLC 1883, 400). First published in 1841 in Philadelphia, *Friendship's Offering* was typical of the annuals and gift books that flooded the market in the 1840s. It combined moralizing verse and prose with a dozen or so illustrative steel engravings. Its first editor, Miss Catharine H. Waterman, argued that such books "elevate the general standard of taste," and that the illustrations helped ensure that the contributions "will be read" (Waterman, iii–iv). But Mark Twain recognized that the books were, in fact, designed as much to be seen as read. When, several years later, he criticized the unnatural speech of certain characters in James Fenimore Cooper's novels, he likened their style to "an illustrated, gilt-edged, tree-calf, hand-tooled, seven-dollar Friendship's Offering" (SLC 1895b, 2, cited by Gribben, 1:246–47).

137.16–17   Henry Clay's Speeches] Probably *Speeches of the Honorable Henry Clay, in the Congress of the United States*, edited by Richard Chambers and published in 1842. Famous for his eloquence and his combativeness, Clay (1777–1852) was closely identified with Kentucky throughout his public career as congressman, senator, and secretary of state. He was an advocate of states' rights and one of the architects of the Missouri Compromise. According to an 1884 biographical sketch written with Orion Clemens's assistance, John Marshall Clemens "believed strongly in Henry Clay" (Holcombe, 915).

137.17–18   Dr. Gunn's Family Medicine . . . if a body was sick or dead] *Gunn's Domestic Medicine, or Poor Man's Friend, in the Hours of Affliction, Pain and Sickness*, first copyrighted by John C. Gunn in 1832. The title page of the eighth edition (1836) gives an account of the book's purpose: "This book points out, in plain language, free from doctors' terms, the diseases of men, women, and children, and the latest and most approved means used in their cure, and is intended expressly for the benefit of families in the western and southern states. It also contains descriptions of the medicinal roots and herbs of the western and southern country, and how they are to be used in the cure of diseases. Arranged on a new and simple plan, by which the practice of medicine is reduced to principles of common sense."

137.22–24   Washingtons, and Lafayettes, and battles . . . "Signing the Declaration."] Engraved reproductions of portraits of George Washington and other Revolutionary War heroes, such as the Marquis de Lafayette, from paintings by John Trumbull (1756–1843), Emanuel Leutze (1816–68), and many others, were very popular in the early nineteenth century. Mark Twain mentioned an engraving of Leutze's "Washington Crossing the Delaware" and two of paintings by Trumbull in chapter 38 of *Life on the Mississippi*. "Signing the Declaration" was almost certainly a reproduction of Trumbull's most famous painting, "The Declaration of Independence, July 4, 1776," completed in 1820 (Cooper, 76).

137.23   Highland Marys] Widely circulated pictures of Mary Campbell, or "Highland Mary," whose early death in 1786 inspired several of Robert Burns's poems, and made her a favorite subject for sentimental painters and engravers in Britain and the United States.

137.24–27   some that they called crayons . . . blacker, mostly, than is common] "Crayon" was the term used for a drawing executed in pastel or paste. In chapter 38 of *Life on the Mississippi*, Mark Twain said that the House Beautiful had "framed in black mouldings on the wall, other works of art, conceived and committed on the premises, by the young ladies; being grim black-and-white crayons; landscapes, mostly . . . name of criminal conspicuous in the corner" (SLC 1883, 403).

137.27–35   a woman in a slim black dress ... Never See Thee More
Alas."] Although new to Huck, this picture would have been familiar to
any middle-class reader. It includes the "stock elements" of standard
nineteenth-century mourning pictures: "the weeping willow, tombstone, and pensive mourner leaning on the monument. Even the style
of dress common in mourning pictures is accurately reproduced" by
Huck's description (Strickland, 228). Huck's allusion to this woman's
"very wee black slippers, like a chisel" is echoed in Mark Twain's char-
acterization, in chapter 38 of *Life on the Mississippi*, of illustrations in
Godey's Lady's Book: "each five-foot woman with a two-inch wedge
sticking from under her dress and letting-on to be half of her foot" (SLC
1883, 400). See the illustrations.

Left: Mourning print, by D. W. Kellogg and Company, lithographers (Hartford,
ca. 1835); the purchaser of the print wrote the name and death date of the deceased on the tombstone. From the collection of Professor Barton Levi St. Armand. *Right:* Mourning print, by William S. Pendleton, lithographer (Boston, ca.
1836), with a handwritten inscription on the tombstone. Courtesy of The Harry
T. Peters "America on Stone" Lithography Collection, Smithsonian Institution,
Washington, D.C.

137.38–138.4   dead bird laying on its back ... tears running down her
cheeks] Magazines such as *Godey's Lady's Book* frequently illustrated
children mourning their dead pets, particularly pet birds: for example,
"The Dead Dove" in the February 1852 issue, or "The Dead Robin" in
The Ladies' Repository (Cincinnati) for May 1855. Engravings de-
picting bereaved women—often using narrative details like the black
sealing-wax—were likewise commonplace. See, for example, "The
Widow" in the 1847 *Friendship's Offering*; "The Empty Cradle" in *Godey's Lady's Book* for 1847; or "Woman's Grief" in the 1842 *Friend-*

ship's Offering, reproduced below. In this case the accompanying verse solemnly indicates that the bereaved woman broods "Over one only thought,—the stunning thought | That *he* was dead, who loved so long and well!" (Esling, 33).

138.18–22   young woman . . . on the rail of a bridge all ready to jump off]
Portrayals of women in despair, appealing to heaven for relief or threatening suicide, were less than commonplace in the ladies' magazines and annuals; nonetheless the genre of even this outlandish drawing can be identified with the following, called "Supplication," in the November 1848 issue of *Graham's Magazine* (Fayette Robinson, frontispiece, 267).

139.8 the *Presbyterian Observer*] The *Presbyterian Observer* (Baltimore and Philadelphia) did not begin publication until 1872, but there were numerous newspapers and magazines with very similar names at the time of the story; for example, the *Christian Observer*, subtitled " 'A Presbyterian Family Newspaper,' founded at Philadelphia in 1813" (Mott, 137), and the *Presbyterian Sentinel*, published in Louisville, 1841–44.

139.12 ODE TO STEPHEN DOWLING BOTS, DEC'D] Sentimental obituary verse was ubiquitous in American magazines, annuals, and gift books at the time of the story. Like many fellow humorists, Mark Twain could not resist the temptation to burlesque this form. He published his first parody of an elegiac poem, "The Burial of Sir Abner Gilstrap," in 1853 at the age of seventeen (*ET&S1*, 106–9). In 1854 he became familiar with mortuary doggerel published routinely in the death notices of the Philadelphia *Public Ledger*, and almost certainly "set up some of that poetry" altered for comic purposes while working as a compositor on the *Ledger* (SLC 1885e). He eventually published two brief articles in 1870 and another in the 1880s on the subject (SLC 1870c; SLC 1870d; SLC [1880?]; Budd 1977, 2). A number of "sources" for this "Ode" have been proposed, ranging from the poetry of Julia A. Moore to the hymns of Isaac Watts to the columns of the Philadelphia *Ledger* itself (Blair 1960a, 209–13; Byers 1971; Branch 1984, 2–3). But Mark Twain's "Ode" is a burlesque of the form, not a parody of any particular obituary verse or writer of such verse, and given his long acquaintance with such poems, it is unlikely that any single "model" can be identified. In his manuscript, Mark Twain originally ended the poem with an additional stanza, which he deleted before publication. It burlesques the diction and exhorting tone of such verse, and echoes the first or last stanzas of typical English ballads (see, for instance, Evelyn Kendrick Wells, 217–19, 272; Bronson 1962, 2:327–29; Bronson 1976, 23, 414):

> Now all young people, come listen unto me:
> So shape ye your varigated lots,
> That you can all die, when you come for to die,
> Like the late sweet Stephen D. Bots.
>
> (MS1, 427½, NBu)

140.1 Emmeline Grangerford] In the library of the Clemens family's Hartford house was an "impressionist water-color" of the "head of a beautiful young girl, life-size—called Emmeline, because she looked just about like that." The Clemenses purchased this portrait by Daniele Ranzoni in Italy in 1878 (AD, 8 Feb 1906, CU-MARK, in *AutoMT1* and *MTA*, 2:73; *N&J2*, 187 n. 50).

141.8–10 They kept Emmeline's room . . . just the way she liked] This procedure, common in the period of the book, received the ultimate en-dorsement in 1861, upon the death of Prince Albert. Queen Victoria kept his room at Windsor Castle unchanged and, like Huck and Mrs. Grangerford with Emmeline's room, visited it and meditated there.

141.17   little old piano, too, that had tin pans in it] The piano may actually have had tin pans in it: "Piano-makers of the early nineteenth century, responding to the programmatic demands of the battle-pieces and to the popularity of Turkish music and instruments, introduced devices for the production of a variety of unusual musical effects. Extra pedals were constructed which permitted the pianist to embellish his performance with the sound of cymbals, drums, and bells" (Slater, 111). See also the note to 141.19.

141.18–19   "The Last Link is Broken"] A sentimental song written by William Clifton in about 1840:

> The last link is broken that bound me to thee,
> And the words thou hast spoken have render'd me free;
> That bright glance misleading, on others may shine,
> Those eyes smil'd unheeding when tears burst from mine.
> (Clifton)

In the margin of the manuscript page on which Sophia Grangerford is introduced, Clemens wrote "Sophia. Last Link." In 1897 he recalled that he associated this song with a Hannibal contemporary of his, Eliza Hyde, and he used it to illustrate his remark that "songs tended to regrets for bygone days and vanished joys" in the days of his youth (*Inds*, 96, 99). In chapter 38, Tom will call it "painful music."

141.19   "The Battle of Prague"] A ten-minute piano piece of program music written in 1788 by Franz Kotzwara (1730–91) of Bohemia. It featured staccato notes to simulate flying bullets and a wailing treble figure to suggest the cries of the wounded. By the 1840s it had become an overworked standard (Slater, 108–9). In 1913, Clemens's childhood friend Anna Laura Hawkins (Laura Frazer) remembered how she and the twelve-year-old Clemens used to climb a hill to visit Mrs. Richard T. Holliday: "Her house, I remember, had a special attraction for us. She owned a piano, and it was not merely a piano; it was a piano with a drum attachment. Oh, 'The Battle of Prague,' executed with that marvelous drum attachment! It was our favorite selection, because it had so much drum in it" (Abbott, 17; Hawkins and Holliday are identified in notes to 47.17 and 1.15–16). In *A Tramp Abroad*—and in an 1878 notebook entry (*N&J2*, 142)—Mark Twain described a performance of this piece by an Arkansas bride which he had heard in a Swiss hotel drawing room:

Without any more preliminaries, she turned on all the horrors of the "Battle of Prague," that venerable shivaree, and waded chin deep in the blood of the slain. . . . The audience stood it with pretty fair grit for a while, but when the can-

sembles General Henry M. Darnall (as he preferred to spell his name),
the family patriarch who figured in newspaper accounts of both incidents and was probably familiar to Clemens's fellow pilots. Darnall, a
wealthy landowner, was chivalrous and hospitable, but also possessed
"a very vindictive temper" (Davidson, 82–84, 93 n. 17, 95 n. 36; Branch
and Hirst, 53–55, 61–80; Cayton, 3).

147.28–31   Next Sunday we all went to church. . . . The Shepherdsons
done the same.] In *Life on the Mississippi* (chapter 26), Mark Twain,
clearly drawing on knowledge of his own, ostensibly quoted a fellow
steamboat passenger who lived in the neighborhood of the Darnells
and Watsons:

> Both families belonged to the same church (everybody around here is religious);
> through all this fifty or sixty years' fuss, both tribes was there every Sunday, to
> worship. They lived each side of the line, and the church was at a landing called
> Compromise. Half the church and half the aisle was in Kentucky, the other half
> in Tennessee. Sundays you 'd see the families drive up, all in their Sunday
> clothes, men, women, and children, and file up the aisle, and set down, quiet and
> orderly, one lot on the Tennessee side of the church and the other on the Ken-
> tucky side; and the men and boys would lean their guns up against the wall,
> handy, and then all hands would join in with the prayer and praise; though they
> say the man next the aisle did n't kneel down, along with the rest of the family;
> kind of stood guard. (SLC 1883, 286–87; Branch and Hirst, 42)

147.35   preforeordestination] Huck's combination of terms for two theological doctrines, predestination and foreordination.

148.13   hogs likes a puncheon floor] In a reminiscence written in 1877,
Clemens recalled the church in Florida, Missouri, near his uncle John
Quarles's farm:

> There was a log church, with a puncheon floor & slab benches. A puncheon floor
> is made of logs whose upper surfaces have been chipped flat with the adze. The
> cracks between the logs were not filled; there was no carpet; consequently, if you
> dropped anything smaller than a peach, it was likely to go through. The church
> was perched upon short sections of logs, which elevated it two or three feet from
> the ground. Hogs slept under there, & whenever the dogs got after them during
> services, the minister had to wait till the disturbance was over. In winter there
> was always a refreshing breeze up through the puncheon floor; in summer there
> were fleas enough for all. (SLC 1877, 2–3)

151.5–8   He ain't ever told me . . . truth."] Jack's subterfuge illustrates the
slaves' need for verbal indirection in encounters with all whites, not
just their legal masters. This "signifying" speech, rooted in African verbal traditions, "can generate two meanings: one appears neutral and
unobjectionable; the other may embody potentially dangerous information and ideas" (Fishkin, 61). For a discussion of Mark Twain's appreciation of this form of speech, see Fishkin, 54–67.

by the regime of a morning "cocktail" made with scotch whiskey, lemon, Angostura bitters, and sugar (SLC to OLC, 2 Jan 74, CU-MARK, in *L6*, 3). While "bitters" might mean almost any kind of alcoholic drink taken in the morning, ostensibly to stimulate the appetite, the Grangerfords' morning tonic appears to be comparable to a "whisky cocktail," which according to the *Century Dictionary* consisted of corn or rye whiskey, "water flavored with bitters, usually also with the peel of orange or lemon, and sweetened with sugar" (6:6906).

146.12–17   a feud . . . takes a long time] On 12 March 1885, Reginald Cholmondeley wrote Mark Twain from England: "I have been reading Huckleberry Finn with delight. You appear to be inexhaustible & evergreen but is it possible that blood-feuds really existed in Arkansas within 50 years[?]" Mark Twain explained that "indeed, feuds existed in Kentucky, Tennessee and Arkansas, of the nature described, within my time and memory. I came very near being an eye-witness to the general engagement detailed in the book. The details are historical and correct" (Cholmondeley to SLC, 12 Mar 85, and SLC to Cholmondeley, 28 Mar 85, CU-MARK, in Blair 1960a, 225). This "engagement" took place in 1859 at Compromise, Kentucky, a steamboat landing at the foot of New Madrid Bend near the border between Kentucky and Tennessee. (Compromise acquired its name in 1852 but eventually, by the early 1880s, was isolated by a sandbar and disappeared from river maps.) In 1882, during his trip down the river, Mark Twain planned to revisit Compromise and New Madrid "& ask about the old feuds" (*N&J2*, 456–57). He discussed this feud with pilot Horace Bixby, recalling that the "row" he nearly witnessed had taken place when he was "on a Memphis packet & at a landing we made on the Kentucky side" (*N&J2*, 567–68). Bixby remembered the feud, and was able to supply the names of the real families—Darnell and Watson. (The Watson territory extended from Compromise upriver toward Watson's Point; the Darnell family lived slightly downriver in Tennessee, in the area around Darnell's Point: see the map on page 371.) Mark Twain relied in part on the notes of this conversation to write his account of the Darnell-Watson feud in chapter 26 of *Life on the Mississippi* (SLC 1883, 286–88; see also the note to 152.9–154.6). For his depiction of the feud in *Huckleberry Finn*, which predated his 1882 research, he must have drawn on his own experience of the events of 1859 at Compromise, along with details he had gleaned from conversations, such as the one he evidently had with John H. "Windy" Marshall, captain of the *John H. Dickey*, who was an eyewitness to the most violent incident at Compromise (Branch and Hirst, 42–45). He may also have read about an 1869 feud incident in eastern newspapers and noted the descriptions of the Darnell family at that time (Branch and Hirst, 73). Colonel Grangerford himself somewhat resembles General Henry M. Darnall (as he preferred to spell his name), the family patriarch who figured in newspaper accounts of both incidents and was probably familiar to Clemens's fellow pilots. Darnall, a wealthy landowner, was chivalrous and hospitable, but also possessed "a very vindictive temper" (Davidson, 82–84, 93 n. 17, 95 n. 36; Branch and Hirst, 53–55, 61–80; Cayton, 3).

147.28–31   Next Sunday we all went to church. . . . The Shepherdsons done the same.] In *Life on the Mississippi* (chapter 26), Mark Twain, clearly drawing on knowledge of his own, ostensibly quoted a fellow steamboat passenger who lived in the neighborhood of the Darnells and Watsons:

> Both families belonged to the same church (everybody around here is religious); through all this fifty or sixty years' fuss, both tribes was there every Sunday, to worship. They lived each side of the line, and the church was at a landing called Compromise. Half the church and half the aisle was in Kentucky, the other half in Tennessee. Sundays you 'd see the families drive up, all in their Sunday clothes, men, women, and children, and file up the aisle, and set down, quiet and orderly, one lot on the Tennessee side of the church and the other on the Kentucky side; and the men and boys would lean their guns up against the wall, handy, and then all hands would join in with the prayer and praise; though they say the man next the aisle did n't kneel down, along with the rest of the family; kind of stood guard. (SLC 1883, 286–87; Branch and Hirst, 42)

147.35   preforeordestination] Huck's combination of terms for two theological doctrines, predestination and foreordination.

148.13   hogs likes a puncheon floor] In a reminiscence written in 1877, Clemens recalled the church in Florida, Missouri, near his uncle John Quarles's farm:

> There was a log church, with a puncheon floor & slab benches. A puncheon floor is made of logs whose upper surfaces have been chipped flat with the adze. The cracks between the logs were not filled; there was no carpet; consequently, if you dropped anything smaller than a peach, it was likely to go through. The church was perched upon short sections of logs, which elevated it two or three feet from the ground. Hogs slept under there, & whenever the dogs got after them during services, the minister had to wait till the disturbance was over. In winter there was always a refreshing breeze up through the puncheon floor; in summer there were fleas enough for all. (SLC 1877, 2–3)

151.5–8   He ain't ever told me . . . truth."] Jack's subterfuge illustrates the slaves' need for verbal indirection in encounters with all whites, not just their legal masters. This "signifying" speech, rooted in African verbal traditions, "can generate two meanings: one appears neutral and unobjectionable; the other may embody potentially dangerous information and ideas" (Fishkin, 61). For a discussion of Mark Twain's appreciation of this form of speech, see Fishkin, 54–67.

dorsement in 1861, upon the death of Prince Albert. Queen Victoria kept his room at Windsor Castle unchanged and, like Huck and Mrs. Grangerford with Emmeline's room, visited it and meditated there.

141.17   little old piano, too, that had tin pans in it] The piano may actually have had tin pans in it: "Piano-makers of the early nineteenth century, responding to the programmatic demands of the battle-pieces and to the popularity of Turkish music and instruments, introduced devices for the production of a variety of unusual musical effects. Extra pedals were constructed which permitted the pianist to embellish his performance with the sound of cymbals, drums, and bells" (Slater, 111). See also the note to 141.19.

141.18–19   "The Last Link is Broken"] A sentimental song written by William Clifton in about 1840:

> The last link is broken that bound me to thee,
> And the words thou hast spoken have render'd me free;
> That bright glance misleading, on others may shine,
> Those eyes smil'd unheeding when tears burst from mine.
> (Clifton)

In the margin of the manuscript page on which Sophia Grangerford is introduced, Clemens wrote "Sophia. Last Link." In 1897 he recalled that he associated this song with a Hannibal contemporary of his, Eliza Hyde, and he used it to illustrate his remark that "songs tended to regrets for bygone days and vanished joys" in the days of his youth (*Inds*, 96, 99). In chapter 38, Tom will call it "painful music."

141.19   "The Battle of Prague"] A ten-minute piano piece of program music written in 1788 by Franz Kotzwara (1730–91) of Bohemia. It featured staccato notes to simulate flying bullets and a wailing treble figure to suggest the cries of the wounded. By the 1840s it had become an overworked standard (Slater, 108–9). In 1913, Clemens's childhood friend Anna Laura Hawkins (Laura Frazer) remembered how she and the twelve-year-old Clemens used to climb a hill to visit Mrs. Richard T. Holliday: "Her house, I remember, had a special attraction for us. She owned a piano, and it was not merely a piano; it was a piano with a drum attachment. Oh, 'The Battle of Prague,' executed with that marvelous drum attachment! It was our favorite selection, because it had so much drum in it" (Abbott, 17; Hawkins and Holliday are identified in notes to 47.17 and 1.15–16). In *A Tramp Abroad*—and in an 1878 notebook entry (*N&J2*, 142)—Mark Twain described a performance of this piece by an Arkansas bride which he had heard in a Swiss hotel drawing room:

Without any more preliminaries, she turned on all the horrors of the "Battle of Prague," that venerable shivaree, and waded chin deep in the blood of the slain. . . . The audience stood it with pretty fair grit for a while, but when the cannonade waxed hotter and fiercer, and the discord-average rose to four in five, the procession began to move. A few stragglers held their ground ten minutes longer, but when the girl began to wring the true inwardness out of the "cries of the wounded," they struck their colors and retired in a kind of panic. . . . She got an amount of anguish into the cries of the wounded that shed a new light on human suffering. (Chapter 32, SLC 1880, 341–45)

141.19–20   The walls of all the rooms was plastered] Plastered walls were thought to be a sign of affluence or sophistication. In an 1870 reminiscence Mark Twain quoted a woman from Fentress County, Tennessee, who expressed the following opinion of what her son and daughter-in-law had done to their house: " 'They've tuck 'n' gaumed the inside of theirn all over with some kind of nasty disgustin' truck which they say is all the go in Kaintuck amongst the upper hunky, & which they calls it *plarsterin'!*' " (SLC 1870a, 7). Mark Twain later adapted this description for Si Higgins's "high-toned" house in chapter 1 of *The Gilded Age* (SLC 1873–74, 21).

142.1–143.3   Col. Grangerford . . . good mannered where he was.] This description, most likely written in 1876 (but conceivably written as late as 1878), is very similar to that of Judge Griswold in Mark Twain's unfinished novel "Simon Wheeler, Detective," written in the winter of 1877–78, which also featured a destructive feud:

He was sixty years old; very tall, very spare, with a long, thin, smooth-shaven, intellectual face, and long black hair that lay close to his head, was kept to the rear by his ears as one keeps curtains back by brackets, and fell straight to his coat collar without a single tolerant kink or relenting curve. He had an eagle's beak and an eagle's eye. He was a Kentuckian by birth and rearing; he came of the oldest and best Kentucky Griswolds, and they from the oldest and proudest Griswolds of Virginia. Judge Griswold's manners and carriage were of the courtly old-fashioned sort; he had never worked; he was a gentleman. . . .
    The Judge was punctiliously honorable, austerely upright. No man wanted his bond who had got his word. He was grave even to sternness; he seldom smiled. He loved strongly, but without demonstration; he hated implacably. (S&B, 313–14)

Both Grangerford and Griswold recall some characteristics of Clemens's own father: Judge Clemens was tall, slim, and smooth shaven, and he had elaborate manners. Like Griswold, he had roots in Virginia and Kentucky, and was stern and unsmiling. Like Grangerford, he often wore a swallow-tailed coat with brass buttons. Grangerford is also a recognizable type: the southern aristocratic gentleman, who appears in scores of nineteenth-century novels in the "plantation tradition" (Blair 1960a, 214–19; S&B, 307–9; see also the note to 146.12–17). Although Grangerford was previously described as "gray and about sixty" (133.19), here his hair is black, presumably a simple oversight.

143.11–17   mixed a glass of bitters . . . sugar and the mite of whisky or apple brandy] In 1874, Clemens proposed to improve his own digestion

152.9–154.6   a couple of young chaps that was behind the wood-rank . . .
found the two bodies laying in the edge of the water] Mark Twain's
model for this incident in *Huckleberry Finn* and in the nearly identical
scene in *Life on the Mississippi* was manifestly the incident at Compromise, Kentucky, a flare-up in the Darnell-Watson feud, to which Clemens told Cholmondeley he had come "near being an eye-witness" (SLC
to Cholmondeley, 28 Mar 85, CU-MARK; Branch and Hirst, 45). This
is how he recalled it in dictation taken down by his secretary Roswell
Phelps in 1882:

> I was on a Memphis packet & at a landing we made on the Kentucky side there
> was a row. Don't remember as there was anybody hurt then; but shortly after-
> wards there was another row at that place and a youth of 19 belonging to the Mo.
> tribe had wandered over there. Half a dozen of that Ky. tribe got after him. He
> dodged among the wood piles & answered their shots. Presently he jumped into
> the river & they followed on after & peppered him & he had to make for the
> shore. By that time he was about dead—did shortly die. (*N&J2*, 568)

158.32   I found a canoe] Mark Twain first wrote "I took the canoe," an error he overlooked until the publisher's proofreader noticed that the canoe had been "lost" in chapter 16 (129.29–30). Because the book was in
page proof, almost ready to print, Mark Twain was obliged to make an
economical correction. He therefore substituted "found a" for "took
the" (see the illustration below). But this solution left a larger problem
unresolved: why, when Huck finds a new canoe, does he say nothing
about going north with it? Mark Twain's wish to write about the Mississippi he knew had, in 1876, collided with the implausibility of Jim's
trying to escape slavery by traveling south. Continuing the journey
south was first made plausible by Huck and Jim's not knowing they had
passed Cairo in the fog, and then, temporarily, by the loss of the canoe,
which caused Huck and Jim to decide to "go along down with the raft"
and look for another canoe to buy for their northward journey. Mark
Twain's next solution, also temporary, was to have the steamboat crash
into the raft, destroying it, and shifting the action ashore (the manuscript reads "she come smashing through the raft & tore it to toothpicks & splinters" [MS1, 394]). He then wrote the end of chapter 16, all
of chapter 17, and a portion of chapter 18 (Huck at the Grangerford
house) before he put the book aside again, the basic problem unsolved.
When Mark Twain returned to his manuscript in 1880, he made a
note about two characters who would eventually provide him with
the solution to his dilemma: "The two printers deliver temp. lectures,
teach dancing, elocution, feel heads, distribute tracts, preach, fiddle,
doctor (quack)." To this note he added parenthetically, "Keep 'em
along." Bringing the tramps aboard the raft, where they could *enforce* a
southward journey, meant Mark Twain could continue to write about
the river he knew, but it also required resurrecting the raft, to which

end he wrote another note to himself: "Back a little, CHANGE—raft only *crippled* by steamer" (see *HF2003*, 484–85, 486–87 [Mark Twain's Working Notes, nos. 2-6, 2-10]). Sometime before publication, he revised his text to read "she come smashing straight through the raft." Having at last devised a plausible motive and means for sustaining Huck and Jim's southward journey, he had forgotten the ostensible reason they were still drifting south: the lost canoe and the need for a new one. When the proofreader caught the inconsistency, Mark Twain concealed the oversight as best he could by the slight change in wording (Henry Nash Smith 1958a, viii–x, 263; Blair 1960a, 250–59).

160.4–9   One of these fellows . . . brass buttons] Although Mark Twain may have had no specific model for this rascal, Walter Blair has noted a resemblance—citing his baldness and gray whiskers, and his coat with slick brass buttons—to Captain Charles C. Duncan of the *Quaker City*, whose picture appears in chapter 60 of *The Innocents Abroad* (1869). Ten years after the voyage, Clemens publicly quarreled with Duncan, calling him a temperance advocate who tippled in secret, "heartless enough to rob any . . . orphan he can get his clutches upon; . . . a canting hypocrite, filled to the chin with sham godliness, and forever oozing and dripping false piety and pharisaical prayers" (SLC to the editor of the New York *World*, 14 and 16 Feb 77, in *MTMF*, 213–14; Blair 1960a, 274–77).

160.15–16   take the tartar off . . . generly the enamel along with it] On 24 August 1871 the *New York Weekly* rejoiced because the peddler of a similar dentifrice made of acid and potash, with an equally disastrous effect, "obtained his deserts by being sentenced to a year's imprisonment" (Jones, 468–69).

160.32–33   they'd tar and feather me and ride me on a rail] Two common mob-inflicted punishments in nineteenth-century America, especially in the South. The first consisted of smearing the victim with hot tar and shaking feathers over him; the second involved transporting him astraddle the sharp edge of a split log, to the accompaniment of jeers and abuse. Both punishments were likely to cause serious injury, even death.

160.37   Jour printer, by trade] The wandering journeyman printer was common in the antebellum South, and a recurrent rascally figure in American humor. In 1886 Clemens would recall from his days in Hannibal "the tramping 'jour' who flitted by in the summer and tarried a day, with his wallet stuffed with one shirt and a hatful of handbills; for if he couldn't get any type to set he would do a temperance lecture. . . . All he wanted was plate and bed and money enough to get drunk on"

Foundry proof for page 160 of the first American edition, revised by the author in response to a proofreader's query. Mark Twain Papers, The Bancroft Library (CU-MARK). See the note to 158.32.

(SLC 1886). Clemens himself had followed this trade from the spring of 1853, when he left Hannibal, until the summer of 1854. Working notes show that Mark Twain had originally planned to make both confidence men jour printers (see the note to 158.32).

160.37   do a little in patent medicines] Itinerant patent-medicine peddlers selling cure-alls regularly appeared in the work of nineteenth-century humorists (see, for instance, "The Erasive Soap Man," in Hooper 1851, 109–11). During the summer of 1883, when Mark Twain was writing and revising *Huckleberry Finn,* he read a typical advertisement from the Magnetic Rock Spring Water Company of Colfax, Iowa, which claimed that their product cured "Rheumatism, Dyspepsia, Liver Complaint, Constipation, Dropsy, Paralysis, St. Vitus' Dance, Delirium Tremens, Diabetes, Stone in the Bladder, Blood Diseases, Scrofula, Ulcers, Female Weakness and General Debility." He thereupon ordered a barrel with the comment, "I do believe that is what is the matter with me. It reads just like my symptoms" (SLC to Magnetic Rock Spring Company, 1 Aug 83, transcript in CU-MARK).

160.38–39   mesmerism and phrenology] Mesmerism, or hypnotism, and phrenology, the reading of character from the shape of the skull, were popular forms of entertainment in the early nineteenth century, often used by traveling "Professors" to exploit the gullible (Field, 129, in Hearn 1981a, 189). Clemens himself had observed practitioners of both as a boy in Hannibal. In his autobiography he recalled acting as a willing and convincing confederate to a traveling hypnotist (AD, 1 Dec 1906, CU-MARK, in *MTE,* 118–25). His 1880 working notes show that he considered having Huck play a similar role: "Do the mesmeric foolishness, with Huck & the king for performers" (see *HF2003,* 486 [Mark Twain's Working Notes, no. 2-9]).

160.39   singing-geography school] In the late 1840s, Benjamin Naylor of Philadelphia introduced his new "system of teaching geography" through public demonstrations and tutorials at various public and private schools. The method used large outline maps:

The teacher with a rod points out the various parts and repeats their names, grouping several together; the class repeats the names after him; after they are somewhat familiarized with the names, they chant or sing them over repeatedly. . . . The children all join in the singing right merrily, keeping their eyes fixed upon the places on the map as he points them out. Mr. Naylor teaches the whole of what is called Geography in thirty lessons. . . . By this system the labour of years is performed, in effect, in a month, the mind is agreeably stimulated, the memory healthfully exercised, the social feeling kindly indulged, while the simple tunes which they chant, blend the class and teacher into the most cordial harmony. (Naylor, 140–41, 143)

Cyrus Edwards (1846–1939) of Kentucky recalled the "old practice of 'Singing Geography' " from his schooldays: "This method of occasionally 'singing lessons' seemed foolish to me in my youth and appears to me now as a little questionable, . . . but I must admit that with a certain class of students, . . . [it] enabled them to retain at least a portion of what they had been taught" (Cyrus Edwards, xiv, 72).

161.36–37   I am a duke!] The duke resembles Clemens's distant cousin Jesse M. Leathers, who claimed to be the rightful earl of Durham. In several letters to Clemens during the composition of *Huckleberry Finn*, Leathers often used a gaudy style similar to the duke's. For instance, "Owing to my impecunious condition I have done nothing to assert the rights of the American heirs," and (in response to Clemens's invitation to visit) "I . . . shall be only too happy if I can bring one little sunbeam to mingle with the pure light which brightens and cheers your humble hearth and home" (Leathers to SLC, 25 and 29 Nov 79, CU-MARK, in *Letters 1876–1880*). Clemens was long fascinated by the subject of the "rightful heir," and during his sojourn in England in 1873 he closely followed the perjury trial of Arthur Orton, who claimed to be the heir to the great Tichborne estate.

162.1–6   eldest son of the duke of Bridgewater . . . I am the rightful duke] Francis Egerton, third and last duke of Bridgewater and one of England's wealthiest and most eccentric peers, died without issue in 1803, an event that eventually led to a long public quarrel about the inheritance and the title. The dukedom was never revived after 1803, and the related earldom of Bridgewater became extinct in 1829 (Gaffney; Falk, 8, 13–14, 176, 180–83, 222–24; Hearn 1981a, 192–93). Clemens had personal knowledge of the intricacies of the Egerton family dispute (see the next note).

163.9   Bilgewater] One of Mark Twain's favorite comic names, found in his notes as early as 1865: "Bilgewater . . . Good God what a name" (*N&J1*, 76). The impulse to conflate the Bridgewater title with the ridiculous "Bilgewater" may have derived from Clemens's unpleasant experience in 1879, when he made a week-long stay at the home of Reginald Cholmondeley, who was married to an Egerton (the heirs to the Bridgewater estate) and was entertaining various members of his wife's family. Clemens saw "two American ladies" rudely excluded from all conversation by the snobbish concentration on "wills & other family matters" (*N&J2*, 336–37). In 1885 when Cholmondeley read *Huckleberry Finn*, he took the satire directed at his relatives in good spirit, offering to present Clemens "to the original Bilgewater." Clemens replied, alluding to his earlier discomfort with Cholmondeley's family: "maybe I can meet the original Bilgewater; and if he is in *your* company, I'll be mighty *glad* to." Mary Cholmondeley (a niece) later explained the reference when she sent Albert Bigelow Paine a copy of Clemens's letter: "Reginald Cholmondeley had invited Mark Twain to meet his brother in law the late Lord Egerton of Tatton. There had been some question of Lord Egerton taking the title of Bridgewater, which Mark Twain miscalls so delightfully" (Cholmondeley to SLC, 12 Mar 85, and SLC to Cholmondeley, 28 Mar 85, transcript by Mary Cholmondeley, both in CU-MARK).

166.12–16   Pike county, in Missouri . . . my brother Ike] Pike County, Missouri, on the Mississippi River below Hannibal, about forty-five miles north of St. Louis. In antebellum lore, this county was the birthplace of some of the most worthless characters on the frontier. A stock character, Ike, appears in popular songs from the Gold Rush days, such as "Sweet Betsey from Pike" and "Joe Bowers."

168.11   the middle watch] The middle watch customarily lasted from midnight to four in the morning.

168.37   Garrick the Younger] David Garrick (1717–79) was a great Shakespearean actor and manager of the Drury Lane Theatre; there was no Garrick the Younger.

169.1   finding water and gold with a "divining rod,"] In 1870, Mark Twain wrote: "I have seen more than four hundred 'gold-finders,' first and last, but I never saw anybody that ever heard of one of them ever finding anything. . . . I recall how for four dreadful weeks I followed step by step in the track of a 'Professor' with a hazel stick in his hand,—a 'divining-rod'—which was to turn and tilt down and point to the gold whenever we came to any. But we never came to any, I suppose" (SLC 1870b; Hearn 1981a, 198).

169.8   sword-fight in Richard III] In the manuscript for chapter 51 of *Life on the Mississippi*, Mark Twain recalled that during his boyhood "a couple of young Englishmen came to the town & sojourned a while; & one day they got themselves up in cheap royal finery & did the Richard III sword-fight with maniac energy & prodigious pow-wow" (SLC 1882, 95–96; in SLC 1883, 503–4). The actor Edmund Kean (see the note to 180.29–30) was largely responsible for the popularity of this flamboyant way of staging the sword fight: "Every personator of *Richard* must fight like a madman, and fence on the ground, and when disarmed and wounded, thrust with savage impotence with his naked hand. . . . Mr. Kean has passed this manner into a law and woe be to him who breaks it" (*Champion*, 16 Feb 17, in Clarke, 15).

170.10–20   little one-horse town about three mile down the bend . . . gone to camp-meeting] This village, later called "Pokeville" (173.3), lies four or five nights' travel (perhaps 150 miles at the average speed) south of the Kentucky-Tennessee border area inhabited by the Grangerfords and Shepherdsons. Mark Twain does not indicate whether it is on the right or left bank of the river and hardly characterizes it. One of his working notes for the book, however, mentions a "Negro camp-meeting & sermon" and is followed by a reference to Walnut Bend, Arkansas, about two hundred miles below the feud area, suggesting that he may have imagined Pokeville as upriver of Walnut Bend or as Walnut Bend itself (*HF2003*, 480–82 [Mark Twain's Working Notes, no. 2-2]).

170.21-22   king . . . allowed he'd go and work that camp meeting] The king's camp-meeting skills have been compared to those of the backwoods confidence man Simon Suggs, in Johnson J. Hooper's sketch "The Captain Attends a Camp-Meeting," included in *Some Adventures of Captain Simon Suggs* (1845). Mark Twain considerably revised his camp-meeting scene before publication. The original manuscript version of the text, and a discussion of the influence of Hooper's story and other camp-meeting descriptions, may be found in Three Passages from the Manuscript (pp. 481–91).

172.7   "It's the brazen serpent in the wilderness! look upon it and live!"] After the wandering Israelites were plagued by snakes, God commanded Moses to make a brass serpent and set it on a pole; those bitten by snakes would be restored by the sight (Num. 21:4–9). This biblical scene was evoked with thrilling effect in sermons by the fiery and charismatic Presbyterian preacher Gideon Blackburn (1772–1838), who was active in Tennessee and Kentucky in the early decades of the century (Sprague, 43, 53–54).

172.10-16   come to the mourners' bench! . . . be at rest!"] At camp-meeting sites, the mourners' bench (also known as the "altar," the "anxious seat," or the "glory pen") was an area immediately in front of the preachers' stand, separated from the congregation, "where sinners under conviction were brought to experience conversion" (Bruce, 71–73). It was the job of the camp-meeting "exhorters," usually ordained ministers, to invite sinners "to enter the pen by reminding them of the prospects of hell and damnation awaiting those who failed to take the step" (Bruce, 75; McCurdy, 160, 172). Mark Twain's preacher uses the conventional language of salvation, reminiscent of Joseph Hart's popular hymn, "Come Ye Sinners" (1759):

> Come, ye sinners, poor and needy,
>   Weak and wounded, sick and sore;
> Jesus ready stands to save you,
>   Full of pity, love and power. . . .
>   (Byers 1977)

Frances Trollope, in her *Domestic Manners of the Americans*, a book very familiar to Clemens, described a minister urging sinners to "come to the anxious bench, and we will show you Jesus!" (1:108; Gribben,

2:713–14). And Harriet Beecher Stowe recorded an exhorter's fierce entreaty to "Come up, come up!" to the mourners' bench, in her 1856 novel, *Dred; A Tale of the Great Dismal Swamp* (1:316).

173.15–16   would he let them kiss him . . . and he always done it] When Clemens saw Kemble's drawings for this episode in June 1884, he told his publisher to "knock out one of them—the lecherous old rascal kissing the girl at the campmeeting. It is powerful good, but it mustn't go in—don't forget it. Let's not make *any* pictures of the campmeeting. The subject won't *bear* illustrating. It is a disgusting thing, & pictures are sure to tell the truth about it too plainly" (SLC to Webster, 11 June 84, NPV, in *MTBus*, 260). Clemens was not alone in his reaction to this subject. Frances Trollope witnessed the plain "truth" of the liberties taken with overwrought young women at both revivals and camp meetings and voiced her disgust in her travel memoir (1:109–111, 239–40). In Hooper's camp-meeting sketch, Simon Suggs observed sourly that the camp-meeting preachers "never hugs up the old, ugly women" (Hooper 1845, 122).

174.12–13   heathens don't amount to shucks, alongside of pirates, to work a camp meeting with] Fund-raising appeals for the conversion of the Indians were found to be especially effective at camp meetings. In 1826, one minister produced a converted Indian chief, Between-the-Logs, who petitioned the congregation in strange broken English. Most fund-raisers, however, were not as successful as the king; collections were "exceedingly modest, often totaling less than five dollars" (Charles A. Johnson, 130, 286 n. 21).

174.22–23   they were going to pay in cord-wood and onions, as usual] Clemens in 1886 recalled that when he worked for his brother Orion's Hannibal newspaper, "The town subscribers paid in groceries and the country ones in cabbages and cord-wood—when they paid at all, which was merely sometimes, and then we always stated the fact in the paper" (SLC 1886).

174.27–28   "Yes, Crush, Cold world, this Breaking Heart"] In the unfinished "Simon Wheeler, Detective" (1877–78), written about two and a half years earlier than this passage, Hugh Burnside wrote a "ten-line deformity" called "The Crushed Heart's Farewell" (*S&B*, 360). At the age of seventeen, Clemens himself wrote a number of highly conventional love poems for Hannibal newspapers (*ET&S1*, 88–90, 92–94, 100–101).

174.32–33   picture of a runaway nigger, with a bundle on a stick, over his shoulder] The duke accurately rendered the typical illustrative woodcut found on fugitive-slave handbills of the antebellum period. A simi-

THE

ANTI-SLAVERY RECORD.

Vol. III. No. VII.   JULY, 1837.   Whole No. 31.

This picture of a poor fugitive is from one of the stereotype cuts manufactured in this city for the southern market, and used on handbills offering rewards for runaway slaves.

THE RUNAWAY.

To escape from a powerful enemy, often requires as much courage and generalship as to conquer. One of the most celebrated military exploits on record, is the *retreat* of the ten thousand Greeks under

From the *Anti-Slavery Record* of July 1837. Courtesy of the Boston Athenæum (MBAt). See the note to 174.32–33.

lar slave-with-bundle motif was used on envelopes to signal the senders' abolitionist sentiments (Jacobs, 136, 143; see also Still 1872, 99, 101, and 103, for examples of other such fugitive-slave stereotype cuts, both male and female). Kemble reused the motif, again following Mark Twain's text, in his sketch of Jim's coat of arms at the beginning of chapter 38.

178.1   Capet] Thomas Carlyle, in *The French Revolution* (one of Clemens's favorite books), reported that after Louis XVI was dethroned, the Revolutionists referred to him as Citizen Louis Capet. The Capets were a ruling family of medieval France.

179.10–39   To be . . . go!] Although the duke claims he is reciting the soliloquy from *Hamlet*, 3:3, he disarranges it, intermingling lines from *Macbeth* and *Richard III*. Scrambled Shakespeare was a staple of nineteenth-century comedy and minstrelsy, and *Hamlet* was the most frequently lampooned Shakespearean play in the popular theater. Charles Mathews (1776–1835), a British comic actor, offered an "irresistibly laughable performance" as Hamlet to London audiences in 1811, and during an 1822–23 trip to America he impersonated a "black tragedian" who tried to recite Hamlet's most famous soliloquy but similarly mangled it (Blair 1976, 6–7, 8). Dan Rice, an American circus clown whose performance Clemens enjoyed as a youth, also made comic use of Shakespeare (Kirkham, 17–19; Browne, 381–83; Wecter, 192). Mark Twain himself attempted several Shakespearean burlesques, including a fragmentary *Hamlet* travesty in 1881 (Berret 1985, 198–99; Hirsh, 254–55; *S&B*, 49–87).

180.8–9   pretty well down the State of Arkansaw . . . little one-horse town in a big bend] Mark Twain originally located this town, later called "Bricksville" (241.20), "in Council Bend" (MS1, 622), which was about 288 miles below Cairo, on the Arkansas side of the river (Bragg, 80, 86–87; James, 3–4). Eventually, probably on the typescript, he substituted "in a big bend" for "in Council Bend." (Council Bend may have seemed too far north to be consistent with the raft's progress, or perhaps Mark Twain again wanted to avoid using real names for places on the river.) He may have modeled Bricksville on Napoleon, Arkansas, 405 miles below Cairo at the confluence of the Arkansas and Mississippi rivers, a busy commercial center with as many as a thousand inhabitants during the 1840s and 1850s (Bragg, 115). The principal evidence for this identification is Mark Twain's working note: "The Burning Shame ,boys give bill of sale of Jim., at Napoleon, Ark." (*HF2003*, 480–82 [Mark Twain's Working Notes, no. 2-2]). Although he planned to locate the "Burning Shame" (the "Royal Nonesuch" of chapters 22 and 23) in Napoleon, he did not ultimately follow his plan to have the king and the duke sell Jim in the same place. In any event, Mark Twain seems to have borrowed some of Napoleon's features for Bricksville: another working note, "an overflowed Arkansas town," describes both. Although Napoleon was still extant when he was a river pilot, he undoubtedly knew that by the early 1870s it had been all but destroyed by the river (*HF2003*, 485 [Mark Twain's Working Notes, no. 2-7]; see the note to 183.37–38). His friend Ralph Keeler included an illustration of Napoleon in an article about the Mississippi, one of a series he wrote for *Every Saturday* in 1871: "You have a faithful representation of what is left of Napoleon, Arkansas. It used to have the reputation of being the wickedest town on the Mississippi; but the streets once vocal with the 'sharp note of the pistol and the pleasing squeak of the victim' have all caved into the river" (Keeler, 284). (The same illustration of Napoleon was appropriated for chapter 32 of *Life on the Mississippi*.) Mark Twain also remembered Napoleon's reputation for lawlessness, describing it in chapter 32 of *Life on the Mississippi* as a "good big self-complacent town twenty years ago.... town of innumerable fights—an inquest every day" (SLC 1883, 363; *L4*, 485 n. 3; Thorpe 1855, 37; Blair 1960a, 305–6; Howell 1970, 199–202).

180.20–181.14   SHAKSPEREAN REVIVAL . . . *cents.*] Mark Twain carefully marked his manuscript to recreate the eye-catching showbills of the period, with their varied type styles and sizes. Most of his markings for capitals, italics, and small capitals did not survive in the first edition, probably because the manuscript was typed on an all-capitals typewriter. His original styling is here restored. See Manuscript Facsimiles, pages 504–5.

180.29–30   EDMUND KEAN THE ELDER, of the Royal Haymarket Theatre] Edmund Kean (1787–1833) was a famous British actor who performed primarily at the Haymarket, Drury Lane, and Covent Garden theaters in London. He was sometimes called "the elder Kean" to distinguish him from his son, Charles John Kean (1811?–68), who was also an actor but considered a lesser talent.

181.35–183.10   loafers . . . gimme the *chaw*, and you take the *plug*] Antebellum travel books and humorous writings were packed with depictions of lazy loafers in sleepy southern towns. Tobacco chewers resembling these occur in an often-reprinted 1844 sketch, "The Mystery Revealed," by William T. Thompson, a Georgia humorist well-known to Clemens (Thompson, 60–61). The chaw and plug incident evidently derives from a western mining-camp anecdote (Eby, 11).

183.37–38   because the river's always gnawing at it] During his piloting years, Clemens undoubtedly saw many towns ravaged by the periodic

Mississippi River floods. He wrote two other descriptions of river towns that were being destroyed by cave-ins. The first, dating from the late 1870s, is in a fragment called "Tupperville-Dobbsville"; the second is in the opening chapter of "Indiantown," an unfinished novel he wrote in 1899 (*Inds*, 24–26, 269–70; *WWD*, 151–55).

186.16–18   Boggs throws up both of his hands . . . Bang! goes the first shot]
The shooting of Boggs by Sherburn was based upon an actual incident that occurred in Hannibal in 1845, when Clemens was nine—the shooting of Sam Smarr by William Owsley. Clemens recalled in 1900, "I can't ever forget Boggs, because I saw him die, with a family Bible spread open on his breast. . . . Boggs represents Smarr in the book" (SLC to Goodrich-Freer, 11 Jan 1900, ViU, noted by Howard Baetzhold). Smarr, whom one neighbor had called "as honest a man as any in the state" though "a little turbulent" when drunk, had on at least one occasion gone through Hannibal shooting his pistol, and had several times publicly insulted Owsley and also threatened his life. After the incident, an eyewitness recounted to Judge John Marshall Clemens that Owsley had called out, " 'You Sam Smar.' Mr. Smar turned round, seeing Mr. Owsley in the act of drawing a pistol from his pocket, said Mr. Owsley dont fire, or something to that effect. Mr Owsley was within about four paces of Mr. Smar when he drew the pistol and fired twice in succession, after the second fire, Mr Smarr fell, when Mr. Owsley turned on his heel and walked off." Smarr was carried into Orville Grant's drugstore, where he died (*Missouri v. Owsley*; Wecter, 106–8; SLC [1900], 14–15).

188.10   The people . . . said he done it perfect] In chapter 23 of *A Tramp Abroad*, Mark Twain recounts an incident he witnessed in Germany, after the fall of a boy: "All who had seen the catastrophe were describing it at once, and each trying to talk louder than his neighbor; and one youth of a superior genius ran a little way up the hill, called attention, tripped, fell, rolled down among us, and thus triumphantly showed exactly how the thing had been done" (SLC 1880, 230).

188.13–16   somebody said Sherburn ought to be lynched . . . to do the hanging with.] Lynching was a common practice in nineteenth-century America, especially in the South during Reconstruction, where it was rationalized as retaliation for alleged crimes, but really was a form of intimidation directed against blacks. Mark Twain had written an editorial in 1869 about the discovery that a young black man who had been lynched for rape was innocent: "A little blunder in the administration of justice by Southern mob-law; but nothing to speak of. Only 'a nigger' killed by mistake—that is all. . . . But mistakes will happen, even in the conduct of the best regulated and most high toned mobs, and surely there is no good reason why Southern gentlemen should worry themselves with useless regrets, so long as only an innocent 'nigger' is hanged, or roasted or knouted to death, now and then" (SLC 1869b). When writing *Huckleberry Finn*, however, Mark Twain was aware that the violence he described was also rooted in genuine frustration with the southern judicial system. In a chapter written for—but excluded from—*Life on the Mississippi*, he wrote that southern juries "fail to convict, even in the clearest cases. That this is not agreeable to the public, is shown by the fact that very frequently such a miscarriage of justice so rouses the people that they rise, in a passion, and break into the jail, drag out their man and lynch him" (SLC 1944, 414). In 1880, before putting his manuscript aside for three years, Mark Twain ended this chapter with two additional sentences, just after the lynch mob arrives at Sherburn's house, clothesline in hand: "But they was too late. Sherburn's friends had got him away, long ago" (MS1, 663; see Manuscript Facsimiles, p. 506). Sometime later, Mark Twain wrote a note to himself, at the bottom of the manuscript page, about taking the episode in a different direction: "No, let them lynch him." When he resumed writing in 1883, however, he decided to delete the two sentences about the colonel's escape and instead began the next chapter with Sherburn confronting the mob.

189.1–27   swarmed up the street . . . Sherburn steps out onto the roof] Sherburn, although portrayed as a villain in the previous chapter, here plays a more sympathetic role, becoming to some extent a spokesman for the author's own viewpoint—a *raisonneur* whose scorn for the mob is nearly identical to feelings Clemens himself expressed in 1901:

> For no mob has any sand in the presence of a man known to be splendidly brave. Besides, a lynching mob would *like* to be scattered, for of a certainty there are never ten men in it who would not prefer to be somewhere else—and would be, if they but had the courage to go. When I was a boy I saw a brave gentleman deride and insult a mob and drive it away; and afterward, in Nevada, I saw a noted desperado make two hundred men sit still, with the house burning under them, until he gave them permission to retire. (SLC 1923, 245)

Many narratives that the author read about the French Revolution recount the quelling of an irate mob by a forceful figure (for instance, Mirabeau, Marat, Robespierre, Danton). Mark Twain told a friend that such reading had confirmed his belief that "men in a crowd do not act as they would as individuals. In a crowd they don't think for themselves, but become impregnated by the contagious sentiment uppermost in the minds of all who happen to be en masse" (Henry W. Fischer, 59).

190.19–20   In the south one man . . . robbed the lot.] Mark Twain used the same example, identifying the highwayman as a Kentuckian, in a chapter on violence in the South that was omitted from *Life on the Mississippi* (SLC 1944, 415; Ganzel 1962a, 415 n. 2).

192.25–26   all through the circus they done the most astonishing things]
The comic acts Huck describes here were a traditional part of the circus in the nineteenth century. Talking clowns were a "key element": Dan Rice (whose circus Clemens may have seen in Hannibal in 1848 and 1852) was famous for his quick rejoinders to the ringmaster, who served as the butt (Carlyon, 5–7). The "flying wardrobe act" in which the circus rider is initially disguised in the audience as a rube, often drunken, was known as "The Peasant's Frolic" and "Countryman" in the early 1800s and thereafter as a "Pete Jenkins" act, after the title given it in the 1850s by the famous comic rider, Charles Sherwood (Thayer). Joe Pentland, another clown and rider "who cracked jokes with the ringmaster," disguised himself as a drunken sailor and

> shouted from the seats that he could ride "that danged fat nag." Amid the jeers of ringmaster and audience the sailor mounted the circus animal, only to fall off repeatedly. But while the audience still jeered at him the sailor doffed his uniform and rode superbly in spangled tights. (May, 70–71)

Descriptions of such traditional circus acts had long been standard material in humorous writings. At least four humorists known to Clemens had written about a purported drunk's disrobing on horseback—William T. Thompson in 1843, William Wright in 1867, George W. Harris in 1868, and Richard M. Johnston in 1881 (see Blair 1960a, 315–16).

195.1–4   Thrilling Tragedy of THE KING'S CAMELOPARD OR THE ROYAL NONESUCH] In his manuscript Mark Twain entitled this skit "The Tragedy of the Burning Shame" and, as he recalled in 1907, it was based on an indecent entertainment he had heard Jim Gillis describe in 1865 in his cabin on Jackass Hill:

> In one of my books—"Huckleberry Finn," I think—I have used one of Jim's impromptu tales, which he called "The Tragedy of the Burning Shame." I had to modify it considerably to make it proper for print, and this was a great damage. As Jim told it—inventing it as he went along—I think it was one of the most outrageously funny things I have ever listened to. How mild it is in the book, and how pale; how extravagant and how gorgeous in its unprintable form! (AD, 26 May 1907, CU-MARK, in MTE, 361)

The tale's title apparently derived from a much earlier term: "burning shame" is defined in Francis Grose's *Classical Dictionary of the Vulgar Tongue* (1785) as "a lighted candle stuck into the private parts of a woman" (Grose, s.v.). Clemens acquired a copy of Grose's dictionary in 1875 and annotated it extensively while working on *The Prince and the Pauper*—a book written concurrently with *Huckleberry Finn*. Gillis's "impromptu" tale may also have been related to a story with the same title, current as recently as the 1930s, in which two traveling players stage a theatrical performance of a naked man on his hands and knees with a candle inserted in his posterior and then lit (Graves, 98). Mark Twain presumably altered the title of the skit for the sake of propriety.

(Many years later, however, when recalling the *Huckleberry Finn* episode in his unfinished novel "Tom Sawyer's Conspiracy," Mark Twain reverted to his original "Burning Shame" title [*Inds*, 205].) The title he finally chose—the "Tragedy of the King's Camelopard or the Royal Nonesuch"—suggests some indebtedness to Edgar Allan Poe's sketch "Four Beasts in One; The Homo-Cameleopard," which describes the antics of Antiochus Epiphanes, a Syrian king of the second century B.C. who capers on all fours before his subjects in the skin of a camelopard, that is, a giraffe. Mark Twain may also have known of the ill-fated giraffe presented to King George IV of England by the pasha of Egypt in 1827. The first of its kind seen in England, the giraffe attracted much attention for a few years, but then wasted away and died. In 1830 King William IV arranged for the skin and skeleton to be preserved and exhibited in London at the museum of the Zoological Society (London *Times*: "Messrs. Gould and Tomkins, of the Zoological Gardens . . . ," 19 Oct 29, 2; "The Giraffe," 15 Apr 30, 5; Berridge and Westell, 8, 182; Blair 1960a, 317–20; Whiting, 251–75; Ellis, 733; Gribben, 1:280; *P&P*, 24; Poe, 2:117–30).

198.1–8   The third night . . . went in.] Mark Twain's account of the final "Royal Nonesuch" performance is similar in tone and detail to a scene in Albert W. Aiken's *Richard Talbot of Cinnabar; or, The Brothers of the Red Hand*, serialized in the *Saturday Journal* from 8 May to 14 August 1880 and published in book form in Beadle and Adams's "Dime Library" series in November 1880. Aiken described an entertainment in a western mining camp by an itinerant actor billed as J. Lysander Tubbs, "The Arkansaw Comedian," late of the Drury Lane Theatre. Like the king and the duke, Tubbs advertises his advent with a comically bombastic handbill, which lists recitations, musical interludes, and scenes from *Hamlet* and *Julius Caesar*, all performed by Tubbs in different guises. The show is attended by "quite a large party of the boys" who come armed "with sundry articles," including potatoes, with which to assault the performer (Aiken, 7–9, in Johannsen, 1:10–11, 207, 440).

198.35   Them rapscallions took in four hundred and sixty-five dollars] An Elizabethan variant of the king and duke's scam occurs in a tale "laid somewhere about 1567." The London swindler, however, absconds with the proceeds and strands his audience in Northumberland Place before giving them even a single performance. John Chamberlain (1553–1627), "the letter-writer," reported that "a precisely similar adventure" actually took place in 1602 (Hazlitt 1890, 203–4).

199.15   Saxon heptarchies] "Heptarchy," or rule of seven, refers to the sixth- to ninth-century kingdoms unified later as Anglo-Saxon England. The heptarchy concept is now known to have been the highly simplified yet convenient invention of a twelfth-century historian (see Keynes).

199.16–23   Henry the Eight . . . Nell Gwynn . . . Jane Shore . . . Fair Rosamun] Although King Henry VIII (1491–1547) did behead two of his wives, neither is mentioned here. Eleanor (Nell) Gwyn (1650–87) was the mistress of Charles II; Jane Shore (d. 1527), the mistress of Edward IV; and Rosamond Clifford (d. 1176), the mistress of Henry II.

199.24–27   tell him a tale every night . . . Domesday Book] Huck confuses *The Arabian Nights' Entertainments* with the *Domesday Book*, a general census and survey of land holdings in England completed in 1086 for William the Conqueror. Neither book concerned Henry VIII, nor did any of the other events or persons mentioned in the rest of the paragraph: the Boston tea party (1773), the Declaration of Independence (1776), the duke of Wellington (1769–1852), or George, duke of Clarence (1449–78), reputedly drowned in a butt of malmsey wine in the Tower of London.

202.8–9   she was plumb deef en dumb] One of Mark Twain's 1880 working notes, which gives a real antecedent for this episode, specifies that the child's deafness was caused by scarlet fever (*HF2003*, 487 [Mark Twain's Working Notes, no. 2-11]). In late 1882 or early 1883 the author noted to himself: "Some rhymes about the little child whose mother boxed its ears for inattention & presently when it did not notice the heavy slamming of a door, perceived that it was deef" (*N&J2*, 510). Clemens had recent personal experience with the ravages of scarlet fever: the Clemens children, particularly little Jean, were ill for several weeks in June and July 1882, and the children of his coachman, Patrick McAleer, were stricken in January 1883 (SLC to Fairbanks, 7 May 83, CSmH, in *MTMF*, 252). In January 1884, when William Dean Howells's son, John, was recovering from the same disease, Clemens recalled the scarlet fever "calamity" and sounded a cautionary note: "I suppose lots of people will say it is safe to let John get out of bed within 6 weeks after he is well; but history does seem to condemn that course. . . . Our Patrick could answer that with a sigh. One of his children is deaf" (SLC to Howells, 7 Jan 84, NN-B, and 20 Jan 84, MH-H, in *MTHL*, 2:460, 465).

204.15–16   the Arkansaw village; and . . . t'other village] These two villages are on "each side of the river" (203.4–5), a day and a night's travel south of Bricksville (Napoleon, Arkansas, or its vicinity). In that stretch of river only Columbia, Arkansas, and Greenville, Mississippi, correspond to this description: the original pre–Civil War Greenville site, across Point Chicot from Columbia, was about seventy-four miles below Napoleon (Howell 1968, 168–70; James, 4, 38, 41; see the map on page 369). That Mark Twain may have had at least their basic geography in mind is also suggested by Huck's later reference to "a big steamboat laying at the shore away up under the point, about three mile above town," which he further says had "been there a couple of hours—taking on freight" (204.27–29). In the manuscript Mark Twain first wrote "taking on cotton"; Point Chicot was the site of a notable cotton plantation.

206.31–32   I'm going in a ship . . . for Ryo Janeero] In 1857 the twenty-one-year-old Clemens started down the Mississippi River to New Orleans, whence he planned to sail to South America to make his fortune (AD, 29 Mar 1906, CU-MARK, in *AutoMT1* and *MTA*, 2:289; *L1*, 70).

208.38–209.1   If gentlemen kin afford to pay a dollar a mile . . . a steamboat kin afford to carry 'em] The king's offer of a dollar a mile was understandably persuasive: in 1857, for example, steamboat fares on the Mississippi, upstream and downstream, ranged from three to six cents a mile, depending on the distance traveled, with a minimum charge of twenty-five cents (Merrick, 167–69). During the 1830s and 1840s, the period of Huck's adventures, the rates were apparently even lower: in 1832, for instance, the fare between St. Louis and New Orleans, a distance of over 1100 miles, was twenty dollars for the downstream trip (Quick, 172).

211.4–6   some of them putting on their coats as they come] In chapter 55 of *Life on the Mississippi* and in "Villagers of 1840–3," Mark Twain recalled a Hannibal saddler who "used to go tearing down the street" to meet the boat, "putting on his coat as he went" (SLC 1883, 540–41; *Inds*, 102). For an acute analysis of the style in the opening portion of this chapter, see Henry Nash Smith 1958a, xiii–xvi; see also Blair 1960a, 328–30.

213.15   hogwash] In a letter to John Horner of Belfast, Ireland, dated 12 January 1906, Clemens stated that this word was "a term which was invented by the night foreman of the newspaper whereunto I was attached 40 yrs ago, in the capacity of local reporter, to describe my literary efforts" (CU-MARK). Clemens had evidently forgotten his discovery that one of his favorite writers, Horace Walpole, used the word in a letter dated 22 March 1796 (Clemens's annotated copy of Walpole, 9:462, CtY-BR; see Baetzhold 1970, 274).

213.20   set up with the ashes of the diseased] The king is speaking figuratively when he refers to Peter Wilks's remains as "the ashes," which can be defined as "a dead body or corpse; mortal remains" (*Century Dictionary*, 1:336).

218.4–5   a word that's made up out'n the Greek *orgo* . . . and the Hebrew *jeesum*] The king's false etymology and pretentious vocabulary were familiar devices in humorous literature. Twice in Oliver Goldsmith's

Vicar of Wakefield, a book Clemens frequently read, sharper Ephraim Jenkinson supports claims to learning by dropping classical allusions (chapters 14 and 25). In Hamilton W. Pierson's *In the Brush; or, Old-Time Social, Political, and Religious Life in the Southwest,* a book whose title Clemens jotted down in his notebook in March 1882 (*N&J2*, 453), a local political candidate tries to settle a contested point and impress his hosts with his erudition: " 'The Greek settles that question. *Blabtow* may not always, in all circumstances, mean 'immerse,' but *blabtezer,* its derivative, means immerse—go in all over—every time. There's no getting away from that'" (Pierson, 137–38). Mark Twain may not have intended "jeesum" to suggest "jism," a vulgar term for semen. He had, however, used the expression "funeral orgies" with pointed intent in 1866 in one of his letters to the Sacramento *Union,* in describing the wild and licentious ceremonies attendant on the death of the king of the Sandwich Islands. "The term is coarse," admitted Mark Twain, "but perhaps it is a better one than a milder one would be" (SLC 1866c; Rasmussen, 345–46).

221.13   William Fourth] William IV, who became king of England in 1830, was succeeded by Queen Victoria upon his death in 1837.

224.5   Honest injun] Although some sources suggest that this expression originated with Mark Twain (in chapter 2 of *Tom Sawyer*), it appeared in the western press as early as 1851 (*ATS,* 15; Burchfield, 2:307; Mitford M. Mathews, 1:825; Ramsay and Emberson, 119; Partridge, 400).

224.10   I see it warn't nothing but a dictionary] During his first trip to England in 1872, Clemens wrote a note about the American consul's requirement: "If you want to ship anything to America you must go there & swear to a great long rigmarole, & *kiss the book* (years ago they found it was a dictionary)" (SLC 1872, in *L5,* 597–98).

232.12–13   He was the softest, glidingest, stealthiest man] In chapter 8 of *Quentin Durward,* a novel Mark Twain consulted when writing *The Prince and the Pauper,* Walter Scott pictures an obsequious barber, councillor of Louis XI, as a little man who conceals his quick glances "by keeping his eyes fixed on the ground, as, with the stealthy and quiet pace of a cat, he seemed modestly rather to glide than to walk. . . . [He] glided quietly back towards the royal apartment whence he had issued, every one giving place to him" (Scott 1823, 1:189–90; Baetzhold 1970, 94–95).

233.1   *"He had a rat!"*] This episode was apparently based on an actual incident that took place while Clemens's close friend the Reverend Joseph Twichell was delivering a Decoration Day (Memorial Day) prayer in Hartford: "The 'He had a rat' story put into a funeral scene, where it actually occurred in this city, will be recognized by a number of Hartford people, who have had many hearty laughs at it in its chrysalis period" ("New Publications," Hartford *Evening Post*, 17 Feb 85, 3, in Victor Fischer, 9). Clemens reminded himself in 1878 and several times thereafter to make use of the story (*N&J2*, 58, 343; *N&J3*, 16, 92).

234.30–31   I can't ever get it out of my memory] Clemens was similarly unable to forget the grief caused by the separation of slave families when they were sold. He wrote about it in "A True Story" (1874), chapter 21 of *A Connecticut Yankee* (1889), and chapter 3 of *Pudd'nhead Wilson* (1894).

237.7   Quick sales *and* small profits] The duke makes sarcastic reference to the common nineteenth-century mercantile maxim, also expressed as "light gains make a heavy purse," that is, "small profits and a quick return, is the best way of gaining wealth" (Brewer, 511; see also Penny, 120; Drake, 120; and advertisements in Richard Edwards, business directory, 62; Timothy G. Turner, 106, 135).

246.24–25   the dreadful pluribus-unum mumps] Huck's source for this impressive diagnosis is the United States motto. In chapter 24 of *The Prince and the Pauper*, Miles Hendon similarly uses irrelevant Latin phrases to frighten a man.

248.27   Here's your two sets o' heirs] A chapter in Fuller's *Noted French Trials: Impostors and Adventurers*, "The False Martin Guerre," tells how an impostor, after passing himself off as a lost relative, disposes of most of the opposition and is about to establish his alleged identity when "a new Martin Guerre" arrives "just at the right time to drag the judges back into uncertainty" (Fuller, 21).

248.28   you pays your money and you takes your choice] This expression seems to have been current in England in the 1840s. Its earliest known occurrence in print was in 1846, in the English humor weekly *Punch*, as a cartoon caption referring to the shift in power from Sir Robert Peel's ministry to that of Lord John Russell (*Punch* 10:17; Wilson, 615).

265.7–10   trees with Spanish moss on them . . . first I ever see it] According to the standard river guides of the period, the growth of Spanish moss (*Tillandsia usneoides*) began at Spanish Moss Bend, near Columbia, Arkansas (Cramer, 146, 178, 267; Conclin, 96, 98; Samuel Cummings, 105; James, 11, 38; see the note to 204.15–16).

266.9–267.7   a shabby village, named Pikesville . . . Silas Phelps's place, two mile below here] In *Huckleberry Finn* Mark Twain does not name the state in which the fictional Pikesville is located, but in other works written between 1884 and 1902, he places the Phelps farm in southern Arkansas, a location supported by references in the working notes to *Huckleberry Finn* (*HF2003*, 505, 507 [Mark Twain's Working Notes, nos. 3-4, 3-6]; "Huck Finn and Tom Sawyer among the Indians" and "Tom Sawyer's Conspiracy" in *Inds*, 33, 197; "Tom Sawyer, Detective" in *TSA*, 107, 112; SLC 1897–98, 37; Ensor, 7). Mark Twain apparently had no actual prototype for Pikesville, and no exact geographical equivalent in southern Arkansas can be determined. Several scholars have nonetheless attempted to determine its location and have noted that if the identification of the Wilkses' village with the vicinity of Columbia, Arkansas, or Greenville, Mississippi, is correct (see the note to 204.15–16), and the raft floats south from there to Pikesville for many days, it should progress well beyond Arkansas into Louisiana (Budd 1959, 234–35; Marx 1967, xli, 324n; Miller, 202–3; Hoag; Sherwood Cummings 1991, 440–47; Rasmussen, 356).

274.15–16   forty mile back here in the country, on the road to Lafayette] Lafayette, like almost all places named in the book, may be fictional. Or it may be Lafayette County, Arkansas, in the southwestern part of the state, about 135 miles away from Mark Twain's intended location for the Phelps farm in southern Arkansas. Despite Mark Twain's persistent identification of Pikesville with southern Arkansas (see the previous note), one scholar has suggested that it was based on Point Coupee, Louisiana, about 175 miles upriver from New Orleans and 1100 miles south of Hannibal—a location consistent with Aunt Polly's statement in chapter 42 (see the note to 358.33–34)—and that the "road to Lafayette" is one that connects Point Coupee to Lafayette Parish, 60 miles away (Sherwood Cummings 1991, 443–47).

276.18   Phelps's was one of these little one-horse cotton plantations] Mark Twain explained in an autobiographical dictation that the model for the Phelps farm was his uncle John Quarles's farm near Florida, Missouri:

> My uncle, John A. Quarles, was a farmer, & his place was out in the country four miles from Florida. . . . I have never consciously used him or his wife in a book, but his farm has come very handy to me in literature, once or twice. In "Huck Finn" & in "Tom Sawyer Detective" I moved it down to Arkansas. It was all of six hundred miles, but it was no trouble. . . . The house was a double log one, with a spacious floor (roofed in) connecting it with the kitchen. . . .
>
> The farm-house stood in the middle of a very large yard, & the yard was fenced on three sides with rails & on the rear side with high palings; against these stood the smoke-house. . . . The front yard was entered over a stile, made of sawed-off logs of graduated heights. . . .
>
> Down a piece, abreast the house, stood a little log cabin against the rail fence. (SLC 1897–98, 36–42)

277.8–10   hum of a spinning-wheel . . . lonesomest sound in the whole
world] In his description of the Quarles farm in his autobiography,
Clemens recalled the family room of the house, which contained a
"spinning-wheel . . . whose rising & falling wail, heard from a distance,
was the mournfulest of all sounds to me, & made me homesick &
low-spirited, & filled my atmosphere with the wandering spirits of
the dead" (SLC 1897–98, 49–50). Henry Nash Smith noted that Mark
Twain used his memory of the farm and the sound of the spinning
wheel to even more telling effect in his fictionalized account of his
brief but traumatic experience as a Confederate militiaman during the
Civil War:

> We staid several days at Mason's; and after all these years the memory of the dull-
> ness, the stillness and lifelessness of that slumberous farm-house still oppresses
> my spirit as with a sense of the presence of death and mourning. There was noth-
> ing to do, nothing to think about; there was no interest in life. The male part of
> the household were away in the fields all day, the women were busy and out of
> our sight; there was no sound but the plaintive wailing of a spinning-wheel, for-
> ever moaning out from some distant room,—the most lonesome sound in na-
> ture, a sound steeped and sodden with homesickness and the emptiness of life.
> (SLC 1885f, 201; Henry Nash Smith 1962, 130–32)

279.19   Lally Rook] A sidewheeler named *Lallah Rookh* operated on the
Mississippi between 1838 and 1847 (Lytle, 109). The name comes from
Thomas Moore's epic poem *Lalla Rookh* (1817), and thus, like the *Wal-
ter Scott*, this boat got its name from a British Romantic.

281   *illustration*] In November 1884, when book agents were beginning
their door-to-door sales of *Huckleberry Finn* with a prospectus containing sheets from the forthcoming first edition, a "glaring indecency"
was discovered in this illustration—Uncle Silas appeared to be expos-
ing himself ("Mark Twain in a Dilemma," New York *World*, 27 Nov 84,
1). The offending pages from the prospectuses were immediately called
in so the sale could continue. Mark Twain's publisher offered a five-
hundred-dollar reward "for the discovery and conviction" of the culprit
who had defaced the engraving, but he was never found. The printers,
using a re-engraved picture, repaired all copies of the first edition so far
in print ("Tampering with Mark Twain's Book," New York *Tribune*, 29
Nov 84, 3; *HF2003*, 742), although one copy of the proofsheets showing
the defaced illustration survives (ViU; the defaced picture is reprinted
in Meine, 32, and *HF2003*, 743). This edition reproduces the repaired illustration, from a first edition in CU-MARK.

282.14   the mouth of White river] Sixteen miles north of the mouth of the
Arkansas River and Napoleon, Arkansas (James, 4); see the map on
page 369.

286.12   Hicksville, Ohio] A village in northwest Ohio, near the Indiana
border.

299.14–15   Baron Trenck, nor Casanova, nor Benvenuto Chelleeny, nor
Henri IV] Baron Friedrich von der Trenck (1726–94), the Prussian soldier and adventurer; Giacomo Girolamo Casanova de Seingalt (1725–
98), the Italian adventurer; Benvenuto Cellini (1500–71), the Italian
goldsmith and sculptor; and Henry IV of France (1553–1610). All made
exciting escapes, and the first three wrote memoirs recounting them.

299.24–25   break your leg . . . nineteen foot too short] "Benvenuto Cellini's rope-ladder was too short. He fell into a moat, breaking his leg,
when he attempted to escape from the castle of S. Angelo" (Olin Harris
Moore, 335).

299.27   Langudoc, or Navarre] Languedoc was a southern province of medieval France; Navarre, Henry IV's inheritance and refuge after his escape, was an ancient kingdom in the Pyrenees.

300.8–9   we can tear up our sheets and make him a rope ladder] An expe-
dient described by Baron Trenck, Casanova, and Cellini, among others.
(Olin Harris Moore, 333–35, cites relevant source passages; see also
notes to 302.2, 302.5–6, and 304.20.)

301.23–24   a shirt . . . for Jim to keep a journal on] In addition to the memoirs of the actual prisoners mentioned above, Tom may have been familiar with one or more books by Alexandre Dumas. In *The Man in the
Iron Mask*, from *Celebrated Crimes* (1839), a prisoner at the Ile Sainte
Marguerite also wrote on a shirt; and in *The Count of Monte Cristo*
(1845), the imprisoned Abbé Faria wrote a political treatise on two
shirts.

301.25   *Jim* can't write] In most slave states, strict laws prohibited the
teaching of slaves, mainly to prevent them from reading abolitionist
literature. In 1836, after a purge of its abolitionist president and faculty
by proslavery forces, Missouri's Marion College forbade its students to
teach slaves to read and write unless they first secured the slaveowners'
permission. In 1847, a Missouri state law was passed which made it a
crime to instruct blacks in reading and writing (Trexler, 82–84; Holcombe, 230).

302.2   the best authorities uses their own blood] A practice followed by
Baron Trenck and Abbé Faria.

302.5–6   write it on the bottom of a tin plate . . . Iron Mask] The Iron
Mask scratched his name on a plate and threw it out of the window of
his cell.

304.20 dig out with a caseknife] Baron Trenck sawed through iron bars with a pen-knife, and Abbé Faria, as Mark Twain recalled in chapter 11 of *The Innocents Abroad*, "dug through the thick wall with some trifling instrument which he wrought himself out of a stray piece of iron or table cutlery" (SLC 1869a, 104).

304.23 Castle Deef] Tom's name for the Château d'If, site of the Count of Monte Cristo's imprisonment and of a brief sojourn for the Iron Mask. Clemens visited it during the *Quaker City* voyage in 1867: "We saw the damp, dismal cells in which two of Dumas' heroes passed their confinement—heroes of 'Monte Christo.' . . . They showed us the noisome cell where the celebrated 'Iron Mask'—that ill-starred brother of a hardhearted king of France—was confined for a season, before he was sent to hide the strange mystery of his life from the curious in the dungeons of St. Marguerite" (chapter 11, SLC 1869a, 104).

304.29 *Thirty-seven year*] Tom exaggerates: after digging for three years the abbé came up, not in China, but in another prisoner's cell.

309.25–27 I said, "Don't do nothing of the kind . . . his way when he'd got his plans set.] Mark Twain added this three-line paragraph on the typescript, or possibly in proof. Probably at the same time, he changed several pronouns in the next paragraph ("we" became "he" or "Tom") in order to make clear Tom's controlling voice in the evasion plan (for details, see *HF2003*, 978–79 [Emendations and Historical Collation]). These changes show that he was well aware of the problem of allowing Huck to be swept along by Tom's cruel enthusiasm for the mock evasion—a problem that has preoccupied critics of the ending increasingly since first publication (for an overview of critical reaction to the ending since 1885, see Richard Hill).

311.8 make them a witch pie] Recipes for this dish (sometimes containing murdered babies or disinterred corpses) were so ancient and obscure that neither Nat nor Tom would know how to make one (Summers, 207).

314.38–39 Matilda Angelina Araminta *Phelps!*] In a footnote to chapter 11 of *The Gilded Age*, Mark Twain explained: "In those old days the average man called his children after his most revered literary and historical idols; consequently there was hardly a family, at least in the West, but had a Washington in it—and also a Lafayette, a Franklin, and six or eight sounding names from Byron, Scott, and the Bible, if the offspring held out" (SLC 1873–74, 109). Matilda is the heroine of Scott's poem *Rokeby* (1813); Angelina is the heroine of Goldsmith's "The Hermit," included in *The Vicar of Wakefield*; and Araminta, the female lead in William Congreve's *The Old Bachelor* (1693), as well as Moneytrap's wife in Sir John Vanbrugh's *The Confederacy* (1705). See also the name of Matilda Phelps's brother (329.9–11).

316.1   Acts seventeen] Silas's biblical namesake preaches with Paul in Acts 17. Mark Twain may have intended an ironic reference to either verse 26 ("And [He] hath made of one blood all nations of men for to dwell on all the face of the earth") or verse 29 ("Forasmuch then as we are the offspring of God, we ought not to think that the Godhead is like unto gold, or silver, or stone, graven by art and man's device"). Either statement can be understood as a condemnation of slavery, a practice which denies the brotherhood of mankind for the sake of economic gain (SLC 1996c, 302; Hearn 1981a, 324; Arner).

321.13–15   lady Jane Grey ... Dudley ... Northumberland] William Harrison Ainsworth's popular romance, *The Tower of London* (1840), recounts the story of Lady Jane Grey (1537–54), her husband Lord Guildford Dudley (d. 1554), and her father-in-law, the duke of Northumberland (1502?–53), whose plot to secure the succession to the throne resulted in her reigning for nine days after Edward VI's death in 1553. All three were imprisoned in the Tower and eventually beheaded. In book 2, chapter 7, Northumberland is described "putting the finishing touches to a carving on the wall. . . . This curious sculpture . . . contains his cognizance, a bear and lion supporting a ragged staff surrounded by a border of roses, acorns and flowers intermingled with foliage."

322.1   coat of arms] Tom's design is described in a hodge-podge of sometimes colliding, though for the most part authentic, heraldic terms (see Birchfield, 15–16). Kemble's illustration on page 320 ingeniously incorporates most of the elements.

322.11   *Maggiore fretta, minore atto*] Literally, "More haste, less action."

326.11   Prisoners ain't ever without rats] Casanova complained of the huge rats in his prison, but Baron Trenck tamed a mouse and taught it to play with him (Olin Harris Moore, 334).

327.21   Pitchiola] *Picciola* (1836) by Joseph Xavier Boniface Saintine. In this highly sentimental novel, a prisoner carefully nurtures a plant and becomes obsessed with its survival; the watering with tears is Mark Twain's embellishment.

329.9–11   Thomas Franklin Benjamin Jefferson Elexander Phelps] Another Phelps offspring named after the "most revered literary and historical idols" of the time (see the note to 314.38–39). Samuel Clemens himself was delivered by a doctor named Thomas Jefferson Chowning; he had a father named after Chief Justice John Marshall, a brother named Benjamin, another named Orion, and even an uncle named Hannibal.

332.8–9   Sometimes it's done one way, sometimes another] Carlyle's *French Revolution*, "Varennes," chapters 3–4, tells of both: a palace chambermaid informed Commandant Gouvion of Louis XVI's plans to escape from the Tuileries, and "a billet" warned "some Patriot Deputy."

332.13–14   it's usual for the prisoner's mother to change clothes with him] Many novels about the French Revolution tell of such exchanges, and for the flight to Varennes the dauphin actually dressed as a girl.

334.25   Ingean Territory] The area known as Indian Territory originally included all the present state of Oklahoma, except the panhandle, and was set aside by the federal government as a home for certain Indian tribes who had been forced to relocate there during the 1820s and 1830s. Never an organized territory, it became a haven for white outlaws.

340.27–28   I wish . . . 'Son of Saint Louis, ascend to heaven!'] Several historians, including Carlyle and Jules Michelet, whose *Historical View of the French Revolution* Clemens is known to have read, emphasized the fact that mistake after mistake occurred during Louis XVI's bungled escape attempt (Gribben, 1:466). The words that Tom quotes were spoken by Abbé Edgeworth just before Louis's execution (*The French Revolution*, "Regicide," chapter 8).

341.13–14   make him swear to be silent . . . and put a purse full of gold in his hand] Tom's suggestions are similar to details in Dr. Manette's story in book 3, chapter 10, of Dickens's *Tale of Two Cities*.

345.32   Well, sister Phelps] Mark Twain wrote in 1898 that "Sister" was a common form of address in the "Methodist, or Presbyterian, or Baptist, or Campbellite church" (*MSM*, 191). For the following description of the Arkansas gossips, Mark Twain may have borrowed some features from a story by Joel Chandler Harris, "At Teague Poteet's," which was published in the *Century Magazine* in May and June 1883, shortly before he wrote this scene. Harris's characters use expressions like "s'I" and "se' she" (for "says I" and "says she") and one of them is even named Hightower (Carkeet 1979, 323–24; Carkeet 1981, 91).

346.4–5   Nebokoodneezer] Nebuchadnezzar (d. 562 B.C.), a king of Babylon who went insane (Daniel 4:33).

346.10   sister Utterback] Clemens was familiar with this unusual name from his childhood, when his mother took him to visit her friend Mrs. Utterback, a faith healer who specialized in curing toothaches (SLC 1897–98, 63–64). He also used it in an 1866 sketch about "Old Mother Utterback," who lived "in the bend below Grand Gulf, Mississippi" (SLC 1866a, 6). See also N&J2, 381.

347.34–35   I reckon they must a *been* sperits] Clemens, who was interested in (but skeptical about) spiritualism, may have read about the strange "haunting" of the Eliakim Phelps family in 1850 and adapted some of the widely reported supernatural occurrences for his tale. These included straw-stuffed dummies, anonymous letters, disappearing sheets and spoons, and "captious nails and candlesticks." The mysterious incidents of 1850 may well have been the work of enterprising, mischievous children (Kerr, 172–81).

352.30–31   he ain't a bad nigger] The expression "bad nigger" had a particular meaning in the antebellum period: it defined the "bold individuals who refused to accept whippings, sauced masters and mistresses with impunity, ran away at the slightest provocation, and even killed masters and overseers who abused them" (Roberts, 176). "Being labeled 'bad' by Southern white plantation owners in the sense of being dangerous, obstreperous, and the like indicated to black people that the individual in question was unwilling to submit passively to the oppression of slavery. Thus 'bad niggers' were Negroes with spirit, Negroes who were willing to fight the system" (Dundes, 581n). In some cases, "behaviors defined by whites during slavery as those of the 'bad nigger' came to be viewed by African Americans after emancipation as the free and open expression of citizenship" (Roberts, 177).

357.7–8   Then what on earth did *you* want to set him free for, seeing he was already free?] In the 1840s, a freedman in Jim's position was still not free: he could not vote, or safely travel at will, and without his manumission papers (easily stolen or held by local authorities), he could be imprisoned and sold into slavery again. Although slavery was abolished in 1865 (eleven years before Clemens began writing this book), after the war conditions worsened for the new freedmen and women, despite the passage of the 14th and 15th amendments to the Constitution. The Freedman's Bureau, established to provide help and legal protection from local abuses, was abolished in 1872, and in 1877 the last of the federal troops were withdrawn from the South. Local authorities were often complicit in the terrorist tactics of mobs and white supremacist groups such as the White Brotherhood and the Ku Klux Klan, and the former "black codes" were replaced by "Jim Crow" practices and laws, restricting the rights of freedmen to vote and threatening them with beatings, fines, and imprisonment for random minor infractions (Litwack 1980, 220 passim). Several scholars have suggested that *Huckleberry Finn*, ostensibly an evocation of the antebellum South, actually reflects the deteriorating social and political situation in the Reconstruction and post-Reconstruction era, when the slave found himself "free at last and thoroughly impotent, the object of devious schemes and a hapless victim of constant brutality" (Schmitz, 60; see also Fishkin, 70–75; Budd 1962, 105–6; Berkove 1994, 213–16; Carrington, 189–92; and Doyno 1996a, 15–16). This thesis is particularly relevant to the concluding "evasion" chapters of the book, where Jim is made to suffer through Tom Sawyer's elaborate scheme to "set a nigger free that was already free before" (360.6–8). The thesis, however intriguing, remains undocumented: Mark Twain nowhere explicitly stated such a purpose for his novel, either at the time of publication or later.

358.33–34   So now I got to go and trapse all the way down the river eleven hundred mile] The actual distance from Hannibal to the southeast corner of Arkansas (the equivalent of the distance from St. Petersburg to Pikesville in Mark Twain's fictional geography) was about 820 miles along the river. A distance of 1100 miles would have put the farm well down into Louisiana or Mississippi, a result which Mark Twain clearly did not intend (James, 3–4; see the notes to 266.9–267.7 and 274.15–16). Mark Twain made two later, somewhat ambiguous, statements about the distance to the Phelps farm. In chapter 3 of "Tom Sawyer Abroad," written in 1892, when Tom announces that the balloon has traveled "close onto eight hundred mile," Huck recalls, "in my experience I knowed it wouldn't take much short of two weeks to do it down the Mississippi on a raft" (*TSA*, 20, 189). And in chapter 2 of "Tom Sawyer, Detective," written in 1895, Mark Twain located the Phelps farm "in Arkansaw . . . not so very much short of a thousand miles" from St. Petersburg (*TSA*, 112, 191–92). Such discrepancies show that Mark Twain was fairly casual about adhering to exact mileage to make his narrative plausible.

361.7   go for howling adventures amongst the Injuns] In the summer of 1884 Mark Twain began the narrative forecast here, "Huck Finn and Tom Sawyer among the Indians," which he never finished (*Inds*, 33–81, 270–72).

GLOSSARY

Among the lasting achievements of *Huckleberry Finn* is the ready accessibility of its language: most of its one-hundred-year-old words and idiomatic expressions still require no gloss. We have, therefore, confined the entries here to words and phrases about which there is likely to be genuine doubt or uncertainty, or about which we have specialized knowledge pertinent to Mark Twain's meaning. When vernacular words or phrases (most oaths, for example) are wholly intelligible, we have not defined them. When words or phrases are to a degree obscure and are not readily found in *Webster's Third New International Dictionary of the English Language,* we have included them. If a word has more than one meaning (for instance, "spread-eagle"), some of which are in *Webster's* and some not, we define only the omitted meaning. A few troublesome dialect spellings are glossed only with the canonical spelling, as an aid to finding the definition in *Webster's.* A few words and phrases have proved more readily defined in the explanatory notes, to which the reader is referred in each case. All entries have been alphabetized letter by letter, always beginning with the first word of a phrase, even when that is a preposition.

The following dictionaries, glossaries, and other sources have been used to prepare the definitions: Bartlett; Bates; Burchfield; *Century Dictionary;* Clapin; Craigie; De Vere; Farmer; Farmer and Henley; Gove; Hunter; Maitland; Mitford M. Mathews; Neilson, Knott, and Carhart; *OED* 1933; Partridge; Ramsay and Emberson; Smyth; Thornton; Watts; Way; Webster [1870], 1884, 1889, and 1894; Wentworth; and Worcester.

allycumpain] Elecampane: hardy, European herb naturalized in the United States and commonly used in folk medicine. A white powder made by boiling the root is applied externally or internally, for lung diseases and for skin disorders, such as psoriasis and eczema. Spelling varied widely in the nineteenth century: elicampene, alycompaine, allicampane.

ash-hopper] Funnel-shaped bin in which wood ashes were leached of their alkali, which was in turn used to make soap.

bar]   Sand bar, any deposit of river sediment that forms a shallow place (shoal) or an island.

beat]   Idler, loafer, good-for-nothing. Short for "dead beat."

beatenest]   Unsurpassable, not able to be "beaten"; hence, most extraordinary, inexplicable, unaccountable.

big water]   The Mississippi River, a translation of the Indian name for the river, from which "Mississippi" is supposed to derive. Huck also says "the old regular Muddy" to refer to the river (129.23).

bitts]   Sturdy posts for securing cables on a steamboat. They were fastened in pairs to the deck. About three feet high, the bitts had a crosspiece above the midpoint, forming an *H*. Kemble has drawn what a riverman would call a "kevel" (illustration on page 89).

blister]   Nuisance, irritating creature, characterized by an overweening, irrational persistence.

boom]   To go at full speed, roar along.

booming]   Splendid, grand, superb (135.16); very, extremely (208.35).

boss]   Term of address used toward ostensible superiors, strangers, often by blacks speaking to whites (103.20); best, first-rate, supreme (215.16).

bottoms]   Alluvial flood plain of a river, the "river bottom" during floodstage. Usually fertile, low-lying, and flat. See Huck's description of the "Illinois bottom" (60.12).

break-down]   See the explanatory note to 111.38–112.1.

by de back]   Thoroughly. Possibly a reference to marked cards, as in *Following the Equator:* "I *know* you—I know you 'by the *back,*' as the gamblers say" (chapter 28).

captain's door]   Door by which the captain entered and left his room in the texas. Huck's description places it in the center of the forward wall. See diagram, page 405.

chimbly-guy]   Chimney-guy: a thin cable or wire used to steady the chimneys (or smokestacks) of the steamboat. See diagram, page 405.

chute]   Narrow channel or bayou outside the main part of the river, navigable only in middle to high water.

close place] Uncomfortably delicate or dangerous position. Huck also says "tight place" (239.6) and "close-fit" (257.15) to mean the same thing.

coarse-hand] Block, as opposed to cursive, lettering. Huck also says "coarse print" (242.20) to mean the same thing.

coase comb] Coarse comb: a comb with large or widely spaced teeth, the opposite of a fine-tooth comb. Used as a crude musical instrument by wrapping it in paper and blowing against the side.

come any such game on] To play any such trick on.

Congress-water] Mineral water bottled at Congress Spring in Saratoga, New York.

cross-hall] Narrow hallway at right angles to the texas hall, opening through a door onto the hurricane deck on both sides of the texas. Usually about two-thirds of the way from the captain's door to the stern of the texas. See diagram, page 405.

crossing] See the explanatory note to 78.23–29.

cross off] To thwart, obstruct, hinder.

dam] To bear young.

dead beat] Worthless idler who never pays his own way, sponger, loafer.

dog my cats] Mild imprecation ("dog" for "damn"), suggesting surprise or annoyance. It can also be found in the contemporary dialect writing of Clemens's friends John Hay and Joel Chandler Harris (Hay 1871, 22; Joel Chandler Harris 1883a, 9).

double-hull ferry boat] Steam ferryboat in which the deck is supported by two distinct hulls, with the paddle-wheel situated between them.

down in de bills] Written down in the specifications, hence predestined, foreordained.

down the banks] Scolding, reprimand.

fox-fire] Rotten wood that emits phosphorescent light (caused by fungi).

freeze] To yearn, long for intensely (169.15); to cling to, hold firmly or tenaciously (282.10).

gabble]   Intimate, eager conversation (264.25); to jabber, prate, talk rapidly and foolishly (274.20).

gars]   Long, spear-like fish of various kinds, commonly deemed inedible.

gone to grass]   Gone to the devil, expired, ruined.

grand bulge]   Most difficult or critical phase of an enterprise.

gumption]   Sense, practical understanding, quick perception of the right thing to do under unusual circumstances.

hark from the tomb]   Serious or earnest reproof, as in Isaac Watts's "A Funeral Thought": "Hark! from the tombs a doleful sound; | My ears, attend the cry—|'Ye living men, come, view the ground | Where you must shortly lie.'"

have it for breakfast]   To save or postpone something.

hive]   To capture, catch, get (14.33); to appropriate, take without permission, steal (225.33).

holt]   Hold, grip, grasp. A "best holt" is one's specialty or title to attention (161.4); "let go all holts" means to relax one's grip, hence to abandon all restraint (284.23).

hollow]   See the explanatory note to 15.3.

horse-bill]   Handbill advertising a stallion available for breeding.

hunch]   To nudge.

jackstaff]   Pole on the bowsprit of a steamboat, used as a steering aid by the pilot, who aligned it with a given point on the horizon. See diagram, page 405.

janders]   Jaundice.

jour printer]   Journeyman printer: one who has completed his apprenticeship and is qualified to practice the trade, usually taking work by the day. See the explanatory note to 160.37.

juice-harp]   Jew's harp.

law]   Lord (also "laws"). "Lawsy" (128.5) derives from "Lordy," "law sakes" (278.6) from "for the Lord's sake"; "laws-a-me" (278.18) and "lawsamercy" (348.38) derive from "Lord have mercy."

meeky]   To move in a retiring manner.

melodeum]   Melodion (or melodium): a reed organ, resembling a small square piano, popular in the nineteenth century. One variety, when the single foot-pump was operated inexpertly, produced a displeasingly uneven sound.

mud-cat]   Variety of catfish abounding in the Mississippi River, not highly prized for eating because of its coarse, muddy-tasting flesh.

mullet-headed]   Stupid, dull. A mullethead is a variety of freshwater fish known for its stupidity.

nigger-head]   Strong, black tobacco of an inferior grade, twisted or pressed into a flat cake or plug.

pat juba]   See the explanatory note to 111.37–38.

pilot house]   Topmost structure on a steamboat, housing the wheel and signaling devices used by the pilot. It was usually situated above the texas, far forward on the texas deck, with windows on all sides—all but the forward side glassed in. See diagram, page 405.

pow-wow]   To hold a meeting for discussion, to confer (14.35); any kind of din, uproar, loud noise or racket (158.22).

quarter]   To sustain a position behind a vessel. The view from any vessel is divided into four parts: the port bow and starboard bow forward, and the port quarter and starboard quarter astern.

sand in my craw]   Pluck, courage, determination. Huck also says "sand" for short (244.11). A bird's craw uses sand to digest hard morsels like seeds; hence, to have "sand in your craw" is to be able to digest or face something difficult.

scoop]   To grab, gather up without ceremony, often surreptitiously (15.7); to vanquish, gain the advantage of, beat (326.24).

scrouch]   To scrooch, crouch, or huddle down.

shake the reefs out of my hind legs]   To put on speed. From the nautical expression "to shake out a reef," that is, to enlarge a sail by unfurling one of its smaller reef sections, thereby increasing speed.

show up]   To present (oneself) for scrutiny or examination.

size their style]   To equal or match their characteristic manner; to estimate correctly their level of sophistication.

skylight]   Short for "skylight roof," the part of the texas deck covering the skylight, a row of transom-like windows (often stained or etched) that ran the length of or even wholly encompassed the main cabin. See diagram, page 405.

slept in our cravats]   Were hanged.

soul-butter]   Pious and sentimental words, perhaps in the sense of unctuous self-flattery.

spread around]   To assume airs, show off.

spread-eagle]   Extravagant (170.7).

stand from under]   To avoid something falling or thrown from aloft, hence to get to a safe place, avoid danger or punishment.

swap around]   To change from one place or subject to another (2.13) (also "swap about," 45.13). To "swap knives" is to change plans or tactics (282.4).

texas]   Officers' cabin of a steamboat, situated on the hurricane deck, usually below the pilothouse and above the main cabin (see diagram, page 405).

tow-head]   Small, recently formed island. Huck defines it as "a sand-bar that has cotton-woods on it as thick as harrow-teeth" (77.25). Mark Twain elsewhere wrote "tow-head (*i.e.*, new island)," a definition for which he recorded the supposed etymology: "Towhead means *infant*— an infant island, a growing island—so it is said" (*Life on the Mississippi,* chapter 23; *N&J2*, 471).

tow-linen]   Coarse cloth woven from spun flax, hemp, or jute.

trot-line]   Long, sturdy fishing line to which shorter hooked lines are attached at intervals. Secured at one end to the river bank, it was used primarily to catch bottom feeders, such as catfish.

up to the hub]   Deeply, fully, without reservation. The reference is to a wheel sunk up to the axle in mud.

valley]   Valet.

whollop]   Wallop.

without a j'int started]   Effortlessly, without strain, without displacing a single joint.

wood-flat]   Raft or barge for transporting wood.

wood-rank]   Stacked firewood, wood-pile.

yaller-jackets]   Gold coins. Huck also says "yaller-boys" to mean the same thing (214.15).

THREE PASSAGES
FROM THE MANUSCRIPT

Mark Twain's Revisions

Three passages from the newly discovered first half of the manuscript, MS1, are reproduced here because of the intrinsic interest of the revisions they contain.

Typically, Mark Twain revised his original handwritten pages, both as he was composing them and as he reviewed them, sometimes more than once. He eventually had this revised manuscript typed, chiefly so that he could continue the process of revision on the typescript. None of these revised typescripts is known to survive for *Huckleberry Finn.* The process of revision and correction might also continue on the proofs of the first edition (of which only a limited number survive, see p. 427), but, with time growing short and the illustrations already in place on the proofs, few changes would have been made at that late stage. Mark Twain never revised *Huckleberry Finn* after its first publication.

The first passage transcribed here, Jim's "ghost" story, was originally part of what became chapter 9, but it was omitted from the first edition. Before Mark Twain had the passage typed, he worked carefully through it using pencil to revise Jim's dialect (the draft itself is in black ink). He doubtless also revised the typed copy of this passage, but because he decided to withdraw it before publication, and because none of that typescript survives, we have no record of those revisions. Except for the "raft chapter" (see the explanatory note to 107.1–123.20), this is the single longest passage cut out of Mark Twain's text. It was finally published in 1995 as "Jim and the Dead Man" in the *New Yorker* and was included in the 1996 Random House edition of *Huckleberry Finn* (SLC 1995; SLC 1996b).

The second passage, the beginning of chapter 19, is Huck's famous description of sunrise on the river. The manuscript itself has relatively little revision, but the published passage shows that dramatic changes must have been made on the typescript and possibly on the proof.

The third passage, from the camp meeting episode in chapter 20, was substantially revised on the manuscript and then, as the published text reveals, revised even more extensively on the typescript and possibly on the proof.

Transcription

The method of transcription used for all three selections is adapted from the "Guide to Editorial Practice" in *Mark Twain's Letters* (see *L5*, 695–722). Canceled text is shown with a horizontal rule ("~~candle~~") or, for solitary characters, a slash mark ("&̸" or "̸"). Inserted words or characters appear enclosed by carets ("ₐlanternₐ"); solitary inserted characters appear with a single sublinear caret ("I̬"). Words that Mark Twain revised internally are transcribed showing the canceled and the revised form separately ("~~ghoses~~ ₐghostsₐ" rather than the more literal but less legible "ghosȩts"). Where Mark Twain interlined an alternate word, without canceling his original choice, a slash mark separates the two readings ("scared/ₐscairtₐ"). If he inadvertently omitted a word, it is supplied within square brackets ("[he]" at 466.36). If Mark Twain inadvertently wrote the same word twice ("& &" at 486.11), the error is corrected because the cause of the error (the line break in the original) is not preserved. Words or characters that Mark Twain misformed, then canceled, are not transcribed. When a compound word is hyphenated at the end of a line, the spelling printed here is Mark Twain's usual or invariant spelling of that compound or similar compounds ("a-yelpin' " at 470.1). When the end of a sentence fell just short of the right margin in his manuscript, Mark Twain often used a brief dash-like mark after the period to fill up the line ("village." at 466.30). He expected his typist to ignore these marks because their sole function was to fill up space, not to signal a pause. They are therefore omitted from the transcription.

Although for the first passage we have no record of the revisions Mark Twain made on the typescript, for the second and third passages we do: it is the text of the first edition. His revisions are identified by comparing the manuscript with the first edition which was set from the revised typescript, now lost. Any differences between them must result from Mark Twain's pen, except when it is more likely that they were volunteered by the typist or typesetter (such as first edition "by-and-by" for manuscript's invariable "by and by"). So for passages two and three we transcribe the handwritten manuscript with its internal revisions on lefthand pages, and provide a parallel text on righthand pages that is essentially a reconstruction of Mark Twain's typed copy of the manuscript with all the revisions he added on typescript or proof. In these reconstructions, canceled readings appear with a horizontal rule ("~~as if~~"); additions or substitutions appear with gray shading ("like"). The ampersand (&) of the manuscript is rendered as "and" because Mark Twain expected the typist to expand abbreviations. But otherwise, if differences between the manuscript and the first edition were manifestly imposed by the typist or the typesetter, the manuscript reading appears unchanged ("by and by" instead of first edition "by-and-by"). For a complete record of all variants between the manuscript and the first American edition, as well as the excerpts in the *Century Magazine*, see *HF2003*, 833–993 (Emendations and Historical Collation).

All of the manuscript pages in this appendix, shown at 70 percent of actual size, are reproduced from the original manuscript in the Mark Twain Room of the Buffalo and Erie County Public Library (NBu). The editors thank the Library and William H. Loos, former curator of the Mark Twain Room, for allowing us to use the digital scans prepared by the State University of New York at Buffalo (NBuU) for *"Huck Finn": The Complete Buffalo & Erie County Public Library Manuscript—Teaching and Research Digital Edition* (SLC 2003).

198

says: "I wouldn't want to be nowhere else than here. Pass me along another piece of fish & some hot corn-bread."

"Well, you wouldn't a ben here, if it hadn't ben for Jim. You'd a ben down dah in de woods widout any dinner, & gittin' most drownded, too, dat you would, honey. Chickens knows when it's gwyne to rain, en' so do de birds, child."

"I ben in a storm here once before, with Tom Sawyer & Jo Harper, Jim. It was a storm like this, too — last summer. We didn't know

Manuscript page 198, written in 1876, shows the beginning of Jim's "ghost" story ("I been in a storm here once before . . ."); the episode ended at manuscript page 214, line 4. It was included in the typescript of the first half of the manuscript which Mark Twain had made in late 1882 or 1883. He deleted the entire story, probably before submitting his typed printer's copy, but in any case some time before publication. Courtesy of the Buffalo and Erie County Public Library (NBu).

JIM'S "GHOST" STORY

A Passage Deleted from Chapter 9

Jim's "ghost" story filled fifteen and one-half manuscript pages and originally followed the paragraph ending at 60.9 ("Well, ... chile."; MS1,
198.16–214.4). Mark Twain wrote these pages in the summer of 1876 as
part of the first long stint (446 pages) on MS1. He subsequently made extensive changes in pencil to Jim's dialect, after which he had the manuscript typed along with the rest of MS1. (No part of this typescript is extant, but Mark Twain's occasional references in notebooks and working
notes to typescript page numbers demonstrate that this particular passage
must have been deleted *after* it was typed.) It was probably among the passages that young Susy Clemens recalled hearing read aloud by her father:

Papa read "Hucleberry Finn" to us in manuscript just before it came out, & then he
would leave parts of it with Mamma to expergate, ... and sometimes Clara & I
would be sitting with Mamma while she was looking the manuscript over, & I remember so well, with what pangs of regret we used to see her turn down the leaves
of the pages, which meant, that some delightfully dreadful part must be scratched
out. And I remember one part pertickularly that Clara & I used to delight in, which
was perfectly fascinating it was so dreadful, & oh with what dispair we saw mamma
turn down the leaf on which it was written, we thought the book would be almost
ruined without it. (OSC 1885–86, 87–88, in OSC 1985, 188–89)

Clemens admitted in 1906 that it was his practice to include a "dreadful"
passage in his manuscript just to elicit the family reaction, and "not with
any hope or expectation that it would get by the expergator alive" (AD,
19 Nov 1906, CU-MARK, in OSC 1985, 189–90). Still, the care he took in
writing and revising the "ghost" story suggests that he originally hoped to
publish it in *Huckleberry Finn*. But by 1883 or 1884, he apparently felt
the passage no longer fit the story as it had evolved since 1876.

Between 1866 and 1897, Clemens made at least four notes to himself
about the core anecdote he relied on for Jim's story (all are in CU-MARK).
On an undated page of notes in purple ink (probably written in the late
1860s or early 1870s) he listed a dozen ideas for stories, including "Uncle
Jim & the corpse." In July 1866, bound from the Sandwich Islands to San
Francisco, he wrote in his notebook, "Jim Lampton & the dead man in Dr.
McDowell's College" (N&J1, 136). Ten years after *Huckleberry Finn* was
published, in November 1895 while on the trip he later described in *Fol-
lowing the Equator*, Clemens wrote in his notebook: "Put in uncle Jim
Lampton's adventure with the corpse in the dissecting room of McDow-

ell's college at midnight" (Notebook 34, TS p. 35). Then again in July 1897, he noted simply, "Jim Lampton dissecting room" (Notebook 41, TS p. 40).

James Andrew Hays Lampton (1824–79) was the much younger half-brother of Clemens's mother, Jane Lampton Clemens (1803–90). He lived next to the Clemenses in Hannibal in about 1845 or 1846, before moving to St. Louis to study at McDowell Medical College. He then settled in New London, just south of Hannibal, but practiced medicine only briefly before abandoning the profession, in about 1849, because he could not stand the sight of blood. While Clemens was in the West in the early 1860s, scattered references to Lampton, then in St. Louis along with Clemens's mother and sister, show that they were clearly friends and kept in touch. Clemens remembered him as a "good fellow, very handsome, full of life" and as a "young doctor without practice, poor" (SLC 1897b, 13–14; *Inds*, 98, 329–30; *L1*, 15 n. 7, 130, 153, 248, 251).

McDowell College, the first medical school in St. Louis and the first west of the Mississippi, was founded in 1840 by the charismatic and eccentric anatomist, Joseph Nash McDowell. It was housed originally in a brick building in the open land southwest of the city, and its facilities included a laboratory, amphitheater, and two dissecting rooms. In 1847 the college became the Medical Department of Missouri State University and moved nearby to a new building, a massive three-story stone structure. Jim's description—" 'Dat college was a powerful big brick building, three stories high, en stood all by hersef in a big open place out to de edge er de village.' " —appears to draw on elements of both structures (Wild and Thomas, 59–60, Plate XII; Norwood, 353–54; Stevens, 2:421–25; Scharf, 1:417–18, 2:1526–27, 1544).

Jim's midnight errand to the dissecting room at the behest of his white master, a medical student, opens a window on the real relations between blacks and nineteenth-century American medical schools, presumably as Clemens learned about them from his uncle Jim Lampton. Many medical schools used blacks as janitors and porters, and it was common for them to accompany students and doctors on nocturnal grave-robbing forays, often among the graves of the recently deceased indigent. Partly for that reason, the cadavers used for instructional dissection were themselves likely to be black. In chapter 15 of *The Gilded Age,* Mark Twain's coauthor, Charles Dudley Warner, acknowledged this fact when he described Ruth Bolton's evening visit by candlelight to the dissecting room of her medical college. Ruth finds the "frightful" corpse of a black man, lying sheeted on a long table. Warner concludes: "the repulsive black face seemed to wear a scowl that said, 'Haven't you yet done with the outcast, persecuted black man, but you must now haul him from his grave, and send even your women to dismember his body?' " (SLC 1873–74, 146–48; French, 61; Plutzky; Shultz, 39; Blanton, 70; Norwood, 400).

The scarcity of cadavers given to or obtained legally by medical schools meant that most cadavers were obtained illegally. Mark Twain was well aware of the traffic in illegal corpses: in chapter 9 of *Tom Sawyer* he described a late night grave robbing by "young Dr. Robinson," Muff Potter, and Injun Joe (*ATS*, 74). He probably knew that Joseph Nash McDowell advocated and practiced body snatching in Missouri in the 1840s. And he may well have known—from local report or from Jim Lampton—of the vandalizing of St. Louis Medical College, in February 1844, by an enraged mob after two boys found body fragments from the school's dissecting room. In the 1870s and 1880s, when he was writing *Tom Sawyer* and *Huckleberry Finn*, there were numerous newspaper reports of body snatchings, including such notorious cases as the 1878 theft of the body of John Scott Harrison, a son of the late president William Henry Harrison, by the Ohio Medical College.

Professional grave robbers typically filled large orders for both local and distant medical schools, well into the 1890s, by robbing graveyards for the poor, and by other illegal means. One detail of Mark Twain's account indicates that he was familiar with this trade: Jim describes " 'a table 'bout forty foot long, down de middle er de room, wid fo' dead people on it, layin' on dey backs wid dey knees up en sheets over 'em.' " The raised knees suggest that the corpses were obtained illegally, for to avoid detection, grave robbers embalmed their corpses before shipping them, not in coffins, but in small boxes or barrels which required that the knees be flexed (Shultz, 34–35, 38–39, 59–66, 90–91; Blanton, 71–72; Doyno 1996b, 374).

Some details of Jim's description—the cadaver's eyes snapping open and the sudden movement of the toes and legs—are not explicable as normal signs of decomposition. They are, however, typical features mentioned in the voluminous literature about vampires and revenants, which derived in part from misunderstandings of normal postmortem changes. Disinterred bodies were sometimes found to have changed their position or appearance in ways that seemed clearly animate, but were actually the result of movement caused by decompositional gases.

The corpse in Mark Twain's story, however, does not seem to be decomposed: Jim even comments that it looks "pretty natural." In the absence of refrigeration, cadavers were necessarily dissected as soon as possible after death. If dissection were delayed, the corpse would be injected with a concoction of beeswax, tallow, resin, and turpentine (the most popular formula) which arrested decay and preserved a natural appearance. Jim is clearly dealing with an illegally acquired, embalmed corpse whose startling movements have a perfectly rational explanation ("Mars. William said I didn't prop him good wid de rollers") (Timbs, 429; Barber, 41–43, 102–9, 117–19; Ross, 3–5; Shultz, 18–19; medical information courtesy of Alameda County Deputy Coroner Kevin Hinkle and the Pathology Department of the University of California at San Francisco).

Jim's story is not a "real sure-'nough" ghost story, as Huck ultimately points out, but its grotesque effect and grisly humor are heightened by the realistic setting and the grounding in contemporary medical school practice (Shultz, 85–86; Blanton, 71–72; Flexner, 221–24, 278–79; Long, 97; Scharf, 2:1545, 1835–36; see Doyno 1996b, 372–76).

"I been in a storm here once before, with Tom Sawyer & Jo Harper, Jim. It was a storm like this, too—last summer. We didn't know about this place, & so we got soaked. The lightning tore a big tree all to flinders.[1] Why don't lightning cast a shadow, Jim?"

"Well, I reckon it do, but I don't know."

"Well, it don't. *I* know. The sun does, & a candle does, but the lightning don't. Tom Sawyer says it don't, & it's so."

"Sho, child, I reckon you's mistaken 'bout dat. Gimme de gun—I's gwyne to see."

So he stood up the gun in the door, & held it, & when it lightened the gun didn't cast any shadow. Jim says:

"Well, dat's mighty cur'us—dat's oncommon cur'us. Now dey say ~~ghosts~~ ₐa ghos' don't cas' no shadder. Why is dat, you reckon? Of course de reason is dat ~~ghoses~~ ₐghosts₍ₐ₎ is made ~~out of~~ ₐout'n₍ₐ₎ lightnin', or else de lightnin' is made out'n ~~ghoses~~ ₐghosts₍ₐ₎—but I don't ₐknow₍ₐ₎ which it is. I wisht I knowed which it is, Huck."

"Well I do, too; but I reckon there ain't no way to find out. Did you ever see a ghost, Jim?"

"Has I ever seed a ghos'? Well I reckon I has."

"O, tell me about it, Jim—tell me about it."

"De storm's a rippin' ~~an'~~ ₐen₍ₐ₎ a tearin', ~~an'~~ ₐen₍ₐ₎ a carryin' on so, a body can't hardly talk, but I reckon I'll try. Long time ago, when I was 'bout sixteen year old, my young Mars. William, dat's dead, now, was a stugent in a doctor college in de village whah we lived den. Dat college was a powerful big brick building, ~~&~~ ₐthree stories high, ~~&~~ ₐen₍ₐ₎ stood all by ~~herself~~ ₐhersef₍ₐ₎ in a big open place out to de edge ~~of~~ ₐer₍ₐ₎ de village. Well, one night in de middle of winter young Mars. William he tole me to go to de college, ~~an'~~ ₐen₍ₐ₎ go up stairs to de dissectin' room on de second flo', ~~&~~ ₐen₍ₐ₎ warm up a dead man dat was dah on de table, ~~&~~ ₐen₍ₐ₎ git him soft so he can cut him up—"

"What for, Jim?"

"I don't ~~do~~ know—see if [he] can find ~~suffin~~ ₐsumfin₍ₐ₎ in him, maybe.

Anyways, dat's what he tole me. ~~An'~~ ₐEnₐ he tole me to wait dah tell he come. So I takes a ~~candle,~~ ₐlanternₐ ~~&~~ ₐenₐ starts out acrost de town. My, but it was a-blowin' ~~&~~ ~~an'~~ ₐenₐ a-sleetin' ~~an'~~ ₐenₐ cold! Dey wan't nobody stirrin in de streets ~~an'~~ ₐenₐ I could scasely shove along agin de wind. It was ~~most~~ ₐmos'ₐ midnight, ~~an'~~ ₐenₐ dreadful dark.

"I was mighty glad to git to de place, child. I onlocked de do' ~~&~~ ~~an'~~ ₐenₐ went up ~~star~~ stairs to de dissectin' room. Dat room was sixty foot long ~~an'~~ ₐenₐ twenty-five foot wide; ~~an'~~ ₐenₐ all along de wall, on bofe sides, was de long black gowns a-hangin', dat de stugents wears when dey's a-choppin' up de dead people. Well, I goes a swingin' de lantern along, ~~&~~ ₐenₐ de shadders ~~of~~ ₐerₐ dem gowns went to spreadin' out ~~&~~ ₐenₐ drawin' in, along de wall, ~~&~~ ₐenₐ it ~~scart~~ ₐscairtₐ me. It looked like dey was swingin' dey han's to git 'em warm. Well, I never looked at 'em no mo'; but it seemed like dey was a-doin' it behind my back ~~jist~~ ₐjis'ₐ de same.

"Dey was a table 'bout forty foot long, down de middle ~~of~~ ₐerₐ de room, wid ~~four~~ ₐfo'ₐ dead people on it, layin' on dey backs wid dey knees up ~~&~~ ₐenₐ sheets over 'em. You could see de shapes under de sheets. Well, Mars. William he tole me to warm up de big man wid de black whiskers. So I unkivered one, ~~&~~ ~~an'~~ ₐenₐ he didn't have no whiskers. But he had his eyes wide open, ~~an'~~ ₐenₐ I ~~kuv~~ kivered him up quick, I bet you. De next one was sich a gashly sight dat I ~~most~~ ₐmos'ₐ let de lantern drap. Well, I ~~sh~~ skipped one carcass, ~~an'~~ ₐenₐ went for de las' one. I raise' up de sheet ~~an'~~ ₐenₐ I says, all right, ₐboss,ₐ you's de chap I's ~~after~~ ₐarter,ₐ. He had de black whiskers ~~an'~~ ₐenₐ ~~I~~ was a rattlin' big man, ~~an'~~ ₐenₐ looked wicked like a pirate. He was naked[2]—dey all was. He was a layin' on round sticks—rollers. ₐiust in his shroud—do' it was a pooty cold night,[3] ~~I rolled him~~ I took de sheet off'n him ~~an'~~ ₐenₐ rolled him along feet fust, to de ~~end~~ ₐen',ₐ ~~of~~ ₐerₐ de table ~~before~~ ₐbefo',ₐ de fire place. His ~~legs~~ ₐlaigs,ₐ was ~~spread open~~ ₐapartₐ ~~an'~~ ₐenₐ his knees was cocked up some; so when I up-ended him on de ~~end~~ ₐen',ₐ ~~of~~ ₐerₐ de table, he sot up dah lookin pretty natural, wid his feet out ~~an'~~ ₐenₐ his big toes stickin' up like he was warmin' hissef. I propped him up wid de rollers, ~~an'~~ ₐenₐ den I spread ₐde sheet,ₐ over his back ~~an'~~ ₐenₐ over his head to help warm him, ~~an'~~ ₐenₐ den when I was a tyin' de corners under his chin, by jings he opened his eyes! I let go ~~an'~~ ₐenₐ stood off ~~an'~~ ₐenₐ looked at him, ~~a-feelin'~~ ₐfeelin'ₐ

---

[2]Below the words 'He was naked', in the margin of his manuscript page (MS1, 205), Mark Twain scrawled what appears to be the word 'leave' followed by a wavering line or flourish that could be a note in shorthand. A few pages later, he inscribed another wavering line in the margin above the words 'all naked' (468.6 in this text). His marks may have been related to his decision to modify the cadaver's nakedness with a reference to his "shroud" (see the next note).

[3]Mark Twain interlined these words ('iust . . . night') in pencil, without a caret, and in an erratic, crabbed hand, below 'a layin' on round sticks' and above '—rollers. I rolled him' (MS1, 206). The initial word, perhaps an attempt at a dialect rendering of 'just', is doubtful. He may have intended the words as an addition or as an alternative to his text; in either case their placement is ambiguous.

mighty shaky. Well, he didn't look at ~~nothin'~~ ∧nuthin∧ particular, ~~an'~~ ∧en∧ didn't do nuffin', so I knowed he was good ~~an'~~ ∧en∧ dead, yit.

"But I couldn't stan' dem eyes, you know. It made me feel all-overish, ~~you know, just~~ ∧jis'∧ to look at 'em. So I pulled de sheet ~~clear~~ ∧clerr∧ down over his face ~~&~~ ∧en∧ under his chin, ~~an'~~ ∧en∧ tied it hard—~~an'~~ ∧en∧ den dah he sot, all naked in front, wid his head like a big snow-ball, ~~an'~~ ∧en∧ de sheet a-kiverin' his back ~~an'~~ ∧en∧ fallin down on de table behind. So dah he sot, wid his ~~legs~~ ∧laigs∧ spread out, but blame it he didn't look no better'n what he did befo', his head was so awful, somehow.

"But dem ~~eyes~~ ∧eyes∧ was kivered up, so I reckoned I'd let him stan' at dat, ~~an'~~ ∧en∧ not try to improve him up no mo'. Well, I ~~too~~ stoop' down between his ~~legs~~ ∧laigs∧ on de hathstone, ~~an'~~ ∧en∧ took de candle out'n de lantern ~~an'~~ ∧en∧ held/∧hilt∧ it in my han' so as to make ~~more~~ ∧mo'∧ light. Dey was some embers in de fire place, but de wood was all to de ~~other end~~ ∧yuther en'∧ ~~of~~ ∧er∧ de room. ~~While~~ ∧Whils'∧ I was a stoopin' dah, gittin' ready to go ~~after~~ ∧arter∧ de wood, de candle flickered, ~~an'~~ ∧en∧ I thought de ole man moved his ~~legs.~~ ∧laigs.∧ It ~~kind o'~~ ∧kind er∧ ∧kinder∧ made me shiver. I put out my han' ~~an~~ ∧en∧ felt ~~of~~ ∧o'∧ his ~~leg~~ ∧laig∧ dat was poked along pas' my lef' jaw, ~~an'~~ ∧en∧ it was cold as ice. So I reckoned he didn't move. Den I felt ~~of~~ ∧o'∧ de ~~leg~~ ∧laig∧ dat was poked ~~past~~ pas' my right jaw, ~~an'~~ ∧en∧ it was powerful cold, too. You see I was a stoopin' down right ~~betwixt~~ ∧betwix'∧ 'em.

"Well, pretty soon I thought I see his toes move; dey was ~~jus jist~~ ∧jis'∧ in front ~~of~~ ∧er∧ me, on bofe sides. I tell you, honey, I was gittin' oneasy. You see dat was a great big old ramblin' bildin', ~~an'~~ ∧en∧ nobody but me in it, ~~an'~~ ∧en∧ dat man over me wid dat sheet roun' his head/∧f∧ over his face∧,[4] ~~an'~~ ∧en∧ de wind a wailin' roun' de place like sperits dat was in trouble, ~~an'~~ ∧en∧ de sleet a-drivin' agin' de glass; ~~an'~~ ∧en∧ den de clock struck twelve in de village, ~~an'~~ ∧en∧ it was so fur away, ~~an'~~ ∧en∧ de wind choke up de soun' so dat it only soun' like a moan—dat's all. Well, thinks I, I wisht I was ~~out of~~ ∧out'n∧ dis; what *is* gwyne to become ~~o'~~ ∧er∧ me?—~~an'~~ ∧en∧ dis feller's a-movin' his toes, I *knows* it—I can/∧kin∧ *see* 'em move—~~an'~~ ∧en∧ I ~~can~~ ∧kin∧ ~~jist~~ ∧jis'∧ feel dem eyes ~~of~~ ∧er∧ his'n ~~an'~~ ∧en∧ see dat ole dumplin' head done up in de sheet, ~~an'~~ ∧en∧—

"Well, sir, ~~jus jist~~ ∧jis'∧ at dat minute, ~~down he comes,~~ ∧down he comes,∧ right a-straddle ~~of~~ ∧er∧ my neck wid his cold ~~legs,~~ ∧laigs,∧ ~~&~~ ∧en∧ kicked de candle out!"

"My! What did you do, Jim?"

"Do? Well I never done ~~nuffin',~~ nuffin', only I ~~jist~~ ∧jis'∧ got up ~~&~~/∧en∧ heeled it in de dark. *I* warn't gwyne to wait to fine out what he wanted. No

---

[4]Mark Twain wrote the single character 'f' above 'head', apparently because he was considering writing 'face' as an alternative to 'head'. He then interlined an alternative phrase ('over his face') above his original inscription ('roun' his head'), leaving the 'f' in place but effectively canceled.

209

more light. Dey was
some embers in de
fire place, but de wood
was all to de ⁿᵘᵗʰᵉᵈ other en'
of de room. While I
was a stoopin' dah, sit-
tin' ready to go ᵃʳᵗᵉʳ after de
wood, de candle flick-
ered, 'ⁿ an' I thought de ole
man moved his, ˡᵃⁱᵍ ᵗᵉᵍˢ
It kind o' made me
shiver. I put out my
han' 'n an' felt of his
ˡᵃⁱᵍ dat was poked along
pas' my lef' jaw, 'n an'
it was cold as ice. -
So I reckoned he didn't
move. Den I felt of
de ᵗᵉᵍ ˡᵃⁱᵍ dat was poked
pas' my right jaw, 'n an'
it was powerful cold.

Manuscript page 209 with Mark Twain's revisions of Jim's dialect, in both ink and pencil. Courtesy of the Buffalo and Erie County Public Library (NBu).

sir; I ~~jist~~ ₍jis'₎ split down ~~star~~ stairs ~~an'~~ ₍en₎ linked it home a-yelpin' every jump."

"What did your Mars. William say?"

"He said I was a fool. He went dah ~~an'~~ ₍en₎ found de dead man on de flo' all comfortable, ~~&~~ an'/₍en₎ took ~~an'~~ ₍en₎ chopped him up. Dod rot him, I wisht I'd a had a hack at him."

"What made him hop on to your neck, Jim?"

"Well, Mars. William said ~~I'd~~ I didn't prop him good wid de rollers. But I don't know. It warn't no way for a dead man to act, anyway/₍nohow₎; it might a scared/₍scairt₎ some people to death."

"But Jim, he warn't ~~a~~ rightly a ghost—he was only a dead man. Didn't you ever see a real sure-'nough ghost?"

"You bet I has—lots of 'em."

"Well, tell me about them, Jim."

"All right, I will, some time; but ~~the~~ ₍de₎ storm's a-slackin' up, now, so we better go ~~an'~~ ₍en₎ tend to de lines ~~an'~~ ₍en₎ bait 'em agin."

HUCK DESCRIBES SUNRISE ON THE RIVER

A Revised Passage from Chapter 19

Chapter 19 begins with this passage, first drafted in 1879–80 (MS1, 498.1–514.16), then revised extensively on the typescript in 1883–84. Huck's "rhapsody" about life on the river, as Walter Blair called it, is one of the most famous passages in *Huckleberry Finn* (Blair 1960a, 258). In 1957, Leo Marx analyzed its style to explain how the excellence of *Huckleberry Finn* "follows from the inspired idea of having the western boy tell his own story in his own idiom":

> There are countless descriptions in literature of the sun coming up across a body of water, but it is inconceivable that a substitute exists for this one. It is unique in diction, rhythm, and tone of voice. . . . The scene is described in concrete details, but they come to us as subjective sense impressions. All the narrator's senses are alive, and through them a high light is thrown upon the preciousness of the concrete facts. Furthermore, Huck is not . . . committed to any abstract conception of the scene. He sets out merely to tell how he and Jim put in their time. Because he has nothing to "prove" there is room in his account for *all* the facts. Nothing is fixed, absolute, or perfect. The passage gains immensely in verisimilitude from his repeated approximations. . . . Both subject and object are alive; the passage has more in common with a motion picture than a landscape painting.
>
> . . . Much of the superior power of *Huckleberry Finn* must be ascribed to the sound of the voice we hear. It is the voice of the boy experiencing the event. Of course no one ever really spoke such concentrated poetry, but the illusion that we are hearing the spoken word is an important part of the total illusion of reality. . . .
>
> . . . [T]he vernacular method liberated Sam Clemens. When he looked at the river through Huck's eyes he was suddenly free of certain arid notions of what a writer should write. It would have been absurd to have had Huck Finn describe the Mississippi as a sublime landscape painting. . . .
>
> . . . Clemens not only fashioned a vital style, he sustained it. Its merit was the product not so much of technical virtuosity as of the kinds of truth to which it gave access. (Marx 1957, 129, 138–40, 143)

For further, similar analysis, see also Henry Nash Smith 1958a, xxv–xxvi, Hearn 1981a, 184–85, and Angell.

The discovery of the first half of the manuscript in 1990 provided the first opportunity to compare how Mark Twain conceived the passage originally with how he revised and ultimately published it. One surprise was how many of the stylistic virtues Marx and others identified were achieved only by patient revision: the "vernacular" details of "bull-frogs a-cluttering," breaking the otherwise total silence, and of rotting fish on the shore, for example, were clearly added on the typescript. The revisions show that Clemens was not "suddenly free" when he looked at the Mississippi through Huck's eyes: the truly vernacular style had to be achieved in stages and took, perhaps, more "technical virtuosity" than Marx or others suspected.

Revision occurred in two stages, designated here as: **Manuscript Text**—on lefthand pages, Mark Twain's 1879–80 manuscript draft with its internal revisions; and **Final Text**—on righthand pages, that same revised passage as it was typed and then further revised in 1883 and 1884, with possibly some changes also made on proof. These two stages are published here, side by side, for the first time.

5-07

~~Some~~ A scow or a raft went by so close to us that we heard them talking & laughing — heard them just as plain as if they had been ~~eight at ten~~ *only five steps off;* ~~races~~; but we couldn't see the faintest sign of them; it made me feel crawly, it was so like ~~so they are spirits~~ ghosts or spirits ~~flutter~~ talking & & laughing in the air; & the voices drifted off & faded out, just the same as if they had been

Manuscript page 507. Mark Twain made only a few changes here, but he revised these lines extensively on the typescript of 1883–84. Courtesy of the Buffalo and Erie County Public Library (NBu).

Manuscript Text
Mark Twain's first draft with his revisions

CHAP.

Two or three days & nights went by; I reckon I might say they *swum* by, they slid along so quiet & smooth & lovely. ‚Here is the way we put in the time.‚ It was a monstrous big river down there—sometimes a mile & a half wide; we run, nights, & laid up & hid, daytimes; soon as ~~day~~ night was ~~no m~~ most gone, we ~~would quit~~ ‚stopped‚ navigating, & tied up—nearly always in the dead water under a tow-head; & then cut young cottonwoods & willows & hide the raft with them. ~~But I'll tell what we done & what we saw for *one* day,‚ & night,‚ & that will do for all—for all the days & nights was about alike.~~

~~Well, we hid in a towhead~~

Then we set out the lines. ⨍ Next we slid into the river & had a swim, so as to freshen up & cool off; then we set down on the sandy bottom where the water was about knee deep, & watched the daylight come. Not a sound, anywheres—perfectly still—just as ‚if‚ the whole world was dead asleep. The first thing to see, looking away across the water, was a kind of a dim, dull line—that was the forest on ~~'tother~~ t'other side—you couldn't make anything else out; then a pale place in the sky; then more paleness, spreading around; then the river softened up, away off, & wasn't black‚ any more, but gray; you could see little dark spots drifting along, ever so far away— trading scows, & such ~~things—~~ ‚things;‚ & long, black streaks—rafts; sometimes you could hear the screak of a sweep, or jumbled sounds of voices, it was so still, & sounds traveled so far; now you could begin to see the ruffled streak on the water that the current ~~from~~ breaking past a snag makes; next, you would see the lightest & whitest mist curling up from the water; pretty soon the east reddens up, then the river reddens, & maybe you make out a little log cabin in the edge of the forest, away yonder on the bank on ~~other~~ t'other side of the river; then the nice breeze would spring up, & come fanning you from over the water, so cool & fresh, & so sweet to smell, on account of the woods & the flowers; next you'd have the full day, & everything shining in the sun, & the song-birds just agoing it!

> **FINAL TEXT**
> *Mark Twain's final revisions on typescript or proof*

~~CHAP.~~ Chapter XIX.

Two or three days and nights went by; I reckon I might say they ~~swum~~ swum by, they slid along so quiet and smooth and lovely. Here is the way we put in the time. It was a monstrous big river down there— sometimes a mile and a half wide; we run, nights, and laid up and hid, daytimes; soon as night was most gone, we stopped navigating, and tied up—nearly always in the dead water under a tow-head; and then cut young cottonwoods and willows and hid the raft with them. Then we set out the lines. Next we slid into the river and had a swim, so as to freshen up and cool off; then we set down on the sandy bottom where the water was about knee deep, and watched the daylight come. Not a sound, anywheres—perfectly still—just ~~as if~~ like the whole world was ~~dead asleep.~~ asleep, only sometimes the bull-frogs a-cluttering, maybe. The first thing to see, looking away ~~across~~ over the water, was a kind of ~~a dim,~~ dull line—that was the ~~forest~~ woods on t'other side— you couldn't make ~~anything~~ nothing else out; then a pale place in the sky; then more paleness, spreading around; then the river softened up, away off, and ~~wasn't~~ warn't black any more, but gray; you could see lit- tle dark spots drifting along, ever so far away—trading scows, and such things; and long, black streaks—rafts; sometimes you could hear ~~the screak of a sweep,~~ a sweep screaking; or jumbled ~~sounds of~~ up voices, it was so still, and sounds ~~traveled~~ come so far; ~~now~~ and by and by you could ~~begin to~~ see ~~the ruffled~~ a streak on the water ~~that the current breaking past a snag makes,~~ which you know by the look of the streak that there's a snag there in a swift current which breaks on it and makes that streak look that way; ~~next,~~ and you ~~would~~ see the ~~lightest and whitest~~ mist ~~curling~~ curl up ~~from~~ off of the ~~water,~~ water, and ~~pretty soon~~ the east reddens up, ~~then~~ and the ~~river reddens,~~ river, and ~~maybe~~ you make out a ~~little~~ log cabin in the edge of the ~~forest,~~ woods, away ~~yonder~~ on the bank on t'other side of the ~~river,~~ river, being a wood- yard, likely, and piled by them cheats so you can throw a dog through it anywheres; then the nice breeze ~~would spring~~ springs up, and ~~come~~ comes fanning you from over ~~the water,~~ there, so cool and fresh, and ~~so~~ sweet to smell, on account of the woods and the flowers; but sometimes not that way, because they've left dead fish laying around, gars, and such, and they do get pretty rank; and next ~~you'd have~~ you've got the full day, and everything ~~shining~~ smiling in the sun, and the song-birds just ~~agoing~~ going it!

A little smoke couldn't be noticed, now, so we would take some fish off the lines, & cook up a hot breakfast. After we had ~~a~~ had a smoke, we would watch the awful lonesomeness of the river, & kind of dream along, & be happy, not talking much, & by & by nod off to sleep. Wake up, by & by, & look to see what done it, & maybe see a steamboat, coughing along up stream, so far off towards the other side that she didn't seem to belong to this world at ~~I~~ all, hardly; then ₍for₎ about an hour there wouldn't be a sound on the water, nor a solitary moving thing, as far as you could see— just solid Sunday & lonesomeness. Next you'd see a raft sliding by, away off yonder, & maybe a man on it, chopping; you'd see the axe flash, & come down—nary a sound, any more than if it had sunk into butter; you'd see that axe go up again, & by the time it was above the man's head, *then* you'd hear the sound, sharp & clean—it had took all that time to travel over the water. So we would put in the day; dozing, dreaming, & listening to the stillness. Once there was a thick fog, & the rafts & things that went by ~~were~~ ₍was₎ beating tin pans to warn steamboats to keep off & not run over them. ~~Once~~ A scow or a raft went by so close to us that we heard them talking & laughing—heard them just as plain as if they had been ~~right at our noses;~~ ₍only five steps off;₎ but we couldn't see the faintest sign of them; it made me feel crawly, it was so like ~~go ghots or spirits~~ ghosts or spirits ~~fluttering~~ talking ₍I & laughing in the air; & the voices drifted off & faded out, just the same as if they had been on the wing. Jim said he believed it *was* spirits; but I says, ¶ "No, spirits wouldn't say, 'Dern the derned fog.' "

Soon as it was night, out we shoved; when we got her out to about the middle, we let her alone, & let her float wherever ~~I~~ the current wanted her to; then we lit the pipes & dangled our legs in the water ~~(we was al~~ & talked about ~~religion~~ all kinds of things—we was always naked, day & night, whenever the mosquitoes would let us—the new clothes Buck's folks made for me was too good to be comfortable, & besides I didn't go much on clothes anyway.

FINAL TEXT
Mark Twain's final revisions on typescript or proof

A little smoke couldn't be noticed, now, so we would take some fish off ~~of~~ the lines, and cook up a hot breakfast. ~~After we had had a smoke,~~ And afterwards we would watch the ~~awful~~ lonesomeness of the river, and kind of ~~dream~~ lazy along, ~~and be happy, not talking much,~~ and by and by ~~nod~~ lazy off to sleep. Wake up, by and by, and look to see what done it, and maybe see a steamboat, coughing along up stream, so far off towards the other side ~~that she didn't seem to belong to this world at all, hardly,~~ you couldn't tell nothing about her only whether she was stern-wheel or side-wheel; then for about an hour there wouldn't be ~~a sound on the water, nor a solitary moving thing, as far as you could~~ nothing to hear nor nothing to see—just solid ~~Sunday and~~ lonesomeness. Next you'd see a raft sliding by, away off yonder, and maybe a ~~man galoot on it, chopping,~~ it chopping, because they're most always doing it on a raft; you'd see the axe flash, and come down—~~nary a sound, any more than if it had sunk into butter,~~ you don't hear nothing; ~~you'd~~ you see that axe go up again, and by the time ~~it was~~ it's above the man's head, ~~then you'd~~ then you hear the ~~sound, sharp and clean~~ *k'chunk!*— it had took all that time to ~~travel~~ come over the water. So we would put in the ~~day, dozing, dreaming, and~~ day, lazying around, listening to the stillness. Once there was a thick fog, and the rafts and things that went by was beating tin pans ~~to warn~~ so the steamboats ~~to keep off and not~~ wouldn't run over them. A scow or a raft went by so close ~~to us that~~ we ~~heard~~ could hear them talking and cussing and laughing—heard them ~~just as plain as if they had been only five steps off,~~ plain; but we couldn't see ~~the faintest~~ no sign of them; it made ~~me~~ you feel crawly, it was ~~so~~ like ~~ghosts or~~ spirits ~~talking and laughing~~ carrying on that way in the ~~air, and the voices drifted off and faded out, just the same as if they had been on the wing.~~ air. Jim said he believed it ~~was~~ was spirits; but I ~~says,~~ says:

"No, spirits wouldn't say, 'Dern the ~~derned~~ dern fog.' "

Soon as it was night, out we shoved; when we got her out to about the middle, we let her alone, and let her float wherever the current wanted her to; then we lit the pipes and dangled our legs in the water and talked about all kinds of things—we was always naked, day and night, whenever the mosquitoes would let us—the new clothes Buck's folks made for me was too good to be comfortable, and besides I didn't go much on ~~clothes anyway.~~ clothes, nohow.

> **MANUSCRIPT TEXT**
> *Mark Twain's first draft with his revisions*

Well, sometimes we'd have that whole monstrous river all to ourselves, for hours. Yonder was the dim banks & the islands away off ~~across~~ ‸acrost‸ the water; & now & then a spark—which was a candle in some cabin window—some family was at home, there, and they could see our lantern, of course, & so it was kind of sociable-like, & friendly; & ẅ sometimes, away down the river, or away up it, we could see a spark or two—on a raft or a scow, you know; & maybe we would just hear the faintest scraping of a fiddle or sound of a song coming over the water from one of those crafts. ~~Lordly,~~ Lordy, ~~its~~ it *is* lovely to live on a raft. We had the sky, up there, all sprinkled thick with stars, & we used to lay on our backs & look up at them, & discuss about whether they was made, or only just happened— Jim he allowed they was made, ~~a purpose~~ but I allowed they happened; I judged it would have took too long to *make* so many. Jim said the moon could have *laid* them; well, that looked kind of reasonable & natural, so I didn't say nothing against it, because I've seen a frog lay most as many, so of course it was plain enough it could be done. We used to watch the falling stars, too, & see them streak down the sky & trail their sparky tails behind them. Jim reckoned they had got spoiled & was flung out of the nest.

About once or twice a night we would see a steamboat slipping along ‸in the dark,‸ away over on t'other side, like a long string of glow-worms, & now & then she would belch a whole world of sparks up out of her chimneys, & they would trail off & rain down in the river & look awful pretty; then the boat would turn a corner & her light would wink out & her powwow die down & leave the big river all to us again; & by & by the wash of her waves would travel to us, long after she was gone, & joggle our raft a bit, & after that we would have the dead quiet ~~again.~~ once more.

> **FINAL TEXT**
> *Mark Twain's final revisions on typescript or proof*

~~Well, sometimes~~ Sometimes we'd have that whole ~~monstrous~~ river all to ourselves, for ~~hours.~~ the longest time. Yonder was the ~~dim~~ banks and the islands, ~~away off acrost~~ across the water; and ~~now and then maybe~~ a spark—which was a candle in ~~some~~ a cabin window—~~some family was at home, there, and they could see our lantern, of course, and so it was kind of sociable-like, and friendly,~~ and sometimes, ~~away down the river, or away up it, we~~ on the water you could see a spark or two— on a raft or a scow, you know; and maybe ~~we would just~~ you could hear ~~the faintest scraping of~~ a fiddle or ~~sound of~~ a song coming over ~~the water~~ from one of ~~those~~ them crafts. ~~Lordy, it is~~ It's lovely to live on a raft. We had the sky, up there, all ~~sprinkled thick~~ speckled with stars, and we used to lay on our backs and look up at them, and discuss about whether they was made, or only just happened—Jim he allowed they was made, but I allowed they happened; I judged it would have took too long to *make* so many. Jim said the moon could ~~have a~~ *laid* them; well, that looked kind of ~~reasonable and natural,~~ reasonable, so I didn't say nothing against it, because I've seen a frog lay most as many, so of course ~~it was plain enough~~ it could be done. We used to watch the ~~falling stars,~~ stars that fell, too, and see them streak ~~down the sky and trail their sparky tails behind them.~~ down. Jim ~~reckoned they had~~ allowed they'd got spoiled and was ~~flung~~ hove out of the nest.

~~About once~~ Once or twice of a night we would see a steamboat slipping along in the dark, ~~away over on t'other side, like a long string of glow-worms,~~ and now and then she would belch a whole world of sparks up out of her ~~chimneys,~~ chimbleys, and they would ~~trail off and~~ rain down in the river and look awful pretty; then ~~the boat~~ she would turn a corner and her lights would wink out and her pow-wow ~~die down~~ shut off and leave the ~~big~~ river ~~all to us~~ still again; and by and by ~~the wash of~~ her waves would ~~travel~~ get to us, a long time after she was gone, and joggle ~~our~~ the raft a bit, and after that ~~we would have the dead quiet once more.~~ you wouldn't hear nothing for you couldn't tell how long, except maybe frogs or something.

582

Some of the old women
was knitting, & some of
the young folks was
courting on the sly.

The first shed we
come to, the preacher
was lining-out a hymn.
He lined out two lines;
every body sung it —
roared it out, they did, in
a most rousing way:

"Am I a soldier of the cross,
A follower of the Lamb,"—

— Then the preacher lined
out the next two:
"And shall I fear to own his cause,
Or blush to speak his name?"

Manuscript page 582, in the account of the Pokeville camp meeting. Mark Twain changed his mind about which lines to quote from the hymn "Am I a Soldier of the Cross?" Later he would drop the hymn entirely (see the note on page 484). Courtesy of the Buffalo and Erie County Public Library (NBu).

THE POKEVILLE CAMP MEETING

A Revised Passage from Chapter 20

The camp-meeting scene as published differs considerably from the original manuscript version written in 1880 (MS1, 579.1–600.8). Mark Twain carefully edited the episode at the typescript stage—shortening it, toning down the racial and religious satire, and reducing its similarity to Johnson J. Hooper's 1845 sketch, "The Captain Attends a Camp-Meeting."

As a child, Clemens may well have attended camp meetings with his family. He attended a Methodist Sunday school until 1841 when his mother joined the Presbyterian church, which maintained a site for an annual encampment three miles outside of Hannibal. Clemens also had firsthand experience of the intense revival preaching of the period, for in about 1850, while he was a printing apprentice on the Hannibal *Missouri Courier,* he witnessed a Campbellite revival at which Alexander Campbell himself preached. "All converted but me. All sinners again in a week," he commented later (SLC [1897?]; *Inds,* 350; Sweets, 4, 17, 51–53; AD, 29 Mar 1906, CU-MARK, in *AutoMT1* and *MTA,* 2:279; [Bacon], 39; *L4,* 86 n.1).

Camp meetings were at their height in Missouri during the first half of the nineteenth century. Hundreds, even thousands, gathered at the camp sites, often traveling for miles, and bringing bedding and tents. "Many anticipated a profound conversion and religious experience; some came only to jest, swear, or be amused by the emotional excesses for which the meetings were known; others came to see the condition and prospects of the matrimonial market" (Windell, 256). Early meetings were associated with some immorality and rowdyism, as well as extraordinary physical manifestations of religious fervor, such as the "holy laugh," the "jerks," and the "falling exercise" or "holy toppling" (Charles A. Johnson, 54–62, 93; Windell, 259–61). Slaves and free blacks attended the meetings along with white worshipers; there were many accomplished black preachers, as well as white. Although certain areas were designated for the black congregation, and the sexes were also segregated, it is clear that race and gender barriers were not strictly observed (Bruce, 73, 89; Windell, 253–55, 261, 263, 266–67; Charles A. Johnson, 46, 113–18, 242–46; McCurdy, 156–60, 167).

While Mark Twain probably drew on his own personal knowledge in writing his camp-meeting episode, he was undoubtedly also aware of the numerous literary treatments of the theme. The general influence of

Johnson J. Hooper's backwoods sketch "The Captain Attends a Camp-Meeting" has long been known. Hooper's shifty rogue, Captain Simon Suggs—like the king in Mark Twain's scene—comes to the mourners' bench, feigns conversion, and then gulls the crowd by collecting funds for a spurious church. The rediscovered manuscript version of Mark Twain's camp-meeting scene reveals a more specific debt to the Suggs sketch: Mark Twain's "fat nigger woman" who in her religious fervor would "tackle" and "smother" the white mourners, recalls Hooper's "huge, greasy negro woman" who falls on another mourner, yelling "Gl-o-*ree!*" (Hooper 1845, 121; Blair 1960a, 279–81; DeVoto 1932, 255; see also Doyno 1996b, 379–81). Mark Twain excised this passage before publication, probably realizing that its coarse humor was too reminiscent of Hooper's sketch.

Camp-meeting descriptions were commonplace in the travel memoirs and fiction of the period. All provided details of the camp sites, the style and language of the sermons and exhortations, the fervent hymn singing, and the frenzy of the congregation. Among the accounts that Mark Twain may have seen are the following: Frederick Marryat's *Diary in America* (1839), chapter 32; Frances Trollope's *Domestic Manners of the Americans* (1832), chapters 8 and 15; Fredrika Bremer's *Homes of the New World* (1853), letter xiv; and Harriet Beecher Stowe's *Dred; A Tale of the Great Dismal Swamp* (1856), chapter 23. (The works by Marryat and Trollope are among those he consulted while writing *Life on the Mississippi*.) Descriptions of village revivals and backwoods preaching can also be found in three of Edward Eggleston's novels—*The Hoosier School-Master* (1871), *The Circuit Rider* (1874), and *Roxy* (1878)—as well as in Hamilton Pierson's *In the Brush* (1881), a title that Clemens jotted down in his notebook in March 1882 (*N&J*2, 453; Ganzel 1962a and 1962b; Kruse 1981, 49, 166).

Revision occurred in two stages, designated here as: **Manuscript Text**—on lefthand pages, Mark Twain's 1879–80 manuscript draft with its internal revisions; and **Final Text**—on righthand pages, that same revised passage as it was typed and then further revised in 1883 and 1884, with possibly some changes also made on proof. These two stages are published here, side by side, for the first time.

587

a-coming-ah! — one more shake, sister, one more shake & your chains is broke-ah! [Glory hal-lelujah!] O, come to the mour-ner's bench! [Come, black with sin! — . Come, sick & sore! [Amen!] come, lame, & blind & halt! [Amen!] come, pore & needy, sunk in shame! [A-a-men!] come all that's worn, & guilty & suf-ferin'! — come with a bro-ken spirit! come with a contrite heart! come in your rags & sin & dirt!

Manuscript page 587. Mark Twain ended up deleting or revising most of the material on this page when he revised the typescript. Courtesy of the Buffalo and Erie County Public Library (NBu).

> **MANUSCRIPT TEXT**
> *Mark Twain's first draft with his revisions*

We got there in about a half an hour, sweating like sin, for it was ~~an~~ ₐa most₍ awful hot day. Everything was a-booming. There was as much as ~~two~~ a thousand people there, from twenty ₍forty₎ mile around. The woods was full of teams & wagons, hitched everywhere₍, feeding out of the wagon troughs & stomping to keep off the flies. There was sheds made out of poles & roofed over with branches, where they had lemonade & ginger-bread to sell, & piles & piles of ~~water-millions~~ ₍n̸ ~~watermillions~~ ₍water-melons₍ & green corn & such-like truck.

The preaching was going on under the same kind of sheds, only they was bigger & held crowds of people. The benches was made out of outside slabs of logs, with holes bored in the round side to drive sticks into for legs. They didn't have ~~no~~ ₍any₍ backs. The preachers had high platforms to stand on, at one end of the sheds. The women had on sun-bonnets; & some had linsey-woolsey ~~from~~ frocks, some gingham ones, & a few of the young ones had on calico. Some of the young men was barefooted, & some of the ~~good~~ children & good-sized boys didn't have on any clothes but just a tow-linen shirt. Some of the old women was knitting, & some of the young folks was courting on the sly.

The first shed we come to, ∅ the preacher was lining-out a ~~hymn,~~ hymn. He lined out two lines; everybody sung it—roared it out, they did, in a most rousing way:

> ~~"Shall I be carried to the skies,~~
> ~~On flowery beds of ease—"~~
> ₍"Am I a soldier of the cross,
> A follower of the Lamb,"—₍

—then the preacher lined-out the next two:

> ~~"Whilst others fight to win the prize,~~
> ~~And sail through bloody seas?"~~
> ₍"And shall I fear to own his cause,
> Or blush to speak his name?"⸀₍[1]

---

[1] Mark Twain here substitutes the first for the second verse of "Am I a Soldier of the Cross?" written by Isaac Watts in 1709 (Amos R. Wells, 82–84). He had already used the second verse in chapter 5 of *Tom Sawyer*, where it is read "with relish" by the St. Petersburg minister. Watts's hymns were a staple of the camp-meeting reper-toire, and "Am I a Soldier of the Cross?" in particular, was well known as the "re-cruiting song of Methodism" (Eggleston 1874, 226; Charles A. Johnson, 57, 123, 192, 194). After the manuscript was typed, Mark Twain deleted the Watts hymn entirely (see the facing page), perhaps because the words were too familiar to be "lined": "The practice of 'lining the hymn' . . . [was] especially helpful to the many in the au-dience who were illiterate. In this procedure the preacher read two lines and then

> ### FINAL TEXT
> *Mark Twain's final revisions on typescript or proof*

We got there in about a half an hour, ~~sweating like sin,~~ fairly dripping, for it was a most awful hot day. ~~Everything was a-booming.~~ There was as much as a thousand people there, from twenty mile around. The woods was full of teams and wagons, hitched everywheres, feeding out of the wagon troughs and stomping to keep off the flies. There was sheds made out of poles and roofed over with branches, where they had lemonade and ginger-bread to sell, ~~and piles~~ and piles of watermelons and green corn and such-like truck.

The preaching was going on under the same ~~kind~~ kinds of sheds, only they was bigger and held crowds of people. The benches was made out of outside slabs of logs, with holes bored in the round side to drive sticks into for legs. They didn't have ~~any~~ no backs. The preachers had high plat-forms to stand on, at one end of the sheds. The women had on sun-bonnets; and some had linsey-woolsey frocks, some gingham ones, and a few of the young ones had on calico. Some of the young men was bare-footed, and some of the children ~~and good-sized boys~~ didn't have on any clothes but just a tow-linen shirt. Some of the old women was knitting, and some of the young folks was courting on the sly.

The first shed we come to, the preacher was lining-out a hymn. He lined out two ~~lines,~~ lines, everybody sung ~~it—roared it out, they did, in a most rousing way:~~

> ~~"Am I a soldier of the cross,~~
> ~~A follower of the Lamb,"—~~

~~—then the preacher lined-out the next two:~~

> ~~"And shall I fear to own his cause,~~
> ~~Or blush to speak his name?"~~

---

everyone sang them; he continued in this way until all the verses had been sung. If the selection was as popular as Isaac Watts's 'Am I a Soldier of the Cross?' prompting was not necessary" (Charles A. Johnson, 195–96).

MANUSCRIPT TEXT
Mark Twain's first draft with his revisions

—& so on. The people woke up more & more, & sung louder & louder; & towards the end, some begun to groan, & some begun to shout. The preacher begun to preach, & he warmed up, right away, & went a-weaving ~~up~~ first to one side of his platform & then ~~to~~ to t'other, & then a-leaning down over the front of it, with his arms & his body a-going it all the time, & sing-songing his words out ~~so~~ with all his might & main, so you could a heard him a mile; & every now & then he would hold up his open Bible, & kind of pass it around this way & that, shouting, "It's the brazen serpent in the wilderness-ah! look upon it & ~~live!"~~ live-ah!"[2] & people would sing out, "Glo-o-ree!—A-a-men!" & so on, & next he would lay the Bible down & weave about the platform, & work back to the Bible again, pretty soon, & fetch it a ~~whack~~ ₐbangₐ with his fist & shout *"Here* it is! the rock of salvation-ah!" And so he went on a-raging, & the people groaning & crying, & jumping up & hugging one another, & *Amens* was popping off everywheres. Every little while he would ~~tal~~ preach right *at* people that he saw was stirred up:

"The sperrit's a workin' in you brother—don't shake him off-ah! Now is the accepted time-ah! [*A-a*-MEN!] The devil's holt is a weakenin' on you, sister—shake him loose, shake him loose-ah! One more shake & ₐtheₐ vict'ry's won-ah! [*Come* DOWN, **Lord!**] Hell's a-burning, the kingdom's a-coming-ah!—one more shake, sister, one more shake & your

---

[2]The Reverend Hamilton Pierson, in his memoir of 1850s ministerial life in the "wilds" of Tennessee and Kentucky, described in detail a similar "sing-songing" style of delivery:

Scarcely a sentence in the sermon was uttered in the usual method of speech. It was drawled out in a sing-song tone from the beginning to the end. The preacher ran his voice up, and sustained it at so high a pitch that he could make but little variation of voice upward. The air in his lungs would become exhausted, and at the conclusion of every sentence he would "catch" his breath with an "ah." As he proceeded with his sermon, and his vocal organs became wearied with this most unnatural exertion, the "ah" was repeated more and more frequently, until, with the most painful contortions of face and form, he would with difficulty articulate, in his sing-song tone:

"Oh, my beloved brethren—ah, and sisters—ah, you have all got to die—ah, and be buried—ah, and go to the judgment—ah, and stand before the great white throne—ah, and receive your rewards—ah, for the deeds—ah, done in the body—ah."

From the beginning to the end of his sermon, which occupied just an hour and ten minutes by my watch, I could not see the slightest evidence that he had any idea what he was going to say from one sentence to another. While "catching his breath," and saying "ah," he seemed to determine what he would say next.

FINAL TEXT
Mark Twain's final revisions on typescript or proof

it, and it was kind of grand to hear it, there was so many of them and they done it in such a rousing way; then he lined out two more for them to sing—and so on. The people woke up more and more, and sung louder and louder; and towards the end, some begun to groan, and some begun to shout. ~~The~~ Then the preacher begun to ~~preach, and he warmed up, right away,~~ preach; and begun in earnest, too; and went ~~a-weaving~~ weaving first to one side of ~~his~~ the platform and then ~~to t'other,~~ the other, and then a-leaning down over the front of it, with his arms and his body ~~a-going it~~ going all the time, and ~~sing-song~~ing shouting his words out with all his ~~might and main, so you could a heard him a mile,~~ might; and every now and then he would hold up his ~~open Bible,~~ Bible and spread it open, and kind of pass it around this way and that, shouting, "It's the brazen serpent in the ~~wilderness-ah! look~~ wilderness! look upon it and ~~live-ah!"~~ live!" and people would ~~sing~~ shout out, ~~"Glo-o-ree!—A-a-men!"~~ "Glory!—A-a-*men!*" ~~and so on, and next he would lay the Bible down and weave about the platform, and work back to the Bible again, pretty soon, and fetch it a bang with his fist and shout "Here it is! the rock of salvation-ah!"~~ And so he went ~~on a-raging,~~ on, and the people groaning and ~~crying, and jumping up and hugging one another, and Amens was popping off everywheres. Every little while he would preach right at people that he saw was stirred up:~~ crying and saying amen:

~~"The sperrit's a workin' in you brother—don't shake him off-ah! Now is the accepted time-ah! [A-a-MEN!] The devil's holt is a weakenin' on you, sister—shake him loose, shake him loose-ah! One more shake and the vict'ry's won-ah! [Come DOWN, Lord!] Hell's a-burning, the kingdom's a-coming-ah!—one more shake, sister, one more shake and your~~

There was no more train of thought or connection of ideas than in the harangue of a maniac. And yet many hundreds of such sermons are preached in the Brush, and I am sorry to add that thousands of the people had rather hear these sermons than any others. This "holy tone" has charms for them not possessed by any possible eloquence. As the preacher "warms up" and becomes more animated in the progress of his discourse, the more impressible sisters begin to move their heads and bodies, and soon all the devout brethren and sisters sway their bodies back and forth in perfect unison, keeping time, in some mysterious manner, to his sing-song tone. (Pierson, 3, 73–74, 313–14, 320)

In his 1871 novel *The Hoosier School-Master*, Edward Eggleston also included such a sermon, characterized by "the see-sawing gestures, the nasal resonance, the sniffle, the melancholy minor key" and the repeated "ah" of the "holy tone" described by Pierson (Eggleston 1871, 104–7). In his final revision of this scene, Mark Twain shortened the sermon and deleted all the "ahs" found in the manuscript version.

MANUSCRIPT TEXT
Mark Twain's first draft with his revisions

chains is broke-ah! [*Glory* HAL-*lelujah!*] O, come to the mourner's bench!
Come, black with ~~sin-ah!~~ sin! ₍[*Amen!*]₎ come, ~~sich~~ sick & sore! ₍[*Amen!*]₎
come, lame, & blind & halt! [*Amen!*] come, pore & needy, sunk in shame!
[*A-a-*MEN!] come all that's worn, & guilty & sufferin'!—come with a broken spirit! come with a contrite ~~heart,~~ heart! come, in your rags & sin &
~~dirt, & dont~~ dirt! the waters that cleanse is free, the door of heaven stands
open—O, enter into the everlasting rest!" [*A-a-*MEN! *Glo-o-ry-glory!*
Come DOWN, *Lord!*]

And so on. You couldn't make out what the preacher said, anymore, on
account of the whooping & shouting & crying that was going on. Folks got
up, everywheres in the crowd, & worked their way, just by main force, to
the mourner's bench, with the tears a-pouring down their faces, & folks
hugging them & crying over them all the way. And it was worse than every
when all the mourners had got up there to the front benches in a gang.
They hugged one another, & shouted, & flung themselves down on the
straw, & wallowed around, just plum crazy & wild. One fat nigger ~~wench~~
₍woman₎ about forty, was the worst. The white ~~mour~~ mourners couldn't
fend her off, no way—fast as one would get loose, she'd tackle the next one,
~~& most~~ & smother ~~him!~~ him. Next, down she went in the straw, along
with the rest, & wallowed around, clawing dirt & shouting glory hallelujah same as they did.

Well, the first I knowed, the king got a start. He begun to warm up, & by
& by he ~~just~~ laid over them all, for whooping & hugging & wallowing. And
when everything was just at its boomingest, he went a-charging up onto
the platform & flung his arms around the preacher & went to hugging him
& kissing him, & crying all over him, & thanking him for saving him. The
preacher felt so good about it, that he begged the king to speak to the people, & he done it. He warmed them up, too—told them he ₍'d been a~~ was a
pirate—been a pirate for thirty years, out in the Indian ocean, & his crew
was ~~killed off~~ thinned out considerable, last spring in a fight, & he was
home, now, to take out some fresh men, & thanks to goodness he'd been
robbed last night & put ashore from a steamboat without a cent, & glory
hallelujah he was glad of it, it was the blessedest thing that ever happened
to him, because he'd got ~~converted~~ ₍religion₎ to-day, & was a changed man
& happy for the first time in his

FINAL TEXT
Mark Twain's final revisions on typescript or proof

~~chains is broke-ah! [*Glory* HAL-*lelujah!*]~~ "O, come to the ~~mourner's~~ mourners' bench! Come, black with sin! [*Amen!*] come, sick and sore! [*Amen!*] come, ~~lame, and blind and halt!~~ lame and halt, and blind! [*Amen!*] come, pore and needy, sunk in shame! [*A-a-*MEN!] come all that's worn, ~~and guilty and sufferin'!~~ and soiled, and suffering!—come with a broken spirit! come with a contrite heart! come in your rags and sin and dirt! the waters that cleanse is free, the door of heaven stands open—O, enter ~~into the everlasting rest!" [*A-a-*MEN! *Glo-o-ry-glory! Come* DOWN, *Lord!*]~~ in and be at rest!" [*A-a-*MEN! *Glory, glory hallelujah!*]

And so on. You couldn't make out what the preacher said, ~~anymore,~~ any more, on account of the ~~whooping and~~ shouting and ~~crying that was going on.~~ crying. Folks got up, everywheres in the crowd, and worked their way, just by main ~~force,~~ strength, to the ~~mourner's~~ mourners' bench, with the tears ~~a-pouring~~ running down their ~~faces, and folks hugging them and crying over them all the way. And it was worse than ever~~ faces; and when all the mourners had got up there to the front benches in a ~~gang. They hugged one another,~~ crowd, they sung, and shouted, and flung themselves down on the straw, ~~and wallowed around,~~ just ~~plum~~ crazy and wild. ~~One fat nigger woman about forty, was the worst. The white mourners couldn't fend her off, no way—fast as one would get loose, she'd tackle the next one, and smother *him*. Next, down she went in the straw, along with the rest, and wallowed around, clawing dirt and shouting glory hallelujah same as they did.~~

Well, the first I knowed, the king got ~~a start. He begun to warm up, and by and by he laid over them all, for whooping and hugging and wallowing. And when everything was just at its boomingest,~~ agoing; and you could hear him over everybody; and next he went a-charging up onto the platform and ~~flung his arms around~~ the preacher ~~and went to hugging him and kissing him, and crying all over him, and thanking him for saving him. The preacher felt so good about it, that~~ he begged ~~the king~~ him to speak to the people, and he done it. He ~~warmed them up, too—~~ told them he was a pirate—been a pirate for thirty years, out in the Indian ocean, and his crew was thinned out considerable, last spring in a fight, and he was home, now, to take out some fresh men, and thanks to goodness he'd been robbed last night and put ashore ~~from~~ off of a steamboat without a cent, and ~~glory hallelujah~~ he was glad of it, it was the blessedest thing that ever happened to him, because ~~he'd got religion today, and~~ he was a changed man now, and happy for the first time in his

MANUSCRIPT TEXT
Mark Twain's first draft with his revisions

life; &, poor as he was, he meant to start right off & work his way back to
the Indian ocean & put in the rest of his life converting pirates & turning
them into the true path; for he could do it better than anybody else, being
acquainted with all the pirate crews in that ocean; & though it would take
him a long time to get there, without money, he would *get* there, anyway,
& every time he converted a pirate, he would say to him, "Don't you thank
me, don't you give *me* no credit, it all belongs to them dear people in Pokeville camp meeting, & that dear preacher that spoke the words that set my
soul afire & saved it from that other fire that burns foreverlasting—glory
hallelujah!"

And then he busted into tears, & so did everybody; & he hugged the
preacher & cried on him again, & everybody hugged one another & sung
out "A-a-MEN! & all that sort of thing. Then somebody sings out "Take up
a collection, take up a collection for the pore soul!" Well, a half a dozen
made a jump to do it, but somebody sings out, "Let *him* pass the hat
around!" Then everybody said it, the preacher, too.

So the king went all through that crowd with his hat, a-crying, & a-
swabbing his eyes, & blessing the people & praising them & thanking
ˌthemˌ for being so good to the poor pirates away off there with nobody to
give them a lift & show them the way to the light; & every little while the
~~pretty~~ prettiest kind of girls, with the tears a-running down their cheeks
would up & ask him would he let them kiss him, for to remember him by;
& he always let them; & ~~sometimes he~~ some of them he hugged & kissed
as many as five or six times—& he was invited to stay a week; & everybody
wanted him to live in their ~~houses.~~ houses, ⅋ & said they'd think it an
honor; but he said as this was the last day of the camp meeting he couldn't
do no good, & besides he was in a sweat to get to the Indian ocean right off
& go to saving pirates.

When we got back to the raft & he come to count up, he found he had
collected eighty-seven dollars & seventy-five cents. And he had fetched
away a three-gallon jug of whisky, too, that he had found under a wagon
when we was ~~coming home~~ starting home through the woods. The king
said, take it all around, it laid over any day he'd ever put in in the missionarying line. He said it warn't no use talking, heathens didn't amount to a
dern, alongside of pirates, to work a camp meeting with.

> ## FINAL TEXT
> *Mark Twain's final revisions on typescript or proof*

life; and, poor as he was, he ~~meant~~ was going to start right off and work his way back to the Indian ocean and put in the rest of his life ~~converting pirates and turning them~~ trying to turn the pirates into the true path; for he could do it better than anybody else, being acquainted with all the pirate crews in that ocean; and though it would take him a long time to get there, without money, he would ~~get~~ get there, anyway, and every time he ~~converted~~ convinced a pirate, he would say to him, "Don't you thank ~~me,~~ me, don't you give ~~me~~ me no credit, it all belongs to them dear people in Pokeville camp meeting, natural brothers and benefactors of the race—and that dear preacher ~~that spoke the words that set my soul afire and saved it from that other fire that burns foreverlasting—glory hallelujah!"~~ there, the truest friend a pirate ever had!"

And then he busted into tears, and so did ~~everybody, and he hugged the preacher and cried on him again, and everybody hugged one another and sung out A-a-MEN! and all that sort of thing.~~ everybody. Then somebody sings out "Take ~~up a collection, take~~ up a collection for ~~the pore soul!"~~ him, take up a collection!" Well, a half a dozen made a jump to do it, but somebody sings out, "Let *him* pass the hat around!" Then everybody said it, the preacher, too.

So the king went all through ~~that~~ the crowd with his hat, ~~a-crying, and a-swabbing~~ swabbing his eyes, and blessing the people and praising them and thanking them for being so good to the poor pirates away off ~~there with nobody to give them a lift and show them the way to the light,~~ there; and every little while the prettiest kind of girls, with the tears ~~a-running~~ running down their ~~cheeks~~ cheeks, would up and ask him would he let them kiss him, for to remember him by; and he always ~~let them,~~ done it; and some of them he hugged and kissed as many as five or six times—and he was invited to stay a week; and everybody wanted him to live in their houses, and said they'd think it was an honor; but he said as this was the last day of the camp meeting he couldn't do no good, and besides he was in a sweat to get to the Indian ocean right off and go to ~~saving~~ work on the pirates.

When we got back to the raft and he come to count up, he found he had collected eighty-seven dollars and seventy-five cents. And then he had fetched away a three-gallon jug of whisky, too, that he ~~had~~ found under a wagon when we was starting home through the woods. The king said, take it all around, it laid over any day he'd ever put in in the missionary-ing line. He said it warn't no use talking, heathens ~~didn't~~ don't amount to ~~a dern,~~ shucks, alongside of pirates, to work a camp meeting with.

MANUSCRIPT FACSIMILES

In 1882, the year before Mark Twain finished his manuscript draft of *Adventures of Huckleberry Finn*, he described the first half as "a book I have been working at, by fits and starts, during the past five or six years" (SLC 1883, 42). That first half of the manuscript, written between 1876 and 1880, was missing and thought permanently lost until 1990, when it was discovered in a Los Angeles attic. Readers and scholars with access only to the second half, written in 1883, had long tried to determine when Mark Twain wrote each part of the story, which portions he revised or added later, what his original ideas were about the characters and plot, and exactly how the known half and the "lost" half of the manuscript fit together. The following pages from the entire manuscript—its two halves united at the Buffalo and Erie County Public Library since 1992—illustrate the physical evidence which answers some of those questions.

The manuscript breaks into three distinct sections, each representing a major period of composition separated enough in time from the others so that Mark Twain was using different inks and stationery. The pages he wrote wholly or mostly in 1876 (1–446) are in black ink on embossed Crystal Lake Mills paper; the pages he wrote in 1880 (447–663) are in purple ink on white wove paper; the pages he wrote in 1883 (title page, 81-A-1 through 81-60, 160–787) are in blue-gray ink on watermarked Old Berkshire Mills paper. Mark Twain had the 1876 and 1880 pages typed before he began writing the 1883 pages, which were numbered to follow (or to be interpolated into) the typescript pages. Although the typescript is lost, the manuscript pages below show where the breaks between stints occurred and where the interpolations go.

On these pages are examples of Mark Twain's revisions, sometimes in pencil, showing the author's attention to even the smallest details of his text, and also a sample of his careful markings for emphasis which were lost in the transmission of the text to the first edition. In addition, several pages show notes Mark Twain wrote to himself in the margins. Because composition was often interrupted, for a day or for years, he used these notes to review and plan the book's characters and incidents.

The manuscript text does not, of course, correspond exactly to the critical text presented in this edition, in which all errors have been corrected, all revised readings from the first edition that can be considered authorial have been incorporated. For a brief history and overview of the book's composition and structure, see the Note on the Text. For a full history of composition and a record of all variants between the text of the manuscript and that of the first American edition, see *HF2003*, 664–744 (Introduction), and 833–993 (Emendations and Historical Collation). All of the manuscript pages in this appendix, shown at 62 percent of actual size, are reproduced from the originals at the Mark Twain Room of the Buffalo and Erie County Public Library (NBu).

ADVENTURES

OF

HUCKLEBERRY FINN

Tom Sawyer's Comrade.

[OVER]
          ^

By Mark Twain.

=

New York:

Chas. L. Webster & Co.

1885.

Title page, 1883 and 1884. Most of this page, including the instruction to the printer on the verso, probably dates from the summer of 1883 when Mark Twain completed the second half of the book and decided on his final title. After it was typed, Mark Twain continued to tinker with it, apparently adding information about "Scene" and "Time" on his typescript, but not on this manuscript page. But in July 1884, months after he had submitted his typescript for publication, he decided to further modify the title page. He sent his changes to his publisher in a letter and brought this page (probably his own record copy) up to date, adding the publication date and the first two lines on the verso (see the next facsimile).

Scene: The Mississippi Valley.
Time: Forty to fifty years ago.

Follow general style of
Prince & Pauper — &
send no proof.

SLC

over again

Title page verso, 1883 and 1884. This page reflects Mark Twain's decision, in July 1884, to alter the time of the book's action from "forty years ago" to "Forty to fifty years ago" (see the explanatory note to vii.8). Since the book's publisher, Charles L. Webster, already had in hand the typed printer's copy, including a typed and revised title page, this handwritten title page was probably Mark Twain's own record copy. As instructed, Webster generally matched the title page style of *The Prince and the Pauper*, published in 1881 by James R. Osgood.

"Notice" page, late June 1880 or after. This page is on the same paper Mark Twain used between late 1879 and mid-June 1880, but in the blue ink that he only started using in late June 1880 and that he used throughout the 1883 manuscript. The canceled notes at the top of the page include a version of the working title he had used since 1876, " 'Huckleberry Finn'—Autobiography," and a direction to place the "Notice" "under preface of to 'Huck.' " Ultimately, the "Notice" would precede the "Explanatory," which was the book's only "preface." Mark Twain left uncanceled a penciled reminder to himself about his preferred dialect forms for ampersands ("en") and "of" ("er" and "o' ") in Jim's speech (for a sample of his dialect revisions, see the facsimile of manuscript page 209 in Three Passages from the Manuscript, p. 469). He replaced "book" with "narrative," "this book" with "it," and considered replacing "Ordnance" with "Artillery" but ultimately did not (see the explanatory note to page xxxi.*title*–6).

Page 1, 1876. Mark Twain began work on *Huckleberry Finn* in the summer of 1876, but he almost certainly added the penciled working title, "HUCK FINN" (which he altered to "HUCKLEBERRY FINN") and the attribution, "Reported by MARK TWAIN," in 1880 or after. Although uncanceled here, this title and attribution were superseded in 1883, by the formal title and author credit as they appear on the manuscript title page and in the first American edition (see page 379). Mark Twain twice revised the often-quoted opening line of the book: he altered "You will not know about me" to "You do not know about me" and finally settled on "You don't know about me." (Later, on his typescript, he added a final clause to the sentence.) The lower right corner of the manuscript page is now torn, obliterating parts of the words "nothing" and "anybody."

2 80

every little chimney-guy
clean & clear, & a chair
by the big bell, with an old
slouch hat hanging on the
back of it.
We judged that ~~two~~
three
nights more would fetch
us to Cairo, at the bottom
of Illinois, where the
Ohio river comes in, &
that was what we was
after. We would sell the
raft & get on a steam-
boat & go away up the
Ohio amongst the free
States, & then be out of
trouble.
Well, the second night
a fog begun to come on,
& we made for a tow-head
to tie to, for it won't do
to try to run in fog. but

Page 280, 1876. In the summer of 1883, seven years after he had written what would be the twelfth chapter of the book, Mark Twain decided to expand Huck and Jim's early adventures, writing sixty pages (about two and a half chapters) of new manuscript containing the account of the *Walter Scott* wreck and Huck's conversations with Jim. The 1876 portion of the manuscript had been typed by this time, and the text of manuscript page 280, where he wished to interpolate his new pages (the new passage would have fallen between 280.5 and 280.6), was now on typescript page 81. So he numbered the new pages as 81-A-1 through 81-60 to accord with the typescript (see the facsimile on the facing page). In the second paragraph of this page, Mark Twain originally wrote "two nights more would fetch us to Cairo," altered it to "two or three nights," and then finally settled on "three nights" (see the explanatory note to 99.1–2).

Page 81-A-1, 1883. This is the first page of the sixty-page *Walter Scott* passage, which Mark Twain added to the typescript of the first half of the book, and numbered to follow typescript page 81. The canceled page number ("18"), at the top of the page, is either a miswriting for "81" or evidence of an earlier numbering sequence. Mark Twain wrote "Whirp-powILL!" in pencil in the top left corner, probably to remind himself of the association of the wreck "laying there so mournful and lonesome" and the fate of the men on the *Walter Scott* with the whippoorwill's call or death portent that Huck heard in chapter 1 (see the note to 4.20–22). He canceled "naturally," interlined "a felt," above canceled "feel" and "slink" above canceled "spy."

Page 362, 1876. This is the last of almost 54 manuscript pages about Huck's encounter with the raftsmen, the so-called "raft episode" which was dropped from the first edition of *Huckleberry Finn* (see the next facsimile and the explanatory note to 107.1–123.20). The notes in the top margin suggest that page 362 may mark a break or a pause in the book's composition. The marginal notes are prospective ("negro sermon," "Twichells clothes—p. 58," "80," "A town 80," "ball 96," "House 236," "Remarks at a funeral"), intended to remind the author of incidents he might use in the next chapters. The associated page references have not been explained. Mark Twain did make use of an incident involving his friend, Reverend Joseph Twichell (see the explanatory note to 233.1).

Page 363, 1876. This page immediately follows the raft episode. When the episode was dropped from the first edition, the first two sentences on this page ("I had . . . sorry."), as well as the chapter break, were likewise dropped (see the note to 107.1–123.20). "Eddy," which Mark Twain wrote in the top left margin, is one of the names given "Ed" by his skeptical mates in the raft episode (see 119.16 and 119.29). Mark Twain did not make use of the other note ("child with rusty unloaded gun *always* kills.").

446

"What's the feud?"
"Why where was you
raised? Don't you know
what a feud is?"
"Never heard of it
before — tell me about it."

Page 446, 1876. This is the last page written in black ink on Crystal Lake Mills paper. When Mark Twain resumed work on his manuscript, probably in late 1879 or early 1880, he switched to purple ink and new paper. In the top right margin (in faint pencil) and on the next page as well, Mark Twain reminded himself that this chapter began at manuscript page "408."

408)

447

Chap.

"Well," says Buck, "a feud is this way. A man has a quarrel with another man, & kills him; then that other man's brother kills him; then the other brothers, on both sides, goes for one another; then the cousins chip in — & by & by everybody's killed off, & there ain't no more

Page 447, 1880. This is the first of over 200 pages written in purple ink on wove paper. Mark Twain eventually redivided and renumbered his chapters and suppressed this chapter break entirely—this passage now occurs in the middle of chapter 18 (146.12).

624

good chance. The duke hired the court house, & we went around & struck up our bills. They read like this: SHAKSPEREAN REVIVAL!!! Wonderful Attraction! For One Night Only! The World-renowned Tragedians. David Garrick the Younger, of Drury Lane Theatre, London, and Thomas Kean the Elder, of the Royal Haymarket Theatre, White-Chapel, Pudding Lane, Piccadilly, London, & the Royal Continental Theatres.

Page 624, 1880. This is the first of three pages (two are reproduced here) on which Mark Twain carefully marked the handbill for the king and the duke's Shakespearean performances, using single underlines for italics, double underlines for small capitals (or capitals and small capitals), triple underlines or block capitals for full capitals, and inscribing centered rules he meant to be typeset. The handbill appeared in the first edition with almost all of this styling dropped, probably because the manuscript had been typed on an all-capitals typewriter, which made difficult the transmission of capitals, small capitals, and italics. Mark Twain's distinctive styling has been restored in the present edition.

625

In their sublime Shakesperean
Spectacle entitled
The Balcony Scene
in
Romeo & Juliet!!!

Romeo . . . . Mr. Garrick.
Juliet. . . . . Mr. Kean.

Assisted by the whole strength
of the Company!
New Costumes, New Scenery,
New Appointments!
Also:
The thrilling, masterly & blood curdling
Broad-Sword Conflict
in Richard III.!!!
Richard III . . . . Mr. Garrick.
Richmond . . . . Mr. Kean.

Page 625, 1880. The second of the handbill pages marked
up by the author.

663

treated him.

Well, by & by somebody said Sherburne ought to be lynched. In about a minute every body was saying it; so away they went, mad & yelling, & snatching down every clothes line they come to, to do the hanging with. But they was too late. Sherburn's friends had got him away, long ago.

No, let them lynch him.

Page 663, 1880. This is the last of the pages in purple ink and the end of the first half of the manuscript. It shows the original ending of what became chapter 21 (which ends at 188.16 in the present edition): "But they was too late. Sherburn's friends had got him away, long ago." Mark Twain's penciled note at the bottom of the page ("No, let them lynch him.") indicates that he continued to question the resolution of the Sherburn episode. When he resumed work on his manuscript three years later (see the next facsimile), he chose to take the episode in a new direction, with Sherburn scornfully facing down the lynch mob.

160

They swarmed up the street, towards
Sherburn's house, a-whooping
& yelling, like Injuns, & everything had to clear the way or get
run over & tromped to mush,
& it was awful to see. Children
was heeling it ahead of the mob,
screaming & trying to get out
of the way; & every window
along the road was full of
women's heads, & there was
nigger boys in every tree, &
bucks & wenches looking over
every fence; & as soon as the
mob would get nearly to
them they would break & shaddle

Page 160, 1883. By the time Mark Twain returned to work on *Huckleberry Finn* in the summer of 1883, after a three-year hiatus, the first half of the book (663 manuscript pages) had been typed and comprised 159 typescript pages, so he picked up the pagination at that point. On the second and third lines of this page, he originally wrote "a-whooping & a-yelling," later added "& a-raging," and finally revised it to read "a-whooping & yelling & raging." Below, he replaced "or" with "&" and canceled a comma following "it."

786

Tom's most well, now, & got his bullet around his neck on a watch-guard for a watch, *& is always seeing what time it is, and so* there ain't nothing more to write about, & I'm *rotten* ~~cussed~~ ~~blame'~~ glad of it, because if I'd a knowed what a trouble it was to make a book I wouldn't a tackled it & ain't agoing to any more. But I reckon I got to light out for the Territory ahead of the rest, because *aunt Sally she's* ~~they're~~ going to adopt

Page 786, 1883. The final paragraph of *Huckleberry Finn* begins on this page, with Huck's particular voice and viewpoint very much in evidence. On line 4, to emphasize Tom's calling attention to his bullet, Mark Twain replaced "&" with "& is always seeing what time it is, and so." Finding the right intensifier for Huck took several attempts: he first wrote "powerful glad," altered it to "cussed glad," then "blame' glad," and finally "rotten glad." On the last line of the page he replaced "they're" with "aunt Sally she's."

787

me & sivilize me & I can't stand it, I been there before.

The end, yours truly Huck Finn.

Page 787, 1883. The final page of the manuscript. In the first edition, the last line ("THE END, YOURS TRULY HUCK FINN.") was changed to "THE END. YOURS TRULY, HUCK FINN."—almost certainly not by Mark Twain—and became the caption for Kemble's illustration of Huck doffing his hat in farewell. This edition capitalizes and punctuates the last line the way Mark Twain wrote it, and restores it to its proper place as the last line of the text.

REFERENCES

This list defines the abbreviations used in this book and provides full bibliographic information for works cited by the author's name, or by name and publication date. Any edition listed here known to be the one that Clemens owned is identified by an asterisk (*)—except for editions of his own works.

Abbott, Keene. 1913. "Tom Sawyer's Town." *Harper's Weekly* 57 (9 August): 16–17.

AD. Autobiographical Dictation.

Aiken, Albert W. 1880. *Richard Talbot of Cinnabar: or, The Brothers of the Red Hand.* Citations are to the reprint edition in *The Dime Library* 82 (August 1901), New York: M. J. Ivers and Co.

Ainsworth, William Harrison. 1840. *The Tower of London. A Historical Romance.* London: R. Bentley.

Alden, William L.
   1885a. Letter to SLC, 28 February, CU-MARK.
   1885b. Letter to SLC, 15 March, CU-MARK.

AMT. 1959. *The Autobiography of Mark Twain.* Edited by Charles Neider. New York: Harper and Brothers.

Anderson, Frederick, and Hamlin Hill. 1972. "How Samuel Clemens Became Mark Twain's Publisher." *Proof* 2:117–43.

Anderson, Frederick, and Kenneth M. Sanderson, eds. 1971. *Mark Twain: The Critical Heritage.* New York: Barnes and Noble.

Andrews, William L. 1981. "Mark Twain and James W. C. Pennington: Huckleberry Finn's Smallpox Lie." *Studies in American Fiction* 9 (Spring): 103–12.

Angell, Roger. 1995. In "Huck, Continued." *New Yorker* 71 (26 June and 3 July): 130–32.

*Arabian Nights. 1839–41. *The Thousand and One Nights, Commonly Called, in England, the Arabian Nights' Entertainments.* Translated by Edward William Lane. 3 vols. London: Charles Knight and Co.

Arac, Jonathan. 1997. *"Huckleberry Finn" As Idol and Target: The Functions of Criticism in Our Time.* Madison: University of Wisconsin Press.

Arner, Robert D. 1972. "Acts Seventeen and *Huckleberry Finn:* A Note on Silas Phelps' Sermon." *Mark Twain Journal* 16 (Summer): 12.

Ashmead, John. 1962. "A Possible Hannibal Source for Mark Twain's Dauphin." *American Literature* 34 (March): 105–7.

ATS. 1982. *The Adventures of Tom Sawyer.* Foreword and notes by John C. Gerber; text established by Paul Baender. The Mark Twain Library. Berkeley, Los Angeles, London: University of California Press.

AutoMT1. 2010. *Autobiography of Mark Twain, Volume 1.* Edited by Harriet Elinor Smith, Benjamin Griffin, Victor Fischer, Michael B. Frank, Sharon K. Goetz, and Leslie Myrick. Mark Twain Papers. Berkeley, Los Angeles, London: University of California Press.

Ayres, John W. 1917. "Recollections of Hannibal." Letter of 22 August to Palmyra *Spectator,* undated clipping in Morris Anderson scrapbook, Mark Twain Museum, Hannibal. Partly reprinted in Wecter, 149.

[Bacon, Thomas.] 1990. *A Mirror of Hannibal.* Rev. ed. Edited by J. Hurley Hagood and Roberta Hagood. Hannibal: Hannibal Free Public Library. First published in 1905 by C. P. Greene.

Baetzhold, Howard G.
  1961. "The Course of Composition of *A Connecticut Yankee.*" *American Literature* 33 (May): 195–214.

  1970. *Mark Twain and John Bull: The British Connection.* Bloomington: Indiana University Press.

Baker, William. 1985. "Mark Twain and the Shrewd Ohio Audiences." *American Literary Realism* 18 (Spring and Autumn): 14–30.

BAL. 1957. *Bibliography of American Literature.* Compiled by Jacob Blanck. Vol. 2. New Haven: Yale University Press.

Baldanza, Frank. 1955. "The Structure of *Huckleberry Finn.*" *American Literature* 27 (November): 347–55.

Bales, E. G. 1939. "Folklore from West Norfolk." *Folk-Lore* 50:66–75. Citations are to the 1969 reprint edition, Nendeln: Kraus Reprint.

*Ball, Charles. 1837. *Slavery in the United States: A Narrative of the Life and Adventures of Charles Ball, a Black Man, Who Lived Forty Years in Maryland, South Carolina and Georgia, as a Slave.* New York: J. S. Taylor.

Barber, Paul. 1988. *Vampires, Burial, and Death: Folklore and Reality.* New Haven: Yale University Press.

Barker, E. H. 1852. *Literary Anecdotes and Contemporary Reminiscences, of Professor Porson and Others.* 2 vols. London: J. R. Smith.

Bartlett, John Russell. 1896. *Dictionary of Americanisms.* 4th ed. Boston: Little, Brown, and Co.

Bates, Alan. 1968. *The Western Rivers Steamboat Cyclopoedium; or, American Riverboat Structure & Detail, Salted with Lore, with a Nod to the Modelmaker.* Leonia, N.J.: Hustle Press.

Baughman, Ernest W. 1966. *Type and Motif Index of the Folktales of England and North America.* Indiana University Series, no. 20. The Hague: Mouton and Co.

Beaver, Harold. 1987. *Huckleberry Finn.* Unwin Critical Library. London: Allen and Unwin.

Beidler, Peter G.
1968. "The Raft Episode in *Huckleberry Finn.*" *Modern Fiction Studies* 14 (Spring): 11–20.

1990. "Christian Schultz's *Travels:* A New Source for *Huckleberry Finn?*" *English Language Notes* 28 (December): 51–61.

Belden, H. M., ed. 1940. *Ballads and Songs Collected by the Missouri Folk-Lore Society. University of Missouri Studies* 15 (1 January).

Bercovitch, Sacvan. 2002. "Deadpan Huck: Or, What's Funny about Interpretation." *Kenyon Review* 24 (Spring–Autumn): 90–134.

Berkove, Lawrence I. 1994. "Mark Twain's Vision of Truth." *Journal of American Studies* 26 (December): 204–22.

Berret, Anthony J.
1985. "The Influence of *Hamlet* on *Huckleberry Finn.*" *American Literary Realism* 18 (Spring and Autumn): 196–207.

1986. "*Huckleberry Finn* and the Minstrel Show." *American Studies* 27 (Fall): 37–49.

Berridge, W. S., and W. Percival Westell. 1911. *The Book of the Zoo.* London: J. M. Dent and Sons.

Bickerstaff, Isaac. 1981. *The Plays of Isaac Bickerstaff.* Edited by Peter A. Tasch. 3 vols. New York: Garland Publishing.

Bikle, Lucy Leffingwell Cable. 1928. *George W. Cable: His Life and Letters.* New York: Charles Scribner's Sons.

Birchfield, James. 1969. "Jim's Coat of Arms." *Mark Twain Journal* 14 (Summer): 15–16.

*[Bird, Robert M.] 1837. *Nick of the Woods; or, The Jibbenainosay.* 2 vols. Philadelphia: Carey, Lea and Blanchard.

Blair, Walter.

1957. "The French Revolution and *Huckleberry Finn.*" *Modern Philology* 55 (August): 21–35.

1958. "When Was *Huckleberry Finn* Written?" *American Literature* 30 (March): 1–25.

1960a. *Mark Twain & Huck Finn.* Berkeley and Los Angeles: University of California Press.

1960b. *Native American Humor.* San Francisco: Chandler Publishing Company.

1976. "Charles Mathews and His 'Trip to America.'" In Salzman, 2:1–23.

1979. "Was Huckleberry Finn Written?" *Mark Twain Journal* 19 (Summer): 1–3.

Blair, Walter, and Hamlin Hill. 1978. *America's Humor: From Poor Richard to Doonesbury.* New York: Oxford University Press.

Blair, Walter, and Franklin J. Meine, eds. 1956. *Half Horse Half Alligator: The Growth of the Mike Fink Legend.* Chicago: University of Chicago Press.

Blanck, Jacob.

1939. *A Supplement to "A Bibliography of Mark Twain."* New York: Privately printed.

1950. "In Re *Huckleberry Finn.*" *New Colophon* 3:153–59.

1960. "'Mark Twain & Huck Finn' Reviewed." *Antiquarian Bookman* 26 (28 November): 1931–35.

Blanton, Wyndham B. 1933. *Medicine in Virginia in the Nineteenth Century.* Richmond: Garrett and Massie.

Blathwait, Raymond. 1891. "Mark Twain on Humor." New York *World*, 31 May, 26.

Bliven, Bruce, Jr. 1954. *The Wonderful Writing Machine.* New York: Random House.

Boewe, Mary. 1985. "Twain on Lecky: Some Marginalia at Quarry Farm." *Mark Twain Society Bulletin* 8 (January): 1–6.

Bontemps, Arna, ed. 1969. *Great Slave Narratives.* Boston: Beacon Press.

Bowen, Elbert R. [1959]. *Theatrical Entertainments in Rural Missouri before the Civil War.* University of Missouri Studies, vol. 32. Columbia: University of Missouri Press.

Bradley, David. 1996. "Introduction." In *How to Tell a Story and Other Essays.* New York: Oxford University Press.

Bragg, Marion. 1977. *Historic Names and Places on the Lower Mississippi River.* Vicksburg, Miss.: Mississippi River Commission.

Branch, Edgar Marquess.
1983. "Mark Twain: Newspaper Reading and the Writer's Creativity." *Nineteenth-Century Fiction* 37 (March): 576–603.

1984. "Three New Letters by Samuel Clemens in the Muscatine *Journal.*" *Mark Twain Journal* 22 (Spring): 2–7.

Branch, Edgar Marquess, and Robert H. Hirst. 1985. *The Grangerford-Shepherdson Feud . . . with an Account of Mark Twain's Literary Use of the Bloody Encounters at Compromise, Kentucky.* Berkeley: The Friends of The Bancroft Library.

Brand, John. 1877. *Observations on Popular Antiquities.* London: Chatto and Windus.

Bremer, Fredrika. 1853. *The Homes of the New World; Impressions of America.* Translated by Mary Howitt. 3 vols. London: Arthur Hall, Virtue, and Co.

Brewer, Ebenezer Cobham. 1882. *Dictionary of Phrase and Fable.* 14th ed., rev. London: Cassell, Petter, Galpin and Co.

[Bridges, Robert.] 1885. "Mark Twain's Blood-Curdling Humor." *Life* 5 (26 February): 119. Reprinted in Da Ponte, 79, and Anderson and Sanderson, 126–27.

Bronson, Bertrand Harris, ed.
1962. *The Traditional Tunes of the Child Ballads.* 4 vols. Princeton: Princeton University Press.

1976. *The Singing Tradition of Child's Popular Ballads.* Princeton: Princeton University Press.

Brown, Spencer. 1967. "*Huckleberry Finn* for Our Time." *Michigan Quarterly Review* 6 (Winter): 41–46.

Browne, Ray B. 1960. "Shakespeare in American Vaudeville and Negro Minstrelsy." *American Quarterly* 12 (Fall): 374–91.

Bruce, Dickson D., Jr. 1974. *And They All Sang Hallelujah: Plain-Folk Camp-Meeting Religion, 1800–1845.* Knoxville: University of Tennessee Press.

Bruchac, Joseph. 1993. *The Native American Sweat Lodge: History and Legends.* Freedom, Calif.: Crossing Press.

Budd, Louis J.
1959. "The Southward Currents under Huck Finn's Raft." *Mississippi Valley Historical Review* 46 (September): 222–37.

1962. *Mark Twain: Social Philosopher.* Bloomington: Indiana University Press.

1977. "A Listing of and Selection from Newspaper and Magazine Interviews with Samuel L. Clemens, 1874–1910." *American Literary Realism* 10 (Winter): i–100.

1982. "Who Wants to Go to Hell? An Unsigned Sketch by Mark Twain?" *Studies in American Humor*, n.s., 1 (June): 6–16.

1985. "'A Nobler Roman Aspect' of *Adventures of Huckleberry Finn*." In Sattelmeyer and Crowley, 26–40.

1992. *Mark Twain: Collected Tales, Sketches, Speeches, & Essays, 1852–1890.* The Library of America. New York: Literary Classics of the United States.

1999. *Mark Twain: The Contemporary Reviews.* Cambridge: Cambridge University Press.

*Bunyan, John. [1678] 1875. *The Pilgrim's Progress as Originally Published by John Bunyan, Being a Fac-simile Reproduction of the First Edition.* London: Elliot Stock.

Burchfield, R. W., ed. 1972–86. *A Supplement to the Oxford English Dictionary.* 4 vols. Oxford: Clarendon Press.

Buxbaum, Katherine. 1927. "Mark Twain and American Dialect." *American Speech* 2 (February): 233–36.

Byers, John R., Jr.
1971. "Miss Emmeline Grangerford's Hymn Book." *American Literature* 43 (May): 259–63.

1973–74. "Mark Twain's Miss Mary Jane Wilks: Shamed or Shammed?" *Mark Twain Journal* 17 (Winter): 13–14.

1977. "The Pokeville Preacher's Invitation in *Huckleberry Finn*." *Mark Twain Journal* 18 (Summer): 15–16.

Camfield, Gregg. 1992. "'I Wouldn't Be as Ignorant as You for Wages': Huck Finn Talks Back to His Conscience." *Studies in American Fiction* 20 (Autumn): 169–75.

Cardwell, Guy A. 1953. *Twins of Genius.* [East Lansing]: Michigan State College Press.

Carkeet, David.
1979. "The Dialects in *Huckleberry Finn*." *American Literature* 51 (November): 315–32.

1981. "The Source for the Arkansas Gossips in *Huckleberry Finn*." *American Literary Realism* 14 (Spring): 90–92.

*Carlyle, Thomas. 1856. *The French Revolution: A History.* 2 vols. New York: Harper and Brothers.

Carlyon, David. 2007. "Twain's 'Stretcher': the Circus Shapes *Huckleberry Finn*." *South Atlantic Review* 72 (Fall): 1–36.

Carrington, George C., Jr. 1976. *The Dramatic Unity of "Huckleberry Finn."* Columbus: Ohio State University Press.

*Casanova de Seingalt, Giacomo Girolamo. 1833–37. *Mémoires de Jacques Casanova de Seingalt.* 10 vols. Paris: Paulin.

Cassidy, Frederic G., ed. 1985–. *Dictionary of American Regional English.* 4 vols. to date. Cambridge: Belknap Press of Harvard University Press.

Cayton, Frank M., comp. 1879. *Landings on the Mississippi River, Showing Locations, Etc.* St. Louis: Woodward, Tiernan and Hale.

CCamarSJ. St. John's Seminary, Camarillo, California. Formerly home to the Estelle Doheny collection (now dispersed).

Cellini, Benvenuto. 1851. *Memoirs of Benvenuto Cellini, a Florentine Artist.* Translated by Thomas Roscoe. New York: George P. Putnam.

Century Dictionary. 1889–91. *The Century Dictionary: An Encyclopedic Lexicon of the English Language.* Prepared under the superintendence of William Dwight Whitney. 6 vols. New York: Century Company.

Cervantes Saavedra, Miguel de.
1855. *The Exemplary Novels of Miguel de Cervantes Saavedra.* Translated from the Spanish by Walter K. Kelly. London: Henry G. Bohn.

1992. *Don Quixote de la Mancha.* Translated by Charles Jarvis, with an introduction by E. C. Riley. Oxford: Oxford University Press.

Champion, Laurie, ed. 1991. *The Critical Response to Mark Twain's "Huckleberry Finn."* Westport, Conn.: Greenwood Press.

Childs, Marquis W. 1982. *Mighty Mississippi: Biography of a River.* New Haven and New York: Ticknor and Fields.

Clapin, Sylva. 1902. *A New Dictionary of Americanisms.* New York: Louis Weiss and Co.

Clarke, Asia Booth. 1882. *The Elder and the Younger Booth.* Boston: James R. Osgood and Co.

Clemens, Olivia Susan (Susy). See OSC.

Clemens, Samuel L. See SLC.

Clifton, William. [1840?]. "The Last Link Is Broken. A duet composed and arranged for the piano forte, by Wm. Clifton." New York: Firth and Hall. The Lester S. Levy Sheet Music Collection, Johns Hopkins University.

CLjC. The James S. Copley Library, La Jolla, California.

Colwell, James L. 1971. "Huckleberries and Humans: On the Naming of Huckleberry Finn." *PMLA* 86 (January): 70–76.

Conard, Howard L., ed. 1901. *Encyclopedia of the History of Missouri.* 6 vols. New York: Southern History Company.

Conclin, George, comp. 1848. *Conclin's New River Guide; or, A Gazetteer of All the Towns on the Western Waters.* Cincinnati: George Conclin.

Cooper, Helen A. 1982. *John Trumbull: The Hand and Spirit of a Painter.* New Haven, Conn.: Yale University Art Gallery.

Couch, W. T. 1934. *Culture in the South.* Chapel Hill: University of North Carolina Press. Citations are to the 1970 reprint edition, Westport, Conn.: Negro Universities Press.

Covici, Pascal, Jr. 1960. "Dear Master Wattie: the Mark Twain–David Watt Bowser Letters." *Southwest Review* 45 (Spring): 104–21.

Craigie, Sir William, ed., with James R. Hulbert. 1936. *A Dictionary of American English on Historical Principles.* 4 vols. Chicago: University of Chicago Press.

*Cramer, Zadok. 1817. *The Navigator, Containing Directions for Navigating the Monongahela, Allegheny, Ohio and Mississippi Rivers.* 9th ed. Pittsburgh: Cramer, Spear and Eichbaum. [Cramer's book was in Clemens's library (Gribben, 2:914), but it is not known which edition of the twelve published between 1801 and 1824 he owned.]

CSmH. Henry E. Huntington Library, San Marino, California.

CtHMTH. Mark Twain Memorial, Hartford, Connecticut.

CtY-BR. Beinecke Rare Book and Manuscript Library, Yale University, New Haven, Connecticut.

CU. Charles Franklin Doe Memorial Library, University of California, Berkeley.

CU-BANC. The Bancroft Library, University of California, Berkeley.

CU-MAPS. Map Collection, Earth Sciences and Map Library, McCone Hall, University of California, Berkeley.

CU-MARK. Mark Twain Papers, The Bancroft Library, University of California, Berkeley.

Cummings, Samuel. 1854. *The Western Pilot; Containing Charts of the Ohio River and of the Mississippi, from the Mouth of the Missouri to the Gulf of Mexico; Accompanied with Directions for Navigating the Same, and a Gazetteer.* Corrected by Capts. Charles Ross and John Klinefelter. Cincinnati: J. A. and U. P. James.

Cummings, Sherwood.
    1989. *Mark Twain and Science: Adventures of a Mind.* Baton Rouge: Louisiana State University Press.

    1991. "Mark Twain's Moveable Farm and the Evasion." *American Literature* 63 (September): 440–58.

Current, Richard N. 1954. *The Typewriter and the Men Who Made It.* Urbana: University of Illinois Press.

CY. 1979. *A Connecticut Yankee in King Arthur's Court.* Edited by Bernard L. Stein, with an introduction by Henry Nash Smith. The Works of Mark Twain. Berkeley, Los Angeles, London: University of California Press.

Da Ponte, Durant. 1959. "*Life* Reviews *Huckleberry Finn.*" *American Literature* 31 (March): 78–81.

*Darwin, Charles. 1871. *The Descent of Man, and Selection in Relation to Sex.* Vol. 1 of 2. New York: D. Appleton and Co.

David, Beverly R.
1974. "The Pictorial *Huck Finn:* Mark Twain and His Illustrator, E. W. Kemble." *American Quarterly* 26 (October): 331–51.

1982. "Mark Twain and the Legends for *Huckleberry Finn.*" *American Literary Realism* 15 (Autumn): 155–65.

David, Beverly R., and Ray Sapirstein. 1996. "Reading the Illustrations in *Huckleberry Finn.*" In SLC 1996a, editorial back matter, 33–40.

Davidson, Loren K. 1968. "The Darnell-Watson Feud." *Duquesne Review* 13 (Fall): 76–95.

Davis, Chester L. 1955. "Mark Twain's Personal Marked Copy of *History of European Morals* by William Edward Hartpole Lecky (Continuation)." *Twainian* 14 (September–October): 1–4.

*Defoe, Daniel. 1747. *Life and Strange Surprising Adventures of Robinson Crusoe.* London.

De Forest, J. W. 1872. "An Independent Ku-Klux." *Galaxy* 13 (April): 480–88.

Den Hollander, A. N. J. 1934. "The Tradition of 'Poor Whites.'" In Couch, 403–31.

De Vere, M. Schele. 1872. *Americanisms; the English of the New World.* New York: Charles Scribner and Co.

DeVinne, Theodore Low. [1883] 1926. *Manual of Printing Office Practice.* Reprint, with an introductory note by Douglas C. McMurtrie. New York: Press of Ars Typographica.

DeVoto, Bernard.
1932. *Mark Twain's America.* Boston: Little, Brown, and Co.

1942. *Mark Twain at Work.* Cambridge: Harvard University Press.

1946. *The Portable Mark Twain.* New York: Viking Press.

DGU. Georgetown University Library, Washington, D.C.

Dickens, Charles.

    1842. *American Notes for General Circulation.* New York: Harper and Brothers.

    *1866–1870. *The Works of Charles Dickens.* Household Edition. 55 vols. New York: Hurd and Houghton.

    *1882. *A Tale of Two Cities.* New York: J. W. Lovell Co.

    1970. *A Tale of Two Cities.* Penguin English Library. Harmondsworth, England: Penguin Books.

DLC. United States Library of Congress, Washington, D.C.

Dorson, Richard M., ed. 1967. *American Negro Folktales.* Greenwich, Conn.: Fawcett Publications.

Douglass, Frederick. 1997. *Narrative of the Life of Frederick Douglass, an American Slave, Written by Himself.* Edited by William L. Andrews and William S. McFeely. A Norton Critical Edition. New York: W. W. Norton and Co.

Doyno, Victor A.

    1996a. "Afterword." In SLC 1996a.

    1996b. "Textual Addendum." In SLC 1996b.

Drake, Samuel Adams. 1875. *Nooks and Corners of the New England Coast.* New York: Harper and Brothers.

Dresser, Amos. 1836. *The Narrative of Amos Dresser with Stone's Letters from Natchez, an Obituary Notice of the Writer, and Two Letters from Tallahassee, Relating to the Treatment of Slaves.* New York: American Anti-Slavery Society.

Drew, Benjamin. 1882. *Hints and Helps for Those Who Write, Print, or Read.* Boston: Lee and Shepard; New York: Charles T. Dillingham.

Dumas, Alexandre.

    [187-]a. *The Count of Monte-Cristo.* London: G. Routledge and Sons.

    [187-]b. *Novels and Tales.* 14 vols. London and New York: George Routledge.

Dundes, Alan. 1990. *Mother Wit from the Laughing Barrel.* Jackson: University Press of Mississippi.

Eby, Cecil D., Jr. 1960. "Mark Twain's 'Plug' and 'Chaw': An Anecdotal Parallel." *Mark Twain Journal* 11 (Summer): 11, 25.

Edwards, Cyrus. 1940. *Cyrus Edwards' Stories of Early Days and Others.* Edited and compiled by Florence Edwards Gardiner. Louisville, Ky.: The Standard Printing Company.

Edwards, Richard, ed. 1855. *Statistical Gazetteer of the State of Virginia.* Richmond: Richard Edwards.

Eggleston, Edward.

1871. *The Hoosier School-Master: A Novel*. New York: Orange Judd and Co.

1874. *The Circuit Rider: A Tale of the Heroic Age*. New York: J. B. Ford and Co.

1878. *Roxy*. New York: C. Scribner's Sons.

Eliot, T. S.

1950. Introduction to *Adventures of Huckleberry Finn*, by Samuel L. Clemens (Mark Twain). London: Cresset Press.

1953. *American Literature and the American Language*. Washington University Studies, Language and Literature, n.s., 23. St. Louis, Mo.: Committee on Publications, Washington University.

Ellis, James. 1991. "The Bawdy Humor of *The King's Camelopard or The Royal Nonesuch*." *American Literature* 63 (December): 729–35.

Ellison, Ralph. 1970. "What America Would Be Like Without Blacks." *Time* 95 (6 April): 54–55.

Engle, Gary D. 1978. *This Grotesque Essence: Plays from the American Minstrel Stage*. Baton Rouge: Louisiana State University Press.

Ensor, Allison. 1969. "The Location of the Phelps Farm in 'Huckleberry Finn.'" *South Atlantic Bulletin* 34 (May): 7.

Esling, Catharine H. W., ed. 1842. *Friendship's Offering*. Boston: E. Littlefield.

Estes, David C., ed. 1989. *A New Collection of Thomas Bangs Thorpe's "Sketches of the Old Southwest."* Baton Rouge: Louisiana State University Press.

ET&S1. 1979. *Early Tales & Sketches, Volume 1 (1851–1864)*. Edited by Edgar Marquess Branch and Robert H. Hirst, with the assistance of Harriet Elinor Smith. The Works of Mark Twain. Berkeley, Los Angeles, London: University of California Press.

ET&S2. 1981. *Early Tales & Sketches, Volume 2 (1864–1865)*. Edited by Edgar Marquess Branch and Robert H. Hirst, with the assistance of Harriet Elinor Smith. The Works of Mark Twain. Berkeley, Los Angeles, London: University of California Press.

Falk, Bernard. 1942. *The Bridgewater Millions: A Candid Family History*. London: Hutchinson and Co.

Farmer, John S., comp. and ed. 1889. *Americanisms—Old & New*. London: Privately printed by Thomas Poulter and Sons.

Farmer, John S., and W. E. Henley. 1905. *A Dictionary of Slang and Colloquial English*. Abridged from the seven-volume work, entitled *Slang and Its Analogues*. London: George Routledge and Sons.

Fatout, Paul.
  1960. *Mark Twain on the Lecture Circuit.* Bloomington: Indiana University Press.
  1976. *Mark Twain Speaking.* Iowa City: University of Iowa Press.

Field, J. M. 1847. *The Drama in Pokerville; The Bench and Bar of Jurytown, and Other Stories.* Philadelphia: T. B. Peterson and Brothers.

Fischer, Henry W. 1922. *Abroad with Mark Twain and Eugene Field: Tales They Told to a Fellow Correspondent.* New York: Nicholas L. Brown.

Fischer, Victor. 1983. "Huck Finn Reviewed: The Reception of *Huckleberry Finn* in the United States, 1885–1897." *American Literary Realism* 16 (Spring): 1–57.

Fishkin, Shelley Fisher. 1993. *Was Huck Black? Mark Twain and African-American Voices.* New York: Oxford University Press.

Fleming, Walter L. 1906. *Documentary History of Reconstruction.* 2 vols. Citations are to the 1960 reprint edition, Gloucester, Mass.: Peter Smith.

Flexner, James Thomas. 1937. *Doctors on Horseback: Pioneers of American Medicine.* New York: Viking Press.

FM. 1972. *Mark Twain's Fables of Man.* Edited with an introduction by John S. Tuckey, text established by Kenneth M. Sanderson and Bernard L. Stein. The Mark Twain Papers. Berkeley, Los Angeles, London: University of California Press.

Foner, Philip S. 1958. *Mark Twain: Social Critic.* New York: International Publishers.

Freedman. Collection of Samuel N. Freedman.

French, Bryant Morey. 1965. *Mark Twain and "The Gilded Age": The Book That Named an Era.* Dallas: Southern Methodist University Press.

Fry, Gladys-Marie. 1975. *Night Riders in Black Folk History.* Knoxville: University of Tennessee Press.

*Fuller, Horace W. 1882. *Noted French Trials: Impostors and Adventurers.* Boston: Soule and Bugbee.

Gaffney, W. G. 1966. "Mark Twain's 'Duke' and 'Dauphin.'" *ANS Notes* 14 (September): 175–78.

Ganzel, Dewey.
  1962a. "Samuel Clemens and Captain Marryat." *Anglia: Zeitschrift für Englische Philologie* 80: 405–16.
  1962b. "Twain, Travel Books, and *Life on the Mississippi.*" *American Literature* 34 (March): 40–55.

Gardner, Joseph H. 1968. "Gaffer Hexam and Pap Finn." *Modern Philology* 66 (November): 155–56.

Gates, William Bryan. 1939. "Mark Twain to His English Publishers." *American Literature* 11 (March): 78–80.

Genovese, Eugene D. 1974. *Roll, Jordan, Roll: The World the Slaves Made.* New York: Pantheon Books.

Gerber, John C. 1985. "Introduction: The Continuing Adventures of *Huckleberry Finn.*" In Sattelmeyer and Crowley, 1–12.

Gibson, William M. 1976. *The Art of Mark Twain.* New York: Oxford University Press.

Giddings, Robert, ed. 1985. *Mark Twain: A Sumptuous Variety.* London and Totowa, N.J.: Vision Press and Barnes and Noble Books.

Gilder, Richard Watson. 1916. *Letters of Richard Watson Gilder.* Edited by Rosamund Gilder. Boston and New York: Houghton Mifflin Company, Riverside Press.

Gneiting, Teona Tone. 1977. "Picture and Text: A Theory of Illustrated Fiction in the Nineteenth Century." Ph.D. diss., University of California, Los Angeles.

*Goldsmith, Oliver. 1882. *The Vicar of Wakefield, a Tale.* New York: John W. Lovell Co.

Goodyear, Russell H. 1971. "Huck Finn's Anachronistic Double Eagles." *American Notes & Queries* 10 (November): 39.

Gordon, Robert Winslow. 1927. "Negro 'Shouts' from Georgia." *New York Times Magazine,* 24 April. Reprinted in Dundes, 445–51.

Gove, Philip Babcock, and the Merriam-Webster editorial staff. 1961. *Webster's Third New International Dictionary of the English Language, Unabridged.* Springfield, Mass.: G. and C. Merriam Company.

Graff, Gerald, and James Phelan, eds. 1995. *"Adventures of Huckleberry Finn": A Case Study in Critical Controversy.* Boston and New York: Bedford Books of St. Martin's Press.

Graves, Wallace. 1968. "Mark Twain's 'Burning Shame.'" *Nineteenth-Century Fiction* 23 (June): 93–98.

Gribben, Alan. 1980. *Mark Twain's Library: A Reconstruction.* 2 vols. Boston: G. K. Hall and Co.

*Grose, Francis. 1785. *A Classical Dictionary of the Vulgar Tongue.* London: S. Hooper. PH of Clemens's own copy, with marginalia, in CU-MARK, courtesy of Justin G. Turner and Howard Baetzhold.

Gunn, John C.
   1836. *Gunn's Domestic Medicine, or Poor Man's Friend, in the Hours*

of Affliction, Pain and Sickness. 8th ed. Springfield, Ohio: John M. Gallagher.

1867. *Gunn's New Family Physician: or, Home Book of Health.* 100th ed. Cincinnati, New York: Moore, Wilstach and Baldwin.

Hale, Sarah J., and Louis A. Godey. 1856. "The Art of Making Wax Fruit and Flowers." *Godey's Lady's Book and Magazine* 52 (January): 20–22.

Hall, Edward H. 1867. *Appletons' Hand-Book of American Travel.* New York: D. Appleton and Co.

Hapgood, Olive C. 1893. *School Needlework.* Boston: Ginn and Co.

Hardwick, Charles. 1872. *Traditions, Superstitions, and Folk-lore.* Manchester, England: A. Ireland and Co.

Harris, Joel Chandler.
1883a. *Nights with Uncle Remus.* Boston: Houghton Mifflin Company.

1883b. "At Teague Poteet's. A Sketch of the Hog Mountain Range." Parts 1 and 2. *Century Magazine* 26 (May and June): 137–50, 185–94.

1885a. Letter to SLC, 1 June, CU-MARK.

1885b. "To the Editors of the Critic." *Critic,* n.s. 4 (28 November): 253.

Harris, N. Dwight. [1904] 1969. *The History of Negro Servitude in Illinois and of the Slavery Agitation in That State, 1719–1864.* Reprint. New York: Negro Universities Press.

Hay, John M.
1871. *Pike County Ballads and Other Pieces.* Boston: James R. Osgood and Co.

1872. "Mark Twain at Steinway Hall." New York *Tribune,* 25 January, 5.

1885. Letter to SLC, 14 April, RPB-JH.

Hazlitt, W. Carew.
1890. *Studies in Jocular Literature: A Popular Subject More Closely Considered.* London: Elliot Stock.

1905. *Faiths and Folklore: A Dictionary.* 2 vols. London: Reeves and Turner.

Hearn, Michael Patrick.
1981a. *The Annotated Huckleberry Finn.* New York: Clarkson N. Potter.

1981b. "Mark Twain, E. W. Kemble, and *Huckleberry Finn.*" *American Book Collector* 2 (November–December): 14–19.

Heitman, Francis B. 1903. *Historical Register and Dictionary of the United States Army, from Its Organization, September 29, 1789, to March 2, 1903.* 2 vols. Washington, D.C.: Government Printing Office.

Helper, Hinton Rowan. 1857. *The Impending Crisis of the South: How to Meet It.* New York: Burdick Brothers. Citations are to the 1968 reprint edition, edited by George M. Frederickson, Cambridge: Belknap Press of Harvard University Press.

Herkimer County Historical Society. 1923. *The Story of the Typewriter: 1873–1923.* Herkimer, New York.

HF1988. 1988. *Adventures of Huckleberry Finn.* Edited by Walter Blair and Victor Fischer, with the assistance of Dahlia Armon and Harriet Elinor Smith. The Works of Mark Twain. Berkeley, Los Angeles, London: University of California Press.

HF2003. 2003. *Adventures of Huckleberry Finn.* Edited by Victor Fischer and Lin Salamo, with the late Walter Blair. The Works of Mark Twain. Berkeley, Los Angeles, London: University of California Press. Also online at *MTPO.*

HH&T. 1969. *Mark Twain's Hannibal, Huck & Tom.* Edited by Walter Blair. The Mark Twain Papers. Berkeley and Los Angeles: University of California Press.

HHR. 1969. *Mark Twain's Correspondence with Henry Huttleston Rogers, 1893–1909.* Edited by Lewis Leary. The Mark Twain Papers. Berkeley and Los Angeles: University of California Press.

Higginson, Thomas Wentworth. 1870. *Army Life in a Black Regiment.* Citations are to the 1960 reprint edition, Michigan State University Press.

Highfill, Phillip H., Jr. 1961. "Incident in Huckleberry Finn." *Mark Twain Journal* 11 (Fall): 6.

Hildreth, Richard. 1856. *Archy Moore, The White Slave; or, Memoirs of a Fugitive.* New York: Miller, Orton, and Mulligan. Citations are to the 1969 reprint edition, New York: Negro Universities Press.

Hill, Hamlin. 1964. *Mark Twain and Elisha Bliss.* Columbia: University of Missouri Press.

Hill, Richard. 1991. "Overreaching: Critical Agenda and the Ending of *Adventures of Huckleberry Finn.*" In Graff and Phelan, 312–34.

Hilton, G. W., R. Plummer, and J. Jobé. 1976. *The Illustrated History of Paddle Steamers.* Drawings by Carlo Demand. Lausanne: Edita; New York: Two Continents Pub. Group.

Hirsh, James. 1992. "Samuel Clemens and the Ghost of Shakespeare." *Studies in the Novel* 24 (Fall): 251–72.

Hirst, Robert H. 2000. "Who Was 'G.G., Chief of Ordnance'?" *Bancroftiana* (Fall): 8, 11.

Hoag, Gerald. 1989. "The Delicate Art of Geography: The Whereabouts of the Phelps Plantation in *Huckleberry Finn*." *English Language Notes* 26 (June): 63–66.

Hoffman, Daniel G. 1960. "Jim's Magic: Black or White." *American Literature* 32 (March): 47–54.

*Holcombe, R. I. 1884. *History of Marion County, Missouri*. St. Louis: E. F. Perkins.

Hooper, Johnson J.
    1845. *Some Adventures of Captain Simon Suggs, Late of the Tallapoosa Volunteers; . . . and Other Alabama Sketches*. Philadelphia: Carey and Hart.

    1851. *The Widow Rugby's Husband*. Philadelphia: T. B. Peterson and Brothers.

Howell, Elmo.
    1968. "Huckleberry Finn in Mississippi." *Louisiana Studies* 7 (Summer): 167–72.

    1970. "Mark Twain's Arkansas." *Arkansas Historical Quarterly* 29 (Autumn): 195–208.

Howells, William Dean. 1910. *My Mark Twain: Reminiscences and Criticisms*. New York: Harper and Brothers.

Hughes, Langston, and Arna Bontemps, eds. 1958. *The Book of Negro Folklore*. New York: Dodd, Mead, and Co.

Hundley, Daniel R. 1860. *Social Relations in Our Southern States*. New York: Henry B. Price. Citations are to the 1979 reprint edition, edited, with an introduction, by William J. Cooper, Jr., Baton Rouge: Louisiana State University Press.

Hunter, Louis C., with Beatrice Jones Hunter. 1949. *Steamboats on the Western Rivers: An Economic and Technological History*. Cambridge: Harvard University Press.

Hunting, Robert. 1958. "Mark Twain's Arkansaw Yahoos." *Modern Language Notes* 73 (April): 264–68.

Hurd, John Codman. 1858–62. *The Law of Freedom and Bondage in the United States*. 2 vols. Boston: Little, Brown and Co.

Hyatt, Harry Middleton. 1965. *Folk-lore from Adams County Illinois*. Memoirs of the Alma Egan Hyatt Foundation. 2d rev. ed. Hannibal, Mo.: Harry Middleton Hyatt.

ICRL. Center for Research Libraries, Chicago, Illinois.

Inds. 1989. *Huck Finn and Tom Sawyer among the Indians, and Other Unfinished Stories*. Foreword and notes by Dahlia Armon and Walter

Blair. Texts established by Dahlia Armon, Paul Baender, Walter Blair, William M. Gibson, and Franklin R. Rogers. The Mark Twain Library. Berkeley, Los Angeles, London: University of California Press. Also online at *MTPO*.

IU. University of Illinois, Urbana.

Ives, Sumner. 1950. "A Theory of Literary Dialect." *Tulane Studies in English* 2:137–82.

Jackson, Bruce, ed. 1967. *The Negro and His Folklore in Nineteenth-Century Periodicals*. Austin: University of Texas Press.

Jacobs, Donald M., ed. 1993. *Courage and Conscience: Black and White Abolitionists in Boston*. Bloomington: Indiana University Press.

James, U. P., comp. 1857. *James' River Guide*. Cincinnati: U. P. James.

Janows, Jill, and Leslie Lee. 2000. *Born to Trouble: "Adventures of Huckleberry Finn."* Part one of the four-part Public Broadcasting System series, *Culture Shock*. Videocassette, produced by the WGBH Educational Foundation, Boston.

JLC. Jane Lampton Clemens.

Johannsen, Albert. 1950. *The House of Beadle and Adams and Its Dime and Nickel Novels*. 2 vols. Norman: University of Oklahoma Press.

Johnson, Charles A. 1955. *The Frontier Camp Meeting: Religion's Harvest Time*. Dallas: Southern Methodist University Press.

Johnson, Merle. 1935. *A Bibliography of the Works of Mark Twain*. Rev. and enl. New York and London: Harper and Brothers.

Jones, Joseph. 1946. "The 'Duke's' Tooth-Powder Racket: A Note on *Huckleberry Finn.*" *Modern Language Notes* 61 (November): 468–69.

Jussim, Estelle. 1974. *Visual Communication and the Graphic Arts: Photographic Technologies in the Nineteenth Century*. New York and London: R. R. Bowker Company.

Keeler, Ralph. 1871. "From Vicksburg to Memphis." *Every Saturday*, 16 September, 284–86.

Kemble, E. W. 1930. "Illustrating *Huckleberry Finn.*" *Colophon*, Part 1 (February): [41–48].

Kerr, Howard. 1972. *Mediums, and Spirit-Rappers, and Roaring Radicals: Spiritualism in American Literature, 1850–1900*. Urbana, Chicago, London: University of Illinois Press.

Keynes, Simon. 1999. "Heptarchy." In *The Blackwell Encyclopedia of Anglo-Saxon England*, edited by Michael Lapidge et al. Oxford: Blackwell.

King, Moses. 1893. *King's Handbook of New York City.* 2d ed. Boston: Moses King.

Kirkham, E. Bruce. 1969. "Huck and Hamlet: An Examination of Twain's Use of Shakespeare." *Mark Twain Journal* 14 (Summer): 17–19.

Kiskis, Michael J., ed. 1990. *Mark Twain's Own Autobiography: The Chapters from the "North American Review."* Madison: University of Wisconsin Press.

Koundakjian. Collection of Theodore H. Koundakjian.

Kruse, Horst H.
    1967. "Annie and Huck: A Note on *The Adventures of Huckleberry Finn.*" *American Literature* 39 (May): 207–14.
    1981. *Mark Twain and "Life on the Mississippi."* Amherst: University of Massachusetts Press.

Kuralt, Charles. 1985. Quoted in Edward Ziegler, "Huck Finn at 100," *Reader's Digest* 126 (February): 101.

L1. 1988. *Mark Twain's Letters, Volume 1: 1853–1866.* Edited by Edgar Marquess Branch, Michael B. Frank, Kenneth M. Sanderson, Harriet Elinor Smith, Lin Salamo, and Richard Bucci. The Mark Twain Papers. Berkeley, Los Angeles, London: University of California Press. Also online at *MTPO.*

L2. 1990. *Mark Twain's Letters, Volume 2: 1867–1868.* Edited by Harriet Elinor Smith, Richard Bucci, and Lin Salamo. The Mark Twain Papers. Berkeley, Los Angeles, London: University of California Press. Also online at *MTPO.*

L3. 1992. *Mark Twain's Letters, Volume 3: 1869.* Edited by Victor Fischer, Michael B. Frank, and Dahlia Armon. The Mark Twain Papers. Berkeley, Los Angeles, London: University of California Press. Also online at *MTPO.*

L4. 1995. *Mark Twain's Letters, Volume 4: 1870–1871.* Edited by Victor Fischer, Michael B. Frank, and Lin Salamo. The Mark Twain Papers. Berkeley, Los Angeles, London: University of California Press. Also online at *MTPO.*

L5. 1997. *Mark Twain's Letters, Volume 5: 1872–1873.* Edited by Lin Salamo and Harriet Elinor Smith. The Mark Twain Papers. Berkeley, Los Angeles, London: University of California Press. Also online at *MTPO.*

L6. 2002. *Mark Twain's Letters, Volume 6: 1874–1875.* Edited by Michael B. Frank and Harriet Elinor Smith. The Mark Twain Papers. Berkeley, Los Angeles, London: University of California Press. Also online at *MTPO.*

Landau, Sidney I. 1984. *Dictionaries: The Art and Craft of Lexicography.* New York: Charles Scribner's Sons.

Landon, Melville D. [Eli Perkins, pseud.]. 1891. *Thirty Years of Wit.* New York: Cassell Publishing Co.

[Lathrop, George Parsons.] 1883. "Mark Twain's Life on the Mississippi." *Atlantic Monthly* 52 (September): 406–8.

Leary, Lewis. 1974. "Troubles with Mark Twain: Some Considerations on Consistency." *Studies in American Fiction* 2:89–103.

*Lecky, William Edward Hartpole. 1874. *History of European Morals from Augustus to Charlemagne.* 2 vols. New York: D. Appleton and Co.

Leonard, James S., Thomas A. Tenney, and Thadious M. Davis, eds. 1992. *Satire or Evasion? Black Perspectives on "Huckleberry Finn."* Durham, N.C.: Duke University Press.

Letters 1876–1880. 2007. *Mark Twain's Letters, 1876–1880.* Edited by Victor Fischer, Michael B. Frank, and Harriet Elinor Smith, with Sharon K. Goetz, Benjamin Griffin, and Leslie Myrick. Mark Twain Project Online. Berkeley, Los Angeles, London: University of California Press. To locate a letter text from its citation, select the Letters link at http://marktwainproject.org, then use the Date Written links in the left-hand column.

Litwack, Leon. 1980. *Been in the Storm So Long: The Aftermath of Slavery.* New York: Vintage Books.

LLMT. 1949. *The Love Letters of Mark Twain.* Edited by Dixon Wecter. New York: Harper and Brothers.

LNT. Howard-Tilton Memorial Library, Tulane University, New Orleans, Louisiana.

Long, Esmond R. 1962. *A History of American Pathology.* Springfield: Charles C. Thomas.

Lorch, Fred W. 1968. *The Trouble Begins at Eight: Mark Twain's Lecture Tours.* Ames: Iowa State University Press.

Lott, Eric. 1995. "Mr. Clemens and Jim Crow: Twain, Race, and Blackface." In Forrest G. Robinson, 129–52.

Lucas, E. V.
1910. "E. V. Lucas and Twain at a 'Punch Dinner.'" *Bookman* 38 (June): 116–17.

1929. Notes dated 1 February 1929. John Hay Library of Rare Books and Special Collections, Brown University, Providence, Rhode Island.

Lynn, Kenneth S.
1958. "Huck and Jim." *Yale Review,* n.s., 47 (Spring): 421–31. In Lynn 1961, 211–15.

1961. *"Huckleberry Finn": Text, Sources, and Criticism.* New York: Harcourt, Brace and World.

Lytle, William M., comp. 1952. *Merchant Steam Vessels of the United States, 1807–1868.* Edited by Forrest R. Holdcamper. Publication no. 6. Mystic, Conn.: Steamship Historical Society of America.

MacCann, Donnarae, and Gloria Woodard, eds. 1985. *The Black American in Books for Children: Readings in Racism.* 2d ed. Metuchen, N.J.: Scarecrow Press.

McCullough, Joseph B., and Janice McIntire-Strasburg, eds. 1999. *Mark Twain at the Buffalo "Express": Articles and Sketches by America's Favorite Humorist, Mark Twain.* DeKalb: Northern Illinois University Press.

McCurdy, Frances Lea. 1969. *Stump, Bar, and Pulpit: Speechmaking on the Missouri Frontier.* Columbia: University of Missouri Press.

McDougall, Marion Gleason. 1891. *Fugitive Slaves.* Publications of the Society for the Collegiate Instruction of Women, Fay House Monographs, no. 3. Boston: Ginn and Co.

McIlwaine, Shields. 1939. *The Southern Poor-White from Lubberland to Tobacco Road.* Norman: University of Oklahoma Press.

Mackay, Alexander. 1849. *The Western World; or, Travels in the United States in 1846–47.* 2 vols. Philadelphia: Lea and Blanchard.

MacKellar, Thomas. 1882. *The American Printer: A Manual of Typography.* 13th ed. Philadelphia: MacKellar, Smiths and Jordan.

MacKethan, Lucinda H. 1984. "Huck Finn and the Slave Narratives: Lighting Out as Design." *Southern Review* 20 (April): 247–64.

McKinney, John. 1981. "Tom Sawyer's Island." *Islands* 1 (October–November): 60–65.

Mailloux, Steven. 1989. *Rhetorical Power.* Ithaca, N.Y.: Cornell University Press.

Maitland, James. 1891. *The American Slang Dictionary.* Chicago: R. J. Kittredge and Co.

Manierre, William R. 1968. "On Keeping the Raftsmen's Passage in *Huckleberry Finn.*" *English Language Notes* 6 (December): 118–22.

*Marryat, Frederick. 1839. *A Diary in America, with Remarks on Its Institutions.* New York: William H. Colyer.

Martin, Francis, Jr. 1976. "Edward Windsor Kemble, a Master of Pen and Ink." *American Art Review* 3 (January–February): 54–67.

Marx, Leo.
1957. "The Pilot and the Passenger: Landscape Conventions and the Style of *Huckleberry Finn.*" *American Literature* 28 (January): 129–46.

1967. Introduction and notes. In SLC 1967.

Masterson, James R. 1946. "Travelers' Tales of Colonial Natural History (Concluded)." *Journal of American Folklore* 59 (April–June): 174–88.

Mathews, Anne. 1838. *Memoirs of Charles Mathews, Comedian.* 4 vols. London: Richard Bentley.

Mathews, Mitford M., ed. 1951. *A Dictionary of Americanisms on Historical Principles.* 2 vols. Chicago: University of Chicago Press.

Matthews, Brander.
1885. "Huckleberry Finn." *Saturday Review* 59 (31 January): 153–54. Reprinted in Anderson and Sanderson, 121–25.

1922. "Memories of Mark Twain." In *The Tocsin of Revolt and Other Essays.* New York: Charles Scribner's Sons.

May, Earl Chapin. 1932. *The Circus from Rome to Ringling.* New York: Duffield and Green.

MBAt. Boston Athenæum, Boston, Massachusetts.

MCo. Concord Free Public Library, Concord, Massachusetts.

Meine, Franklin J. 1960. "Some Notes on the First Editions of 'Huck Finn.'" *American Book Collector* 10 (June): 31–34.

Mencken, H. L.
1909. "Novels and Other Books—Mostly Bad." *Smart Set* 28 (August): 156–57.

1910. "The Greatest of American Writers." *Smart Set* 31 (June): 153–54.

Merrick, George Byron. 1909. *Old Times on the Upper Mississippi: The Recollections of a Steamboat Pilot from 1854 to 1863.* Cleveland, Ohio: Arthur H. Clark Company.

MH-H. Houghton Library, Harvard University, Cambridge, Massachusetts.

Michaelson, L. W. 1961. "Four Emmeline Grangerfords." *Mark Twain Journal* 11 (Fall): 10–12.

*Michelet, Jules. 1848. *Historical View of the French Revolution.* Translated by Charles Cocks. London: H. G. Bohn.

Mieder, Wolfgang, ed. 1992. *A Dictionary of American Proverbs.* New York and Oxford: Oxford University Press.

Miller, Michael G. 1980. "Geography and Structure in *Huckleberry Finn.*" *Studies in the Novel* 12 (Fall): 192–209.

Minor, Mary Willis. 1898. "How to Keep Off Witches (as Related by a Negro)," in "Notes and Queries." *Journal of American Folklore* 11 (January–March): 76.

Minstrel Gags. 1875. *Minstrel Gags and End Men's Hand-Book.* New York: Dick and Fitzgerald.

Missouri v. Owsley. 1845. *State of Missouri v. William P. Owsley*. File 3873, Marion County Circuit Court, Palmyra, Missouri.

Moody, Richard, ed. 1966. *Dramas from the American Theatre 1762–1909.* Cleveland and New York: World Publishing Company.

Moore, Chauncey O. 1964. *Ballads and Folk Songs of the Southwest.* Norman: University of Oklahoma Press.

Moore, Julia A. 1928. *The Sweet Singer of Michigan.* Edited by Walter Blair. Chicago: Pascal Covici.

Moore, Olin Harris. 1922. "Mark Twain and Don Quixote." *PMLA* 37 (June): 324–46.

Morris, Courtland P.
  1930. "Philadelphia Business Man Original 'Huck' Finn of E. W. Kemble's Drawings for Mark Twain's Classic; Posed as Other Characters in Parents' Old Clothes." Clipping from an unidentified newspaper, conjecturally dated 18 May 1930, PH in CU-MARK; courtesy of Louis J. Budd and the Rare Book Room of the University of Illinois at Urbana-Champaign.

  1938. "The Model for Huck Finn." *Mark Twain Journal* 2 (Summer–Fall): 22–23.

*Morrison, D. H., ed. 1882. *The Treasury of Song for the Home Circle: The Richest, Best-Loved Gems.* Philadelphia: Hubbard Brothers.

Morrison, Toni. 1996. "Introduction." In SLC 1996a.

Mott, Frank Luther. 1931. *A History of American Magazines, 1741–1850.* Cambridge: Harvard University Press.

MoU. University of Missouri, Columbia.

MS. Manuscript.

MS1. The first half of the *Huckleberry Finn* manuscript, comprising pages numbered 1–663, written over a four-year period, 1876–1880. Paper and ink differences distinguish two subsections of MS1: MS1a (1–446), all or most of which was written in June–September 1876, and MS1b (447–663), written in March–June 1880. The manuscript was believed lost until 1990, when it was discovered in a Los Angeles attic. Now at the Buffalo and Erie County Public Library (NBu).

MS2. The second half of the *Huckleberry Finn* manuscript, written in the summer of 1883, comprising pages numbered 160–787 (continuing the pagination of TS1, the typescript made from MS1) and pages numbered 81-A-1 through 81-60. Now at the Buffalo and Erie County Public Library (NBu).

MSM. 1969. *Mark Twain's Mysterious Stranger Manuscripts.* Edited by William M. Gibson. The Mark Twain Papers. Berkeley and Los Angeles: University of California Press.

MTA. 1924. *Mark Twain's Autobiography*. Edited by Albert Bigelow Paine. 2 vols. New York and London: Harper and Brothers.

MTB. 1912. *Mark Twain: A Biography*. By Albert Bigelow Paine. 3 vols. New York and London: Harper and Brothers.

MTBus. 1946. *Mark Twain, Business Man*. Edited by Samuel Charles Webster. Boston: Little, Brown and Co.

MTE. 1940. *Mark Twain in Eruption*. Edited by Bernard DeVoto. New York and London: Harper and Brothers.

MTH. 1947. *Mark Twain and Hawaii*. By Walter Francis Frear. Chicago: Lakeside Press.

MTHL. 1960. *Mark Twain–Howells Letters*. Edited by Henry Nash Smith and William M. Gibson. With the assistance of Frederick Anderson. 2 vols. Cambridge: Belknap Press of Harvard University Press.

MTL. 1917. *Mark Twain's Letters*. Edited by Albert Bigelow Paine. 2 vols. New York: Harper and Brothers.

MTLBowen. 1941. *Mark Twain's Letters to Will Bowen*. Edited by Theodore Hornberger. Austin: University of Texas.

MTLP. 1967. *Mark Twain's Letters to His Publishers, 1867–1894*. Edited by Hamlin Hill. The Mark Twain Papers. Berkeley and Los Angeles: University of California Press.

MTMF. 1949. *Mark Twain to Mrs. Fairbanks*. Edited by Dixon Wecter. San Marino, Calif.: Huntington Library Publications.

MTPO. *Mark Twain Project Online*. Edited by the Mark Twain Project. Berkeley, Los Angeles, London: University of California Press. Launched 1 November 2007. http://marktwainproject.org.

MTS.
　　1910. *Mark Twain's Speeches*. Edited by Albert Bigelow Paine. New York and London: Harper and Brothers.

　　1923. *Mark Twain's Speeches*. Edited by Albert Bigelow Paine. New York and London: Harper and Brothers.

MTTB. 1940. *Mark Twain's Travels with Mr. Brown*. Edited by Franklin Walker and G. Ezra Dane. New York: Alfred A. Knopf.

MU. University of Massachusetts, Amherst.

*Murray, Charles Augustus. 1839. *Travels in North America during the Years 1834, 1835, & 1836*. 2 vols. London: Richard Bentley.

Musick, Ruth Ann. 1948. "The Tune the Old Cow Died On." *Hoosier Folklore* 7 (December): 105–6.

N&J1. 1975. *Mark Twain's Notebooks & Journals, Volume I (1855–1873)*. Edited by Frederick Anderson, Michael B. Frank, and Kenneth M.

Sanderson. The Mark Twain Papers. Berkeley, Los Angeles, London: University of California Press.

N&J2. 1975. *Mark Twain's Notebooks & Journals, Volume II (1877–1883).* Edited by Frederick Anderson, Lin Salamo, and Bernard L. Stein. The Mark Twain Papers. Berkeley, Los Angeles, London: University of California Press.

N&J3. 1979. *Mark Twain's Notebooks & Journals, Volume III (1883–1891).* Edited by Robert Pack Browning, Michael B. Frank, and Lin Salamo. The Mark Twain Papers. Berkeley, Los Angeles, London: University of California Press.

Nathan, Hans. 1962. *Dan Emmett and the Rise of Early Negro Minstrelsy.* Norman: University of Oklahoma Press.

Naylor, Benjamin. 1851. *Naylor's System of Teaching Geography.* Philadelphia: T. Ellwood Chapman.

NBu. Buffalo and Erie County Public Library, Buffalo, New York.

NBuU. State University of New York at Buffalo.

NcD. Duke University, Durham, North Carolina.

Neider, Charles, ed. 1961. *Mark Twain: Life as I Find It.* Garden City, N.Y.: Hanover House.

Neilson, William Allen, Thomas A. Knott, and Paul W. Carhart, eds. 1945. *Webster's New International Dictionary of the English Language.* 2d ed., unabridged. Springfield, Mass.: G. and C. Merriam Co.

NN. New York Public Library, New York City.

NNAL. American Academy of Arts and Letters, New York City.

NN-B. Henry W. and Albert A. Berg Collection, The New York Public Library, Astor, Lenox and Tilden Foundations.

NNPM. Pierpont Morgan Library, New York City.

Northup, Solomon. 1853. *Twelve Years a Slave.* Auburn, N.Y.: Derby and Miller.

Norwood, William Frederick. 1944. *Medical Education in the United States before the Civil War.* Philadelphia: University of Pennsylvania Press.

NPV. Jean Webster McKinney Family Papers, Francis Fitz Randolph Rare Book Room, Vassar College Library, Poughkeepsie, New York.

O'Connor, William Van. 1955. "Why *Huckleberry Finn* Is Not the Great American Novel." *College English* 17 (October): 6–10.

Oe, Kenzaburo. 1994. Quoted in Carlin Romano, "Nobel to Japanese writer; Oe's political themes evoke a deep unease," Houston *Chronicle,* 14 October, A20, and in Teresa Watanabe, "Japanese Writer Wins Nobel in Literature," San Francisco *Chronicle,* 14 October, A1, A9.

OED.

1933. *The Oxford English Dictionary.* Prepared by James A. H. Murray, Henry Bradley, W. A. Craigie, and C. T. Onions. 13 vols. Oxford: Clarendon Press.

1989. *The Oxford English Dictionary.* 2d ed. Prepared by J. A. Simpson and E. S. C. Weiner. 20 vols. Oxford: Clarendon Press.

Oehlschlaeger, Fritz H. 1981. "Huck Finn and the Meaning of Shame." *Mark Twain Journal* 20 (Summer): 13–14.

OHi. Ohio Historical Society, Columbus.

OLC. Olivia Langdon Clemens (née Olivia Louise Langdon).

OLL. Olivia Louise Langdon.

OSC (Olivia Susan [Susy] Clemens).

1885–86. Untitled biography of her father. MS of 131 pages, ViU. Published in OSC 1985.

1985. *Papa: An Intimate Biography of Mark Twain.* Edited by Charles Neider. Garden City, N.Y.: Doubleday and Co.

Ottley, Roi, and William J. Weatherby, eds. 1969. *The Negro in New York: An Informal Social History, 1626–1940.* New York, Washington, London: Praeger Publishers.

Paine, Albert Bigelow. 1923. Introduction to *What Is Man? and Other Essays,* by Samuel Langhorne Clemens. Vol. 26 of *The Writings of Mark Twain,* Definitive Edition. New York: Gabriel Wells.

PAM. Pamela Ann Moffett.

P&P. 1979. *The Prince and the Pauper.* Edited by Victor Fischer and Lin Salamo, with the assistance of Mary Jane Jones. The Works of Mark Twain. Berkeley, Los Angeles, London: University of California Press.

Partridge, Eric. 1967. *A Dictionary of Slang and Unconventional English.* 6th ed. New York: Macmillan Company.

Pasko, Wesley Washington. 1894. *American Dictionary of Printing and Bookmaking.* New York: Howard Lockwood and Co. Citations are to the 1967 reprint edition, Detroit: Gale Research Company.

Paulding, James Kirke. 1832. *Westward Ho! A Tale.* New York: J. and J. Harper.

[Pease, Lute.] 1895. "Mark Twain Talks." Portland *Oregonian,* 11 August, 10. Reprinted in Budd 1977, 51–53. Pease later admitted that he had supplied some of Mark Twain's words after the interview was unavoidably cut short, but that Mark Twain had later telegraphed him "You said it better than I could have said it myself" (Shirley M. Friedman, "Mark Twain's Favorite Reporter," *Editor & Publisher* 82 [19 February 1949]: 10).

Penick, James Lal, Jr. 1981. *The New Madrid Earthquakes.* Rev. ed. Columbia and London: University of Missouri Press.

Pennington, J. W. C. 1849. *The Fugitive Blacksmith; or, Events in the History of James W. C. Pennington.* In Bontemps, 193–267.

Penny, Virginia. 1863. *The Employments of Women: A Cyclopedia of Women's Work.* Boston: Walker, Wise, and Co.

Pettit, Arthur G. 1974. *Mark Twain & the South.* Lexington: University Press of Kentucky.

Pierson, Hamilton W. 1881. *In the Brush; or, Old-Time Social, Political, and Religious Life in the Southwest.* New York: D. Appleton and Co.

Pike, Martha V., and Janice Gray Armstrong. 1980. *A Time to Mourn: Expressions of Grief in Nineteenth Century America.* Stony Brook, N.Y.: The Museums at Stony Brook.

Pitcher, E. W. 1991. "Huck Finn as Sarah Williams: A Precedent for the Discovery Trick." *Notes and Queries,* n.s., 38 (September): 324.

Plutzky. Unpublished article and personal communication by Dr. Jorge Plutzky, Boston, Mass.

Poe, Edgar Allan. 1978. *Collected Works of Edgar Allan Poe.* Edited by Thomas Ollive Mabbott. 3 vols. Cambridge: Belknap Press of Harvard University Press.

Pond, James B. 1900. *Eccentricities of Genius.* New York: G. W. Dillingham Company.

Powers, Lyall. 1985. "Mark Twain and the Future of Picaresque." In Giddings, 155–75.

Puckett, Newbell Niles. 1926. *Folk Beliefs of the Southern Negro.* Chapel Hill: University of North Carolina Press. Citations are to the 1968 reprint edition, New York: Negro Universities Press.

Quarles, John A. 1855. Deed of Emancipation. Recorded 14 November by George Glenn, Clerk, Monroe County Circuit Court, Paris, Missouri. Monroe County Deed Records, Book O, 240.

Quick, Herbert, and Edward Quick. 1926. *Mississippi Steamboatin'.* New York: Henry Holt and Co.

Radford, E., and M. A. Radford. 1969. *Encyclopedia of Superstitions.* Westport, Conn.: Greenwood Press.

Railton, Stephen. 1987. "Jim and Mark Twain: What Do They Stan' For?" *Virginia Quarterly Review* 63 (Summer): 393–408.

Ramsay, Robert L., and Frances G. Emberson. 1963. *A Mark Twain Lexicon.* New York: Russell and Russell.

Rasmussen, R. Kent. 1995. *Mark Twain A to Z.* New York: Oxford University Press.

Reade, Charles. 1861. *The Cloister and the Hearth.* London: Trübner and Co.

Redpath, James. 1859. *The Roving Editor: or, Talks with Slaves in the Southern States.* New York: A. B. Burdick. Citations are to the 1968 reprint edition, New York: Negro Universities Press.

Reed, E. J., ed. 1861. *Transactions of the Institution of Naval Architects.* Vol. 2. London: Institution of Naval Architects.

Reilly, Bernard F., Jr. 1993. "The Art of the Antislavery Movement." In Jacobs, 47–74.

Reviews. 1883–85. Reviews and commentary on *Adventures of Huckleberry Finn* quoted in Foreword. "February Magazines," Boston *Herald,* 1 February 1885, 17; Lathrop, 406; "Huckleberry Finn," St. Louis *Globe-Democrat,* 17 March 1885, 1; "Mark Twain's Bad Boy," New York *World,* 2 March 1885, 6; "Adventures of Huckleberry Finn," San Francisco *Examiner,* 9 March 1885, 3; Bridges; Matthews 1885, 153; "Mark Twain's Readable New Story," San Francisco *Chronicle,* 15 March 1885, 6; "Huckleberry Finn," Hartford *Courant,* 20 February 1885, 2. Partially reprinted in Victor Fischer, 4, 7, 9, 12, 14, 17.

Revised Statutes.
1835. *Revised Statutes of the State of Missouri, Revised and Digested by the Eighth General Assembly.* St. Louis: Printed at the Argus Office.

1845. *The Revised Statutes of the State of Missouri, Revised and Digested by the Thirteenth General Assembly.* St. Louis: Printed for the State, by J. W. Dougherty.

Roberts, John W. 1989. *From Trickster to Badman: The Black Folk Hero in Slavery and Freedom.* Philadelphia: University of Pennsylvania Press.

Robinson, Fayette. 1848. "Supplication." *Graham's American Monthly Magazine of Literature and Art* 33 (November): frontispiece, 267.

Robinson, Forrest G., ed. 1995. *The Cambridge Companion to Mark Twain.* Cambridge: Cambridge University Press.

Rodney, Robert M., ed. 1982. *Mark Twain International: A Bibliography and Interpretation of His Worldwide Popularity.* Westport, Conn.: Greenwood Press.

Ross, Joan M. 1937. *Post-Mortem Appearances.* 3d ed. London: Humphrey Milford, Oxford University Press.

Roueché, Berton. 1960. "Annals of Medicine: Alcohol, III—The Bird of Warning." *New Yorker* 35 (23 January): 78–106.

Rubin, Louis D., Jr. 1967. *The Teller in the Tale.* Seattle: University of Washington Press.

Rulon, Curt Morris. 1967. "The Dialects in *Huckleberry Finn.*" Ph.D. diss., University of Iowa, Iowa City.

Saintine, Joseph Xavier Boniface. 1848. *Picciola. The Prisoner of Fenestrella; or, Captivity Captive.* Philadelphia: Lea and Blanchard.

Salm. Collection of Peter A. Salm.

Salzman, Jack, ed. 1976. *Prospects.* New York: Burt Franklin and Co.

S&B. 1968. *Mark Twain's Satires & Burlesques.* Edited by Franklin R. Rogers. The Mark Twain Papers. Berkeley and Los Angeles: University of California Press.

Sattelmeyer, Robert, and J. Donald Crowley, eds. 1985. *One Hundred Years of "Huckleberry Finn": The Boy, His Book, and American Culture.* Columbia: University of Missouri Press.

Scharf, J. Thomas. 1883. *History of Saint Louis City and County.* 2 vols. Philadelphia: Louis H. Everts and Co.

Schirer, Thomas. 1984. *Mark Twain and the Theatre.* Nuremburg: Hans Carl.

Schmitz, Neil. 1971. "Twain, *Huckleberry Finn,* and the Reconstruction." *American Studies* 12 (Spring): 59–67.

Schultz, Christian. 1810. *Travels on an Inland Voyage through the States of New-York, Pennsylvania, Virginia, Ohio, Kentucky, and Tennessee . . . Performed in the Years 1807 and 1808.* 2 vols. New York: Isaac Riley.

Scott, Arthur L. 1955. "The *Century Magazine* Edits *Huckleberry Finn,* 1884–1885." *American Literature* 27 (November): 356–62.

Scott, Walter.

    1822. *The Fortunes of Nigel.* 3 vols. Edinburgh: Archibald Constable and Co.

    1823. *Quentin Durward.* 3 vols. Edinburgh: Archibald Constable and Co.

    1827. The Poetical Works of Sir Walter Scott. 5 vols. Philadelphia: J. Maxwell.

    1842–47. Quentin Durward. Vol. 8 of The Waverley Novels, Abbotsford Edition. Edinburgh: R. Cadell.

    1871. The Lady of the Lake. Edinburgh: John Ross and Co.

Seabrook, E. B. 1867. "The Poor Whites of the South." *Galaxy* 4 (October): 681–90.

Shapiro, Michael Edward. 1985. *Bronze Casting and American Sculpture 1850–1900.* Newark, N.J.: University of Delaware Press.

Sharp, Cecil J. 1932. *English Folk Songs from the Southern Appalachians.* London: Oxford University Press.

Shaw, George Bernard. 1907. Letter to SLC, 3 July, CU-MARK. In *Bernard Shaw: Collected Letters, 1898–1910*, edited by Dan H. Laurence, 697. London: Max Reinhardt, 1972.

Shultz, Suzanne M. 1992. *Body Snatching: The Robbing of Graves for the Education of Physicians in Early Nineteenth Century America*. Jefferson, N.C.: McFarland and Co.

Siebert, Wilbur H.
[1898] 1967. *The Underground Railroad from Slavery to Freedom*. Reprint. New York: Russell and Russell.

1947. "Beginnings of the Underground Railroad in Ohio." *Ohio State Archaeological and Historical Quarterly* 56 (January): 70–93.

Simpson, F. A. 1929. *The Rise of Louis Napoleon*. London, New York, Toronto: Longmans, Green and Co.

Slater, Joseph. 1949. "Music at Col. Grangerford's: A Footnote to *Huckleberry Finn*." *American Literature* 21 (March): 108–11.

SLC (Samuel Langhorne Clemens).
1851 [*attributed*]. "The New Costume." Hannibal *Western Union*, 10 July.

1862. "Petrified Man." Virginia City *Territorial Enterprise*, 4 October. Reprinted in *ET&S1*, 159.

1864. "Whereas." *Californian* 1 (22 October): 1. Reprinted in *ET&S2*, 88–93.

1865. "Jim Smiley and His Jumping Frog." New York *Saturday Press* 4 (18 November): 248–49. Reprinted in *ET&S2*, 282–88.

1866a. "Captain Montgomery." San Francisco *Golden Era* 14 (28 January): 6. Reprinted in Taper, 177–99.

1866b. "An Open Letter to the American People." New York *Weekly Review* 17 (17 February): 1.

1866c. "Scenes in Honolulu—No. 13." Letter dated 22 June, number 14 in the sequence. Sacramento *Union*, 16 July, 3, clipping in Scrapbook 6:118–19, CU-MARK. Reprinted in *MTH*, 328–34.

1867. "Letter from 'Mark Twain.'" San Francisco *Alta California*, 26 May, 1. Reprinted in *MTTB*, 141–48.

1868. "Cannibalism in the Cars." *Broadway: A London Magazine*, n.s.1 (November): 189–94. Reprinted in Budd 1992, 269–77.

1869a. *The Innocents Abroad; or, The New Pilgrim's Progress*. Hartford: American Publishing Company.

1869b [*attributed*]. "Only a Nigger." Buffalo *Express*, 26 August, 2. In McCullough and McIntire-Strasburg, 22–23.

1869c. "The 'Wild Man' 'Interviewed.'" Buffalo *Express*, 18 September, 1. In McCullough and McIntire-Strasburg, 53–56.

1870a. Untitled autobiographical reminiscence. MS of thirteen pages, CU-MARK. Published as "The Tennessee Land," in *AutoMT1* and in *MTA*, 1:3–7.

1870b. "A Big Thing." Buffalo *Express*, 12 March, 2. In McCullough and McIntire-Strasburg, 161–66.

1870c. "Post-Mortem Poetry." *Galaxy* 9 (June): 864–65.

1870d. Untitled article in "Memoranda." *Galaxy* 10 (November): 735.

1872. English travel diary. Partial MS of 100 pages, CU-MARK. Published in *L5*, 583–629.

1873–74. *The Gilded Age: A Tale of To-day.* Charles Dudley Warner, coauthor. Hartford: American Publishing Company. Early copies bound with 1873 title page, later ones with 1874 title page: see *BAL* 3357.

1874. "A True Story, Repeated Word for Word as I Heard It." *Atlantic Monthly* 34 (November): 591–94.

1875a. "Old Times on the Mississippi." Articles 4 and 5. *Atlantic Monthly* 35 (April and May): 446–52, 567–74.

1875b. Letter to William Dean Howells, 5 July, NN-B. In *L6*, 503–6.

1876a. *The Adventures of Tom Sawyer.* Hartford: American Publishing Company.

1876b. Letter to William Dean Howells, 9 August, NN-B. In *MTHL*, 1:144, and in *Letters 1876–1880.*

1877. Untitled autobiographical reminiscence. MS of eleven pages, NNAL. Published as "Early Years in Florida, Missouri" in *AutoMT1* and in *MTA*, 1:7–10.

1880. *A Tramp Abroad.* Hartford: American Publishing Company.

[1880?]. "A Few Epitaphs: Mark Twain Unfolds a Few Striking Specimens." Interview printed in the Hartford *Post* of unknown date, clipping, marked "80s," in CU-MARK.

1881a. *The Prince and the Pauper: A Tale for Young People of All Ages.* Boston: James R. Osgood and Co.

1881b. "A Curious Experience." *Century Magazine* 23 (November): 35–46.

[1882?]. Untitled speech. MS of sixteen pages, CU-MARK. Published as "Advice to Youth" in *MTS* 1923, 104–8.

1882. Draft of chapter 51 of *Life on the Mississippi.* MS of thirty-seven pages, NNPM.

1883. *Life on the Mississippi.* Boston: James R. Osgood and Co.

1883–84. Unused dedication for *Adventures of Huckleberry Finn* entitled "*To the Once Boys & Girls.*" MS of one page, with a note by Charles L. Webster ("Never used."). Tipped into a copy of SLC 1885a, with the following note on the flyleaf: "This copy of 'Adventures of Huckleberry Finn' was bound by J. F. Tapley Nov. 26th 1884, and is the *first* copy ever bound. | Chas. L. Webster | Publisher." PH in CU-MARK.

1884a. "Hunting for H——." New York *Sun*, 24 August, 2. Reprinted in Budd 1982, 11–15.

1884b. "An Adventure of Huckleberry Finn: With an Account of the Famous Grangerford-Shepherdson Feud." *Century Magazine* 29 (December): 268–78.

1885a. *Adventures of Huckleberry Finn.* New York: Charles L. Webster and Co.

1885b. *The Adventures of Huckleberry Finn.* 2 vols. Leipzig: Bernhard Tauchnitz.

1885c. "Jim's Investments, and King Sollermun." *Century Magazine* 29 (January): 456–58.

1885d. "Royalty on the Mississippi: As Chronicled by Huckleberry Finn." *Century Magazine* 29 (February): 544–67.

1885e. Speech delivered at the Actors Fund Fair at the Academy of Music, Philadelphia, on 9 April 1885. In *MTS* 1910, 265, as "Obituary Poetry" (misdated) and Fatout 1976, 194.

1885f. "The Private History of a Campaign That Failed." *Century Magazine* 31 (December): 193–204.

1886. Speech at the Typothetae Dinner, Delmonico's, New York, on 18 January, as reported in "The Typothetae," Hartford *Courant*, 20 January, 1. Reprinted as "The Compositor" in Fatout 1976, 200–202.

1889. *A Connecticut Yankee in King Arthur's Court.* New York: Charles L. Webster and Co.

1893–94. "Tom Sawyer Abroad." *St. Nicholas: An Illustrated Magazine for Young Folks* 21 (November 1893–April 1894): 20–29, 116–27, 250–58, 348–56, 392–401, 539–48.

1894. *The Tragedy of Pudd'nhead Wilson and the Comedy Those Extraordinary Twins.* Hartford: American Publishing Company.

1895a. Annotation for public reading of *Adventures of Huckleberry Finn.* In volume 1 of *The Adventures of Huckleberry Finn.* 2 vols. Leipzig: Bernhard Tauchnitz, 1885 (with November 1893 advertisement on back cover). Author's personal copy in CU-MARK. Volume 2 no longer extant. Pages annotated by Clemens are reproduced in *HF2003*, 622–54, and at *MTPO* (Revisions for Public Reading, 1895–1896).

1895b. "Fenimore Cooper's Literary Offences." *North American Review* 161 (July): 1–12.

1895c. List of selections for public reading. Notebook 35, TS page 6, CU-MARK.

1895d. Draft introduction to public reading selection, "Small-pox & a lie save Jim." Notebook 35, TS pages 34–36, CU-MARK.

1896. "Tom Sawyer, Detective." *Harper's New Monthly Magazine* 93 (August–September): 344–61, 519–37.

[1897?]. Autobiographical notes. MS of one page (beginning "Camp-meeting. . . ."), PH in CU-MARK. Formerly acquisition no. A-1392, CCamarSJ. Sold as lot 1198, *Estelle Doheny Collection . . . Part IV*, 17 and 18 October 1988, Christie, Manson and Woods International; present location unknown.

1897a. "A Little Note to M. Paul Bourget." In *Tom Sawyer, Detective, As Told by Huck Finn, and Other Tales*, 225–46. London: Chatto and Windus.

1897b. "Villagers of 1840–3." MS of forty-three pages, CU-MARK. Published in *Inds*, 93–108.

1897–98. "My Autobiography. [Random Extracts from it.]" MS of seventy-five pages, CU-MARK. Published as "Early Days" in *AutoMT1* and, with omissions, in *MTA*, 1:81–115.

[1900]. "Scraps from My Autobiography. Playing 'Bear.' Herrings. Jim Wolf and the Cats." MS of forty-two pages, CU-MARK. Published in *AutoMT1* and in *MTA*, 1:125–43.

[1902]. Autobiographical notes. MS of one page (numbered "3" and beginning "Seek & get measles . . ."), CU-MARK.

[1906?]. Notes glossing OSC 1885–86. MS of thirty-two pages, ViU. Published in OSC 1985.

1906a. "A Family Sketch." MS of sixty-three pages, CLjC.

1906b. "William Dean Howells." *Harper's Monthly* 113 (July): 221–25.

1907. "Chapters from My Autobiography." *North American Review* 186 (October): 161–73. Reprinted in Kiskis, 210–20.

1909a. *Extract from Captain Stormfield's Visit to Heaven.* New York: Harper and Brothers.

1909b. *Is Shakespeare Dead?* New York: Harper and Brothers.

1909c. Autobiographical MS of six pages, dated 25 March, CU-MARK. Published in SLC 1909b, 144–50.

1923. "The United States of Lyncherdom." In *Europe and Elsewhere*, edited by Albert Bigelow Paine, 239–49. New York and London: Harper and Brothers.

1942. *Adventures of Huckleberry Finn.* Edited by Bernard DeVoto. New York: Limited Editions Club.

1944. *Life on the Mississippi.* Edited by Willis Wager. New York: Limited Editions Club.

1958. *Adventures of Huckleberry Finn.* Edited, with an introduction and notes, by Henry Nash Smith. Boston: Houghton Mifflin Company, Riverside Press.

1962. *Adventures of Huckleberry Finn.* A Facsimile of the First Edition. With an introduction by Hamlin Hill. San Francisco: Chandler Publishing Company.

1967. *Adventures of Huckleberry Finn.* Edited, with an introduction and notes, by Leo Marx. The Library of Literature. Indianapolis: Bobbs-Merrill Company.

1982. *The Adventures of Tom Sawyer . . . A Facsimile of the Author's Holograph Manuscript.* Introduction by Paul Baender. 2 vols. Frederick, Md., and Washington, D.C.: University Publications of America and Georgetown University Library.

1983. *Adventures of Huckleberry Finn . . . A Facsimile of the Manuscript.* Introduction by Louis Budd; afterword by William H. Loos. 2 vols. Detroit: Gale Research Company.

1995. Previously unpublished excerpt from the manuscript of *Adventures of Huckleberry Finn,* printed as "Jim and the Dead Man." *New Yorker* 71 (26 June and 3 July): 128–30.

1996a. *Adventures of Huckleberry Finn.* Foreword by Shelley Fisher Fishkin. Introduction by Toni Morrison. Afterword by Victor A. Doyno. The Oxford Mark Twain. New York: Oxford University Press.

1996b. *Adventures of Huckleberry Finn.* Introduction by Justin Kaplan. Foreword and addendum by Victor A. Doyno. New York: Random House.

1996c. *The Adventures of Huckleberry Finn.* Edited by Michael Hulse. Cologne: Könemann.

2003. *"Huck Finn": The Complete Buffalo & Erie County Public Library Manuscript—Teaching and Research Digital Edition.* CD-ROM. Edited by Robert J. Bertholf and Victor Doyno. Designed and developed by The Poetry/Rare Books Collection, University at Buffalo, The State University of New York, for the Buffalo and Erie County Public Library.

Sloane, David E. E. 1988. *Adventures of Huckleberry Finn: American Comic Vision.* Boston: Twayne Publishers.

Smith, Benjamin E., ed. 1902. *The Century Atlas of the World.* New York: Century Company.

Smith, David L. 1984. "Huck, Jim, and American Racial Discourse." *Mark Twain Journal* 22 (Fall): 4–12. In Leonard, Tenney, and Davis, 103–20.

Smith, Henry Nash.
1958a. Introduction to *Adventures of Huckleberry Finn.* Boston: Houghton Mifflin Company, Riverside Press.

1958b. "Mark Twain's Images of Hannibal: From St. Petersburg to Eseldorf." *Texas Studies in English* 37: 3–23.

1962. *Mark Twain: The Development of a Writer.* Cambridge: Belknap Press of Harvard University Press.

Smith, Herbert F. 1970. *Richard Watson Gilder.* New York: Twayne Publishers.

Smith, Solomon. 1868. *Theatrical Management in the West and South for Thirty Years.* New York: Harper and Brothers.

Smyth, W. H. 1867. *The Sailor's Word-Book: An Alphabetical Digest of Nautical Terms.* London: Blackie and Son.

Spaulding, Henry G. 1863. Excerpt from *Under the Palmetto.* In Jackson, 64–73.

Sprague, William B. 1858. *Annals of the American Pulpit; or, Commemorative Notices of Distinguished American Clergymen of Various Denominations.* Vol. 4. New York: Robert Carter and Brothers.

Stevens, Walter B. 1911. *St. Louis: The Fourth City, 1764–1911.* 2 vols. St. Louis: S. J. Clarke Publishing Company.

Stevenson, Burton, ed. 1934. *The Home Book of Quotations, Classical and Modern.* New York: Dodd, Mead and Co.

Stevenson, Robert Louis.
1885. Letter to J. A. Symonds, February. In *Letters and Miscellanies of Robert Louis Stevenson,* edited with notes and introduction by Sidney Colvin, 414–15. New York: Charles Scribner's Sons, 1911.

1888. Letter to SLC, April, CU-MARK. Quoted in *MTB,* 2:794.

Stewart, A. A. 1912. *The Printer's Dictionary of Technical Terms.* Boston: School of Printing, North End Union.

Still, William.
1872. *The Underground Rail Road.* Philadelphia: Porter and Coates.

*1883. *The Underground Rail Road.* Rev. ed. Philadelphia: William Still.

Stowe, Harriet Beecher.
1853. *A Key to "Uncle Tom's Cabin"; Presenting the Original Facts and Documents upon Which the Story Is Founded.* Boston: John P. Jewett and Co.

1856. *Dred; A Tale of the Great Dismal Swamp.* 2 vols. Boston: Phillips, Sampson and Co.

Strickland, Carol Colclough. 1976. "Emmeline Grangerford, Mark Twain's Folk Artist." *Bulletin of the New York Public Library* 79 (Winter): 225–33.

Summers, Montague. 1946. *Witchcraft and Black Magic.* London: Rider and Co.

Sweets, Henry H., III. 1984. *The Hannibal, Missouri Presbyterian Church: A Sesquicentennial History.* Hannibal: Presbyterian Church of Hannibal.

Tadman, Michael. 1989. *Speculators and Slaves.* Madison: University of Wisconsin Press.

Taper, Bernard, ed. 2003. *Mark Twain's San Francisco.* Berkeley: Heyday Books.

Thayer, Stuart. 1974. "A Short History of Three Equestrian Acts." *Bandwagon* 18 (March–April): 8–10.

Thomas, Daniel Lindsey, and Lucy Blayney Thomas. 1920. *Kentucky Superstitions.* Princeton, N.J.: Princeton University Press.

[Thompson, William T.] 1845. *The Chronicles of Pineville.* Philadelphia: Carey and Hart.

Thornton, Richard H. 1912. *An American Glossary.* 3 vols. Philadelphia: J. B. Lippincott Company.

Thorpe, Thomas Bangs.
    1842. "The Disgraced Scalp Lock, or Incidents on the Western Waters." *Spirit of the Times,* 16 July, 229–30. In Estes, 170–80.

    1855. "Remembrances of the Mississippi." *Harper's New Monthly Magazine* 12 (December): 25–41.

Ticknor, Caroline.
    1914. "'Mark Twain's' Missing Chapter." *Bookman* 39 (May): 298–309.

    1922. *Glimpses of Authors.* Boston and New York: Houghton Mifflin Company, Riverside Press.

Tidwell, James Nathan. 1942. "Mark Twain's Representation of Negro Speech." *American Speech* 17 (October): 174–76.

Timbs, John. 1876. *Doctors and Patients; or, Anecdotes of the Medical World and Curiosities of Medicine.* London: Richard Bentley and Son.

Trelease, Allen W. 1971. *White Terror: The Ku Klux Klan Conspiracy and Southern Reconstruction.* New York: Harper and Row.

Trenck, Friedrich. 1853. *The Life of Baron Frederick Trenck.* Albany: J. Munsell.

Trexler, Harrison Anthony. 1914. *Slavery in Missouri, 1804–1865.* Baltimore: Johns Hopkins Press.

Trollope, Frances. 1832. *Domestic Manners of the Americans.* 2 vols. London: Whittaker, Treacher, and Co. Clemens owned an 1832 edition, complete in one volume (London: Whittaker, Treacher, and Co.; New York: Reprinted for the booksellers).

Trowbridge, J. T. 1864. *Cudjo's Cave.* Boston: J. E. Tilton and Co.

TS. Typescript.

TS1. Typescript, no longer extant, of the first half of the *Huckleberry Finn* manuscript (MS1), probably made in late 1882 or early 1883 and apparently numbered 1–159.

TS2. Typescript, no longer extant, of the second half of the *Huckleberry Finn* manuscript (MS2), made in the late summer of 1883. TS2 became printer's copy for the second half of the book.

TS3. Typescript, no longer extant, of the first half of *Huckleberry Finn,* made in 1884 from TS1. TS3 incorporated Mark Twain's revisions on TS1 and William Dean Howells's corrections, and it became printer's copy for the first half of the book.

TS. 1980. *The Adventures of Tom Sawyer; Tom Sawyer Abroad; and Tom Sawyer, Detective.* Edited by John C. Gerber, Paul Baender, and Terry Firkins. The Works of Mark Twain. Berkeley, Los Angeles, London: University of California Press.

TSA. 1982. *Tom Sawyer Abroad; Tom Sawyer, Detective.* Foreword and notes by John C. Gerber, text established by Terry Firkins. The Mark Twain Library. Berkeley, Los Angeles, London: University of California Press.

Turner, Arlin. 1960. *Mark Twain and George W. Cable: The Record of a Literary Friendship.* [East Lansing]: Michigan State University Press.

Turner, Timothy G. 1867. *Gazetteer of the St. Joseph Valley, Michigan and Indiana, with a View of Its Hydraulic and Business Capacities.* Chicago: Hazlitt and Reed.

TxU. Harry Ransom Humanities Research Center, University of Texas, Austin.

Uk. British Library, London.

Urnov, Dimitri. 1986. Quoted in Diana Ketcham, "Soviet Study at UC Focuses on Twain," Oakland *Tribune,* 28 July, C-1, C-3.

ViU. Clifton Waller Barrett Library, University of Virginia, Charlottesville.

*Walpole, Horace. 1861–66. *The Letters of Horace Walpole, Earl of Oxford.* Edited by Peter Cunningham. 9 vols. London: Henry G. Bohn.

Waterman, Catharine H., ed. 1841. *Friendship's Offering.* Philadelphia: Marshall, Williams, and Butler.

Watts, Peter. 1977. *A Dictionary of the Old West, 1850–1900.* New York: Alfred A. Knopf.

Way, Frederick, Jr.
1943. *Pilotin' Comes Natural.* New York and Toronto: Farrar and Rinehart.

1972. Diagrams, *S&D Reflector* 9 (June): 24.

WEU. University of Wisconsin–Eau Claire.

Webster, Noah.
[1870]. *A Dictionary of the English Language.* Rev. and enl. by Chauncey A. Goodrich and Thomas Heber Orr. 2 vols. Glasgow: William Mackenzie.

1884. *An American Dictionary of the English Language.* Rev. and enl. by Chauncey A. Goodrich. Springfield, Mass.: G. and C. Merriam and Co.

1889. *An American Dictionary of the English Language.* Rev. and enl. by Chauncey A. Goodrich and Noah Porter. Springfield, Mass.: G. and C. Merriam and Co.

1894. *An American Dictionary of the English Language.* Rev. and enl. by Chauncey A. Goodrich. Chicago: Webster's Dictionary Pub. Company.

Wecter, Dixon. 1952. *Sam Clemens of Hannibal.* Boston: Houghton Mifflin Company, Riverside Press.

Wells, Amos R. 1945. *A Treasure of Hymns: Brief Biographies of One Hundred and Twenty Leading Hymn-Writers with Their Best Hymns.* Boston: W. A. Wilde Company.

Wells, David M. 1973. "More on the Geography of 'Huckleberry Finn.'" *South Atlantic Bulletin* 38 (November): 82–86.

Wells, Evelyn Kendrick. 1950. *The Ballad Tree.* New York: Ronald Press Company.

Welsh, Donald H. 1962. "Sam Clemens' Hannibal, 18[4]6–18[4]8." *Midcontinent American Studies Journal* 3 (Spring): 28–43.

Wentworth, Harold. 1944. *American Dialect Dictionary.* New York: Thomas Y. Crowell Company.

Westerhoff, John H., III. 1978. *McGuffey and His Readers.* Nashville: Abingdon.

*White, Gilbert. 1875. *The Natural History of Selborne.* London: Bickers and Son.

Whiting, B. J. 1944. "Guyuscutus, Royal Nonesuch and Other Hoaxes." *Southern Folklore Quarterly* 8 (December): 251–75.

Wild, J. C., and Lewis F. Thomas, ed. 1841. *The Valley of the Mississippi, Illustrated. . . . Drawn and Lithographed by J. C. Wild.* No. 3, September. St. Louis: J. C. Wild.

Wilson, F. P., ed. 1970. *The Oxford Dictionary of English Proverbs.* 3d ed. Oxford: Clarendon Press.

WIM. 1973. *What Is Man? and Other Philosophical Writings.* Edited by Paul Baender. The Works of Mark Twain. Berkeley, Los Angeles, London: University of California Press.

Windell, Marie George. 1943. "The Camp Meeting in Missouri." *Missouri Historical Review* 37 (April): 253–70.

Wolford, Leah Jackson. 1916. *The Play-Party in Indiana.* Indianapolis: Indiana Historical Commission.

Woodard, Fredrick, and Donnarae MacCann.
1984. "'Huckleberry Finn' and the Traditions of Blackface Minstrelsy." *Interracial Books for Children Bulletin* 15:4–13. Also in MacCann and Woodard, 75–103.

1992. "Minstrel Shackles and Nineteenth-Century 'Liberality' in *Huckleberry Finn.*" In Leonard, Tenney, and Davis, 141–53.

Worcester, Joseph E. 1863. *A Dictionary of the English Language.* Boston: Brewer and Tileston.

Workwoman's Guide. 1838. *The Workwoman's Guide. . . . By a Lady.* London: Simpkin, Marshall, and Co.

*Wright, William [Dan De Quille, pseud.]. 1877. *History of the Big Bonanza.* Hartford: American Publishing Company.

WU. University of Wisconsin, Madison.

WWD. 1967. *Mark Twain's Which Was the Dream?* Edited by John S. Tuckey. The Mark Twain Papers. Berkeley and Los Angeles: University of California Press.

Wyeth, John Allan. 1914. *With Sabre and Scalpel.* New York and London: Harper and Brothers.

Yellin, Jean Fagan. 1972. *The Intricate Knot: Black Figures in American Literature, 1776–1863.* New York: New York University Press.

Zellers, John A. 1948. *The Typewriter: A Short History, on Its 75th Anniversary, 1873–1948.* New York: Newcomen Society of England, American Branch.

NOTE ON THE TEXT

This edition of *Huckleberry Finn* is the first ever to be based directly on Mark Twain's complete original manuscript. It replaces the Mark Twain Library edition of 1985, which was able to use only the *second half* of the manuscript for its text, necessarily relying on the first American edition for the remainder. But the discovery in 1990 of the long lost *first half* of the manuscript has made it possible to re-edit the whole text using both halves of the manuscript. As a result, just in the first half of the book alone, this newly edited text departs from the 1985 Mark Twain Library text nearly one hundred times in its wording and nearly eleven hundred times in its spelling, punctuation, and other details. We have also extensively revised the explanatory notes, and we have added two documentary appendixes showing how Mark Twain revised his own text before publication, and illustrating some of the decisive physical evidence for identifying and dating the three main stints of composition.[1]

The story behind this revised edition begins in early 1991, when a truly remarkable rumor swept through the rare book and manuscript world, eventually reaching the Mark Twain Papers in Berkeley: the first half of the *Huckleberry Finn* manuscript, presumed lost or destroyed for more than one hundred years, had been found in a Hollywood attic and was being evaluated for auction by Sotheby's in New York. Another rumor had it that a number of manuscript dealers were pooling their funds to come up with the winning bid (estimated to be as high as $1.5 million) while planning to recover their investment by reselling the manuscript, page by page. Early in February 1991, Sotheby's called the Mark Twain Papers and confirmed that it had recently authenticated a manuscript of some six hundred pages which was clearly the missing part of the *Huckleberry Finn* manuscript. Sotheby's wanted to know if there was any evidence in the files of the Mark Twain Papers bearing on Mark Twain's disposition of this first half, and therefore on who could properly claim to own—or sell—it.

There was. But it was evidence that could be interpreted correctly only

---

[1] The newly edited text is identical in every detail (including pagination) with the text published in the 2003 Works of Mark Twain edition (*HF2003*), which prints a full and detailed apparatus documenting all editorial decisions about the textual evidence, discussed selectively in this edition.

now that these six hundred plus pages had been found. In November 1885, nine months after he published the first American edition of *Huckleberry Finn*, Mark Twain received a letter at his home in Hartford from one James Fraser Gluck, a Buffalo lawyer who was also a curator for the library of the Young Men's Association in Buffalo. Mark Twain had been a member of that association when he lived in Buffalo in 1869–71, as had his friend and partner on the Buffalo *Express*, Josephus N. Larned, who was now superintendent of the library. Gluck wrote to Clemens, in part:

> I can assure you sir, that it would be highly appreciated in this city where you have many readers, if it should seem to you proper to send to the superintendent of the Library Mr. J. N. Larned, or to myself, such manuscript or manuscripts as you might wish to present to the Library. They will be accorded a place of honor and preserved in perpetuo.
>
> If I were asking this for myself, I should expect to be refused, for the compliance with such a request would be merely the gratification of a desire for a selfish possession;—but I ask it in behalf of a large and constantly growing public institution, in one of the largest cities of our country, where such manuscript will be seen daily by hundreds of people, and through the sight of which interest in literature and literary men will be increased and perpetuated. (Gluck to SLC, 7 Nov 85, CU-MARK)

Clemens answered this letter on the day he received it, 11 November, saying in part: "I will comply, as far as I can, with the greatest pleasure—that is, to the extent of 50 per cent. of a MS. book ('The Adventures of Huckleberry Finn.')" He was referring to the *second* half of *Huckleberry Finn*—the half written in 1883. "I have hunted the house over, & that is all I can find," he explained, adding that the first half of the manuscript must have been sent to "the printers, who never returned it" (misdated 12 Nov 85, NBu). Gluck acknowledged this letter on 12 November, offering to show Clemens "how pleasant an abiding place" in the library had been set aside for "the much-abused Huckleberry Finn. When Boston & Concord desert him then the home of the Presidents shall take him up" (CU-MARK). This half of the manuscript was duly shipped and its receipt acknowledged on 14 November 1885: "The manuscript of Huckleberry Finn arrived this afternoon and was at once placed in the Library vault." Clemens annotated the envelope simply, "MS for Buffalo" (Gluck to SLC, CU-MARK). On the envelope of Gluck's first letter he wrote, "Sent what was left of Huck Finn."

There the matter stood, and might have remained, except that some nineteen months later, probably soon after 24 June 1887 when the Clemenses arrived in Elmira for their usual summer stay, Clemens came across some more of his old manuscript. He promptly sent it to his business agent in Hartford, Franklin G. Whitmore, and told him to have it sent to Buffalo. Larned, superintendent of what was by then called the Buffalo Library, acknowledged its receipt on 5 July: "I have received by Express today the first half of the Ms. of 'Huckleberry Finn' kindly sent to us at Mr. Clemens' request (we had the second half of the Ms. already). Please express to Mr. Clemens the thanks of the Library and of myself personally" (Larned to Whitmore, CU-MARK). Just a few days later, Gluck also sent an acknowledgment: "Please accept my thanks for your kindness in forwarding the first part of Mss. of 'Finn' which Mr Larned has just rec'd. The whole can now be bound and placed on exhibition" (Gluck to SLC, 11 July 87, CU-MARK).

To the editors of the Mark Twain Project these letters seemed decisive: Clemens gave the manuscript to the library, and therefore the library was the only entity that could sell it at auction. We sent copies of this correspondence to Sotheby's and also to officials at the Buffalo and Erie County Public Library, where the second half of the manuscript had been since 1885. For it was crucial to the fate of the first half that Buffalo assert a claim of ownership, thus barring Sotheby's from either auctioning it off or returning it to the consignor, at least until its ownership could be legally established. On or about 6 February 1991, lawyers for the Buffalo and Erie County Public Library lodged a claim of ownership with Sotheby's, beginning a legal tussle that would not be completely resolved for a year and a half. On 13 February 1991, the Los Angeles *Times* broke the story of the new-found manuscript, and for the next three months it seemed the entire press corps of the country if not the world was smitten by the Lost-then-Found Romance of the *Huckleberry Finn* manuscript.

Despite these two 1887 letters of acknowledgment, one from the superintendent of the library and one from a curator, the first half of the manuscript was neither deposited nor put on display there. As far back as its records go, the library had no indication that it owned anything except the *second* half, the one sent in 1885. That explains why the real meaning of the 1887 letters was not known until 1991. The pages then at Buffalo actually consisted of chapters 22 through "Chapter the last" (chapter 43), plus sixty pages from chapters 12–14, obviously from the first half of the book. The assumption had always been, therefore, that Mark Twain sent chapters 22–43 in 1885—then found and sent a mere sixty pages from "the first part of Mss." in July 1887. For if he had found and sent the *whole* "first half of the Ms. of 'Huckleberry Finn' " (as Larned's letter certainly seemed to say), surely that large stack of pages would still be in the library.

This view of what must have occurred was understandable, but wrong. For in October 1990, one of James Fraser Gluck's granddaughters, Barbara Gluck Testa, opened a trunk in her Hollywood attic and found a stack of 664 manuscript pages in Mark Twain's handwriting, together with a blue envelope labeled "MSS. of Huck Finn by Mark Twain." She had found the great bulk of the first half, the part that was acknowledged by Larned and Gluck in July 1887. Clearly Mark Twain himself had been wrong about the printers not having returned it (in fact, *neither* half of the manuscript *ever* went to the printers). When James Gluck died suddenly in 1897, at the age of forty-five, he must have had the pages of the first half still in his possession, and they were presumably gathered up and stored along with his other papers. These eventually passed to his daughter, and then to his granddaughters in about 1963. Exactly why *he* still had them instead of the library may never be known. What is clear is that the pages stayed within the Gluck family, tucked away unrecognized in that trunk, until rediscovered by chance in October 1990.

The legal tussle over this new-found document was resolved in June 1992 when the Gluck family agreed to turn the manuscript over to the Buffalo and Erie County Public Library in return for a share of the income derived from its publication. The University of California Press and the Mark Twain Project agreed to set aside their exclusive right to publish its unpublished parts, a right they had by virtue of a 1982 contract with the Mark Twain Foundation, giving them "an exclusive license to publish, and continue to publish, Mark Twain's previously unpublished writings." That concession was made in return for the resolution of the legal fight over ownership, and the Mark Twain Project's right to re-edit and publish the text of *Huckleberry Finn,* so long as any new edition did not appear before July 1997.

All other use of the manuscript was then controlled by an alliance of three interested parties: the Mark Twain Foundation, which owns the copyright in the unpublished materials; the Buffalo and Erie County Public Library, which owns the physical document; and the Gluck family heirs, who found the first half of the manuscript in 1990. Under this arrangement, two trade publishers—the *New Yorker* and Random House—eventually bid for publication privileges. In the summer of 1995, the *New Yorker* published a long episode from the manuscript—a ghost story told by Jim that Mark Twain had removed from his text before the novel was published. And in 1996, Random House issued a text of the novel based on the first edition, into which the editors placed two sections of the manuscript where they would have appeared if Mark Twain had not omitted or replaced them. These were the episode published in the *New Yorker,* and Mark Twain's original description of a camp meeting, which in the book he replaced with a heavily revised version of the same scene (SLC 1995; SLC 1996b).

Both of those rejected drafts are also reproduced here—but in an editorial appendix, not in the text proper. The purpose of this edition is to publish the text as Mark Twain wanted it, using the evidence of the whole manuscript to correct errors, mend oversights, and otherwise restore hundreds of details that were lost during the original process of typing, typesetting, and proofreading his book. This newly edited text is an unmodernized critical edition designed to recover as much as possible of Mark Twain's specific intentions for his text at the time he submitted the printer's copy to his publisher in 1884. It draws textual evidence for constructing that text from the following: (1) Mark Twain's *complete* holograph manuscript, 1,361 leaves (664 new-found pages, plus the 697 pages already known), now in the Mark Twain Room of the Buffalo and Erie County Public Library, Buffalo, New York; (2) the first American edition, published in February 1885 by Mark Twain's own publishing house, Charles L. Webster and Company; (3) excerpts from the novel which Mark Twain published in the *Century Magazine* for December 1884, January and February 1885, which were typeset from first-edition proofs and slightly revised by Mark Twain; (4) a partial set of page proofs for the first edition, corrected by Mark Twain, which have always been in the Mark Twain Papers; and (5) chapter 3 of *Life on the Mississippi* (Boston, James R. Osgood, 1883), which until the discovery of the first half of the manuscript, provided the only text of the "raft episode," a passage written for and submitted with the printer's copy for *Huckleberry Finn*, but removed before publication at the suggestion of Mark Twain's publisher, Charles L. Webster.

Course of Composition. Crucial to any such effort to remove errors and repair damage is having a detailed and accurate understanding of who had opportunity to make changes in the text, and when. It is therefore essential to know how and when Mark Twain wrote his text, and what part he and others played in the process of transforming his manuscript into a book.

Albert Bigelow Paine thought that Mark Twain wrote *Huckleberry Finn* in three stints, "about half" in the summer of 1876; an unspecified portion in the summer of 1880, "writing alternately on *The Prince and the Pauper* and the story about Huck Finn"; and the rest in 1883 (*MTB*, 2:578, 683–84, 754). Bernard DeVoto, who first found and analyzed the *Huckleberry Finn* "working notes" in the Mark Twain Papers, disagreed. He thought the book had been written in only two stints: chapters 1–16 (up to "where Huck's raft is rammed by a steamboat") in July and early August 1876, and the rest—from which a single typescript was eventually made for the typesetter—during the summer of 1883 (DeVoto 1942, 50–81). In 1958 Walter Blair analyzed the physical evidence provided by the working notes, comparing the ink and paper Mark Twain used in letters and other clearly dated manuscripts, and argued that he had written it in three or possibly four stints: chapters 1–16, to where the steamboat crashes into the raft, in the summer of 1876; the last three paragraphs of chapter 16, and chapters 17–18, in 1879–80; chapters 19–21 sometime between 1880 and 1883; and chapters 12–14 and 22–43 during the summer of 1883 (Blair 1958, 6–10, 17–20). Blair further suggested that there might have been not just one, but two, typescripts: the first consisting of "that part of the book written before summer, 1883," the holograph version of which "was destroyed"; the second being the "part written during the summer, 1883," the autograph version of which "was preserved . . . in the Buffalo Public Library" (Blair

1958, 19). In 1988, Blair and Fischer further refined the dating of these three or four stints, proving that there must have been *three* (partial) typescripts. They also showed that the copy from which the illustrator Kemble worked, as well as the copy the typesetters used, were in fact assembled from these typescripts, the first two of which Mark Twain must have extensively revised before using them as printer's copy. That in turn established that no part of the original holograph manuscript ever went to the printers, and therefore could not have been destroyed by them, as Mark Twain mistakenly remembered in 1885 (*HF1988*, xxxi–xxxviii, 432–35, 443–52).

Some of the arguments used in support of these theories were necessarily based on very indirect evidence and on informed speculation. One of the great benefits of having access, at long last, to the first half of the manuscript is that its evidence renders most such speculation unnecessary. The physical evidence of the manuscript is often decisive, showing that there were three principal stints, and also showing beyond reasonable doubt where, and sometimes when, those stints began and ended.

stints	dates	MS pages (*and chapters*)	current pages
Stint 1 MS1a	July–September 1876	Pages 1–446 (*chapters 1–12½, chapters 15–18½*)	1 *title*–80.29, 99.1–146.11
Stint 2 MS1b	March–June 1880	"Notice," pages 447–663 (*"Notice," chapters 18½–21*)	xxxi, 146.12–188.16
Stint 3 MS2	June–September 1883	Title page, pages 81-A-1–81-60, 160–787 (*title page, chapters 12½–14, chapters 22–43*)	vii *title* [see 494–95], 80.30–98.7, 189.1–362.11

■ *Stint 1: July–September 1876.* On 1 August 1876, Clemens said to Moncure D. Conway: "I am booming along with my new book—have written ⅓ of it & shall finish it in 6 working weeks" (PH in CU-MARK). And on 9 August he wrote to William Dean Howells that "a month ago" he had begun "another boys' book—more to be at work than anything else. I have written 400 pages on it—therefore it is very nearly half done. It is Huck Finn's Autobiography. I like it only tolerably well, as far as I have got" (*MTHL*, 1:144).

The first physically distinct part of the manuscript (MS1a), written during the summer of 1876, comprises chapter 1 through the middle of chapter 12, and chapter 15 through the middle of chapter 18. In short, Mark Twain did not stop where the steamboat crashes into the raft in chapter 16 (as earlier supposed by DeVoto, Blair, and others), but continued for two more chapters, stopping only after Buck Grangerford asks Huck if he knows what a feud is and Huck replies, "Never heard of it before—tell me about it." This segment consists of manuscript pages 1–446 (1 *title*—80.29 and 99.1–146.11). Minor changes in inking, and the presence of Mark Twain's working notes in the margins, suggest that there may have been several pauses *within* this 446-page stint, most notably at page 362, the end of the raft episode. But it remains most likely that Mark Twain completed the entire 446 pages during the summer of 1876. If he had reached page 400 by 9 August, as he seemed to say to Howells, he easily had time to complete another 46 pages before leaving Elmira for Hartford with his family on 11 September.

■ *Stint 2: March–June 1880.* Mark Twain's next known reference to the *Huckleberry Finn* manuscript is in a letter to his sister, probably written on 14 November 1880, several months *after* he had completed this second stint. In it he refers to the completed but still unpublished *Prince and the Pauper* and to "Huck Finn's Autobiography," saying

> I have two stories, and by the verbal agreement [with the publisher] they are both going into the same book; but Livy says they're not, and by George I. she ought to know.... I said *two* stories, but one of them is only half done; two or three months' work on it yet. I shall tackle it Wednesday or Thursday; that is, if Livy yields and allows both stories to go in one book, which I hope she won't." (*MTB*, 2:696; see also *P&P*, 6–7)

Livy did not yield, and the two stories were thereby destined for separate publication. Two years later, in 1882, Mark Twain built chapter 3 of *Life on the Mississippi* by importing the "raft chapter" from "Huck Finn's Autobiography," referring to the latter as "a book which I have been working at, by fits and starts, during the past five or six years" (SLC 1883, 42).

This second physically distinct part of the manuscript (MS1b) comprises pages 447–663, the remainder of chapter 18 through the end of chapter 21. It also includes the unnumbered "Notice" page, most likely written in late June 1880 or after (xxxi and 146.12–188.16). As Blair anticipated in 1958, the purple ink and wove paper of this section indicate that the second stint was written sometime during the seven-month period from mid-November 1879 through mid-June 1880. Blair dated the ink from its use in letters and manuscripts between 18 November 1879 and 15 June 1880, and the paper from its use generally and intermittently between September 1879 and 4 June 1881. The paper was used in the sections of the *Prince* manuscript written in 1879 and 1880 (Blair 1958, 7–9). Evidence now suggests March through mid-June 1880, when Clemens took a break from work on *Prince*, as the most likely period of composition for *Huckleberry Finn*.

■ *Stint 3: June–September 1883.* Finally, in 1883, Mark Twain's letters show that he was once again hard at work on *Huckleberry Finn*. He wrote to Howells on 20 July:

> I haven't piled up MS so in years as I have done since we came here to the farm three weeks & a half ago.... I wrote 4000 words to-day & I touch 3000 & upwards pretty often, & don't fall below 2600 on any working day.... I have finished one small book, & am away along in a big one that I half-finished two or three years ago. I ex-

pect to complete it in a month or six weeks or two months more. And *I* shall *like* it, whether anybody else does or not. It's a kind of companion to Tom Sawyer. There's a raft episode from it in second or third chapter of Life on the Mississippi. (*MTHL,* 1: 435)

On 1 September, he completed it, writing to his English publisher: "I've just finished writing a book; & modesty compels me to say it's a rattling good one, too—'Adventures of Huckleberry Finn.' (Tom Sawyer's comrade.)" (SLC to Chatto, in Gates, 79).

The third physically distinct part of the manuscript (MS2) is the entire second half, plus a sixty-page insertion in the first half—in other words, that part of the manuscript which has been in Buffalo since 1885. Written entirely during the summer of 1883, it consists of the insertion numbered 81-A-1 through 81-60, plus pages 160–787. These comprise the text from the middle of chapter 12 through the end of chapter 14, plus chapter 22 through "Chapter the last" (43), and also include the manuscript title page (vii *title,* 80.30–98.7, and 189.1–362.11).

Before Mark Twain began work on stint three of the manuscript, he had his typists transcribe all of stints one and two, pages 1–663. This typescript was probably made using an ALL CAPITALS typewriter, either by Harry M. Clarke and Jakob B. Coykendall, Mark Twain's Elmira typists, sometime in late 1882, or possibly by another, unidentified typist in Hartford. The typing must have been complete before Mark Twain began work on the third stint in June 1883, and it must have been numbered from page 1 through page 159. When Mark Twain began in June, he wrote and inserted the sixty pages of the *Walter Scott* passage (the middle of chapter 12 through the end of chapter 14) at typescript page 81, and he went on to finish the story by writing manuscript pages numbered 160–787. That he began numbering this second half with page 160 (rather than page 664) shows that he had the typescript for the first half in hand. By the end of his summer's work, he also had the newly written portion of manuscript typed, with a carbon copy. He substituted a *typed* copy of the interpolation at page 81 and assembled one complete copy of his text, all in typescript save for the extensive holograph revisions on that typescript.

At this point William Dean Howells offered to read the printer's copy before typesetting could begin, just as he had done for several of Mark Twain's earlier books—*The Adventures of Tom Sawyer, A Tramp Abroad,* and *The Prince and the Pauper.* On 22 April 1884 Mark Twain told Webster, "Yes, I want Howells to have carte blanche in making corrections." By the end of the month, Howells returned the second half of the typescript (the ribbon copy, TS2a, the part that began at page 160), presumably with his suggestions and corrections marked on it. But at the author's request, he held on to the first half (TS1), for which there was as yet no duplicate, in order to have it re-typed (without carbon) for the printer. Howells spent nearly three weeks overseeing this task, proofreading the original (with its many authorial revisions) against the copy so carefully that he considered both equally "ready to go into the printer's hands." The original typed copy of the first half (TS1) plus the ribbon copy of the second half (TS2a) went to the illustrator Kemble. Howells's new typescript of the first half (TS3) plus the carbon copy typescript of the second half (TS2b), onto which Clemens must have copied his own revisions of TS2a, went to the typesetter.

This complex assemblage of copies for transmitting the text to the typesetter significantly increased the opportunity for error, especially in the first part of the book, which was typed and then re-typed. Because none of the typescripts is known to survive, Howells's "corrections" cannot be distinguished from Mark Twain's own alterations. But despite Clemens's grant of "carte blanche," the changes Howells made were very likely limited to simple corrections. Anything more substantial would have been offered more tentatively, as suggestions for Mark Twain to approve or reject.

The first galley proofs came to Clemens in about the middle of June 1884. He was often impatient with proofreading, and his anger was easily stirred by errors he thought should have been eliminated before he was asked to look at any proof. After reading the first eleven or twelve chapters, he wrote to Howells on 28 June: "My days are given up to cursings—both loud & deep—for I am reading the H. Finn proofs. They don't make a very great many mistakes; but those that do occur are of a nature to make a man curse his teeth loose" (*MTHL*, 2:493). By 6 August, he had received galley proofs (already divided into three pages per galley) up through chapter 25. With the arrival of chapters 26 through 29, he erupted in fury before reading another word. He wrote to Howells on 7 August: "I have no doubt I am doing a most criminal & outrageous thing—for I am sending you these infernal Huck Finn proofs—but the very last vestige of my patience has gone to the devil, & I cannot bear the sight of another slip of them. My hair turns white with rage, at sight of the mere outside of the package; & this time I didn't even try to glance inside it, but re-enveloped it at once, & directed it to you. . . . Blackguard me if you want to—I deserve it" (*MTHL*, 2:497). The same day, he wrote Webster: "I miscalculated my fortitude. I *can't* read any more proof. I sent this batch to Howells without glancing at it—except to note that that proofreader had left it to me to mark turned letters under cuts!" (*MTBus*, 271). Although he later asked Webster to re-send these four chapters to him, Mark Twain apparently never did see them in proof. About the next batch, which began with chapter 30, he wrote Webster on 11 August: "Most of this proof was clean & beautiful, & a pleasure to read; but the rest of it was read by that blind idiot whom I have cursed so much, & is a disgraceful mess." And he urged Webster to "insist that the rest of the proofs be *better read*" (*MTBus*, 272). He eventually characterized the process as "the worst & silliest proof-reading I have ever seen. It was never read by copy at all—not a single galley of it" (SLC to Webster, 14 Aug 84, in *MTBus*, 272). In other words, the printer's proofreader read the proof for obvious errors, but did not systematically compare it with the typed printer's copy. Mark Twain himself never read portions of the galley proof at all, and it is likely that he only skimmed the page proof.

Despite his impatience with the proofreaders, they were not all "blind idiots." One alert hand employed by the printer wrote a pointed query on the proofs that prompted Mark Twain to correct an internal inconsistency, replacing "I took the canoe" with "I found a canoe" (see the explanatory note to 158.32). But the first edition did ultimately contain numerous typographical errors, overlooked by both the printer's proofreader and by Mark Twain. They included such things as "enought" for "enough" (31.6) and "see" for "seeing" (183.28), as well as other mistakes that resulted from Mark Twain's own carelessness in the manuscript: "Bessie Thatcher" for "Becky Thatcher" (47.17); "meet again" for "meet" (211.25); and "the nigger woman's gown" for "aunt Sally's gown" (333.10–11). All such obvious errors are corrected in the present text.

It is also obvious that because of its transmission history, the book suffered a good deal of error, the first part somewhat more than the second. Each half of the holograph manuscript has more than 1,700 authorial revisions, including rewritten and inserted passages: 88% of those changes are to words, or to some combination of words, punctuation, capitalization, emphasis, and spelling. These numbers provide a pattern of how Mark Twain typically tended to revise his work. Once the manuscript was typed and Mark Twain had extensively revised the typescript, the number of differences between the manuscript text and the first edition was about 5,800, including some quite complex revisions with several stages. In the first half of the book, only 50% of those differences were to the words (52% in the second half), which means that the remainder were far more likely the result not of the author's hand, but of errors and "corrections" volunteered or imposed by the typist and the typesetter.

Assuming that Howells's changes were limited to correction of errors, we can identify Mark Twain's revisions on the lost typescript by comparing the holograph manuscript with the text as published in the first edition. This process also reveals errors *not* caught by Howells or Mark Twain which originated with Mark Twain's typists, copyists, and typesetters, as well as other changes that probably originated with the printer's proofreader, whose normal task would have been to impose conventional styling on the text.

Among the errors here attributed to the typist are words or phrases omitted in the first edition that were in fact critical to the sense of the passage. For instance, when Huck is still at the widow's and Pap Finn is suing to get him back (chapter 6), the first edition reads:

> That law trial was a slow business; appeared like they warn't ever going to get started on it; so every now and then I'd borrow two or three dollars off of the judge for him, to keep from getting a cowhiding.

But the manuscript for this passage reads:

> That law trial was a slow business; appeared as if they warn't ever going to get started on it; so every now & then, all winter, the old man would lay for me & catch me, & then I'd borrow two or three dollars off of the judge for him, to keep from getting a raw-hiding. (MS1a, 93.4–15)

No one but Mark Twain is likely to have changed "raw-hiding" to "cowhiding," or to have altered Huck's original but too literate "as if" to "like," but the largest change here does not appear to be authorial. It was evidently made by the typist, or possibly the typesetter, who inadvertently dropped the clause that explained the *occasion* for Huck's borrowing money from Judge Thatcher ("all winter, the old man would lay for me & catch me, & then"), probably because he skipped from the first "& then" to the second. The necessary phrase is restored in the present edition.

Similarly, when Huck rows the skiff over to a ferryboat in order to get help (chapter 13), in the first edition he seems to go from his skiff to the deck of the ferryboat as if by magic. This magical effect was probably not intended by Mark Twain, however, but is rather the consequence of the typist's skipping over two sentences that made clear how Huck got from the rowboat to the deck of the ferryboat: "Everything was dead still, nobody stirring. I floated in under the stern, made fast, and clumb aboard" (88.15–16). Partly on the grounds that Mark Twain's typists were demonstrably prone to make just such errors, the two sentences are here restored to the text.

In the manuscript the author carefully marked the various display type lines of the playbill for the "SHAKSPEREAN REVIVAL" (chapter 21). That is, he carefully marked some for italics, some for small capitals, and others for full capitals, simulating the typical printed playbill. All of these fine distinctions disappeared in the first edition text, almost certainly because the typewriter used had no lower-case letters, a limitation that made it impossible to indicate the distinctions Mark Twain made in his manuscript, and that not even he took the trouble to restore (see note to 180.20–181.14 and Manuscript Facsimiles, pp. 504–5).

One major flaw in the text of the first edition arose, paradoxically, from Mark Twain's desire to accommodate his publisher. Webster had been charged with, among other duties, finding a way to publish *Tom Sawyer* and *Huckleberry Finn* as a matched set. Because the two books were of very unequal size (*Huckleberry Finn* was much longer than *Tom Sawyer*), Webster suggested that Mark Twain omit the long passage where Huck visits a lumber raft in order to find out how far he and Jim are from Cairo (the passage he had earlier printed in chapter 3 of *Life on the Mississippi*). Mark Twain replied to this suggestion on 22 April 1884: "Yes, I think the raft chapter can be left wholly out, by heaving in a paragraph to say Huck visited the raft to find out how far it might be to Cairo, but got no satisfaction. Even *this* is not necessary unless that raft-visit is referred to later in the book. I think it is, but am not certain" (*MTBus*, 249–50). Because Mark Twain's decision to omit the episode appears, on the evidence, to have been solely to serve his publisher's practical convenience, and because he clearly intended to include it when he submitted his printer's copy to Webster, we restore the episode here just as we did in 1985, albeit by relying on the holograph manuscript instead of the *Life on the Mississippi* printing. See the note to 107.1–123.20 for more detail about this much-debated crux.

Illustrations. Mark Twain always intended that his text be illustrated, although the illustrations he provided at great trouble and expense have not as a rule survived past the first edition, let alone in modern reprints of *Huckleberry Finn*. Clemens chose Edward Windsor Kemble, a young cartoonist who had published in *Life* and the New York *Graphic*, to draw the illustrations for *Huckleberry Finn*. Although Kemble decided what to illustrate by reading one of the typescripts, Mark Twain asked to see the pictures "by batches of half a dozen or more" as Kemble produced them (SLC to Webster, 22 Apr 84, in *MTBus*, 250). After examining the illustrations for the first twelve chapters and requiring revisions in some of them, Mark Twain could still offer only faint praise: "Some of the pictures are good, but none of them are very *very* good. . . . The pictures will *do*—they will just barely do—& that is the best I can say for them," he wrote to Webster. "Don't dishearten the artist—show him where he has *improved*, rather than where he has failed, & punch him up to improve more" (24 May 84, in *MTBus*, 255–56). But two weeks later when he saw the next batch, which included the pictures from chapter 13 through the middle of chapter 20, Mark Twain was entirely satisfied: "I *knew* Kemble had it *in* him, if he would only modify his violences & come down to careful, painstaking work. This batch of pictures is most rattling good. They please me exceedingly." This batch included the only drawing that Mark Twain is known to have rejected altogether, but through no fault of Kemble's: "you must knock out one of them," Mark Twain wrote Webster, "the lecherous old rascal kissing the girl at the campmeeting. It is powerful good, but it mustn't go in. . . . Let's not make *any* pictures of the campmeeting. The subject won't *bear* illustrating" (11 June 84, in *MTBus*, 260). Later, he had second thoughts about an illustration he had already approved for chapter 13: "It occurs to me, now, that on the pilot house of that steamboat-wreck the artist has put TEXAS—having been misled by some of Huck's remarks about the boat's 'texas'—a thing which is a part of *every* boat" (25 June 84, in *MTBus*, 262). That mistake was eliminated before publication, but some mistakes persisted, despite Mark Twain's close scrutiny: the definite article ("The") in Kemble's rendering of the book's title (chapter 1), for instance (see the notes to vi *frontispiece of Huckleberry Finn*, 1 *illustration*, 91 *illustration*, and 173.15–16). For further detail about the illustrations,

Mark Twain's comments on them, and several newly discovered sources for them, see the explanatory notes.

Edward Windsor Kemble's original pen-and-ink drawings (rather than the first edition photo-engravings) have been used wherever possible to reproduce the illustrations. Thirty-seven of these original drawings are in the Vassar College Library (NPV). Four drawings were generously made available to us by Christie's, New York, and two others by their owner, Peter A. Benoliel. The drawing of the Huckleberry Finn frontispiece is at the Mark Twain House, Hartford (CtHMTH; Stephen Petegorsky photographed it for this edition), and the picture of Harney Shepherdson is in the Mark Twain Papers. When the original drawings were not available, the illustration proofs, also at Vassar, or a copy of the first American edition in the Mark Twain Papers, were used instead. John Harley's illustrations for the raft episode were reproduced from a copy of the first edition of *Life on the Mississippi* in the Mark Twain Papers.

This Mark Twain Library volume, updated for the 2010 printing, has been edited by Victor Fischer and Lin Salamo in collaboration with Harriet Elinor Smith, assisted by Robert Pack Browning, Anh Q. Bui, Michael B. Frank, Sharon K. Goetz, Jon Haug, Neda Salem, Kenneth M. Sanderson, and other members of the Mark Twain Project in The Bancroft Library. Some notes by the late Walter Blair, co-editor of the 1985 and 1988 editions, survive in this edition, and his pioneering work on *Adventures of Huckleberry Finn* is cited throughout. Mark Twain's text, identical to that of the 2001 Mark Twain Library and the 2003 Works of Mark Twain editions, has been established in accord with the standards of the Committee on Scholarly Editions (CSE) and was awarded its official seal in 2002. Editorial work has been supported by generous grants from the Barkley Fund and, for the 1985/1988 editions, the Hedco Foundation, as well as by outright and matching funds from the National Endowment for the Humanities, an independent federal agency.

The text is supplemented by revised and updated explanatory notes and glossary, which derive from the 1985 and 1988 editions and from the 2001 and 2003 editions; and by various maps of the Mississippi River drawn by Mark Ong. We wish to thank all the individuals named above as well as our colleagues at the University of California Press, particularly Laura Cerruti, Lindsie Bear, Sandy Drooker, Sam Rosenthal, and Emily Park, and our typesetters, Wilsted & Taylor, for their contributions.

Victor Fischer
Berkeley, January 2010

The Mark Twain Papers series publishes Mark Twain's private papers—his letters, notebooks, unpublished literary works, and autobiography. All volumes in the series are fully annotated scholarly editions that have been inspected and approved by the MLA's Committee on Scholarly Editions (CSE). For a full list of books please visit http://www.ucpress.edu/books/series/mtp.php

The Works of Mark Twain series publishes authoritative, critical editions of Mark Twain's published works. Based on original manuscripts or first printings, they attempt to repair the textual damage done by the author's original typists, typesetters, and proofreaders; and they restore all of the original illustrations. Each volume is fully annotated and has been approved by the CSE. For a full list of books please visit http://www.ucpress.edu/books/series/mtw.php

The Mark Twain Library series reprints texts from the Papers and Works for students and the general reader. Issued in both paperback and cloth, volumes in the Library always include the original illustrations and explanatory notes, while omitting the textual apparatus and scholarly introduction. The series will eventually include all of Mark Twain's best work. For a full list of books please visit http://www.ucpress.edu/books/series/mtl.php

The Jumping Frogs series brings neglected Mark Twain treasures—stories, tall tales, novels, travelogues, plays, imaginative journalism, speeches, sketches, satires, burlesques, and much more—to readers. Each volume has its own distinctive design and illustrations and is presented by editors selected from Mark Twain's greatest enthusiasts. For a full list of books please visit http://www.ucpress.edu/books/series/jf.php

Mark Twain Project Online offers unfettered, intuitive access to reliable texts, accurate and exhaustive notes, and the most recently discovered letters and documents. Its ultimate purpose is to produce a digital critical edition, fully annotated, of everything Mark Twain wrote. MTPO was launched in 2007 by the Mark Twain Papers and Project of The Bancroft Library, the California Digital Library, and the University of California Press. For more information please visit http://www.marktwainproject.org/